I0788545

THE RYAN CHRONICLES

By
J.E. Taylor

J.E. TAYLOR
SUPERNATURAL SUSPENSE
& DARK FANTASY AUTHOR

THE RYAN CHRONICLES

**Demons, vampires, angels, and the devil.
What the hell kind of nightmare do I live in?**

CJ Ryan was born with enough psychic power to destroy the earth. And Lucifer wants him to do just that.

Raised with a strong moral compass, CJ won't sacrifice innocent lives to protect his own, and that puts him at odds with the devil.

But if he doesn't give in, he and all he loves will become the target of Lucifer's rage.

When CJ gives his twin brother, Tom, a dose of his powers to keep him safe, it puts Tom directly in Lucifer's crosshairs.

As the ultimate battle draws near, what will they have to sacrifice to keep their loved one's safe?

Can they survive the devil's wrath?

THE RYAN CHRONICLES includes these titles:
CJ's Story:
ANGEL GRACE—Book 1
ANGEL HEART—Book 2
ANGEL WRATH—Book 3
Tom's Story:
ANGEL BLOOD—Book 4
ANGEL FIRE—Book 5
ANGEL FURY—Book 6

Fans of Supernatural and Shadowhunters will enjoy this series.

Angel Grace Chapter 1

I STARED OUT THE window at the horror in front of me. The shrill cry of the baby in the background couldn't pull my attention away, not with the fight to the death unfolding on the snow-covered lawn. The battle between my father and Lucifer raged, dredging up a white flurry around the two angels. My heartbeat rammed my throat, drawing my breath in fast pants of anxiety as I watched each mighty blow.

Red splattered white and I bellowed at the vision of my father's head in the demon's grip. My palms banged against the cold windowpane as blood rained down on my father's wings. Even my brother couldn't break through the devastation layering my heart, and my inability to influence Damian's actions just added to my frustration.

A second trembling cry broke through the blackness shrouding me, and I glanced at my brother. Tom's gaze was glued to the scene outside while tears slowly tracked down his cheeks. His lips pressed together, and he grieved in silence, but I felt the darkness grip his heart as surely as it griped my own. Tom's saving grace was the baby in his arms. The child tempered his reaction and the cry of disdain coming from the baby's lips pulled both our eyes to the swaddled bundle; Damian's first born.

I tore my gaze away and refocused on the macabre scene outside. Lucifer decimated three angels in a matter of minutes, and I wondered how, in God's name, Damian could conquer the bastard. Damian held the same vengeful expression my reflection carried and my jaw clenched. My hands followed suit, and my nails drove painful welts into my palms. When Damian's hand shot toward Lucifer's chest, I commanded it to smash through the angel's unbreakable skin. I willed Damian the strength to shatter bone and rip the devil's heart out.

Power leaped from the center of my being like a bolt of lightning and surprise raked through my form when Damian's hand came into view, holding a beating heart. And then Damian did the unthinkable: he took a bite of the bloody muscle. Disgust filtered through me, burning through the horror, and my hand shot over my mouth, clamping down control over my roiling stomach.

The moment the last piece of the bastard's heart disappeared into Damian's mouth, the heavens opened, and a blinding light encompassed him, dropping Damian to his knees. I stared at the man in the midst of the heavenly glow, wondering if the angel grace effect would last. Tom gasped at the spectacle, and I traded a glance with him before refocusing on the bloodied winter scene. The glow faded, and Damian climbed to his feet. The fury etched into his features made me want to shrink away from the glass and I couldn't imagine being the recipient of such wrath.

A blast leaped from Damian, enveloping Lucifer, leaving only torched earth where the devil had stood.

Damian took an unsteady step backwards, reaching for the gazebo post for support as he stared at the same blackened spot. His gaze met mine, and he put the back of his wrist to his lips, paling under the bright moonlight. When Damian finally started toward the house, his gait was steady and he ignored the severed heads sprinkling his path.

As the former vampire passed by my father's head, my gaze locked on the vacant eyes staring at the sky. Anguish encompassed me, numbing my body, and I dropped my chin to my chest, ignoring the birthing process happening less than ten feet away.

I didn't want to be here.

I didn't want to know there were such dark creatures crawling top-side.

I didn't want to experience this type of devastation again.

What I wanted was Sandy.

Sandy had always stood by my side, keeping me sane after my sister died and again many years later when we buried my older brother. She held my hand at my father's funeral and again at my mother's. Losing my brother and then my parents so close together nearly undid me, and Tom was no help during that dark period. He was too busy insulating himself from everyone after being kidnapped and tortured by a madman.

Sandy kept me in line when my world nearly fell to pieces. I couldn't help but blame Steve. Even though I knew it was only the proximity to the former FBI agent that got most of my family killed in that small span of time, it still didn't stop me from feeling he caused the catastrophe. The twist I never saw coming was my father becoming Steve's guardian angel. Because of that, I could hear my father through Steve's mind, and hearing his voice tempered my rage, but not the sense of loss.

Sandy helped fill that void. She was there at every turn, even when her parents forbid her from seeing me. I breezed through college in two years instead of four and had to wait for her to graduate. The past two years seemed to stretch forever, but this spring, she would get her diploma and I planned to pop the question the moment she stepped off the podium.

I hadn't seen her since Christmas break and that disaster was still in the forefront of my mind. Her father had refused to let me in the house and, while I could have forced my way in, I didn't; not with Sandy shaking her head and silently pleading for me not to make another scene.

It was the first time she had truly given into her father's will since she'd turned eighteen and it irked the hell out of me. I left her present in the driveway with the keys in the ignition; and I can still hear her father yelling for me to come get the goddamned car as I trudged away from the house.

It wasn't my worst Christmas, but it came close. I hitched home on Christmas Eve, and Sandy and I didn't talk until New Year's, when she was able to find the time to call without her father standing over her shoulder.

This semester had been tough to deal with. Her course load was insane and with a part-time job and an internship, it made it nearly impossible to catch more than a moment with her by phone and no luck at all with seeing her in person. She kept saying she'd let me know when she had a day off, but it'd been close to two weeks since we actually spoke, and all my messages garnered was a quick text response or an equally brief message in my voicemail box.

I stared at the blood-soaked snow and decided spring was too long to wait.

I needed her now.

The wail of a third baby pulled my attention, and I turned in time to see the little girl swaddled and placed on Naomi's chest. Damian rattled off the names of the boys honoring the fallen angels, my father included, and I gave him a nod of thanks. When Damian and Naomi decided on the name Grace, for their little girl, my lips curved into a ghost of a smile.

Angel Grace Chapter 2

WHEN WE ARRIVED HOME, the feds swarmed around us and the media had already pitched camp outside the gate. I traded a glance with Steve and pulled my keys out of my pocket.

"I'm going to see Sandy." I stepped toward the decimated doors of the garage, ignoring the chaos surrounding our home in Maine.

Steve gave me a nod. "Drive safe," he said before he turned towards his ex-boss, effectively dismissing me.

I didn't envy him; trying to explain the blood-soaked family room and equally stained back yard was going to be difficult and I know the death of his old partner was something that would eat away at him for years. Instead of staying and helping, I bolted, leaving the four of them to clean up the mess. Sliding into my car, I backed it out of the driveway, away from the police and away from the cameras and microphones.

As soon as I hit the highway and the silence descended, the previous night's events hit like a tractor-trailer mowing through a stalled car. My eyes stung and my vision blurred. The road wobbled under the sheen of tears and I swallowed, forcing down the lump wedged in my throat.

"Damn it." I swiped the wetness from my cheeks and pressed the gas pedal, tipping the speedometer into the territory of dangerous. By the time I hit the interstate 84 interchange, my tears had dried up, but my eyes still burned and the emptiness overtaking my soul still threatened.

The rest of the drive into Hartford was quiet, and I concentrated on breathing, on relaxing the coil that had tightened in the center of my chest. My head throbbed as I pulled into the visitor's parking lot outside Sandy's dorm at the University of Hartford. I took a moment and leaned my head on the edge of my steering wheel, trying to get my emotions in check.

I exhaled when I realize I'd been holding my breath and pulled the keys from the ignition, stepping out into the cool night. The slap of cold air cleared my head, and I scanned the parking lot. I really didn't want to have to wait for her in the lobby of her building, or worse, track her down at her job. It took two passes before I located her car and relief settled into my muscles, leaving me unsteady, like I'd had too much to drink. I closed my eyes, willing myself to shake it off.

I was not in the mood for chatting with the resident assistant at the desk while I waited for Sandy to come sign me in, so instead of buzzing in as I had in the past, I silently commanded the doors to open and kept walking past the busy reception desk, like I belonged. No one paid attention to me and I slipped up the stairs, tuning out all thoughts accosting me.

I didn't bother knocking on her door, either, and when the wood swung open, I stopped, frozen in place, with my hand on the handle. Sandy turned from her straddled position and gasped. Neither she, nor the guy she was riding, expected visitors and they certainly did not expect me.

I couldn't move. I just stared, dumbfounded, until my fingers tingled, reminding me I hadn't turned to stone. Reality set in and my heart tumbled to the floor, shriveling to a blackened husk. When I stepped into the room, the door swung behind me and closed with an ominous click.

Sandy pulled the sheet around her, attempting to cover her naked form, and that was the final trigger.

A harsh laugh escaped, one that even I didn't recognize, and I crossed my arms. "So, this is the reason you can't seem to find time for me," I said with a voice that was nothing more than a feral growl, and Sandy's face transformed into a mask of fear.

"Chris. I," Sandy started and turned her back for a minute, but she didn't disengage from the man under her. In fact, I caught the look he traded with her, along with his thoughts, before Sandy turned back. The betrayal ran deeper than just a sordid fuck. It involved feelings, and when she met my glare, I knew it was over.

The ache to strike out ballooned and my fists curled as the fury overrode all senses.

"Don't," she yelled, twisting, so she protected the bastard who stole her heart. Both her hands came up, and her wide eyes shot to my soul, fracturing what little reserve I had left.

I snarled and clenched my teeth, letting the fury snake through my body, poisoning my blood until my skin burned. "You're fucking kidding me. You're protecting that shithead?"

Sandy knew exactly what I was capable of, and her fear blanketed me, stopping me from letting loose. Tears filled her eyes, and she finally slid off him, taking the space next to him on the mattress. She pulled the sheet over her exposed flesh and nodded. "His name is Josh," she said, like that made all the difference in the world.

"You don't need to protect me." Josh sat up.

I twitched, shooting a concentrated blast in his direction. Josh slammed back on the mattress with an audible 'oof'. His hands flew to his throat, clawing at my invisible strangle hold. The fear in his eyes sparked a smile, and I suddenly understood the rush my father always spoke about. He was right. There's nothing quite like scaring the shit out of someone.

"Chris, stop," Sandy yelled, breaking through my concentration.

I let go and Josh gasped for air, his features now holding the same layers of fear as Sandy's.

"What the hell are you?" Josh whispered.

"I'm your worst fucking nightmare," I said, borrowing my father's favorite warning, and then shifted my gaze to Sandy. "Why?" I asked, because I couldn't figure out what this chump had that I didn't.

"I didn't plan on this," she said, wrapping the sheet tighter. "It just happened."

"Do you have any clue how many girls I've fought off over the years?" I started and stopped, shifting my stance and glaring at the floor. "How many times I said no because of you?" I finished and met her teary stare.

"Please," she whispered.

"Please, what?" I snapped. "Don't kill him? Don't make a scene? What?"

"I should have told you," she said.

"Damned right." I crossed my arms again. When she did not explain further, I pressed my lips together against every callous response. When I was certain I wouldn't dig into her and had a solid grip on the need to strike out, I pointed an accusing finger in Josh's direction. "That's what you want?"

She nodded. "Yes," she said in an almost inaudible voice.

Disbelief swept through me. After all, I was CJ Ryan, heir to billions, a fucking Mensa-level genius, and I harbored enough psychic power to destroy the universe. I could offer her the world.

What the hell could he offer her?

The truth almost knocked the wind out of me. Josh could help patch up the rift Sandy had with her father. But knowing the one thing Josh brought to the equation that I couldn't, didn't erase the pain.

"Really? After all these years? This is how it ends?"

She looked at the floor and then back. "Yes."

"Fuck you," I snarled and leveled a deadly glare. It took everything I had to turn and walk out of her room without unleashing hell. A door opened when I was halfway down the hall.

"Chris?"

Her voice stopped me, but I refused to turn, not with her thoughts parading through my mind.

"I'm sorry," she whispered. "This isn't the way..." she trailed off and every muscle in my body stiffened.

I didn't need to ask the questions a normal man would ask. I got everything I needed to know from Josh's thoughts and now Sandy's weren't hidden anymore, either.

"I know you can see," she whispered, and I glanced over my shoulder.

I could see everything that led up to this moment. Everything. The conflict, the fucking love she felt for that deadbeat. Everything.

And everything crushed my heart to a pulp.

"You'd better shut your mind off, because if I get any more of your insane narrative, I'm going to make this entire building implode," I said, and I meant it. I needed to get away now, before I lost control of the raging beast.

I didn't wait; the minute I hit the stairs, I was in full flight mode and the cold air slapped my face a few moments later. I leaned against the cool bricks, counting breaths until my gaze fell on the student parking lot... and her car.

The car *I* bought her and the anger leaped out before I could stop it.

The explosion echoed off the buildings, and I blinked at the damage. Her car was in pieces, burned metal littered the ground, and the cars surrounding hers were now in flames. It felt good to destroy, and I exhaled, letting out a laugh, thankful that losing control only annihilated a car and not the entire university campus. I forced my feet to move forward toward the adjoining visitor's lot.

My car couldn't outrun the onslaught of fury. It couldn't perform fast enough, not through the side streets of Hartford, and certainly not on the highway. When lights and sirens appeared in my rearview mirror, I growled under my breath and considered doing the same damage I did back at Sandy's dorm. The only thing that stopped me was the damned moral compass my mother instilled in me. I have the same high regard for life that she had, and Steve, being a federal agent, just ingrained it further into me. It's the one thing that separated me from my father and despite the disdain careening through me, I slowed my car, pulling over in the emergency lane and dropped the gears into neutral, setting the parking brake before running my hands through my hair.

I knew just how deep in shit I was.

The cop took his time, radioing in the license plate before he finally approached the driver's side door.

I glanced out the window, meeting the officer's questioning gaze.

"Do you know how fast you were going?"

I knew. The needle was buried beyond the 120 mark and I considered saying no, but I nodded instead. My jaw ached from being clenched, and I kept my lips closed against the flurry of sarcastic responses that begged to leap forth.

His features hardened. "Please step out of the car." He straightened, stepping away from the door with his hand on the butt of his gun.

"I haven't been drinking." I glared out the window.

"Please step out of the car."

"Fine," I muttered and stepped out.

"Please put your hands on the car." The officer's tone was now stony.

I had been hauled into police stations more than once and knew the routine, but this time, I was silent, unlike the times in Maine and New Hampshire when I was younger and rebelling against the world with Tom.

After the officer patted me down, he stepped back, assessing me. "Please step to the back of the car.," he said after a few minutes of silence.

I stepped to the back and waited for the sobriety test instructions. Walk in a straight line, touch your nose, and stand on one foot. I did everything the officer instructed until the officer crossed his arms.

"Where's the fire?" he finally asked.

A tractor-trailer zoomed by, creating a breeze that ruffled through my hair, and I met the officer's stare. "Ever catch your girlfriend in bed with another guy?" I asked, and the cop's eyebrows rose. "I guess I let it get the better of me."

The officer rubbed his chin and chuckled. "That's an understatement, son. I'm supposed to haul your ass in for the speed you were going."

I leaned against the car and shrugged. "Do what you gotta do."

I really didn't care. With what had transpired in the last forty-eight hours, a little jaunt in jail wasn't the worst thing in the world, and I almost laughed at the irony.

The officer studied me closer, his eyes narrowing as a new thought dawned, and I rolled my eyes.

"I wasn't trying to kill myself," I said before the officer's thought fully formed. "I'm angry, and I took it out on the road. If you have to arrest me, go ahead. I won't give you any shit."

The officer pressed his lips together; his internal debate broadcasting to me as if he was talking aloud. I waited, trying not to show my impatience or irritation at the pity blooming in the officer.

I knew his decision before he opened his mouth and my muscles relaxed.

"I'm going to give you a break," he said. "But you have to give me your word that you won't tear out of here like a bat out of hell."

I allowed a smile to form and bit down on the first snide remark that entered my mind. Instead, I nodded and said, "Thanks."

"I've been there," the cop added and snapped the ticket book closed. "Just keep it reasonable."

I turned and climbed into the driver's seat, squashing the urge to spin gravel at the squad car. The officer gave me a pass instead of doing his job, which was rare, and judiciousness won out. I started the ignition and pulled onto the road, bottling up the anger.

Angel Grace Chapter 3

THE HOUSE WAS QUIET when I walked in. The drone of the television filtered from the back room and I slapped a lock on my thoughts, guarding them against Steve's unfiltered mind probe. He looked up when I stepped into the family room and his brow scrunched, but I just kept walking, right out into the backyard, crossing through the bloody grass where Damian had annihilated a group of hellhounds, to the rock wall at the far end of the lawn.

I stood, staring out at the churning Atlantic, my jaw clenching and unclenching in concert with my hands. The anger overwhelmed me, and my eyes darted for a source to aim at. Nothing suitable for destroying entered my field of vision and I let out a guttural roar, slamming my fist down on the flat slate rock.

Pain snaked up my arm, and I straightened, pulling my fist to my chest, blinking back the sudden mist covering my eyes. The agony of splintered bones tempered the fury and my chin dropped to my chest.

A hand descended on my shoulder, and I turned, expecting to see Steve, but Jennifer stood at my side. Her green eyes were soft with concern, enough so that when she pulled me into a hug, I allowed it.

"Sandy called?"

"She was worried," Jennifer whispered in my ear.

"I blew her car up." I laid my forehead on Jennifer's shoulder. The admission opened up the wall I'd built around the pain, and it nearly bowed me over. I was so consumed with anger that the reality of losing Sandy hadn't registered until now. Tears started, and she just held me, stroking my back and whispering 'shh' as I cried.

I shifted, knocking my hand against her, and winced before pulling away. "I think I broke my hand," I whispered, and she dropped her gaze to the swollen appendage before giving me a nod.

"I'd venture to guess you did, too," she said.

I wiped the sleeve of my jacket across my face, mopping up the damp tears, before I sniffled and glanced out at the ocean.

"Steve will fix it when you're ready to come in." She gave my shoulder a soft pat and stepped toward the house.

"Jenn?"

She turned, meeting my gaze.

"Did she say why?"

"No, honey. She just said you two broke up and she was worried about you."

"Broke up. That's what she's calling it." I laughed and shook my head, turning toward the water. "It feels more like she put a butcher knife in my chest."

"CJ," Jennifer started, and I glanced over my shoulder.

"I walked in on her fucking another guy."

Jennifer took a step back. Her jaw dropped open before she recovered and stepped closer.

"Yeah, that's the same look I think I wore when I first saw them." I turned back to the ocean. "It felt good to let the power rip. I'm sure some cars are probably still burning."

"Did you..."

"No, I didn't hurt anyone," I cut her off. "I wanted to, but I didn't."

Her hand squeezed my shoulder, and I detested the fact that her show of compassion brought forth more tears. I squeezed my injured hand, welcoming the sharp pain instead of the ballooning agony in the center of my soul.

"Come on, let's have Steve look at that," she said, and I let her lead me back into the house.

Steve's gaze dropped to my hand. "Looks like the slate won."

His response surprised me, and I snorted. "Better my hand than the entire East Coast."

"True." Steve approached me.

I wasn't sure I wanted Steve to fix the broken bones with his miracle healing power. "Maybe I should just go to the hospital." I flexed my hand again, wincing. The pain dulled everything, and I rather liked the diversion.

"Excuse me?" Steve said, stopping short.

I met his gaze but didn't say a word. Instead, I just curled my fist and clamped my jaw tight, sending a smile in Steve's direction.

The silent showdown was broken by the ring of the doorbell. Jennifer traded a glance with Steve before she headed out of the room to answer the door.

Steve reached for my hand, and I stepped back, knocking his hand out of range. Footfalls echoed through the house, pulling our attention to the doorway, and Damian Andreas stepped into view.

"Sorry to interrupt, but I need to grab our stuff from upstairs." Damian hesitated, trading a glance with me. His gaze dropped to my hand and his eyebrows shot up in an amusing arch. "Assuming it's still here." His gaze snapped to Steve.

"The feds left your stuff alone. It's still in the bedroom."

Damian started across the room and slowed to a stop before he got to the stairs. "I'm sorry about your father." His gaze locked on the floor.

Damian's remorse drifted over me. His sense of loss for not only his relatives but for mine as well, made my voice stick in my throat. Instead of responding, I squeezed my fist tighter, sucking air through my teeth.

Damian's gaze shot from the floor to me. "What the fuck are you doing?" he asked, echoing Steve's exact thoughts.

"My girlfriend broke up with me today."

"So, you thought smashing the bones in your hand would somehow make the heartache go away?" Damian asked, filling in the blanks accurately, like he had a special line directly into my mind.

I glared at Damian. "Get out of my head."

"I'm not *in* your head." Damian said. "Besides, it doesn't work for long." He pointed his chin toward my hand before disappearing up the stairs.

"What do you know?" I whispered under my breath.

"A lot more than you." The answer drifted down to me from upstairs.

Steve crossed to the window, pulling the curtain back. When he turned, irritation was written in the lines on his face and he pressed his lips together, waiting for Damian to return.

"You stole a car?" he snapped when Damian stepped into the family room.

Damian shrugged as if it's no big deal. "I couldn't exactly rent or buy without ID." He held up his wallet before tucking it into his pocket. "I'm going to return it," he mumbled and shifted, dropping his gaze.

"There was a car in the garage at the cottage."

"I know. The battery was dead, and it's too small for three car seats. Before Naomi and the kids can leave the hospital, I need a vehicle that will be big enough. I already found what I want, but I didn't have my ID or bank cards on me, so I was shit out of luck."

I couldn't help but smile. Damian's justifications seemed valid, but that little tick over Steve's left eye engaged, and I knew he was pissed.

"You ever hear of a phone?"

Damian glanced at me for help, and I raised my hands, giving him the 'you made this bed yourself' look, and he pressed his lips into a thin line, focusing back on Steve.

"I didn't want to inconvenience you anymore than I already had," he finally said and started for the door.

"CJ, why don't you go with him and make sure he gets that car back to where it belongs," Steve said and turned towards me. He used my shock as his opening and closed the distance before my brain restarted, but it was too late, he planted a quick kiss on my temple and the healing vibe slid from the point of impact, down my arm and into my hand in a progression of pins and needles I was helpless to stop.

"Damn it." I sent a glare his way as a crushing pain surrounded my hand. That's the thing about his healing power. It always hurts like a motherfucker.

He grinned and shrugged, waving me toward the door. Sometimes I hated the man.

"I wasn't put here to make your life easy," he said to my internal commentary.

I bit down on the automatic 'Fuck you' his comment elicited, but his smirk told me he heard it, anyway.

"Go keep Damian from getting into any more trouble, will you?" He pointed to the door.

"I don't..." Damian started, and Steve sent a glare in his direction, silencing him, but I heard the unspoken 'need a babysitter' in his mind.

A layer of irritation surfaced, and I knew exactly what Steve was doing. It wasn't Damian that needed babysitting. It was me.

"Damned straight," Steve said. "You need a diversion." He looked pointedly at my hand and then back to my eyes, using my own thoughts against me. "I figure helping our new friend find a car and a place to live might occupy your mind for a little while."

From the look on Damian's face, he was about as happy as I was about this, but to his credit, he kept his mouth shut.

Angel Grace Chapter 4

R OUTE 4 WAS QUIET at this time of the night, and I stared at the houses as we passed by. Damian was trying to figure out how the hell he and Naomi were going to deal with triplets. Just the ordeal at the hospital was harrowing for him, but the thought of succumbing to a family car brought forth a "humph."

I couldn't help but chuckle. An ancient vampire reduced to a minivan. It was laughable, and he sent a glare in my direction.

"What happened?" Damian asked, turning the tables on me.

"I walked in on her fucking someone else."

Damian had the decency to sigh. "That's rough."

"Yeah, fifteen years out the window like that." I snapped my fingers.

"First love," he whispered and nodded. "That's always the one that kicks your ass." He sent a smile at me. "Be thankful she wasn't your cousin."

I burst out laughing, and Damian met my gaze before I realized he was serious. I choked off my laughter and raise an eyebrow. "Your cousin?"

"You've got the memories. Take a look."

Yeah, I had his memories; twenty-five hundred-years' worth of memories. It wasn't as easy as sifting through one lifetime, but I found the references, and got another viewing of her death at the hands of Lucifer. A shudder ran through me. At least I didn't have to witness Sandy's death. I'm not sure I could have handled that on the heels of my father.

Perhaps Steve was right; hanging with Damian may just be the thing to put my life into perspective.

It was Damian's turn to laugh. "My life won't give you perspective. Nightmares, maybe, but not perspective." He glanced in my direction before taking the exit for Brooksfield. After a few more turns, he pulled into the mall parking lot and came to a stop in one of the farthest parking spots.

"Time to walk." He tucked the keys under the corner of the carpeting on the driver's side floor before opening his door. The wind whipped through the car, and I stepped out into the brutal New Hampshire chill. It was colder than it had been the other night. Either that or my adrenaline had kept me warm during the run from the devil.

"The hospital is this way." Damian nodded toward the road we just drove in on.

I followed him with my hands stuffed in my pockets and my chin tucked into my coat. I wished I'd had the forethought of grabbing a hat, and by the time we got a football length away from the car, I thought my ears were going to fall off from the frigid bite.

Damian sent a sideways glare in my direction.

"It's fucking cold." My voice rose with defensiveness.

"You live in Northern New England. What the hell do you expect this time of year?"

"York is not this cold," I muttered and scrunched my shoulders to cover whatever exposed skin I could.

"The Rockies in the dead of winter is cold. This is balmy in comparison." He continued walking, ignoring my grumbling.

I followed in silence, wondering what the hell was wrong with me. I normally didn't mind the cold. I normally didn't whine. Hell, I normally didn't have the emotional spectrum of a teenage girl.

Damian snorted laughter and looked over his shoulder.

"Fuck you," I muttered under my breath, but he had every cause to laugh. I was a fucking mess. Aggravation snuck in like a cat burglar, at first undetected, but then the silent stalk got sloppy, jumbling my nerves. My eyes stung from more than just the wind, and finally Damian stopped and faced me.

"Think of it this way. There's gotta be something better out there for you."

I stopped and stared at him. "Did you ever have anyone you loved walk away from you?" I tried to decipher his memories. I didn't think that was the case and from the slow shake of his head, he confirmed it.

"It's a little different when they decide you aren't what they want." Bitterness snaked in alongside the aggravation, and I clenched my jaw, blinking away the remnants of mist from my eyes.

"Loss is loss. Mine was just a little more... permanent," he said.

I glared at him, even though his tone wasn't snarky or sarcastic.

"Look, everything happens for a reason." He turned and started walking again. "It took me a long time to accept that," he added when I caught up.

We walked in silence and while I agreed everything happens for a reason, losing Sandy wasn't something I had been prepared for. In some ways, death would have been easier to accept. At least that didn't bruise the ego.

I glanced at Damian and realized I couldn't hear his thoughts.

He smiled at my revelation. "Frustrating, isn't it?" He focused on the building rising from just beyond the trees. "I can't always hear you, either." His brow creased.

The silence hung between us, but it was now layered with the thought-creep of the hospital inhabitants. "We're almost there." He resumed a faster pace.

A sudden urgency gripped me, and I caught up with him, my feet matching his near sprinting pace. I glanced in his direction, and he had the same trepidation carved into his features as I had in the pit of my stomach. I focused on the thoughts and the word tiger surfaced.

I didn't wait for Damian. I turned my sprint into a full-fledged speed contest. The limited experience I had with Naomi and her stellar ability to change into a ferocious tiger had a direct correlation to demons. And if there were demons in the hospital, it meant Grace was in danger.

The air shifted, and a shadow blocked the bright moon overhead. I dodged around an oak trunk and broke out of the tree line before a talon wrapped around my waist. Air sucked out of my lungs as I was lifted off the ground by a giant hawk. We soared above the parking lot, landing on the roof of the hospital. The talon released and before I had a moment to process what just happened, Damian stood beside me, scanning the rooftop for an access door.

"Dude."

He turned toward me and his gaze traveled beyond me. "Door." He pointed and then headed that way. I followed, still unsteady from the experience. I'm not sure Damian knew he transitioned either until he pulled the door open and sent a glare at me.

"We can discuss my ability after we get rid of the demons. Talking our way in would have only wasted time and they're beyond trying tranquilizers. Now, they're talking about killing the tiger."

"Shit," I said, and we took the stairs as fast as possible. Halfway down, Damian reached for the door, bursting into the maternity ward where a collection of officers were plotting how to take down the rabid tiger in the nursery.

Damian scanned the area, his gaze landing on the glass separating the nursery from the rest of the maternity ward. A nurse had her back pressed to the glass, and a tiger stalked back and forth between the nurse and the bassinets. If anyone had been paying attention, they would have understood the tiger was in protection mode, not attack mode.

The nurse took a step forward and the giant cat snarled, swiping a clawed paw in her direction, sending the nurse back into the glass. I exchanged a glance with Damian.

Distaste colored his features and my nose itched with the stench of sulfur filling the ward. The nurse wasn't the only demon on site, and I turned, facing the crowd behind us. At least a half a dozen police officers stared back and their eyes glimmered, revealing the red eyes of demon possession. The others still focused on the hospital schema laid out on the table and beyond the cops were frightened parents and hospital staff.

I glanced over my shoulder, giving Damian a nod. *I got this; you go take care of that bitch.*

Be careful. His thought echoed in my mind, and he started toward the nursery. I turned, just as one of the normal officers called out to Damian to stop.

"He'll be okay," I said, and the demons behind the officer grinned.

Demonic voices filled my head.

Lucifer has plans for you.

I stared at them, and a chill settled over me. What the fuck does the devil want from me?

A smile was the only response, that and the shift of gazes from me to Damian and the nursery beyond. I'm a smart man and my hands curled into fists. If the devil thought he could use me to get to Naomi and Grace, he had another think coming.

Laughter echoed in my head, and I ground my teeth, tempering the need to demolish everything in my path.

"Sir," another officer called, pulling my attention away from hell's collection in the hallway and over my shoulder toward Damian. He had already crossed the distance and stood on the hallway side of the glass case, behind the back of the demonic nurse. He didn't turn, but his reflection in the glass told me enough. He was gearing up and when his gaze met mine, I started counting.

When I hit three, the roll of power expanded from the two of us like a tidal wave, popping overhead lights, and turning demons and their human suits to dust, including the bitch in the nursery. The maternity ward dropped into the black and frightened murmurs echoed on the tile hallway.

It only took a moment before the generator engaged and the red hue of emergency lights bathed the area. I turned toward the nursery. The door next to the window stood open and Damian's back faced us. Arms wrapped around his waist and the stunned quiet broke with the wail of infants. Other than the two of them and a room full of crying babies, nothing else stirred.

The police converged on the open door.

"Where's the tiger?" someone asked, and Damian glanced toward the voice behind him.

"I don't know." He pulled the sleeve of his jacket up, showing the hospital bracelet that gave him access to his children. "My wife's been in here the whole time. She texted me while you guys did shit," he added, turning so they could see Naomi.

The glare he sent at the trooper was enough to pull a smile to my lips, but I pressed them together, staunching the grin. Radios squawked, and they began the search for the missing terror.

"You let that beast out of the room?" the sergeant approached the nursery door, his aggravation making his lips non-existent. "Do you know how much damage a tiger can cause?"

Damian planted a kiss on Naomi's forehead and released his hold on her, turning on the cop. "Would you have preferred letting it snack on the infants?" He waved his hand towards the collection of cribs. This time, a high-pitched laugh escaped from my lips.

Frantic parents filtered into the room, and Damian lifted two fingers, beckoning me into the room.

"I'm taking my wife and children out of here right now." He showed the matching hospital bracelets that allowed him and Naomi access to their kids, and without further conversation, he grabbed Grace and handed her to me. Michael went into Naomi's arms, and he gathered up Gabriel last. He stepped toward the door and rethought his plan, turning and grabbing the three diaper bags sitting under each bassinet.

I followed the two of them with the baby snug in my arms. "Guys, we can't take the babies outside in the cold," I said, and Damian slowed to a stop before we got to the elevator.

"Fuck," he whispered.

I guess I had been designated the voice of reason because the two of them turned to me like I could magically conjure up a car and three infant seats at this time of night. The head nurse intervened, blocking the path out and tried to herd us back into Naomi's maternity room.

"Can you go get us wheels?" Damian asked in exasperation.

I laughed. I didn't mean to, but I couldn't help it. His request was ludicrous.

"Do I look like Harry fucking Potter?" I asked, and for the first time since we stepped onto this ward, his lips twitched into what I assumed was a smirk.

"Fine." Damian allowed the nurse to escort us to the room. As soon as the three of us were alone and the bassinets were lined along the wall with the triplets inside, I turned to leave.

"Where are you going?" Damian asked.

"I'm going to the lake. Why?" I paused at the door. Damian's doubt and unease stretched across the room, and I crossed my arms. "Dude, I'm not staying here." I had no interest in babysitting all night.

"Just keep watch for a little while. We both need some sleep before the babies wake up again, okay?" he asked.

I glanced at Naomi. She was already curled up on the bed, her eyes at half-mast, and her breathing slowing. In a matter of seconds, she was asleep.

"Give me a few minutes." I slipped out of the room. I wanted to be sure demons didn't get close again and headed to the cafeteria. I gathered a half-dozen saltshakers and brought them back to the room.

Damian's eyebrows rose as I trailed salt from one wall to the other, creating a line that kept them reasonably safe. I tossed the last shaker to Damian, and he lined the windowsill and the entry to the bathroom.

"I'll guard the room," I said and grabbed the chair that sat at the small kitchenette table, bringing it outside before closing the door and camping out in front of the entrance.

The floor was quiet and maintenance workers went from light fixture to light fixture, replacing blown bulbs. I watched until my eyelids got heavy. I closed my eyes just for a moment.

When my eyelids fluttered open, I stared at a pair of deep amber eyes. Her mouth was moving but nothing computed, and I blinked, glancing around at the dim hallway.

"Wouldn't you be more comfortable lying down?"

Her question broke through the haze, and I looked at her again. "What time is it?"

"A little after four." She stood when I rubbed my eyes.

A yawn caught me off guard and I stretched, meeting her gaze. I had dozed off for a couple of hours, not minutes.

"I'm good," I finally said after I settled back in the chair. The din of thought lowered, and she scanned me from head to toe, her leer filled with carnal thoughts that made me blush. She sent a sweet smile my way and turned back toward the desk.

"Maybe a place to lie down isn't a bad idea," I said, and she glanced over her shoulder, a smile played on her lips.

"There's a couch in the nurse's lounge," she said. "Come on, I'll show you."

I stood and followed her on feet that felt like I was sinking in quicksand. I shook my head, trying to wipe out the cobwebs. She opened the door just wide enough for me to squeeze through, and pointed toward the couch, but she was so close and made the mistake of licking her lips in such a way that jump started my libido.

My gaze moved from her wet lips to her eyes, and I offered the slightest of smiles and closed the door behind me.

"You're not really concerned with me getting rest, are you?" I said.

The blush that filled her cheeks was my answer.

Damn, it felt good to be wanted, and I reached out, lacing my fingers into the soft hair at the nape of her neck, and pulled her to me.

Doubt passed over her features, and then our lips met. The kiss was different, awkward at first, and then we both relaxed, toying with each other. I pulled away, hornier than I had been in a very long time, and I didn't bother asking her name, not with the flurry swirling inside me.

I pulled the clip holding her hair in place and the long honey locks fell over her shoulders and I couldn't help but grin. Her hands had drifted from around my neck to the buttons of my shirt, unclasping them before searching my eyes. Her warm palms traveled up my bare chest and over my shoulders, peeling my shirt off with the motion.

As I stared at the hunger in her gaze, I remembered Tom telling me it was intoxicating as hell. I never paid much attention to it before, but with the way this nurse was looking at me, I understood the power of being the subject of such raw lust. Intoxicating was an understatement, and I pinned her against the wall, covering her pouty lips with mine.

For the first time in my life, I threw caution out the window and gave in to the carnal desire, turning my blood to liquid fire.

The flurry of clothing lined the path from the door to the couch. I don't remember much beyond the overwhelming sensation of pleasure and heat. I opened my eyes to the ceiling and the cold floor beneath me. Her hair fanned out over my chest as her breath heaved in her chest from exertion, in time with mine.

She raised her head and met my gaze.

"Holy shit," she mumbled and smiled.

I laughed and looked at the ceiling, trying to understand how screwing a stranger could be so bogglingly hot. Now I understood why Tom had gone the slut route. It was liberating, but now I had to try to gracefully exit, and I had no idea how to do that.

Her chuckle pulled my attention back and my post-sex euphoria disappeared. Her eyes shimmered red, and all the heat in the room evaporated. I tried to push her off and scramble away, but the demon bitch was stronger than I expected, and her thighs clamped down on my hips.

"I could give you this type of bliss for eternity," she whispered and slipped her finger in her mouth, seductively drawing it out of those crimson lips while grinding her hips into me.

"Jesus," I gasped and let a mental shove loose. She tumbled off me in a reverse somersault before jumping to her feet. I grabbed the throw pillow and held it in front of my privates, and laughter peeled from her throat.

"Modesty? Now?" she asked, her hands falling on her waist while her perky breasts still glistened with sweat.

The fact I fucked a demon, no matter how hot her host was, turned my stomach into a boiling pit of acid.

"I suggest you leave that girl alone," I said. My voice was a hell of a lot steadier than the quaking in my soul.

"Or what?" she said, raising an eyebrow. She stepped closer, and I moved back, my gaze dropping to my clothing behind her. I put my hand out and my underwear levitated in my direction. She grabbed it out of the air, keeping it from me.

"Goddamnit," I whispered.

"I'll leave her alone if you allow me in," she said, still gripping my shorts.

Her comment left me dumbstruck, but my basic instincts were demanding I run as far and as fast as possible. I knew what I was capable of, and apparently, so did Lucifer. Possessing me would give him everything he ever wanted, and this little seduction was meant to take advantage of my emotional weakness, to disarm me into saying yes.

What she was suggesting was inviting Armageddon to the world's door.

Fiery heat crawled across my skin, and I welcomed the burn of anger. It fanned the power inside, coiling it into a tight ball. I dropped the pillow, balling my hands into fists as I stood tall, leveling a glare in her direction meant to sear.

She smiled, misreading my intention.

I let the power loose and the stench of burned hair filled the room, along with ash drifting on a swirl of air. My trunks dropped to the floor, and I crossed, swiping them from the ashes and slid them on before collecting the rest of my clothing.

I stalked back down the hall and slumped into the chair outside the door. Fury coursed through my blood, and I shifted, leaning my head against the wall in back of me. Seducing me was a low blow, and the bitch of it all was, I could still feel the demanding stroke of her hands and the heat of her mouth on me.

As much as I didn't want to admit it, fucking her had felt damned good.

Angel Grace Chapter 5

NO ONE ELSE CAME near me. The nursing staff gave me a wide berth as I sat with my arms crossed, giving off a definite 'do not approach' vibe. I remained still and awake, unwilling to put myself in another compromising position. When Damian stepped into the hall at a little after seven, he looked more haggard than I felt.

"I didn't get much sleep." He rubbed his face and covered a lingering yawn. "I need to get us out of here. Today," he added and gave a little shake of his head.

I didn't disagree, especially with the nocturnal encounter. I remained seated.

"You can hang in the room while I'm gone."

"I'm fine right here." I met his gaze. He hesitated, glancing at the cracked door. "If she needs help, she can give me a yell. But, honestly, if I'm out here, I can see what's coming."

He gave me a nod. "Don't let them sweep up the salt, okay?"

"No problem. No one is getting through that door," I said, reassuring him and he turned, heading toward the elevator. "Just make sure you get a car big enough to take me home, too," I called after him. His chuckle filled my head and then he stepped into the elevator and his thoughts blended with the rest of the low-grade din.

As the morning went on, the hallway traffic increased, and with it, so did the tension in my muscles, stretching them taut across my chest like an ever-tightening strap. Every face could be a threat, especially since I wasn't a hundred percent on my game and I finally stood, retreating into the room just to catch a break.

Naomi looked up from the chair with a baby at each breast, and my mouth dropped in surprise. I snapped my gaze to the ceiling and spun back towards the door. Her light laughter at my response made me chuckle as well, but I still didn't turn toward her.

"Good morning," she said, her voice full of exhaustion and humor.

"Morning," I said, still facing the door.

"You don't have to stand in the corner like that," she said.

I took a deep breath, turning toward her again, and my gaze kept dropping to the infants latched on her breasts. "Does that hurt?" I asked, forcing my gaze to hers.

"A little." She offered a shrug. "Can you give me a hand?"

I opened my mouth to speak and then closed it because I didn't want to sound like an idiot. Instead, I just nodded and noticed the trembling in her arms as she shifted. I know breast feeding is supposed to be natural and all that, but for a guy, it makes things... uncomfortable. Especially when it was someone as stunningly beautiful as Naomi.

"Please, take Michael. He needs to be burped." She struggled to pull the little guy from her right side.

I paused, and she looked up at me with those big, brown, expectant eyes. As I crossed the room, I kept repeating the silent mantra, this is Damian's wife, and it helped put things into perspective. I gingerly wrapped my hands around the baby's midsection and pulled him toward me, painfully aware of her soft flesh as it brushed against my knuckles. Sucking sounds filled the air and I couldn't help it. My gaze dropped from hers to her fully exposed breast before I turned with the baby in my arms. Heat filled my cheeks, and I brought Michael to my shoulder, ignoring the urge to turn back and ogle.

I got the sense that my behavior amused Naomi.

Cooing in the baby's ear, I rubbed his back and stepped toward the bed, putting some distance between us. When the baby let out a burp in my ear, I chanced turning.

Naomi had her shirt buttoned and Gabriel on her shoulder, coaxing a burp out of Michael's little brother. She was grinning at me like we shared a secret joke, and I rolled my eyes.

"Yeah, I know, it's supposed to be natural," I said, and she shrugged, letting out a soft laugh.

"I'm sorry if I made you uncomfortable. I just needed a hand, and since Damian's gone, you were it." She stood, bringing the baby to one of the empty bassinets, and changed his diaper and swaddled him before turning to me with her hands out. "After yesterday, I don't trust the staff here," she added, and I relinquished Michael.

I couldn't blame her. I had stayed up all night because of the same lack of trust.

"Demons suck," I muttered, and she sent a laugh in my direction.

"Yes, they do." She swaddled Michael, putting him in the third bassinet.

"What about Grace?" I looked at the sleeping child.

"She ate a little while ago, before the boys woke." Naomi climbed onto the bed, yawning. "I am so tired."

I helped her with the covers, tucking her in.

"Thank you," she mumbled, and her eyelids dropped.

I thought about going back to my perch outside the door, but I was tired, too, and at least inside the room, I knew there was a barrier between us and hell's minions. I knew if I sat down, I would follow Naomi's lead. That was dangerous, so I stepped next to Grace's crib, staring down at the perfect little angel.

Her eyes blinked open, like she knew she was being observed, and I smiled. A squeak came from her and instead of waking Naomi, I picked up the little bundle, nestling her in my arms, and slowly rocked her.

The child's eyes were a mix of blue and brown swirls that reminded me of my mother's calico eyes and I sighed, crossing to the window as the sadness hit. Grace squealed, kicking at the blanket swaddling her, and I lifted her to my shoulder, cuddling her soft cheek against mine.

"It's okay," I whispered. "Uncle CJ's just a little sad." I rubbed her back, and she cooed once more before letting out a sigh and settling down with her head nestled against my neck. Her warmth wrapped around me, penetrating layers of despair and a flicker of hope lit in my soul.

I would gladly wipe hell off the map for the little trinity angel in my arms.

Angel Grace Chapter 6

I DON'T KNOW HOW long I stood at the window rocking Grace, but I finally relinquished her to the crib and went back to my post outside the room while Naomi and the babies took a much-needed rest.

A cop wandered by, and I cleared my throat, capturing his attention.

"Did you ever find that cat?" I asked when he stopped in front of the spot of my vigilant watch.

"No." He glanced down the hall toward the operating rooms. "We turned this place upside down, too."

"How do you lose a tiger?" I stretched, rolling my neck to get the kinks out.

The cop chuckled. "I'm beginning to think the guys were pulling my leg." He scratched the back of his scalp and met my gaze. "You know, like an asinine initiation or something." He glanced around and then met my gaze. "The only reason I'm still looking is because a couple of nurses are missing," he whispered.

I swallowed and tried on what I hoped was a shocked expression. "Wouldn't there be some kind of mess if..."

"You would think," he said and straightened. "Watch your back," he added and walked away.

I stared after him and guilt bit at the heels of my conscience. I killed one of those nurses, and Damian killed the other. Of course, they were possessed by demons, so there really wasn't any way around it, at least not one that I was aware of, and none in Damian's history. From what I could glean from his memories, being possessed usually meant the host was dead or had given themselves willingly over to the darkness. They couldn't just take control of a soul at will, which was a good thing in retrospect. Otherwise, I would be Satan's puppet right now.

The elevator dinged, and Damian stepped out with a travel bag slung over his shoulder. I glanced at my watch. It took him three hours to get a car and car seats and he bypassed the room, heading straight to the desk announcing he wanted to have his wife and children released. There really was no leeway in his tone, and the nurse tapped the keyboard.

"What's your wife's name?" she asked.

"Naomi Andreas."

Her fingers flew on the keyboard again. "A-n-d-r-e-a-s?" she asked, spelling the name out, and the muscles in Damian's jaw jumped. He nodded, but I could tell he was getting frustrated.

"I don't have her in the computer," she said, looking up at him.

He pulled up his sleeve and shoved his wrist in her face. "Check again," he said, and I stood, crossing to the desk to intervene.

"She's in the room over there with triplets. I think you were just waiting until they could get a car that held three approved car seats."

She glanced at me offering a smile of thanks and then looked at Damian. "Our records show she was already released. With all the excitement around here, I guess things got a little out of sync." She stood and came around the desk. "I'll do one last verification of your identification tags and then I'll make sure you have enough formula and diapers to hold you over until you can get to a store."

Damian relaxed and gave a nod. "Thank you," he said to her and sent a nod in my direction. The silent thank you resounded in my head as well.

"I'll also need to check the vehicle before you leave," she said as she pushed Naomi's door open.

Damian fished into his pocket, pulling out three tabs and handing them to her. "These were the car seats I ended up getting. They were on your approved list," he said.

She glanced at the make and model on the tag and smiled, nodding and handing them back.

Naomi stepped out of the bathroom, still wearing her hospital gown. The moment her eyes landed on Damian, the tension in her features relaxed. "Home?" she asked, and he nodded even though I knew they didn't have a home right now.

Damian glanced back at me and shrugged. "We're staying with you for a couple of days."

"Really," I said with a laugh, and the seriousness in his gaze shut me up.

The nurse matched up bracelets and checked off items on the clipboard in her hand. Damian put the bag on the bed and began pulling out essentials, like clothing for Naomi and little winter jackets for each of the children. When all was said and done, they had three diaper bags from the hospital stocked with formula and diapers and the travel bag Damian brought.

Naomi dressed, and when she stepped out of the bathroom, I stared at her. If I hadn't witnessed it, I would swear there was no way in hell she had triplets three days ago. I guess transitioning to the tiger really did something incredible to her metabolism.

The nurse stared with the same level of shock and then she flipped through the chart again like something was wrong and her brow wrinkled. "Can I see that wrist band again?"

Naomi held her wrist out again with a smile.

The nurse's eyebrows arched, and she sighed. "I'll be right back with a wheelchair," she said, and when Naomi opened her mouth to argue, the nurse held up her hand. "Hospital policy."

The moment the nurse left, I let out a laugh. "You really don't look like you gave birth to even one child, never mind three." Damian turned toward me. "She doesn't." I shoved my hands in my pocket and glanced out the window, ignoring his probing stare.

His insecurity flared again, and I sighed, sending a look of disdain in his direction. The jackass needed to be a little more confident in how his wife felt about him. He caught my thoughts and irritation flashed in his eyes before he looked away.

"Chill, I'm not making a move on your wife." Although the thought of having a turn at her breasts wasn't something I'd turn down. I just knew the offer would never be extended, at least not while Damian was alive.

He grabbed one bag and threw it in my direction; the glare accompanying the toss meant he got a whiff of my thoughts. I caught the bag and slung it over my shoulder. "Which child do you want me to carry?"

"Why don't you carry Michael," Naomi said, scooping up Grace in her arms.

I stepped to the crib tagged with Michael's name and scooped him up, bringing him to the bed where a winter snuggly was laid out for each child. I slid Michael into the green one. Damian took care of zipping Gabriel into a blue snuggly, leaving the pink one for Grace.

The nurse arrived and our merry little band exited the hospital. After all three kids were hooked into the middle row, I slid into the far back, and leaned back, closing my eyes for the hour-long ride home.

Angel Grace Chapter 7

"CHRIS!"

I sat up in the backseat and stared at the figure standing over me. Damian shifted and pulled the last baby seat from the base.

"We're home." He disappeared out the side of the van.

I rubbed my eyes and stepped out, welcoming the salty tinge in the air. Naomi had already gone into the house and Damian slipped inside as I closed the car door. The gates were clear of lurking media, and I was glad they had deserted their posts. I didn't want to deal with that type of irritation, not with the foul mood brewing under my skin.

The minute I stepped into the house, the level of noise fanned those flames and I gave a nod to everyone in the family room. My gaze lingered on my brother's and even without the benefit of mind reading, I knew he wasn't handling our father's death well. I sent him a nod and escaped into the basement, to our workout area. Specifically, to the punching bag.

I stripped my jacket, tossing it into the corner, and approached the bag, allowing the turmoil inside to curl my hands into fists. The first jab felt good, the scrape of the leather across my knuckles, the slight give of the bag, the rattle of the chains, all fueled me, and my jabs became full punches, each one more brutal than the last.

Scenes from the past few days snapped off in my mind, each punctuated by my fists connecting with the leather. The faster the mind show, the faster my fists flew, and the more my fury bloomed. My breath labored and I finally let out a warrior cry and slammed my right fist in the center of the target with everything I had. The bag flew across the basement, smashing into the far wall, disintegrating into a puff of Styrofoam.

I stared at the mess and then my gaze dropped to my hands, still clenched at the ready. Blood flowed from my knuckles, and I loosened my fists, wincing at the first sign of pain now that I wasn't numb with anger.

"Ah, fuck." I turned toward the stairs and stopped.

"Finished?" Tom signed from his position at the bottom of the stairs.

"What do you think?" I snapped, dropping my throbbing hands to my side. Warm trails of blood dribbled down my fingers, the sensation distracting and calming at the same time.

"I think you're just gearing up," he signed and cocked an eyebrow. "Want to tell me what happened?"

The air went out of my chest, and I shook my head. I didn't want to talk about Sandy, and I sure as hell didn't want to talk about fucking a demon.

"Are you okay?"

I let a bark of a laugh loose. Am I okay? Well, that was the fifty-thousand-dollar question, and I shrugged. "Are you?"

He looked beyond me at what was left of the punching bag and shook his head. When his eyes found mine, they glistened with an unshed layer of tears.

My laughter faded, and I took a closer look, not just at his physical appearance, but at his mind as well. The severed head of my father brought back the nightmare he endured in Georgia, and I crossed, pulling him into a hug. The kid deserved better than what he had been dealt and while he had shut me out at that time of his life; I was the one who he turned to this time.

"I'm sorry I took off," I said when the shakes started, I wasn't sure if it was Tom or me who was trembling, but he was the one crying and holding on like I was the only thing keeping his sanity in check.

Fear radiated from him and without words, I got the litany of nightmares that plagued him these last few nights. Nightmares that he carried alone. Not even Steve had been privy to his sweat-induced terror. Past and present had blended into a carnival of blades and blood, wreaking havoc on everyone he loved.

He couldn't articulate to Raven, not in any way that communicated the depth of the horrors he faced. It had been years since Georgia haunted him and now it was as if the killer had risen in his nightmares, taking vengeance on him for surviving.

"That's not the first time Dad lost his head," I said when the shakes stopped.

Tom pushed me away, his damp face cracking a smile. "You're sick," he signed and then mopped his face with his sleeve.

I grinned and looked at the floor. "Yeah, well, sometimes all you need is a well-placed joke." I glanced up at him.

"Thank you," he signed. "Now that I've unloaded, think you want to tell me what happened with Sandy?"

My smile disappeared, and I looked at the destroyed punching bag instead of my brother. "She found someone else." I grabbed the broom from the closet under the stairs. I crossed and started sweeping the miniature Styrofoam balls into a neat little pile.

When I looked up, Tom wasn't there anymore, but my flash of irritation was short-lived. He trotted down the stairs with the box of garbage bags and another broom. He quietly helped me clean up my mess.

We had the foam cleaned up in no time and I leaned on the broom, staring at the group of full garbage bags, and it occurred to me he had only been dumped once. That travesty had led him to Raven.

"Damian told me everything happens for a reason."

Tom glanced up from tying the last bag. He bit his lip and sighed before his hands slowly signed. "I used to think that was bullshit," he started, and I could hear the words forming in his head as he signed. "But since I met

Raven, I'm not so sure it is." He shrugged and shoved his hands in his pocket, signaling he had nothing to add for the moment.

His answer surprised me, considering the shit he's been through. "So, you really think everything is predetermined?"

He shrugged and picked up a couple of bags, waiting for me to follow suit. I grabbed the remaining garbage and headed upstairs, holding the door for him. The murmuring in the kitchen stopped the moment we appeared. All eyes followed us through the house and into the garage and when I stepped back inside, behind Tom, Jennifer crossed her arms, raising her eyebrow at me.

I glanced at my bloody knuckles and then back at her with a shrug. "I'll live," I said to her silent scrutiny and crossed to the kitchen sink, turning on the cold water. I glanced at the reflections in the window and sent a warning glare as Steve stepped closer.

"Leave it." Stinging pain bit at my knuckles as the water washed away the blood, numbing all other sensations floating through me. I pressed my teeth together, not quite clenching, more like grinding them slowly until the water ran clear. After turning the faucet off, I wrapped a sheet of paper towel over each hand, gripping the ends to keep it in place before glancing at Steve and Jennifer. "My knuckles are only skinned, not broken," I said to Steve. "If they're bothering me tomorrow, I'll let you do your magic."

"Fine," he replied, raising his hands and stepping away.

"If you're going to be a stubborn jackass, at least let me bandage them properly," Jennifer said, grabbing the rarely used first aid kit from under the sink.

I had little choice in the matter. She grabbed my arm and led me to the table, pointing at the chair. Jennifer peeled the paper towel away, wincing at the raw skin, and I glanced beyond Tom at the empty family room.

"Where's Damian and the rest of the gang?"

"They're upstairs. Raven's helping them get settled for the night. I guess they'll be looking for a house tomorrow," Jennifer said, dabbing some antibiotic ointment on my wounds.

The cool sensation soothed the sting and buffered the cuts from the scrape of the gauze she wrapped around my knuckles. When she finished, she looked at the patch job and nodded, pushing back her seat and giving me a quick pat on the shoulder.

"That should prevent you from bleeding all over the furniture."

"Thanks," I mumbled. My phone buzzed. I dug it out of my pocket and laughed at the name on the display, turning it towards Tom. "Do you remember Jenna?"

His eyebrows rose, and he grinned, nodding and meeting my gaze. She was one of the many girls he screwed around with in high school, and his grin told me what I wanted to know.

"Why is she texting you?" he signed.

"I changed my relationship status on Facebook last night." I scrolled through the messages on my social networking page for the first time since I changed it. I chuckled at the sheer number of 'call me' messages and then I brought up Jenna's personal invitation.

"Looks like she's having a party," I said, and met Tom's gaze again.

Tom glanced at Steve and then signed, "I remember her parties being pretty wild."

I could use a little wild right now, especially wild with a non-possessed woman. I typed out a response and moments later, her address appeared on my screen. I knew the area, and I gave Tom a nod. "I'm going out for a bit," I said to Steve and Jennifer and didn't wait for them to intercede. I was out of the house and on the road in a matter of minutes.

Angel Grace Chapter 8

I GLANCED AT THE house and then the address on my phone. It matched, but the house wasn't overrun with people like the few high school parties that we used to crash. Of course, Jenna wasn't in high school anymore, and I crossed to the door, pocketing my phone. I hesitated. The absence of thought raised flags, and I pulled my hand away from the doorbell.

I was no longer sure this was a good idea, but then the door swung open and there Jenna Sylvan stood. In high school, she was one of the prettiest girls, and she had turned into a smoking hot woman. I stared at the skimpy negligee she wore. Stunned into silence, I didn't move. She reached out, grabbed my coat, and yanked me inside.

The door closed and smokey air filtered through the house. I sniffed and found my voice. "Getting high?" I asked as she stripped my coat.

"Among other things." She tossed my coat on the railing, leading me into the living room.

I stopped in the entryway. The coffee table was littered with all manner of drugs, from joints to pills to neatly cut lines of coke, and Jenna wasn't alone. Being a cop's son, I had steered clear of drugs for the most part. I've only experienced a hit of marijuana twice, and nothing like the spread before me. And Jenna wasn't alone. Two former cheerleaders looked up from their position on the floor. Both of them were naked and one was snorting lines off the other's stomach. I don't know whether or not it was a blessing, but I couldn't recall their names.

"Welcome to the party," they giggled, and I glanced at Jenna wondering if Tom knew she swung both ways.

"Don't look so shocked," she said, coaxing me forward and into the lone chair. She handed me a lit joint, and I looked at it, debating. "We have dreamed of having you alone, all to ourselves, for as long as I can remember."

I stared at her stoned eyes and brought the joint to my lips, inhaling a deep pull and holding it, despite the overriding need to cough. "How long have you been doing that shit?" I squeaked out and exhaled, pointing my chin toward the table.

"A few years." Her hands traveled to my belt. I took another hit and reached down, stilling her busy fingers.

"I don't have anything," I said. I hadn't come prepared, and all I needed was to knock up the town slut.

She laughed at me and turned, reaching beyond the drugs to a small bowl, and pulled a strip of condoms from inside, holding them up for me. "We thought that might be the case. You were always so straight-laced in high school. Unlike your brother," she whispered, and I laughed, staring at the package and letting my gaze travel to the two girls exploring each other.

"Damn," I whispered and took a third hit, sucking as the burning embers glowed.

Jenna's eyes focused on the bandages on my knuckles and her hands left my unbuckled belt, choosing to trace the bandages instead. Her gray eyes looked up at me, filled with concern. "You're hurt."

"Nah, just scraped the crap out of my hands. I'll be fine." The pot had started to weed its way into my bloodstream like a numbing agent, and I handed her back the joint. She put it on the table and pulled me to her lips. Her kiss was empty and did nothing to get my engine revved, but when she unbuttoned my shirt and lick her way from my neck to my waistband, I didn't stop her.

She chuckled, and I let her pull my jeans off and accepted the offer of another joint. I smoked the entire thing while the girls took turns blowing me. I had never been this high, this fast, each hit taking me farther into the land of sensations and sex.

"What the hell is this?" I asked, inspecting the stub of a joint between my fingers. Jenna looked up from my lap with a wicked grin.

"Maui laced with a little of everything," she whispered and took me in her mouth again.

I closed my eyes and let them take me to the land of excess.

"OH, FUCK." BRIGHT RAYS of sunshine blinded me. I attempted to roll away, but I was blocked in by bodies draped over me. My head pounded and every muscle in my body ached. Bleached blonde hair covered my chest and I wasn't sure whose head it belonged to.

I blinked, squinting at the ceiling, and the events of the night bled into my memory. I pushed the bodies off and sat up, scanning the family room and the remnants of drugs strewn about, along with the number of used condoms. I think I used up their entire stockpile. Holy shit.

Jenna stirred next to me, her sleepy eyes focused on me for a moment and then her eyelids dropped again, and I hopped to my feet, finding each piece of clothing and pulling it on. For the second time in as many nights, I did the walk of shame, but actually this time, I didn't slink from the place like at the hospital; instead, I stumbled out the door to my car, tumbled into the driver's seat, and fumbled for my keys. My stomach did a slow roll, and I clenched my teeth against the acid burn in my throat, focusing on getting the hell out of there.

Tom had been right. Jenna was kinky as hell and her friends had matched her carnal appetite, leaving me at the mercy of three very stoned, very horny women. I drank it in like a man who had been lost in the desert for days and just stumbled upon an oasis, but during the night, I heard the devil's whisper, promising this type of decadence for the rest of my days if I'd just allow him in.

I swerved to the side of the road and swung the door open, just in time for whatever was in my stomach to purge all over the pavement.

Had I? Jesus, did I say yes?

I shivered, closing my eyes and willing the details out of the fog. What I saw left me shaking with relief, but the shit thing was, I'd considered it. When the devil offered the option of Naomi to me in the same compromising positions as Jenna, I actually considered his fucked-up offer.

I stared out the window, wondering if he had offered Sandy instead of Naomi, would I have said yes?

Angel Grace Chapter 9

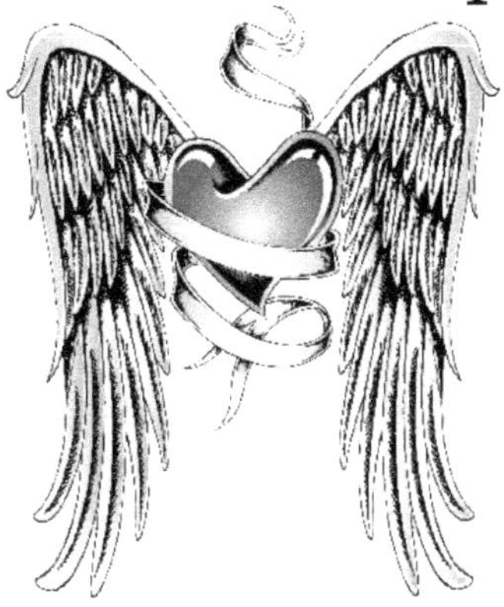

THE HOUSE WAS QUIET, and I glanced at the clock. It was a little after three in the afternoon. I fished out my phone and stared at the home screen. No missed calls. Well, at least they hadn't started a search party. Instead of heading toward the back of the house where Steve and Jennifer's home office was, to see if they were there, I climbed the stairs, heading to the bathroom to clean up. The mint freshness of the toothpaste felt good in my sour mouth, and I stared at my bloodshot eyes. Disappointment raked across my skin, and I dropped my gaze. I didn't want to psychoanalyze my behavior.

I knew I went too far.

The warm water of the shower washed away the dried evidence of a wild night and I stood under the spray, contemplating Steve's reaction to my lapse of judgment. I knew Steve was going to be pissed when he found out I got wasted. I just hoped he wouldn't get a glimpse of my drug induced sexcapades. I shut off the water and wrapped a towel around my waist. I didn't think twice about stepping out of the bathroom in only a towel, but when the door opened and Naomi's surprised gaze met mine, I halted.

"Where is everyone?" she asked.

I shrugged and smiled at the way her eyes bounced from mine to my bare chest.

"What the hell happened to you?"

My smile faded, and I looked at my bare chest for the first time since I left Jenna's. Deep welts crisscrossed my skin, like the girls had raked their nails across me in the heat of our sexual tryst, but the thing that drew breath from my lungs was the five puncture wounds surrounding my heart, just deep enough to penetrate skin, but not deep enough to do lasting damage. It was like someone, or something, had tried to rip out my heart.

Icy terror layered over me, and I snapped my gaze to hers while I reached for the door to steady myself. I didn't realize just how close the devil's bid for my soul had come to succeeding.

"I... uh," I didn't know what to say, and she shifted the baby on her shoulder.

"Who did this to you?" Concern filled her features, causing Grace to let out a wail. Naomi reached for me, her fingers tracing the bloodless welts before her gaze met mine again. "Lucifer?" she asked in a hushed voice.

"I honestly don't know," I said. I had no memory of anything but mind-altering drugs and kinked-out sex. Lucifer's offer surfaced, the seductive whisper, my consideration, the pain... and everything snapped into place.

My eyes widened and my grip on the doorframe tightened.

In a manner of speaking, I had come so close to being royally fucked. The thought produced a high-pitched laugh, and I ran my hand through my hair. Sidestepping Naomi, I headed to my bedroom, closing the door on the questions in her eyes.

No wonder everything hurt. Those girls were possessed by more than just drugs, and the things they did brought me to my knees. Before they turned the tables on me, I ravished the depths of their pussies, their asses, and their mouths, coming more times than humanly possible.

I vaguely remember lounging in the chair, while Jenna sprinkled what I thought was coke in my lap. She put a light layer on her breast and pulled my mouth toward her. The white powder numbed my mouth and brought me back to relative consciousness before sending me into orbit.

They had an array of toys and while I seemed to float in and out of awareness; they played with their toys, pleasuring each other until their moans drenched me. I recall drinking from something they handed me and then whispers filled my world, warning me, telling me to wake up, but I ignored them, letting the numb pleasure take over.

I woke at one point with my wrists tied behind my back and the rope nearly strangling me. Jenna had my ear between her teeth and her hand around my cock while her friend sucked and sucked like I had the secret to immortality hidden in my dick.

My drug induced haze cleared when her hips pressed against my backside, and I realized I was the benefactor of one of her toys. I struggled, choking on the pressure from the bindings, my body tingling back to life from her vigorous thrusts. There was no pain, and a different level of ecstasy gripped me. Jenna's grunts mixed with the others and my entire body seized, my orgasm flooding the mouth of the sucking queen.

Jenna's hands ripped across my chest, drawing the crisscross pattern Naomi saw and she didn't slow her pace. The ominous whisper in my ear, along with the pain in my chest, brought me to another brink; a brink filled with empty promises as her nails slid into my flesh.

How I wanted to say yes, the idea of ravishing Naomi, taking her any way I damned well pleased was so appealing, even though I knew how wrong it all was. I was so close to giving in when another mouth latched onto my hardening member, sucking me into submission.

My father's voice filled my head with a warning that overshadowed everything else, and the rope holding me hostage snapped.

I had the wherewithal to yank her hand from my chest and buck her off before the word "no" slipped from my lips. Jenna's cheeks flushed in anger and then her friend pushed me against the wall, resuming the task of swallowing every inch of me. My eyes rolled back with the next wave.

I remembered nothing after that.

I sat down on my bed, aroused at the memories and disgusted with myself for being such a fucking freak. Demons sure knew how to take advantage of a guy when he's down.

My bedroom door opened, and Tom stared at me, his eyes widening at the raw scrapes crossing my chest.

"Why didn't you tell me she was a drug-crazed bitch in heat?" I asked. I couldn't help the flare of anger that surfaced, and he closed the door behind him.

"Drugs?" he signed and cocked his head.

"Yes. She was a regular fucking drug store." I pulled my pants on, zipping them up before meeting his gaze.

"Like what?"

"Pot. Coke. She had pills, too, but I have no idea what they were." I stared at him and then dropped my gaze. "Hell, they could have been roofies for all I know," I added and opened the bureau, pulling out a sweater and slipping it over my head. "And she wasn't alone."

Tom's lips stretched into a grin that just fueled my anger.

"Did you know she has toys, too?"

His eyebrow shot up in the silent question and I saw a little of his memories as he thought about his experience with Jenna. It was eons tamer than what I experienced, without a toy in sight.

I laughed.

"Compared to last night, your roll in the hay with her was nothing more than a boring workout," I said, and his mouth popped open into a small 'o' of surprise. "Yeah, imagine three girls and every conceivable position you can think of, and then add a half a dozen more that you've never dreamed of," I said, and he grinned. "It's not grin worthy, Tom. Fucking three girls while in a drug-induced haze isn't something to pat me on the back for."

His smile dropped. "You got wasted?"

"Out of my goddamned mind." I ran the brush through my wet hair, slicking it back before turning and facing my brother. "And I'm not sure it was Jenna."

His brow scrunched. "What do you mean?"

"I think she and her friends were possessed by more than just the drugs." I looked out the window at the ocean. "Maybe I was, too, for a bit." When I turned back in his direction, his arms crossed and he waited for more of an explanation.

"It seems the devil wants my soul."

Tom shrugged. "The devil wants everyone's soul," he signed.

I couldn't argue with him there, but he didn't understand exactly why Lucifer was targeting me. "He wants me because I can destroy Damian and deliver Naomi and Grace to the twisted fuck."

Tom's arms slowly unfolded, and his eyes widened as the scope of the devil's tricks unfolded in his mind.

"And the bastard somehow knows I've got the hots for Naomi," I admitted, and Tom laughed.

"She is beautiful," he signed, and his cheeks turned red.

It made me feel marginally better that my brother had the same attraction to the woman. "Yeah, but she's in love with Damian, all the way down to the cellular level, like Mom was with Dad." I leaned against the bed. "Unfortunately, Lucifer knows I'm... vulnerable right now, and he is playing with me."

"How?"

"He's throwing some serious instruments of seduction at me." I met his gaze and saw the confusion in his eyes. Before he could ask, I continued, "There was a nurse at the hospital. I was exhausted, and she showed me to the nurse's lounge."

"What happened?"

I looked up at him. "She was hot." I couldn't help the smile that played on my lips. "After we screwed around, she tried to persuade me to let Lucifer in, just like Jenna did last night. Unfortunately, the nurse had the gall to reveal the demon inside her and I annihilated the bitch."

"Annihilated?"

"Turned her to dust," I said and snapped my fingers. "Gone, dead, whatever."

"You killed a nurse?"

"I killed a demon," I corrected.

He dropped his gaze. His mind jumped to Jenna and his eyes snapped back to mine.

"No, I didn't kill Jenna," I answered the unspoken question. "I probably should have, but I was too far gone. Hell, between the drugs and the mind-blowing sex, I almost said yes to her." I met his gaze. "I think Dad somehow got a warning through to me."

Shock transformed his face. "But…"

"Yeah, I know, he's gone, locked behind the pearly gates with the rest of the fallen angels, but I swear he got a message through to me."

"What did he say?"

I chuckled. "He told me to get my shit together."

Tom smiled. "Sounds like something Dad would say," he signed.

"Yeah." I had nothing else to add to the conversation, so I just shrugged and dug my hands into my pockets, wincing at the scrape of my knuckles on the fabric. I looked at the floor. "Do me a favor?" I asked, without looking up at him.

"Sure?" his voice echoed in my head, and I met his gaze.

"If I fuck up, I want you to be the one to take me out."

His complexion paled, and he shook his head.

"You'd be the only one I'd let close enough, Tom. You're family, and if I screw up for some ungodly reason, you've got to kill me. Otherwise…" My gaze dropped to the ground. I didn't want to entertain what would happen if the devil got his way.

"No." His perfect enunciation pulled my gaze to him. Tom crossed the room and grabbed a fistful of my shirt, pulling me close to his furious features. "You will not screw up." His words came from his mind, not his tightly clamped mouth, and they came with the power of a hurricane, ringing in my ears as his eyes leveled the challenge.

Angel Grace Chapter 10

I ROLLED ONTO MY side and blinked my eyes open. Noise drifted from downstairs, a mixture of babies crying, and people talking, and I stretched, squeezing my eyes closed against the sharp pain behind them. Eventually, I slid out of bed and headed to the bathroom in search of aspirin to take the edge off my headache.

Moving my hands resulted in flares of pain as well, and I leaned my forehead against the pantry door, breathing for a moment before continuing. Opening the bottle presented a challenge, and I was too damned tired to will the thing open, so I headed downstairs.

Conversation stopped when I stepped into the room and held the aspirin up. "Can someone open this for me?" Even my voice sounded haggard and raw.

It was Steve who crossed the space, ripping the bottle from my grip. His angry glare penetrated every fiber and I think I flinched. I know I took a step back.

"I understand you decided, in your infinite wisdom, that drugs were the answer to your problems," he said, shaking the bottle at me like a weird exclamation point.

My gaze bounced from him to Tom beyond and back.

"Tom didn't rat you out," he said, clenching his teeth, and he stepped closer. "Banging everything in a skirt isn't the answer, either." This time there was less bite to his words, and I met his gaze. He had been there before. In both places, and I gave him a sheepish nod.

"I didn't…" I started and studied the patterns in the carpet at my feet. "I didn't intend to get wasted." I forced myself to meet his gaze.

Steve could be intimidating when he wanted, and he knew how to push the guilt buttons. I had to give him a great deal of credit for taking us in and raising us like we were his own, and I hated like hell to disappoint the man. But that's exactly what I saw in his eyes. Disappointment. And it made me feel like I was ten years old again.

"Can you just open the aspirin?" I whispered, hating the pathetic lilt in my voice.

"I should just let you suffer," he muttered, and his lips pressed together. Instead of opening the container, he pulled my forehead to his lips, opting to give me one more dose of excruciating pain before the tingling started in my hands, my chest, and behind my eyes.

"Damn it, I didn't ask you to fix it. I asked you to open the fucking aspirin." I stepped back, grabbing the stair railing to steady the after-shakes of his healing power.

"Next time, I'll beat the shit out of you." He pointed and turned away, leaving me huffing against the wall.

Silence blanketed the room, and I slid to a seat on the steps, cradling my head while Steve's power magically erased the pain. After a few seconds, the crew resumed their conversations, and I glanced between my splayed fingers.

Only one person focused on me, his glare sharp over the edge of his laptop, and I dropped my gaze, avoiding Damian's silent rage. I stood, unsure of where to go to get away from the commotion and his justified anger. I had nearly sold his family out, and instead of confronting it head on, I slipped out the back door and took a seat on one of the lounge chairs, letting the cold wind saturate my clothing.

The door opened, and I stiffened, meeting his gaze as he took the seat next to me and handed me a beer. He didn't speak at first, just stared out at the open ocean, and drained half the bottle.

"I get it," he said after a while.

"You get what?"

"Naomi. I get why you might be tempted to trade your soul for her."

I sighed. "No offense, but I really wouldn't trade my soul for her." I took a sip of beer. "There just isn't that 'I gotta have her' connection." I met his gaze. "I was high and horny, and I guess getting a viewing of her chest the other day at the hospital put some unsavory thoughts in my head." I shrugged.

Damian chugged the rest of his beer, the knuckles on his hand gripping the bottle turning white as he squeezed the glass. "You what?" he asked, planting the bottle on the cold concrete.

"She needed help breast feeding the boys while you were out getting a car." I tried not to smirk, but it appeared anyway.

His face turned red, and his hands clenched.

"Look, I told you the first night you were here, I wasn't interested in making a play for her," I said. "I'm still not."

He took a deep breath, calming the coil inside, and I waited, gearing myself up for an attack. Damian surprised me by getting up and crossing to the rock wall, where he swung a leg over the wall and took a seat. He stared out at the Nubble Lighthouse in the distance, blocking me from the thoughts going through his mind.

His expression told me nothing, and I waited and wondered how much of my sordid evening he got wind of. His head turned toward me and the muscles in his jaw jumped.

"You made the mistake of leaving them alive," he said, too quietly to carry over the distance, but his voice was loud and clear in my head.

His penetrating glare painted a picture in my mind, and I shot to my feet, approaching him. "What did you do?"

He stared me down and then looked out at the ocean.

"Damian," I snapped, even though I had a clear idea.

"I took care of it," he said.

"You killed them?" A shiver spread through me and then I thought about the DNA evidence strewn all over the family room. Evidence that would point to me.

"It's all gone. The demons, the drugs, the fucking house. It's just a pile of dust and burning embers."

"I'm not sure they were all possessed," I balked. "Jenna, sure, but her friends, I didn't know, and I couldn't take the chance of killing innocents."

"And I couldn't take the chance they weren't."

I stared at him, popping my mouth closed. His cavalier attitude toward killing reminded me of my father. He was a master at justifying it, too. "What gives you the right?"

He swung his leg back and stood, crowding me. "Twenty-five hundred years of dealing with demons. Knowing how they operate, how they manipulate their victims. If I'd let them live, they would have ditched the meat suits and gone onto someone else. Maybe someone you wouldn't have had the ability to say no to." He stepped closer, his gaze hard and unyielding. "And you would have been implicated in whatever they left behind."

I gave him some space and shoved my clenched hands into my pockets.

"If they can't get you to say yes, they ruin your life to the point you don't give a damn. Either way, they win." He stopped and took a deep breath. "I was not only protecting my wife and kids, but I was also protecting your ass, too."

I kicked a patch of frozen grass and scanned the cold ocean. I didn't like what he did, but it was no different from what I did to the nurse, and I eventually nodded. "Are you sure there isn't a way to exorcise a demon?" I needed to know if there was a way we could save the souls they pillaged.

"Without killing the host?" Damian sighed and shook his head. "No."

I took a moment to scrutinize his memories. What I came back with was confirmation, and I turned back toward the house, trudging across the lawn, and sat back in the lounge chair. The chill in the air had been

replaced with a chill in my soul, and a dark fear
encompassed me.

What if they ever got a hold of Sandy?

Angel Grace Chapter 11

"DID YOU FIND A house?" Jennifer asked when everyone was settled at the dinner table. She passed the rolls and focused on Damian.

"Yes," Damian said, digging into a pile of pasta on his plate. "It's actually just down the road. I negotiated a move in date on the first of next month." He glanced across the table at Steve. "In the meantime, we'll grab a hotel room after tonight."

"You are welcome to stay here until the closing," Jennifer said, rocking Grace in her arms. The two boys were sound asleep in new strollers near the table.

I exchanged a glance with Tom. Our nice quiet home had become a mini-day care, and I took a bite of the spaghetti. He gave me that 'it isn't that bad' look and slid his gaze to Raven. She was enamored with the babies as much as Jennifer was.

Damian opened his mouth to answer, and his cell phone rang, interrupting the conversation. He looked at the display and said, "Excuse me," before taking the call. Damian's face paled as he held the phone to his ear and his gaze traveled to mine. The panic written in his irises gave me pause and I closed my eyes, pulling the gist of the conversation from his fragmented thoughts. I opened my eyes when he ended the call.

"What's going on?" Naomi asked, pulling him out of his broken thoughts and reading the concern in his face accurately.

"Ted says there's a problem at the hospital." His voice cracked.

"Is Valerie okay?" Naomi asked.

Damian laughed and looked at the ceiling, his eyes glazing over in a way I hadn't seen.

I took a moment to scan his memories for the name Valerie and came up with a wealth of information. He had known Valerie from the day she was born and considered her the closest thing he had to family. He felt responsible for letting a demon get to her, and her uncle Ted shared that feeling, asking Damian to leave their home after the attack on his niece nearly took her life.

I equated the kinship Damian felt with Valerie with what Steve and Jennifer felt for us and instinctively knew he would have never left her if he thought she was in danger. Both he and her Uncle Ted thought being safely tucked away in Hartford Hospital would keep her away from Lucifer's greedy grip.

Damian blinked his eyes clear and focused back on his wife. "For now, but Ted has a feeling come nightfall they'll send something that can breach the salt line.

Naomi looked at the fading sun outside the family room windows, blanching the way Damian had. She didn't need to say what the fearful look in her eyes meant, and Damian didn't either, but one word resounded in both their heads. Vampires.

"Is he armed?" she asked.

Damian shook his head. "I have to get there as fast as I can."

He glanced at me, and I knew that his chosen mode of transportation involved nothing that encased him in metal. His fastest bet was taking on the hawk form and from his expression, he didn't know if he could pull that off.

His gaze moved to Steve, and he looked at the phone in his hand, zeroing in on the man's unique gift set. "Can you really do that two places at once, shit?"

Steve traded a glance with Tom and Raven before meeting Damian's gaze. "Yes."

"Can you do that and still wipe out anything that tries to hurt them?"

Steve slid his gaze to Jennifer and nodded. "Yeah, I can still smoke a demon," he said to Damian's worried train of thought.

"Can you stay with them until I get there?"

This time, Steve hesitated and put his fork down. "I don't know if I'll be able to hold the connection for that long." It wasn't so much what he said, but the underlying fear that if he left his own family unprotected, bad things might happen.

"We can make sure the house here is protected," I said. "Besides, I have a feeling Damian will get there within an hour."

Steve silently debated, and some of it filtered through to me. When he met my gaze, I shrugged a shoulder, giving him a what-the-hell gaze. He drew a deep breath, his chest expanding before he blew a stream of air through his lips. He turned to Damian and gave a quick nod before wiping his mouth with a napkin. He excused himself from the kitchen table and crossed to the new leather recliner, and settled in before meeting Damian's gaze.

"I need a connection. Do you mind calling your friend back and leaving your phone here with me?"

Damian fumbled with the phone, and I covered a smirk with my hand, trading glances with Tom and Jennifer. They wore the same amused smile I was covering. Damian glared at us and then held the phone to his ear.

"Ted, I've got some help coming. He's one of the good guys," he said and held the phone out for Steve.

"Hi, Ted. My name is Steve, and I need you to take a seat and keep the phone line open no matter what, okay?"

After a moment, all the animation left Steve. Damian stared at Steve's waxy figure sitting stalk-still. After a few stunned blinks, Damian traded a glance with Naomi and his eyebrows rose in a 'get a load of this shit' way that forced a chuckle from my throat.

Their minds both broadcast the word "Freak."

"Oh, come on," I said to Naomi. "You change into a fucking tiger, for God's sake." Then I turned toward

Damian. "And you, you're just as much of a freak of nature as he is."

Damian let a huff of a laugh and gave Naomi a quick peck on the forehead. "I'll have Steve give you the phone when I get there," he said before he bolted out the front door.

Naomi waited for a few moments and then met my gaze, her eyebrows scrunching together in a question. "I didn't hear the car."

"Seems Damian still has that hawk gene." I sent a wink in her direction and refocused on my meal.

"You're kidding?"

I shook my head. "He actually gave me a lift to the roof of the hospital the other night when you turned tiger in the nursery. It was a little unsettling."

"Oh. He didn't say anything," she said and stared at her food.

The hurt in her voice took me and everyone else at the table by surprise. I finished the last bite on my plate and wiped my lips with my napkin before I replied. "You two kind of have your hands full," I said, waving towards the three kids. "I'm not sure he's had more than a couple of hours of sleep in the last few nights."

"I'm just as tired as he is," she said, her voice took on a defensive lilt. Raven put her arm around Naomi's shoulders and gave her a little squeeze.

"Men," she whispered and added an eye roll that pulled a ghost of a smile to Naomi's pouting lips.

I stood and cleared my plate. "I'm not saying you aren't just as tired. I'm just saying he was a little more concerned with your safety than mentioning his ability had resurfaced."

She nodded and glanced at Steve. "What do we do with him?"

"Just leave him be," Jennifer answered and cleared the rest of the empty plates.

I sat down next to the living corpse and turned on the television, flipping through the channels while Jennifer and Raven helped Naomi with the babies. Tom wandered in and took a seat on the other couch.

"I'll never get used to that," he signed, and I huffed, glancing at Steve's waxy complexion.

I'm not sure I'll ever get used to astral projection, either. It's one ability I'm glad I don't have. It's beyond disconcerting, but it comes in handy at times like these when Steve needs to be in two places at once, especially when there is a lag time between the distress call and when the cavalry rides in.

When my mother used to do this, I could still read her thoughts, but whenever my father or Steve projected, I lost the contact. In other words, I was in the blind. Which is not the most comfortable place to be when I knew he was in danger. I shifted and then decided maybe we should be a little more pragmatic.

"Jen, did you buy salt at the store?" I asked over my shoulder, my gaze traveling to the darkening sky outside.

"I bought half a dozen canisters," she said, and I returned my gaze to hers, picking up the haunting thoughts resounding in her head.

"Mind throwing me one?" I stood and waited, catching the Morton's when she tossed it. Without explanation, I lined the doors and windows, creating a demon buffer for the occupants in the house. I considered getting Steve's gun out of his room along with the platinum rounds, but I didn't think Jennifer would be very keen on that with the infants around. It was one thing to have Steve carrying. He was an expert shot, but as far as we were concerned, she didn't have the same blind faith.

I set the nearly empty container on the counter and shot a smile in their direction before returning to my seat. The salt provided a safety net that made me feel marginally better about getting lost in the television program.

The babies were fed and put down in their infant car seats and Jennifer, Raven, and Naomi settled into the couches with us. The knot between my shoulder blades loosened a fraction with everyone in close proximity. I handed Jennifer the remote and let her drive the entertainment for the evening.

Halfway through the latest sitcom, Steve winced, pulling air between his teeth in a hiss, and our gazes jumped from the television to him. Every muscle was taut and the blood vessels in his neck became a relief map of blue against the pallid skin.

"Oh, shit," Naomi cursed and jumped off the couch, grabbing Steve's exposed forearm. Thin lines of blood flowed from two puncture wounds in the meat of his forearm. Before I understood what she was doing, she ripped her belt off and looped it around his upper arm, tightening the makeshift tourniquet.

I didn't understand all the to-do about the small punctures in his arm until Naomi dropped to her knees and covered them with her mouth and sucked. Without warning, she pulled away and spit a bloody glob on the floor. It reminded me of someone sucking poison from a snake bite, and I shivered.

I tuned Jennifer's panicked questions out, along with the infant wail that filled the room. Instead, I spun and stalked to the bar, reaching over and grabbing the Grey Goose Vodka and returning to Naomi and her suck, spit routine. When she pulled away to spit, I doused his arm with the alcohol, hoping it would kill the vampire poison traveling in his bloodstream.

He didn't reanimate either, which told me more than I wanted to admit. It meant he was still battling whatever was attacking them and it had to have attacked without warning. Otherwise, Steve would have gotten the drop on the bastards.

Steve's waxy pallor turned almost gray, a feat I didn't think possible, and I traded a glance with Tom, praying that my mounting panic wasn't as visible as his. Before I could say anything to appease his fears, Naomi grabbed the bottle from me, taking a swig and spitting it out, diluting the small puddle of blood on the floor.

Raven rocked with Grace in her arms, the baby flailing for her mother and crying like a siren warning of the coming darkness. Jennifer gripped Steve's unmarked hand, the slow progress of tears marring her perfect features.

Naomi wiped her mouth and then put her hand on Jennifer's shoulder and squeezed. Without a word, she stood, crossing into the kitchen to grab paper towels and Clorox Wipes to clean and disinfect the floor.

"He's still alive and bleeding. That's a good sign. From what I understand, the shadow virus kills fast. I think if he was going to die, he would have by now," Naomi said, wrapping the soiled paper into a ball and tossing it into the garbage.

I narrowed my eyes into a glare. She was lying through her teeth, and she flicked her gaze to me and then back to Jennifer, forming a fake smile that Jennifer bought. While relief flooded through Jennifer, my muscles clenched painfully as the thought of Steve suffering a long, slow death stunned me.

My gaze landed on the oozing puncture wounds, and I forced myself to swallow the bile lining my throat. I reached and pulled the phone from his hand, listening to the chaos on the other line. Glass crashed, and Damian's snarl echoed through the room.

And then silence blanketed the phone line.

"Fuck," Steve muttered and pulled his arm to his chest, curling over in the seat, resting his forehead on his knees.

"Is Damian all right?" Naomi asked, kneeling by the side of the chair.

"Yes." He turned his head toward her.

"And Valerie?"

"Damian has her," he said, his voice strained, and he sat up again, breathing through clenched teeth like a man in excruciating pain.

The tension coiled in Naomi relaxed.

"What did you do to my arm?" Steve asked, glancing at the oozing wounds.

"I attempted to suck the poison out and used your bottle of Gray Goose to sterilize it the best I could."

His gaze dropped to the tourniquet. "I think you may have saved my life," he said and looked at her. "Ted wasn't so lucky." He grimaced and closed his eyes. "I wasn't... prepared for an attack."

Steve was intentionally blocking my ability to read his mind and see what really happened. I sensed something deeper had occurred, and my gaze dropped to the wounds. He hadn't healed himself. "Why didn't you fix that?" I asked, pointing, and he opened his eyes, meeting my gaze.

"Because when I healed Valerie, my powers transferred to her."

Motion in the room stopped. Even Grace quieted, and everyone stared at Steve.

Shock skittered through my blood, creating an uncomfortable warmth that painted every cell in my body in a suffocating squeeze. "What?"

"I figured it would be easier transporting a healthy woman and not someone still listed in serious condition," he said, meeting my gaze. "So, I was a little preoccupied with the results of doing that when they struck." His eyes dropped to the floor and Jennifer kissed his cheek. "I didn't know if I was going to make it back," he whispered and glanced at her.

"She stole your powers?"

He shook his head. "No, it was more like what happened between Eric and me. Completely unintentional and a hell of a surprise."

"Like when I healed you in Georgia?" Jennifer asked.

"Exactly, except she passed out," Steve said and reached his good hand to the makeshift tourniquet, unhooking the belt. He winced and continued, "At least I'm a black belt. Even with their strength, it gave me enough of an advantage to defend myself. I thought for sure I was dead when that shit bit me."

It took Naomi a good five minutes of sucking, spitting, and sterilizing before she stopped. I met his gaze.

"How did you get away?" I asked. My brain stalled at the fact Steve wasn't supercharged anymore. He had been that way since my father died thirteen years ago and I wondered how he would do being normal.

"Ted," he said. "That bastard drained him while I was trying to figure out how the hell to get Valerie out of his reach before I died from the virus burning in my arm. If

Damian hadn't shown up when he did, that thing would have done the same to me. Valerie never woke to witness the attack. She was still unconscious when Damian took Ted's car keys and phone and scooped her up. The last thing I saw before I opened my eyes here were giant talons holding her body as he jumped from the window."

Naomi's eyes glazed with tears and the sudden swell of sorrow in her heart blanketed me. I stepped to her and wrapped her in a warm hug. She allowed it and I ran my hand over the back of her head, whispering "shh" in her ear as she openly cried. Grace joined her, pulling my attention to the infant in Raven's arms.

Naomi pulled away from me, wiping her face. She reached for Grace and Raven gave the baby to her mother. The child snuggled under Naomi's chin, her cries turning to soft whimpers that seemed to soothe her mother's sorrow. Naomi glanced at me and planted a kiss on the back of Grace's head.

"Your friend is going to freak out when she wakes up," I said, and Naomi cracked a smile.

"Valerie doesn't freak out."

Angel Grace Chapter 12

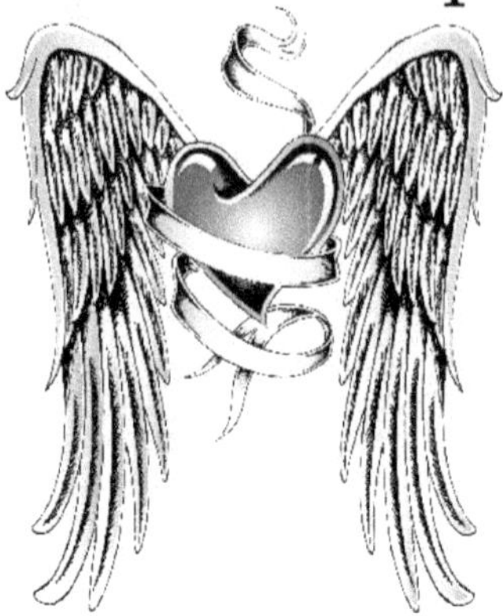

THE MORE I THOUGHT about Naomi's comment, the more intrigued I was to meet this girl.

I collected the guns and set them on the coffee table along with the arsenal of platinum bullets and then grabbed a few beers, handing one to Tom and Steve while Jennifer patched his arm up. He had paled a little after the tourniquet was removed and the blood flow returned to his arm, but he hadn't dropped into a screaming ball on the floor like some of Damian's vampire memories suggested.

Naomi had indeed saved his life and relief loosened the fearful grip on my heart. I'm not sure I could deal with losing Steve on the heels of losing both my father in angel form and Sandy. I said a silent prayer of thanks and traded a glance with Tom, sending a nod in his direction. The tension in his face loosened at my silent acknowledgement of Steve's condition.

Someone upstairs was looking after us tonight.

I picked up the gun, making sure the safety was on before focusing on the back door. The front had the deadbolt on it, and while I knew someone with a vampire's strength could break through it or choose to crash through the windows just as easily, I figured they would come from the direction closest to their victims.

My phone buzzed, and I glanced at the latest requests coming through on Facebook. The number of women in the area sending friend requests was unsettling, and I turned my ringer off. There was no one I wanted to talk to right now. The people I held close were all present in this room and the only other person I might be inclined to talk to knew our home phone number.

Instead of letting my mind drift in that direction, I kept watch out the window and started shuffling through Damian's memories to understand just who Valerie was. Memories tagged with her name came forth in a wave, fronted with Damian's last memory of her as they wheeled her away. Her bloody and pale form sent chills through me, and I was amazed she'd pulled through that ordeal.

Damian knew her from birth until her near death. Only five years had separated them and those were the years he spent in Colorado with Naomi, hiding from the devil. Inspecting the memories, I got a flavor for the girl and only glimpses of the young woman since their return. She was brash and bold and fearless, but even with all she'd been presented with in her life, I was sure the realization of Steve's abilities would throw her for a loop.

I wondered if she got the download of his life as well. I glanced at Steve as he nursed a tall glass of scotch. His hands held a slight tremble and my closer than normal inspection of him pulled his attention away from the television. His eyebrows creased and frustration etched into the new creases in his face. I also noted the appearance of gray at his temples. I guess not having that magic healing mojo really opened the door for aging.

"What?" he asked.

"Did you get the memory transfer as well?" I asked, knowing that was a normal side effect of the power transfers.

He nodded and glanced back at the television, still blocking me.

Before I could press him for details, the wail of a baby set the girls in motion. Before they got to Michael, both Gabriel and Grace had started crying, too. I glanced at the clock, calculating the time since they were last fed. They were going at a clip of two hours between meals. That had to be brutal on Naomi. This time, she chose bottled formula instead of breastfeeding and whether I wanted to admit it; I had a moment of letdown. Tom's face gave away his disappointment as well, and we traded a smirk that Raven didn't catch. If she had, it would have earned him a punch in the arm.

Once the babies were cared for, the cuddle fest started in earnest. I ended up with Gabriel in my arms. He cooed and squeaked and for a few glorious moments I forgot danger lurked. I had never been swayed one way or another as far as children go, but after playing with Gabriel and having him settle into my arms, trusting me enough to fall asleep, my mind was made up. I wanted a child someday, even with the distinct possibility that my child could outshine my unique gift set.

I relinquished a sleeping Gabriel to Jennifer and the three women tucked the children into their car seats, lining them up in full view on the floor in front of the television.

"We'll have to get them cribs," I said as Naomi settled onto the couch across from me.

"Damian already ordered them for the house." She glanced at the clock on the wall.

I followed her gaze and calculated the timing. Depending on how fast he was driving and if he didn't get pulled over for speeding, he should be home any time now.

"Why hasn't he called?" Worry laced her words.

"He's probably driving like a bat out of hell and doesn't want to risk their lives by trying to dial Ted's antiquated flip phone," Steve answered.

Naomi pressed her lips together and nodded. The mention of Ted's name caused another flare of pain in her.

"Tell us a little about Valerie," I asked, purposely trying to keep her mind occupied with something other than death.

Lights crossed the room, and she popped out of her seat, running to the window and peering out. The tickle of a mind scan made me smile, and I clamped down on my thoughts.

"It's Damian," I said and stood, crossing to the door and opening it for him, careful not to break the semi-circle of salt that outlined the entry.

Damian shut the car off and stepped out, meeting my gaze before walking to the passenger door. It opened and the sensation of a chill caressed my skin. I scanned the yard to make sure he was alone and saw nothing that would explain the shiver that gripped me. Damian stood with Valerie in his arms. The thin hospital gown billowed around her, and each pass of wind brought another chill, and I realized I was feeling the wind as it blew against her skin.

Her gaze locked on mine and stayed locked, even when they crossed the threshold, and I closed the door. The minute her feet hit the ground, Naomi was hugging her. Valerie blinked and pushed her away, staring at Naomi's flat stomach. A whirlwind of thoughts danced in her mind and her eyes saddened.

"She had the babies," Damian said from behind her, and her stunning eyes went wide.

It took me a moment to place where I saw eyes like that and when the answer came, my jaw popped open. Her eyes were the same calico storm as my mother's and Eric's eyes.

"Who's Eric?" Her gaze jumping to me instead of what Damian said and then she shook her head, clearing the diversion, trying to catch up with everything she'd missed.

I didn't bother to answer. Her mind was hitting mach ten, snapping through some of Steve's memories that had been transmitted along with his power. She stared at me, coming up with the answer on her own. The depth of sadness in her eyes shot straight to my heart, like she knew what those memories did to me inside.

Valerie refocused on Naomi's flat stomach, still coming to terms with the progression of memories accosting her. "How long was I out?" she finally asked.

"Not as long as you're thinking," Damian said, and his gaze flicked to mine. A shadow of irritation passed over his features, but nothing broadcast with it. I supposed he wanted to ease her into the different layers of her powers, and I backed off.

"Turning tiger accelerated their growth," Naomi said. "You want to see them?"

The woman blinked. "How long was I out?" she repeated, meeting Naomi's stare. Her scientific mind wasn't able to grasp the tiger angle.

Naomi looked over her head at Damian, trying to calculate the passage of time in her own mind. Before she could speak the number, Valerie's eyes widened.

"Two weeks? Are you telling me you went from being a little over four weeks pregnant to delivery in two weeks?"

"It was ten days from when the demon attacked you."

She looked at me like I could shed light on the anomaly. I just shrugged, keeping her gaze. A strange sensation crawled under my skin, making my entire form tingle. This was one of Michael's descendants, just like Naomi. A moment of awe encompassed me.

Her confusion seemed to disappear as we stared at each other, and then she blinked and looked away, breaking the overwhelming spell she had over me. She turned and the back of the hospital gown gave me a view of her ass that made me grin.

Damian stepped in front of my view and glared in my direction. This time his glare came with a thought. *"Don't even think about it."*

"Maybe you should get some clothes for Valerie before we parade her into the family room with the rest of the people," Damian said to Naomi.

The blush in Valerie's cheeks heightened, and she reached in back of her, gathering the sides of the hospital gown together, making the gap disappear. When she met my gaze, I couldn't help the grin that stayed plastered on my lips. I looked at the ground and then stepped away, heading into the family room while Naomi retrieved some more appropriate clothing.

When she stepped into the room dressed in jeans and a t-shirt Naomi gave her, and her gaze locked with mine, all thought ceased. She was more stunning than

Naomi, and I actually forgot to breathe. The feeling passed as soon as her eyes dropped to the three car seats lining the floor, and Tom nudged me.

I turned my attention to him, and his eyebrow rose in that silent challenge. I rolled my eyes at him, and he covered a smirk with his hand. Sometimes just a look was enough for my brother and me to communicate.

"Did Damian tell you what happened at the hospital?" Steve asked, as Valerie made a beeline to the babies.

She slowed and stopped, the smile on her face fading before she turned toward Steve. "My uncle died?" The question in her voice was enough of an answer, and Steve nodded. Tears filled her pretty eyes, and she turned towards Damian. "Why didn't you tell me?"

"I was concentrating on getting us here as fast as I could," he said.

Her hands shot to her hips and the frown that formed on her lips made me want to cover them with mine. I shoved my hands in my pockets and dropped my gaze to the ground, wondering what the hell was wrong with me.

"Look..." he started.

"Don't give me that shit, Damian. You know I can handle it; you just didn't want to deal with it yourself."

The challenge in her voice drew my gaze back to her, and I focused, reaching into her mind and drawing out some memories she had associated with Damian. I had all of his, along with the overwhelming guilt he felt for ruining her life. Her gaze shifted to me for a moment and then returned to Damian's.

"Why do you constantly feel the need to protect me?" Everyone fell silent. The aggravation projecting from her made everyone shift in their seats.

"Because it's my job," he said. "It has been since you were born."

"Why? Because Michael is my blood?"

"No, because you're *my* blood," he said, staring her down like an overprotective big brother. "And because there's no one else to do it now."

I huffed, breaking the tension and pulling all eyes to me. "She's perfectly capable of protecting herself. Or hadn't you noticed?" I said, but the look in her eyes, and the knowledge that swarmed her brain, made her wobble.

Damian stared at her, blinking like he didn't understand she had all of Steve's gifts. He wasn't there when Steve healed her, and he looked at me. His mouth popped into a little 'o', too preoccupied with this new information to notice Valerie's sway, or the fact her eyes just rolled back in her head.

I was faster than Damian. I caught her as she fell. The moment my skin came in contact with her, it was like being stuck in a wind vortex. Her eyes locked on mine and memories merged. Our powers combined, splitting into destructive and redemptive halves of a coin. I gasped as the darker force melded with my cells, increasing the power within me a thousandfold. The air around her sparkled as the healing forces settled into her and the calico patterns in her eyes swirled.

"Michael's dead?" she asked me, her voice soft and subtle, like a gentle caress.

For the first time in my life, I understood what drove my father to do anything for my mother. I understood the overwhelming connection between my parents. I always thought Sandy was the one, but I was dead wrong.

The woman staring at me with the stormy eyes was my soul mate.

"Yes," I said, and the wind silenced. "So is Lucifer."

She pulled out of my arms and climbed to her feet, sending a glare in Damian's direction. "You could have given me a heads up."

"I figured you'd find out soon enough..." he trailed off. "But if you got his memories like I did, you should have already known," he finished; the unsure crevice between his eyes announced his confusion.

"You should have told me." She gawked at him. "Besides, I didn't just get his memories. I got everyone he's downloaded as well, so how the hell would I know what happened, with the sheer volume of shit in my head?"

She had a point. Steve had my parent's memories, Eric's memories and an assortment of others from his FBI days, and now with twenty-five hundred years of Damian's memories on top of that, there was no rhyme or reason to the flood in his memory banks. It was enough to make you think you were schizophrenic. Now she had mine on top of that, just like I had all the above and hers. I couldn't help the chuckle and she turned that fierce glare in my direction.

"If you look closely enough, you'd know that Damian stole a little piece of my talents," I said. "He can hear your thoughts just as easily as I can."

"Then why can't I hear either of you?"

"I'm a master at blocking people from getting in my head," I grinned, and her eyes narrowed. Her 'fuck you' resounded in my head, although she kept it from escaping her mouth.

Damian smirked. "I figured it out from the memories," he said.

Steve cleared his throat, calling our attention back to him. "CJ, Valerie can have your room tonight. You'll stay down here on the couch."

I know he was just trying to diffuse the budding argument, but the blank stares he received from everyone just left him the focal point of our attention. It was only a little after nine and the real entertainment had just begun.

"I imagine everyone's tired. It's been a hell of a day and I need to get some rest."

Damian's stare dropped to his arm. "You didn't heal that bite yourself like I assumed, did you?"

"No. I didn't," Steve said, and a shadow drew across Damian's face, his eyes jumping to Steve's, looking for signs of the disease overtaking him. "Your wife sucked the poison out and saved my life."

"I figured it was worth a try," Naomi said. "And it worked."

Damian opened his mouth and closed it, his eyebrows arching. He apparently never thought to do something like that. Of course, he was usually the one administering the bite, so it wouldn't dawn on him to suck the poison out, not when his goal was to drain his victims dry.

"I'm going to bed," Steve mumbled and headed upstairs.

Damian's gaze followed Steve, and then he glanced at Jennifer. "Keep an eye on him tonight," he said.

"I thought..."

"He probably is, but just in case, keep an eye on him. If he spikes a fever or starts hallucinating, come get me."

"Actually, come get me," Valerie interrupted. "I'm the one in med school."

Jennifer looked between the two of them and nodded, taking her leave as well.

Instead of dwelling on the situation, Valerie refocused on the babies, crouching down and running the tips of her fingers over each little face, mesmerized by their perfection.

"Naomi, your children are beautiful," she said, looking over her shoulder.

"Thank you," she said and promptly yawned. "I think we'll take them upstairs and try to get some sleep before they wake up again," she said, and Damian hesitated, leveling a glare in my direction.

"I'm not a child, Damian," Valerie said.

"I know you're not, but I don't trust him." He pointed at me.

Valerie rolled her eyes, which only endeared me to her more. "Go help your wife with your children," she ordered, pointing toward the stairs.

He only hesitated a moment and then he grabbed the last two car seats, following Naomi upstairs, leaving the four of us alone in the family room. I waited for a minute and then turned to Valerie.

"Hi, I'm CJ," I said, putting my hand out and going through the formalities that Damian forgot.

"I know," she said, but took my hand anyway. "Do you mind if I call you Chris? I like that better than your nickname."

Her grip was firm and warm and sure, and even though Sandy was the only one to ever call me by my real name, I smiled and nodded in response. "This is my brother Tom, and his wife Raven," I waved to the two of them on the couch and Valerie exchanged handshakes and salutations before taking a seat in the chair that Steve vacated. She quietly studied her hands.

"I'm sorry for your loss," Raven said, her Irish lilt presenting itself.

Valerie tried to smile, but a tear belied the attempt, sliding down her cheek and making me want to hold her and wipe the sorrow out of her eyes.

Raven moved first, taking Valerie's hands, her eyes sincere and warm, welcoming Valerie to the family without words. I knew Valerie was close with Naomi, but I had a feeling Raven would be her ultimate confidant. Raven had a way of keeping secrets, even from Steve and me, and I think it had to do with some of her weird wiccan hexes, either that or Tom taught her the basics of blocking thought, which probably made more sense, but I was never sure.

As far as a sister-in-law goes, she was pretty cool, and she made Tom happy, so I dealt with the natural separation that had occurred between Tom and me as he relied on her more and more. Valerie seemed to take to her as well and ended up in her arms, while Tom and I sat by like awkward onlookers.

When her tears dried, she pulled away and wiped her face. "I'm sorry."

"Don't be," I said, thinking about how badly I'd handled my most recent loss. A brief bout of tears was as graceful as it gets compared to my complete meltdown. She met my gaze and offered a half-hearted smile.

"Did you want me to show you where you're sleeping?" I asked.

"In a little while. I'm not tired right now," she said.

"Tom and I are heading up, and I'll leave you some pajamas and a change of clothes for the morning," Raven said. "Maybe we can go shopping tomorrow to get you whatever you need."

"Thank you," Valerie said, and we watched them head upstairs. She turned to me. "You wouldn't have a laptop, would you?"

"Yes." I said and left her alone in the family room while I ran up to my room. While I was up there, I grabbed a sheet, blanket and pillow for the couch and brought that downstairs along with my laptop, piling the bedding on the loveseat before handing her the laptop.

"Mind if I turn on the television?"

"Go ahead. I need to see just how far behind I've gotten with all this." She waved at her side and propped open the laptop.

I studied her profile with the remote in my hand, forgetting about the television and she sighed, sliding her gaze to me. Her fingers paused over the keyboard. Her exasperation with my acute observation of her made me smile.

"I'm sorry." I turned the television on, feeling her eyes still on me.

"How much of my life did you see?" she asked, pulling my attention back to hers.

"All of it. The same as you saw of mine."

She nodded and refocused on the computer. Her forehead creased in concentration, ignoring me as she tabbed through the assignment list. Finally, she snapped the laptop closed and handed it to me.

"Making up two weeks of classes and labs is going to kill me," she muttered and ran her hands through her hair. "Never mind internship hours." Her arms crossed and her frown deepened. "I hate demons," she added, turning her glare in my direction. "They always seem to fuck up my life just when I think I have my shit together."

I laughed and put the remote on the table. Instead of agreeing with her, I stood, crossing to the sliders, staring out at the cold evening. The demons I had encountered were more interested in seduction than destruction. But maybe that was by design. I wasn't cut from an angelic bloodline like she was. However, Lucifer wanted me just as much as he coveted the offspring of angels. My smile faded as shadows stretched under the moonlight. I took a couple of steps away from the door and closed my eyes, building a barrier around the house like I had once done around our car when I was four. Any beast that tried to reach the house would fry like a bug in a bug zapper.

I thought the scale would be a problem, but with the darkness fully charged inside me, it was much easier than protecting the car had been. I knew it would stop a human. I just hoped like hell it would stop whatever monsters Lucifer commanded.

Valerie stepped next to me, staring out at the moon playing on the water. "It's beautiful here," she said.

"It's home."

Her silence pulled me out of the trance I'd put myself in, and I glanced at her.

"You look like Damian."

"You look like Naomi," I countered.

"She's blood, so it makes sense, but you and Damian aren't related, so it's a little weird. Of course, your hair isn't nearly as dark, but your eyes are the same striking blue."

"Striking?"

She smiled, and I felt a need stir inside me and it had nothing to do with my heart, or soul, for that matter.

"You really let a demon tie you up?" Dimples appeared in her cheeks and mine bloomed with heat.

I shifted, focusing back on the darkness beyond the glass, suddenly uncomfortable and unable to look at her. I swore my face must be the shade of a bright red kickball. "I wasn't exactly myself," I said without looking at her.

She chuckled.

The kind of chuckle that was meant as a turn on and I slid my gaze to her. "You like your men tied up?" I raised an eyebrow. It was her turn to blush, and she grinned, shrugging and looking back outside. Before I could explore more of this conversation, she paled and took a step back, dragging me with her.

There must have been a dozen pale creatures slinking across the backyard. I gave her hand that gripped my upper arm a gentle pat and she turned her frightened gaze to me.

"They won't get through." My voice held confidence, but deep inside, I was trembling just as much as she was. Damian, Steve, and I had wiped out more than this at the cove, but that was three of us and, of course, Paradise Cove probably had a lot to do with it.

We both focused on the approaching horde and, without thinking, I slung my arm around Valerie's shoulder and pulled her close. It was time to concentrate on the deadly quality of the wall I put up. I wasn't sure of how much sizzle to put into it.

"I want to see them burn," Valerie said, answering my silent contemplation, and a chill ran up my spine.

She had every right to hate these creatures as much as demons, and I concentrated, glaring at the approaching danger. Saliva ran from their lips and their teeth gleamed in the moonlight. My heart pounded in my chest, sending throbbing vibrations through my skin. The harder my heart beat, the hungrier the approaching vampires looked.

"Just a few more feet," I muttered, focusing on the entire perimeter of the house because I wasn't as much of an idiot as they thought. This wasn't the only line of assault. Still, when they advanced, I took a cautious step backward, pulling Valerie with me. The power inside me grew and I couldn't tell whether it was the adrenaline or the power raking across my skin like a hundred finely manicured nails. The sensation grew, moving from the land of pleasure into the world of discomfort, and I gritted my teeth.

"Come on, you motherfuckers," I growled, loud enough for their acute hearing to pick up. I moved Valerie behind me and positioned myself in a fighting stance, waving them in with my leading hand. The results were memorable.

They all launched towards the glass slider and the moment they hit my invisible barrier, each vampire burst into a ball of flame. The roar of fire drowned out their screams, but I heard them, and the dark part of my soul reveled in it.

Valerie let out a high-pitched laugh, and I glanced back at her, smiling.

She met my gaze with a measure of awe. "The only one I ever saw do something that impressive was Michael."

Being compared to an archangel was humbling, and I glanced outside at the black dust that spun on the wind. "I'm not an angel."

"Oh, I gathered that." She stepped away.

I turned towards her. "What do you mean by that?"

"You're more recent activities?"

I shoved my hands into my pockets and stared at the floor, shamed by the fact she was privy to my more decadent actions. Instead of apologizing, I lifted my gaze to hers, studying her memories of past events, especially the times after the more traumatic events. Naomi was right about one thing. The girl never freaked out. Ever.

And therein lay the challenge.

I let a grin slowly surface and narrowed my eyes, stepping closer. "So, you want to try out some of those 'activities' with me?"

She laughed. The kind of laugh that bruised a man's ego and when she went into the gale realm, I crossed my arms, my good humor turning sourer by the second. I didn't have anywhere to storm off to. I was tempted to tell her she could sleep on the couch, but I knew Steve would be pissed.

"You know I'm rich, right?" I said, feeling more than just a bruised ego now. Most girls threw themselves at me, but this one was aloof in a way that pissed me off.

Somehow, my comment made her laugh even harder. "I couldn't give a rat's ass how much money you have," she sputtered through the laughter and settled into the couch, holding her stomach as her laughter wound down.

I didn't know what to do. Being rejected had been a truly foreign concept until Sandy cut me loose and it just didn't seem natural.

"I'm sorry if I hurt your ego," she said with the light of humor still dancing in her eyes.

"Right," I said, delivering the sarcasm I was famous for before stalking to the refrigerator to grab a beer. "You want one?" I asked.

"Sure," she said.

I wasn't sure why I still wanted to be in her presence, especially after that harsh shoot down, but I did, just like a pathetic puppy following its master around, hoping for a treat. I grabbed a beer for her and returned to the couch. After I switched the television on and opened the beers, I handed her both the beer and the remote, settling into the far side of the couch.

"You don't have to stay," she said, and I raised my eyebrows, waving at the linens on the other couch. She was the one encroaching on my temporary bedroom.

"Oh, sorry." She took a sip of beer and the mad shuffle through the channels began and I glanced at her after two rounds of channel changing.

"Make up your mind."

The glare she shot me made me raise my hands in surrender. She finally snapped the box off and tossed the remote on the table. When she brought her beer to her lips, her hand was shaking. She noticed too and put the beer on the table.

"Are you okay?"

She just stared at her hands in her lap, her hair obscuring my view of her face. I reached out and pushed her hair back.

"Oh, babe," I whispered at the sight of her tear-stained cheeks. When her gaze met mine, I felt her world crumbling around her and moved closer, pulling her to my chest. She covered her face and leaned into me, silently crying. Losing her uncle hit harder than she expected.

When her shaking stopped, I threaded my fingers through her hair with my palms gently pressed to each cheekbone and pulled her away from my chest. Her misty eyes met mine and I couldn't help it. I leaned in for a kiss. Instead of her lips, like I intended, her fingers pressed against my lips, and she moved out of my grip.

"No."

Such a simple word, but devastating in its own right.

"Why not?"

"Because everyone I come to care about dies."

Stunned to the point of silence, I just stared at her. I knew the feeling, but I'd rebelled against it for so long that I just couldn't accept the reason. Hell, I felt the attraction, her attraction, not just mine, and I leaned back. The fact that she was scared didn't negate the sting.

"And if I promised I wouldn't die?"

"Michael, the archangel, died. What hope do you have if he can be destroyed?"

"Michael's not dead, he's just locked in heaven. Just like Lucifer is locked in hell," I said. "Damian saw to that, and Lucifer was *possibly* the only force on this planet that could have destroyed me, and I'm not a hundred percent sure even he could have." I knew it sounded cocky as hell, but it was the truth.

"You're not a god."

"No shit. I bleed when I'm cut and break when I'm punched. I'm flesh and blood, just like you."

"I can't take the chance," she whispered, piling onto my frustration.

"I know damned well you feel the current between us just as acutely as I do," I said, and the sincerity in her eyes morphed to anger.

"It doesn't matter."

"What? Are you going to insulate yourself from all human emotions? Just wall it up and become a walking zombie?"

"Fuck you! You know nothing about me," she spit out, leaning towards me in her anger.

I laughed and tapped my temple. "Oh, yes, I do." I mentally yanked her toward me. Unfortunately, I yanked a little too hard and our foreheads met, dazing both of us.

"Ouch." She held her forehead.

I covered the sting of mine as well and met her gaze.

"Smooth, CJ," she said and broke into a genuine smile.

I started laughing, and she followed. As they say, the third time is the charm, and this time I didn't mentally or physically man-handle her. I just leaned in and kissed her cheek, tasting the dried-up tears on her skin.

"Thank you," I whispered on her skin.

She turned her lips into mine and the first genuine attempt was sweet and awkward and nothing like I imagined. I pulled back, meeting her gaze and the second time we closed the distance, not just with our mouths, but our bodies, like molded magnets, came together with all the pent-up electricity sparking between us. She felt damned good in my arms, and I lost track of time, of where we were and of everything else that happened in the last few days. I fell into blissful nothingness where only her tongue reigned.

She broke the kiss first, and I pulled away, settling onto the couch, forcing my breathing back to normal. Kissing Sandy didn't consume me the way that kiss did, and I stared at the dark television, wrestling with the urge to tear every stitch of clothing off her.

"Maybe that's what I need," she said, and my head snapped in her direction.

"I'm a guy, don't tempt me," I said, running my hand through my hair, unsure if she was serious or not. I also knew Steve was no longer privy to what was in my head, and she was supposed to be sleeping in my bed, anyway.

"What if I said I really wanted to tie you up?" she grinned, her eyes sparkling with the type of mischief I knew would land me in a world of trouble.

I crawled the few feet toward her, pushing her down on the couch under me. "What if I wanted to tie *you* up?" I said and didn't wait for an answer. I settled on top of her and licked her sweet lips again. They parted, and I dropped into heaven.

Before I knew it, both our shirts were balled up on the floor and I was exploring the bounty of her chest with my mouth. God, she was delicious, and I moved my way back up her neck to her lips. This kiss was slow and seductive and playful and damned if I wasn't harder than an oak tree.

I wanted it all, every inch of her soft skin. I wanted to drink her like wine, and I wanted her delectable mouth to swallow every inch of me. When the kiss broke, I stared into her stormy calico eyes and pulled away.

With the want still pounding through my veins, I said. "You need to go to bed."

"What?" she asked.

Her voice carried the husky rasp of lust, and I almost gave in, ripping the rest of her clothes off and just taking her here. But this was not a rush fuck.

Valerie deserved better than that. Besides, if I screwed her here on the couch, letting the frantic need in both of us loose, it would be the end of whatever started here tonight.

"You need to go upstairs before we do something you'll regret in the morning." I couldn't believe I was being the voice of reason, and she certainly didn't take too kindly to it. She huffed and put her shirt on, except it wasn't her shirt, it was mine, but I don't think she figured it out until she was upstairs and by then, I was sure she was too mad to come back down.

I folded her shirt neatly on the table along with my jeans before tucking the sheet around the couch cushions. I crossed to the downstairs bathroom and splashed cold water on my face to tame the hunger still present. The hunger that almost made me march upstairs, consequences be damned, but the chill of the icy splash tempered it. The fact I didn't act on my impulses tonight gave me hope I wasn't a total jackass.

I stretched out on the couch, concentrating on the barrier around the house, willing it to remain until the sunlight broke the horizon.

Angel Grace Chapter 13

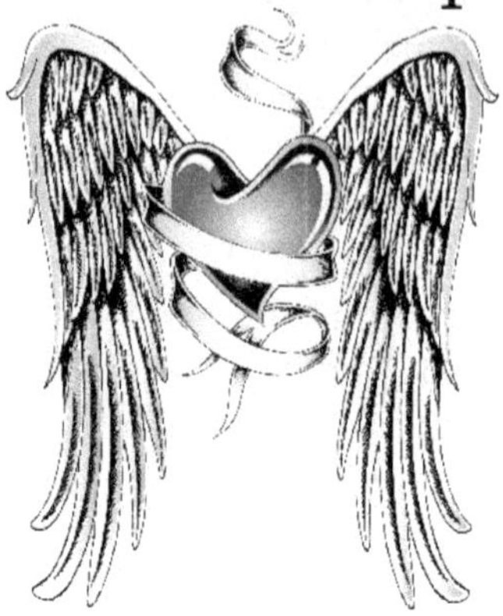

THE SCRUNCHING OF BAGS pulled me out of sleep and I wiped the drool off my chin and turned onto my back, covering my eyes with my forearm. "What time is it?"

"It's a little after three," Steve's voice announced from nearby.

"In the afternoon?" I tilted my head back, peering under my arm. Steve was seated in his recliner with the newspaper in his hands. He glanced in my direction and nodded. I sat up and rubbed my face. "Why didn't someone wake me?"

"Valerie said you held a force field around the house until dawn. I figured you needed the sleep." He folded the paper.

I scanned the kitchen for the noises that woke me and found it empty. I swung my legs over the side of the couch. "Where is everyone?"

"The girls just came back from shopping. Tom's working out, and I have no idea where Damian went." He stared at me. "Interesting combination there." He pointed his chin toward the folded clothing and tossed the paper onto the side table.

I said nothing. Instead, I reached for the jeans and slipped them on before I got out from under the covers. "Do we know how long we'll have house guests?" I asked, folding the blankets neatly. The answer would drive whether I stowed these in the washing machine or on the ottoman in the corner of the room for tonight.

"I don't know, but Jen extended the invitation for them to stay until they close on their house. She seems to enjoy helping with the babies."

"Raven likes helping, too," I said, and then headed to my room to get a clean pair of clothing. Without thinking, I opened my door and got an eyeful of satin and lace.

"Get out!" Raven snapped, but it wasn't her I was staring at.

Valerie turned towards me in only a bra and panties. I wasn't sure if the dress she held was going on or coming off, but I didn't care. The view was outstanding.

"Christopher James," Raven said again, calling my attention away from Valerie.

I blinked and stepped into the room. "I need a change of clothes. Besides, she's got more coverage than some of the chicks we see on the beach." I didn't wait for the okay. Instead, I crossed to my dresser, pulling out a pair of jeans and clean underwear before walking out. It took everything I had not to try for another quick glance before the door closed behind me.

I dialed the shower into the warm zone and stripped, stepping in after brushing my teeth and using the toilet. The soap smelled fresher this morning than I remembered, and I wondered if it was just the fact I had a good night's sleep or if it was something else heightening my senses. I mused over that while I did my hair and then I just stood under the spray with my palms on the cool tile, letting the water cascade down my back. The sensation was hypnotizing.

The curtain rattled and my eyes snapped open. I stood, getting a face full of water, and coughed out the spray that had gone into my mouth. Valerie tilted her head at me.

"Since you decided walking in on me was okay, I thought I'd take my turn at getting an eyeful."

She went to close the curtain, and I grabbed her wrist, pulling her under the spray with me before she could escape. The jeans and t-shirt she'd donned soaked through in seconds and I raised an eyebrow.

"Chris!" she shrieked and tried to break my grip.

"You made the questionable decision to come into the bathroom. You're fair game now." I pushed her into the corner and blocked her escape from the warm water by planting my arms on either side of her. "Want to play doctor?" I said and grinned.

She smacked my chest, and the corners of her lips twitched into an unwanted smile. "Don't be an ass. Just let me out of here."

I glanced at her wet attire. "I think you'll have to take that off in here. No sense in dripping all across the house." I was enjoying this game.

She reached for the controls, and I gasped when the water turned frigid, jumping away from her and out of the spray.

"That was mean," I said, and she flashed a wicked grin at me and slid out of the shower, leaving me to dance around the cold spray in order to turn off the water. When I pushed the curtain aside, I fully expected an empty bathroom. Instead, Valerie was peeling her jeans off.

She turned and threw the wet denim at me.

"You mind hanging those from the shower rod for me?" The grin that danced on her lips was enough to spark an interest, and it didn't go unnoticed. I dropped the jeans on the floor and reached for the towel, but she snatched it off the rack first.

"Uh-uh. 'Mr. I'm too sexy for my shirt'. Hang the pants first, then maybe I'll give you the towel."

Damn it all to hell. Now I was self-conscious and aware I was naked and responding to being near her. My lack of control was embarrassing, and she was enjoying toying with me the way I had toyed with her in the shower.

I scooped up the wet fabric and wrung it out over the shower drain and neatly hung it from the curtain bar before turning back to her.

"You have an exceptionally nice ass," she grinned and handed me the towel.

I chuckled and rolled my eyes, even though her brazenness caught me off guard and my face flushed with heat. "So do you," I said, and wrapped the towel around my waist.

She peeled off her shirt and tossed it to me. "Can you hang that as well?"

I wrung the shirt out and repeated hanging it neatly over the bar. When I turned back, she had a towel wrapped around her and two more wet garments that she deposited in my hand before leaving me with her soaking underwear. I slung them over the rod and shut the bathroom door.

This time I locked it.

Angel Grace Chapter 14

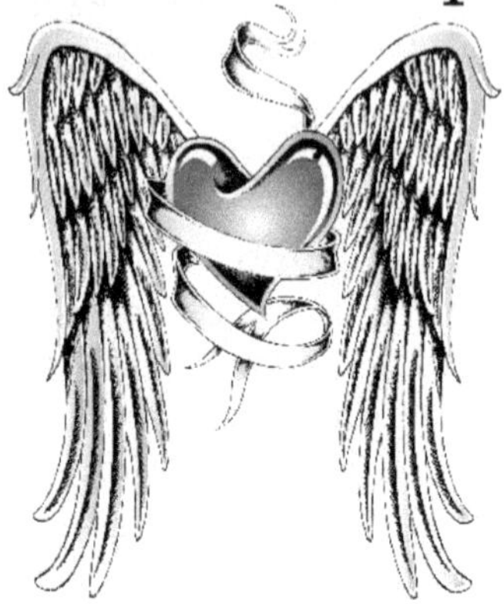

I DIDN'T REALIZE I could strut, but that's exactly what I did. I fucking strutted with my shirt hanging open, right up to Valerie and Naomi, standing by the refrigerator. The game was on, and I didn't care who took notice. I reached for the handle, pulling the ice box open and reached for a soda. When I closed the refrigerator, I faced Valerie with a hint of a grin.

I didn't wait for a reaction, instead I ducked back into the family room and switched on the television, propping my feet up on the table. I cracked the can open and the stupid thing sprayed all over me. I couldn't believe it and the incessant laughing behind me told me they saw it too, so I couldn't just brush it off.

Steve snorted laughter, looking at me over his Kindle like I was the world's biggest idiot. I guess my dating practices were rusty, hell; they were non-existent, and this was all trial and error on my part. I had Sandy for fifteen years and never had to try to get a girl before, and now I just looked like a ridiculous peacock ruffling his feathers.

I guess I missed the 'how to be cool' class in high school, and it certainly wasn't on the college curriculum. I took the hem of my shirt and wiped my face, settling into the couch with no intention of calling any more attention to myself than I already had.

I had already embarrassed myself to the point of no return. Their laughter just sealed my fate.

"Oh, come on, Chris?" Valerie said. "Can't you see the humor in this?"

I slid my gaze to Steve, and he was silently laughing so hard his face was red. "Fuck you," I whispered, and he pointed his finger at me, the admonishment for my language lost in his laughter.

"What'd I miss?" Raven asked, stepping into the family room.

"CJ thought he'd be all cool and cocky until he opened his soda and it sprayed all over him," Steve said, his laughter winding down.

Raven smiled, but God bless her, she didn't laugh.

"It's really okay to laugh," I said. "It was funny."

"I won't laugh at your sad attempt to woo the girl," she said, waving toward Valerie and, as only Raven can, she silenced the room for exactly three heartbeats, and then laughter erupted.

As for me, I ducked down farther into the couch, wishing like hell I could disappear. Valerie came into view, and I met her gaze when she squatted in front of me.

"What?"

She smirked and raised an eyebrow. *Do I have to go get some rope?*

The question resounded in my head, and I clamped my lips together against a smirk. *Maybe.* I sent the thought back and received an all-out grin.

"Want to go grab something to eat?" she asked me directly, and my smile faded.

"When Damian gets back, I'd love to go grab some food with you." My gaze flicked to the sliders and back and her smile disappeared.

"We're never going to be safe, are we?" Naomi asked.

I turned and stared at Naomi. "I don't know, but you're a hell of a lot more prepared now than you were before you met us."

"What about me?" Valerie said.

"It's my personal mission in life to make sure you're safe," I said.

"Now *that's* how you woo a girl," Raven said, pointing at me.

I glanced up at her in the darkest way possible, broadcasting just by way of my expression, for her to shut the hell up. She chuckled and disappeared into the workout room to find her husband. My quiet and borderline boring home had now become a mecca of activity and I just wanted the quiet back.

As if reading my mind, the three babies started crying all at once.

"For the love of..." I didn't finish the sentence; instead, I trudged up to my room and closed the door, throwing myself on my neatly made bed.

The creak of the door interrupted my mope, and I turned, staring at the last person I wanted to see. Valerie shut the door and crossed, taking a seat next to me, and I turned my head toward the wall. I didn't want to give her the satisfaction of seeing my full-blown irritation.

"What you said was really sweet."

I grunted my response.

"I'm not very good at this dating thing," she admitted, and I rolled to my side, facing her and propping myself up on my elbow.

"I obviously suck at it," I said.

"Not really. It's quite entertaining." She smiled in that emboldened way that made me want to strip her down again.

"You realize when you smile at me like that, I just want to rip your clothes off."

She shrugged. "You've only known me for less than a day."

"I'm aware of that, but the memory sharing shit makes it seem like I've known you all my life." I reached up and tucked the stray strands of hair behind her ear. "Which is kind of a mind fuck, you know?"

"A big-time mind fuck," she agreed. "Especially since I think love at first sight is a crock of shit."

We stared at each other for a moment, and then her words sank in. "I wasn't a believer either. Sandy and I knew each other since we were born and at first, she annoyed the hell out of me, but then my father died, and she was there and for the first time I saw her as an individual and not as Uncle Danny's annoying kid."

Her brow creased, and I gave her the time to inspect my memories. When she made the correct connections that told her he was only an uncle by name and not relations, her features relaxed.

"I know, weird as hell, but we always called him Uncle Danny. I don't think my mother knew how to explain all the connections she had before my dad."

"She hurt you," Valerie said and threaded her fingers through mine.

"Yes. And I did not handle it well." I sighed. "I'm still not handling things well."

"You're a smart guy. You'll figure it out." She gave me a smirk, and I squeezed her hand.

"You know…"

"I know. You're a genius and you're richer than God and you've got mega-freaky powers that could blow this earth to bits as easily as you dispatched of those vampires. But here's the thing, I really don't care about those things."

I opened my mouth, and she put her finger over my lips, stopping my retort.

"What I do care about is how you treat others. How you conduct yourself in life. Why do you think I went to medical school?"

"To help kids," I said. I didn't need to search her memories for answers. I had already taken a long look while night crawled into dawn.

"So, let me ask you a question. Besides teaching Karate class once a week, what exactly do you want to do with your life?"

I stared at her and shrugged. I had no clue of what I wanted to do. I had a computer science degree and tooled around putting together video games for giggles, but nothing serious and she was right. I had more money than I knew what to do with and Tom and Raven could have moved out a long time ago, but this was home, and the only remaining connection Tom had to our parents.

They had discussed moving into the house on Nubble Road when the current lease ran out, but that wasn't for another four months, and Steve and Jen hadn't broached the subject about moving to either New York or their place in New Hampshire. I think they were waiting until Sandy and I got married.

"I will figure something out." I didn't want to discuss what my future held. I kind of liked doing what I wanted, when I wanted. But I also love teaching the little kids how to defend themselves. "Maybe I'll increase the number of classes I teach," I added.

Her eyes pierced through me and without speaking, she passed judgment on me.

"I told you, I'm not an angel."

"I know, but you could do so much with your gifts," she started, and I shut her down.

"If word ever got out, you think I'd ever be safe? You think governments would allow me to roam free?" I shook my head. "They'd hunt me down hoping to lock me up until I agreed to become their weapon of mass destruction. If you think it's bad running from demons and vampires, try adding the vilest of humans to that list."

Her face paled as the realization came to her. The reality that her power was not for public consumption hit and with it, the hopes of healing the world crashed and burned.

"If you decide to help someone, you can't blatantly do it. Look at Steve's memories, on how he used the healing power. Granted, he wasn't a doctor, but he saved a few people in his stint as an FBI agent."

"But..." she started and closed her mouth. Her mind filtered to a scene from a movie she once watched, where hordes of people bombarded a famed healer. "I'd become a sideshow trick, wouldn't I?"

I nodded, and she hung her head. "I just want to help sick kids."

I hooked my finger under her chin and forced her to look at me. "You still can. You just have to use medicine unless the only way to save them is by using the power."

"Assuming I still have it," she said, and I grinned.

"I think it's probably safe to assume you'll have it for a while." I pushed myself up and pulled her into a gentle kiss. When the kiss broke, the colors in her eyes swirled, slowing and settling as the air cooled between us.

"You really know how to fuck with my mind," she said.

"I love it when you talk dirty," I purred, wrapping my arms around her waist and shifting her onto her back. "Now, I think you may have mentioned... bondage?"

She laughed and wrapped her hands around my wrists and spread her arms wide. I surrendered and let her hold my arms in place. I found the curve of her neck and nibbled. She giggled under me, and I slid my gaze from her throat to her eyes. My playfulness faded, replaced by the certainty that she would be beyond fantastic in bed.

Her cheeks bloomed, and she smiled at me. "I'd be the best you ever had," she said.

I thought about the wild drug induced sex fest of the last few days and raised an eyebrow.

"I'd still be the best," she said, but this time the conviction waned.

"I'm thinking you're full of shit," I said, twisting my arms from her grip and wrapped them around her. "Remember, I have all your memories," I whispered in her ear. "My little virgin girl."

I pulled back and grinned.

Her smile faltered. "You knew?" she asked, and then she rolled her eyes. "Of course you knew."

"Yes. I knew. And I could have been an insensitive bastard last night, too, but I'm not. I was never like Tom, or my father, for that matter." I pecked her lips and propped up on my elbows. "Although I went to Jenna's houses for some action. I just didn't expect the triplets from hell, and I can't lie. The physical side of the equation was out of this world, but it wasn't worth the shitty feeling the next day."

"The walk of shame?"

"Yep. Sucks," I said and slid off her, propping up on my elbow again.

"You don't think I'm a freak for—"

I shook my head before she finished. "You had your reasons, and I respect that."

She stared at me for a while and did a pretty good job at blocking her thoughts.

"I don't understand how she could let you go?"

"Sandy?"

"Yes."

"Well, I think it was a couple of things. Distance being one and her father being the other driver. You see, her father hated my father. I can't really blame him, either. My father was diabolical in his younger years until he kidnapped my mother." I sighed and fell on my back, staring at the ceiling. "My dad did some pretty messed up things, and it poisoned Sandy's father's opinion of me. He tolerated me until he caught us in bed together. Ironically, that was our first time."

She chuckled, scanning over the memory. "You are so lucky he didn't own a gun."

"I know." I couldn't help but smile. Sandy's father had had one major conniption. I propped myself up and stared at Valerie. "Damian has a gun. Should I be worried about him popping a cap in my ass?"

"Are you planning on popping my cherry?" she asked, an impish glint danced in her eyes.

I laughed. "I think that may be a distinct possibility."

"Then I think you'll have to battle Damian for my honor." She batted her eyes at me and grinned like the Cheshire cat just as the door swung open.

"What the hell do you think you're doing?"

"Speak of the devil," I said, and his nostrils flared. Damian had a protective streak a mile wide where Valerie was concerned, and seeing her in a nearly compromising position didn't help my case.

"Get off her," he growled.

"I'm not 'on' her," I countered, and when she went to get up, I pressed my hand to her shoulder, holding her in place. I glanced at her. "Do you want to get up?"

Her eyes darted to Damian, and she shrugged. "It might be best."

I lifted my hand and let her go. As soon as she was out the door, I sat up and leveled a glare at Damian. "I wasn't doing anything with her."

"Damned right," he said.

His macho, high-and-mighty attitude needed to be taken down a few pegs, and I hopped to my feet. "If I was, there isn't a goddamned thing you could do about it."

Damian stepped farther into the room and closed the door behind him before turning towards me. Aggravation tensed the muscles in his jaw and narrowed both his eyes and lips.

"You're crossing a line," he growled, and I grinned.

"And here I thought you'd breathe a sigh of relief, considering your massive insecurities where your wife is concerned." I knew I was poking the bear, but I needed some release for the building anger inside me. And who better to take it out on than someone on an equal plane?

The mental shove came, and I stepped back, catching myself in a ready stance. "You don't really want to wage that kind of war with me." I warned. If I let go on that front, I'm not sure if anyone would be left standing, and Damian reconsidered.

He glanced around the room and then directly at me. "Backyard," he said through clenched teeth.

"After you," I waved at the door.

He hesitated a moment and then turned and I followed. It was going to feel really good pummeling the shit out of him. He sent a glare over his shoulder as he rounded the corner and, with a sweep of his hand, the sliders opened. We passed by the rest of the family, leaving them staring with slack jaws.

I closed the door behind me in the same manner as he opened it. The patio bricks were cold on my bare feet and the air settled a chill over me. Damian slipped off his shoes, tossing them by the lounge chairs, and turned on me.

I shifted to the ready, waving him in like I had the vampires the night before. His face turned red, and he stepped forward, taking on the same form. When his face transformed into a grin, I had a second to wonder if this was a wise decision.

I could almost hear my father saying "Hajime!" and we both stepped into the ring. With my thoughts blocked, I let myself react. Damian threw a punch, and I parried, stepping in and pulling him off balance. He recovered in time to counter my foot sweep and he spun out of my hold. His foot came around and before I could block it, he connected with my abdomen, sucking the air from my lungs and knocking me on my ass.

I scrambled to my feet, forcing my breath in slowly, ignoring the throbbing pain in my diaphragm. He didn't let me catch my breath and launched into his next attack and damned if he wasn't fast. I blocked nearly everything and finally an opportunity presented itself and I hooked his arm, rolling him over my hip and onto his back, and I remembered to let go instead of protecting him like I would have in the dojo. His breath escaped in an 'oaf' as he hit the slate square, his head bouncing on the hard stone before he could stop it.

His daze only lasted a moment, and he sat up, climbing to his feet. He glanced at the sliders, at the audience I knew was there but refused to focus on, and that was a grave mistake. I spun and my foot connected with his chest, knocking him on his back. This time, he didn't get up right away. He blinked and wheezed, staring at the sky before his gaze traveled to me.

"Shit," he coughed and rolled onto his knees, slowly getting to his feet. "That's going to leave a bruise," he said.

"Never. Ever. Take your eyes off your sparring partner." I pointed at him. "First fucking rule, dude. First fucking rule." I gave a quick bow and walked away. I had the benefit of the reflection on the glass, so when he launched his next attack, I got the drop on him, ducking under his kick and sweeping his leg out from under him.

I hopped to my feet and stared down at him with enough distance between us to counter any strike he attempted.

"Are you done yet?" I asked, knowing just how frustrated he was. After all, I was just this twenty-four-year-old kid, and he was closer to three thousand years old.

"You need to stay away from Valerie," he said from his position on the ground.

I laughed and the door behind me opened.

"Are you two done with your testosterone contest?"

I didn't turn towards Valerie, not with Damian still in fight mode. When her hand landed on my arm, I met her gaze.

"Enough," she said, and I relaxed, dropping my hands to my sides.

Damian got to his feet, and I bowed out, turning and heading back inside, leaving her to deal with him. As I passed Steve, I got a nod of approval, which meant I did well on my forms. It meant a lot coming from him, since he picked up teaching Tom and me when my father died.

I knew Damian had studied several arts under some of the most talented masters over the millenniums, but he'd never studied under *my* mentors.

Angel Grace Chapter 15

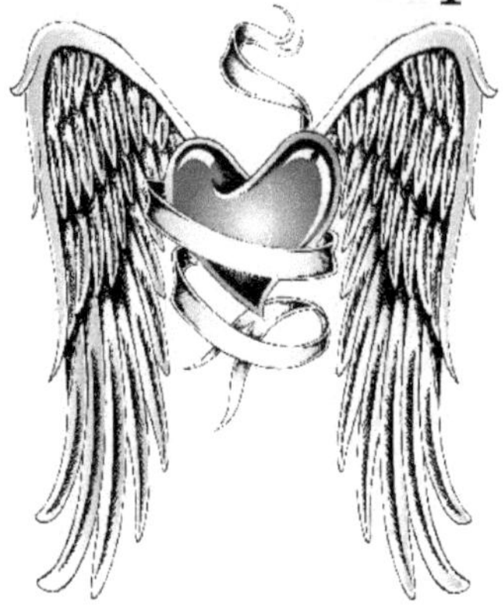

I LEANED AGAINST THE wall with the silent square in my hand, waiting for it to light up and vibrate, announcing a table was available. I glanced at the gorgeous brunette sitting on the bench, her calico eyes scanning the crowd like she expected an assassin to jump out. I leaned close to her ear.

"I promise, you're safe tonight."

Valerie met my gaze and offered a tight smile.

"I promise."

The second time seemed to ease her mind a little and the stress in her shoulders relaxed.

"How'd you convince him to let us go out alone?"

Her lips stretched into a smile. "I told him it was his turn to man up. You stood watch last night and deserved some down time. When he argued about you having enough downtime, I said I wanted dinner and you had offered."

"So, you basically told him he had no choice."

"That sounds about right."

"I'm sure he wasn't happy." I focused on the crowd again. The unit in my hand buzzed, and I showed her. "Our table." I waited for her to stand and gather her coat and purse before approaching the hostess.

When we were seated, Valerie sighed. "I don't want to be your rebound."

The softness in her voice tore at my chest. I damned well didn't want that and instead of agreeing; I focused on the wood grains in the table, questioning my intentions. This was all conveniently placed in my lap when I needed something to lift me up out of the hurt and anger.

Was I using her to get back on my feet?

After all, that's the definition of rebound. I met her gaze and blew out my breath.

"Then maybe we should just start as friends," I said.

She stared at me, her lips pouting as she turned over my response. "What if we are incapable of just being friends?"

"By we, you mean me?" I pointed at my chest and raised my eyebrows.

She shrugged a single shoulder and her gaze shifted as the waitress set two glasses of water on the table and I rattled off an order for two steaks, medium rare, Caesar salads and a blooming onion and boneless buffalo wings as appetizers.

"Do you want anything to drink?" I asked after I finished ordering for us.

"This is fine for now." She picked up her water and took a sip, waiting until the waitress was out of range. "I'm capable of ordering for myself," she said.

"I know, but I figured it would save time. Unless you were going to change your mind again?"

She smirked and shook her head. "The fact that's what I was going to order is neither here nor there."

"Okay. From now on, I'll let you order for yourself."

"Thank you," she dipped her head in acknowledgement.

"Now, back to the original conversation. You think I can't keep my hands off you?" I leaned back in the seat and crossed my arms. The smirk was back, and then she slowly shook her head. Well, okay, maybe she was right, but I'd play this game out. I leaned my elbows on the table.

"Game on, baby." I smiled.

The smirk morphed into a grin and that gleam returned to her eyes. I could tell this was going to be a hell of a difficult game to win, but I vowed any time I got the urge to jump her, I'd double-check the underlying reasons, and if Sandy entered my mind in any way, I'd back off.

"So, you were muttering about being behind in your schoolwork last night. What's involved in becoming a doctor, beyond gross anatomy?"

I swear that statement opened Pandora's box. She perked up and started enlightening me about her classes, her challenges, the gross things she's experienced, and while I could almost picture each instance she told me about, the memories didn't do them justice the way she described things. Dinner came and went and when the check was placed on the table, I ignored it, enjoying really laughing again.

I didn't realize how long it had been since I'd laughed with someone instead of laughing out of necessity or sarcasm. It was refreshing as hell.

*

Angel Grace Chapter 16

"**Y**OU THINK EVERYTHING AT home is okay?" Valerie asked, as I opened the car door for her.

The light mood fizzled at the reminder of the darkness that shrouded our lives, and I glanced at the dark sky. "No one called, so that's a good sign." I closed the door and scanned the parking lot before I slid into the driver's seat.

Instead of starting the car, I sat contemplating if I could do what Steve did, now that I had the rest of the mojo fused in my blood.

"Try it," she whispered.

I sighed, tempted. "Here isn't the place." I turned the car on and headed home. "I'll try at home." I didn't need to explain why. Just the darkening of my mood was enough.

The question of whether we would ever be able to truly relax and enjoy life settled into my bones. "There's got to be a way to get hell's legions to back the fuck off."

She burst out laughing. "I'm not sure that's possible."

Unfortunately, I agreed with her. I had too much information downloaded into my brain and just couldn't abide by some mutants and monsters that existed. Suddenly, what I really wanted to do with my life overwhelmed me. Instead of sitting by waiting to be attacked, it was my turn to hunt those motherfuckers and put them down.

"I think I should take up hunting." I glanced at Valerie and her eyes widened.

"You can't…"

"Yeah, I can. Damian ran all his life. Look what that got him. It wasn't until he fought back that he won. It wasn't the martyrdom that broke the cycle, it was the attack." I refocused on the road. "I'm better suited to attack than look over my shoulder for the rest of my life."

"Are you out of your fucking mind?" Valerie spouted at my epiphany.

"Seriously, think about it. Everything so far has been defensive maneuvering. It's time to gear up and go on the offensive. Make the monsters run from us for a change."

"Why? Why would you put yourself in that kind of situation?"

I knew she'd had run-ins with some pretty evil assholes, and almost didn't live to tell about it, but she didn't see the beauty in the solution, nor did she get the real reason behind my epiphany. "Someone has to save those kids from a life of running and fear." I refocused on the road in front of me, stopping at the next set of lights. "If Damian isn't prepared to do it, I certainly am."

"Why would you risk your life for someone else's children?"

She really didn't get the scope of what would happen to our world if Lucifer got his hands on Damian's little girl. "Because saving Grace from Lucifer should be a priority for all of us."

"And the boys?"

"Lucifer can't build an army of trinities with them. At least not an army of his offspring, one that he can control. Naomi's at risk too, but I have a feeling if he ever got hold of her, she'd destroy herself before she let him use her for his evil spawn. Besides, there's something special about Grace. Something compelling that makes me want to put my life on the line for her." I bit my lip and turned onto the highway, trying to pinpoint what made the child stand out more than the other two. "It's much more than just the consequences of Lucifer getting his slimy hands on her. It's something deeper." I glanced at Valerie. "You and Naomi have a hint of the same power, albeit much less intense."

"You think it might be our angelic bloodline?"

"Maybe, but I don't feel the same compulsion to protect Damian."

We drove in silence over the Piscataqua River Bridge into Maine. "I'm not sure if it was Damian's innocence or Naomi's specialness, for lack of a more appropriate word, which drove Steve to take a stand with them." *Or if it was just his sense of justice, combined with his untainted moral compass that drove it.*

"Why did you?"

"I wasn't going to let Steve stand alone against what was coming. He's family."

"Damian's my family," she said under her breath.

The last thing I wanted was another Sandy situation, even if it only involved a friend. "I guess that means we'll have to call a truce, then."

Valerie's hand slid over mine and gave a little squeeze and I traded a glance with her and then looked down at my hand covered with hers. She removed her hand, and the absence of her flesh against mine made me sigh. Shutting off access to my thoughts, I stared at the road ahead of me, wondering how in the world I was going to continue playing this game when any time our skin touched it sparked a fire in my soul.

Angel Grace Chapter 17

THE HOUSE WAS DARK when we pulled in and Damian's van was gone, along with Steve's truck, and I slowed to a stop in front of Tom's car. Valerie and I exchanged a glance, and she reached for the door. I grabbed her arm.

"Not yet," I said and pulled my phone out of my pocket and dialed. Holding the phone to my ear, I waited, feeling the unease snake into my skin. The call dropped to voicemail, and I ended the call, trying another line.

"Hello?" Raven's Irish brogue came through the line, and I exhaled.

"Hey Raven, where is everyone?"

"You aren't the only one who can decide to grab a fine dinner out on the town," she said over the background noise.

"So, nothing weird happened at the house?"

"No. We let Damian and Naomi experience Wild Willy's while it's slow."

I let out a laugh. "Wild Willy's is never slow."

She laughed too. "I know, right? Anyhow, we're just getting ready to head out."

"Okay, see you in a few."

I folded the phone. "They went out to eat."

"I heard," Valerie said, and we both stepped out of the car.

The chill tonight wasn't as biting as it had been the past few nights, and I hoped that meant spring wasn't far off. I waited on my side of the car for her to join me before heading toward the front door. Halfway down the path, my intuition prickled, and instead of running from whatever stalker had invaded our property, I stopped and mentally told Valerie to stop as well. Taking a moment, I glanced at her and willed the protective bubble around both of us.

We both turned, slowly enough for me to get a whiff of her perfume, the sweet scent grounding me and reminding me I wasn't the only one facing off against whatever it was. When we faced the approaching beast, Valerie threaded her fingers through mine, pulling my attention to our hands and then her eyes. I smiled and gently squeezed her hand, giving her the strength to not scream at the sight before us.

The rabid vampire bear stood on its hind legs and roared. This wasn't a human I could intimidate, nor was it a demon or vampire that had a sense of reason. This was a killing machine, and it was hungry.

I let out a snarling roar of my own, wishing the beast into dust. A swirl of fire engulfed the beast like a destructive tornado until all that was left was fine gray ash.

"Impressive," Valerie said.

The protective field still encompassed us, and I turned toward the house, flipping my phone open again and redialing, keeping Valerie by my side.

"Raven, everyone is with you, right?"

"Yes, we didn't want to leave anyone at home alone."

"Good call." I folded the phone and closed my eyes. "Can you smell them?" I whispered, as my nostrils filled with a foul mixture of brimstone and blood. Her hand tightened on mine, and I opened my eyes, focusing on the downstairs window and the grin that met my gaze.

I pointed. "Come here."

His smile fell into shock as his body stepped into sight.

"What are you doing?"

"Leaving one alive." I glanced at her and when the door opened. I inhaled, putting a duplicate layer of protection around the fiend stepping out of our house. And then I let loose, killing every non-living, pseudo-living and live being from our property line to the ocean breakers at the bottom of the small cliff outside the rock wall. Mini-fire tornados engulfed flesh, leaving the physical property intact as if nothing happened. The only hint of destruction was the gray dust raining to the ground.

The lone demon standing on the stoop stared at me, his face paling, and the first hint of fear gripped his eyes. I released control of his physical form and the protective cocoon around him.

"Let your friends know that I'm coming after them," I said.

He waved his hand and the spark of contact hit our protective barrier. I think he thought he could toss me around like a rag doll, but I was truly supercharged. In kind, I waved my hand toward the gate, tossing him halfway across the lawn. He scrambled to his feet with the front of his jeans now soaked with piss.

"And whoever has the gall to step on this property will end up being roasted alive. Understand?"

The demon nodded, turned tail, and ran out the open gate. I turned back to Valerie with a smirk dancing on my lips.

"You should have torched him as well."

The venom in her tone pulled my gaze to her, and my heart dropped into my stomach. I searched the collective memory banks for some redemption, and there was none. Demon red eyes peered out from Valerie's beautiful face, and I dropped her hand, stepping away.

She had been right next to me all night. And then it occurred to me. She had gotten up and gone to the bathroom. The thing possessing Valerie opened the blazer, showing me the bloodied shirt covering her right side.

"The bitch passed out, and I took over."

I couldn't destroy her, but I could contain her, and I created a force field box around her. One that would stun but not kill the body this prick inhabited.

"Inside," I said, pointing to the opened door. I blocked my thoughts, focusing on the blood, wondering if this shit knew she had the power to heal. My chest hurt as I forced her across to the chair at the head of the table, tying her arms to the hand guards and her legs to the legs of the chair.

I backed into the wall across from her, forcing my breath in and out, keeping the need to scream and tear my hair out at bay.

"I'll let her go if you'll be a dear and let me in," it said.

I covered my mouth, wondering what the hell Damian was going to do. He destroyed the last demon nest without a thought, but this was Valerie. The girl he saw grow from an infant to the beautiful woman before me.

I regained my composure and stalked right up to her. "Get out of her, you bastard," I growled, but I didn't know the first thing about exorcism. I knew if I could get the shit out of her, then she had more of a chance of survival than anyone on earth. Hell, she might be unconsciously mending as I stood and stared.

The door opened, and the family filtered in, chatting away until the tiger growled. Naomi stepped around the car seat she had the presence of mind to put down before she changed, and Damian's gaping stare met mine.

"She went to the ladies' room right before we left," I said. "I... I didn't know. When I got here, the house was infiltrated, and I destroyed all but one. Well, two." I waved at Valerie. "And after the last one ran with his tail between his legs, this one..." I ran my hand through my hair. "That was when this one made its presence known."

Naomi hissed, pacing a trail blocking Valerie from her children.

I met Tom's gaze and signed for him to take Jen, Steve and Raven upstairs along with the babies. He nodded, and Damian didn't stop them when they disappeared upstairs.

"I couldn't..." I said after everyone else left. Damian's thoughts were sporadic and stinted. He collapsed on the closest ottoman and glanced at the broken lines of salt all over the house. His jaw tightened, and he got up, crossing into the kitchen and disappeared with the salt container. When he came back, he fixed the last three entry points and drew a line across the lowest stair. The last grains fell, and he chucked it across the house, roaring with the same frustration that pounded my muscles.

He grabbed another container and circled the chair. Slamming the container on the table before coming even with me. His shoulder faced me and then his hand shot out, clamping around my throat as he slammed me against the wall. Fury lined his face and Naomi rubbed against his leg, trying to calm the wild beast raging inside him.

I didn't fight back. Whatever he did to me, I deserved it. I was supposed to protect her, and I failed in epic fashion.

His grip loosened and his chin dropped to his chest.

"Don't," I whispered as the power coiled into a tight ball inside him.

"I have to."

"No. You don't. Valerie is still in there. You can't kill her."

He shook his head. "She's not."

"What if it was Naomi," I said and the muscles in his jaw jumped. "There has to be a way."

"She's already dead."

"No. She just passed out, and that gave that thing an opportunity to get in."

"But," he started.

"I don't have everything," I whispered, and his eyes narrowed. His grip loosened more, and he finally dropped his hand as understanding dawned in his eyes. "But I don't know the first thing about exorcism."

"Neither do I," he said.

Naomi continued to pace in agitation.

"You may not know about such things, but I have a potent banishment spell we can try."

Both Damian and I turned toward the stairs where Raven stood, leaning on the railing, her squinting gaze meeting mine and averting Damian's blinding aura.

"Bullshit," Damian said.

Valerie cackled from the seat, her gaze bouncing around the room from the aggravated tiger to Damian and me, and finally landing on Raven. "Your pathetic spells won't work on me," she said, her voice transitioning between demon and Valerie's in an eerie stereo quality.

Raven flipped her hair back with her hand and gave the demon inside Valerie the evil eye. "You'd be surprised at what my spells can achieve," she said and turned, heading upstairs to gather what she needed.

"If this doesn't work, I'm flying her out to the middle of the Atlantic and leaving her there," Damian said.

I couldn't help staring at him, and then I said two words that made Valerie pale.

"Salt water."

Damian nodded, and I closed my eyes, hanging my head. If he did that, hypothermia would kill her before she had a chance to do anything else. There were limitations to the healing power, and while I liked to think what gifts we had made us invincible. The reality was we still had vulnerabilities. A surprise shot to the heart would kill us, same with a bullet in the brain. Our human frailties existed, and there are some people and things that could get the drop on us no matter how diligent we were. Valerie could heal her wound, but the cold water would stop her heart.

I pulled up a chair next to the bound demon and sighed, nodding to Damian.

If what Raven cooked up, didn't work, Valerie would have to be sacrificed.

Angel Grace Chapter 18

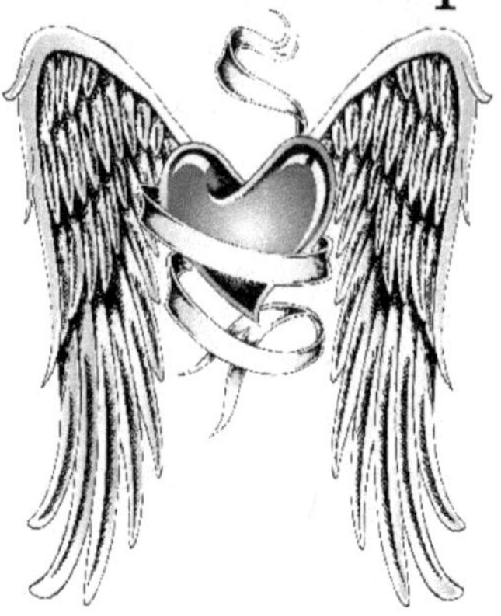

RAVEN CAME DOWN WITH a duffel bag and set it on the table, turning towards Damian and the wild tiger.

"Please, take everyone but Valerie, CJ and me, somewhere while I do this."

A hand banged on the railing, pulling our attention to the stairs. Tom shook his head and pointed to his chest and then the floor, conveying his stance without the flurry of sign language.

"No. I..."

Tom put his palm out, stopping her. I knew that stubborn set of his jaw. There was no way he was leaving her if there was any hint of danger. Besides, his ability to see and even intercept spirits might come in handy.

"Fine," she said and turned back to Damian. "Take Steve, Jen and your wife and kids and go."

"I don't..." Damian started, and Naomi hissed again, this time at him.

He hesitated, and Raven stared him down. "The fewer people here, the better."

There was something more to the warning. She was concerned about the children. About the demon taking over one of their impressionable minds and Damian blanched when Raven's thoughts broadcast her concerns. He nodded, turning and bolting up the stairs.

A few minutes later, he came down with Jennifer and Steve, each carrying a car seat and a diaper bag.

"Keep us informed," he said and opened the garage door, letting Naomi take the lead.

Raven waited until the lights disappeared and the gate closed, locking us in. Then she turned, looking between Tom and me. "Are you two ready for a storm?"

Tom nodded without hesitation, and I followed suit. I was ready to brave a hurricane to save Valerie.

Raven started unpacking the duffel bag, setting jewelry, and what looked like fancy paperweights, on the table along with candles and oils and a big sea-salt grinder. She turned and tossed a necklace to me. The black wiccan star reflected in the light, and I raised an eyebrow.

"Just put it on," she said and looked from me to Tom. "Do you have yours on?"

Tom unbuttoned his shirt, showing her the necklace she gave him back in high school for protection against a crazy ghost. It worked back then, and I don't think he'd taken it off since.

I slipped it around my neck and waited while she finished setting up the table. Raven turned and walked into the living room, away from the demon, beckoning to us to follow.

"Block your thoughts," she said.

I consciously put up the wall in my head and nodded, glancing at Tom and then Raven where only static resided. "We're blocked," I said.

She looked at Tom. "The only reason I let you stay is because I may need your special skills."

He started to sign, but she shook her head, stopping him.

"You told me you once put your father's spirit back in his body."

Tom nodded and glanced at me.

"Well, I might need you to do that with Valerie. Okay?"

"Okay," Tom signed.

Raven turned to me. "Do you think your protective shield can repel demon spirits?"

I shrugged. "I don't know."

"Well, let's hope that's the case, because the moment the spirits separate from her physical form and Tom has Valerie's, I'll need you to block anything else from getting to her. Or us, for that matter. She'll still be vulnerable until her spirit is put back in her body. If we fail and the demon gets in there first, she will be lost to us. Understand?"

The layer of doubt that blanketed me must have reflected in my eyes, because Raven's face hardened.

"Understand?" she said, more forcefully this time.

"Yes. I understand," I said. "How do you know this will work?"

"I've seen it done before," she whispered. "But we didn't have the benefit of a ghost whisperer or a psychic shield."

"Did it work?"

She stared at me for a long moment and then shook her head. "No."

"What happened?" I asked, unable to get the details from her mind.

"My father happened," she said and turned away, storming back to the kitchen, leaving Tom and me staring at each other. A chill settled over me and I looked toward the kitchen. Her father was rotting in jail for two consecutive life sentences for the crimes he committed as the Windwalker.

"What do you mean?" I stalked into the kitchen after her, with Tom following.

"We can discuss that later. You know what I expect of you." She turned back to the table and Valerie chuckled. The demon quality of it left me cold.

"I want Val back," I growled at the thing holding her hostage.

"Maybe we can trade?" it said, raising one of her manicured eyebrows.

"As tempting as that sounds, I think I'll see what Raven can do with you first."

A shadow passed over her face and her teeth clenched as she focused on Raven's array of potions and precious rocks on the table.

Raven turned to me. "Can you hold her still for a minute?"

I nodded and wrapped a mental straight jacket around Valerie's body. The demon roared and tried to thrash, but the physical form it inhabited wouldn't budge under my power. The beast within Valerie roared when Raven slipped a bloodstone necklace over her head. The red jewel rested on her chest, right above her heart and the skin under it singed, sending off a waft of steam.

Raven stepped out of the salt ring, visibly shaken by the scorching skin. She glanced at Tom, and he gave her a nod of encouragement. With a deep breath, she arranged four pyramid shaped stones at the north, south, east and west spots inside the circle and stepped back.

In the teak bowl, she mixed salt, some fine black powder and added a drop of green, red, and yellow potions to the mixture. Raven paused and glanced at me, waving me forward. I stepped to her side, and she took my hand. With no explanation, she raked a knife across my palm.

"Squeeze," she said, holding my hand over the mixture.

As bizarre as it sounded, I did what she said and after three drops of blood hit the mixture; she moved my hand away and gave me some sterile gauze. I wrapped the cut and stepped away as she mixed the cocktail and muttered an incantation.

"Mháthair a chara, cruthaitheoir go léir, cabhrú liom banish an Demon as an cailín. Cabhraigh léi a fháil ar ais ar a anam. Dhíbirt an olc as a corp. Cabhraigh léi a fháil ar ais ar a anam. Demon a bheith imithe!"

The mixture bubbled and sizzled, and she turned toward Valerie.

"Repeat after me, boys," Raven said as Valerie started thrashing in the chair. "Spiorad olc saoire an gcomhlacht seo. Demon a bheith imithe!"

Tom and I repeated the foreign chant. "Spiorad olc saoire an gcomhlacht seo. Demon a bheith imithe!"

Raven flung a spoonful of the mix at Valerie and the scream that followed tore at my soul.

When Valerie looked at me and whispered, "Help me." I nearly came undone, but the darkness that flashed over her eyes told me it was a demon trick and not the girl I was willing to lay my life down for.

"Again," Raven ordered and moved to Valerie's side.

We repeated the chant and Raven flung another spoonful at Valerie. This time, the mixture produced scorching welts in her skin, and I stepped towards Raven to stop her from scalding Valerie again, but Tom grabbed my arm and opened his mind. What I saw stopped me. The struggle of souls coming from her writhing form gave me hope and when Raven ordered us to speak the incantation again, I didn't hesitate.

The third time brought forth a wail of pain that made me want to cover my ears. The earth around us rumbled to the point the jars on the counter rattled. The dishes in the cabinets shifted, knocking open cabinet doors and sending plates and glasses crashing to the counter. Even the refrigerator door opened, crashing contents to the floor in a mad swirl.

The fourth time, Tom let go of my arm and stepped forward, grabbing onto something I couldn't see, but his command of "Now" in my head along with the vision of what he held set me in motion and I directed a capsule of protection around the four of us.

Tom took the invisible ghost in his arms and slammed it back into Valerie's body. The melding of spirit to skin arched her back, and she took a deep wheezing breath. Her eyes locked on mine, and she moaned in pain. I glanced at the bloody wound on her side and then back at her.

"Will yourself to heal," I whispered, and her eyes widened and then dropped closed. She sagged in the chair, and I kneeled next to her, untying her arms and legs that had held her in place.

The surrounding air sparked, and Tom glanced up. A black cloud attacked my shield, trying to get back into the body it had been expelled from, and I looked up, using Tom's vision to direct me. With all the anger burning my skin, I sent my wrath toward the demon, willing it to burn. Flames licked the protective bubble and blackened the ceiling and then an explosion rocked the kitchen, blowing the window over the sink open and obliterating the salt line protecting that exit. What was left of the demon spirit fled through that portal, sending a plume of black smoke out into the yard and into the night sky.

Silence fell over us and Tom stepped out of the circle toward the banging window and closed it, replacing the salt line before he turned back to us.

"Is it gone?" I asked, knowing deep down it was, but I didn't trust my instincts right now. They were too colored by my worry for Valerie.

"Yah," Tom said.

I relaxed, sending the protective bubble around the house in case another barrage of creatures attacked.

"Give Steve a call and tell them they can come back," I said to Raven. "And have them call when they get to the gate," I added as I picked Valerie up and brought her to the couch. The scald burns had already faded, and I lifted the hem of her shirt, watching as the stab wound mended.

"It's done. I'll explain when you get home," Raven said into her phone and then pocketed it. She and Tom started the onerous task of cleaning up the mess the demon created.

"Why my blood?" I asked, and Raven turned toward me.

"Only love's blood works," she said and offered me a fleeting smile before continuing to sweep up the glass covering the kitchen floor.

I stared at the blood-soaked bandage around my hand and then at Valerie. I knew I'd die for her, but love? Really? The rational side of my brain scoffed, and I wiped the hair out of her face, ignoring the pounding of my heart and the relief saturating my muscles. Instead, I retrieved a wet washcloth and gently began wiping the blood from her now unmarred side.

Her eyes fluttered open, and she met my gaze.

"Hey," I whispered, and continued cleaning the evidence from her skin.

She pressed her lips together and covered her mouth with the back of her hand. Tears immediately sprang from her eyes, and she focused on the ceiling. Her entire form shook, and I dropped the cloth and pulled her into my arms. She clung to me, trembling and sobbing at the horrors she experienced during the demon possession.

"I killed..." she whispered in my ear.

"No, you didn't," I said, pulling away and wiping her face.

"The waitress. The one who stabbed me. I... I..." she trailed off and swallowed. "I saw everything," she added. "Oh, God, Chris. If you had tried that thing in the car..." she shuddered. "I was so terrified you were going to and kept screaming for you not to. If you had, it would have gotten you. It would have stolen your body."

I smiled and smoothed her hair back. "Well, then, it's a good thing I didn't try now, isn't it?"

Her chin quivered, and she nodded, throwing her arms around me, and burying her face in my neck. I rubbed her back and cooed "shhh" as she started crying again. The phone rang and Tom picked it up, muttering hello in his unintelligible way. I traded a glance with him, and he gave the thumbs up. Concentrating, I opened a gate in my protective barrier until I heard the car pull into the garage and then the opening slammed closed.

Damian charged in the house with Naomi running after him in human form. His gaze jumped from the destroyed kitchen to the couch where I held Valerie and he stopped. Naomi bumped into him with one of the boy's car seat on her arm.

Steve and Jennifer stepped into the house behind them and closed the garage door. The babies were relinquished to their parents and Jennifer stared at the damage, crossing to the kitchen with her mouth drawn in a frown. I couldn't help but laugh. Jennifer and the kitchen were fleeting connections. She couldn't cook worth a damn, and I would have expected Steve to be more distraught.

"What…" Jennifer said and waved toward the glass speckled counters and the swept piles of debris.

"It could have been worse," I said. "The demon could have blown up your stove."

Jennifer's head snapped in my direction. As soon as my words sank in, her face transformed into a smile, followed by a small giggling laugh. Being privy to the joke, Steve, Tom and Raven joined her.

Yeah, leave it to me to crack up the crowd.

Damian was not at all amused, but I guess he wouldn't be. He never had to endure anything Jennifer cooked. Valerie pulled away from my chest and wiped her face before turning toward him.

"You're really okay?" he asked, taking a tentative step towards us.

"Yes. Raven has quite the talent for banishing demons," she said.

"Oh, that reminds me," Raven said and propped the broom against the wall. She rifled through the duffel bag, pulling out four more pendants. She crossed, handing one to each of the adults, and then her gaze fell on the children.

"I think I might actually have something to protect them as well," she said and marched back to her bag of tricks. She dug around in the bag and pulled a little pouch out.

We all watched as she pulled out half a dozen crocheted bracelets with gems embedded in the designs. She peeled off three of the smallest ones and crossed to the babies, tying the bracelet on each ankle for a loose fit that wouldn't slide off.

"That will do for a while," she said, looking up at us.

"What are these?" Naomi asked, turning her pendant over.

"They're tourmaline pendants. They'll protect you from evil spirits," Raven said and crossed back to the kitchen. Instead of grabbing the broom, she went to the table and started packing up her bag of tricks.

"They work," Tom signed.

He knew firsthand, but a ghost was much different from a demon and I wasn't sure it would protect us from a demon attack the way it did with Tom and his crazy ghost.

"I know they work on ghosts, but..."

Raven snapped her gaze to mine and stopped packing. "It wards off evil."

"So, I can take down the protective barrier?" I waved towards the roof and her gaze jumped from me to the outside and back. Hesitation colored her face, but eventually she nodded.

"If you want to test the theory, be my guest."

I most certainly did not want to put my family at risk, so I left the barrier in place.

Damian studied his pendant and then let it drop to his chest. "I've seen a couple of these along my travels, but it does nothing to deter a hungry vampire," he said, bringing the point home. "I'm not sure about demons," he added with a shrug.

Raven waved toward Valerie. "It certainly helped her," she said and zipped up her bag, lugging it back upstairs.

I couldn't argue with that, although I think it was the entire ritual that helped, not just the necklace. Valerie turned toward me, and her gaze dropped to my hand.

"I think this was the magic ingredient," she whispered and brought my palm to her lips.

I clamped my teeth together, offering a tight smile as the healing pain took hold.

Angel Grace Chapter 19

THE HOUSE WAS QUIET, and I glanced at the clock on the wall. It was only three in the morning and I was exhausted. Despite that, I forced my eyes to remain open and the force field outside to stay intact. It was only a few more hours until dawn and then I could let my guard down.

The stair creaked, and I rolled onto my side, meeting Valerie's gaze.

"I couldn't sleep," she said.

I wished that was my problem. I was having a hard time staying awake. I just sent a smile in her direction instead of voicing my thoughts.

"Are you okay?" I sat up as she approached, making space for her on the couch.

"Not really." She plunked down next to me and wrapped her arms around my arm, using my shoulder as a headrest. "Thank you."

"Why are you thanking me?"

"Because if you hadn't convinced Damian to give Raven's mojo a try, I'd be dead right now."

I remained silent and covered her hand with mine. "I didn't do it for you," I said after a few minutes of soul searching. "It was a matter of self-preservation."

She lifted her head and looked at me. "What do you mean?"

I let out a small laugh. "I was responsible for that demon getting to you. If I didn't try, and I had let Damian take you out to sea..." I pulled out of her grip and slid out from under the covers. The moonlight danced on the water outside and I stared at the hypnotizing patters the waves made before continuing. "If I let you die without trying to save you, I would have lost faith in winning this war."

She joined me at the window, wrapping her arms around my waist from behind. "You wouldn't have given up," she whispered in my ear.

I focused on the reflection in the window, on her calico eyes. She didn't know how close to the edge I really was. "Babe, I'm a disaster away from falling apart."

The admission raked its weak nails across my skin, leaving a gradual burn that turned in my stomach. I didn't like being on the edge. It was not a comfortable place for me and my volatile gifts.

She reached out, cupping my cheek, and turned my head towards her. I met her gaze and shifted to face her. "No, you're not," she said and pulled me to her lips before I could correct her.

Time stopped, and I think I stopped breathing with it. Her kiss captivated me like nothing else ever had. Her hands slid from around my neck, down my chest, and around my waist. Just the feel of her fingertips on my skin lit a fire inside me and the t-shirt she wore wasn't enough to save her from the need ripping through me.

It was animalistic and fierce, and I tore the fabric from her body in a fit of uncontrollable lust. I maneuvered her past the couch and up the stairs, our lips only parting in order to take a breath. Before I knew it, I was on top of her on my bed with my hands caressing her breasts and my mouth savoring her hard nipples. She clutched a fistful of my hair and pulled me back to her lips.

I shifted and traced the lines of her stomach down to her underwear, smiling at the sudden appearance of goose bumps all over her flesh. The thin fabric between her legs was damp, and I broke the kiss, moving down her body, teasing her with my tongue.

Valerie made a sweet noise of surrender when I pressed my mouth to her underwear, blowing a breath through the fabric. I didn't wait for acknowledgement, instead; I ripped the underwear from her body and tossed it to the floor.

She followed the progression of the ruined fabric and then looked at me. "I just bought those," she whispered.

"So?" I said and pushed her thighs apart. The moment my tongue parted her, I think all her thoughts and retorts disappeared. She sighed and twirled a lock of my hair in her fingers, enjoying the spoils of my mouth. I gently slid my finger inside her, and she moaned softly, further fueling the fire inside me.

I tapped into her mind, reading the things that she liked and those that were 'eh'. She wanted more, more of me, and I followed her desires, bringing her over the brink more than once before I worked my way back up to her mouth.

The urge to tear off my shorts and fuck the daylights out of her took hold, but I resisted. Valerie shifted, pushing me onto my back and then she broke the kiss, traveling down my body with her lips, teasing me in a way I never knew existed.

She pulled my shorts to my knees, and I propped up on my elbows. "Val," I warned, and then her mouth swallowed the tip of my cock and I forgot all about my warning. Instead, I watched her suck and lick and swallow me whole. She was fucking fantastic.

She shifted again, and I smiled when she planted her knees on either side of my head. She might be a virgin, but damned if she didn't know the art of oral sex. I pulled her toward me and fucked her with my tongue and fingers, making her moan around my cock. She came again and again, and I forced myself to hold off, to prolong the heaven that was her mouth. Each stroke of her lips brought me closer to my climax and, finally, I let go.

My entire body went rigid with the power of it, and I sucked her harder, groaning against her soaking pussy. Valerie didn't pull away; instead, she swallowed, gently sucking until I said okay.

She shuffled into the crook of my arm, and we stared at the ceiling, unable to speak. Hell, I have no idea how she could move, because I certainly couldn't right now.

"That was fucking brilliant," she whispered.

I couldn't help it. I laughed. "Brilliant?" I turned my head toward her.

She grinned. "Fucking brilliant."

I had never been referred to as fucking brilliant in bed, but then again, I really only had Sandy as a reference and nothing we ever did compared to this.

"You were fucking brilliant," I smiled.

"I'm not sure about that." Her cheeks turned crimson, almost glowing in the darkness.

"This surpasses anything I've experienced to date. You were fucking brilliant." I leaned towards her and grabbed a kiss.

"So, I'm better than a houseful of demons?" she teased.

"Worlds," I said. "Even without the bondage."

She covered the laughter with her hand, stifling the sound. I chuckled softly, wondering just how mind blowing that would be. The only thing more satisfying than what I just experienced would be making love to the girl. My smile faltered, and I stared at the ceiling again as the thoughts stirred me back to life.

I started to slide out from under her before I did something she didn't want, and she pushed me back down.

"Don't go."

"Val, hon, if I stay, I'm going to pin you to this bed and..." I inhaled and went to sit up. This time, she pushed me down and swung her leg over me, coming up into a straddle position. I stared into her eyes, the swirling pattern as hypnotizing as the ocean's moon dance.

"Val," I said, again, as her hips slowly swirled, grinding me back to life. "Ah, fuck, Val," I whispered and pulled her to my lips.

The sweetness of sliding inside her overwhelmed me and she winced, stiffening for a moment before settling down on top of me. She met my gaze and offered a forced smile and I put my hands on her thighs, holding her in place.

"Relax," I said, and little by little, she did.

She started with slow hip grinding circles, and I moved my thumb to her clit, circling lightly enough for her to forget the pain. I let her set the pace, keeping eye contact with her through it all, and prayed she wouldn't regret this in the morning light.

She smiled down at me, rolling her hips in circles in time with my thumb.

"You like that?" I asked, raising an eyebrow.

"Yes." The breathless quality of her voice reached into my heart, taking another piece of it with her.

Valerie started sliding herself up and down my shaft in concert with her hip twirls, and I thought I had died and gone to heaven. She was hot and wet and so fucking tight. I wanted to flip over and take control, but I didn't want to hurt her again, and I was sure my control meant complete loss of such, so I let her get off with the slow ride.

I gripped her hips, moving her a little faster, until I felt the buildup start. She arched into me, covering her own moan with her hand as she contracted, squeezing the cum right out of me. She shuddered, twirled her hips a couple of more times and collapsed on top of me while my body trembled with aftershocks.

"Holy Christ," she whispered in my ear, and I wrapped my arms around her, planting a kiss on her cheek.

"Complete and utter mind fuck," I said, and she pushed away, meeting my gaze.

She didn't understand what I meant, and the hurt in her eyes made me sigh.

"I'm now sure," I said.

"About what?"

"You are *not* a rebound."

Her head tilted.

"Everything before you was."

Her hands fluttered to her mouth and her eyes filled with tears. Valerie's mind was open enough for me to know they weren't tears of sadness. I'd touched her in a way she had never felt before.

So, we were pretty much even in that respect.

Angel Grace Chapter 20

SUNSHINE STREAKED THROUGH THE room, and I blinked, wiping the sleep from my eyes, and looked down at the head of brown hair resting on my chest. I turned toward the clock and stared at the numbers as they changed from 12:59 to 1:00.

"Shit," I whispered and tried to shuffle out from under her, but my arm was dead weight, sound asleep underneath Valerie. "Val," I whispered, and she stirred, lifting her head. She stared at me and then at us, still naked and entwined and then back at me, with arched eyebrows.

"Yeah, it wasn't a dream." I grinned.

"Holy crap." She moved her gaze to the clock. I sensed the panic and when her gaze came back to mine, it was there. Thoughts of what Damian would do surfaced in her mind and then on the heels of that. She looked down at me and covered her mouth.

My smile faded. We didn't use protection. It never even entered my mind last night; or hers, for that matter. I blinked and slammed my head back into the pillow. Pregnancy was a complication neither of us needed right now.

"I'm sorry." I tucked the hair behind her ear.

"It's not entirely your fault. I didn't think of it either." She dropped her head to my chest.

"Still think it was fucking brilliant?"

She looked up at me and grinned. "A complete mind fuck."

I chuckled, and she did too.

"Utterly impractical of both of us." Dimples appeared in her cheeks. "Who would have thought?"

"Raven, actually," I said, thinking about the blood sacrifice needed for the spell. "She knew I loved you before I did."

Valerie pulled the sheets around us before refocusing on me. "How?"

"Beats the shit out of me, but she said only love's blood made the spell work."

"Sounds like a fairy tale," she scoffed and rolled her eyes.

"Yes, it does," I said, and I really didn't mind as long as the fairy tale had a happy ending.

Her brow creased. "That's sappy as hell," she said to my train of thought.

"Come on. And you don't want a happy ending?" I prodded.

She stared at me and then moved her gaze to the window and the bright sky beyond. "I didn't think I was destined for it, with all that's happened." When she brought her gaze back to mine, doubt laced them.

"And now?"

"I'm still afraid of the big bad wolf." She offered a hint of a smile. "We need to get moving." She slid off me, crossing to the bags on the floor.

I stared at her beautiful form and sighed as she pulled on a bathrobe and collected her clothing and headed toward the bathroom, leaving me alone with my thoughts.

I rolled onto my side, squeezing my fist open and closed as pins and needles struck. I hated the feeling of a limb coming back to life. and gritted my teeth, shaking the feeling back into my arm. I rolled out of bed and grabbed a pair of clean underwear and jeans, sliding both on before straightening out the bed and headed downstairs.

Steve sat in his chair with the paper again, but this time, he folded the corner over and stared at me. I didn't need to read minds to get that he was not pleased with me. Damian stepped into the kitchen from the living room with a baby in his arms. The look on his face was ten times more damning than Steve's.

"We're both adults," I said, clamping down on the urge to say she started it. I put my hand out to stop whatever wrath the ex-vampire was planning on sending my way.

Raven sat at the table opposite Naomi, feeding the other two children. Both women wore the same "I told you so" shit-eating grins.

"Under my roof?" Steve said, and I shot a glare in his direction. It was enough to shut him up, but he folded the paper and set it down on the table next to her shredded night shirt. He picked it up and held it out to me.

I stared at the ripped fabric and uttered a laugh. "Oops," I said and shrugged. Tom snorted laughter from the loveseat, looking up from the book he was reading, and gave me a silent high five.

"You..." Damian began through a set of clamped teeth.

"He loves her," Raven said, announcing my secret to the world and diffusing a potentially explosive situation. Well, the only world of people that counted, anyway.

I shifted and looked at the floor, sliding my gaze to hers, and then rolled my eyes and crossed into the kitchen. I figured I was safe from Damian's wrath while he held a baby in his arms.

"You're not out of the doghouse yet," he whispered as I walked past and I stopped, turning on him.

"We can take it outside again if you'd like," I said, leveling a glare at him. "Because that worked out so well for you before."

His jaw tightened, and he turned, stomping back into the living room. I smiled and grabbed a glass of orange juice, thinking about how I would feel had the tables been turned. My smile faded and because the jackass meant a lot to Valerie, I headed into the living room and took a seat opposite Damian.

"When did you know you loved Naomi?" I asked, and he glared at me. I knew the answer, but I wanted him to say it.

"When I bit her," he finally said.

"So pretty much at first taste."

His lips pressed into a thin line, and his gaze hardened. "It wasn't the same as seducing a virgin," he growled.

"Oh?" My eyebrows shot up, and I leaned forward. "Wasn't she a virgin when you swept her away?" I didn't think it was possible for the man to get redder, but his face transitioned to the beet color of fury, and I felt the waves wash over me. "Besides, *I* didn't just take her virginity in the heat of the moment." I tilted my head, making my point.

"That still doesn't make it right. You took advantage..." he trailed off, glaring at me a second before his gaze moved to the entry.

Valerie stood with her arms crossed, sending her own glare. But this time it wasn't aimed at me.

"He really didn't have a choice in the matter," she said and stepped into the room.

It wasn't entirely true; I probably could have stopped if I wanted to.

She shot her loaded gaze in my direction, raising her eyebrows in jest, to my train of thought. I offered a one shoulder shrug and then she shot her dagger-like eyes back to Damian. "So, if you're going to go on one of your tirades, it better damned well be directed at me, not him."

Holy hotness, she was a fireball, and I couldn't help but smile and be thankful her fury wasn't aimed at me.

"Besides, he was the one who bet on me. You were ready to write me off."

Ah, the real reason for her wrath, and I leaned back in my chair watching the show unfold, wondering if it was going to be a comedy or tragedy.

My analogy drew a smirk on Damian's face, and he slid his gaze to me. The redness in his face had tempered a bit, and he pulled the bottle from the baby's mouth, propping him on his shoulder for a burp before meeting Valerie's stark stare again.

"You have to understand…" he started.

Colossal mistake.

"I don't have to understand a fucking thing," she growled. "I've known you all my life, and you gave up. I've only known him for what, three days? Three days and he had enough faith to believe saving me was possible."

"Faith has nothing to do with it. He wanted to get you into bed. That's it."

"Bullshit!" she yelled. "He chose to save me. You didn't. What would Michael think of that?"

Damian winced. She nailed a nerve, and he looked down at the angel's namesake with an expression full of regret.

"Or did you just choose to give up on him, too?" she asked, her fury pulling the low blow.

"Wait a minute, Val, that's not fair," I piped in. "I was there. What Michael and Gabriel did was to save Naomi and the babies regardless of the consequences."

"You don't need to defend me," Damian said.

I glanced at him. "You didn't kill them. You didn't kill my father, either. They made the choice. As much as we'd like to take the blame, it was their choice."

"Yes. But she's right. I gave up on her and you didn't. It was my choice, and I chose my children."

His words were like a blow in Valerie's mid-section, and she reached for the wall. A blend of aggravation and understanding ran through her as her gaze moved from him to his child.

"I would have made the same choice if it had been Naomi," he said, and her gaze jumped back to his. "I didn't believe banishment spells worked and you're damned lucky it did because I would have dropped you in the middle of the Atlantic otherwise." His mouth curled into a frown. "I would have hated myself forever, but I would have done it."

Her mouth dropped open and her eyes glazed over with tears.

"You'll understand someday," he said and stood, leaving us alone in the living room.

Her horrified gaze snapped to me, and I stood, crossing and taking her in my arms. Her last vestige of family ties unraveled, and she hugged me tightly, retreating into herself and she rebuilt the wall I broke down last night.

"Please, don't shut me out," I whispered, feeling her pull away.

She tilted her head up, meeting my gaze.

"How can I trust anyone?"

I smoothed her hair back and gazed into her eyes. When I kissed her, I opened up my mind to her. Everything I kept locked in the dark corners, things that didn't transfer with my memories. My fears, the hurt, the betrayals, the loneliness, everything that molded me into the man I was. Things I didn't even share with Tom. I shared with her and when the kiss broke, she stared at me.

"Colossal mind fuck," she whispered.

I smiled and shrugged. "Now you know me better than anyone on earth, better than even my brother."

She cupped my cheek and gave me a small peck on the lips, knowing just how much I opened up, but her eyes still held doubt.

"What do I need to do?" I asked, my smile fading at the blockade building between us.

"I don't know," she said and pulled out of my arms.

I stared after her as she walked back inside the house with the rest of the family. Instead of following, I went upstairs and jumped in the shower to wash off the irritation building under my skin. It wasn't easy for me to open up, either, and to get so brutally shot down, just fed into my insecurities. And I hated I had insecurities to begin with.

The shift of air interrupted my destructive train of thought.

"I didn't shoot you down," Valerie said.

"Then what was that?" I gestured toward the main part of the house.

"That was me freaking out." She leaned against the wall. "It doesn't happen often." A dimple appeared in her cheek. "But since I've met you, I've had my fair share of freak outs."

I finished rinsing my body and turned the water off, reaching for a towel before addressing her comment. "I thought you didn't freak out." It wasn't a question, just an open-ended statement.

"You unhinge me," she said, and I couldn't help but laugh. "Stop laughing at me," she snipped and turned toward the door.

I grabbed her arm. "Then we're even," I said, and she spun toward me. I cornered her against the door. "Unhinged is as good a word as anything to describe what I'm like around you." I stepped closer. "I have a bitch of a time forming a coherent thought and become a bumbling fool when I'm near you. I'm a fucking genius for god's sake, and yet, with you, I feel like I have an I.Q. of an infant." I was mad now.

"Calm down," she said and put her palms on my chest. Just her touch shut my brain down for a moment and I stepped back, giving us both some breathing room so I could get my thoughts together from jumble land.

"I opened up to you, and you shut down on me."

"I'm not very good at this," she said.

"No shit." I couldn't help the sarcasm. It was my favorite default, and she knew it.

Her arms crossed and her stormy eyes darkened. "You aren't exactly the smoothest, either."

I laughed and took another step back. I knew it was a way to psychologically put distance between us, and her eyes narrowed. She called it before the words formed and I put my hands up in surrender.

"You started the barricade. I'll finish it because I don't want to be crushed beyond recognition."

She stepped toward me, and I steeled myself against the need to give in. She froze and drew her hand back slowly.

"You could destroy me," I said, meeting her gaze, not really understanding how it could be such a solid fact with so little time invested. I didn't want this type of dependency. I guess mind fuck was really an appropriate term to put to this overwhelming certainty.

Valerie let a nervous laugh escape, but her eyes didn't break away from mine. Instead, she crossed the distance, blocking me in. I flinched when she went to touch me, knowing I'd lose my ability to distance myself if her skin connected to mine.

The closer she got, the more the storm colors in her eyes swirled, and when her hands connected with my chest, I lost control of my reserve.

"Don't do this if you have no intention of following through," I whispered, and she pressed the rest of her body against me, taking full advantage of my weakness. Her hand threaded through my hair, and she pulled me to her lips.

A shadow passed over my vision and I closed my eyes, drinking in her vulnerabilities, her fears, her sorrow and uncertainties. She opened everything to me, including her deadly fear of losing me to my past or worse, to the devil. When the kiss broke, I opened my eyes, meeting hers and I let a small smile of understanding form.

I walked some of the same pathways, had the same fears, and only God knew why we were thrown together, but I took a moment to say thank you. He could have let me wander like a lost nomad, but he delivered her to my door, gift wrapped in sass and strength.

I glanced up at our surroundings and then back down at her. "We have to stop meeting in the bathroom."

She grinned. "I like having you in nothing but a towel. It makes you vulnerable. And you're adorable when you're vulnerable."

Just what a guy wants to hear. I ran my hand through my wet hair and chuckled. "I thought you just liked the view."

"Well, that, too," she said, and I sidestepped around her, heading to the bedroom for a change of clothes. She followed, closing the door behind her. At first, I thought she was going to make another move on me, but she took a seat at my desk and stared out the window instead.

"What's up?" I asked after I had a pair of jeans on. I pulled a flannel shirt on and started buttoning it before I glanced at her contemplative profile.

She turned away from the window, meeting my gaze. "How's this going to work?"

I shrugged. "How's what going to work?"

"Us. This." She pointed at her chest, then me. "I've still got another year of med school and then two years in rotations, followed by residency. It's going to be a few years before I get any kind of break."

"Would you consider something closer?" I asked. I really didn't want to leave my family high and dry right now, nor did I want to leave her alone, even with her home as secure as Fort Knox. She still had to go out, no matter where she was. My gaze dropped to the necklace Raven had given her and then back to her eyes.

"Where?" she finally said, not wanting to shoot my ideas down after the last twenty minutes of strife we conquered.

"How about somewhere in Boston? That's closer than Farmington."

She scoffed at me. "What? Like Harvard?"

"It is the number one medical school in the country." I raised my eyebrows.

"I can't afford that," she said.

I pressed my lips together, suppressing the smile. "I can."

"I don't want your money," she said and stood up.

"Would you like a medical degree from Harvard?" I asked, keeping my voice soft and reasonable. And her eyes sparked with interest.

"I can't afford it, so it's not an option."

"Can you get into Harvard?" I purposely kept using the name of the school and every time I did, I saw the inclination to keep me pushing.

"Of course I can," she snapped, her hands finding her hips. "I may not be a fucking genius, but I'm damned smart."

"I never said you weren't," I smiled. "And you damned well know you want a degree from the best school in the country." I stepped closer. "Transfer and I'll foot the bill just to have you closer."

She opened her mouth to say no, but closed it just as quickly, studying me. "If I say no, you'll come to Connecticut with me, right?"

The conflict between my family and her brewed inside me, but I nodded, anyway. If that's what she insisted on, I'd follow her. After all, I was just tinkering and could do that anywhere. Same with teaching self-defense. It didn't tie me to a place like the path to what she wanted to do.

"Harvard?" she asked after a few minutes of silence.

"If that's what you want."

"What about my house?"

I shrugged and looked at the ceiling. "This is legally mine now that I'm over twenty-one."

"What about Tom?"

"He's got a place in New Hampshire and an option to take the house across town once the lease runs out."

"And Steve and Jen?"

"They've got a place in New Hampshire and New York."

She got quiet, studying me in a way that made me wonder what was churning behind those beautiful eyes.

I loved this quaint little town. It was home, and I really didn't want to leave it behind. It was all I had left of my parents. I waited for her to decide, and then she nodded.

"Connecticut is probably not the best place for either of us to be right now," she said, and her eyes darkened. "Besides, my house is one of Lucifer's prime targets, so a change would probably be in order."

"So, Harvard?" I asked.

"I guess I can at least apply," she conceded. "But when things blow over here, I will need to take a ride to pick up some things."

"That's no problem. I'd really like to see Michael's artwork."

Her smile faded. "Didn't Damian booby trap the basement?"

I grinned. "I'm a fucking genius, remember?" Damian was borderline genius, but I could get around his computer programming as easily as an adult could snatch a piece of candy from a child.

She laughed and turned toward the laptop on my desk. "Do you mind?"

"Not at all," I said and turned it on, typing the passcode in and relinquishing the computer to her. I went to leave when a familiar voice came through the speakers.

My blood chilled, and I kept my back to the Skype screen that was set to automatically come up when she called.

"Who the hell are you?" Sandy said.

Valerie didn't speak, she just got up and gave me a sideways glance as she passed, leaving me alone with the video screen of my ex.

"Val, you don't have to leave," I said, and she turned at the door, meeting my gaze. The fear present in her eyes shut down my voice. She gave me the slightest of nods before disappearing down the hallway. The hurt in her eyes haunted me and set my fury switch on high.

"Chris, who was that?"

"None of your fucking business," I said, still refusing to turn. I stared at the empty hallway and my heart pounded in my chest.

"I'm sorry, Chris. I fucked up."

My hands clenched into fists, and I glared over my shoulder. Her hazel irises were surrounded by red lines, like she had been crying. It dug under my skin, but whatever I may have felt for the girl died the moment that door opened.

"You're too late for apologies."

"Please..."

"No. I didn't fuck around on you with the first girl who threw herself my way, and honey, I had a lot of girls propositioning me over the years. But you, you jump into bed with the first guy that turns on the charm just to get in your pants. Was he the first one or just one of many?" The anger blew wide open, and I knew the dig was wrong, but I couldn't help it.

135

I shouldn't be reacting like this, but the callous way she let me loose really burned my ego. The fact I had Valerie didn't make a difference where Sandy's shitty treatment was concerned. I leaned over, planting my fists on the desk. The fury encompassing me was a massive beast, and I almost lost control of it until a hand landed on my shoulder.

I looked at the hand's owner and my fury reined in. Valerie's touch tempered the wild beast, and I refocused on Sandy.

"You're right, you fucked things up beyond the ability to ever fix."

Tears welled up in her eyes.

"I was wrong," she whispered, and then the screen tilted, widening the shot.

I took an involuntary step back, bumping into Valerie. A sick understanding swept through my gut as I stared at her possessed boyfriend and the knife he held to her throat. Three days ago, I would have been on my knees begging for her life, but now, I just stared at her, with a total sense of loss raking my skin.

"That's not your boyfriend," I said softly, and a crease appeared between her eyes. "I mean it was, but now he's possessed by one of hell's demons."

"He's right," Josh whispered in her ear, his red eyes shined in the camera. "And he's going to either trade his soul for you or watch you die."

Sandy paled, and her eyes widened. As much as she'd hurt me, she really didn't deserve to die for it. The anger flooded back into my skin, and I shook my head.

"My soul is not a bargaining chip," I said and concentrated, opening my hand and envisioning it wedged between the knife and her throat.

Tears sprang to Sandy's eyes, and she shook as fear blazed through her slight form.

"Say goodbye," the demon said, and the knife sliced flesh.

Pain and anger fueled me, and I took a step right into her room. Both their eyes widened, and I pushed out a blast of power along with the roar of fury that escaped my lips. Josh, and the demon possessing him, exploded.

The sound of it was wet and vile, followed by the sound of metal on tile as the knife hit the ground.

I stared at Sandy's shocked gaze and stepped back into my room, blinking at her image on the screen and the blood-soaked room behind her. She shook in the seat, just staring at me. I dropped my gaze to my hand and the gash splitting the skin to the bone. Throbbing pain resonated up my arm, and I moved my gaze back to Sandy.

"Are you okay?" I asked.

She shook her head, on the verge of hysteria. "Did you say demon?" she asked, her voice shaking as much as her body.

"Yes." I glanced at Valerie. "Think you can go get me one of Raven's stone necklaces?" I asked her and she nodded and left the room. I focused back on Sandy. "A lot has happened in the last couple of weeks." I refrained from saying she'd know what was going on had she not been fucking that asshole when I came by.

She let out a high-pitched laugh and her gaze dropped to the knife.

"He... he," she gulped and brought her gaze back to mine.

I raised my hand into view, and she stared at the ugly gash. Her chin trembled, and tears snaked down her cheeks. Valerie stepped to my side and handed me a necklace with one of the smaller black pendants.

I took it in my good hand and met her gaze. The hurt there burned in the pit of my stomach. "Watch my back, okay?" I asked, and she nodded without speaking. I refocused on the monitor and stepped forward.

This time, the tingling sensation of the transition overtook me, and I stepped into her dorm room, opposite the desk she sat at. Her gaze bounced from the monitor to me, and I moved around the desk to her side, unclasping the necklace in my hand and putting it on her. When she moved to throw her arms around my neck, I caught them and shook my head, pushing her gently back into the chair.

"I was serious before. It's over and there's no backtracking. I just want to make sure you're safe," I said and let go of her arms. My blood stained her forearm, and she looked at the blotch and then my hand.

"You really saved my life," she said, and I stood, stepping back to the front of the desk.

"Yeah," I said and let the transition take hold.

Sandy stared at me on the monitor and her gaze dropped to her arm and then the necklace before returning to mine.

"Why?" she asked as the shakes quelled.

"Because no matter how angry I am at you, you don't deserve to die."

She blinked and made the mistake of looking over her shoulder. "Oh, god," she gasped, and her hand shot over her mouth, but not quickly enough to stop the flow of vomit.

"Sorry about the mess," I said, and she gagged and spit before looking back at me. "Wear the necklace. It'll keep you safe," I added as her gaze transitioned from horror to panic.

"How am I supposed to explain this?" she asked, pointing her thumb over her shoulder.

I looked at the dripping walls and shrugged. "Freak accident?"

She burst out laughing, but it was that 'I've gone over the edge' laugh that would transition to a scream any second.

"I gotta go. I need my hand fixed," I said, and she nodded, still laughing that edgy laugh. I shut down the session before she started screaming and turned toward Valerie.

"Are you okay?" My concern for her was greater than it had been for Sandy.

"Yes. Are you?" she asked, and I knew damned well she didn't mean my hand.

"Honestly, I'm numb right now." I wasn't sure when my actions would catch up to me, but right now I was still riding the adrenaline high that kept real feelings at bay.

She reached down and took my wounded hand. "Have you ever done this before?"

I just raised an eyebrow. She had the memories; she knew this was the first time I'd put myself between a blade and someone I cared about. Whether or not I wanted to admit it, I cared about what happened to Sandy. It was in my nature to protect those close to me, and Sandy had been one of those people for fifteen years.

"Okay, stupid question," she said and pulled my palm to her lips.

Pain magnified. "Oh, fuck, that hurts," I whispered.

She smiled, wiping the blood stain from her lips. "Not numb anymore, eh?"

I rolled my eyes and squeezed my hand, pressing it to my chest. "At least I don't pass out from the fucking pain," I snapped and turned away, trying not to double over. A deep wound hurt worse than broken bone and I forced my breath into shallow pants, repeating the word fuck with every exhale. The springs on my bed creaked, and I glanced over at Valerie.

She seemed to be highly amused by my pain.

"What are you smiling at," I hissed.

"You." She crossed her arms. "The ultimate hero acting like a major wuss."

"It fucking hurts," I growled.

"I'm sure, but you're dancing around like a kid having a tantrum."

"No, I'm not," I said and straightened. Okay, maybe I had been, but in my defense the pain made me nutty. I've had broken bones mended along with scrapes and bruises, but never to-the-bone slices before. It was more than just unpleasant, and I glanced at her side and then back to her eyes. No wonder she passed out cold.

The pain abated, replaced by that weird pins and needles sensation that drove me equally insane. I started flexing and squeezing my hand until it passed, and then I took a seat next to her, staring at my closed monitor.

With the numbness gone, the full impact of everything I'd done hit and I dropped my chin to my chest. "Oh, man," I whispered just as the shakes took hold and my stomach started that slow roll that sent me running. I made it in time, spilling the contents of my stomach into the toilet bowl.

Valerie kneeled next to me and rubbed my back. I spit, flushed, and then met her gaze.

"I blew her boyfriend to bits," I whispered. "He was all over her walls." My words didn't do justice to the horror I felt. Cold dread wrapped around my body, plummeting me into a shivering mass of flesh and bone.

Steve stepped into the bathroom doorway. "Damian said you might need me," he said, looking between the two of us before his gaze landed on my bloody hand. "What happened?"

"The demon attacked in a different way," I said, and his brow creased. It took a second and then his brow smoothed over.

"They went after Sandy?"

I nodded, pushing myself to my feet, and crossed to the sink, cleaning out the vile taste in my mouth before I started scrubbing the blood from my hand.

Steve hadn't said anything; he let me get myself in presentable order before he spoke.

"Tell me what happened."

"The bastard didn't possess her," I said to his concerned look and his shoulders relaxed.

"Thank god," he said and leaned on the doorframe waiting for the rest.

"He possessed her boyfriend," I said, and Steve straightened again, concern retracing the lines in his face. I looked at my healed palm. "He tried to bargain for my soul. When I said no, he slit her throat." I met his gaze and held up my clean palm. "Except I blocked it and then I stepped into the dorm room and blew him to bloody bits."

I held his gaze as he processed the information.

"And Sandy?"

"She's going to be a disaster for a while, but she's alive and now has one of Raven's necklaces to ward off evil spirits." I dropped my hand to the buttons on my ruined shirt, stripping it off and dumping it in the trash before heading to my room again. I stopped in the entry and stared at the droplets of my blood staining the carpet and turned toward my closet, pulling out another shirt. I wasn't sure what I was feeling right now.

Both Steve and Valerie left me at the entrance to my bedroom, heading downstairs and letting me have a little space to deal with what had happened. If I hadn't witnessed Raven's successful exorcism, I wouldn't be second guessing myself right now. Before that, a demon possession was certain death for the host, but knowing there was a way to save the guy, well, it just compounded the guilt and made me wonder if all my wrath was aimed solely at the demon. I probably could have vaporized him into dust, but I made a choice, however subconscious it was, to make a bloody fucking mess.

Angel Grace Chapter 21

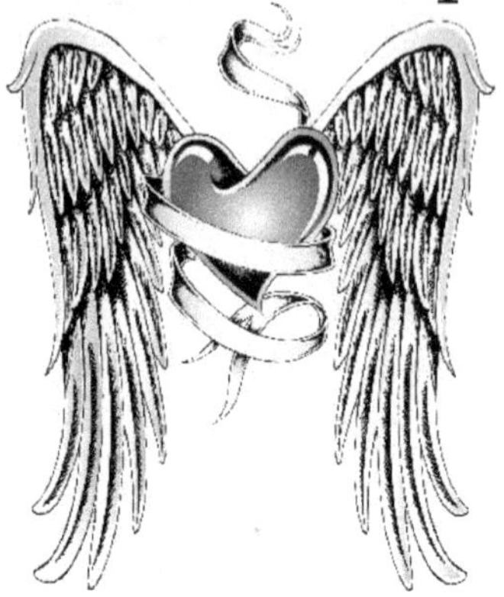

"THIS HAS TO END. Now," I announced when I walked into the family room where everyone was sitting, enjoying each other's company. Silence blanketed the room, and all eyes locked on me. Valerie shook her head.

"You don't want to do what you're thinking," she said.

I ignored her, focusing on Damian. "How are the demons getting through from hell?"

He blinked at me and shrugged, and I moved my gaze to Steve's.

"If Paradise Cove is a portal to heaven, then Black Cove must be a gate to hell."

He paled, and so did Jennifer. "We closed that," he said, but the hesitation in his words belied the confidence in his statement.

"You killed one demon," I said. "But did you really close that gate?"

"I don't think it's one location," Damian said, thinking back on how easily Michael showed up wherever he was called. Lucifer could do the same before he was vanquished to hell.

"Demons aren't angels," I answered his train of thought. "They have to be escaping by some means, and from your memories, they existed back when you were turned. But they haven't overrun the earth, so they have to have limited access topside."

"They aren't escaping. They're following orders," Damian said.

"Either way, they're getting here through some sort of portal. It isn't through the same means that an angel has of just popping in whenever they damned well feel like it."

Faces stared at me with vacant eyes and the anger in my soul flushed a heat over my skin that scalded. I had to stop this madness. I would not live in fear for the rest of my life and the only way to do that, was to do what I had said to Valerie in the car.

I was going hunting.

I turned toward the closet and pulled out my coat. "They want a fucking war. They got one."

Steve shot to his feet and grabbed my arm before I got out the garage door.

"Don't," he started, and I yanked the fabric out of his grip.

"I have to. We…" I twirled my finger around, pointing to everyone in the house. "We will never know peace if I don't do this."

"Chris," Valerie said, approaching me.

I turned my angry gaze in her direction. "I want the fucking fairytale."

She stopped her approach and just stared, pleading with her beautiful eyes, and I gritted my teeth.

"It's hunting season," I growled, repeating the words my father had said many years ago. I glanced at the sudden paleness in Steve's cheeks before turning away. I didn't wait for a reaction; I stormed to my car and slid inside, willing everything in my way to yield. When the garage door opened, I had a clear path out of the house and I punched the gas, leaving a spray of gravel, dirt, and exhaust in my wake.

Each mile that passed ratcheted my anger and people on the highway gave me a wide berth, and in some ways, I felt like Moses parting the Red Sea. The power smashed through my veins in time with my heartbeat and throbbed in my temple. By the time I pulled into the driveway at the cottage, I was in an all-out frenzy.

I had never ventured to Black Cove and the only way I knew how was by following the small brook from Paradise cove. I trudged across the snow toward the lake and slowed at the singe spot, growling low in my throat at the sight of it. He was still messing with our lives, and I was damned if I'd allow that.

I stomped through the trodden path to Paradise cove where the moss was still clear and the ice at the edge of the water was thinning enough to see the water underneath. I turned my back on the beautiful prisms in the water and focused on the stream trench that disappeared to the right of the entrance.

"You will not win with that much anger ruling your emotions," the voice broke over the cove like soft rain, shocking every nerve in my body. I turned and swallowed the sudden lump in my throat.

"I have to try," I said, staring into my father's preternatural eyes and he smiled that knowing smile that bit under my skin.

"I know you do. But you've got to get a handle on your fury, otherwise, they'll use it against you. I really don't want to see you up here yet... if you get my drift. Neither does your mother. She wants grandkids," he said and flashed that smile again. "So do I."

Just seeing him reinforced my belief that the portals exist.

"Is Black Cove the only one?" I asked, and he shook his head.

"There aren't many, just a few dozen around the world," he added. "But trust me when I say they're harder to find than Black Cove is," he said with a sigh. "I know they exist, but I don't know where they are."

I nodded and turned away, stepping toward the woods.

"Son?"

I glanced back at him.

"I'm proud of you," he said.

"I haven't done anything, yet," I said, and he faded into the layer of fog that crawled across the ground. Leave it to my father to make me feel completely inadequate when I needed strength. I stepped off the moss into the snow, willing the thick brush to yield to my passage. I couldn't have cut a cleaner path had I had a machete in my hand, and I used the time to build the power and temper the fury to the point rational thought ruled.

As I got closer to Black Cove, the air thickened. Unwelcomed fear licked my skin, leaving it tacky under my coat, and I shifted. If my father could show up in Paradise Cove, could Lucifer appear in Black Cove? I glanced down at the chain holding the pendant over my heart and prayed that if Lucifer appeared, that chunk of rock would protect me from having my heart ripped out.

The combination of fear and fury does funny things to a man. With each step, my heart drove faster, and the evilness of the landscape penetrated my coat, chilling me and drawing sweat from my pores. I knew the distance was a little under a mile, but in the thick brush, it seemed longer, and I had a new appreciation for Steve.

He'd carried Jennifer's unconscious body the entire way, without the benefit of any supernatural powers, to cut a clear path. He ran on tenacious willpower alongside the drive to get her to safety, and he nearly bled out.

The forest echoed with unfamiliar noises, some sounding more like screams of the dead than forest creatures, and I slowed, knowing I was approaching the perimeter. The stench of brimstone settled on the air, and I put my hand to my nose to stop an unwanted sneeze. The last thing I wanted to do was announce my presence in the area.

I closed my eyes, pulling the details of the landscape from Steve's sketchy memories. If I mapped out my approach correctly, I would come in on the narrow path next to the sinkhole. There was no maneuverability if I was attacked there, and I had a feeling that sink hole wouldn't be a pleasant place to fall into.

I thought about just sending out a rolling wave of destructive power across the landscape, clearing it clean; but that was unreasonable, especially if I miscalculated and went farther than the reach of Black

Cove. Killing a human being wasn't on my to-do list. I had done it once, granted it was warranted, but it still haunted me to this day.

Which left me the option of cutting through the thick woods until I was parallel with Black Cove's rotting moss bed. A twig snapped to my left, and I froze. Demons weren't the only things Lucifer commanded, and I set a deadly cocoon around me. If anything grabbed for me, they'd find themselves roasted to a crispy corpse.

I slogged my way through the woods, quietly carving the path. I'm sure my electrified safety net was enough of a disturbance to announce my presence, but I kept my thoughts masked. I curved back towards the cove, ignoring the drop in temperature. My adrenaline acted as a body warmer, setting my blood on overdrive enough so that even my palms were covered in a light sheen of sweat.

The dense forest thinned, and I saw my first slivers of the setting sun penetrating the trees. A thread of fear bit into me. I really didn't want to be here after dark and looking at the progression of the dying rays, I knew I wouldn't have a choice. Twilight was on the horizon and with it would come things just as nasty as demons.

Angel Grace Chapter 22

THE MOMENT I STEPPED onto the black moss, I knew I'd made a mistake coming alone. There must have been fifty demons just waiting for me and when I breached their domain, they parted, one by one, stepping to the side until I faced Lucifer's back.

Every memory of Damian's flooded my brain, terrifying me, and when he turned in my direction, I had to get a hold of the fear, otherwise I was going to pee my pants like a scared little kid. My gaze dropped to the gaping hole in his chest, and I shivered.

When the first demon reached out and actually touched my shirt, my heart leaped in my throat. My safety net was gone, and now I was at their mercy. Muscle memory guided my every move, parrying blows away, executing throws and kicks powerful enough to kill an ordinary man. I don't know how many I took down, but they just kept coming and my knuckles were scraped and bloodied by the blows I got in.

The muscles in my arms burned, but I kept going, snapping bone and dropping demons. But they didn't stay down long. It was like battling a horde of zombies from World War Z and I was one in a sea of many.

Most of them didn't know the art of self-defense, so I had that going for me, but that's where my benefits ended. These fuckers were strong and relentless. The demon spirits in their bodies were not susceptible to the frailties of the human body. Unfortunately, the same couldn't be said for me.

I faltered, and the first actual blow hit my kidney, driving me to my knees. I rolled into an empty space and dodged another blow, trying like hell to let loose some of the destructive power locked within my flesh. Nothing happened and the first tendrils of panic settled in, making my strikes less effective and my blocks either too early or too late. I couldn't seem to regain my center and each blow that connected had one goal; to break what it hit. I missed the next block, and a fist connected with my ribs, cracking at least two of them by the crushing pain.

I bellowed my pain, striking out and breaking a nose before stumbling back with my arm locked over my side to protect them from being hit again. I didn't get my arm up in time and a fist smashed my lips, splitting both of them and loosening several teeth, but I remained on my feet, shaking off the shock.

I knew if I went down, that would be the end; I wouldn't get back up.

The next blow smashed my cheek, and I stumbled, losing the battle with gravity. I landed on the side with the cracked ribs and yelled out. Pushing to my hands and knees, I tried to dodge the kick coming at me and served only to give someone on the other side a better shot of my back.

I curled and covered my head, screaming through the pain as over a dozen boot clad feet connected with my body. And then everything stopped. For a moment I thought I'd died. Then hands grabbed my arms, lifting me and bringing me back with a ferocious dose of agony.

Each step they took sent a jolt through my body and I couldn't help the tears. I'd welcome blacking out right now, but I knew if I did that, Lucifer would take control over my body, knocking my soul who knows where and the world would end.

They dropped me on the ground in front of Lucifer and I struggled to my hands and knees. One of his lackey bastards grabbed a fistful of my hair and pulled my head back.

"You're on my turf now, boy, or hadn't you noticed?" Lucifer asked, and I just stared at him. He crouched down in front of me. "You can end this. All you have to do is surrender," he said in a perfectly reasonable tone. He tilted his head and studied me like a poor lost stray.

"Fuck you," I hissed, spraying blood with my words.

"You sure about that? You think you're in pain now. I can make it infinitely worse." He stood, towering over me.

A cloud passed over the path of the dying sun, creating a dark shadow on the trees behind Lucifer that reminded me of an eagle... or a hawk, and I blinked the sudden vertigo away. I let out a raspy laugh at what must be a last-ditch hallucination. I was sure I was one punch away from death anyway, and if I died, my powers went with me.

"Game on, motherfucker," I glared through my only open eye, energized by the strength of my voice. It reminded me of my father and his steel nerves.

Lucifer gave a nod and the hands holding me disappeared. I dropped to my hands and knees and a painful flare from impact seized my muscles and I groaned. My forehead dropped to the ground, landing on the scratchy moss. Instead of clenching my eyes closed, I scanned the number of shoes surrounding me and forced an inhale. Too many for me to fight off, but I would not die kneeling on the ground. Lucifer's black steel toe boots circled me, and I pushed up, forcing myself to my feet, blocking the pain from overriding me. When he appeared in my peripheral vision, I turned my gaze toward him, stepping into form. I spit a wad of blood on the ground and glared in his direction.

If I couldn't influence matter around me, I damned well could look inward. The power was still there, brewing in my chest, filling my skin with the ability to remain standing. Tapping my mental reserve, I filled every inch of my broken body with strength and narrowed my good eye at him.

"Let's see what you got."

He tilted his head and my pinky snapped, pulling a groan from my chest that I clamped between my teeth.

I glanced at my pinky, willing the bone to reset, and damned if it didn't. It was still broken, but not at an angle. I couldn't curl into a fist. I did just that and smiled my best 'fuck you' smile.

"I may not be an archangel, but I'm a force to be reckoned with."

Lucifer leaned his head back and laughed and I threw a punch aimed at his throat. My fist stopped less than an inch away and my arm slowly twisted, peeling a growling scream from my throat when both my ulna and radius snapped. Flashes of light filled my vision, and I blinked them away even as he continued to twist.

"Your powers are useless here," he smiled as I kneeled helplessly at his feet, watching the skin tear around the breaks.

"His may be, but mine aren't," a familiar voice rocked the landscape, and the smell of singing moss filled my nostrils. The crowd surrounding us evaporated to dust, leaving Lucifer, Damian, and me on the playing field.

Lucifer let go of my arm and I collapsed to the ground, pulling the pieces to my chest. My breath wheezed in and out and I did the same thing I did with my finger, screaming my pain to the heavens. I clung to consciousness by a thread as the last direct rays of the sun disappeared.

Lucifer's boot pressed down on my throat and black spots filled my vision. My father's words echoed in my head and tears leaked from the corner of my eyes. He would be so disappointed in me for dying like this.

Something inside me broke, and with it whatever wall blocked my ability to harness and wield the power engulfing me shattered into a million pieces, and I let loose like I have never done, knocking Lucifer across the Cove. I struggled to my feet, unable to harness this fury or the fire ripping through my skin.

Damian's expression matched the absolute shock on Lucifer's face. The ground shook under us, crumbling under Lucifer's feet. Trees started toppling, sucking into the sinkhole, scraping the evil off the land and filling it with white light.

I had a moment, a quick glimpse through Damian's eyes, and what I saw fueled the power. I shined like a celestial being, one made to purify the land, and I was hell bent on destroying this portal, even if I lost my life doing it.

If I could destroy Lucifer in the process, that was just a bonus.

He charged at me, and I put my hand up like a traffic cop, targeting the power. I don't think he knew what hit him and he went down into the giant crack like a fly slapped in a hurricane. Trees amassed over the crevice, crackling and snapping as the white light surrounded us, peeling away the evil and scrubbing the land from edge to edge. Every bit of shrub and moss scraped down to the dirt, and the debris slid into the giant whirlpool where the sink hole had been, slipping through the crack until there was nothing left, and then the crack slammed closed, fused with light, closing this portal to hell forever.

The light faded, and I stared at the perfectly round, perfectly flat, and perfectly clean patch of land that reminded me of those strange alien crop circles in the mid-west. None of the devastation remained and what was left waited for a harvest of new life. I turned my gaze to Damian.

"So that's what happens when I lose control," I whispered, and then everything went black.

Angel Grace Chapter 23

MUFFLED SOUNDS AND DARKNESS.
Sobbing, then silence.
Bright light, then blackness, again.
A steady machine-like beep.
Hushed whispers.
Music.
Moments lost in the dark.
Where the hell was I?
Who the hell was I?
All fractional pieces of the puzzle that my brain couldn't wrap around.
There were no answers, just darkness and silence and nothing.

Angel Grace Chapter 24

I OPENED MY EYES, and everything around me was a blur. After a few blinks I stared at a hanging bag of liquid. The slow drip captivated me.

Drip, drip, drip.

I peeled my eyes away and turned my head. Lights bounced across a screen, just as hypnotizing as the drip above me. Spike up, back down, pause, spike again over and over like an endless steady earthquake. It took a few minutes for me to connect the timing of the spikes to the pounding in my chest. I moved my hands to the source and a hard smooth object lay in the spot I thought my heart should be and then my fingertips slid off whatever it was onto warm skin.

My brain was slow to understand, and it was a struggle to think clearly.

My nose tickled, and I reached up to scratch it, pulling small tubes from my nostrils. I stared at the thing, blinking as air flowed into my eyes. Why was it so hard to know the words for things? I turned my head away from the machines and they landed on a man slumped in a chair.

I didn't recognize him, just like I didn't recognize names for the things around me. Should I know him? Logic wasn't working, and I shifted uncomfortably in the bedding. His eyes blinked open, and he stretched, rubbing his scruffy face. Then his gaze landed on me, his eyes widened and met my gaze, and then widened some more.

"EA?" he said, and my brow creased. "O o ow whe oo a?" he asked, and his hands moved along with his speech, none of which made a lick of sense.

I blinked, hoping something would compute, but nothing came, and I just stared at him, unable to decipher what the hell he was saying.

He pulled something from his pocket and tapped the screen before turning it to me. It was covered with unfamiliar symbols strung together. Nothing registered.

Distant whispers filled my head, and I glanced around the room for the source and then back at the man. I shook my head slowly.

"Do you know where you are?" the question formed in my head an unfamiliar voice along with my own broken narrative. The man's mouth didn't move, and I glanced around the room, looking for the source.

He took my hand and my gaze snapped to him as I tried to pull my hand away.

He let go and pointed to his chest. *"CJ, it's me, Tom."*

I licked my lips and tried out the last word of the sentence. "Tom?" It came out in a harsh croak, and he smiled, nodding. It didn't hold any meaning, and I glanced around again for what made the words inside my ears.

Liquid sloshed, and I glanced back at him as he moved something clear with a thin plastic rod toward my mouth. I backed away, uneasy by the offering. The complete unfamiliarity of everything was pushing me closer to the freak out zone.

"Take a small sip," the voice said as the plastic touched my lips.

I hesitated, unsure of what a sip was, and the man pulled the liquid away slowly, plugging one end of the plastic with his finger and placing the long straight end against my lips. He lifted his finger and cool liquid seeped into my mouth, quenching the dryness. I swallowed and closed my eyes, licking the remaining liquid from the corner of my lips.

"Do you know where you are?"

The voice announced again, and my eyes opened, scanning what I could see of the room before slowly shaking my head and dropping it back on the soft pillow.

"*You're at the hospital,*" the voice echoed softly in my mind, but his lips still didn't move. Again, I looked for the voice in my ear, but only the man stood in the room with me.

"Hos...pit..tal?" I tried the word out and it didn't come as smoothly as in my head. His smile faded.

"*Do you know who I am?*" the voice whispered and behind it resided pain that I couldn't identify. The man patted his chest when I didn't answer, his eyes pleading for a reaction that I couldn't give.

I stared at him and shook my head. The devastation in his eyes squeezed my heart, and he sat down slowly in the chair. That's when I realized he was the one talking in my head.

"*I'm your brother,*" his voice whispered.

"Broth...ther?" I asked, the meaning lost to me. I didn't know why it was so damned hard to speak or to understand things; it was like my brain wasn't firing on all cylinders.

He nodded. "*Do you know who you are?*" his voice invaded my mind again.

This time, I met his worried stare. "Bro...ther?" I said, because I had no idea what the right answer was.

He covered his mouth and his eyes glossed over with a watery sheen. When his eyes closed, some of the liquid leaked out, rolling down his cheeks. He opened his eyes and turned away with the device in his hand, tapping away at the screen for what seemed like ages. When he was done, he set his shoulders and turned, offering a smile meant to reassure, but it just scared the shit out of me.

Everything about this scared the shit out of me. Not being able to smoothly answer the questions or understand where I was scared the shit out of me, and my gaze darted around the room, looking for an escape route.

He reached over and picked up a stick that lay near my hand and pressed a red button on the top. I stared at the magic wand in his hand, trying to understand how I knew the button was red, or the fact that it was a button, for that matter.

The door opened and a woman with a white coat came in. She had her hair pulled back and her eyes, her eyes captivated and calmed me. The colors in her eyes swirled as she crossed the distance. The warmth in her gaze wrapped around me like a security blanket and I knew with her I was safe.

"Chris?" she asked in such a tender way that my heart ached for her. When she sat on the edge of the bed and took my hand in hers, I stared at the union of our flesh, and heat tingled from the point of contact through my form, from my head to my toes and everywhere in between. A living connection between the two of us created a warmth deep in my soul and even though I didn't remember her, I remembered this overwhelming and pure sensation.

"Hi," I croaked and blinked again. That word came from nowhere and the reaction seemed to sadden her.

Water sprang from her eyes, and then the right word popped into my head. She was crying, and those glistening drops were tears. I don't know why, but I sat up and pulled her into my arms. Holding her felt like home, and I closed my eyes, inhaling her sweet scent.

"Jesus, Chris, I didn't think you'd ever wake up," she whispered in my ear.

"Je..sus. Chri..is?"

She stiffened in my arms and slowly pulled away, the same concern present on her face as the man who called himself brother. She unwrapped from me and put her hand on my chest.

"Chris, that's your name," she said, blinking away the tears. She took my hand and placed it under the ornate necklace onto her flesh. "Valerie. I'm Valerie."

I stared at my hand on her chest. Underneath the soft warmth, her heart beat against my hand, echoing my own, and I knew this girl had a piece of my soul. It wasn't from a memory or familiarity; it was as natural as the air and just as essential to my survival.

And best of all, I knew the word to describe it.

"Val...er...ie." I glanced into her eyes. "Lo...ove Val...er...ie."

She got the meaning right away despite my stilted speech, and her eyes filled with tears. Her hand fluttered to her lips, and she nodded before leaning forward and placing a kiss on my forehead.

A strange tingle encompassed my head along with flashes of pain, of white light, of angels. The tingles cascaded down my body all the way to my toes and another word surfaced.

I tilted my head.

"Ha...avad?"

She let out a musical laugh and squeezed my hand. "Yes. I'm going to Harvard Medical School. I've already finished the classroom portion, with straight A's mind you, and now I'm in my second year of clinical rotations at the Children's Hospital."

She positively beamed, but something didn't compute right in my mind. Some important piece of information was missing, and I needed it to fix this awful dread in my stomach. I glanced at the man again and something clicked.

"Gr..grace?" I asked, and my brows rose. I wasn't sure the meaning, but it seemed important enough for me to voice.

"She's fine," Valerie said, and while my shoulders relaxed, it didn't stop the building trepidation. She glanced at the gadget on her wrist. "They should be here in an hour or so." She picked up my wrist and stared at the same band she did a minute ago and then sighed, meeting my gaze again. "You don't remember much, do you?"

I tilted my head and put my hand back on her chest. "Love. I re..mem...ber." My tongue wasn't articulating as quickly as I wanted, and Tom moved his hands again.

"I don't know," she said, meeting his gaze.

"Don...'t know?"

"If you'll ever regain your memory," she answered, and her eyes misted again.

I thought about her words and looked around the room, specifically at the pictures covering the opposite wall. "Ho...ow lo...ong?" I pointed to the bed.

She took my hands and met my gaze. "A little over two years."

I blinked, unsure of what that really meant. I'm sure what she said would mean something sooner or later, but right now it had all the sense of what an hour was.

"Mind fuck," I said, clear as day, pleased that something came out without the halting lilt, and she actually giggled.

"Big time," she said and leaned in, pressing her lips to mine. Everything stopped, no sound, no sensation other than her lips on mine and it felt right as rain. When the kiss broke, I smiled. The little machine clipped to her pocket beeped, and she glanced at the scrolling symbols.

"I have to go, but I should be back before everyone gets here, okay?" She palmed my cheek.

I took her hand and put it on my chest, forcing the question out. "Lo...ove Chri...is?"

She stared at her hand and then my eyes and I swallowed with the sudden understanding her answer to my question was where the dread originated. If she didn't, I might as well crawl back into the nothingness that came before this room.

She leaned close and kissed my cheek.

"Yes, Chris. I still love you. I always will." When she pulled away, I bit my lip and nodded, fearing the sting in my eyes.

She caressed my cheek and smiled. "I have to go now, okay?"

"O...kay."

The minute she left the room, an emptiness filled me like the other half of my soul was now gone and I looked at the man. "Valer...ie?"

"Ya," he said.

I searched for the words. "Come...back?"

He folded his hands in his lap and nodded. I got a whiff of a memory from him. He'd had to relearn how to communicate, too, and my gaze dropped to his hands, and I closed my eyes.

"Sign?" I said and popped my eyes open.

"Ya," he said and pointed to his mouth. "*No tongue. I had to learn sign language. It was a bitch not being able to talk,*" he thought. "*But at least you didn't have to wait for me to go through the pains of trying to spell shit out with my hands.*"

I nodded but didn't really understand, and then I put my hand to my chest. "Chri...is."

He nodded and put his hand on his chest. "*Tom.*"

The connection to the first time he referred to the name clicked, and I said, "Tom. Bro...other."

"Ya," he said aloud and took the seat. "*Do you understand what brother means?*"

Before I told him I didn't, the door opened and a man wearing the same type of thing Valerie wore walked in.

"Hi," I said, and he glanced at the chart in his hand.

"Welcome back, Mr. Ryan," he said.

I put my hand to my chest. "Chri...is," I forced the word out.

His gaze traveled from mine to Tom's and Tom's hands started speaking their language. The doctor nodded and took the pen out of his pocket, scribbling on the chart before focusing on me again.

"Your brother said you're having a problem remembering things and difficulty speaking. That's quite normal for people waking from extended comas." He approached and did the same thing with my wrist that Valerie did. "Since you seem to be awake now, I can remove some of the tubes attached and we can see if you can walk, okay?"

"Okay," I said and shrugged.

He checked a bag attached to the bed and then looked at me. "You're going to feel a little pressure," he said and then folded the sheets back. He pulled on a pair of gloves and handled me, gently pulling on the tube that seemed to grow out of me.

Pressure, holy fuck, it was more like a burning fire line. "Oww," I said and then was rewarded with relief when the plastic thing disappeared. He straightened the sheet back into place and snapped the gloves off.

"Not the most comfortable of things, I'm sure, but it was necessary. I'm going to leave the I.V. in until we see how you do with food." He pointed to the bag.

"O...kay," I said.

"Do you think you can get up?"

"U...p?" I asked, not sure of what he meant. The fact that I should know this stuff just added a low level of frustration.

The doctor sat on the edge of the bed and then straightened. "Up."

I nodded and swung my legs over the side of the bed. He put his hand out for support and I stared at it a second before pushing off the bed myself. My feet landed on the floor and the chill of the tile seeped through my socks. I straightened like he had.

His brows creased. "Take a step." He showed me what he meant.

I did as he asked.

"Another."

I took another step, and he flipped open the chart, scribbling again. With no more direction, I crossed toward the pictures on the wall, but I was stopped by something in my arm. I stared at the tube holding me to a minimal distance from the bed. It ran from my arm to the bag of liquid.

"Out?" I asked, pointing at the thing and meeting the doctor's gaze.

"Not yet," he said and went back to scribbling.

Irritation flushed through me, and I stared at it again. "Pft," I said and yanked the blue connector. The tube separated, and I dropped the end onto the bed, crossing to the wall and tracing the pictures with my fingers.

"Mr. Ryan, we need to put the IV back in," the doctor said, and I met his gaze, shaking my head. He stepped toward me, and Tom put his hand up, stopping the doctor. Whatever his hands conveyed, the doctor gave a curt nod and left us alone.

Tom stepped next to me. *"Damian's kids drew those for you."* he thought, and I met his smiling gaze with no reference point to understand his commentary. *"Grace did this one."* he pointed to a vibrant angel drawing.

"Gr...ace?" I ran my hand along the waxy surface.

He nodded and his smile faded. *"I've got a little girl now, too,"* he thought. *"Her name is Hannah."*

"Han..n...ah?"

His eyes swam in a sheen of tears. *"I wish you had been awake when she was born."*

Tom turned away, and I grabbed his arm, struggling for the right word to say, and then the light bulb went off. "Con...gra." I closed my eyes, frustrated that I was having so much difficulty. I focused on the word, concentrating. "Con...grat...tu...la..tions." I smiled and opened my eyes.

He pressed the tips of his fingers to his lips and brought them down into the palm of his other hand. *Thank you* resounded in my head. A layer of comfort settled over me as I stared at him. I still remembered nothing, but I felt the kinship in his heart.

"I'm so...rry I..." I couldn't think of the right string of words that came after that and I looked at the ceiling for a little help. "There?" I glanced at him and bit the side of my lip.

He didn't speak, instead he pulled me into a hug. I awkwardly patted his back and when he pulled away, he crossed to the window and wiped his face. Glancing one more time at the wall, I sighed and headed back to the bed, climbing in and looked at the dripping tube.

"Help?"

Tom turned, and I held up the tube. He reached and pushed the red button again.

A few minutes later, a nurse came in and her eyebrows arched at me sitting up in the bed. "You're awake," she said, and I nodded without rolling my eyes at the obvious. I held up the IV lead in one hand and showed her the base plug in my hand, raising an eyebrow, hoping she'd know what the hell I was trying to convey. My thoughts seemed to come together more, but the trigger to my mouth was still shoddy at best.

She seemed to recover and crossed, her gaze moving to Tom's back at the window.

"Well, since you seem to be moving, maybe we can get you cleaned up? Would you like that?"

"Cl...ean?"

She paused, and Tom turned. I met his gaze, and he gave me a slight nod. *She's asking if you want to take a shower. It's probably not a bad idea.*

"Okay," I said. I seemed to have mastered that word and my assent pleased her.

"We can leave that out until we're done," she said.

"We?" I blinked as she helped me to my feet.

"Well, I can't leave you in there by yourself," she said in a perfectly reasonable tone.

I glanced at Tom for help, but he just smirked and turned back toward the window.

"I...my...self," I said with a little more force and stepped away from her.

She studied me standing on my own and then met my gaze. "I'll let you wash yourself, but I need to be in there with you."

"N...no."

"I," Tom said, pointing to his chest and crossing the distance. He spoke with his hands.

"If something happens," she argued, and his hands flew through another explanation I didn't understand.

She looked at me. "Your brother will stay with you in the bathroom, and I will wait just outside the door. Does that work for you?"

I nodded and trudged into the room she pointed to and stared at the open stall and the dials on the wall beyond the entrance. The logistics of taking a shower seemed foreign, and I glanced over my shoulder at Tom.

He sighed and closed his eyes, sending me a picture of what he did in a shower. It seemed reasonable, and I peeled the hospital gown off and pulled the paper undergarments off as well as my socks, leaving it on the floor and stepped inside the shower stall, waiting.

Tom reached beyond me and touched the control. *Pull and turn this way for hotter water,* he thought and hooked his thumb toward the entrance, *and that way for cooler water.* He pointed toward the back of the shower. He picked up a bottle. *Shampoo for your hair.* And after putting that down, he pointed at the small square bar. *Soap for your body. Got it?*

"Thi...ink so." I said and waited until he stepped away and then pulled the knob, turning it toward the entrance. Warm rain fell from the spout, but it got hot enough to scald, and I realized I was turning the knob the wrong way and quickly dialed it the other way. I was rewarded with frigid water. Shivering, I slowly turned the dial back until the water hit the perfect temperature.

I stepped under the stream, closing my eyes and letting the water pound my face and chest. Sensations returned along with a glimpse of another shower at another time. My eyes shot open, and I tried to force the memory. The penalty for trying to pull blood from a stone was the slam of vertigo. I reached for the wall and Tom's hand grabbed my wrist, giving me a steadying hold.

I sent a weak smile in his direction and repeated the hand gesture he used to say thank you. He gave me a nod and released his grip with his eyebrows rising in a question. I nodded. I would be okay as long as I didn't pry my mind open with brute force.

Another inconvenient truth occurred after the shampoo suds flowed into my open eyes. It was a stinging lesson to always close your eyes when you're rinsing shampoo from your hair. The grin that formed on Tom's lips prompted me to raise my middle finger at him. It was an automatic reaction, and I stared at my finger as he broke out into a snorting laugh. I turned and rinsed my stinging eyes out before making sure no stray soap was still in my hair. When it squeaked between my fingers, I gathered it was clean.

Once I seemed to have cleaning my hair mastered, I took the bar of soap in my hands and ran it over my chest. The clean scent filled the steam-filled enclosure, and I followed the silent instruction Tom had given me.

When I was done and the soap returned to the dish, I just stood under the spray, letting it pelt my back.

I sent a smile to Tom, and he returned it before twirling his finger. I knew the gesture, but I wasn't sure what it meant. I tilted my head and scrunched my brow.

Wrap it up.

I pushed the knob, and the water shut off. Tom handed me a towel, and I dried off with little instruction. I even wrapped the towel around my waist without help. We stepped back into the room.

"Cl...ean." I said to the nurse.

"Did you brush your teeth?" She pointed to her teeth, and I shook my head. She grabbed me by the elbow and led me back into the bathroom. A tube and a little brush sat on the counter, and she picked it up, lining it with a dab from the tube and handed it to me. I pulled it to my mouth and followed the motions she was doing with her finger on her own teeth.

The minty taste filled my mouth, creating a pleasant tingle.

"Now spit in the sink and rinse the brush."

I spit and tentatively reached for the controls on the faucet. When I successfully turned it on and did what she said, I replaced the brush where she picked it up.

She grabbed a towel and wiped my lips before swiping it across the steamy wall, revealing her reflection along with Tom near the door and another man. It took me a moment to realize the blue eyes glued to the reflection were mine.

The nurse handed me another utensil, and I studied the thin tool.

"It's a comb. For your hair." She took it from my hand and ran it gently over the top of her hair from brow to crown and I nodded, taking it from her and doing the same until my hair was knot-free and slicked back. It wasn't much longer than Tom's and easy to manage.

"That's good. Let's see if we can find you something clean to wear, okay?"

I nodded and followed her into the room where Tom had already laid out a pair of underwear on the bed, along with thin pants and a shirt. Studying the different articles of clothing, I figured out the correct way to put the underwear on, along with the pants. I left the pull tie loose because after a couple of attempts; I didn't get how it clasped together.

The shirt slid on over my shoulders with buttons on the front, but I left it open.

The nurse stepped forward, reaching to help, and I stopped her.

"Not...co...old."

"All right," she said and led me back to the bed, helping me under crisp sheets.

I pointed to the bed. "Cl...ean?"

"Yes, I changed it while you were in the shower." She picked up the IV line and reattached it. "There you go," she said and patted my hand. "If you need to use the bathroom, this can roll with you now." She showed me I was no longer tied to the bed.

"Th...ank.....you," I said, along with the proper hand gesture.

She left with a smile, and I turned to Tom.

"Th...th.....is st..stut.....r.....g sucks."

He laughed and nodded. "Ya wo a mi." *Yeah, worse than mine.*

I raised my eyebrows. "De...b.....te." I inhaled, forcing the rest out. "Able."

He sat down and folded his hand over his fist, leaning it on his grinning lips.

Before I formulated another response, the door slammed open in a flurry of activity. The noise and chaos shocked fear into my blood and I pulled my knees closer to my chest in response, wrapping my hands around them and staring as a group of people poured in.

"Uncle CJ!" a little voice pierced the room and a small child broke free of her mother's hand, her coat flying off and landing a few feet away as she jumped, grabbed onto the rail, and climbed onto the bed.

Paying no mind to my raised knees, she squeezed between my chest and legs and plunked down in my lap, clapping her hands with joyful glee.

I didn't know whether to be horrified or humored by this, and I stared into the hauntingly dark eyes and smiled as her little hands cupped my cheeks.

"Grace, get off him," the woman from whom she broke free said.

"Gr...race," I said, and she nodded emphatically. "I like.. pic..tu...re," I added, pointing towards the wall.

She patted my cheeks and turned. "Mommy. Uncle CJ!"

I pulled my gaze away from the happy child on my lap and glanced at the group still piling in the door. Tom had joined a pretty red head holding a little swing from her arm. It took a second, but the word car seat came to my mind. Behind the red head stood a man who looked a great deal like Tom and confusion clouded my mind.

The sudden chaos overwhelmed me, and I didn't know where to look. I recognized no one and my heart started the fast pump of an unfathomable fear. Even the little girl bouncing on my lap presented mental challenges that made the room spin.

Grace placed her hands on my cheeks again, pulling my attention to her. There was no more smile gracing her lips, just a sad expression that further clouded my judgment and breathing got harder. Everything twisted into prisms, and I blinked. My vision righted, but small lines of heat rolled down my cheeks.

"It's okay," the child whispered.

"Guys!" the familiar voice cut through the noise.

My gaze snapped to Valerie standing in the doorway, a tray balanced on one hand and her other propped on her hip with an expression I wouldn't want aimed at me. Her gaze met mine and locked on there for a minute. The way they traveled down my chest and back up gave me that warm tingly feeling and I sent her the hand signal for thank you.

"Guys, you're overwhelming him," she said, stepping inside and closing the door behind her. She crossed and messed up Grace's hair before setting the tray on the little table to my right. "I brought you something to eat," she said before taking my hand and turning to the group. "Chris is awake, but he's suffering from regressive amnesia. He doesn't remember a thing before waking up here."

I opened my mouth to argue, and she shot me a 'shut up until I'm done' glare. I closed my mouth, meeting Grace's gaze. The smile was back, but it was tempered by my unease.

"That is also affecting his ability to speak," she added, and I nodded.

"Wo...ords h...ha...hard," I added, scanning the six adults standing at the foot of my bed. I glanced at Tom and the woman with the red hair. He had his arm around. His attention wasn't on me, it was on the baby in her arms.

"Han...nah?"

Tom looked up and smiled, taking the baby from the redhead and bringing her to me. *My daughter,* he thought, and Grace moved to my side while Tom placed the baby in my arms. It was so small and wiggly. I shifted and found a comfortable hold and she settled down, making a little squeal before Tom put a small pacifier in her mouth.

"Beau...bu." I closed my eyes. I knew what I wanted to say, but it was too complex for my mouth to form.

"Beautiful," Valerie whispered, and I opened my eyes, nodding, meeting her gaze. "Chris, this is our family." she gestured toward the now silent crowd.

"F...fam...il..ly?"

"Yeah, babe. Family."

"Oh," I replied and tried to remember. Even one memory would be a blessing, but it was a big black hole. I shifted the baby to my hands, handing her back to Tom.

"Don't force it, hon. It'll come."

What if it didn't? What if I never remembered my past with these people?

I closed my eyes for a minute and the sensation of falling hit. I jerked on the bed, grabbing the edges. My eyes popped open, and the panic came alive in my veins.

Valerie turned to the group. "I think maybe we should do this another day."

I didn't argue, dropping my gaze to my hands, fidgeting with the edge of the blanket as Valerie ushered them out, exchanging hushed whispers about my condition. She stepped back in and crossed the distance, taking a seat and pulling the tray closer.

"So...ory," I whispered, feeling as small as Grace.

She reached under my chin, tilting my head so I'd meet her gaze. "Never apologize for being overwhelmed."

"Wha.." I stopped and clenched my fists. "What if I nev..ver..."

She put the tips of her fingers on my lips, stopping me. "It takes time."

The mention of time got me thinking. "H..how...m...man...y hours," I paused a moment and took a breath to force the rest of my question out. "i...is tw...two ye...years?"

She sighed and her lips moved as she silently calculated it for me. "17,520 hours. You've been in a coma for a little over twenty thousand hours."

My brain couldn't wrap around that now that I knew what an hour felt like. I covered my face, running my fingers into my hair, trying to grasp it. Valerie stood and headed toward the door. I didn't want her to leave, and I glanced at the open door. It slammed closed. Something had leaped from my chest and the door closed.

I stared with my mouth open, and Valerie turned, propping her hands on her waist and gave me a look that reduced me to shame.

"I wasn't leaving. I was going to close the door."

"Oh," I studied my hands.

When she returned to my bedside, she pushed the tray aside and shooed me over on the mattress, taking a seat so she faced me. "The fact you survived was a miracle," she started and stopped, her eyes dropped to the spot right in front of her.

It was my turn to lift her chin.

"Even my ability to heal took time to put you back together," she said when our eyes met.

"Why d...on't I re...mem...ber you here?" I asked and tapped my head. "Wh..hen I re...mem...ber you here." I pointed to my heart. I didn't really expect an answer, so when she spoke, I moved, pulling her to me and crushing her lips against mine.

This time, her lips parted, and I followed her lead. Our tongues entwined in the most sensual kiss. Slow and lazy and breathless. She pulled away when my hand dropped to her breast, caressing her through the thin fabric.

"Someone could walk in," she said.

I looked at the door and then the ceiling as I searched for the word I was looking for. "Lo...ock." The word hiccupped from my lips but was perfectly enunciated in my head and the click of the lock on the door engaging made me smile and I turned back to Valerie.

A smile gained traction on her lips.

I reached out and pulled the elastic out of her hair before running both of my hands through her dark satin locks. The silky feel of it caressed my hands. I traced her face, memorizing the lines, burning every sensation into my brain, so if I ever lost my way again, I would know her anywhere. When my thumb ran over her lips, she kissed it and met my gaze.

"Are you going to kiss me or what?" she whispered, her swirling eyes sparkled.

I licked my lips and curled my hand around the back of her neck, guiding her toward me. Sensations billowed over my skin, covering me with a need that drove my actions. The kiss I delivered started tentatively, stirring the molten lava in the center of my being. I moved from her lips to under her jaw, finding a spot that made her shiver.

Running my hands under the lab coat, I peeled it off, revealing a sleeveless V-neck shirt. I pulled her into my lap and turned, laying her against the pillow before continuing my exploration of her. Each layer I peeled off of her brought more delights, and she never interrupted my studies. My fingers memorized her curves, and my tongue memorized her taste. Her spring-like musk tickled my nose and her soft purr recorded into my mind forever. She filled every one of my senses with awe.

Time meant nothing to me right now. All I wanted was this goddess.

I crawled back from my inspection of her finely painted toes with a hunger I couldn't categorize. She smiled at me and guided my hand between her legs. I circled the wet folds with my fingers, watching her mouth part and head tilt back when they ran over a certain spot. The effect her pleasure had on me was irresistible.

She widened her legs, and I smiled, leaning over and covering the area she liked best with my mouth, circling my tongue over the flesh.

"Oh, God, Chris," she said in a throaty sigh that coaxed me to continue the motion.

Her hand threaded into my hair, guiding me to the spot that quickened her breath. I slid my index finger inside her wet folds, slowly because I wasn't sure exactly what I was doing, but it all felt surreal and my senses were highly attuned to her.

"Faster," she whispered, and it took me a moment for the word to compute, but instead of honoring her request, I wasn't ready to set aside the physical study of what drove her crazy. I smiled and purposely slowed down. Sucking her in a way that pulled a moan from her chest.

"That's not faster," she said, her eyes half-crazy with delight.

"I know," I said, still rolling my tongue around her. The fact the words didn't stutter wasn't lost on either of us. My gaze dropped from her stormy eyes to her hard nipples, and I left my post between her legs, kissing my way up her body, much to her chagrin.

I kept my hand between her legs, circling the spots my tongue had while I covered each nipple with my mouth, sucking gently, and she arched into me, pulling me closer to her bosom.

When I found her lips, she kissed me with a fervor that sucked the air out of my lungs and left me as breathless as she was.

"Make love to me," she whispered when our lips parted.

"I am."

She peeled my shirt off, nipping at my neck as her fingers fumbled with my pants and couldn't quite reach to do anything more than shift the waistline. "Take your pants off," she said.

I leaned back on my knees and pushed them down as she instructed and stared at my hard member. I glanced up at her, unsure whether or not to be alarmed. Valerie smiled and reached for me, her hand gentle and soft around my skin as she stroked.

I entered the next stage of heaven when she guided me inside her. I stretched out, and she wrapped her legs around me, our hips moved in slow exquisite circles, my body entered sensory overload and I took her breast in my mouth, speeding up the sensations until I thought my heart was going to pound right out of my chest.

A wave started in my toes and rocketed up my legs, seizing every muscle and I groaned, burying my head into the crook of her neck. Spasms clenched me, making my body tremble all at once and then my muscles acted like I had been hit with a tranquilizer dart, slowly relaxing until all that was left was a trembling mass of flesh.

I lifted my head and met her gaze, and she pulled me to her lips. I moved the necklace and pressed my ear to her chest. The drum of her heart made my eyelids droop.

"Chris?"

"Mmm," I looked up at her.

"I need to get up," she said and pointed to the bathroom.

I rolled off her and watched as she slid off the bed, gathering her clothing. She headed into the bathroom without looking at me, and my euphoria faded. I pulled up my pants and tightened the strings, but again I couldn't figure out what to do with them.

The toilet flushed, but she didn't come out right away and I wondered if I had done something wrong. Instead of waiting, I slid off the bed and grabbed the rolling IV bar. I rounded the corner, and she stood leaning on the sink with her head down. Her shoulders shook.

"Val?" the shortened version rolled off my tongue easily, and she stiffened. Her head rose enough for me to catch a glimpse of her tear-stained face. "Di...id I do so...some...thi...ing wro...ng?"

She turned and shook her head. "You did everything right," she said.

I closed the distance. "Th...then wha...at?" I wiped the tears with my thumbs, searching her eyes for answers.

She let out a laugh. "You unhinge me,"

"So...or...ry"

"Please don't apologize for being perfect," she said.

It was my turn to laugh. Perfect? I knew what that meant, and she had to be the one with brain damage. I wasn't perfect by any means. I couldn't remember my family or even my full name and I couldn't speak worth a damn.

"Christopher James Ryan."

"Huh?"

"Your full name. Your family calls you CJ for short. I like your real name as opposed to the nickname. It's softer, sweeter." Her cheeks turned red, and she sniffled and turned back to the sink, splashing water on her face and then patting it dry with the towel.

"I think you'll be able to go home in a few days if you continue to do this well."

When she turned towards me, I stepped closer, looking down into her eyes, and pressed my palm to the warm flesh over her heart. "I am home."

Angel Grace Chapter 25

I WOKE TO A darkened room, disoriented. It took me a second to place where I was, and another to realize I was alone. Valerie was no longer in my arms like she had been when we fell asleep. I turned to the chair, expecting to see her curled on the cushion, but it was empty, and my heart skipped and pounded in my throat.

Pressure pushed down on my chest, and I glanced at the door. The lock wasn't engaged, and I slid out of bed, unsure of which direction to go. My body made the choice for me when the sudden urge to piss overshadowed my desire to find Valerie. I headed toward the bathroom and relieved myself, like Valerie had instructed last night. Before starting my search, I brushed my teeth and ran the comb through my unruly hair, putting it in some semblance of order. My gaze dropped to the medallion, and I ran my fingers over the black and red star before meeting my gaze. I studied my reflection, not finding any noticeable scar on my face or chest that would warrant dropping into the black for two years. With a shake of my head, I turned, collecting my pants off the floor and put them on before I ventured beyond the only environment I had a memory of.

Hesitation stalled my muscles as I opened the door to a brightly lit hallway. Quiet permeated the floor, but I could hear soft voices in the distance. I just wasn't sure which way they were coming from. I ducked my head out, looking both ways for a sign of where she would have gone. Given the choice of two non-distinct directions, I turned to my right, studying the symbols on the doors and the brightly colored lines on the floor. Artwork speckled the walls, most drawings by young hands, and I smiled as I passed a collection that reminded me of Grace's art.

The voice grew as I got closer to where the hall opened up to a bright area. A collection of nurses stood behind a desk on the left side of the atrium watching as a candy striper read to a group of children. I leaned on the entryway, listening to the story as the girl read. Halfway through the next page, she glanced up and her voice faltered as her gaze fell on me.

Some children looked over their shoulder at me, their heads in varying states of hair loss or covered with hats. Those that saw me turned back when the girl continued the story. To the right of the entrance was a large object that I couldn't find the right word for and in front of it sat a small bench. I crossed and took a seat, still able to see the girl, but my gaze dropped to the black and white ivory keys in front of me.

One child in the back got up and crossed to where I sat. She leaned on the edge or the instrument and asked, "Do you play?"

"I d...don...t know." My speech was still a crap shoot, and I offered a halfhearted shrug. "Wha...at is i...it?"

"It's a piano," she said and, shooed me aside.

I moved, giving her space on the bench and watched her place her thin fingers on the keys. "This is middle C." She pressed the note. I grinned at the melody of that one note and then she enthralled me more by playing a progression up and down the scale for me.

"My mom used to make me practice all the time." She ran through the scales and then pulled her fingers away and stared at me. "What's wrong with you?"

I shrugged and tapped my head. "No mem...m...or...y." Instead of trying to articulate the same question, I pointed at her and raised my eyebrows.

"Cancer," she said. "They think the chemo will help this time."

"I ho…pe so."

"Thank you. I gotta get back." She slid off the bench just as the girl closed the book.

My gaze dropped to the piano keys, and I placed my fingers on them, closing my eyes. My fingers moved of their own accord, filling the atrium with the slow cadence of music. I played the tune and then repeated it. Words flowed in time with the melody, softly at first and then drifting over the children. When I got to the chorus, more voices than my own joined me, singing Hallelujah, and I opened my eyes.

I didn't know where the words or the music were coming from, but I had no stutter and the rapt attention of everyone in the vicinity made me smile. I slid my gaze to the entryway that I had come from, and Valerie stood in the center with cups in her hands and her mouth open in surprise.

The children and some adults came closer. I continued, even as a rash of gooseflesh crawled up my arms and before long, everyone was singing with me. The rush of it created a heat in my cheeks and when I finished, silence blanketed the room for a minute before the clapping started.

I stared at my hands and then the people prompting me to play something else. Even the little girl who had told me this was a piano was egging me on. I glanced at Valerie and her paralysis broke. She crossed the distance.

"Okay, kids, Chris needs to go back to his room now," she said, and eyes turned to her.

"But Dr. Denongalis," one child whined, and she raised an eyebrow. The group collectively whined "aww" and disbursed.

"I didn't know you played," she said, staring at me before she handed me the cup.

I shrugged. "I di…dn't know, eith…ther."

Her eyebrow cocked. "That's my favorite song."

"Oh."

"And you sang it flawlessly." She took my elbow, leading me back toward my room. "Come on. You need to have some tests today to make sure everything is okay."

"Okay." I followed her back to the room, studying the walls again as I passed. "Why here?" I asked, pleased when the simple words came out without a stutter.

She glanced over her shoulder. "I wanted you where my rotation was. So, you're at Dana Farber in the children's section."

I thought about our escapades last night and heat filled my face. If I had known we were in the children's ward... ah hell, I still would have indulged. When we stepped into the room, the man who looked similar to Tom turned from his station at the window. My smile faded.

"You never told me Chris could play the piano," she said to him.

He let out a small laugh. "He doesn't."

With that, I was now the focal point of both sets of eyes.

"How did you do that?" she asked in just a small whisper.

I raised a shoulder. "I heard it in my head."

With a couple of blinks, she turned toward the man. "Chris, this is Steve. He's your father."

"I adopted you after your parents died," he added, clarifying his role further. "You and Tom have called me Uncle Steve ever since."

I gave him a nod, and my gaze dropped to the floor. "I don't remember you," I said, but the words didn't flow as smooth from my mouth as they did in my head. At least now the single syllable words didn't pause and restart like a stuck recording like the rest. I hated the fact that I was still struggling.

"It's okay," he said, his voice soft and low, and I looked up into his blue irises. "Valerie asked me to come because, if the tests show nothing to be alarmed about, she said, I can take you home."

I stepped back and my gaze slid to Valerie.

"If everything checks out, you can't stay," she said, the conflict in her eyes hammered against my chest.

"But?"

"I will see you at home when this rotation ends." Her stern eyes met mine in the same way she scolded the children a few minutes ago, but I knew under the sternness was hesitation.

It should have made me feel better that she didn't want me to go, but it didn't. As a matter of fact, I didn't like this at all. This was familiar and calm and the only normal I knew. Being with her was home. "How long?"

"I have another six weeks here."

"How man...ny hours?" I said because six weeks didn't mean squat to me.

"There are twenty-four hours in a day and seven days in a week." She crossed her arms.

The calculation in my head took the same time as it took her to cross her arms. "A thousand hours?" I gawked.

"One thousand and eight, to be exact," she said. "You can visit on weekends if you want," she said, and I nodded while the center of my body slowly twisted into a knot. "And we'll have to get you a piano."

The heat rose in my cheeks. I still didn't understand how I did that, but the way she looked watching me was worth going out and buying a hundred pianos. "When you come home," I said.

She sent a smile my way and handed me the shirt that hung over the end of the bed. "Time for us to take a look at your magnificent brain," she said, and I didn't meet Steve's gaze, but he did chuckle and took a seat in the chair, opening a tablet and settled in.

The machine was loud, and I had to stay still while it rattled around me. Valerie's voice kept telling me I was doing well, appeasing my unease with soft assurances every time the anxiety ratcheted up. The whispers of thought tickled my mind and while I didn't understand the terminology being used, I got the awe and excitement at what they saw.

I stared at the white plastic and the more I thought about leaving, the more the knot in my stomach clenched. The machine finally silenced, and Valerie came in, pulling me out of the scanner. Her gaze told me I was more than fine, and I closed my eyes. Sighing.

As we walked back to the room, I asked. "Before. How long did we..."

She slowed to a stop and met my gaze. "How long were we together before you got hurt?"

"Yes."

She sighed. "Three days."

"Three days?" The declaration sent a wave of chills through me. "What the fuck?"

She pulled me into an empty room. "Neither of us expected it at all. And in case you hadn't noticed, neither of us is what you would call normal. Normal people can't heal with a kiss or read minds or lock doors with a thought."

I crossed my arms and stared down at her, unconvinced. Even without much of a memory, I knew three days didn't make this kind of connection. It had to have been more.

"We shared memories," she finally said. "When we first touched, we got a download of each other's lives. It was a real mind fuck because, in a matter of seconds, it was like we were lifetime friends with a hell of a physical connection."

"How..." I didn't know how to articulate the question and stepped back, clenching my fists in frustration. "Three days?" I asked instead.

She nodded. "You were my first," she said, and I looked at her, blinking, trying to catch up. "Last night was my second time, ever." Her voice softened. "You aren't imagining the connection. I was lost for the last two years, walking around like half my soul was gone."

"But three days to be this..." I paused and swallowed, targeting the right word. "De...pen...dant?"

"It's not logical. But then again, you playing a song that I played at least a dozen times a week when you were in a coma, like you performed it a thousand times, isn't logical. You nearly dying..." she pressed her lips together and her mind closed with a slam.

"What happened to me?"

"You saved our lives," she said and stepped around me to the door.

I grabbed her arm, and she met my gaze.

178

"Seeing you so broken..." Tears filled her eyes, and she shook her head, unable to speak for a minute as her locked down memories overtook the conversation. She took a deep breath and continued, "I'm in love with you, Chris. I have been since you first kissed me. For me, it wasn't the memory download, it was that kiss. Time stopped and nothing existed but you and as much as I didn't want to, you stole my heart by believing in me like no one else ever had. I waited for you, not knowing if you'd ever wake up."

Tears painted her face. "You became home to me."

"You're my home." I leaned in and kissed her gently and accepted our bizarre attachment. I really had no choice. The thought of navigating life without her left me terrified.

Angel Grace Chapter 26

STEVE NAVIGATED THE CAR out of the parking lot and wound his way around the city until we pulled onto a wider road. Signs with symbols hung on the overpasses and we eventually turned off the two-lane highway in favor of a wider stretch. I still couldn't read, and I wondered just how long it would be until that ironed itself out. Instead of trying to study the roadways and signs that were as foreign to me as anything else, I studied the scenery for a while.

"Piano?" he said after a while.

"Yeah," I said.

"Huh," he huffed, shaking his head like that was the damnedest thing.

"What happened?" I asked, pushing the stilted words out.

Steve sighed and continued staring out at the road. "A lot," he finally said and glanced at me before focusing on driving.

I waited for more, but it was obvious nothing was coming. All I heard was a low-level static from him. "Are you really my uncle?"

He smiled and shook his head. "No. I met your father while I was on a case and we kind of grew on each other. Unfortunately, he was killed in the crossfire and your mother died later that same year. Murdered by the same wacko who nearly killed your brother."

"What do you do?" I stuttered, now more nervous to be around someone associated with so much death.

"I used to be a special agent with the Federal Bureau of Investigation. A cop," he added when I raised an eyebrow.

"Cop?"

He bit his lip, and the space between his eyebrows creased. "A cop keeps the peace and goes after the bad guys. Their job is to keep people safe," he said, trying to boil it down into simplistic terms.

"Valerie said I saved everyone's life. Does that make me a cop?"

"No. You aren't a cop." He glanced at me. "You're just a kid who stepped into something far worse than you could handle alone, and we nearly lost you."

"Why is everyone being so cryptic?"

He laughed. "It's our turn to keep you safe," he said and met my gaze. "Valerie doesn't think you're ready yet, and I have to trust the doctor's instincts."

I crossed my arms and sank farther into the seat, opting to watch the other cars on the road instead of engaging in any further conversation.

"Give it time," he said, pulling my gaze back to him. "It's been a rough road for all of us and we'd just like the chance for you to get to know us before we walk you through what happened. Okay?"

I caught the sheen of tears in his eyes, and he blinked them away without shedding any.

"Okay," I agreed.

He glanced at me. "You're doing a little better talking than you were yesterday," he said.

"Yes." I continued watching the scenery. "Small words work, the rest, not so much."

"Val said you still had an issue reading. Do you recognize any letters on the road signs?"

I glanced at the green signs with white symbols and shook my head. "No."

"Well, we'll have to work on that."

His matter-of-fact statement made me shift in the seat. "I don't understand how the words are in my head, but I can't remember what they look like."

"The brain is a funny thing." He glanced at me. "I assume you can still do some things you did before?"

I stared at him, hesitating for a moment before nodding. If Valerie trusted him enough to let him take me out of the hospital, then perhaps I should put some trust in the man.

He gave me a soft smile. "I used to have some of that magic mojo," he said and sighed. "The illusion of invincibility was a comfort most of the time and reading Jen's mind was always an adventure." He laughed. "It's been an adjustment not having it anymore."

"What happened?"

Steve sighed. "Valerie. She was sick and in order for Damian and me to get her out of danger, I had to heal her." He was quiet for a bit. "It was kind of the same thing that happened to me when I first..." he trailed off, searching for the right word. "Absorbed your older brother's powers. It was as much of a shock to him as it had been for me."

"Tom?" I asked, focusing in on the word brother.

"No, Eric. He died the same year as your parents."

"You sure seem to be around a lot of dead people," I said.

He laughed. "True, and some stick with you longer than others." His laughter wound down and there was an emptiness about him that etched into the lines of his face. "Silence is another thing I've had to get used to."

"Huh?"

"The constant undercurrent of thoughts of those around you?" He sent a knowing glance at me. "It's white noise until you focus and then it's like being invisible in the middle of a private conversation. But now that I'm back to normal, I don't have that and I never thought I'd say this, but between you and me... I miss it."

"I thought it was normal," I muttered.

He chuckled. "No. It took some getting used to for someone who has never had any ability to speak of. I remember the first night. I was at Quantico with a training class and the noise drove me bat shit. Your brother hadn't given me any instructions on how to lower the thought assault from an overwhelming roar to white noise. Instead, he found my struggle amusing, but I can't blame him. I wasn't all that happy when everything I had transferred to Valerie."

"I bet." I wouldn't be very comfortable with someone depleting my powers, either. Although, I wasn't sure of the realm of gifts I possessed. I just knew it felt like a ball of pure energy at the center of my body that snaked through every membrane of my form, creating a constant hum in my skin.

We both got quiet, and I watched the green scenery pass.

"Why me?" I asked as I turned the conversation over in my head.

"Why what?" he asked as we approached a scenic bridge overlooking a water way.

"Why do I have these... powers?"

He shook his head and shrugged. "I don't know. I think your mother was naturally blessed, along with your older brother, but their powers didn't really trigger until your mom met your father." Steve navigated from the high-speed lane to the right-hand lane, slowing down a little. "You were born out of that union of love and power and because of that, you're unique in ways a lot of us can't comprehend." He glanced at me and then set the blinker, taking the exit ramp. "In some ways, your uniqueness reminds me of Grace."

I lost focus on the conversation, studying the quaint town we drove through, and the glimpses I had of the water on a few of the curves. Steve pulled down a side road and approached a large home surrounded by a black iron fence and an immaculately manicured lawn. The fence looped around both sides of the house, blockading the residence from the bordering properties until it met up with a low stone wall and the water beyond. It was an impressive piece of oceanfront property.

Steve pressed the remote attached to the visor and the gates slowly opened, leading to a short driveway and a three-car garage. "This is your home," he said and something about the way he stressed the word your pulled my gaze to him. He stopped and turned off the car before meeting my gaze. "Your parents left it to you. We've been living here with you since you were nine years old."

"Oh," I said, and stepped out of the car when he did. The house was quiet when we entered. The garage attached to an open family room-kitchen concept that was warm and inviting. Beyond the sitting area stood sliding glass doors and an enviable view of the ocean. I crossed to them and stared out at the large, pristine pool. It all looked inviting and utterly foreign.

"Did you want to see your room? I'm sure your swim trunks are still in the drawers somewhere," Steve said, and the thought of jumping in that water turned me on my heels. I followed him up the stairs and we turned to the left. Steve showed me where the bathroom was and across the hall, he opened the door to what he said was my bedroom.

I stepped inside, hoping for some reference of familiarity and it just felt strange. Pictures on the shelves clearly contained me in them, along with some of the people who had come into the room yesterday. I picked up one of Tom and me, leaning together in formal attire, our champagne glasses raised, and grins plastered on our faces.

"Tom's wedding," Steve said when I turned to him. "You two had a little too much to drink."

I put the frame back on the shelf and picked up another one with three pictures. The center was a man in a suit who looked a lot like me and a stunning woman in a white dress. On one side, the woman stood with four children and on the other; the man sat with two boys on his knees.

"My parents?" I stuttered and got a nod in response.

"You remember them?" The hopeful arch of his brow hit a nerve, and I put the picture back on the shelf. It was a nice-looking family, but I didn't have any recollection of them.

"No. I look a lot like my father," I replied, pointing.

"Yes, you do." He stepped closer and pointed to one of the older children. "That's your brother, Eric. He was my partner at Quanitco. And that's Emily, your older sister. I never got the chance to meet her."

I stared at the picture. "Only Tom and I are alive?"

"Yes." He sighed and opened the top drawer of the bureau under the shelf of pictures. "Your swim trunks are in here. I'm going to enjoy the rest of the afternoon by the pool." He crossed to the door. "I'll bring my tablet out and we can start re-learning how to read and get you some basics of sign language so you and Tom can communicate."

"We talked just fine yesterday," I said, glancing at him and tapped my temple.

"You may have heard him without an issue, but he struggled to understand you, so having the sign language as a backup will help him. He can't read minds."

"Oh," I said, and he left me standing in what should have been a comfortable room, but I just wanted to be with Valerie, not here, feeling empty and lost.

Angel Grace Chapter 27

THE SUMMER HEAT HIT me when I stepped out on the patio. I crossed to the chairs and took a seat on the lounge chair next to where Steve's things were stacked. He was in the pool swimming laps. I squinted, scanning the oceanscape beyond the rock wall.

A tablet sat on the table between the chairs, and I picked it up, swiping my finger across the screen like Valerie had with my chart. It came to life, and I stared at all the icons, unsure of what to do next. None of the symbols meant anything to me and instead of trying to figure it out, I placed the tablet where I picked it up and lowered the back of the chair, closing my eyes in the warmth of the sunshine.

Pain gripped me, and I sat up with my breath ripping at my chest. Steve pulled himself out of the pool. Concern traced the lines in his face and his sharp gaze was locked on me. I glanced around the empty backyard with my heart pounding in my throat, not understanding the panic that overwhelmed me.

"Are you okay?" he asked, approaching me.

I shook my head, afraid to speak. My gaze continued to dart around, like I expected a monster to appear from the shadows.

"Just take a deep breath," he said and sat on the end of the adjoining chair.

I did as he said, and my head cleared.

"Take another breath," he said when I glanced at him.

Fragments of my dream surfaced, and I winced, shrinking into the chair at the intensity.

"You fell asleep," he said, and I nodded.

"Nightmare," I whispered in my broken way. The scratchy fear in my voice flipped the irritation switch. "I'm okay. Just thirsty," I said, forcing my muscles to relax.

Steve reached over the side of his chair and opened a cooler. He handed me a bottle of chilled water and I sucked it down, the coolness quenching my thirst and calming my nerves.

"You might want to jump in the pool to cool off."

I couldn't argue with his offer, and I drained the bottle before I approached the pristine water. The breeze ruffled through my hair, and I closed my eyes, letting the wind dry the layer of sweat on my skin. Before I jumped into the pool, the sliders opened, and a woman stepped out. The smile that formed warmed me. It took me a moment to place her name and then Steve filled in the blank without knowing it.

Jennifer. Steve's wife and, by default, my mother. She crossed the distance with a tentative gait, and I turned toward her instead of the welcoming pool.

"I'm glad you're home," she said, looking up at me, and then she stepped in and gave me a warm hug. "We've missed you," she said, and pulled away when I didn't reciprocate the hug.

"Thank you," I said and turned away, diving into the cool water. The chill of the water brought me to life, and I surfaced, shaking my head and flipping my wet hair out of my face. It refreshed in a way that soothed my hot nerves.

I climbed the ladder to the edge of the pool just as the rest of the crew came rolling out the door. Tom gave me a wave, and I sent a nod of acknowledgement in his direction. The quiet of the backyard erupted into activity, and I found a towel and dried off before the chaos got to me. I excused myself and headed into the house.

"CJ?"

I stopped with my foot on the first step and glanced at the door. A man filled the doorway, and I couldn't recall his name, but he was the man Grace had run to at the hospital.

"I never got to say thank you," he said.

I had no idea what to say, so I just nodded and headed upstairs without another word. In the bedroom, I slipped on dry shorts and turned on the laptop on the desk and picked up the piece of paper Valerie had given me just before I left the hospital. She had drawn the instructions of how to call her using the computer and I followed the pictures, plugging in the symbols on the keypad in the order they were drawn. The program buzzed, and I waited.

When her picture filled the frame, I exhaled and closed my eyes, hanging my head with the overwhelming relief.

"Hey. Are you okay?" her tender voice caressed me.

"Yes." I opened my eyes to her beautiful face. "I just miss you."

She glanced down at the desk in front of her and then back at me. "I miss you, too," she said and folded a notebook closed.

When she stretched, I just wanted to wrap my arms around her, and I shut my eyes. When I opened them, I stood in the room right behind her. The image on the computer was an eerie version of me, with a layer of milky white over my naturally bright eyes. Even with my non-existent memory, I knew this was not normal.

Valerie turned towards me and stood, running her hands up my chest with eyes filled with wonder. She grinned and wrapped her arms around my neck, pulling me to her lips. The sweetness of the kiss drew my breath from my lungs, and I was the one who broke free first. I traced her face with my fingertips and met her gaze.

"What the hell am I?" I whispered, looking between her and her computer screen.

"You are a very special man." She cupped my cheek, running her thumb gently over my lips before meeting my gaze.

I laughed softly. Special? This was more in the land of a freak than I cared to understand.

"Whatever runs through your blood gave you the ability to recover. A normal human would not have come back from the amount of raw damage you were brought to me with. It scared the living daylights out of me. My magic healing infusions brought your body back from the edge of death, but you had such severe brain damage that none of the doctors thought you'd ever regain the ability for coherent thought, never mind the ability to speak again. I like to think I had a little to do with your being able to function, but I think it was more about your inherent gifts than mine." She reached up on her tiptoes and kissed me gently.

"Speaking is debatable," I stuttered, and she smiled.

"I'm on call right now, so you have to go back." She pointed toward the computer monitor.

"How?" I didn't even know how the hell I got there in the first place.

"Just release the connection. Let go."

I hesitated and then dropped my arms, stepped back, and closed my eyes. The sensation of being pulled overtook me and I opened my eyes to my room and her smiling on the computer screen.

"Now, do you understand why I wasn't as concerned as you about not being in Maine?"

I slowly nodded. "I can do that whenever we talk?"

She put her palm on the screen and I covered it with mine, staring into her swirling irises. "Not necessarily. Popping into a roomful of people wouldn't be cool, so you have to wait until I give you the all clear, okay?"

I saw her point and nodded, dropping my gaze to the floor.

"Chris, no matter how much physical distance separates us, you can always step across it. You know why?"

I shook my head.

"Because we're connected. Not only by this unnatural power we both possess, but by the depth of love in our hearts."

I couldn't help but smile. "That's the corniest thing I've ever heard," I said.

"Yeah, well, you're a real mind fuck." She grinned and for the first time since I woke up, I wasn't worried about whether or not I would regain my memory, as long as I had her by my side.

The End

Continue CJ's story with Angel Heart on the next page.

Angel Heart Chapter 1

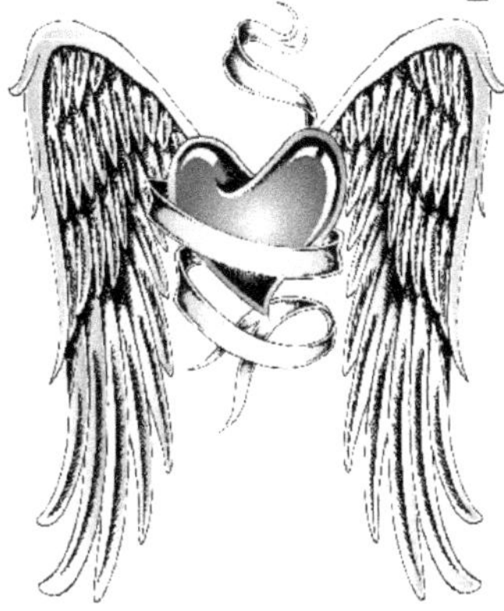

THE HOT SUMMER SUN beat down on my closed eyelids and the sounds of the ocean lulled me into a state somewhere between the sheets of sleep. Valerie rubbed her foot against mine in the sand and I opened an eye, peeking over at her.

She looked up from her tablet, smiling at me as she swiped to the next page. The August heat had rolled in just about the time her rotation ended, and she was on a two-week break, opting to spend it with me here in York instead of her apartment in Boston.

"Chris?" The questioning lilt pulled my attention from Valerie to the blonde standing a few feet away on the beach. I lifted my glasses, studying her. It wasn't anyone I recognized, so I glanced at Valerie, raising my eyebrows for a little help.

Valerie rolled into a sitting position, but the look on her face was enough to shoot my gaze back to the stranger.

"I'm s...sor...ry," I stuttered, aggravated with the lack of control over my speech. It seemed the only time I mastered words was when I sang. "I don't re...mem...member you." It was my failsafe quote when I ran into someone who knew me from before the accident.

The blonde's face fell, and her hazel eyes became sad as they moved from me to Valerie and back, as if she felt out of all the people that could have switched my memory back on, it would have been her.

"Chris was in an accident a few years ago," Valerie said.

"I know. Steve told me he was in a coma," she said to Valerie, her eyes narrowing in a way that was a blatant challenge, and then she turned to me. "He wasn't sure if you would ever wake up," she said, focusing on me. Her eyes filled with a particular wonder that made me squirm, and I shifted in the seat.

"This is Sandy," Valerie said after a few beats of silence. "Your ex-girlfriend."

I stared at Valerie, recognizing the flare of insecurity in the tightness of her features, before moving my gaze back to Sandy.

"Nice to meet you," I said with a nod, but I didn't offer my hand. Something told me Valerie would not like me touching this girl in any manner, and I respected her unannounced wishes. "San...dy."

A profound sadness filled her as I stuttered out her name, and underneath it was a layer of pity that rubbed my skin raw. I may stutter like a fool, but I wasn't an imbecile.

My gaze hardened, and she caught it, her face flushing with embarrassment at my penetrating stare. "The connection between my brain and my mouth doesn't always work, but that doesn't mean I'm simpleminded." I forced the words out, the stutter making it slow and stilted, but my aggravation was clear.

"I didn't mean to offend you," she said. "It's just..." She looked down at the sand and glanced toward the ocean before swinging her hazel eyes in my direction again. "You still look the same." Longing filled her eyes, and she shrugged.

"How long were we...?" I asked, and Valerie looked away, her features distant and tense as Sandy sent a soft smile at me.

"Fifteen years," she said, and the impact of the words hit like a face full of sand.

Questions swarmed my mind, and I glanced in Valerie's direction. She was still looking out at the ocean, at something far away, with her poker face expression that I knew was hiding a new level of turmoil underneath.

"Fifteen years?" I sent the question back to Sandy, now understanding the level of hurt in her eyes. I guess, being with someone that long, it had to be like a sucker punch that I didn't have a hint of recollection.

"Yeah, if I hadn't screwed up, we'd probably be married right now," she said, and her gaze jumped to Valerie before settling back on me.

"Really," the word actually came out without a stutter, and this time Valerie met my amused gaze. I couldn't envision anyone else I wanted to share my life with besides Valerie, so Sandy's comment struck me as funny, and the girl caught the sarcasm that bled through in my tone.

Sandy sucked her bottom lip and shook her head slowly. "Still wielding sarcasm like a weapon." She cocked an eyebrow, and I shrugged. "Some things will never change," she said, and her gaze traveled over my exposed flesh like a loving caress before she turned and trudged off into the distance.

"That was interesting," I muttered and glanced at Valerie. She was still staring after Sandy with worry lines creasing her forehead. I reached out and turned her face toward me. "I'm yours." This time the words were clear, powered with all the conviction I felt in my heart.

Angel Heart Chapter 2

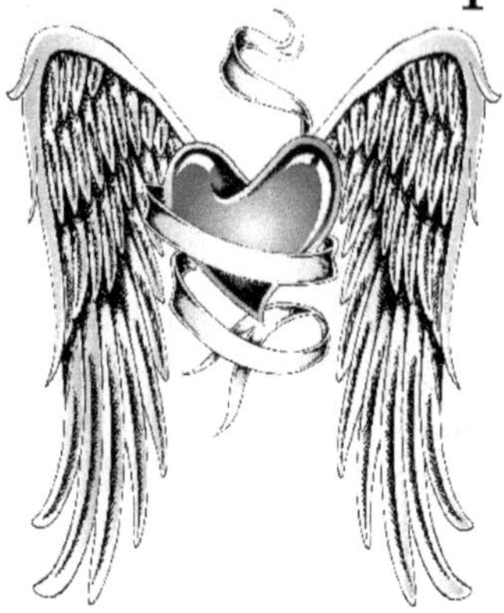

"I WANT TO REMEMBER my life." I stood looking out over the ocean in our backyard with a beer in my hand. I figured after two months, I should remember something, but it was all still a blank slate. Steve and Jennifer taught me the letters of the alphabet, and now I was working on recognizing strings of simple words. It was more than frustrating because my brain worked, my thoughts produced words without question, but the minute I saw a string of letters, I blanked.

"Give it time." Raven's Irish lilt pulled my attention away from the ocean vista. The rest of the family was on the patio, where Steve was grilling steaks for dinner. But she had approached me, leaving her daughter in Tom's capable hands. My sister-in-law was a pistol, and I knew she had ulterior motives for cornering me.

"Valerie's a little unhinged, isn't she?" I asked, and Raven nodded.

"She's scared."

I raised an eyebrow. "Why?"

"Because history is history." Raven shrugged. "I told her there was nothing to worry about. Even if you regain your memory, it wouldn't matter, because she's the one. She was before the accident and has been since you woke up, but that doesn't seem to make her feel any better."

"What happened to me, Raven?" I asked, meeting her stare.

"Only Damian knows the details," she said, and I glanced over my shoulder. Damian and his wife Naomi sat at the mini picnic table monitoring their kids, who were madly scribbling in coloring books. As always, whenever I looked in their direction, Damian's gaze was drawn to mine.

I moved my attention back to Raven, still not fully comprehending the connections of all the people here. I knew Tom was blood. He was my brother, and while I couldn't remember anything else, the kinship with him was stronger than with anyone else.

I had grown a healthy respect for Steve in the short time I had been back. His knowledge and patience reminded me of a caring father, and I wondered if my real father had been as genuine. Jennifer was sweet and had the biggest heart in the world. I knew her concern stemmed from love and it didn't just encompass me, its umbrella included everyone in the yard, from Steve to Tom's little girl, Hannah. Jennifer was the mamma bear of this family and God help anyone who took a stand against us. I think she would tear their head off with her bare hands.

The relationship with Damian was one I wasn't sure about. He, Naomi, and Valerie were related in some fashion, but even that was sketchy, and Damian and I had some weird psychic connection, like he was an extension of me. With Valerie, our connection was natural and right, as if we were compatible pieces of a puzzle meant to fit together, but with Damian, it was just unsettling.

Raven was easy. She was family by marriage and she and Valerie were the closest of friends. The way she looked at Tom made me smile; it was like a light shined brighter in her eyes at the sight of him. I took a minute to study her pretty profile before the wind swirled her auburn hair over it. There were times her gaze wandered far away, and her smile faltered, but then she'd shake her head and the darkness disappeared.

There were secrets in this family. Secrets beyond just my abilities. Secrets so dark that they all masked their thoughts whenever I was in the vicinity. I glanced towards the beach, realizing Sandy had done the same thing today, like a protective reflex.

"Did you know her?"

"Sandy?"

I nodded.

"Not that well. I only met her a couple of times," she said and shrugged. "She was sweet, but it just never seemed like the right fit for you."

"She said I was with her for fifteen years," I said, not understanding how I could have such a long-standing relationship without Raven really knowing the girl.

"Aye," she said. "But Sandy lives in Connecticut, so most of the time you saw each other, it was on the computer screen."

Raven stood and turned, looking out at the water before glancing at the family. "We're all damaged in one way or another. That's why we work so well together. And I think it's why we'll gladly stick our necks out for each other," she said, and then her gaze traveled to mine. "That's really all you need to know."

"Damaged?" Of course, the word didn't come out nearly as smoothly as in my head.

She stared at the family. "Yes. Myself included, but being a part of this family has healed the wounds more so that anything Valerie's healing power could ever do. It's a kinship that goes deeper than blood. You may not remember it, but you do feel it."

I turned and let my gaze travel over each member before settling back on Raven. "Yes. I feel it," I said, succumbing to her wisdom.

"Well, there you go." She clicked the neck of her beer against mine and I couldn't help but chuckle. "Why do we all wear these?" I said, tracing the black and red stone that lay on my chest. Even Sandy had one, and I met Raven's gaze.

Her smile disappeared, and she sighed. "It protects us," she said and walked away before I could pry more information out of her.

Protection.

Damaged.

Secrets.

And a few of us had the power of the gods.

197

Angel Heart Chapter 3

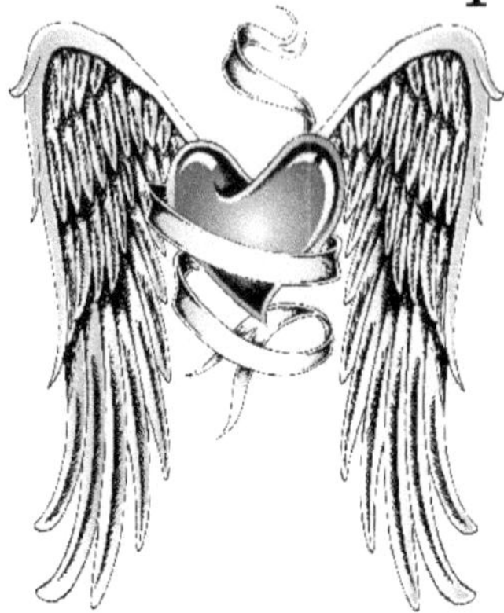

I STARED AT THE ceiling, twirling a piece of Valerie's hair around my finger. Her breath rose and fell in the cadence of sleep, but I couldn't stop the litany of questions today dredged up. Sleep wasn't in the cards for me, so I slid out of bed and put on a pair of shorts and a t-shirt.

With a pair of flip-flops on my feet, I snuck out of the house, easily finding my way to Long Sands Beach. The full moon tempered the darkness, and I climbed down the stairs to the sand and started walking the beach.

I strolled, not worrying about the time or the tide; it was low, so the expanse of beach was at its widest and the water was seasonably warm. I followed the sand from one end of the beach to the other and turned back. Damian stood ten feet away with his arms crossed.

"You scared the hell out of Valerie," he said, his voice carrying on the night air and his expression one of stern unhappiness.

I stopped and turned toward the water.

"What happened?" I asked and turned my hard stare in his direction.

Damian let out a laugh and stepped into place next to me. "You aren't ready for it, kid."

"I'm only a couple of years younger than you. Why are you always so fucking condescending, like I'm a child and you're some ancient old man?"

Damian crossed his arms and stared out at the water for a few minutes. Just when I thought he would not dignify my outburst with an answer, he slid his gaze to me. "That's because I am."

"You are what?"

"I'm old. Older than you can fathom." He looked back toward the house. "You're only operating on hours, days, and years right now."

"You're twenty-seven, right?" I asked. That's what it said on his driver's license; he turned back toward me, shaking his head. "So, what, you're like, thirty?" I guessed.

He laughed and started toward our homes. Naomi and Damian lived next door to us in an equally secluded fortress. I caught up with him.

"Do you know what your brother and I do?" he asked.

I shook my head. They were in and out, but I never thought to ask what they did. I knew what I did lately. I spent my days relearning the English language and the basics of self-defense.

"We own a private detective agency that specializes in paranormal activity," he said without breaking stride. He slowed after a few paces. "Do you understand what that is?"

I stared at the sand, trying to decipher the word, and I looked up at him. "You research things… like me," I said.

"No. You are psychic. That's different from the things we look into."

"Oh," I said and stopped. "What does this have to do with your age?"

Damian stopped as well. "Everything," he said. "As far as my age is concerned, think beyond your limited understanding of time. Think decades and centuries."

I narrowed my gaze and clenched my teeth. "I don't appreciate you messing with me." I stalked off.

"Monsters are real," he said, and I stopped, spinning around and staring him down. "Monsters, ghosts… other things," he added.

My hand went to the pendant under my shirt, and my conversation with Raven crossed my mind. Damian's gaze dropped to it.

"Raven's hex pendants do protect us."

"I'll ask one more time. What the fuck happened to me?" The anger inside was building and my body started shaking with the ballooning power.

Damian stared me down. "You took on Lucifer yourself."

My brain stalled and pain bit through my skin, dropping me to my knees and crushing the air from my chest. My hands clamped the sides of my head, trying to stop the freight train bearing down on my mind, and I had the sensation of being lifted into the air just before everything went black.

Angel Heart Chapter 4

MY EYES OPENED TO the star-speckled sky, and an argument brewing just outside my range of vision. It took me a few moments to recognize the setting. I was in my backyard lying on one of the lounge chairs.

"What the hell were you thinking?" Valerie's voice carried across the yard.

"He asked, so I figured..."

"I told you what would happen. Any time a memory so much as flickers to the surface, he has a seizure. But no, you figured you knew better," Valerie snapped, her tone laced with enough venom to turn my head in her direction, just in time to see her swat Damian's chest. "You are an asshole," she added.

"I didn't think..." Damian started, flustered by her fury.

"That's right, you didn't think," Valerie cut him off.

"Val?" I said, interrupting the escalating fight. She spun in my direction and nearly sprinted the distance, dropping to her knees next to me. She ran her hand over my forehead and into my hair before leaning in for a gentle kiss. I stared at her stormy eyes when she pulled away.

"Hey," she smiled, running her thumb over my forehead in a gentle caress.

"Seizure?" I asked.

She dropped her gaze to the ground before sighing. "Yes," she said with a nod, bringing her beautiful eyes back to mine. "Which is the reason no one has talked to you about what happened."

"What does that mean?"

"It means your brain is overloading and shutting off whenever something triggers a memory."

My mouth dropped open as what she said sank in. "Fuck," I muttered and closed my eyes. What the hell kind of memories did I have that caused my mind to shut down?

"It was traumatic, babe. There's no rhyme or reason to how the mind reacts to trauma. You just have to wait until you're ready to handle the information."

"And what if it never gets better?" I searched her eyes, praying whatever lay beyond my reach wouldn't tear down what I had built with her. Her eyes softened, and she leaned in for another kiss. This one was as gentle as her thumb stroking my forehead.

"Chris, you're still you, even without the memories or the flawless speech pattern." She cupped my cheek. "You have not changed."

I had nothing to compare it to, and my gaze moved to Damian. The conversation on the beach was fuzzy and my brow scrunched. "Weren't we on the beach?"

"You collapsed, and I brought you back here," he said and covered a yawn. "I need to get back home before Naomi sends out a rescue party."

Valerie gave him a nod, and he slipped into the house. Something didn't sit right with me, and I stared after him before turning my gaze to Valerie. If he brought me home, why wasn't I inside?

"The kids kept asking when you were going to come back and sing for them," she said, changing the subject. "You made a hell of an impression."

"I only know one song," I said. I had no clue how I knew the notes to play on the piano, or the words to the song for that matter, but I had sung 'Hallelujah' without a flaw right after I came out of the coma, and the performance delighted a group of young cancer patients at Dana Farber.

"We can always test out my theory," she said. "I played quite a few songs over the two years you were out."

Ah. Her theory. She thought my comatose mind absorbed the music. Neither Steve nor Tom had ever seen me play the piano before, so her theory seemed like the most logical answer, considering the absence of any prior musical training. Personally, I think she just wanted to see me do it again.

I slowly pushed myself up, despite the head-heavy sensation. The movement left me disoriented to the point I had to grip the edge of the chair. "Is there anything you can do to stop the seizures?" I asked, returning to the original subject.

"No, not to my knowledge. At least, nothing that doesn't risk permanent brain damage." She took a seat next to me and slid her hand into mine.

I stared out over the water, at the moonlight dancing on the waves.

"Damian said monsters are real." I slid my gaze from the ocean to her and she huffed a laugh, her gaze dropping away from mine. I inhaled at her little tell and glanced back at the ocean.

A flash of annoyance heated my skin, and I stood, choosing to head inside instead of continuing the conversation. I slowed as I passed the bar, turning back and reaching in, pulling the bottle of vodka out.

"You probably shouldn't drink right now."

I sent a glare in her direction and poured a glass, filling it to the top and chugging it down despite the burn. I pressed my teeth together and shuddered as the liquid hit my stomach and a slow fire spread from my center to my fingertips.

"You just lied to me," I said, squaring off.

"Chris," she started, and I turned away, ignoring her, and poured another drink. She tried to intercept the glass, and I pulled it out of her reach.

"What the fuck was Damian talking about?"

She huffed in exasperation. "Chris," she started in that calm manner that drove me crazy; and for the first time since I woke, I felt the bite of anger.

"Don't coddle me." I stepped back, putting distance between us. "I'm not a fucking child," I growled out, getting more pissed by the second at my irritating stutter. I downed the second glass before she could grab it out of my hand.

She stopped, pressing her lips together. "So help me," she started, and I narrowed my eyes, slamming both the cup and the bottle on the counter.

I stepped closer, glaring down into her equally furious face. "I get that you're trying to protect me, but goddamn it, don't treat me like an idiot."

The fire in her eyes fanned the coal the alcohol set alight, and I didn't know whether to shake her or kiss her.

"What was Damian talking about?" I asked through clenched teeth.

She stared at me, the muscles in her jaw tightening. "Inhuman killers," she said in a way that chilled my anger; and I cocked my head, waiting for more explanation. She didn't disappoint. "The kind nightmares are made of."

My memory didn't allow for any explanation, and I shrugged. "What is out there?" I waved toward the window.

"Vampires, demons, hybrid killers."

I blinked and took a small step backwards as my brain slowly combed over the conversation I had with him on the beach. At least, the little I could recall, and I crossed my arms. "Is Damian... human?"

She smiled and kept eye contact this time. "Yes."

I sensed more was coming, but she just kept her mouth and her mind closed.

"But?" I asked when she didn't continue.

"He wasn't for a very long time."

The second alcohol bomb hit my stomach, and I reached for the counter to steady myself. I wasn't sure I heard her right. "What?"

"Damian was born five hundred years before Christ."

If anything should short circuit my brain, that fact should have, but I just stared at Valerie, trying to break down the timeframes. When I couldn't, I asked the obvious question. "How?"

She chuckled. "Damian was a vampire until two and a half years ago. I've known him since I was born, and he hasn't changed at all. He hasn't aged a day."

I crossed to the table and sat down, trying to find the meaning of vampire among the cobwebs in my head. She might as well have told me he had been a rock since the dawn of time, and I glanced up at her. "What exactly is a vampire?"

"He existed on blood, but he differed from the rest of the lot. He didn't become a mindless killing machine."

"Why not?"

"That's a long story. One I really don't want to get into at three in the morning." She covered a yawn. "Can we go back to bed now?"

"Does Naomi know?"

"Oh yeah," Valerie said and took my hand, pulling me to my feet. "Bed, now."

"I have more questions," I said as she navigated me through the family room, turning off the lights as we went.

"You will have to wait until I get some sleep."

We climbed the stairs, and I excused myself, stepping into the bathroom to do my business and brush away the bitter taste in my mouth. I raised my gaze to my reflection and my expression soured. "Fucking memory," I muttered and sent a glare at the image before retiring to the bedroom.

Valerie was already curled up on her side and I slid under the covers, spooning her, and letting the alcohol numb my senses to sleep.

Angel Heart Chapter 5

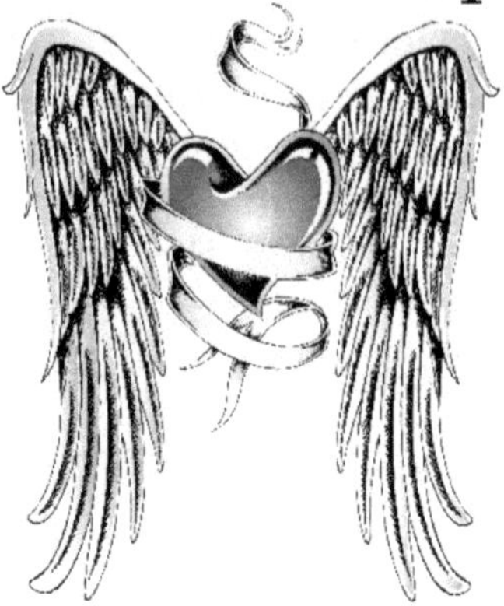

THE HOUSE WAS QUIET, and I rolled, glancing at the clock. I let out a laugh at the blinking time. We had slept half the day away. Usually, Steve hauled my ass out of bed to start our studies, but he and Jennifer had taken a ride to their lake house for a much needed weekend alone.

I slid my arm from underneath Valerie and climbed out of bed. My head hurt and I didn't know if it was from the alcohol binge or the seizure. Either way, it was miserable, and I ducked into a hot shower, hoping the steam would ease some of the pounding.

Unfortunately, it did nothing to dull the pain, and I wandered downstairs, pilfering the cabinets for medicinal relief. Frustration clawed at my skin as I looked at the foreign words on each bottle. I still couldn't decipher the different medicines and I slammed the cabinet closed. My mood soured to match my stomach, and I took a seat on the couch, picking up the tablet and pulling up the latest list of words Steve had gone over with me earlier in the week.

What I really wanted was to do some research on what a vampire was, but even if I could figure out how to spell the damn word, any search engine result would be just as much of a mystery to me as the medicine bottles. I tossed the tablet on the table and growled my discontent.

My gaze landed on the phone and the list of names and numbers next to it. I bit my lip in contemplation, wondering just how much my brother would know about these things.

"What the hell," I whispered. If he and Damian were in business together, I guess he would know a thing or two. I crossed to the phone and moved my finger down the list, looking for my brother's name. It took me two passes to recognize the T, and I picked up the phone, pressing the numbers listed next to his name.

"Hello?" an electronic voice answered.

"Tom?"

"Yes. Is everything all right?"

"Yes. I just had some questions about..." I paused and sighed. "About vampires."

Silence filtered over the line. "Give me a half hour and I'll be down," he said.

"Okay." I hung up the phone and settled onto the couch with the television clicker in hand, waiting for Tom to arrive or Valerie to come down.

Nothing interested me on television, so I clicked it off and stood, crossing to the bookcase where photo albums lined the shelf. I pulled one of the earlier ones down and took a seat. The photos were of the man and the woman Steve said were my parents; I realized I had a unique key to my life lining the shelves.

In this album, my mother's belly protruded in the distinct form of pregnancy; and the way my father beamed at her told me enough about how happy he was at the thought of being a father. The way he seemed to take her in was familiar, and I glanced at the ceiling, thinking of Valerie. I like to think I held the same expression of adoration when I looked at her. With each page, I got a flavor for how much they loved each other; it was written in every gaze, and sadness stretched over me.

As the pages progressed, babies came into the picture, and I recognized Tom's eyes in one of the infants. Through the years, his eyes never changed. They held the same strength and kindness that I had seen in him since I woke from the coma.

Seeing pictures of us at a lake, both holding fish up for the camera, made me smile. There was a connection in the way we played together and stood for pictures. His admiration of me was clear, and I nearly laughed.

There were pictures of the other people as well. My half-sister and half-brother. The same ones in the wedding photo upstairs; the girl stopped showing up in pictures by the time I turned five. There seemed to be sadness in my mother, and her eyes didn't light up like they had before, although she and my father still looked at each other in a way that burned off the page.

The mood changed dramatically around the time we were nine. At least that's what the dates represented. The few pictures in that timeframe showed my mother barely able to hold a smile and my father wasn't present.

A distinct gap of time occurred and the next set of photos of Tom and me showed pained eyes and subdued demeanors. Tom was a shell of his former self and I always looked angry. Every now and then, either Steve or Jennifer would be in the picture, but overall, it was Tom and me. Once high school started, Tom was with a different girl in almost every picture and he had a devilish grin all the time, like he was on the edge of trouble. Me, I was with the blonde we saw on the beach, or alone.

I closed the latest album and placed it on the coffee table when Tom walked into the house. "Are there any videos of us when we were little?" I asked.

Tom nodded. "I have some at our lake house," he signed. "Maybe a change of scenery would be good for you." He looked around the room and then back at me, offering a shrug.

I bit my lip and had dropped my gaze to the photo album when the creak of the stairs pulled our attention.

Valerie stepped into view; her hair crumpled, and wearing an oversized t-shirt. When her gaze landed on Tom, her cheeks bloomed pink and she stepped backwards, using the knee wall as a shield against her naked legs.

"Hi, I didn't realize you were here," she said, covering a yawn.

"I asked him to come by," I said, drawing her attention. "I figured he'd fill me in on vampires since you shut me down last night."

Tom blew out a stream of air, his gaze bouncing between Valerie and me as he accurately pieced together the current situation. The look he leveled at me was one of reproach and he crossed his arms, unhappy that I put him in the middle.

"Damian was a vampire," I said, and Tom glanced at Valerie for her permission to either confirm or deny my statement. When he glanced back at me, he nodded.

"But he's not anymore, and we've all been immunized against the shadow virus as well," he signed and articulated in his mind.

That was a new twist, and I glanced at Valerie, because what she said last night didn't jive with an inoculation. I cocked my head to the side, prompting her for more information without the words.

"I took samples of Damian's and Naomi's blood, along with Grace's, and I was able to make a serum that makes us just as toxic to vampires as both Damian and Naomi," Valerie said, and my eyebrows rose.

"Toxic?"

"Yes. If a vampire bites us, they die and we don't. We are immune to the virus."

"Oh," I said, resorting to my fail-safe one-word response. My logical mind wasn't piecing this together gracefully, and I sighed. Instead of pursuing the information, I let it sink in and opted to return to the original conversation with Tom. "Lake house?"

"Yeah," he signed. "We can take a boat ride around the lake, too, if you want."

The thought was extremely appealing, and I turned my attention to Valerie. "Mind if we go?" I asked, wondering if she'd let me go somewhere that might trigger a memory or two, and her gaze landed on the photo album before returning to mine with a sigh.

"Sure," she said.

Tom grinned. "You might want to pack something for the night and leave a note for Steve and Jen," he signed. "I'll go grab Raven and Hannah and be back..." He glanced at his watch. "In a half hour?"

I nodded, and he turned, leaving Valerie and me to pack an overnight bag.

I focused on her, taking in her rumpled hair and her bare legs, as she stepped into view. Packing could wait. She grinned as I closed the distance and pulled her into my arms.

"We need to pack," she said, trying to level a stern look, but it didn't quite work with the dimples still carved in her cheeks.

"We will. Eventually," I said and picked her up, carrying her to my bedroom and planting a determined kiss on her lips. Losing myself in the feel of her, I closed my eyes, letting all sensation drive me. Making love to Valerie always felt like home, as if it was predestined that I be in her arms.

"I love you," I whispered and snuggled into her.

"Chris," she said, and I raised my head, meeting her gaze. She just cocked an eyebrow at me.

"Oh, yeah, packing," I said and pulled away, grumbling as we uncoupled and she slid out of bed.

"Yes. They're going to be here any minute and we haven't done a thing," she said, rushing around the bedroom in a flurry that plastered a grin on my face.

"They can wait a minute or two," I said, when she sent an exasperated 'get your ass up' glare in my direction. It earned me a pair of underwear pitched in my face. Begrudgingly, I slipped them on and pulled on a pair of shorts before helping her pack the duffel bag she hauled from the closet. "You might want to run a brush through your hair," I said, studying the knotted mess.

Valerie glanced in the mirror and uttered a laugh before grabbing her sundress and crossing to the bathroom with her travel bag. I finished packing for us, making sure I had both our bathing suits and night clothing along with clothes for tomorrow. When she stepped into the room, I hesitated. She really was a beautiful woman, and for the hundredth time since I woke up, I wondered why she stayed with me.

"Because you're rich," she said in response to my thoughts and delivered a wink and a smile.

"So, they tell me." I zipped the bag and her smile faltered.

"You know I'm just joking, right?"

I took a minute to study the sincerity in her face. "I'm a stuttering idiot," I said and hauled the duffel over my shoulder. "You staying with me because I have money makes much more sense than you staying because you love me."

She put her suitcase on the bed and took the duffel bag from my hand before cupping my face between her palms. "I have never cared that you had money, or that you have a brilliant mind, or even that you have all these mystical powers. Even if you were poor and powerless, I would still love you for what's in your heart."

I rolled my eyes and her stare hardened.

"I'm serious."

My good humor faded a notch. "Then open your mind and let me see the way I can see into a stranger's head."

Her expression transitioned into a guarded frown; she dropped her hands to her sides. "I can't do that," she whispered.

"Why not?"

"Because that much information will probably blow all your circuits and push you right back into a coma," she said and stepped away. "I can't take that chance."

Frustration edged in and I grabbed the bags, circling around her, ignoring her huff. I stopped in the hallway and glanced back at her. "Maybe it's not up to you." I didn't wait for an answer before descending the stairs.

I wanted answers. The more things that were revealed, the more I wondered what the hell I was and why everyone was so damned quiet about my past.

Angel Heart Chapter 6

I SAT IN FRONT of the television staring at the home movies while Tom, Raven and Valerie prepared dinner. It was weird seeing myself as a little kid and even stranger seeing my brother talking and laughing. The scenes displayed on screen seemed like a very happy, well-adjusted family and when the camera turned on my parents, you could see the electricity between them and the depth of their commitment in their eyes; their adoration of us was just as clear.

Sadness folded its arms around me, and I wished like hell I could remember. I finally clicked the television off and left through the porch, taking a seat on the steps of the dock and staring out at the haunting sunset.

Tom had given me the grand tour of the place, and it was a beautiful piece of property. The boat tour around the lake was equally pleasant, but none of it made so much as a chip in the wall blocking me from the rest of my life.

The door to the porch squeaked behind me and I didn't bother turning until the unlaced sneakers appeared in my peripheral vision. I glanced at Tom as he took the seat next to me. He didn't speak or send words into my head. Instead, he just stared at the same serene scene I was watching. I turned my attention back to the lake, remaining silent.

"I miss them," he said. His voice was quiet in my head, and he kept his hands clasped on his knees. "I don't know how much Steve told you, but Mom's death..." his voice trailed off and I glanced at him.

He didn't continue. His gaze dropped to his hands and then turned to me. "The psycho who cut my tongue out, cut off her head and propped it on the end of the surgical table he had me chained to."

My eyes widened and my jaw slowly fell open.

"Raven's father is a serial killer who thought he owned her. When she fell in love with me and rebelled against him, he set out to kill her," he added, keeping my gaze and adding to my discomfort. "And Valerie's family was slaughtered by monsters. So, we're all damaged in some way or another."

I turned back to the scenery and remained quiet. "Where was I?" I finally asked, meeting his gaze again. "Where the hell was I when all that shit happened?"

Tom's hands moved, signing as his voice whispered in my head. "No one knew where I was. If either you or Steve had figured it out, it would have been over like that." He snapped his fingers and then his hands stilled for a moment and squeezed into tight fists. He took a deep breath and stretched his fingers out before he continued. "Steve was doing his best, but he didn't piece it together in time to save her."

"As far as Raven's concerned, you were in Washington, D.C. testifying on Steve's behalf when her father attacked us."

"And Valerie?"

He met my questioning stare. "We didn't know Valerie until a few days before your..." His hands stilled again. "Accident," he finished.

Silence fell between us, and I sighed.

"There are some things that are not worth remembering," he signed.

"But..."

"And there are some things I wish like hell I could forget."

His statement silenced me, and I glanced at him. He offered me a stiff smile and climbed to his feet, leaving me alone on the dock. My mind lingered on the facts Tom just laid out for me, as well as the videos of us as kids. We seemed to be a hell of a way off the beaten path from the happy family we were when we were seven.

His revelations didn't dissuade me from wanting my life back. I still wanted my memories. I still wanted to know who the hell I was. I sighed and climbed to my feet, trudging back into the main house just as Raven announced dinner was ready.

The table was set for a feast, and I stared at the gourmet spread, impressed by the culinary skills of our host. The filet mignon tasted as good as it looked.

"This is delicious." I stumbled over the words, but Raven got the gist and beamed.

"Thank you," she said, and Tom leaned over, delivering a kiss on her cheek. I guess it was his way of thanking her for taking the time to whip up the meal on short notice. Just as she sliced into her steak, Hannah started whining in her crib. She closed her eyes and exhaled before setting her silverware down. Tom covered her hand and shook his head, pointing from her to her food.

His plate was already nearly cleared. He gave us a nod and placed his napkin by his silverware, disappearing into the kitchen for a minute before coming out, shaking a bottle of formula. He settled onto the couch with his daughter in his arms, taking the time to feed her so Raven could enjoy our company. Well, enjoy Valerie's company. I remained quiet and let the girls talk.

"Chris thinks I'm just hanging around because he has money," Valerie said after they finished a majority of the meal.

Raven laughed and glanced at me. "You're kidding."

I shook my head. "Makes more sense than anything else."

Raven's laughter faded, and she stared at me. "Sometimes you can be a true jackass," she finally said. "The girl is your soul mate. That's something that you cannot ignore, ever." She picked up her glass and toasted me. "It was meant to be," she added after the last of the wine passed through her lips.

It was my turn to laugh, and Valerie's eyes narrowed. The particularly tight set of her lips told me she was aggravated with me, and I was sure I'd hear about it when we went to bed in the guest cottage tonight.

Instead of dignifying her with any other response, I cleared my plate and began tackling the pile of dishes in the kitchen. Valerie stepped into place beside me with a dishtowel in her hand. I handed her the pot and met her sharp gaze.

"What?"

"What is your issue?" she asked and put the dried pot on the clean counter.

I stopped washing and stared out the window, formulating the words in my head. "There are too many unanswered questions." I stumbled through the audible delivery and met her gaze. "And it's making me..." I pressed my lips together at my inability to articulate, and I really had no frame of reference for the unease settling into my skin. Valerie wasn't the source; neither was my lack of memory, but a warning like a storm siren was starting in the center of my body. "Crazy. It's making me crazy." I finally said and refocused on the dishes. "And something's coming. I don't know what, but it has me..." I paused and handed her another clean plate. "...unhinged."

We finished the dishes in silence and, as soon as I dried my hands, Valerie put the cloth down and wrapped her arms around my neck. The expression in her eyes gave me pause, and I cocked my head, trying to identify the right word for it. She pulled me closer, laying her head on my chest without explanation, and the word popped into my head. She was afraid.

"Val?"

She didn't move at first and then she just unclasped her arms and turned, trudging into the living room and leaving me with no answers. I crossed the distance just as she took a seat on the couch and put her arms out for Hannah.

"Let me see that sweet girl," she said, and Tom relinquished his daughter.

"Tell me about vampires." I pulled out a chair from the table and took a seat.

Everyone turned towards me like I interrupted some silent after dinner ritual.

"They're nasty creatures." Raven translated Tom's moving hands and met my gaze. "They live off the blood of their victims."

The idea of drinking blood soured my thoughts of dessert. I waited for more, and when I realized it wasn't coming, I crossed my arms. "That's it?" My gaze moved over the three of them. "Valerie already told me that last night."

Tom met my frustrated stare. "Since Valerie immunized us, they don't bother us anymore." His voice echoed in my head, and he turned away, ending the conversation. I got the distinct impression that was going to be the extent of information I was going to receive tonight, and I glanced out at the deepening night.

Despite the early hour, both Raven and Tom's eyes drooped, and their yawns became more prevalent as Valerie and Raven continued their small talk about Hannah and motherhood. Tom's eyes dipped closed, and I glanced at my watch. It was a little before ten, early by the standards I had been used to since I woke from my coma but, then again, I didn't have a baby.

"Maybe we should let you two get some rest," Valerie said, and Tom's eyes snapped open.

"We're okay," Raven said as Valerie handed Hannah to her.

Valerie laughed and hooked her thumb at Tom. "You may be, but he's falling asleep on us."

"Sorry," Tom signed, but exhaustion came off him in waves.

"I could use some sleep," I said, even though it was the farthest thing from my mind. I knew they didn't want to appear rude, and the kinks in their necks loosened a notch at my declaration. They didn't know about my nightmares, so they had no way of knowing I didn't like going to sleep, especially in a strange place like this. I was likely to wake in the same pain that paralyzed me at the beach. Like I did most nights.

It took a minute and then the slow realization sank in. Perhaps the nightmares were memories tripping seizures, and that's why all I remembered about the dream was crushing pain.

Valerie met my gaze, and a shadow passed over her eyes before she dropped them to Tom and Raven. "I'm going to take him over to the cottage." She offered a shrug.

"Be careful, it's dark out there," Raven said and then they both stood, giving Valerie a hug goodnight. "Goodnight, CJ," Raven said, and Tom just gave me a nod before they disappeared down the back hall.

Valerie took my hand and led me across the dark lawn to the tiny guest house bordering the private stretch of beach. Instead of going inside, I pulled her beyond the cottage toward the beach. I wasn't in the mood for sleep or even a quiet night in front of the television. I wanted a little adventure and as soon as we stepped on the sand; I slipped my shoes off and stripped my shirt, dropping it on the pile.

"What are you doing?" Valerie whispered, but even her whisper hung on the water.

"I'm in the mood for a swim." I dropped my shorts. The evening air hovered around eighty degrees, and I was certain the water would be warmer than the ocean in Maine. When she didn't take her clothing off, I slipped out of my underwear, smiling at her and grabbed the hem of her shirt, stripping it off without permission. The tear of fabric echoed across the lake and her mouth opened to protest.

I took the opportunity and covered the start of her admonishment with my lips. *If you don't take the rest of your clothes off, they're going to get wet*, I thought, and she pulled away, meeting my hungry stare.

I was ravenous, but food wasn't the special on the menu that sparked my interest. She shook her head, pressing her lips together against the smile forming. When she didn't budge, I scooped her in my arms and plunged into the water. She didn't scream, but she squeaked her disdain as the lake enveloped us.

"I told you to strip," I said as we surfaced.

"Chris," she whispered in that harsh tone meant to scold, but her eyes danced with as much mischief as was coursing through my blood.

"Val," I whispered back and grinned.

"Let go," she said softly, and I loosened my grip, placing her on her feet on the sandy bottom. She took a step back and unbuttoned her shorts, pushing them down and then grabbing my arm to steady herself as she slid them off. Valerie flung them toward the shore where they slapped on the sand and then she turned back to me with only her bra on.

I raised my eyebrows, waiting for the rest of her clothing to come off. She sighed and unhooked, flinging her bra in the same direction as her wet shorts. She was beautiful in the moonlight, and I stepped closer, wiping the wet strands of hair from her face.

"I love you," I whispered without stuttering, and she smiled up at me in the way that always stole my breath. Valerie wrapped her arms around my waist and kissed my chest, sending waves of heat from the spot her lips touched through my entire being.

Instead of looking up at me, she peeled out of my arms and dove under the water, swimming out toward the deeper part of the lake. I watched how gracefully she cut through the water until she stopped and pulled herself up on something just below the surface. The flash of her teeth in the darkness hinted at the grin I was sure graced her face, and I stared in her direction.

I reached the oversized boulder and hauled myself up next to Valerie. "You..."

"Shush," she whispered. "Just be quiet for now."

"Make me," I challenged, speaking clearly enough for the words to echo.

She covered my mouth with her hand, meeting the challenge, just not in the way I expected. I kissed her palm and pulled her hand away. I thought about placing it in my lap, but I knew that would earn me a swat.

Instead, I wrapped my arm around her shoulders and stared out at the glasslike water.

Silence, broken only by the sweet sounds of nature wrapped around us.

"It's beautiful here," she whispered after a while.

"Mhm," I agreed, sliding my arm down her back to her waistline. She met my gaze when I leaned over and slung my other arm under her knees, pulling her into my lap. She met my lips with the same fervor, the kiss as hot and frantic as the starry night.

Her kiss always stopped time. Like the gods paused to watch the spectacle below, and whenever our tongues intertwined, the heat in my soul flashed into a burning need. I took my time, slowing the pace and sliding my hand between her thighs. Her mind echoed the soft sigh as I started the slow and insistent circles over her clit. Even though we had only fooled around a dozen times since I woke, it was as if I knew just how to play all the right chords on her body to awaken the sexual beast within her.

She shifted into a straddling position over me and, damn it all to hell, when she slid onto my hard cock, I nearly lost it. Making love on a rock in the middle of the lake wasn't the easiest thing in the world. Challenging was a better description, but that only added to the flame. Thankfully, this rock was flat and pretty big and just a few inches under the water's surface.

Valerie wrapped her arms around my neck and her legs around my waist and we moved together, creating a never-ending ring of waves that spread out from us. The water lapped at us, enhancing the sensations rocketing through me. She clamped her mouth over mine to stifle a moan that was building in her chest, and I chuckled under my breath. I loved it when she lost control and out here, it would echo for miles.

She stiffened, and the moan flowed from her mouth into mine and I responded, the heat pooling in my belly circling along with her hips until it burst forth, erupting through me and pulling a rough groan into my throat. My heart pounded, thumping through my entire body, and all I wanted to do was fall backwards and slip into oblivion. Instead, I wrapped my arms tightly around her, pulling her close, and rested my head on her shoulder until I caught my breath.

"I don't know if I can swim back to shore," I whispered.

"You'll make it." She peeled away from me, dropped back into the water, and did a slow crawl back to shore. I sat for a few more minutes before sliding into the water all the way. I followed her until my feet could touch the sand and then I stood and slowly walked ashore.

Valerie twirled her hair, ringing the water out as she watched me approach. Her lips formed in that contemplative faraway look, and I wished I could unlock her mind. Her eyes cleared up and met mine, and her dimples made an appearance.

"Where were you just then?"

She shrugged, and I swore I could see the blush rise in her cheeks.

"What?" I whispered, approaching her.

"I was thinking about our first time," she said.

"Ah," I replied and shook the sand from my underwear before slipping them on without another word. Her comment soured my mood. I wasn't able to recall even that, and her reaction to it just made me feel more lost than usual.

I scooped up the rest of my clothing and headed back toward the cabin. Valerie followed and kept quiet until we stepped inside.

"Why do you do that?" she asked and rummaged through our suitcase, pulling underwear and a nightshirt on before turning to me.

"You have those memories. I don't," I muttered and dropped to the bed.

She climbed on the mattress beside me and propped herself up on her elbows, looking down at me. "Someday, when I know you won't drop into a seizure, I'll let you see that, okay?"

"Let me see it now," I demanded, and a small dose of willpower went along with it. Valerie's eyes widened and the flow of that first time hit with all the force of a hurricane. I saw enough to know it was special, to know

I was her first, and I inhaled, preparing for the pain, but her mind locked down, shutting me off from anything further. When the pain didn't come, I met her angry glare. Of course, the memory was hers, not mine, so perhaps that's why I didn't drop into a universe filled with agony.

She blinked, and her eyes narrowed. "Christopher James," she said through clenched teeth. "You can't do that."

"You were a virgin?" I asked, surprised. Her memory painted the experience as painful at first, but then an all-encompassing pleasure took over, confirming that I was the one she had been waiting for all her life. It was a liberating memory and gave me a little bit of understanding of where she was coming from in our relationship.

At least her memory didn't paint me as an insensitive, virgin-busting bastard.

"Yes." She was still unhappy that I forced her to relinquish the memory, but the fact I didn't have a seizure tempered her anger.

I just gave her a smile and pressed my lips to hers. "Sorry," I whispered when I pulled away. I really had no idea I could make people do things they didn't want to, and the reality of that sparked a world of opportunity.

"You can't just go around forcing your way into people's minds," she said, reading my thoughts accurately. "It's not right."

"No harm," I started, and she put her finger on my lips.

"Just don't do that, okay?"

I took a deep breath and exhaled, nodding my agreement. Valerie curled up in the crook of my arm, draping herself over me, and I stared up at the ceiling, inspecting her memory while she fell into a soft snore.

Seeing it through her eyes was strange, like a window to her soul, but the way I looked at her was consistent with how my father looked at my mother in Tom's videos. Maybe Raven was right. Maybe we were meant to be.

Angel Heart Chapter 7

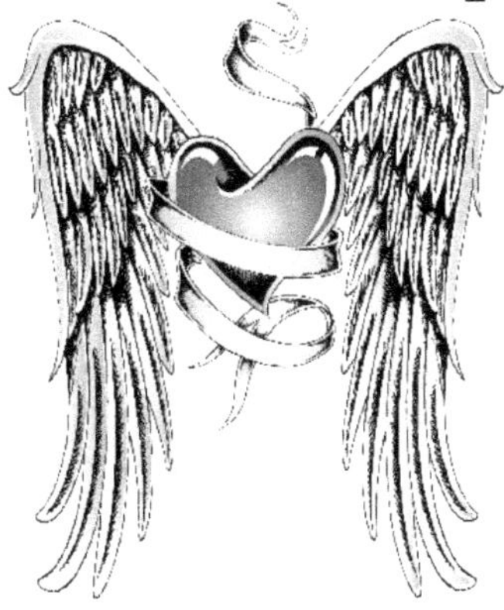

THE NIGHT SURROUNDED ME, and I finally gave up and pulled out of bed. I found my shorts and slid them on, retreating to the quiet sandy beach where I took a seat. The silence of the pre-dawn lake was soothing, and I scavenged up some rocks, tossing them at the flat surface and listening as they skipped the water. The gentle lapping of waves calmed the nerve bundle in the back of my neck.

It was time to unlock the labyrinth of my mind. I concentrated on breathing, on the steady drum of my heart. Each beat brought me closer to a calm state, and I closed my eyes, imagining an endless hallway lined with doors. Each door represented a memory, and I approached the first one.

The handle turned easily, but the door didn't budge, and I studied it closer. My gaze fell on the deadbolt lock, and I muttered under my breath, searching my pockets for a key, but I came up empty.

"Damn it." I found the same setup on every door but the last one. I reached for the doorknob, but a warning siren went off inside me and I pulled my hand away. Instead of opening the door, I placed my palm flat against the surface, trying to gauge the level of danger beyond the barrier. What passed into me made me yank my hand away and step back. The layer of evil streaming through the door chilled me to the core and my eyes flew open to the dark horizon.

"What the hell happened to me?" I asked the moonlit sky.

A shuffle behind me caught my attention, and I climbed to my feet, turning. I thought the imaginary door in my mind chilled my blood, but the air went frigid as I stared at the feral, snarling thing behind me. I wasn't sure what it was, but the saliva dripping from its sharp canines was enough to make me step back in the sand. The report of gunfire in the big house pulled my attention away, and the thing leaped at me.

I really don't know where the reaction came from, but the minute it hit me, I twisted and tossed him over my shoulder, sending the thing splashing into the water. The next thought that scrambled through my head was Valerie, and I stepped in that direction, but the diseased monster charged again, and I snapped my head in its direction, angered by his tenacity. I think I might have snarled too, but the pooled-up power in my chest shot out and the thing turned to dust.

I stared for a minute and then broke out in a run, barreling into the little cottage and willing every light on in the area. It took a moment to understand the screaming wasn't Valerie, but she stood to the side with her hand over her neck and bloodstains on her nightshirt.

An unquantifiable anger let loose, and the beast burst into flames. Valerie looked at me and then beyond and I spun, ready to strike again, but I reined it in at the sight of Tom with a gun in his hands.

You two all right? He thought, and I glanced back at Valerie. She nodded, and I followed suit.

"What was that?" I asked.

Vampires. Tom's thought echoed in my head.

"Does Raven or Hannah need me?" Valerie said, stepping next to me, her face forming a mask of worry.

Tom's gaze landed on her scar free neck, and he shook his head. *I got it before it could do any damage.*

"How many this time?" Valerie asked, and Tom held up two fingers.

"Three," I corrected. "One attacked me on the beach."

They both turned my way, and I shrugged.

224

"I couldn't sleep," I said to their probing stares.

"Damn." Valerie stared at her bloodstained hand. "They haven't bothered us for a while. Why now?"

Tom's gaze drifted in my direction and then back to her, but his mind was closed tight and so was hers. The now guarded expressions told me more than words, and I turned and stomped back out of the house, opting for the open gazebo at the end of the point instead of the beach. I climbed up on the railing, straddling the thick wooden post, and leaned on the side beam. Neither of them came after me, and I was both thankful and endlessly frustrated at their insufferable silence.

I stared at the moon-dance on the still lake, wondering yet again what the hell kind of world I lived in. It wasn't until the soft shuffle of feet reached my ears that I focused my attention on the dark entry.

"Chris?" Valerie whispered, stepping into a streak of moonlight.

"Why would it be my fault?" The bite of the words came through in my harsh tone. She dropped her gaze before stepping next to me and looking out at the water. "Val?" I asked when she didn't explain.

Her sigh gave me chills, and when she looked at me, I stifled the need to recoil. "It isn't your fault." She said nothing more, but she slid her hand in mine and squeezed.

I swung my leg over and stood facing her. "Then why did Tom look at me that way?"

She met my probing stare. "Because they're still trying to use us to get to you."

Her answer wasn't what I expected, and my brow rose. "Me?"

She let out a strained laugh. "Yeah, you dummy, you're the goddamn brass ring."

I didn't understand the reference and my head cocked to the side, trying to frame her words in something equatable. "Brass ring?"

She stared at me, and I could tell she was debating on how to answer.

"Chris, as I've told you before, you're special. There are some forces out there that would like to manipulate you to do their bidding, and what they want you to do is pure evil."

My gaze moved to the beach and the reality of what I did to both vampires hit like a gale force wind. A layer of gooseflesh traveled over my skin, and I understood her meaning. In the wrong hands, I could be this world's worst nightmare.

Angel Heart Chapter 8

WE GATHERED OUR STUFF from the small cottage and met Tom and Raven in the big house, holing up in the living room, and taking turns keeping watch through the remainder of the night. At first light, we piled into the car for the hour-long ride back to the shore.

Silent and tense, everyone except me kept vigilant watch on everything around us. Valerie held my hand. But she was as distracted by the sparse traffic as Tom and Raven, like they were expecting the neighboring vehicles to ram us off the road. I figured I'd get some sort of heads up if danger revealed its ugly head, so I focused on entertaining Hannah with the toys hanging from her car seat.

She cooed and kicked until we reached the halfway mark and then she gave a heavy sigh and slipped into sleep. How I wished I could just drop into sleep like a baby. I wasn't sure if I got any sleep last night at all; and from the looks of Tom, Raven, and Valerie, I don't think anyone else did, either.

"Maybe after we take a nap, we can head down to Boston and entertain the kids a little." Valerie yawned as we pulled into the driveway. I just nodded. Every sensation of exhaustion settled into my skin, from the ache in my muscles to the heaviness of my eyes. I didn't have enough energy to yawn, and the quick trip from the car into the house felt like I was trudging through quicksand. My movements were beyond sluggish, but Valerie led me inside and tucked me into bed, curling up next to me.

She started snoring before sleep finally claimed me.

The scraping of a chair snapped my eyes open, and I turned my head. Valerie stood, stretching, in front of the computer and my gaze landed on the clock. It took a few moments to identify the four. The following numbers were slower to materialize in my head, but Valerie turned in my direction, pulling my attention away from the clock.

"How are you feeling?"

"I slept for nine hours?" This was the longest I had slept in one go without waking from horrible nightmares. As a matter of fact, I didn't recall any dreams.

"Yep," she said, pulling her arms back to her sides.

"Wow." I blinked and rubbed my face, sitting up and stretching. My back and neck made various cracking sounds, and I offered Valerie a smile before swinging out of bed and heading for the bathroom.

The shower washed the cobwebs from my brain and by the time I finished cleaning up, my energy level skyrocketed. I paused at the bedroom door, listening with both my ears and my mind. Jennifer and Steve hadn't come back yet, and I focused on my room. Stepping inside, I closed the distance and pulled Valerie into my arms, covering her protest with my mouth.

I loved how her mind went fuzzy every time we kissed. For me, time stopped, and it was just the two of us; every cell in my body ached for her. I wasn't sure if this was a natural byproduct of love, or if it was because of the connection we had, but it was unnaturally natural.

She broke the kiss first.

"Chris, we don't have time for this," she said, meeting my gaze.

I just raised an eyebrow, silently challenging her.

"Later," she whispered and wiggled out of my arms.

"No one is home." I chose simple words that flowed instead of multi-syllable ones.

She glanced at the clock. "We don't really have time," she stressed, but she still reached for the towel wrapped around my waist, yanking it away with a playful grin. "Get dressed," she added and snapped the towel at me.

The corner caught my thigh, stinging as it whipped across my flesh. I jumped back out of range and sighed.

"You sure?" I asked, spreading my arms out with the question.

She threw the towel at me this time. "Traffic is going to be a bitch, and we only have a few more hours left before visiting hours are over."

Exasperation snaked into my skin. I dressed quickly and ran a comb through my hair before turning toward her. "You owe me." I pointed and got a sly smile in return.

"I promise I'll make it up to you."

The lilt of her voice promised a great deal of pleasure when we got back, and I succumbed to her will, letting her drag me out of the house.

"Can I drive?" I asked.

She stopped, looking between the keys and the car. When her gaze met mine, she shook her head. "Not yet."

"Come on, live dangerously," I stuttered out.

She sighed and I could see her resolve waning, so I put my hand out for the keys. Her brow furrowed, and she shook her head, bypassing me and settling in the driver's seat before I could respond.

I stomped around to the passenger side, dejected. I wanted to be self-reliant again, with or without my memory.

"If you had a seizure while driving..." She trailed off and started the car, finally meeting my gaze. "You could kill us both," she finished, and my irritation disappeared. I couldn't care less about my well-being, but if it put her in danger, well, I wasn't willing to do that if I could help it.

"Okay." I settled in.

Traffic was heavy, but I passed the time reading the signs. Valerie drilled me on numbers and letters and pronunciation, so the ride went much faster than it would have if I had resorted to sulking.

"Maybe I can take you driving in one of the school parking lots tomorrow," she said as we pulled into the garage across from the hospital. She glanced at her watch. "We're just in time for evening story time."

The reception we received when we stepped off the elevator warmed my soul, and I traded a glance with Valerie. The children surrounded us, more than excited to see Valerie, but equally excited to see me. I scanned the faces, looking for the little girl who had taken a seat by me the last time I warmed the piano bench and, when I couldn't find her, I glanced at Valerie. The small shake of her head constricted my throat, and I had to force the smile to remain on my lips.

"Are you going to sing for us?" a little girl with big green eyes and a colorful bandana asked.

"I'm going to try," I said in my less than smooth way, but none of the children seemed to mind my stuttering. If I could have waved a magic wand and healed every one of them, I would. Instead of harping on their illnesses, I turned toward the piano, biting my lip as I approached. Nerves jumbled in my belly, and I wondered if I'd be able to perform as flawlessly as I had the last time.

I sat on the bench and sent my most dazzling and confident smile toward the children, but truth be told, I was terrified. Inhaling, I placed my fingers on the keys, running up and down the keys, listening to the tones like I had that first time.

"You ready?" I asked the crowd and cracked my fingers after the loud chorus of 'yes' echoed in the atrium. With a quick glance at Valerie, my fingers started the slow and haunting rhythm of *Hallelujah* to the delight of the children.

As I started signing, I glanced at Valerie and the rapture in her expression fueled the power of my voice, carrying it through the atrium like an offering to heaven above. The heightened color in her cheeks made me grin because I knew damn well when this was over; she'd give me one hell of a show of her own.

I refocused on the kids surrounding me as their sweet voices joined mine in the chorus. The last note hung on the air and then I lifted my fingers off the keys, smiling at the crowd.

"Play something else!" a little boy with tufts of hair begged, his little hands still clapping in anticipation.

I closed my eyes and hung my head a moment, hoping something else would surface. I had no idea what the hell would come forth when my hands found the keys again, but as soon as they began moving, words miraculously spouted from my mouth. The kids knew this one too, and a quick glance at Valerie told me her hypothesis was correct.

Whispers from above pulled my attention away from the kids, but it didn't stop the performance. I stared at the camera pointed in my direction for longer than I should have before returning my gaze to the crowd singing the song with me.

"More!" they chanted when I finished the final note. Their enthusiasm was intoxicating, and I grinned, stretching my fingers before dropping them to the keys for another mysterious song. This time, my hands weren't as quick to pick a song, and I glanced at Valerie. She gave me a shrug and my fingers found an appropriate tune. Silence blanketed the room as the lyrics to 'Angel' came rolling off my tongue. Slow and deep and the children swayed with the melancholy tune. Both the words and the music sent shivers through me, and I met Valerie's intense gaze.

Tears filled her eyes, and she sent a strained smile in my direction before dropping her lips to the head of the child sitting in her lap. A cascade of sparkles drifted over the child, and I almost lost my place in the song, but my hands and mouth were on some different wavelength. They continued until the last note faded in the atrium.

After a beat of silence, the clapping started. I pulled my hands away from the keyboard, pushing the bench back a few feet, offering the crowd an uncomfortable smile. Humbled was the best word to describe the reaction, and I dropped my gaze to my hands, wondering where the music was coming from. Before my brain wrapped around my silent question, a voice broke through my reverie.

"Mr. Ryan?" a voice called from the hallway, and I turned, looking directly at a camera and a man with a microphone. He moved closer toward me with the cameraman tagging along.

"Mr. Ryan, we understand you woke from a coma recently," he started, and my eyebrows rose. I glanced at Valerie, but she had her back to me and was preoccupied with setting the child in her arms down.

"Yes," I said, turning back to him.

"Can you tell us what happened?"

I shook my head, and before he hurled another question in my direction, Valerie intercepted him.

"Mr. Ryan isn't giving any interviews," she said, blocking the reporter.

"He seems perfectly capable," the reporter started and tried to step around her, but she blocked his path again.

"Do I have to call security?" she asked, and the reporter snapped his gaze to hers. "You know damned well you aren't supposed to film the children here without parental consent."

He pulled a piece of paper out of his pocket, handing it to her.

"We got permission."

Valerie handed him the paper. "Fine, you can film the kids, but Chris Ryan is not available for an interview," she said, and I stared at the tense form of her back.

"Do you mind talking to us for a few minutes?" the reported called over her shoulder and she sent a warning glare in my direction. I glanced at the dispersing kids and then back at the camera, offering a shrug.

"I have nothing to say," I stuttered and the reporter's hand holding the microphone dropped a fraction, along with his jaw. My gaze flitted to Valerie's and back and her relief actually stroked my skin from ten feet away.

"But..."

"Enough," Valerie snarled, catching the reporter's attention. "I will call security."

His lips tightened, and I stood, crossing to Valerie.

"We should go," I said, wrapping my arm around her waist before she got ornery. I led her away even as the reporter and camera followed. When we stepped into the elevator, I put my hand up, stopping them with my open palm and nothing else. When the elevator doors shut, I glanced at Valerie. "What was the problem?"

"Reporters can be royal assholes," she said and offered nothing more. The good mood from earlier seemed to be gone now, and a level of disappointment settled into me.

We crossed to the car in silence, and it wasn't until we hit Interstate 95 North that she sighed.

"I'm sorry," she said, glancing at me before turning back to the road. "You did fantastic, by the way," she added.

"Thanks." I kept my gaze out the window until her hand landed on my thigh. I covered her petite fingers with mine and then glanced at her.

"I almost lost my place when you kissed that little girl's head. It looked like a shower of sparkles fell over her."

Valerie let out a small laugh and chanced a quick look in my direction. "That's my healing magic," she said and sent a wink in my direction. "Amber is going to have a miraculous recovery. It'll stump the doctors, and they will round up specialists, but they won't find a thing wrong with that little girl. It'll almost be like that impromptu concert of yours..." She drifted off. "Shit."

"What?" I was still digesting the healing magic conversation. I mean, I knew she could read minds and talk to me in my head, but I had no basis to understand the exact extent of her unique power set. She had said several times she tried to heal me when she arrived at the hospital, but I never really connected the dots until now.

"I may have put you in the miracle maker crossfire."

I shrugged, again not connecting the pieces together.

"The reporters are going to latch onto that when they find out, and I'm afraid of what that will do to you."

I still didn't get her aversion to reporters. "Why didn't you let me talk to them?" I asked.

"Because they could have triggered a seizure, and I figured you wouldn't want that broadcast over all the news stations in the tri-state area."

She had a point, and I squeezed her hand. "You really think I did well?"

The grin that formed on her lips, along with the return of the light in her eyes, told me everything I needed to know, and I couldn't wait to get her alone for that rain check.

Angel Heart Chapter 9

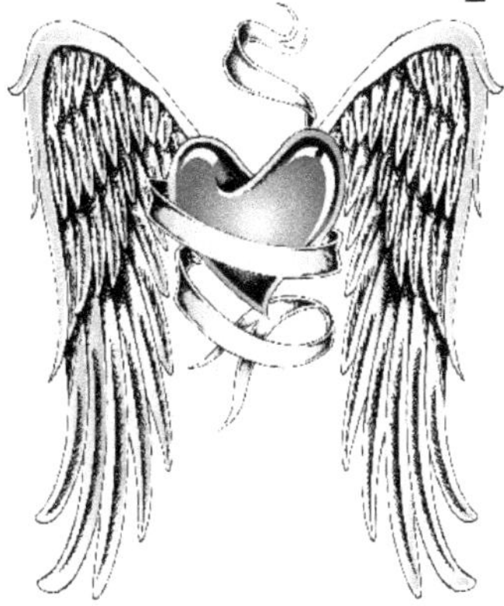

THE SETTING SUN CAST, a pink glow over the water. I sipped the soda in my hand, just staring at the ocean while Valerie chatted with Jennifer. The house was not empty when we got home and that soured my mood a fair amount, but I put on the benign smile, and we joined Steve and Jennifer on the patio.

The phone buzzed, and Steve answered. When his gaze jumped to me before he disappeared in the house, my curiosity peaked, and I followed him in. He flipped to the Boston channel, and there I was in high-definition glory singing *Hallelujah* with all the children gathered around the piano.

"Damn," both Steve and I whispered for very different reasons. Mine was based on actually hearing myself sing. It did not sound anywhere near the mediocre melody I heard in my ears. What came out of the television speakers was a voice, pure and strong, that rivaled most current day pop stars. I glanced at the door where Valerie now stood; her gaze locked on the television, with that special, heightened color filling her cheeks, and understood why she got that hornier-than-thou look when I sang.

Our awe was short-lived as the news story cut from me singing to video footage from a past I didn't remember. Steve reached for the remote.

"Leave it on," I said as the facts surrounding my family unraveled. My father was a kidnapper and murderer, and my mother had been his last victim. They speculated my parent's marriage had to be Stockholm syndrome, or he completely duped her into thinking he actually was Christopher Ryan. References to another chilling incident after a major motion picture premier were made and then videos of Tom and me covered in blood being escorted out of a warehouse filled the screen. My mother's death was highlighted next, and the near death of my brother. That was the first mention of Steve and the question of his motivations in raising us. A more recently banged up version of both Tom and me stood at the front door glaring out before I slammed the door shut.

However, none of these images really sank in. Not until the last image appeared. I reached for the couch at the picture of the bloodied and broken man wheeled in from a heliport. His face was unrecognizable through the swelling and bashed bones, but Valerie's panicked gaze and her deathlike grip on the man's hand made me turn toward her. Her eyes were wide, clearly registering the same horror flashing in my blood. That form was me and, as the voiceover announced, this was the last footage they had of me until this afternoon.

According to the story, I should not have been breathing when they wheeled me in, and my chances of survival were slim. It was a miracle that I survived, never mind recovered to the point of being able to put a coherent sentence together. The newscaster joked that he'd have to get the name of my plastic surgeon.

So much for a human-interest piece highlighting cancer victims. I sank to the couch, soaking in the information, and my gaze moved to Steve. The ex-FBI agent.

His jaw tightened at the speculations drawn regarding our family. This time when he pointed the remote, I didn't stop him from shutting off the drivel. Silence hung over the room.

"Did you know?"

Steve met my gaze and nodded at my question. "Yes," he said and placed the remote on the coffee table. He took a seat and rubbed his face before issuing a sigh. "I knew what your dad was when I met him."

"And you... killed him?" I asked because that would be the one reason I could think of why he would take us under his wing. Guilt.

Steve didn't answer right away. "I didn't kill him. I leveraged his skills to track another serial killer, and he was caught in the crossfire. Your father..." He stopped and dropped his gaze. "Your father offered to help because he wanted the killer as much as I did. At the time, Jen was in a coma, and I had nothing to lose. Not only was your father a computer genius, but he also had a piece of the power in your veins." He leaned back in the chair. "I should have hauled your father in, but I wanted to nail the bastard who nearly ruined my life more than I wanted to follow protocol."

"But my father was a serial killer?" I still couldn't wrap my head around that. The idea of taking an innocent life made me feel physically ill.

Jennifer came into view and opened a cabinet, scanning the contents before pulling out a Digital Video Disk. She turned and extended it to me. "If you really want to know the story of your father and mother, it all starts here."

I took the case and stared at the title. A few of the letters made sense, and it took me a half dozen times to sound out the words, but finally I stuttered, "Survival Games?" and looked up at Steve. He gave a curt nod.

"It's not pretty," he said. "The script is based on video evidence of what he was involved in, but it doesn't show everything that happened. There were things that occurred that never made it into the script because your father wiped out all record of his brother's involvement. The rest is pretty accurate based on his memories." Steve tapped his temple and shrugged.

"You have my father's memories?"

"Yes. That came with the supercharge." He glanced at Valerie, and I turned my head in time to catch her warning glare. She was protecting me again, and a new level of anger burned through my disbelief.

"What is it?" I snapped in her direction. "What are you so fucking afraid I'll remember?"

"Watch your language," Steve warned, and all the muscles in my back contracted.

Instead of hitting this tension head on, I stood with the movie in my hand and headed up to the silence of my room, slipping the disc into my laptop. I propped the computer on the nightstand, but before I could press play, Valerie opened the door.

"Just leave me alone for a little while, okay?" I asked, keeping my voice reasonable and calm even though a storm was brewing under my skin. There were too many questions and not enough answers, and I was hoping the video would clue me in to some of my locked past. I didn't really care if it prompted a seizure at this point. I just wanted those doors to open.

Valerie paused at the door, looking dejected. "I want to..."

I shook my head, stopping her. "Let me watch it alone. Please." I didn't leave any leeway in my answer, and the sudden tension in her clamping jaw, coupled with the bright sheen in her eyes, made me sigh.

"If it's as bad as Steve says..."

Her gaze dropped to the ground before it moved to the pictures on the wall. "The movie doesn't do justice to the reality." She brought her stormy eyes back to mine. "And I'm sure it's going to make you question a great deal of things."

She didn't know the half of it, and I raised my eyebrows.

She closed the door and stepped closer. "I know you already have questions, but as Steve said, what you're going to watch isn't the full picture. I might be able to help fill in the blanks if you need it."

I tilted my head at her comment and considered the ramifications. "You have the memories, too?"

She grinned and the color in her cheeks bloomed. "I have so much shit in my head that it's amazing I don't short circuit." She crawled on the bed, curled up next to me, and reached over, hitting play on the computer screen.

If the movie hadn't been based on the true story of my father, I might have enjoyed it. It certainly was a steamy suspense, and I couldn't quite grasp the fact it was about my parents. The actor playing my father was the spitting image of Tom and my gaze moved from the screen to the picture of my family when I was a kid. I was the one who looked like my dad.

"You and Tom are only half-brothers," Valerie whispered in my ear, and I turned to look at her. She pointed at the screen. "That's his biological father. He and your mom got married after all that shit happened."

"Aren't we twins?"

"Yes. You shared the same womb, but you were conceived by different fathers."

"Oh," I whispered and concentrated on the movie.

"Why didn't my father use his powers?" I asked when the scene transitioned to him as a prisoner.

"He didn't have any. That was all your mother. There is a whole other side of things that this movie doesn't show, one that Tom's biological father didn't disclose when they were writing the script, but he was down there with them. I can't imagine going back to the place you were meant to die in." She shuddered in my arms.

I couldn't agree with her more. If I had been given the choice to relive such horrors just for a paycheck, I would have passed a hundred times over. I gave her a squeeze, and she glanced over her shoulders at me, offering a hint of a smile before we both refocused on the movie.

As the last scene faded, I stared at the rolling credits; not comprehending the ordeal, or even how my father walked out of that place. "I thought Steve said my father died in the crossfire of one of his cases?"

"He did."

"But..." I waved at the screen, and she rolled towards me.

"Your older brother, Eric, was the one responsible for giving him another fifteen years on this earth. Eric and your mom had the same power that flows through my veins now. The power to heal. Your mother also had the powers in you. They balanced out in your parents. Sort of the way they do in us. I guess Steve held onto a lot of it until he met me and the fates dictated we were now the two sides of the coin."

"What two sides?"

"Light and dark." She pulled me into a kiss. "Healing and destruction," she said when our lips parted.

I stared into her calico eyes, still unable to grasp the whole thing. My father had killed for fun and got away with it. He was arrogant and smooth, manipulative and controlling, and despite all that, if the movie held true, he had to be one of the bravest sons of bitches I've ever seen.

Was I the same way? Is that why no one would let me unlock my past?

Her head shook as my thoughts paraded through her mind. "No. You aren't manipulative and controlling, and your sense of right and wrong is so deeply ingrained, you're definitely like your mother in that respect."

"So, you think I'm arrogant?" I stuttered, and she grinned.

"And brave," she added.

"And smooth?" I lifted an eyebrow.

She laughed and shook her head. "No, you aren't smooth, babe. You're more like a bumbling genius when you try to be smooth."

I couldn't help but grin and when she went to sit up, I pushed her back on the bed, covering her protest with my mouth. The lock clicked on the door at my direction, and I pulled away, offering her my best salacious grin. "I can be smooth," I purred and lowered my lips to her neck.

"Chris," she whispered in admonishment, but her tune changed as I drifted lower, pushing the thin t-shirt up and over her head and tossing it on the floor.

I just gave her a sideways glance and had to admit some of the scenes we had just watched had lit a match in my libido. I was tempted to bind her wrists and try that type of seduction on her just to see how it felt to have her at my mercy.

The color in her cheeks turned crimson, and she bit her lip.

"You want to play that kind of game?" I asked, kind of surprised by the rise in her heart rate at the thought of it.

Her one shouldered shrug made me chuckle.

"Do you want me to tie you to the bedpost?" I asked, curious what her answer would be.

Again, that slight rise of her shoulder, but the heightened color told me more than the shoulder roll.

I slid off her and headed toward the closet.

"Chris," she whispered, and I turned to see her sit up.

"Lie down," I said, and she did as I directed, her expression registering a bit of shock at the forced command. I knew I didn't need physical bonds to keep her in place, but the idea of seeing her wrists wrapped in satin sashes just fueled my kink level.

I grabbed the sashes off two of her dresses and slowly crossed towards her, rigging slipknots in each sash before I got to the bedside. Before I bound her, I stripped her bra, taking a moment to study her sexy form. Her nipples were already hard, and I slid the sash around her wrist, tightening it before tying the other ends to each of the head posts, leaving her splayed on my bed like my personal captive.

The overwhelming power of the situation hit as I stripped her shorts and underwear, leaving her naked on the bed. My heart pounded as I crawled over her, looking straight down into her eyes.

I licked my lips and forced my arms to stop shaking. "Beg," I whispered, adopting the line from the movie just to see how it felt to completely dominate her.

"No," she whispered, drawing a smile.

I lowered my mouth to within a fraction of hers, feeling her excited pants fall on my face, and then I just grinned, moving away from her succulent lips to the line of her throat. Only my tongue touched her skin, and she sighed that breathless sigh that turned the flame into a roaring inferno.

She tasted like honey. Sweet and soft as my lips traveled to her breasts, playing with her nipples until she let out a soft moan with my name on it. Being in control like this was more intoxicating than a fifth of Jack Daniels, and I continued my quest lower until my mouth settled between her legs.

She was so fucking wet already, and now her hands were squeezing the bindings, pulling on them as she writhed under my manipulation. God bless her. She was trying so hard to be quiet when that first orgasm hit; I thought her eyes were going to get stuck rolled back in her head. I didn't stop there either, even though she was truly begging for me now. I kept going, bringing her from one orgasm to the next until I couldn't hold out any longer.

My shorts came off in a flurry and I didn't think about what I was doing. I just slammed my hips to hers, riding her hard and fast into the land of rapture.

Angel Heart Chapter 10

WE LAY SIDE-BY-SIDE IN silence, just staring at the ceiling.

"Next time, I get to tie you up," Valerie whispered, her voice hoarse and raw with spent energy.

I laughed and turned my head, meeting her gaze. "I'm game," I said, with an equally spent voice.

"How'd we get from watching that movie to this?" she asked and slowly untied the satin from her wrists, dropping the fabric to the floor before she rolled into the crook of my arm.

"I don't know, but I'm a little ashamed to admit I think I understand the lure of that kind of power over someone had on my father." I kissed her forehead. "Especially if it's tied up in feelings."

"Pardon the pun?" she asked, grinning.

I just rolled my eyes. "I still don't get it. How could my mother forgive him for that crap? How could she ever marry that guy?" I sat up, staring at the blank computer screen.

"I don't really have the answers. Even the memories don't answer that question. She saw underneath his cold exterior and she fought so hard to not give in to him, but the two of them together..." She trailed off and sat up, swinging her legs over the edge of the bed next to mine. Valerie sighed and looked at me. "It just made sense. They balanced, like everything clicked into place in the universe when they were together."

The statement made me scoff. It just didn't settle right. There had to be some level of manipulation on my father's part to make her fall for a killer. "I want their memories," I said, staring her down with the command.

Valerie flinched and growled—"No"—forcing the wall surrounding her memory banks to hold against my silent assault. "Stop, Chris," she whispered, and her hands flew to the sides of her head.

I blinked, letting go of whatever door I was trying to force open in her mind. She crumpled to the bed, her breath labored, and she glared up at me.

"You can't do that." She swatted my leg.

Instead of apologizing, I leaned over and pressed the keyboard on my computer. The root menu on the disc appeared, and I scanned the other options, debating on looking at the special features or not. Valerie decided for me. She closed the laptop.

"I need to grab something to eat." She slipped out of bed, gathering her clothes and throwing mine to me.

My stomach growled in agreement. We both ran brushes through our hair, and I grabbed the disc out of the computer, returning it to the case before we descended to the family room. Steve and Jennifer looked up from the kitchen table, where they were engaged in a card game.

I dropped the movie on the coffee table and passed to the refrigerator without a word. Their eyes burned holes in my shoulder blades, and I sighed, grabbing two beers before turning toward them.

"What?" I asked, as I twisted each top off and handed one to Valerie.

"Are you okay?" Jennifer asked, and the concern in her voice was as clear as the view from our backyard.

I took a minute to think about how to answer her. It hadn't had time to really settle in, not with the romp Valerie and I had, and I'm sure it was my deliberate defense, so I wouldn't have to think too hard about the man who sired me.

"I don't know." I raised my gaze back to hers.

"Take a seat." Steve pointed his chin at the chairs lining the table.

I slid into the chair next to Jennifer and took a swig of the beer, waiting for Steve to impart some wisdom. He looked at the cards in his hand and placed a discard on the deck, fanning the cards out with a smile.

Jennifer muttered under her breath and slammed her cards face down. I wasn't sure if the glare she sent in Steve's direction was real or just part of losing the card game.

"I love you," Steve said, grinning.

"So, why couldn't you let me win from time to time?" She swiped the cards into a pile and shuffled them together with Steve's before she slid them into the cardboard box. "I'll let you two talk," she said, and gave Valerie a nod to follow.

Valerie lingered for a moment, trading a worried glance with Steve.

"I'll be fine," I said, and she leaned over, planting a kiss before she stepped out on the patio with Jennifer.

Steve retrieved the scotch from the bar and took a seat after he filled a glass with ice. He took his time, pouring and capping the bottle before he focused on me. "I'm not going to lie to you. Your father could be a royal asshole, and his views on human life were questionable at times, but, and this is a huge but, he, for the most part, had the right reasons for most everything he did. The only time he turned his back on morality completely was the time his stepbrother was manipulating him." He took a sip of his drink and leaned back in the seat. "Your dad..." He trailed off and took another sip, glancing around the room before his gaze landed back on me, like he half expected something from the great beyond to talk to him. "Your dad ended up being, probably, the closest friend I ever had."

"How long did you know him?"

Steve was quiet, and he looked down into his drink. "I worked with him for a month on the Winslow case." When he raised his eyes to mine, I got chills, and I wasn't sure I wanted to know anything more. "And he was with me for close to ten years after he died."

I just stared at him, the words sinking in like a drug, the meaning still lost on me.

"Your father's penance was being assigned as my guardian angel."

I laughed out loud. He had to be fucking kidding me and yet his stoic gaze didn't alter, and I could see the truth in his eyes, but it was as insane as the vampires that attacked us at the lake.

"Why?" I whispered, when I found my voice.

He huffed a laugh. "He needed me alive."

I shrugged to say what the hell did that have to do with anything?

"He needed me to make sure you turned out the way you did." Steve leveled a look in my direction that turned my insides to ice.

"And what way is that?" I asked, dreading the answer.

Steve's expression softened, and he smiled. "Honorable and courageous, along with a moral compass that is pure and ethical."

It wasn't what I expected, and I sat back in the chair, blinking. "You make me sound like an angel."

This time, he did laugh. "Well, you had your moments of rebellion like every kid does, although some of it could have gotten both you and Tom into a world of trouble."

"So, I'm not like my father?"

He was a little slower in responding to that than the other questions. "You are in a great deal of ways, but the thing that separates you from him is you have never compromised your morality. Sure, you stole a car once and got hauled in for trespassing and reckless driving, but you were side-by-side with your brother and I'm pretty sure most of that shit was his idea and you just went along to make sure he didn't kill himself."

I looked into my beer, wishing I could remember these things.

"CJ," Steve said, and I met his gaze. "You're one of the brightest and kindest men I know. You also can be cocky as hell and have a razor-sharp sense of humor. Most of those qualities came from your father. Your sense of right and wrong comes from your mother and I like to think I may have reinforced some of that, but..." he shrugged.

"Did money have anything to do with why you took us in?"

Steve shook his head. "No. Your father helped finance a victim's fund, and he made sure I got a hefty cut of it. I had no clue he would do that, either. Nor did I know he had made arrangements that Jen and I would become your guardians when your mother died. He made me independently wealthy, and I haven't touched a cent of either yours or Tom's trust funds."

"What about my medical expenses?"

He tilted his head. "I covered it. You've been my kid since you were nine. And if you haven't figured it out yet, there's pretty much nothing Jen and I wouldn't do for you and Tom."

I dropped my gaze and swallowed the sudden lump in my throat.

The phone rang, and Steve didn't move to answer it. I stood.

"Leave it, it's probably the press. The phone hasn't stopped ringing since the news story aired."

I dropped back into my seat. And the dial tone rang through as soon as the answering machine picked up. "Thanks," I said after the phone cut off.

"For?"

"For giving me a little more insight into my past."

"I figured you didn't drop into a seizure watching the movie," he said and shrugged. "So, what was the harm in talking to you a little about your father? Besides, if the media corners you, at least you'll have some clue and won't be taken off guard. That could be a disaster."

"So, there are such things as angels?" I asked, returning to his prior statement.

He nodded. "Yes. However, that's really not a conversation for right now. Okay?"

The clear warning in his tone gave me pause. I wasn't sure whether or not to push him on the issue, but by the hard expression, I figured the conversation was now over.

"Okay," I conceded. "Think we should join Jen and Val?" I hooked my thumb over my shoulder toward the patio and Steve gave a nod, topping off his glass with scotch before storing the bottle away. I followed him outside.

"You okay?" Valerie asked when I took the seat next to her.

I gave a nod before I took a swig of my beer and scanned the dark horizon. That same sense of foreboding that I experienced at the lake house crawled over my skin and I shivered in the summer heat.

"Something's coming," I said, and Jennifer hissed out a breath, pulling our attention to her. Her usually clear green eyes were opaque, like the dead, and my vision clouded over.

My blood turned to ice, making my entire body numb. The edge of a blade pressed against Valerie's throat, and I stared into fire-red eyes, eyes that didn't belong in Raven's face.

"Jennifer," Steve's voice rocketed through me and whatever visual nightmare accosted me shattered into the silence surrounding us. But what I had seen couldn't be erased.

Jennifer's eyes were wide, but back to normal and they locked on mine. "You can't take the deal," she whispered. "No matter what." Her eyes rolled back in her head, and she slumped in the chair.

I thought the vision was chilling, but her words frightened me into silence. When I turned my glance to Valerie, her eyes held a sadness I didn't understand.

"She's right. If we find ourselves in that situation, you have to say no, no matter what. You understand?"

I just stared at her. If that was a glimpse of the future, there was no way in hell I'd sacrifice her. Not for me. Not for anything on this earth.

Angel Heart Chapter 11

THE SHRILL RING OF the phone interrupted the tension outside and I got up to answer it this time, just for the sheer need to get away from the three of them.

"Hello?" I managed without a stutter.

"Is Mr. Chris Ryan available?" the formal voice inquired.

"This is he," I answered, sticking with one-syllable words.

"My name is John Anderson. I'm with KMR Associates in New York and based on the national news story coming out of Boston this evening, we'd like to sit down and talk to you about signing with our agency."

"Ex...cuse me?" This time the stutter was prevalent, and I turned back toward the sliders.

"You were filmed singing at the Dana Farber Cancer Institute," he said.

"And?"

"You have an incredible talent that we would like to represent."

"Are you kid...ding me?"

Valerie stepped inside and put her hand out for the phone, and I narrowed my eyes, turning away. I could handle this.

"No. I am not kidding you. I'm prepared to hop on the first commuter jet out of JFK in the morning to discuss terms of representation."

"Why?"

"Because you have the specific star quality we have been searching for."

I laughed. "You know I was in a co...ma for the last two years, right?"

"It doesn't matter. I have never seen a roomful of both men and women swoon at a voice like that. You have the raw talent to be bigger than Elvis or The Beatles. I want to represent you and make you a star."

"I couldn't care less about being a star." I enjoyed singing for the kids, but it wasn't a passion the way being a doctor was for Valerie.

"You could impact millions of people. It could change your life."

"No dis...re...spect, sir, but I don't need an ent...ter...tain...ner plat...form to do that," I struggled to get the words out. I knew I was rich beyond most people's wildest dreams and could do a lot of good in the world with the money. I also knew from my limited exposure to entertainment that stars never had privacy, and I had a feeling that, with the talents both Valerie and I possessed, privacy was more critical for us than the average Joe.

"You could reach a lot more sick children," he said, very softly, trying to appeal to my humanity. I got a strange sensation, one that chilled me the same way that the vision had, and I turned back to Valerie.

A familiar voice overrode all my senses.

"CJ!" Tom's voice barreled through my head, and I dropped the phone, covering my ears at the decibels.

Valerie picked up the phone. "Sir, I'm sorry, but we are late for an appointment. If you would be so kind as to call back during normal business hours, either Chris or I would be glad to discuss this further." She didn't wait for a response; she just hung up the phone and grabbed my arm, yanking me toward the car.

"Tell him we're coming," she said.

I closed my eyes.

"No!"

My eyes snapped open, and I stared at her.

"No, don't jump the distance, not right now."

"But he sounded terrified."

She nodded. "The reason he is terrified is also the reason you can't leave yourself open. Just trust me." She pushed me into the passenger seat and nearly slid over the hood to the driver's side. She hit the gas, sending the little sports coup barreling toward the slowly opening gates. I had a moment to gasp and then I mentally pushed the gates faster, so we wouldn't crash into the solid iron. "Open a path for us, Chris. I'm not slowing down."

She wasn't kidding, either. Thank God it was late enough in the evening that the summer traffic had thinned to a reasonable rate. There were only a handful of cars that I had to push over into the parking spots. Pedestrians were a different thing. Any I saw hit a wall and couldn't progress or became speed demons as they crossed the road faster than humanly possible. I would have loved to see their faces, but I didn't have time to check out the complete shock; I was still concentrating on keeping the path clear.

We squealed into Tom's driveway less than five minutes after she dragged me out of the house and both of us were out of the car and sprinting for the door before the engine's last click sounded. I didn't bother with knocking; instead, I opened the door with a thought and skidded to a halt in the living area.

My brother's wide eyes met mine and my brain just stalled. He sat in a chair, his arms bound at the elbows and his wrists sliced open. The cascade of blood shocked me into motion.

"Valerie," I said and turned to let her pass.

The vision I had seen through Jennifer's eyes was standing before me. A red-eyed Raven held a knife to Valerie's throat and my jaw dropped. I knew I should do something, but again my brain stalled, and fear froze me in place.

"Are you ready to let me in or do I have to slice up this bitch too?" Raven said in a voice that could only be categorized as right from the bowels of hell.

"Don't you dare," Valerie said, her eyes broadcasting a warning I didn't understand.

"Will you let them go?" I asked with a voice that shook with raw fear.

Raven's eyes narrowed, and she sent an evil smirk my way.

Please don't kill her, Tom's voice echoed in my head with such pain that I took a second to glance back at him. If I didn't do something soon, he'd bleed to death.

Is Hannah okay? I sent the thought, and he gave a small nod.

The demon hurt Raven, though, so she needs help. He looked directly at Valerie, and I turned, trying to grasp what was happening. Valerie turned her head enough to plant a kiss on the hand grasping the knife.

Layers of fear drove through me as the tip of the knife pressed farther into the flesh of Valerie's neck. A thin line of blood dripped from where the blade broke skin. Underneath the fear bloomed a righteous anger and my hands curled into fists.

"Let her go," I issued the command in a growl I didn't recognize, and the knife came away from her throat.

It was only a second, but the command gave Valerie enough time to turn in to Raven's elbow, away from the blade and drop her to the ground. The minute she was clear, she sprinted to Tom's side and delivered the healing kiss to his temple.

A horrific cry of pain came from his chest and Valerie met my gaze, and then her eyes darted beyond me. I turned back to Raven, raising my hand as if I was directing traffic. The knife stopped an inch from my palm and clattered to the ground when I let the barrier surrounding me down.

"Keep her there, Chris," Valerie said, and in my mind, I cast a net over Raven to hold her in place.

"What is wrong with her?" I asked, turning back to Valerie and my now unconscious brother.

"She's possessed."

Motion outside the window caught my attention. A giant shadow landed on the lawn outside and I nearly lost control of the thing that had control over Raven.

Valerie turned the moment the door blew open. Damian stood outside, his eyes dark and his features tense.

"It's about time," Valerie snarled, and he sent a glare in her direction.

"I have three kids," he said, like that accounted for his less than desirable arrival time.

I knew it wasn't the time to ask how he got to the house from the ocean side; instead, I turned back to Raven, still holding her snarling form against the wall like a trapped wild cat. The red of her eyes kept transitioning back to the bright blue of Raven's eyes, and terror lay behind those irises. I got fragments of her thoughts before the dark presence put a gag order on her.

The scrape of a chair behind me pulled my attention in that direction, and Valerie pulled the other armchair onto the tile lining the foyer and met my gaze.

"Make her sit here."

I nodded and focused back on Raven, forcing her body to cross the distance to the chair in stiff steps. Making her sit took a little more effort. Whatever was in her was a powerful force, but not as strong as I seemed to be. Once she was sitting, Valerie dumped a line of salt around the chair and then stepped in the circle, binding Raven's wrists to the armrests.

When she stepped out of the salt barrier, she reached for the wall to steady herself.

"You can let go," she whispered to me, and I pulled the imaginary net away before stepping to Valerie's side and wrapping my arms around her.

"What the fuck?" I whispered, because, really, what the hell else was there to say?

Valerie let out a nearly hysterical laugh and pulled out of my arms. Her palms found each of my cheeks, and she held my face. "You can never, ever, give in to them, you hear me? Even if it means my life. If you do, the world will end."

"Why don't you poison the boy's mind some more," the thing inside of Raven purred, and I tried to turn my head to look, but Valerie held me still.

"Do you know who Lucifer is?" she asked me, and the world shook. "Chris?" her cry followed me into the blackness.

Another argument filtered in, and I kept my eyes closed this time, still trying to get my bearings. A cool cloth swiped over my forehead, but I knew it wasn't Valerie. She was going at it with Damian again, but this time it was Damian reading her the riot act.

I blinked open my eyes and Tom's bloodshot gaze met mine. He looked haggard and nearly ten years older than when we left the lake. He tried to smile at me, but it only succeeded as a sad contortion of his lips. His fingers touched his lips and then lowered into his other palm. That was one sign I knew, even without the soft voice thanking me.

I gave him a nod and looked beyond him at Raven cackling in the chair like a raving lunatic.

"She triggered another seizure, didn't she?" I whispered, trying not to draw Valerie's attention and Tom nodded, handing me the wet rag. That's when I noticed he was in different clothes, and I glance around the room. Whatever stains had been on the floor were gone. "How long was I out?"

Tom glanced at the clock on the wall and sighed before he held up six fingers.

"Six hours?" I shot up to a sitting position.

He broke out in an amused smile. "Ya," he said. "Fu up."

"Did you just call me a fuck up?"

This time the smile reached his eyes, and he shook his head. He twirled his finger. *I meant this whole thing is fucked up.*

I relaxed and agreed with him. The morning twilight seemed to break, and he followed my gaze outside.

"How long have they been going at it?"

I hooked my thumb at Valerie and Damian, standing toe-to-toe in a heated exchange.

Tom put up all six fingers again and rolled his eyes. I got it even without words.

"Do you know what to do with her?" I pointed to Raven.

He rocked his hand on the air in the universal code for sort of. *I really need you to remember the exact sequence of things we did for Valerie.*

I stared at him, disbelief and remorse centered in my chest. I hoped like hell their cure didn't lie with my memory being miraculously restored, because if it did, he was in for a hell of a disappointment.

Valerie and Damian were still going at it, and I sighed, meeting the gaze of the demon possessing Raven.

"What if I trade?" I asked and moved my gaze to Tom's.

The conflict there tore at my heart, and he slowly shook his head. "I can't let you," he signed and met my gaze.

The bitch in Raven had the audacity to laugh. "Lucifer said you were no more than a vegetable," she said, and I stared at her, blinking rapidly.

"Who the hell is Lucifer?" I asked, and the back door opened.

Valerie glared at the demon and then turned her sharp gaze toward me. "He's the one who put you in the hospital." The level of venom in her voice shocked me more than her statement. What surprised me even further was the fact I wasn't jerking around on the floor, like a fish out of water, at the hint of what happened. Maybe this was a breakthrough. Minor, but still, the name didn't trigger a seizure.

"That's all you're going to tell the poor man?" Raven's mouth said, but the voice sounded like a host of evil beasts growling the words instead of a human.

"Shut up," Damian said, and Raven's mouth clamped closed.

Valerie moved to my side, carefully guarding her thoughts now that I didn't drop into a slobbering mess. The way she was handling me was both amusing and irritating. I climbed to my feet and met her halfway.

"I'm not going to fall apart," I said, meeting her gaze. "Despite what everyone thinks."

"I know, but as much as I'd like your memory to come back, I also know forcing it could land you back in the hospital." Her hand palmed my cheek, and she pressed her lips to mine.

"Stop protecting me," I said when she pulled away.

"Chris," she started, and I pressed my finger to her mouth.

"Who has the clearest memory of what I need in order to help Raven?"

Her eyes jumped to Raven before they moved to Tom. "Your brother has the best recollection."

"I'm going to need that memory," I said and went to turn, but she stopped me.

"Chris." This time, her voice was little more than a whisper, and I met her gaze.

"I will be fine," I assured her, even though I was clueless how this would affect me. "I've got to try."

Tom looked up at me from his position on the couch.

"I don't know if I can do the selective memory thing," he signed. The worry in his eyes matched that of Valerie. But his was tempered with the need to help his wife.

"Don't worry; I can command the memory if I know what it is."

"It was when I was possessed," Valerie said, and I met her gaze for a moment, digesting her words before my gaze slid to Raven.

I could only imagine what kind of basket case I would be if that was Valerie in the chair, and I had to give props to Tom for keeping it together as much as he was. I had no clue how he could be so damned calm right now. I'd be climbing the walls.

I took a seat next to him and focused on my hands for a minute, collecting the power I needed to command him. When the skin of my stomach burned with the force inside me, I turned and met his gaze. "Show me what happened when Valerie was possessed." The command came in perfectly formed words and along with a hint of a growl.

His eyes widened in shock and then the images encompassed everything, drowning out reality and taking me back a little over two years ago, from Tom's perspective.

"Are you two ready for a storm?" Raven asked, and I nodded. CJ was a little more cautious, but he nodded after a second.

Raven started unpacking the duffel bag, setting jewelry, and what looked like fancy paperweights, on the table, along with candles and oils and a big sea-salt grinder. She turned and tossed a necklace to CJ. The black Wiccan star reflected in the light, and he raised an eyebrow.

"Just put it on," she said and looked from CJ to me. "Do you have yours on?"

I never go anywhere without it, and I unbuttoned my shirt, showing her the necklace that had saved my ass back in high school.

When she finished setting up the table, she turned and walked into the living room, away from the demon, beckoning to us to follow.

"Block your thoughts," she said.

I consciously put up the wall in my head and CJ confirmed our thoughts were masked.

She looked at me. "The only reason I let you stay is because I may need you're special skills."

I started to sign but she shook her head, stopping me.

"You told me you once put your father's spirit back in his body."

I nodded and glanced at CJ. He had been there; he knew damned well what I could do.

"Well, I might need you to do that with Valerie. Okay?"

"Okay," I signed.

Raven turned to CJ. "Do you think your protective shield can repel demon spirits?"

"I don't know."

"Well, let's hope that's the case, because the moment the spirits separate from her physical form and Tom has Valerie's, I'll need you to block anything else from getting to her. Or us, for that matter. She'll still be vulnerable until her spirit is back in her body. If we fail and the demon gets in there first, she will be lost to us. Understand?"

CJ blinked a couple of times, and I don't know if he realized it, but his mouth dropped open a little, like it does when he's going to argue a point, but Raven's face hardened.

"Understand?" she said more forcefully this time.

"Yes. I understand," CJ said. "How do you know this will work?"

"I've seen it done before," she whispered. "But we didn't have the benefit of a ghost whisperer or a psychic shield."

"Did it work?" CJ asked.

She stared at him for a long moment and then shook her head. "No."

"What happened?"

"My father happened," she said and turned away, storming back to the kitchen, leaving CJ and me staring at each other. A chill settled over me and I looked toward the kitchen. Her father was rotting in jail for two consecutive life sentences for the crimes he committed as the Windwalker.

"What do you mean?" CJ asked when we got back into the kitchen.

"We can discuss that later. You know what I expect of you." She turned back to the table and Valerie chuckled, the demon quality of it left me cold and I traded a glance with CJ.

"I want Val back," CJ growled at the thing holding her hostage.

"Maybe we can trade?" it said, raising one of her manicured eyebrows.

"As tempting as that sounds, I think I'll see what Raven can do with you first."

A shadow passed over her face and her teeth clenched as she focused on Raven's array of potions and precious rocks on the table.

Raven turned to CJ. "Can you hold her still for a minute?"

The demon snarled and tried to thrash, but the physical form it inhabited wouldn't budge under CJ's power. The beast within Valerie roared when Raven slipped a bloodstone necklace over her head, the red *jewel rested on her chest, right above her heart and the skin under it singed, sending off a waft of steam.*

Raven stepped out of the salt ring, visibly shaken by the scorching skin. She glanced at me, and I gave her a nod of encouragement. With a deep breath, she arranged four pyramid shaped stones at the north, south, east and west spots inside the circle and stepped back.

In the teak bowl, she mixed salt, some fine black powder and added a drop of green, red, and yellow potions to the mixture. Raven paused and glanced at CJ, waving him forward. She took his hand and raked a knife across his palm.

"Squeeze," she said, holding his hand over the mixture.

After three drops of blood hit the mixture, she moved CJ's hand away and mixed the cocktail, whispering an incantation.

"Mháthair a chara, cruthaitheoir go léir, cabhrú liom banish an Demon as an cailín. Cabhraigh léi a fháil ar ais ar a anam. Dhíbirt an olc as a corp. Cabhraigh léi a fháil ar ais ar a anam. Demon a bheith imithe!"

The mixture bubbled and sizzled, and she turned toward Valerie.

"Repeat after me, boys," Raven said, and Valerie stared thrashing in the chair. "Spiorad olc saoire an gcomhlacht seo. Demon a bheith imithe!"

CJ repeated the foreign chant, clearly enunciating over my tongue-less mutter. "Spiorad olc saoire an gcomhlacht seo. Demon a bheith imithe!"

Raven flung a spoonful of the mix at Valerie and the scream that followed tore through me. From the look on CJ's face, he was a breath away from freaking out.

"Again," Raven ordered and moved to Valerie's side.

We repeated the chant and Raven flung another spoonful at Valerie. This time, the mixture produced scorching welts on her skin and the struggle of souls began writhing together in a fight to the death. Whatever my wife was doing was working. CJ stepped towards Raven, but I grabbed his arm and opened my mind, letting him see what I was seeing.

He traded a glance with me before we refocused on the struggle. When Raven ordered us to speak the incantation again, neither of us hesitated.

The third time brought forth a wail of pain that made me want to cover my ears. The earth around us rumbled to the point the jars on the counter rattled. The dishes in the cabinets shifted, knocking open cabinet doors and sending plates and glasses crashing to the counter. Even the refrigerator door opened, crashing contents to the floor in a mad swirl.

The fourth time, I let go of CJ and stepped forward, grabbing onto Valerie's spirit like Raven had instructed, and sent the command "Now" out to CJ, along with what I was seeing.

I knew CJ had put up that barrier just with the electrical quality in the air, and I forced Valerie's spirit back into her body. The melding of spirit to skin arched her back, and she took a deep wheezing breath. Her eyes locked on CJ's, and she moaned in pain.

"Will yourself to heal," CJ whispered, and her eyes widened and then dropped closed.

I glanced up at the black cloud trying to attack us and sent the vision to CJ. The mask of anger that transitioned his features froze my blood, and I prayed I'd never be the recipient of his wrath, ever. It was ten times scarier than the demon trying to breach his protective barrier. Flames licked the protective bubble and blackened the ceiling. An explosion rocked the kitchen, blowing the window over the sink open and obliterating the salt line protecting that exit. What was left of the demon spirit fled through that portal, sending a plume of black smoke out into the yard and into the night sky.

I blinked, back in my own skin with my own thoughts and I met Tom's wide-eyed stare. "Holy shit," I whispered and slumped into the cushions, running my hands through my hair. Tom gave me a crooked smile and raised an eyebrow.

"I got it," I said and exhaled. "Do you have her bag?"

Tom nodded, and we both stood. Before he stepped away, he pulled me into a hug.

"Thank you," his thought echoed in my head.

"I haven't done anything yet," I said, and he pulled away, disappearing down the hall. When he came back, he carried the same duffel bag from his memory. He handed it to me, and I crossed to the table, emptying the contents, inspecting each element and setting them in two piles. One that corresponded to the memories and one that didn't. I looked through the jewels, looking for the same type of stone, and when I came up empty, I glanced at Valerie and my hand went to the pendant around my neck.

"No," both Valerie and Tom said at the same time. Tom stepped forward and pressed his hand over the star lying on my skin. He shook his head. Even without words, he said everything with his eyes. I still needed the protection just as much as Raven. He reached beyond me and picked up a different emblem.

"This is also made of blood stone, even though it isn't red. Not as potent as the one around your neck, but it will do," his thoughts rang in my head, and I took the offering.

I picked up one of the pyramid stones. "Do you know which direction true north is?"

"Facing her, it's at ten o'clock," Damian said.

I tried to remember what he was referencing, and finally I held out the stone. "Can you put this in the right place just inside the salt line?"

Damian's lips pressed together, and he grabbed the pyramid, putting it on the ground just to the left of center behind her. I could place the rest now that I had the right reference. After all four stones were placed, I clasped the necklace around her neck, despite the hissing coming from Raven's lips. A welt immediately seared the exposed skin of her neckline, and I met the demon's fiery gaze.

"Don't worry, I'm planning on sending you back to hell," I stumbled on the words, prompting a chuckle from the demon possessing Raven.

"You know you have to speak the words precisely for the spell to work," it said and laughed.

I leaned close. "I may stutter like a fool when I speak, but I'm flawless when I sing."

I stepped out of the salt ring and back to the table, ignoring the incessant cackling. I scanned the bottles I had put aside. Half of them were ruled out just based on color, and now I was presented with a challenge. Concocting the serum she made would not be as easy as she made it look and I closed my eyes, going step-by-step through the memory. With each ingredient, I inspected Tom's memory, matching symbols on the canisters before I added it to the mini cauldron. It took me a little over a half hour before I got to the point of adding the three drops of blood.

I picked up the knife and positioned my hand over the mixture.

"No," Tom said; his voice clear in my head, he stepped next to me, offering his hand instead, and I paused, meeting his gaze.

"True love's blood," his thought announced, and I started laughing. It was too fairytale for me, but the seriousness in his stare gave me pause.

"Okay," I said. "Just three drops," I added, and he nodded. This part he remembered, and when I drew the blade across his palm, he squeezed. The blood sizzled on contact and after three drops, he withdrew his hand, wrapping it in one of the cloth diapers folded in the clean laundry basket in the corner.

I took a deep breath and stirred the mixture, letting my vocal cords relax and, in a haunting melody, I recited the incantation Raven had whispered.

"Mháthair a chara, cruthaitheoir go léir, cabhrú liom banish an Demon as an cailín. Cabhraigh léi a fháil ar ais ar a anam. Dhíbirt an olc as a corp. Cabhraigh léi a fháil ar ais ar a anam. Demon a bheith imithe!"

The mixture bubbled, and I traded a glance with Valerie before turning toward Raven. "Repeat after me," I said, and Raven thrashed in the chair. I spattered her with a spoonful of the mixture and sang the spell. Damian, Valerie, and Tom repeated it without the melodic flow. "Spiorad olc saoire an gcomhlacht seo. Demon a bheith imithe!"

My voice echoed off the walls as I repeated the phrases, the power of it penetrating the demon and Tom opened his mind as he had done before, but the struggle was less pronounced, it was almost as if my voice actually hypnotized the demon right out of Raven. The thrashing and cries were weak compared to what possessed Valerie. When Tom stepped forward and grabbed Raven's spirit, I could have sworn she placed a gentle kiss on his lips.

Instead of focusing on his tender moment, I closed my eyes and let the sudden swell of anger eviscerate the thrashing demon hovering just outside my protective bubble.

This time, when the demon screamed, Tom's gaze afforded me the fruits of my labor. The bastard didn't escape this time. I made damn sure it perished in the ball of flame. As soon as the fire dissipated, I let my guard down and glanced at Raven.

The awe in her bright eyes made me shift my stance, and I shoved my hands into my pockets, opting to stare at the floor.

"You have the voice of the angels," she said in a thick Irish lilt, and I moved my gaze back to hers, letting the absurdity of her statement peel a laugh from my throat. She kept my gaze for all of two seconds before her eyes rolled back and she slumped in Tom's arms.

Valerie stepped to her side and delivered another dose of healing via a kiss on her forehead before she turned to me.

"Are you okay?"

I shrugged and met her gaze, the entire ordeal leading me to question so much more about my past. "Who is Lucifer?" I asked again, returning to my earlier question. "And how the hell could he put me in a coma for two years?"

"Chris," she sighed.

"Lucifer is the devil," Damian said, and I met his gaze. "He's the fallen archangel and his level of power probably rivals yours when he is in angel form."

For the first time since I woke up, a vision surfaced that didn't throw me into a twitching mess. It was only a moment, but the face I saw was my father's and it wasn't human. His white wings spanned the small clearing and his preternatural eyes fell upon me.

I blinked and stumbled back, reaching for the wall.

"My father was an angel?" I gasped and my gaze landed on Tom.

He issued a sharp laugh and shook his head. "No. Dad wasn't an angel," he signed. "The news stories were accurate. He was a badass for most of his human life. When he died, well, I guess he was assigned a job as penance for his less than moral deeds."

I cocked my head, and my brow furrowed in confusion.

"Talk to Steve. He can tell you more of the details, but Dad was assigned to keep him out of trouble."

Steve's conversation with me the other day came barreling forward, along with the vision of my father with wings. "I remember Dad with wings," I said and all motion in the room stopped.

"You remember?" Valerie said, approaching me.

"I guess so," I said. "I saw my father with angel wings." I crossed to the couch and took a seat before my legs gave out from under me. "So, is that somehow related to why Lucifer tried to kill me?"

"No," Valerie answered. "Lucifer wants to possess you, and you refused. He needs you in order to defeat Damian and get to Naomi and Grace."

"Why?"

"Naomi is a descendant of two archangel bloodlines. Michael and Raphael. I've got Michael's bloodline, so I'm on Lucifer's hit list just because he considers the heart of Michael's descendants a delicacy." She paused and glanced at Damian. "Damian is Gabriel's son, so when he and Naomi hooked up, they had the possibility of creating a true trinity for the first time in over two thousand years. Their children are trinities. Do you understand the significance of that?"

I just stared at her. The only thing I correlated was what I got out of the Sunday morning services that Jennifer and Steve took me to, and I just couldn't wrap my head around it. The boundaries of good and evil, which I understood from church. God and the devil, I understood and even the son of God made sense, but Damian's children, trinities like Jesus? I just couldn't grasp that.

"Yes. Grace is a trinity, and Naomi can create more. That's why Lucifer wants them. He is interested in breeding an army of dark trinities so he can rule the earth and I am standing in his way," Damian said.

I couldn't help it. I started laughing. Demons, vampires, angels and the devil. What the hell kind of nightmare did I live in?

"One where you are the white knight," Valerie said to my train of thought. "You went up against the devil and lived. The only other person I know who faced off against him and survived is in this room." She turned to Damian.

He shrugged. "Naomi's the one who nearly killed him."

"And you stole his grace," Valerie clarified.

"I couldn't have done it without CJ." He tapped his temple and met my gaze. "You gave me the extra edge I needed to steal Lucifer's grace."

Tom placed Raven's unconscious form on the couch and then met my gaze. "Thank you," he signed and offered me a hint of a smile. But it wasn't his signing or his voice that sounded in my head that caught my attention. It was the memories swarming in his mind that triggered my own of the same situation.

My throat constricted, and I couldn't pull a breath. The room disappeared along with everyone's voices and what replaced it was a snowy scene and a black-winged man with a severed head in each hand. He dropped them on the ground so they faced the window Tom and I stood at, and then the bastard wiped his hands together as if they were nothing more than dirt and grime.

The face was familiar and drew a level of fury to the surface, pulling at my mind and for a moment, I felt the jolt of each muscle in my body clenching, but I ignored the obvious signs of seizure and clung to the memory.

The two angels charged, slamming into each other and creating an explosion that rattled the window. I stared at the horror in front of me; the shrill cry of the baby in the background couldn't pull my attention away, not with the fight to the death unfolding on the snow-covered lawn. The battle between my father and Lucifer raged, dredging up a white flurry around the two angels. My heartbeat rammed my throat, drawing my breath in fast pants of anxiety as I watched each mighty blow.

Red splattered white and I bellowed at the vision of my father's head in the demon's grip. My palms banged against the cold windowpane as blood rained down on my father's wings. Even my brother couldn't break through the devastation layering my heart. A second trembling cry broke through the blackness shrouding me, and I glanced at my brother. Tom's gaze was glued to the scene outside, while tears slowly tracked down his cheeks. His lips pressed together, and he grieved in silence, but I felt the darkness grip his heart as surely as it gripped my own.

White light drowned all thought, and then blackness pulled me under.

Angel Heart Chapter 12

I STOOD AT THE wall overlooking the ocean with my back to the house. The day's events rattled around my brain like a ping-pong ball, and blew my definition of normal to hell and back; but then again, I wasn't sure what the hell a normal family was.

Saving Raven opened doors I wished to God had stayed closed, and I wondered just what kind of nutcase I really was to go up against the devil.

"Uncle CJ!" the childish screech pulled my attention away from the water and I turned to see the three-year-old making a beeline across the yard with her arms spread wide. Setting my drink down on the rocks, I crouched, mimicking Grace's pose, and when she launched, I caught her in mid-air, twirling her around like a rocket, taking off for the stars. Her laughter was infectious, and I joined in long enough to soften the heartache in my chest. She placed a sweet butterfly kiss on my cheek, and then her laughter faded.

Her bright blue eyes met mine and her little hands cupped my cheeks. The transformation of her features, from a child into a wisdom-infused being, gave me pause. She pressed her lips together in a sad smile. "Give it time. It will all make perfect sense when you remember everything."

Even her voice sounded ancient and a chill bit my back. Her little hands gave each cheek a pat and then her eyes cleared, and she was back to the fidgety three-year-old I remembered. I put her on the ground, and she ran back to her parents.

My gaze met Damian's, and he gave a halfhearted shrug. Grace was a natural trinity and for the first time since I came out of the coma, I really understood all the ramifications of that label. Damian shared the same destiny, except he acquired his grace through inheritance and thievery, just like he gained the seed of my power.

I turned back toward the ocean. The vastness of the water calmed my nerves. It made me feel much smaller than the world, even though I knew somehow I played a very important part in the world's survival. The responsibility left me breathless and more unhinged than I had been since I woke from the coma.

Tom's decision to share the demise of our father wasn't a conscious one. All the talk about Lucifer and angels prompted his memory, and he didn't have enough time to put up the barrier to keep me from it.

Of course, this time the seizure took hold, but for the first time since I came to, I had the full recollection of it and not some vague shadow of a memory. It wasn't just Tom's memory, either. My thoughts and feelings intertwined with his like a snake curling around a magical staff. The level of pain and anguish that scene caused still held on, and the sense of loss was so great, I wasn't sure I could hold it together for the impromptu family barbeque.

"Hey," Valerie's voice intercepted my thoughts, and I glanced at her. "Are you okay?"

I laughed and scanned the endless blue before me. "I am no longer sure I want my memory back."

"Chris," she whispered and slid her hand in mine.

"How many people out there know these things really exist?" I waved my free hand toward the crowded beachfront in the distance.

"Not many. You didn't know these things existed until a couple of years ago. Before that, you may have dealt with a ghost or two, as well as a guardian angel, but other than that, you were just as clueless as the general population."

I turned and met her gaze. "What else is out there?"

She shrugged. "I don't know. I've only been exposed to vampires, demons, and angels, but I gather from some of Damian's memories there are other things that we haven't had the misfortune of running into."

"Great," I said with all the enthusiasm of a rock.

"The good news is you can destroy most anything that comes after us," she said.

I rolled my eyes. That wasn't really what I wanted to hear. "So, basically, I am as much of a freak of nature as all those things out there that go bump in the night."

"No..." she started, and I sent a glare in her direction, shutting up whatever argument she was going to launch. She yanked her hand out of my grip and crossed her arms. "Don't forget to include me in that category, too," she added with a level of sarcasm I had yet to encounter.

"Oh, I haven't forgotten," I said and had to suppress a smirk at the full-blown fervor now etched into her tight features. I was really pushing her buttons today and, to be honest, it was a major tension release. If I didn't let off some steam, I might have a goddamned melt down.

God knows how much I loved Valerie, but at the moment, I wanted to see just how irate I could get her. When she turned to leave, I exercised a little of my freakish strength and willed her to remain at my side. The fire that lit up her eyes brought forth a smile.

"Sorry, babe," I whispered, and she muttered some foul curses aimed at me.

"Tsk, tsk. There are young ears in the vicinity."

Her face turned that explosive red that should have reduced me to shame, but it had the opposite effect, and I chuckled.

"Let me go," she hissed through clenched teeth.

My eyebrows rose and my chuckle turned into a full guffaw. The more she cursed me out, the harder I laughed.

"Next time you're jerking on the ground, I'm going to laugh while you drool," she growled, and the mental image those words gave me didn't help corral my laughter. In fact, I actually dropped into a crouch and held onto the rock wall to steady myself.

"You are such an ass," she said.

I looked up at her. "I love you," I said through the laughter.

"Fuck you," she whispered, but her lips twitched and those adorable dimples appeared.

I didn't have a chance to explore that comment. Steve hollered my name, and I released Valerie, looking in his direction as I climbed to my feet. He wasn't alone and all the motion in the back yard stopped. Every pair of eyes shot to the woman standing next to Steve.

She looked like the hot teacher in one of those old rock and roll videos as she strutted across the lawn in stiletto heels. "Mr. Ryan, I presume," she said as she approached.

I traded a glance with Valerie and then nodded in her direction.

"I'm Sam Cole, the vice-president of acquisitions at KMR Associates." She jutted her hand out in my direction and I just stared at it before meeting her gaze.

"I'm sorry, Ms. Cole, but as I told your ass...oc...i...ate, I'm not interested."

She dropped her hand. "Boy, you have a natural talent that needs to be shared with the world," she said as her hands found her hips.

I chuckled. "I beg to differ."

Steve joined us. "Hear her out," he said, and I cocked an eyebrow in his direction before refocusing on Ms. Cole.

"Thank you," she said to Steve and then drew in her breath. "KMR would like to represent you."

That's all she said, and Steve's lips thinned to the point I knew she had snowed him to get in the door.

"What did you tell my uncle that made him let you in the house?"

She sighed. "I told him we want to hire you for charity events."

I crossed my arms, staring her down. "Why?"

"Because you could bring in a tremendous amount of money for different charities," she said and left the implications hanging.

"Which means you'd get a sizeable chunk," I stuttered out and doubt crossed her features.

"Well, as your representative, we would get a cut," she said and shifted her weight. Her heels had sunk in the grass. This wasn't the normal high-powered boardroom scene this woman was used to, and I took a seat on the rock wall, facing her.

"Tell me how that makes a difference, in, say, a child's life?" I wanted to see if there was any form of a heart in this woman. So far, I hadn't seen anything more than a self-serving, money-hungry publicity whore.

She leveled a glare at me. "It could make the difference between a life-saving treatment and a cold box in the ground."

Okay, I had to admit, that was a good comeback, and I slid my gaze to Valerie. Her study of the woman intrigued me, and I got a whiff of the budding rivalry and perhaps a twinge of jealousy. When she realized I was studying her, she dropped her gaze to the ground.

I focused back on Ms. Cole. "I don't know how to read music," I said, and the surprise that formed a small 'o' of her mouth pulled a smile to my lips. "As a matter of fact, I don't really know how to read, period."

"Excuse me?" She glanced between Steve and me, and then her gaze landed on Valerie.

"He's learning, but he's nowhere near the point where you could give him sheet music and he could read the words, never mind translate it to song," Valerie said.

Ms. Cole pressed her lips together and stared at me. "After the performance I saw on television, you're telling me that was a fluke? I don't buy it."

"I'm sorry, but I am really not interested in signing with you, ma'am," I said, knowing the salutation would piss her off, and I offered my best apologetic smile to soften the blow. If I was going to help a charity, I would sing for free, not be whored out by a pimp masquerading as an agent.

She glanced at the open water beyond me and blew a slow stream of air from between her lips. When her gaze returned to mine, I knew exactly what she was going to say next.

"I can't leave here without signing you," she said and crossed her arms, digging in.

"Well, then you might as well ditch the stilettos and pull up a seat because you're going to be here for a very long time." I stuttered through the words, but Valerie got the gist and started laughing.

I gave a nod and stepped away, leaving Ms. Cole with Valerie to either drill her for more details or escort her to the door. I took a seat at the picnic table next to Grace and help her color one of the Disney princesses in her coloring book.

I glanced at Raven, who sat quietly in one of the lounge chairs nursing a drink. After the day she had, I got she needed a stiff drink, and she cocked her head, silently questioning what the lady on the lawn wanted.

"She wants to represent me," I said, and the crease between her eyes made me smile. "She saw the news story and wants to make me her singing monkey," I clarified, and a smirk appeared.

"That could be fun," she said, and winked. "But I think Valerie might get a wee bit jealous of all the harlots throwing themselves at your feet." Her Irish brogue was thicker with the free rein of alcohol running amok in her system.

"Harlots?" I raised an eyebrow and smirked.

Raven made out as if she was going to pitch her glass at me and broke out laughing. "You'd be a fool to walk away from that girl," she said, tipping her head toward Valerie, who had corralled Ms. Cole and was leading her into the house.

"I agree with you there," I said and refocused on the coloring book.

"Thank you," Raven said after a few minutes of silence, and I met her gaze.

"For what?"

"For saving both of our lives."

I gave her a nod and finished coloring in Sleeping Beauty's dress. Staying in the lines was more of a challenge than I thought it would be, and I concentrated. Grace placed her hand over mine, stilling my movement.

"It isn't over yet," she whispered and then looked out over the ocean. Darkness crept across the water, turning the twilight sky into the deep colors of night, and the full moon crested the horizon like a giant white saucer.

A chill swept down my spine like a bitter winter wind, and I shot to my feet, turning toward the house with only my internal alarms raging.

Before I knew it, I was sprinting through the family room, dodging furniture until I made it to the open front door. Valerie stood by the passenger window and glanced back at me. "I'm going to take a ride with Ms. Cole. She has some interesting thoughts about raising funds for the children's hospital; instead of just directing her to the best hotels, I'll accompany her. I should be back in a little while, okay?"

Something told me to say no, but I just nodded like an idiot, and she climbed into the car. The last glimpse I got was Valerie in the passenger seat, sending a wave in my direction and I closed the front door, even with the warning bells inside me screaming like a banshee.

Angel Heart Chapter 13

THEY MOVED THE GATHERING inside to get away from the relentless mosquitoes. The family room and kitchen were an abundance of activity, and the three kids kept running around like they had sixteen pieces of candy and were riding the sugar high.

Despite the relaxed atmosphere, a mounting panic pierced my soul; and I couldn't sit still as long as Valerie was off somewhere in town with that piranha. I guess the charity bit the agent laid out must have really suckered her in, and I slid into the kitchen chair closest to the family room where Tom, Raven, Steve, Jennifer and Naomi were talking.

Damian stood with his back against the counter, drying his hands on a dishcloth, regarding me with an amused smile.

"What?" I snapped.

"You don't know what to do with yourself when she's not here."

I opened my mouth to argue, but then just snapped it closed and crossed my arms on the table. He was absolutely correct, and I wondered if the panic biting my skin had more to do with that than some ominous cloud waiting to shoot me down with a bolt of lightning.

He laughed and glanced at Naomi. "You about ready, babe?"

"Yeah, want to grab the kids while I pack up our stuff?"

It took them fifteen minutes to gather their things and head out. The absence of chaos settled over us all in a heavy sigh, and I joined Tom and Raven on the couch. Hannah was tucked into the playpen in the corner, sleeping peacefully.

"It's been a hell of a day." I glanced at the clock. Valerie had been gone for over an hour and I pulled my cell phone out, pressing the phone icon and finding her name. Her phone rang and the buzzing behind me pulled my attention. Her phone vibrated on the counter, and I sighed. I wasn't sure if the burn on my skin was aggravation or just some weird precognition, and I shook it off.

"Are you okay?" Steve asked as Raven collected a couple of the glasses and turned toward the sliders.

Glass crashed on the floor, snapping our attention to Raven. Shock radiated off her like a dark layer of fog and she stepped backwards. Everyone turned toward the sliders and immediately jumped to their feet at the sight of the man standing in the entry, a sharp hunting knife in his hand. His crazed gaze locked on Raven and the sadistic smile that had formed chilled me to the core.

When her stalled brain restarted, her memories plowed over me like a two-ton truck. Fear blanketed the room, radiating off all of them like an airborne disease. Even Steve sported a skittish look that I had never seen, and he inched toward the bookcases and the gun hidden behind a false front.

The man's gaze moved from Raven's to his and he sent an evil chuckle.

"Special Agent Williams, I would think twice before going for that gun," he said with a hellish growl that pulled goose pimples to the surface of my skin.

"How did you get out?" Steve asked, his hand pausing before he took another step toward what he deemed their best chance at protection. He obviously forgot I was in the room.

"I guess you missed the news story," the man said and stepped across the threshold. That simple act removed the possibility that this was a demon. He successfully crossed the line of salt protecting the doorway. "There was a fire and a handful of us escaped." He grinned. "And I figured it was time to collect." His gaze narrowed and moved to Raven.

"I think you'd better leave," I said, stepping next to my brother, who was just as frozen to the spot as Raven. His thoughts were a mass of blood and pain and panic, and I had to shut it off in order to focus on the current situation.

"Just as soon as I carve up this ungrateful bitch and her mute boy-toy," he said and pointed the knife at Raven.

Tom reached for her, pulling her behind him, and then he stepped in front of her, blocking the psycho from reaching her. He shook his head, his face hardening, and the blaze in his eyes ballooned into a hostile storm.

Bits and pieces of what this man did came forth from my family, and my fists clenched. "I don't think so."

His lunatic gaze turned to me. "Who the hell are you?"

"I'm your worst fucking nightmare," the words slipped out in perfect form, shocking me as much as everyone else in the room, but I recovered quicker than the rest and narrowed my eyes to make my point.

He laughed, and Steve reached for the shelf where he had hidden his service revolver. The man shot his gaze in Steve's direction and pushed his hand against the air. Steve went flying backwards, slamming into the wall hard enough to knock him out. Jennifer ran to his side, and I turned back to the man, wondering just what the hell he was.

When the asshole's gaze fell on me, he whispered, "I said yes, and he promised me revenge." Then he flashed the evilest smile I have ever seen.

"Run," Raven whispered, pulling my attention to her. "CJ run," she repeated.

"No," I said and shook my head. I would not sacrifice my family to a psycho just to save my ass.

The man's scrunched face transitioned into an expression that tickled a memory and the knife pointed in my direction. "You and I will have a long talk just as soon as Raven's father gets his just desserts."

The voice chilled me, and I could feel the memories clawing at my consciousness. I knew the moment I let them break through; I wouldn't be able to help my family, so I put up a protective barrier in my head, shutting off the hurricane.

I focused on the crazy demon-seed in front of me and let the power swirl until it became as sharp as the knife he carried. For every step he took inside the house, Tom, Raven and I retreated. The front door opened, and feet shuffled toward the family room, but I couldn't split my concentration just yet.

It wasn't until Valerie stepped into view that the tight coil inside me fizzled. Two red-eyed demons dragged her into the room. One had a gun to her head; the other had one against her back, right in line with her heart. I wasn't sure I could prevent both bullets from ending her life and I froze in place, unable to decide how to deal with this new threat. Valerie wouldn't recover from either shot, even with her healing power.

The hiss behind Raven's father captured our attention and my gaze dropped to the snarling white tiger in the doorway. Everything happened so fast, I didn't have a chance to digest what I was looking at, but I said a little prayer of thanks for the diversion. When the tiger launched at Raven's father, the barrel of each demon's guns shifted away from Valerie, giving me the opening I needed. I let the anger fly at the same moment the tiger's jaw clamped down on Raven's father's knife-wielding arm.

Burning flesh filled the air and Valerie fell to her knees, away from the dust storm created by the annihilated demons.

Raven's father screamed, and I didn't know where to focus my remaining fury.

Raven touched my arm, and I met her gaze.

"The tiger is Naomi," Raven whispered.

I think my eyebrows rose and I know my jaw dropped open, but it snapped closed just as quickly when I refocused on the tiger attack unfolding before me.

Somehow, Raven's father got the knife into his other hand, and it was falling in a deadly arc aimed at the tiger's neck.

Power shot out of me like a bullet, and it hit the knife with the force of a home run swing, sending the blade clattering out the door onto the concrete patio.

The man's gaze jumped from the attacking tiger to me, his face transitioning from a mask of anger to one of pain, and he threw his head back with a roar. A trail of thick black smoke ballooned from his mouth and snaked out the door into the sky like a retracting tornado.

The man collapsed on the floor, screaming until the tiger relinquished his arm and stepped back, still baring its teeth, but no longer in attack mode. He seemed smaller now, more fragile, even with the murderous thoughts raging in his head.

He scrambled to his feet and lunged at Tom, still roaring with anger and pain.

Tom's fist smashed into the man's throat with such force, I actually heard the crack of bone. It took a second to realize it wasn't his hand that broke. His punch destroyed Raven's father, collapsing his windpipe and snapping his spine in one brutal blow.

There was no remorse in Tom as he looked at the twitching corpse, just a visceral satisfaction that I could identify with based on his memories. He met my gaze and gave a nod before turning and wrapping his arms around Raven, just holding her while Steve blinked his dazed eyes at the horrifying scene.

I glanced toward the doorway and Naomi stood where the tiger had been, her chin dripping with thick blood. She wiped her mouth and turned her dark eyes in my direction.

"You would have found out what I can do eventually," she said, and I uttered a laugh.

The barrier in my brain gave like a weakening dam and the memories flooded my head, dropping me to my knees. Pain slammed into my eyes like a dozen knives, and I cried out just before the dark yanked me into oblivion.

Angel Heart Chapter 14

IN THE DARKNESS, A succession of visions hit. Each one more debilitating than the last, and I bellowed with pain, but my cries were soundless in this horrifying black pit. Death intruded in many forms, starting with my sister and then my older brother. My mother and father were next, and my heart thundered in agony.

Some memories were mine, but many were sourced elsewhere. Memories of a concrete prison blanketed me, and the deaths in that place were just as violent as my mother's. Other memories layered over my parents' memories, and until I saw an infant fitted with an explosive onesie and Jennifer's wide eyes, I realized I was seeing the more devastating moments in Steve's life. His experiences were even more painful than mine.

A blood mist blanketed the room along with a sound that pressed on my eardrums, sending a shot of torture through my entire form.

I sat up screaming, the sound like rough sandpaper drawn over lead escaped from my throat. Valerie stood next to my bed with a syringe in her hand and a panicked look on her face, like the devil had just jumped out of the closet.

I couldn't catch my breath, not with the dozens of deaths now emblazoned in my memory. When the room spun, I dropped my head to my knees, forcing myself to breathe, despite the energy each labored breath drew.

A cool sensation covered the back of my neck and I turned, meeting Valerie's much calmer gaze. She removed the washcloth and dipped it in the bowl of cool water before pressing it against my skin again.

"How long this time?" I asked.

She uttered a hysterical laugh and met my gaze.

I glanced around at the surroundings, confirming I was still at the house and then back at her. I sat up slowly, wincing at the deep ache present in every muscle. That alone gave me a clue it was more than just a couple of hours. "How long?" I said, this time with more force.

"A couple of weeks," she whispered. "And your heart stopped twice." Her eyes filled with tears, and she showed me the syringe. "I thought I'd have to use this again."

"What is that?" I asked, homing in on the long, nasty looking needle.

"Adrenaline shot to restart your heart," she said. "My healing powers did nothing this time."

"Holy shit," I said and rubbed my face, trying to grasp the current situation through the clutter of so many horrific memories. "What happened after I passed out?" I asked without the thick stutter. It seems the connection between my brain and mouth wasn't as bad as it was before I dropped into memory land.

She bit her lip, and tears formed again. "Tom was hauled in for killing Raven's father."

"What?" I snapped, clearly recalling the entire situation. If anything, it was self-defense.

"They came to the same conclusion," Valerie said, reading my thoughts. "I was the only solid witnesses. Steve hadn't fully come to at that moment and Jennifer focused her attention on him, not the situation. Of course, both Raven and Tom were biased, based on what that bastard did to them, and you were knocked out cold. They wanted to bring you to the hospital, but I explained I was a doctor, and you had already been under home care for seizures. They left me in charge of your case as long as we had the local visiting nurse in daily. The only thing we really couldn't explain were the bite marks. We just said he arrived with those wounds."

I gave a nod and rubbed my face again, before swinging my legs over the side of the bed. That's when the IV line tugged, and I glanced down at the back of my right hand. I gave Valerie a raised eyebrow.

"You needed nutrients," she said and gave me a shrug. "I didn't know how long you'd be out, and I certainly didn't want you to starve to death."

I offered what I hoped was a smile and her head dipped to her chest. The shake of her shoulders clued me in on how difficult the last two weeks had been for her. She thought she'd have to go years without me again, and I reached out with my un-tethered hand and pulled her into my arms.

"Shhh," I cooed in her ears while she trembled and sobbed. When she finally stilled, I held her a few minutes longer, smoothing the hair away from her face before I pulled away. "I think I know who possessed Raven's father, but I thought Damian killed him," I said, and she met my gaze.

"You remember?"

"Yes. Some things, but not everything. There are still some big ass gaps and I think those are my true memories."

"You aren't stuttering nearly as much anymore," she whispered and sniffled.

I couldn't help the smile that surfaced. "You sound disappointed."

"No, just surprised." She peeled out of my arms, crossed to the box of tissues on my dresser, and used one before turning back to me. "How far back did the memories go?"

I sighed and put my hand out for her to remove the IV while I figured out the first memory from the clutter in my head. She stepped next to me and began pulling the tape off, and with it, any hair that had grown on the back of my hand. It took me a moment to pinpoint the timeframes of the memories. It all blended, folding in on each other like a complex puzzle, but I think the first memory was that of my grandfather's funeral. "I only saw death and destruction," I said, meeting her gaze. "Starting with my father's dad's funeral and ending with my mother's death."

She nodded like she understood.

"Coupled with the vision I had at Tom's, I'd say that brings me up to date."

She paused and looked at me, her features filled with skepticism, and the laugh she uttered told me I had only scratched the surface.

"I think I was looking at my mother and father's memories." I rubbed my hand after she pulled out the last of the tube. "I also saw the things Steve has seen," I said.

"Okay," she stretched the word out like there was more.

"Besides my own, whose memory am I missing?"

She just stared at me and then turned away.

"Yours?"

She nodded and glanced over her shoulder. "When we first touched, the powers that Steve transferred to me reshuffled, leaving me with only the healing thing and you with everything else. When that happened, we swapped memories." She gave me a shrug.

"Wouldn't that have been part of my memory, too?"

Her eyebrows arched as she considered this before nodding.

"Is that all?"

She slowly shook her head. "You said you only saw the deaths. If you had gotten everything, the first death you would have seen would have been from over twenty-five hundred years ago."

I blinked, and my jaw slowly opened. "I have Damian's memories?"

"Yep. And so do I. There's a lot of shit in our heads."

"Whose heads?"

"Damian, Steve, Jennifer, you, and me." She shrugged and took a seat on the bed next to me. "If your parents were alive, they'd probably be in the memory share category as well."

"And yet, I still don't know why two years of my life were spent in the dark," I said and hopped off the bed.

The adult diapers I was wearing had to go, and I needed to feel clean after the litany of deaths I witnessed. With a pair of boxers and shorts in hand, I crossed to the bathroom, leaving Valerie to do whatever she needed to restore my bedroom from the sick room it had become.

The hot shower felt good, but after expending the energy to clean every inch of my body, my reserves were drained. I shut off the water and pulled the shower curtain back. I was tapped, and I sat down on the edge of the tub before I collapsed.

The door opened, and I looked up at Valerie's soft gaze. She didn't need to ask if I needed her help. She already knew and slipped inside the steamy room. The towel she draped across my shoulders felt good, and I leaned into her when she put her arm around me.

"I should have warned you," she said, and I huffed.

I didn't remember being this exhausted when I woke from my coma. "I am so damned tired."

She helped me dry off and get into my shorts before aiding me back to the bedroom. Valerie guided me into the chair, and I stared at the stripped bed, wishing it was made and I could just crawl into it and curl up around her.

"What you need is food," she said and pointed to the desk next to me.

The small serving of soup did nothing for me, but I sighed and picked up the bowl, forgoing the spoon. The moment the warm broth hit my stomach; you would have thought I hadn't eaten in years. Like a switch had turned on, my exhaustion morphed to a ravenous need for sustenance. Not only did I forget about being tired, but the soup revived me from the core out, and I drained the bowl, suppressing the urge to lick the china clean.

Valerie let out a stifled laugh, and I met her gaze.

"I'm hungry," I said, stating the obvious, since my stomach was now making a grumbling racket.

"Let that settle, and if you're still hungry in a few minutes, we can go downstairs. I just want to make sure it's not going to decide to come up."

I rolled my eyes and put the bowl back on the desk. A yawn caught me off guard and I stretched with it. In the middle of my stretch, my stomach clenched, sending a horrific cramp that pulled me into a ball, freezing my breath in my lungs.

Breathing was not something that I could live without, and I fought for air while my chest resisted. Each breath drawn amplified the pain until my seized muscles recognized the oxygen flowing and loosened.

I glanced up at Valerie. Her features remained neutral, waiting for me to recover. She had warned me, so I had no recourse but to thank God I hadn't barreled downstairs and raided the cabinets. This was from soup, and I couldn't imagine how excruciating it would have been had I continued stuffing my face.

Slowly, I unfolded and leaned back in the chair, out of breath, but no longer in crippling pain.

"Damn," I whispered.

She leaned in to brush my cheeks with her lips. The warmth left behind settled my stomach and I sighed, watching her as she continued making my bed for me.

"I don't think I need any more rest for a while," I said when she folded the sheets back. The bed now looked like those fancy hotel turn down services and she glanced over her shoulder at me with a grin.

"I'm just making it for later, silly."

I forced myself to my feet, shuffling the short distance between us, and wrapped my arms around her waist. She smelled as delicious as the soup and my lips found their way up her neck.

Before I could maneuver her around and catch a kiss, the bedroom door opened. I turned and took in my guardian. Steve's eyebrows rose, and then the initial surprise etched into his face stretched into a smile.

"You're awake." He stepped into the room.

"Ap...parently," I said, pleased that I only screwed up one of the four syllables in the word.

"It sounds like your speech pattern is improving as well." He walked into the room and pulled me into a hug. He gave my back a quick pat and then he stepped away, meeting my gaze. "How are you?"

I shrugged. The amount of pain and horror this man had experienced left me speechless, especially since I could see the depth of caring in his eyes.

"I remembered some things." I looked at the floor. "Some... disturbing things."

"Your life hasn't always been a picnic," he said, and my gaze bounced to his.

"My memories are still locked up tight."

The truth slowly dawned on him, and he pointed at his chest, raising an eyebrow.

"Yeah. And not the good parts, either."

He pressed his lips together in a tight smile and gave me a nod. The shrug accompanying it was more a way to let the memories slide than to acknowledge the hell he'd been through. "I lived."

"I'm glad." I had seen him through my father's eyes and his own and they had polar opposite views. My father thought Steve was a man of honor and truth and as close to a living saint as one could get. Steve, well, he'd always beaten himself up for not being fast enough to stop the bad guys. Sure, he'd made some mistakes, but I would have to side with my father on this one.

Steve laughed. "You saw everything?"

I inhaled and shook my head. "No," I said with an exhale. "I only saw the... bad things." I chose my words carefully and shrugged. "Same with the memories of my mother and father. Only the devastating circumstances presented."

"That sucks," Steve said, and I couldn't help but laugh.

"Pretty much. I'm sorry about your kids."

A cloud of sadness passed over his features before they cleared. "I was lucky enough to get a second chance." With a nod in Valerie's direction, he turned and headed out of the room, closing the door behind him.

With my stomach settled and my hunger now manageable, I turned my sights on Valerie, and a different hunger brewed.

"If I recall correctly, it's my turn to be tied up."

"Chris," she sighed.

I stepped closer, looking down into her upturned face. "It's only fair," I whispered and tucked the stray hairs behind her ear. She tilted into my touch and closed her eyes. Her lips parted in that way that sparked my needs and all I could think of was those lips stroking me and sucking until I came.

"If you have that kind of energy, I think we should use it to get you a little more food," she said, although the color in her cheeks bloomed.

"You don't want to tie me up and have your way with me?" I teased and covered her protest with my lips. I sat on the edge of the bed, breaking the kiss and looking up at her. A grin played on my lips, and she rolled her eyes. When I put my arms out for her and raised an eyebrow, she grabbed onto my wrists and pushed me back on the clean bedding. Her eyes lit up in that playful gaze that raised more than just my heart rate.

"You really want me to tie you up?" she asked in a husky whisper.

I nodded. Being at her mercy created a sizzle in my loins that neither of us could ignore. She climbed off me and crossed to the closet to retrieve the sashes I had hung after our last experience.

Valerie tied the sashes tightly around my wrists, much tighter than I had bound her, and she gave me a crooked smirk as she tied my right wrist to the farthest post and my left to the closest one to the bedside. She stretched me out to the point of discomfort on purpose.

"You know damned well I can break these," I said.

She pulled the bindings tighter, creating an unpleasant burn in my wrists. Valerie stepped back and assessed her work before meeting my gaze. "I know you can, but you won't."

"I didn't tie you up this tight." I couldn't even shift my weight without my shoulders screaming in protest. The reality of being bound to the bed lost its appeal, even when she stripped my shorts. I was still so focused on my discomfort that it didn't spark the flickering flame.

It wasn't until she slid my cock in her mouth that everything else disappeared. The juxtaposition of discomfort and heaven consumed me. Her pace was painfully slow, and each stroke of her mouth tugged me farther into bliss.

"Faster," I gasped, and she just kept on doing that slow, long stroke, bringing me to the brink and then she'd pause and blow a stream of air on the tip of my cock, sending chills through every pore.

Every ounce of energy I had pooled in my lower abdomen, building up the pressure with each pass of her mouth.

She glanced up at me through her lashes, sending a chilling smile in my direction before swallowing my entire cock. The low hum in the back of her throat rippled through me.

"Ah, fuck," I whispered and tilted my head back, clamping my mouth shut against the groan building just as frantically as the energy inside me. My muscles tightened, and the release barreled from my core, sending a torrent down her throat, drowning that heavenly hum.

After shocks ripped through me as she swallowed and sucked until there was no more.

"Okay," I whispered as she passed her tongue over my sensitive slit. I couldn't move to stop her, and she chuckled, ignoring my plea. Each pass of her tongue sent shockwaves through me, and I couldn't help the low growl that rumbled in my chest. "Val," I said more forcefully and lifted my head.

She batted her fucking eyes at me and grinned. "You wanted this, babe," she said and flicked my cock with her tongue.

I dropped my head back on the mattress and stared at the ceiling, debating on whether I should break the bindings holding me in place or order her to stop. She climbed her way up my chest and looked down at me.

"Don't you dare," she said.

Just her scolding tone narrowed my eyes, and the wicked gleam in hers clinched my decision. The fabric bindings shredded to bits, along with every stitch of her clothing, and I grabbed her arms and twisted my body, pulling her underneath me. The utter surprise in her wide eyes and dropped chin made me smile.

"Never is...sue a dare like that," I said. "Not when I can do this." I willed her arms into the same position mine had been.

"Christopher James," she said, and her terse tone pulled forth something akin to a giggle.

I ignored her protest and licked, nipped and kissed my way down her body. By the time I reached my destination, her protests had morphed to pleas. I teased her the way I had before and when she had soaked the sheets beneath her, I moved up her body with the same care, and thrust inside the sweet wetness, losing myself in the very essence of Valerie.

Angel Heart Chapter 15

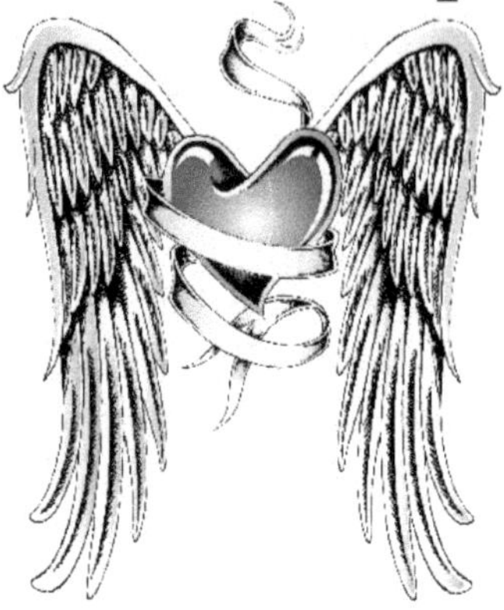

W E STUMBLED DOWNSTAIRS IN search of food, and the glare Steve leveled in my direction made me pause and cock my head in question.

"The rules," he said.

I pressed my lips together against the grin that begged to surface. "I'm twenty-three," I said, opting not to remind him that this actually was my house on paper, not his.

"You could at least turn on a radio or something," he mumbled, and went back to the book he was reading.

I glanced outside at the backyard and the misty rain layering the landscape. If it had been nice out, he would have been on the patio. We tried to keep quiet, but I guess both of us forgot this past go round.

"Sorry," I muttered back and crossed to where Valerie was raiding the refrigerator, pulling out sandwich meat and all the fixings. When she met my gaze, her cheeks were already the color of a crisp red apple.

"Beyond the fallout of that night, did I miss anything else?" Valerie and I obviously hadn't talked for the last hour, so beyond what she told me before my shower, I had no clue of what went on with Lucifer.

Steve traded a guarded look with Valerie and then shook his head. The glance alone told me more than anything else.

"I don't need protecting, or haven't you figured that out yet?"

Valerie dropped the knife she held and spun in my direction, pointing her finger at me. "I have every right to try to prevent what happened the last couple of weeks from happening again."

"Whoa, babe, calm down," I said, putting my hands in front of me against her venomous tone.

"Calm down? Are you out of your ever-lovin' mind?"

I guess that was the wrong thing to say, and I dropped my gaze to the floor, feeling more like a scolded puppy than a man. I pushed my hands into my pockets and sighed before meeting her sharp glare.

"Val, I know you were... freaked out, and I'm sorry. However, you can't keep buffering me from things. Not when I can help." She opened her mouth to argue, and I leveled an equally dangerous glare. "You can't."

"Damian found another portal," Steve said, and stood, facing us.

"Damn it, Steve," Valerie snarled. "Do you want to kill him?"

"No. But he has a right to know, especially now that the memories are creeping back. You know damned well that Lucifer wants him catatonic. If the memories don't kill him, Lucifer just might, and now that the devil's topside, and possessing at will, we don't have a prayer unless CJ knows what kind of hell is coming."

I had the benefit of my father's memories, but Steve's building anger projected in his voice, landing over both of us like an exclamation point. Valerie stared at him with her jaw hanging open, and instead of consoling her and easing her fears, I hit them head on.

"Tell me what I need to know."

"You don't need to know right now," she said, spinning in my direction.

Her eyes held a frantic panic that I could identify with. I had felt that when I first woke from my coma, not knowing who I was, never mind the people around me. However, Valerie's fears were more personal, more intertwined with my destiny than I cared to admit. I didn't want to hurt her, but I also didn't want to be blindsided again.

"I get Lucifer isn't dead. That was obvious from the other night." I waved at the family room where the skirmish with Raven's father occurred. "I get that I somehow went up against him after Damian stole his grace, and Lucifer put me in a coma. But what I really need to know is what I did, or didn't do, that landed me in that hospital."

The slider opened and Damian stepped inside, his clothing and hair soaked from the downpour outside. His appearance whenever I spoke of things really was unnerving.

"Steve asked me to come," he said, and my gaze shot to Steve. I hadn't heard the request broadcast from his mind.

Steve held up his cell phone. "I texted him. He's the only one who knows what happened that day."

"No," Valerie stepped in front of me. "You can't."

"I need to know, Val." I softened my voice and met her gaze. "I'm going to have to take him on again, whether you want me to or not."

"But..."

I planted my lips on hers, stopping the rest of her argument. "Sounds like any way we look at it, I'm screwed, so I'd rather walk into this with my eyes wide open." I cupped her shoulders and moved her out of my way before focusing on Damian.

Damian wasn't looking at me; he was focused on Valerie and waited for her go ahead.

"Tell me what happened," I commanded, and his eyes shifted to mine. A sarcastic smile appeared, along with an edge of a chuckle.

"Your commands don't work on me."

"Why not?" I asked.

"I'm Gabriel's son, not some distant angel descendant. That overrides the mind control aspect of your gift."

I mulled that over as he and Valerie went back to their silent debate. I caught hints of her thoughts but none of his, so I met Steve's glance. "I can't control angels, can I?"

He shook his head. "No. You can't."

Pieces started clicking into place slowly. "I can't decimate them like I can a demon or vampire."

"No."

I didn't need Damian to fill in the blanks. I was smart enough to figure this one out.

"I don't have the power to destroy an archangel, do I?" It was more of a statement than a question, and Steve slowly shook his head. "So, what the fuck was I thinking?"

Steve let out a laugh and shrugged.

"When you lose control, you have enough power to push Lucifer back to hell and close the portal. Forever." Damian interrupted, throwing a wrench into my thought process, and I turned toward him, ignoring my girlfriend's silent rant. "There are a finite number of portals, too."

"So, how many have I closed?"

"Just one."

I reached for the kitchen chair and took a seat. "And it put me in a coma for two years?"

"No. Closing the portal didn't put you in a coma," Damian said. He didn't continue, and his gaze slid to Valerie before returning to me. "Lucifer and his pack of demons beat you to within a breath of life before I got there."

This additional fact settled, and no one spoke while I studied my hands. My mind wrapped around the facts, and I glanced back at Damian. "If I was injured, why didn't he just take me over like the demons did to Valerie and Raven?"

This time Damian just chuckled, and his eyebrow rose. "A demon tried once at the hospital, but it didn't work out so well for him. Even in your comatose state, you toasted that fucker."

"No shit?" Surprise rippled through me like an electric shock.

"Seriously." He nodded.

I glanced at Valerie and despite her crossed arms and closed-off stance; she offered a single shoulder shrug confirming what Damian was telling me.

"They need you to say yes," he said, pulling my attention back in his direction. "In order to defeat me and get to my wife and daughter, you have to say yes."

"That'll never happen," I stuttered. The sigh that escaped him wasn't reassuring in the least.

"Lucifer knew we were hunting for the rest of the portals. He waited for you to come to before he passed through. But he's not sporting a body, so he's hunting for a loaner until he can get his hands on you. Now that you're awake, he's going to send everything he's got at you." His gaze moved to Valerie. "And at everyone you love. No one you care about is safe."

A chill hit me in the center of my chest, spreading numbness through every cell, and I shivered, thankful I was already sitting down. Had I been standing; I probably would have dropped to my knees.

With sudden certainty, my motives for going on a suicide mission finally made sense. "That's why I went after him, isn't it?" I asked, looking for a confirmation I really didn't need.

"Yes," Valerie answered, and I turned to her. Her arms fell to her sides and her chin dipped to her chest. She turned away and stared out the window at the steady rain. "You didn't want us to be on the run all our lives."

I dropped my head in my hands. The conflict nestling in my chest tightened, and I pushed at the barrier in my brain that was locking me from the rest of the puzzle pieces. It was like poking a bear and knowing the outcome would not be pleasant, but the alternatives were even more devastating. At least, if I dropped into a coma again, the people around me would be safe.

Unfortunately, the bear I was poking must have been a teddy bear because the wall blocking my memories remained intact. The sliders engaged, and I turned in time to see Damian close the glass behind him and head back to his adjoining property.

Valerie took the seat across from me and slid the sandwich she'd made in front of me. She sniffled despite the absence of tears in her bloodshot eyes. "On a different note, we never got to talk about that charity gig," she said, and her gaze dropped to the sandwich before her.

"You really want me to become a performing monkey?" I picked up her offering of sustenance. She cracked a smile and glanced up at me.

"Ms. Cole had a piano delivered as a token of her sincerity. She hasn't stopped calling since I left her at the Anchorage."

"A piano?"

"And sheet music. She wants to book you down at the Wang Theater in Boston for a fundraiser they are putting on for St. Jude's. You aren't the only performer, so she just has a couple of songs she wants you to sing, including *Hallelujah*. I've been stalling, but she needs an answer as soon as possible because the telethon is this coming weekend."

I stopped with the sandwich halfway to my mouth. "Like, in a few days?"

"Yes," she said and took a bite. "She's trying to hold a spot for you, but if you don't get back to her by tomorrow, she has to find someone else to fill in."

"And that's my problem, how?"

Valerie's lips tightened, hinting that her level of annoyance in me had risen another notch. "You could convince an awful lot of people to donate," she said. "It's for cancer research," she added and dropped her sandwich on the plate. "You saw those kids in Boston. The research St. Jude's does has helped thousands of kids survive."

"Fine. You really want me to do this?"

"Yes."

"Then call her and tell her okay," I said and a slow smile appeared on her face. I guess she really wanted me to sing. "Where's the piano?"

"In the living room."

I scoffed down the sandwich and dropped both our dishes in the dishwasher before heading into the other room. I stopped in the doorway at the beautiful baby grand piano nestled in the far corner by the window.

Walking over to the piano, I picked up the sheet music piled on the bench. *Hallelujah, Drops of Jupiter, I Don't Want to Miss A Thing, If Everyone Cared*, and a couple that made my eyebrows raise; *The Story* and *Angel*, both sung primarily by women. I went to toss them all back, when I froze in place and stared at the papers.

With a spark of excitement igniting in the center of my chest, I spun around, facing Valerie.

"I can read," I said, opening the top pamphlet and licking my lips as the words and music formed in my head with each scan of my eyes. It came alive and I let out a laugh of joy, dropping the rest of the sheets on the floor, and propping the one I'd arbitrarily opened on the piano.

My hands rested on the smooth ivory keys as I scanned the music again, and then I closed my eyes and let my fingers create something amazing. When I opened my mouth, the words flowed just as effortlessly as the tune on the piano. Of course, my first attempt at singing *The Story* was more of a baritone growl than the high feminine pitch of Brandi Carlile. I stopped, cleared my throat and started again, choosing the right octave to start that would give me the ability to hit the high notes without screaming. I didn't want to replicate her version, but I didn't want to stray so far that the audience wouldn't know what I was singing.

Halfway through, I glanced up, meeting Valerie's gaze. Her jaw was open, and beyond her stood both Steve and Jennifer with the same shocked expression. I stopped playing and stared back at them.

"Don't stop," Valerie whispered, recovering enough to speak.

"All of you could have been masquerading as fly traps a few seconds ago," I stuttered. "Was I that bad?"

"No. On the contrary. That was beyond exceptional," Jennifer said and crossed the distance. She moved the discarded sheets of music and took the seat next to me.

"Start from the top," she said. "And stay in the octave you were just singing."

I stretched my fingers and placed them on the keyboard, closing my eyes once again. With a big inhale and exhale, to settle my nerves, I began again and when I opened my mouth; the words flowed in that same key. Jennifer's voice penetrated my concentration almost making me lose my place. I opened my eyes and glanced at her; her voice complimented mine in a way that produced goose bumps up my arms. Our voices filled the room, layering the tune and giving it depth I lacked. I glanced at Valerie and Steve, who now stood together at the far side of the piano.

When we finished, their clapping created a swell of pride in my chest and I shifted on the bench, a little intimidated by the adoration in all their gazes.

"You have a beaut...i...ful voice," I stuttered, moving the focus to Jennifer. I couldn't recall hearing her sing since I woke from the coma, and I was impressed by the pureness of her voice.

"Thank you. So do you," she said and gave me a one-armed squeeze.

"Sing this with me this weekend at the telethon?"

Jennifer grinned, lighting up like I had never seen her. "I would love to."

"Oh, good, feed the applause junkie," Steve muttered, and Jennifer sent him the kind of 'shut up' glare I was used to seeing from Valerie.

"You're going to come, right?" I asked, feeling more like a little kid searching for approval from his father than a grown man. It was one thing to sing for the kids at the hospital, but on live television, well, let's just say the butterflies had already set in, leaving my stomach a roiling mess.

Angel Heart Chapter 16

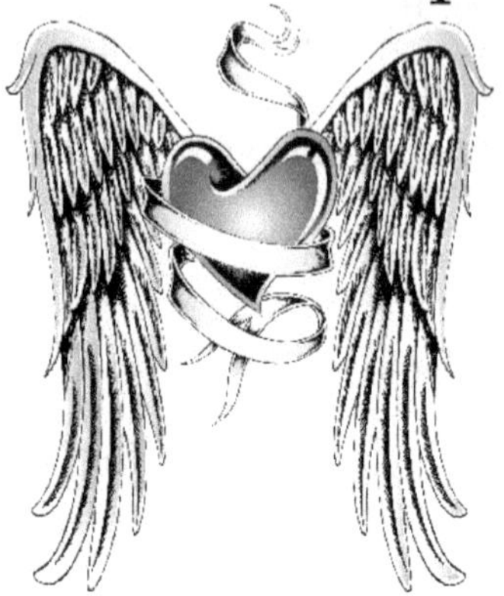

I SAT IN WHAT they referred to as the red room, with Jennifer. My mouth felt like I had stuffed it with cotton and no amount of water seemed to quench the dryness. I shifted in the seat again and Jennifer put her hand on my knee, pulling my attention from the monitor to her.

"Relax. You're going to be fantastic," she said with a calm smile.

"Wh...hat if I s...screw up?" I said, frustrated that the stutter was back in full force due to the nerves eating away at my mid-section.

"If you do, so what?"

I blinked at her casual attitude swallowing the lump of fear in my throat. "But..."

"Look, I've been on stage many times before, and having a fit of nerves beforehand is normal. Just trust me when I say the minute you walk out on that stage it all disappears."

"Yeah, well, I'm not so sure..."

"CJ, I promise you will be in your element. You used to love the sound of the crowd when you walked out on the football field in high school. You thrived on the attention just the way I do. From what I saw of that news story, you had that same glow when you were singing to those kids."

"Those were special kids," I mumbled.

"There are kids here, too. And Steve and Valerie are in the VIP section within your line of sight. The rest of the family is somewhere in the audience as well," she said.

Before I could respond, the light flashed in the room and the door opened. A production assistant with wild red hair poked her head into the room.

"We are ready for you, sir," she said, making me feel ancient, when in reality, I might have been only a year or two older than she was.

I put on what I hoped was a smile and not a terrified grimace, but she paused, and her face softened.

"First time?"

I nodded and Jennifer stood, pulling me to my feet.

"I saw that news story. You have nothing to worry about," the production assistant said, and then propped the door open for us.

"That's what I've been trying to tell him all morning," Jennifer said, and I think my smile was more genuine this time.

My stomach did a few flips as we walked down the narrow hall, but I was able to keep it in check. The production assistant parked us just off stage right, and I peeked out at the crowd and then at the telethon board and finally at the grand piano being wheeled out while the MC jabbered on about donations and goals.

The goal was set for a million dollars, and they were a little less than halfway to their goal.

"What time does this end?" I asked the production assistant, and she glanced at her watch.

"In another thirty minutes."

"What time did you start?"

"We went on air at nine this morning and are due to wrap up at five."

I glanced at the progress and then back at her. "You're not ev...ven halfway."

"You win some, you lose some. People are tight these days."

With a big inhale, I nodded, realizing I was set up as the clincher; the mule that has the last run at the goal, and it put even more responsibility on my shoulders, making my nerves rattle my bones. Jennifer gave my arm a gentle squeeze, and I closed my eyes, letting the sounds of the crowd fill my mind. The overwhelming noise of a couple of hundred thoughts drowned out my hesitation, and when the MC announced my name, I opened my eyes and stepped onto the stage.

Jennifer was right. The limelight was exhilarating, and I grinned and waved at the audience before extending my hand to the MC. After we shook hands, I put my hand out for the microphone and the MC hesitated until I raised an eyebrow.

"Hel...lo, Bost...ton!" I said, smiling through the stutter. I pointed toward the tally and then at the crowd. When my gaze landed on the camera, I continued, "I'll make you all a deal, what...ev...er that board says at the close of the show to...night, I'll match. Twice." The crowd cheered. "So, if we can get to that goal, I'll kick in an...nother two million. Let's get those do...nat...tions...cra...nk..ing."

I handed the stunned MC the microphone and made my way to the piano as the crowd cheered. It took a moment, but once my eyes adjusted to the bright lights, I could see Valerie just beyond the stage, with Steve clapping next to her. I sent her a wink and settled into the seat.

"You ready?" I said, grinning toward the camera and the phones started ringing in the background. With an inhale, I placed my fingers on the ivory and closed my eyes for a moment before the music came. My voice filled the auditorium and I let my mind flow with it. When the audience started singing along with the familiar tune, I smiled.

This rush was something I could get used to. By the time I finished *Hallelujah,* the progress had almost doubled. They were now within reach of the telethon's goal. As the last note faded, I glanced at the boards and then the camera, before dropping my gaze to a couple of the children in the first row. "This one's for all of you," I said and pointed at the kids they paraded across the camera all day before launching into *I Don't Want To Miss A Thing.* By the time I finished my modified version of the Aerosmith tune, the tally had run up beyond a million and I glanced at Jennifer waiting in the wings.

"For my last song, I'd like to bring out the woman who took my brother and me in after our parents passed away. Ladies and gentleman, give a warm welcome to Jennifer Williams." I waved toward where she stood, and she stepped onto the stage. "Thank you for giving us a loving home," I said as she crossed with a sparkle in her eye that I could fully identify with. Being in the spotlight, even with the stutter I had, was intoxicating.

The crowd's applause was polite, nothing like what they had given me, but the moment we launched into *The Story*, they fell silent. Awe layered the coliseum, mingling with our voices and, for a moment, my soul filled with pride.

The phones went nuts, and when we finished singing, the crowd followed suit.

I stood and gave Jennifer a hug before looking at the final tally. In the last twenty minutes, the amount had nearly tripled.

"Hey, look at that." I smiled at the board and turned back to the camera. "Thank you all for supporting such a worthy cause," I stuttered and turned toward the MC. "And because I'm more of a round number kind of guy, why don't you just add, oh... another five million to your tally."

The crowd went wild, and I successfully flustered the MC. He stammered a bit, like he had never seen such a large donation by one person before. St. Jude's was a fundraising machine, so I was sure there were other large benefactors out there, maybe just not one like me.

"Hey, I'm the one with the stutter," I said, and the crowd laughed right along with the MC. It gave him time to regroup and take control of the show again.

As soon as the lights dimmed, and the crew started disbursing, I glanced back toward where Valerie and Steve had been sitting. All my good humor faded. Valerie's seat was empty, and Steve was slumped in the seat next to her vacant one.

My gaze scanned the crowd until I zeroed in on Tom and Raven making their way down to the VIP section against the crowd. He met my gaze across the theater and then his gaze moved to Jennifer. His proud expression crumbled, and his gaze dropped to Steve. His polite maneuvering stopped, and he barreled through the crowd, his face showing the same sense of panic throbbing in my veins.

He dropped to his knees next to Steve, and his fingers pressed against the soft flesh of Steve's neck. Tom's relief washed over me, and I glanced at Jennifer. In all the chaos, I hadn't focused on her until now. Her waxy expression and glazed eyes sent a chill that made my teeth clench. With the crowds still in range, it took me a minute to focus on what horrors were playing through her ever-clairvoyant mind.

What I saw made my knees tremble to the point I had to take a seat back on the piano bench. Valerie was now in the hands of the devil.

Angel Heart Chapter 17

I HAVE NO IDEA how we got out of the auditorium without making a major scene. All I know is every fiber of my body was in panic mode. For the life of me, I don't know how Jennifer remained calm and focused enough to give the details necessary to fund my pledge. I somehow managed a gracious exit.

Jennifer, Tom, and Raven sat in the car with Steve, trying to wake him from the stupor he was in, and I just leaned on the hood staring at the traffic jamming the exit lane, trying to piece together what had happened. The spot next to ours was empty, a reminder that someone had yanked her out of that theater, and she hadn't sent me any sort of warning.

My stomach clenched tighter, and I closed my eyes, hanging my head as both frustration and aggravation mounted. None of us were sure what they had given Steve and I could only surmise that they had given Valerie the same thing, otherwise she would have let me know there was danger in the house.

The bastard used me as the diversion. Everyone's focus was on me. No one saw them take her out of the VIP section, so I don't know if she walked out or was carried out. All I knew was that Lucifer had his pawn. He had the leverage that would bring me to my knees.

The cell phone in my pocket vibrated, and I pulled it out, staring at the words that comprised the text. The fact I could read no longer provided a thrill, especially with the instructions outlined. I slid the phone back into my shirt pocket.

Tom stepped by my side, and I didn't look his way. The instructions were simple. I had to follow them alone.

"Are you okay?" he signed, and I just shook my head. He stepped into my line of sight and crossed his arms. "He contacted you, didn't he?" Tom's voice filled my head, and I brought my gaze to his.

"What do you think?" I couldn't help the snide tone. It was a dumb question, one Tom should have known, and I could see from the sharpness in his gaze, he didn't appreciate my sarcasm.

"You can't go alone."

I just stared him down.

"I saw you take out your phone. Lucifer sent you a message, didn't he," he signed, and I exhaled, nodding. "You cannot go alone. The last time almost killed you," he signed, and his words echoed in my head.

I broke eye contact and dropped my gaze to the stained concrete, contemplating what would happen if I showed up with the cavalry. Lucifer made it clear. He assured me I'd get a front-row seat to her death, and it would be brutal.

"He's going to kill her if I don't do what he says."

"He's going to kill her, anyway."

Tom's statement was enough to pull my attention to him. I shook my head slowly. "Not if I can help it."

"That's exactly how he wants you to react," Tom signed and echoed in my head.

"And if you were in my place?"

Tom glanced behind me at Raven and exhaled before bringing his gaze to mine. "I would do the same thing you're about to do," he said in my head without the use of his hands. "Barrel off and get myself killed just to prove I'm her knight in shining armor." He shrugged and gave me that half-hearted smile that I was getting familiar with. It was his 'I know where you're standing—I've been there' look.

I let out a soft laugh. "You'd go running just as fast as I'm going to." I met his gaze, and he nodded. "So, what do you propose?" I took a mental step backwards to see if he had a viable alternative.

He stepped next to me and leaned on the car, crossing his arms. Instead of reaching into his mind to see what he was thinking, I waited while he chewed on his lower lip in contemplation.

"The way I see it, you've only got one choice to save Valerie and keep Grace safe." His voice rang softly in my head. "You have the capability of transferring your power." He glanced at me. "You have to give it all to Valerie and then say yes to Lucifer."

I raised my eyebrows. "But wouldn't he figure that out?"

Tom shrugged and glanced at the traffic patterns. "Not if you do it in such a way that he doesn't know, and there isn't enough time between the transfer and his possession. Then your biggest task would be to keep him locked inside you until Raven can banish him."

"And if he kills me?"

Tom grinned. "Then he'd be killing himself. He won't do that."

His proposal sounded reasonable, except for one little thing. Saying yes to the devil would lock an evil entity in my skin. One that could still create havoc topside even without my powers, especially if he could snow everyone the way I would have to have snowed him.

"What if Raven can't banish him?"

Tom's sigh sent a shiver through me, and his grin disappeared. "Then I'd lose my brother." His voice carried the dread vibrating from him and when his gaze met mine, it was filled with a sheen of tears.

The traffic started moving more steadily now, and I glanced at Tom. "And if we just think Raven banished him?"

Tom's cheeks paled, and he swallowed hard. "I don't even want to think about that," he signed and then shoved his hands in his pockets.

Another thought pattern started itching at my mind, and I glanced over my shoulder. "Steve's coming around." I turned toward Tom. "I'm going to need a head start, so he really thinks I'm alone."

"No." Tom said, his voice enunciating the word correctly and his head shook.

"Yes." I said. "Give me your phone."

Thankfully, he didn't hesitate, and I typed in the address I was given. It wasn't anywhere near Boston, and I had to figure out a means to get there since my car had been stolen by the bastard.

"Get Steve home and then head down to Connecticut."

This time, he hesitated. I stared him down.

"Take Steve and Jen to their place in New Hampshire," I commanded, and the red of anger flitted over Tom's face, but he grabbed his phone and retreated to the car. Once he was behind the driver's seat, I engaged the locks and he glared at me as he pulled out of the parking spot, nearly clipping an oncoming car.

"Damn you," his voice resounded in my head.

"I love you, too, Tom," I said aloud and slipped out the side door. I was complying with the rules and would arrive without back up. However, I was going to time it so that backup wouldn't be more than a good ten or fifteen minutes behind.

Or so I thought until my phone buzzed, and I glanced at the next text.

The longer you take to get here, the more fun I'm going to have with her.

I stared at the photo he attached, and my skin crawled with the flush of anger. They were in a limousine, and he had her wrists bound to the straps on either side of the car. Her pretty silk shirt was ripped open, and her skirt was nowhere in sight. At least the matching lace bra and panties were still on, but the terror in her eyes told me they might not be for long.

If you harm her in any way, the deal is off. I stared at my response and then hit send.

So, you're considering saying yes, to save this vixen?

I am considering it. But only if I know she is safe and left untouched.

I pocketed the phone, not waiting for the response. When it came back, I slowed on the street, reading the words. *You have exactly two hours. If you are late, I will make sure you get an explicit viewing, much like Damian got all those years ago.*

A memory started clawing at the wall in my head and I shut it off, glancing around at my choices. Parked cars lined the street. I crossed to an Audi and glanced around before reaching for the door. With a breath, I willed the car to unlock and disengage the security system. The telltale beep-beep filled the street. I hadn't driven since I woke from the coma, but that didn't matter. I'd figure it out pretty quickly and I willed the machine to start. The engine revved, and I pulled out the phone, switching to the GPS and typed in the address he gave me in New Fairfield, on Candlewood Lake.

I waited for the directions to load because every time we had been in Boston, Valerie cursed under her breath at how the traffic patterns in this city were laid out. She believed they designed it just for the fun of confusing drivers. Once the instructions came online, I peeled out of the parking space and navigated through the streets like a racecar driver.

For me, it wasn't a confusing maze and by the time I hit the Mass Pike; I was cruising. The car had one of those monitors that allowed me to drive through the tollbooth without paying and I used every ounce of power I had to create an open path I could fly down.

The GPS said it was over a two-and-a-half-hour drive. I could see that, if I remained at the speed limit and didn't manipulate the traffic, but the slowest I drove was eighty, and that was through the toll itself. When a cop pulled out after me, I sent the silent command to ignore me, and the lights flipped off a moment later.

The more I pushed, the more I knew I couldn't let Lucifer get hold of this power. He would use it to destroy everything good and pure on this earth.

They had an hour on me, even with the time I cut off the clock, and when I pulled into the long driveway, a group of demons, and a text warning not to do anything stupid, met me. There was something about the house that tickled my memory, and I clenched my teeth, resolved not to crumble into another seizure. That would be the ultimate suck.

"Don't fucking touch me," I said when the main demon went to grab my arm. "I can walk," I spit out the warning and he backed off, but they surrounded me, escorting me into the house. The minute I stepped over the threshold, it felt like a blanket draped over me.

The lead demon reached out and grabbed my upper arm, yanking me toward the living room. I mentally pushed, growling the command to let me go, but nothing happened. He just laughed at me.

"You're on Lucifer's ground. You have no power here." He pushed me forward, and I faltered, stopping in my tracks at the spectacle before me.

I put a lockdown on my mind, my thoughts, everything I could lock up, and I took a deep breath. Tom and Raven wouldn't be anywhere in the vicinity for another two hours, minimum, and Lucifer stood facing Valerie. My Valerie. In chains, splaying her out for him to play with.

Anger scrolled down my spine, and I glared at the devil.

"I understand she likes to be tied up," he said, and sent a chilling grin in my direction. The human he'd donned was not the model of physical physique that Lucifer was used to, and even I couldn't help but cringe as he stepped closer to her.

I moved fast. Faster than he expected, and I had the advantage of surprise. I jumped and my feet connected with his chest, sending him flying into the wall. I landed on my feet, now occupying the spot where he had stood, blocking him from Valerie.

"I told you the deal was off if you touched her." I said without fail and took the ready form Steve had taught me.

Lucifer slowly got to his feet and gave a nod to the demons in the room. I didn't have enough memory of how to fend off multiple attackers and they overwhelmed me. Forced to my knees by a dozen demons, I glared at Lucifer.

"Say yes or I will let everyone in the room have their way with her," Lucifer said, crouching in front of me. "And you'll get to see her struggle and hear her scream."

I shivered and glanced at Valerie as the fear stuffed my mouth with a metallic blend that made me want to spit. She shook her head adamantly.

"Don't," she whispered, and her voice shook with the fear quaking her bound form. Fear that matched my own.

I glanced back at Lucifer. "I will, but I have two conditions before you get hold of me," I stuttered.

He pressed his lips together, and I honestly thought he was going to say no. I thought I was going to have to say yes, with no concessions of my own, in order to save Valerie.

"I owe you a world of hurt, son," he said and licked his lips. "But just for giggles, what are your conditions?"

"I get to kiss her goodbye and as soon as she is clear of this property, I will say yes."

"I'll let you kiss her goodbye, but the moment she is clear of this property, I lose my bargaining chip."

"Then send a demon with her," I said. "And you can call the bastard off once you have me."

"No, Chris!" Valerie struggled against the bonds, her breath hitching in a way that made me want to break the eye contact I had with Lucifer, but I resisted.

Lucifer rubbed his chin as he studied me. "If you doublecross me, I will have her brought back here and I will do the most heinous things to her while you watch, until I lose interest, at which point I will kill her."

I nodded. "I know. As soon as she is clear, you've got what you want."

He stood and gave me a nod. The hands holding me in place receded, and I climbed to my feet.

"Give her her clothes, too," I said, and Lucifer raised his eyebrow. "Please," I added, and he handed her the shirt once she was out of the bonds.

"Kiss him goodbye," Lucifer directed and pushed her in my direction.

Tears flowed down her cheeks, and she fell into my arms. I held her and touched my forehead to hers. "I love you, Valerie," I said, and she met my gaze. The power swirled in the center of my chest, and I closed my eyes and pulled her parted lips to mine. Our tongues mingled and I willed every ounce of magic I possessed into her. The kiss lingered and my grip on her tightened. So did hers, but to her credit, she didn't gasp or give away anything that transpired between us. Memories flashed like a slide show, and I pulled them into the vault in my mind where everything else was stored. I didn't have time for that just yet, and I didn't want to tip my hand.

When I pulled away, hot wetness traced down my cheeks, and my vision blurred. I removed the necklace from around my neck and slipped it over her head, offering her more than double the protection against the demon horde. I pressed it to her chest despite her protests.

"I love you, now go," I whispered and stepped away, pointing at the door.

She shook her head, sobbing and shaking. "I can't leave you," she whispered.

"You can, and you will." I wiped my face and nodded toward the door.

One of the appointed demons grabbed her arm and escorted her out of the house.

I followed and stood at the door. "Let her drive," I said and got a nasty glance from the demon, but he pushed her into the driver's seat and shuffled to the passenger seat. She glanced in the rearview mirror just before she took the gentle curve out of sight and I swallowed the lump that formed, turning away from my future and everything I loved.

The slam of the front door felt more like a casket closing, and I returned to the living room without the help of the henchmen following me. A blanket of despair covered me, and I paused in the entryway, collecting my courage before I stepped into Lucifer's line of sight. I needed to steel my nerves in order to pull this off.

"If you don't hear from me in five minutes, bring the bitch back," he said into the phone and then ended the call.

The fact he called Valerie a bitch made my fists clench, and I met his gaze. "One more condition," I said, and his jaw tightened. "You leave my family alone. Valerie included, otherwise this isn't happening."

He crossed his arms and glared at me.

"Do we have a deal?" I asked and adopted the same stance, hardening my features and forcing the shake out of my limbs.

His gaze rose to the crowd of demons behind me, and the first hint of genuine fear stripped my voice for a moment. They converged, dropping me to my knees. One of them took a handful of hair and yanked my head back.

Lucifer stepped in front of me. "Say yes," he growled, his hands balling into fists.

"Do we have a deal?" I asked again through clenched teeth.

"Yes," he said. "We have a deal."

"Then my answer is yes."

Black smoke flowed from every pour of the soul he possessed, covering the room in a fog that swirled into a tight mass until every bit exited the man's body. With nothing animating the man, his former husk dropped to the ground, stone dead from the horrific experience.

The cluster darted at me, drowning me. An inhuman wail filled the space, and it took me a few moments to realize the sound was coming from me. His possession was not the smooth transition of a demon; it was a complete mind rape. Bitterness filled my soul, wringing it with agony. Every cell screamed as his essence overwhelmed me and I doubted I would survive an exorcism. Evil settled in, trying to eject me from my body, but I held firm despite the raw pain.

I retreated into the locked space where my memories were housed, hoping for asylum from the pain and fear now chasing after me, but it only succeeded in making me a prisoner in my own skin. His power, diluted from his angel form, still was a force to be reckoned with, although it felt nothing near the power that had once raged in my blood.

When my eyes opened, I could see what he saw and feel everything he felt. He mentally bucked a few times, but I held on. If I didn't, I would be lost forever.

"I'm not leaving, and neither are you," I said.

He turned toward a mirror and my face stared back.

"You little shit," he said.

I couldn't help but laugh at the anger flaring my nostrils and making my eyes daggers of fury.

"Where is it?"

"Where is what?" I replied, toying with him despite the agony fleecing my soul.

"Your powers," he growled.

"Oh, that. Well, that wasn't part of the deal."

He roared and punched the glass. It shattered and the skin of my knuckles broke open, spraying blood all over the remaining shards. The phone came out, and he slammed his index finger on the redial button.

"Bring her back," he snarled.

"I'm sorry, but your demon henchman has been reduced to a pile of dust," Valerie said into the phone in the same polite tone she would have used when asking someone to leave a message. I made a mental note to kiss her and never stop if I ever got out of this jam.

The rage that filled my form was so black that I had to retreat farther into the safe haven in my mind. The last trap I had wouldn't be sprung until I got word the rest of the cavalry arrived and then I'd blow the wall holding the floodgates of memories, sending my taxed brain into another seizure and rendering the devil unconscious, or at least a spastic mass that couldn't function.

At least, that was my hope.

I still had some control and, when he turned his anger on the demons in the room, I encouraged their destruction.

By the time his little shit fit was over, blood and gore covered the walls and me. Lucifer made a bid for control, and I gave it to him, retreating to a place he couldn't seem to reach.

"I swear I will make you eat her heart," he growled, his gaze locked on the mirrored shards sending me a broken reflection of outright fury.

Angel Heart Chapter 18

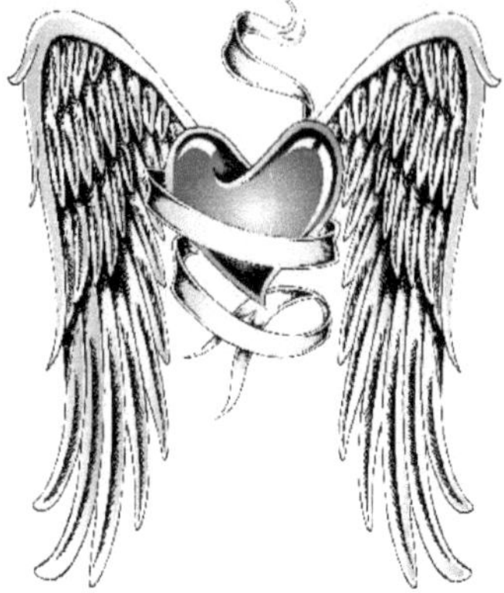

THE PHONE RANG AND Lucifer rummaged through the carnage to find it. He pressed the speaker button and her voice filtered through the room.

"I have a deal for you," Valerie said, her voice soft and timid.

Unfortunately, I was privy to his thought process and what was going on there made me shiver. Whatever her deal, it would end with my hand pulling out her bloody heart. I tried to intervene, but in the half hour that he had been silent and still, he seemed to have built a fortress around my motor skills.

"What are you offering?" he asked, in my smoothest voice possible. The one we both knew she couldn't resist.

"If you meet me at the Starbucks in town, I won't kill you."

"You won't kill me as long as I am in your boyfriend's skin."

"I wouldn't bet on that. You killed my family, I have a score to settle and as far as I'm concerned, Chris is dead, so I have no qualms about taking your life."

He was silent, and I went bat shit trying to break through, exhausting my mental capacity until I sat down huffing, as if I had run a marathon. She had to know I still existed. She had to know the plan by now. I put my head in my hands and waited for Lucifer to speak, to coerce her with my voice.

"So, why the deal?"

Silence prevailed, and when I didn't think she'd answer, she sighed. "I want to see him."

"He's dead," Lucifer whispered. "Shoved out into the ethereal world. Forever lost to you."

"I need to see for myself." Her voice hardened.

"Fine. But the deal stands. If I show up, you don't kill me," he said, plotting his own attack, relishing the visions he showed me which jumped from a quick death to a slow, agonizing one where he took every advantage of her physical form before delivering the final blow. He drew correlations to my different escapades with her, allowing me to see every brutal detail of his attack. "Give me a half hour. I need to make myself...presentable."

"Fine."

The line went dead, and he chuckled. "I hear you rattling about. Don't worry, I'll let you participate in the fun."

"Fuck you," I growled, but it didn't reach my vocal cords and I wondered what the hell was happening.

He stopped in front of the bathroom mirror. "I'm absorbing you." He grinned, and a flush of goose flesh covered the body we shared. "You didn't bet on that, did you?"

No. I didn't bet on that at all, and I couldn't tell if he was giving me a line of bull just to give himself a leg up on this battle of wills or not. All I knew is the moment we stepped into that Starbucks and confronted Valerie, the memory wall I was struggling to hold at bay would tumble, so I kept quiet, biding my time.

Lucifer showered, shaved, and prettied himself up just for Valerie's benefit, and then he glanced in the mirror. "I wonder if I can fool her into thinking you've won the battle of wills?"

Fuck. That was not what I wanted to hear.

"You wouldn't dare," I said, and this time the voice came out. He grinned and winked before stepping out. Whistling, he grabbed a pair of keys off the peg by the door and stepped into the garage.

When he settled into the driver's seat, he looked into the rearview mirror. "Boy, I'm going to have fun with this."

I roared and nearly unloaded the wall of memories, but I knew it wasn't time. If I did it now, I risked wasting the element of surprise.

His quiet chuckle burned, and I sat back for the ride. Whether or not I wanted to admit it, I wanted to see Valerie. The thought of her made my pulse increase, and he noticed the building desire.

"I'm used to my mules being devoid of emotion, but you're just a plethora of sensations," he said, and I remained quiet, trying to buffer my emotions from surfacing.

It took a few minutes of twisting roads before we rounded the lake to the small town. The Starbucks was another quick turn and before I had time to contemplate the proximity; he stepped out of the car, locking it behind him like a normal citizen. He glanced at our reflection and smirked before inhaling and taking on the shell-shocked expression. He adjusted his breathing as well.

The bastard was a master at portraying something he wasn't, and he ran his hand through our hair and headed inside with the borderline panicked expression. Eyes darted from corner to corner, and Valerie was nowhere in the vicinity. He turned toward the parking lot and then looked at the time on the phone before heading to the counter.

The salesgirl perked up like the Christmas tree lighting in Rockefeller Center at the sight of me. Women always do and Lucifer sent a full-on smile in her direction and leaned on the counter. He ordered a grand cafe mocha and took a seat, waiting for Valerie to enter.

With each minute that passed, he got more irritated. I guess he never had to wait for a woman in his entire existence, and it made me chuckle.

"Shut up," he whispered, and the lady at the table next to him sent a worried gaze in his direction.

He looked at the last text, calculating the time again, like it would suddenly render a different outcome. She stood us up. He stood, and the ground rumbled. The glass cups on the shelves behind the counter clinked together, and the lights swayed as the mini earthquake rocked the small town.

Lucifer didn't panic. In fact, he didn't really register the anomaly at all, but as time passed, he began grinding his teeth in frustration. "Where the hell is she?" he asked and glanced at the time again. He started drumming his fingers on the table, slowly at first, but it quickened to a frantic pace and the woman sitting at the adjoining table moved away, her face painted with lines of unease.

"Screw this," he finally said after an hour went by. "This is beyond fashionably late," he muttered as he stood. He swept the half-empty cup off the table and deposited it in the trash before heading out to the car.

"She just upped the ante," he growled and glanced in the mirror. "I swear she'll be begging for death when I'm done with her."

I kept my silence and the vigilant lockdown on my thoughts. That earthquake had to have some significance and as we got closer to the lakeside mansion, I noted the abundance of afternoon light coming through the thick canopy of trees. Something had changed and when we turned into the driveway, I knew the landscape had been altered.

I think Lucifer did, too, because the burn in the center of my chest shifted from anger to apprehension; he slowed around the last bend and stopped the car when the lake came into view. The area where the house had been was a perfect circle of cleared dirt.

He blinked, scanning the odd devastation before his gaze locked on a lone figure in the middle of the dusty clearing. I'd recognize that back anywhere and the fact she had changed into one of my favorite sundresses didn't go unnoticed.

His mood quickly transitioned from the numbing shock weighing heavily on his hands to the raw burn of fury that clenched his fists around the steering wheel. He revved the engine, and Valerie glanced over her shoulder. Even from this distance, I could see the tears tracking down her cheek.

The roar of the engine lowered as he saw the same. The word opportunity blossomed in his head, and I had to staunch a reaction. If he got hold of her, I wasn't sure I could stop him from harming her.

What he did next made me want to scream, but I held onto my mental sledgehammer, just waiting for an opening to smash the memory wall.

Lucifer put the car in park and stepped out, using the car door to prop himself up.

"Valerie?" he asked with just the right note of hesitation. It was enough to trace doubt in her features, and she turned.

The flash of hope in her eyes singed, and Lucifer took full advantage. He cleared the door and took a couple of steps in her direction. What he didn't realize was that he had crossed onto the dirt.

She took a step in his direction and then stopped. "How do I know it's you?" she asked and sniffled, running her wrist across her nose.

"Why was I at a cof...fee shop?" Lucifer said and purposely stuttered and took another step forward.

"Bastard," I whispered, but it didn't reach my vocal cords.

He ignored me, playing the game that was putting Valerie in danger. She blinked and covered her mouth. More tears cascaded down her cheeks, and she took a stumbling step in our direction before falling to her knees in a sob.

"I thought you were dead," she said and glanced around. "I felt the earthquake and came here instead of going to the shop and I found this." She waved at the flattened land. "And the car you came in was still in the driveway." Her hand pointed to the car I stole in Boston. "And..." she covered her face. Her shoulders shook and the sobs that escaped slammed straight into my heart.

Lucifer, on the other hand, had no sentimental reaction, but boy did he put on a show.

"Ah, babe," he said and made my voice crack at just the right spot. My eyes misted over, and he moved closer to her kneeling form. His caution was waning in favor of viewing her as the perfect victim. One he could use to derive a significant victory over me, but he didn't know what I knew.

He didn't know she was the one that harbored my power.

Valerie didn't move from her spot, even when my hand brushed her hair. I thought I was going to have to scream a warning, but then she looked up with the hardest stare I've ever seen.

"Now," she said, and I knew she directed the command at me.

I swung with every ounce of mental strength at the wall bulging with memories. When my imaginary hammer hit, it shattered with the force of a tidal wave.

I laughed as Lucifer dropped into a twitching, convulsing mess before the memories overrode all logical thought, pulling both of us into the abyss.

Angel Heart Chapter 19

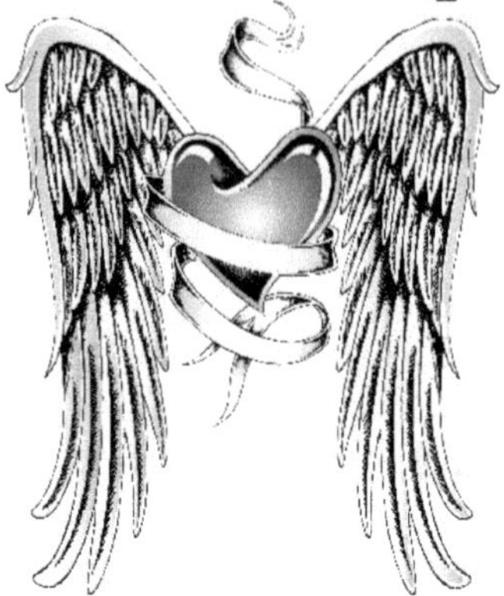

LUCIFER STIRRED AND SO did I. I glanced around at the unfamiliar room, and over at Valerie sitting in the chair beyond the bed, her face drawn and pale as she scanned a book in her hand. It looked like we were in a forest of white birch trees, but the air didn't have a woodsy quality. It had almost a stale, dry smell that indicated we were in a desert or inside.

My guess was inside, but I didn't have a clue where.

Lucifer tried to move, but the bindings held him to the bed, rattling enough for her to sigh and turn to the next page in the book.

"Let me go," Lucifer growled, and she shook her head without looking up from her reading material, as if this was a routine they had walked through many times before.

"No," she said and folded the book onto her lap, meeting my gaze. "Let me speak to Chris."

"I told you; pretty boy is dead and gone," he said, and he stretched my lips into a toying smile.

"Bullshit," I said, and she sat up straighter in the chair. The paperback slipped to the floor, and she didn't bother picking it up. She just stared, searching the face of the man bound on the bed, looking for a hint of me in his eyes.

The mood of my host darkened, and he clenched his teeth against anything else that might slip past his internal defenses.

"Chris?"

"He's gone," Lucifer insisted, but the fact I was able to get a word out sparked hope in her eyes and she glared at the bastard inhabiting my form.

I had no idea how long we had been tied to the bed, but I had survived the waterfall of memories. I think I had them all straight and based on the last memory assault that incapacitated me; I gauged I had been out of it for at least a month. Maybe more. The surroundings weren't familiar at all, but it wasn't a hospital setting, like when I woke from the coma.

"Where are we?" Through sheer force of will, I pushed the words out.

Valerie let out a little laugh and her hand shot over her mouth. She reined in the sudden onslaught of giddiness, composing herself before she spoke. "This is Damian's underground quarters in my house," she said. "We brought you here from the house in New Fairfield. You gave us just enough time to sedate Lucifer, and I wasn't sure if you survived or not. I didn't give up on you, despite this asshole's insistence that you were dead." She picked up the book and put it on the table next to her. "You're probably wondering how long you've been... gone."

I tried to nod, but I only got a fraction of the movement I intended before Lucifer locked down my ability to physically maneuver my body.

"Five months."

Her words landed with a thud, and I stared at her. I'm not sure if my mouth popped open or not, but five months was a long ass time to be tied anywhere.

"Lucifer has had control for the entire time, but we were able to get him here and bound before he regained all his faculties. And he has promised to do some pretty nasty shit if he ever gets out of those bonds. He isn't very pleasant," she said and winked.

My chuckle at her understatement welled to the surface for a minute before he grabbed control again. The slam down was swift and hard enough to knock the wind from my control, and I growled my dissatisfaction.

"I'll make him watch," Lucifer whispered capturing her attention. "When I get a hold of you, I will make sure he has a front-row seat to your pain and suffering."

"I think I'll take a rain check on that," she said and stood. The way she stretched sent a tingle of longing through me I know she saw reflected in my eyes. Even if it was only fleeting, the recognition that flashed in her eyes made me feel like I just won a major battle. She lowered her arms and sighed. I couldn't read her thoughts, but her expression matched the ache in my chest. She offered a tight smile and left the room.

In the silence, Lucifer recounted his plans, contemplating the vile things he'd do to her, and voicing them in such detail that my stomach clenched. If I lost this battle, there was nothing on this side of heaven that could help her.

Angel Heart Chapter 20

"VAL TELLS ME CHRIS is finally awake," Damian said, staring me down from the end of the bed. "He's a lucky man. If I had my way, I would have toasted your ass until there was nothing more."

"Great," I said, but nothing escaped my lips.

"Fuck you," Lucifer growled and fought against the chains.

"Your power doesn't work here." Damian offered with a voice dripping with sarcasm. He gave Valerie a quick nod. She stepped in with a needle and the burn of whatever she plunged into my arm made me wince.

Lucifer glared. "You don't have the will to destroy me," he said, his voice heavy with whatever drug Valerie fed us.

"She might not have a choice. Regardless of how much she loves Chris, if we can't make him whole, I get to have the pleasure of making sure *you* can never come back." He pointed at me before crossing his arms. The sadistic smile that formed sent a shiver down my spine.

I think my body broke out in gooseflesh, but Lucifer just sneered at him.

The drugs rendered both of us a mass of heavy limbs and lax muscles. When Lucifer couldn't form a coherent sentence, they unbound his arms and legs and carted our body up to a living room that looked out at a sun-drenched back yard. The barren trees in the distance gave me an indication of the passage of time from the

August heat I last experienced to what looked like late fall in New England.

They tied me to the chair and set up the familiar salt ring. My head lolled.

"Bitch, you are going to regret this," Lucifer slurred, and Valerie glared at him.

The doorbell rang, and Damian stepped away, leaving me with Valerie. I watched her as she stood with her back to me. Her reflection told me more than I really wanted to know. I recognized the pain in her scan of the yard and when she refocused on my reflection; she stiffened.

Before she could turn and address me, Tom stepped in the door with Raven and her infamous bag of tricks. I actually smiled at the welcomed sight. I didn't know if I'd survive this, but I was sure whatever was coming was better than living in this mental prison.

Raven didn't waste any time. She pulled out the crystals and pulled out a compass, which was a new edition since the last time I played exorcist. Using the compass, she set the stones in the proper places. Raven glanced around at the group.

"I don't know if this will work. It's meant for exercising a demon, not an angel, and I'm afraid these hexes aren't going to do a thing." She nodded to the symbols above the doorways and continued, "Those will trap him here, so you'd better make sure you do your magic and turn his black spirit to ash."

Damian nodded. "That'll be my pleasure," he said, and Lucifer laughed.

"You don't have the power," he growled, forcing my head upright against the liquid muscles.

"That's where you're wrong. Who the hell did you think Chris gave all his power to before he made the deal?" he asked, and his lips formed a smile that scared the shit out of me.

That tidbit shocked both of us, sending a fiery strip of electricity up my spine, but for very different reasons, and I kept my reasoning under wraps. The element of surprise is always a good thing to have when you're on the devil's hit list.

Doubt sank into my bones, and I tried not to revel in Lucifer's budding fear. There was too much at stake for me to fuck up right now.

"Bullshit," he finally whispered, and Damian gave him a grin that called his bluff.

"You'll find out soon enough."

Raven turned to Valerie. "I need your blood," she said, and Valerie didn't hesitate. She didn't even wince when the knife opened her palm. What surprised me was when she held out her hand to Damian. He glanced at it and then back at her.

"Please fix it," she said and understanding smoothed the lines on his forehead. He dipped down and placed a kiss on the wound. Light sparkled and Valerie winced. Her calico eyes shifted and then settled back in place, and I knew it was all a ruse—an expertly played snow job.

Lucifer bought it, and for the first time in his existence, he squirmed. I started chuckling and a little of it bled through. Enough to pull everyone's attention.

Tom signed. "Love you, bro. Just hang tight and we'll get you back."

I forced a nod to come through. Even though his thoughts were clear, his eyes held doubt. Tom's conviction wasn't as solid as it had been with Raven's demon banishment.

Raven turned to the group and picked up the brew she'd concocted. Her hands trembled as she turned toward the king of hell masquerading as her brother-in-law. I wanted to say thank you, even if this didn't work, but she started her magical chant. This time she didn't fling the mixture; instead, she dipped her finger in it and started drawing on my face, as if she was applying war paint.

She didn't stop there. On my chest she drew a hex and covered my arms with streaks of the mixture. Curiously, my skin bubbled under the brew, but it didn't hurt. At least, not at first. As the group chanted and she loaded my exposed skin with the bitter smelling liquid, it burned.

Both Lucifer and I gasped as it flashed over, turning my skin into a molten-lava relief map of pain. The urge to flee overwhelmed me, even though I knew I should try to hold on for as long as possible. Lucifer had the same idea, but he had more willpower than I did, and more of a marriage to my cells than I thought he had, especially since he had only been an inhabitant of my body for a small sliver of time.

We bellowed as the burn increased into an inferno. I caught sight of Tom looking like a deer in the headlights as his gaze moved from one spot to another above me. The indecision in his gaze told me more than I wanted to know. Lucifer must have fashioned his ghost in the same form as mine, and Tom didn't know which one to pick.

He had a fifty-fifty chance and when he stepped in; I said a small prayer through the throes of pain. Unfortunately, the gods must not have heard it because he grabbed Lucifer, pulling him back down into my useless shell of a body.

I tried to get back, but the bubble of protection Damian and Valerie set up was impenetrable, and the pain escalated to the point I couldn't voice Tom's mistake. I screamed and writhed and then everything turned white.

Angel Heart Chapter 21

"NO, NO, NO," I repeated, fighting the arms that held me in place. "He's going to kill her!"

"There's nothing you can do," my father's voice penetrated my struggle, and I turned, looking into his bright blue eyes before surveying the landscape behind him.

When my gaze fell on my mother, the strength in my legs gave out, but my father's arms held me in place.

"It's going to be okay, CJ," he whispered in my ear.

"No, Dad. I failed. It's never going to be okay," I said and found the strength to push off him. Heaven didn't look like anything I ever imagined. There were no pearly gates or fluffy clouds. It was lush, filled with tropical fruits and grains and lakes dotting the land all the way to the horizon. There were people and animals, and even birds soaring through the impossibly blue sky. The focal point was a giant tree that provided shade to a great deal of the inner sanctuary with its multiple groups of branches. Behind me, a great turquoise sea stretched out with small waves gently lapping the white sands. Ancient and immaculate houses dotted the land.

It reminded me of pictures of Greece. It was beautiful. More beautiful than I imagined the Mediterranean to be. Nevertheless, it did nothing to settle my unease.

Faces I recognized appeared in our group with smiles and hellos, but I just couldn't accept that I was dead.

Not with Lucifer firmly housed in my body, and certainly not with my family in danger.

"We're your family, CJ," my mother said, and I turned my gaze to hers.

I hadn't seen my mother since I was eight and my eyes welled up with tears. My father let me go, and I took a seat on the ground, putting my head in my hands.

I thought being in Heaven would have calmed the building panic, but it just fanned the tension. "I'm not supposed to be here," I said and looked up at the gathering crowd. My father. My mother. My half brother and sister all gathered, along with the archangels Michael and Gabriel.

My father crouched down next to me. "I feel your pain, but we're all slaves to the choices we make." He offered a shrug and my teeth clenched.

"Do you know what he is going to do?" I said and my gaze traveled to Michael's. "You know better than everyone here." I pointed and climbed to my feet. "You know what a sick bastard he is." My voice rose, calling the attention of the closest patrons to our little group.

Michael was not intimidating in this setting. Perhaps it was the absence of wings, or just the fact that he lacked grace, but I figured if there was anyone who could change things, it was him.

"You can change this," I said. It was more of a demand than a question.

Michael crossed his arms. "Watch your tone."

I stepped closer, pushing the boundaries of propriety, and people were noticing. The murmurs of my distant family members fled on the gentle breeze.

"No," I replied, silently daring him to take a swing. I had pulled the lockbox of memories with me, every last one, leaving Lucifer empty. With all the memories at my disposal, I had the benefit of Damian's, and he knew how to push Michael's buttons, so I pulled a page from his book and moved closer, crowding him.

Everyone paused and stared at us as Michael puffed out his chest with his own challenge. I narrowed my eyes, but before I could cause a scene on Heaven's serene landscape, a hand landed on my shoulder.

"Dad, back off," I said, without breaking eye contact with the archangel.

"CJ," my mother's voice cut through my building anger, and I stood down, stepping back and meeting her gaze before dropping mine to the ground in shame.

"Sorry." I hung my head. Her arms wrapped around me. I couldn't have counted the number of times I wished for her arms for comfort when I was mortal, but this wasn't one of them. I didn't want to be here. The only place I wanted to be was in Valerie's arms, but they were probably wrapped around that twisted fuck.

"You need to let go," she whispered.

I stepped out of her grasp. "I can't, Mom." I met her concerned gaze. "I need to figure out how to get back and warn them. I know it can be done. Eric's made it through and so has Dad. I'm not asking to take my body back..." I glanced down and then over at my father. "Okay, maybe I am, but if that isn't an option, let me at least get a warning through."

"There isn't a portal from heaven," Michael said, and I turned toward him.

"Yes, there is. It's called Paradise Cove."

Silence settled over the group, and Michael inhaled, nodding. "The loophole with that is you can't leave the confines of the cove."

"You did."

He let out a small laugh. "I'm an archangel. You would do well to remember that."

I ground my teeth in frustration and my fists clenched.

"Walk with me," my father said. It wasn't an invitation, and I glanced at him before I nodded ascent.

I paused next to my mother. "It is good to see you," I said to her and offered a conciliatory smile.

"I love you." She brushed my cheek with her lips before she nodded for me to head off with my father.

"Love you too, Mom." I gave a small wave to my half-brother and sister and then followed my father toward the shoreline.

We walked in silence through the lush gardens, and he slipped off his shoes and set them on the grass at the edge of the sand. I followed his lead. The soft, warm sand sifted through my toes as we walked. He stopped where the waves and grains met and took a seat, patting the spot next to him.

"It's been a hell of a couple of years," he said slid his gaze to me. "I missed you, boy."

I bit my lip and stared out at the water. "I've been in a coma for the better part of the time since Lucifer..." I trailed off. I couldn't even say it.

"Since I lost my head?" he asked, sending a sly smirk my way.

I chuckled and sifted sand through my hands. "Yeah. Not one of my better jokes, but it made Tom laugh."

"You've always been good at watching out for him."

"Thanks. He was the only family I had left, so..." I shrugged, scanning the water. "Can I ask you a question?"

"Sure," he said, digging welts in the sand with his right heel.

"Were you the one who slapped some sense into me at Jenna's house?"

"You were too fucked up to think straight, so yeah, I got a warning through."

"How?"

He didn't say anything at first, just kept digging a ditch and letting more water pour into the small hole he created.

"How did you even know?"

He met my gaze. "I can still... see," he said, and his sigh caused ripples in the water. "You and I both know I don't belong here, either."

He let the silence build and sent a glance over his shoulder before he continued. "Heaven tolerates me because of your mother, and when I finally got here, the reasons why she and I are special were laid out in frightening detail. It explains why you are special, too."

"Why?"

He sighed. "Michael, Gabriel and Raphael weren't the only archangels to harvest blood lines. Uriel had a few flings over the years... along with others." He stopped and sifted the sand through his fingers.

"So, I'm part of an angel bloodline?"

"Lucifer doesn't know about these bloodlines. Hell, Metatron had a bitch of a time keeping track, but he was able to show us where each bloodline originated. It was quite impressive," he said, still sifting the sand and digging trenches with his heel. "Here's the kicker. Both your mother and I are a bit like Naomi," he said, and I stared at him.

"What?"

He turned to me. "Being near me activated your mother's gifts because we both have two angel bloodlines running through us. We share one of the lines."

His less than enthusiastic statement blanketed me with dread.

"Uriel?" I asked, targeting the one bloodline I had no clue about and hoping like hell that was the right one because, from the look on his face, he was a much darker breed.

He laughed. "I wish," he said and sifted more sand. "Apparently, Lucifer had some flings in his early days, too."

I shivered. "Are you seriously telling me I have his blood running through my veins?"

My father nodded. "You're a trinity." He glanced at me. "I'm surprised he didn't pick up on it," he said with a shrug.

I wanted to vomit, and I cradled my head in my hands.

"A combination of Uriel and Raphael... and a double dose of Lucifer." He let out a laugh. "Your mother gets a pass somehow, but as I said, they only tolerate me because of her. I crossed the line, and they don't understand why I was forgiven. Frankly, neither do I, but maybe they figured between Steve and me, we could keep you on the righteous path."

"I'm a dark trinity?" I asked.

He didn't say anything for a few minutes and the sinking feeling in the pit of my stomach expanded.

"No." He paused, licking his lips and sighing. He took a moment to scan the horizon again like he was waiting for someone or something to intervene on this conversation. His gaze finally met mine. "No, you are not a dark trinity. You've always been blessed with a pure streak that guides you, just like your mother. Even in your darkest moments, you always held on to your humanity."

I huffed and focused on the sand. "Not always," I said, thinking of the insane sexual romp I had with Jenna and her friends, and then to my unfortunate agreement with Lucifer.

"Making mistakes and forsaking your humanity are two very different things, son."

His words pulled my gaze to his.

"You never turned your back on being a decent human being," he clarified. "You never killed for the pure rush of killing."

I had the memories. I knew exactly what he was referring to. His life wasn't exactly one to model, and I had nothing to add to his assessment of himself.

"Will you help me get a message to Tom?" I asked, knowing my brother had the unique ability to converse with ghosts.

"Why?"

"Two reasons. To keep Valerie safe and to give me a fighting chance to get back into my body."

My father let out a laugh and glanced at me. "I don't think either of those things is possible." He climbed to his feet and wiped off the sand from his trousers before offering me a hand.

"I'm serious," I said, looking up at him. I didn't take his offer of help and stood of my own accord.

"So am I."

"You've cheated the system, Dad. Help me do the same." I squared off in front of him as the frustration bloomed inside me.

"What's your plan," he asked in that mocking tone that grated on my nerves, as if I wasn't a Mensa-level genius like he was.

"Paradise Cove." I locked my eyes on his and crossed my arms to see if he could thread the pieces together on his own.

His brow creased as he contemplated the idea and eventually, he started tapping his lips as if he was running through a task list and counting the steps. Finally, he dropped his hand. "That might work."

He turned and bowed his head, closing his eyes and clenching his fists in concentration.

The beat of wings above yanked my attention away from my father and the angel that descended made me blink. He could have passed for my father's twin, and I completely understood why Lucifer had called my father Uriel the first time he saw him.

"What are you doing?" he said to my father.

"Getting a message through," my dad said and glared at the angel. "Uriel, this is CJ. CJ, this is one of your bloodlines," he said and closed his eyes again.

Uriel studied me to the point I shifted my stance, nervous that he was going to smite me or something. He glanced at my father. "You are not supposed to do that," he scolded.

Dad just opened an eye and gave him his sarcastic smile before his eyelid shut again, and the concentration crease between his eyes deepened.

"I need to go back," I said and pulling Uriel's questioning eyebrow in my direction.

"Impossible."

"Nothing's impossible," I replied. "Even stopping Lucifer isn't impossible."

He crossed his arms and shifted, leaning back and appraising me again, but this time it wasn't like he was studying a useless bug.

"You realize you carry his bloodline as well," Uriel said, his tone more condescending than I would have liked.

"No shit, Sherlock," I said. "But that won't stop me from putting him back in his cage." The words slipped out, dripping with sarcasm, and I knew deep down I should show some respect, but I was too motivated to get back to Valerie to worry about how I came across to my ancestor.

"He's just as ornery as you are."

My father's dimples appeared. "Like father, like son." He opened his eyes and glanced at his doppelgänger with wings. "Apple doesn't fall far from the tree and all that shit," he added and the ghost of a smile that appeared on Uriel's lips gave me an indication that these two had somehow made peace.

"I never disrespected my elders," he said, and my father scoffed.

"That's bullshit and you know it," he muttered and glanced at me. "The message got through."

A dark wrath spread over Uriel's face, and his glance darted to mine. "What message?"

"That it isn't me in my body down there and to get that dickhead to Paradise Cove so I can bounce him the hell out of it."

Uriel's eyebrows arched and then he started laughing.

"He's a trinity," my father said, crossing his arms and staring down Uriel.

"Yes, but a trinity without grace is about as good a weapon as a baby halibut against Lucifer."

"Lucifer doesn't have his grace, either," I said.

"Lucifer without grace is still a force of nature," he clarified. "Or don't you recall the damage he is capable of?"

My teeth clenched, grinding together to get my temper in check. "I know what he is capable of on his turf and off his turf, but Paradise Cove is a different landscape. One he doesn't stand a chance on, or am I incorrect in that assumption?"

A spark lit in Uriel's eye, and he grabbed my shirt, pulling me close to his angry features. "Your assumption is flawed." He pushed me away and his wings fluttered. "I suggest you keep him in line," he said to my father and then lifted, leaving us in the sand swirl of his wings.

"Charming," I said and kicked at the sand. "Are all archangels dicks?"

My father laughed and nodded before heading back to where the rest of the family still milled about.

I didn't follow; instead, I wandered down the beach to the water and stepped in, the warmth of it more foreign than the chill of the ocean in Maine. A restlessness gripped me, and I turned toward the far outcrop of rocks that held a few glistening tide pools. As a kid, I always enjoyed searching for sea creatures with Tom, so I headed in that direction looking for a distraction.

Angel Heart Chapter 22

THE TIDE POOLS HELD treasures like I never dreamed of. Beautifully intricate cameo shells and starfish and even sea horses graced the small pools. I played with them, chasing the sea horses with my fingers. It brought a genuine laugh from me, and I sighed, pulling my hand away.

I stood, and a tide pool near the rock ledge caught my eye. The darkness radiating from it pulled me closer, scratching at my curiosity, and it wasn't until I stood looking down at it that the mild air of Heaven could no longer keep my soul warm.

I stared, unable to comprehend the visual details of the inside of the car. My car. With Valerie in the passenger seat holding the hand of the driver. The hand raised, pulling hers with it and lips pressed against her skin.

"Maybe we should find a safe place to pull over," he said, and my hands clenched.

Lucifer.

Lucifer had her in my car and from the look on her face, she thought it was me.

I glanced over my shoulder and my father was a few feet away, crossing the distance with purpose.

"You really don't want to watch," he said meeting my gaze.

"Is this how you saw?" I framed the word saw with finger quotes.

"Sort of. Each time something bad was unfolding, I couldn't sit still, like I was hard-wired to you somehow. I found this almost as fast as you did, but it's just a looking glass."

"Can I get a warning through to her?"

He shook his head. "No, at least not from here. It only reflects, it doesn't allow you to interact. It gave me the ability to watch over you when you were in a coma, too." His hands disappeared into his pockets and his gaze dropped to the ground before looking back toward the grass.

None of the others came this way.

I followed his gaze. "Do they know this is here?"

My father chuckled and glanced at me. "Besides archangels, you and I are the only ones who have stepped on this beach since I arrived. I'm not sure they can cross onto the sand."

The statement sent a skitter of shock down my spine.

"Maybe only those who have danced with the devil can see this," he waved toward the glass-like water. "It's like he left a mark on us that allows us to see when he steps into the mix."

The thought of forever seeing Lucifer's transgressions left me unhinged, and I glanced back at the water in time to see the reflection of the car pulling out of the snow into a warehouse. The door rattled closed behind them and my face chilled even further. "Shit."

"What?"

"I think he has her on his turf, now." The unfolding deception made my legs collapse under me, driving me to my knees. I just had a quick glimpse at the interior, and I knew exactly where he had taken her. It was the hellhole where Naomi almost defeated him.

Valerie didn't catch on; she seemed distracted like she couldn't place the scenery until Lucifer pulled her to his lips. Her shoulders relaxed and the purr that escaped pissed me off.

"How could she not know that isn't me?"

"He's good at fooling people, CJ, and right now, she wants to believe it's you."

"Tom got the message, right?" I met my father's gaze.

"Yes, and he'll do what he can..." He trailed off as he glanced at the reflection. "There's nothing we can do but wait and hope they get to her in time," he said.

I opened my mouth to speak, but there really was nothing I could say and the agony that formed in the center of my being nearly ripped me apart.

Lucifer convinced her to get out of the car to watch the sunset on the water, but they never got to the window. He slowed, letting her ahead, and the minute she stepped between the poles holding the ancient chains, they came to life. Valerie jumped and tried to get clear, but the shining shackles on the ends of the rusted chains snapped closed around each wrist, yanking into a tight position as if they were on an automatic spring.

The horrified gasp that escaped set my teeth on edge.

Lucifer ducked under the nearest chain and took a few steps toward the window before he stopped.

"I wanted him to be alive to watch the creative tortures I have in store for you," he said and turned toward her. "To feel the agony each mutilation created in his soul." He stepped toward her. "But you want to know what I wanted most?"

She shook her head, shivering from more than the chilly air in the warehouse.

"I wanted to feel his soul shrivel when I made you come," he whispered. The tone of his voice was a match to the one I used to seduce her.

"You bastard," she hissed, struggling against the chains, even though they held her arms out as wide as they could go without popping a shoulder.

He just grinned my salacious grin. The one I knew sent a tingle of anticipation up her spine. Whether or not she realized it, the way he stalked closer to her made her body respond. Her breath shortened and her lips parted, but the flush creeping up her neck was the decisive factor, and I was sure if he took her clothing off, her nipples would be rock hard.

My likeness did that to her, even with the knowledge I wasn't the one possessing it.

"Get away from me," she said in that breathy quality that used to make me twitch in anticipation.

I glanced at my father. "I have to figure out a way to end that fucker."

He just nodded and turned his back, opting to lean against one of the large rocks and stare out at the ocean. Unfortunately, the soft waves didn't drown out the sounds coming from the portal to hell.

I couldn't help watching the horrifying scene as Lucifer stripped Valerie. He removed each article of clothing slowly, as if this was a grand seduction instead of a prequel to murder. Valerie's chest rose and fell in a shaky cadence that belied the tears flowing freely. The loss of hope in her eyes ate through my resolve and my vision wobbled.

When she was naked and exposed, he stepped behind her, pressing his body against her. The fabric of his shirt whispered across her skin, and he ran his hands over her, tenderly, like a lover, and I wanted to scream. From the conflict in her features, she didn't know whether to scream or moan.

He cupped her breasts and kissed the nape of her neck.

"Don't worry, darling," Lucifer whispered. "As soon as I treat you to that orgasm, the fun will begin." He grinned against her neck and one hand traveled lower.

Valerie slammed her head back, catching Lucifer square in the nose.

"Fuck!" his angry curse filled the warehouse, and the shadows came to life. Demons crawled forward, looking hungrily at Valerie as they gathered closer to the bizarre scene.

"Not yet," he snarled, and the masses slunk back, becoming one with the shadows again.

The chains rattled as shakes gripped Valerie, now that the demented seduction had turned into her worst nightmare. I think I was shaking just as much. His violation of her stripped me of any sense of sanity and her unintended moan sent me directly into the realm of insane.

"No!" My bellow rattled the stones and rolled over the water in an unending echo of my cracked mind.

My father pulled me away and wrapped his arms around me, holding me against his chest to keep me from seeing any more.

"I've been there," he whispered in my ear. "It's better if you don't see."

That's when she began screaming.

Angel Heart Chapter 23

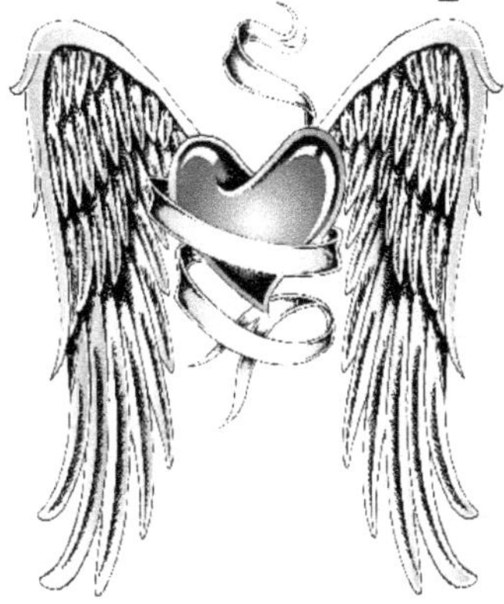

MY FATHER SPARED ME of the vision, but he couldn't buffer me from her screams or the choked gags that alternated. I struggled to get out of my father's grip, but he clamped down.

"Trust me," he said in a tone that forced me to look at him.

"Let go," I whispered, my voice shaking and raw.

He gave me the saddest smile and shook his head. "You'll know if he succeeds," he said, and tears blurred my vision again.

I didn't want Valerie to die and come to this benign place. She had a life; one I didn't want Lucifer to steal. One I wanted to share, and I buried my face in his chest. The shakes took hold and I think he was the only thing that was holding together what was left of me.

After what seemed like forever, the screams cut off and I stiffened, pulling my face away from the wet fabric and glancing over my shoulder at the sunny fields, expecting to see Valerie standing and gazing around with the same level of confusion I had.

I stepped closer to the pool and my fists clenched along with my teeth. Lucifer had one hand around her throat and his other hand in that familiar claw-like formation over her heart. She was still conscious, but her face was borderline purple as he cut off both her airway and the blood flow to her brain. Her body sported bruises and cuts from the demons having their way with her. And now Lucifer was following through on the final promise he made to me.

His hips slammed her in the fast pace of a building climax, and I covered my mouth in horror. A sound like an air puff rose above the rattle of the chains and I blinked at the dart embed in Lucifer's bare ass. His motion slowed, and both hands dropped to his side before he slid down her body and crumbled on the ground.

A whirlwind circled around the warehouse, torching every demon shadow, and finally the chains holding Valerie disappeared in a puff of smoke. She dropped to her knees, unable to support herself after the abuse she endured. I couldn't see outside the warehouse, but the flap of wings gave me an indication of who had just saved her ass.

When Tom dropped to the warehouse floor with a tranquilizer gun slung over his shoulder, my hand dropped from my mouth, and I turned my gaze to my father. He was watching as well, his expression one of fierce pride in the way his younger son took fearless action.

Tom crossed, peeling off his coat as he approached Valerie. He wrapped her in the fabric and picked her up, heading toward the car. I was so focused on her that I didn't even take note of where Damian was.

Valerie's eyes widened. "Don't!" she yelled over Tom's shoulder, and he spun back toward where Lucifer lay unconscious. My gaze followed.

Damian stood over the prone figure of Lucifer with a sword poised to sheer off Lucifer's head. His face altered from the furious intensity of the kill to shock as he glanced up at her. Snow fell over them and I realized Damian had leveled the place, leaving only Valerie, Tom, and Lucifer alive.

Tom shook his head.

"Tom says we have to bring him to Paradise Cove, it's the only chance we have to get Chris back."

"You two saw what we did to him. There's no way he survived and I'm not letting this bastard have another go at any of us," Damian said, lifting the blade.

"No," Valerie growled with such ferocity that Damian paused again, but this time, his muscles strained against the invisible force holding the blade at bay. "If it was Naomi, you would try everything under the sun."

The trembling in his arms stopped, and he closed his eyes. Lowering the sword to his side and straightening up. He inhaled and glared at her.

"If it doesn't work, I get to destroy him," he said, and both Tom and Valerie nodded.

My hands relaxed the tight grip on the edge of rock surrounding the pool. I hadn't realized I had the stone so tightly clamped, but with the relief came the loosening of tension and I glanced at my father.

"What now?" I asked as they packed my body in the trunk of the car, where every sigil known to Damian was scribed on the interior. So if Lucifer awakened, he would be temporarily pinned in place.

"We figure out a way to get you back," he said.

"I may have an idea on that," a voice pulled both of us around. Michael was only a few steps behind us. I hadn't heard him approach, but from the stoic expression on his face, and the fire blazing in his eyes, he had seen enough of the details to spark a fair amount of fury.

After all, Valerie was his descendant, and they had a special bond. Knowing Lucifer violated Valerie in every manner set me ablaze. I couldn't imagine what it did to her great grandfather.

"He must be stopped," Michael said through clenched teeth. "But, as Uriel pointed out, a trinity without grace is as good as dead going up against Lucifer." His gaze slid from me to my father. "Even with grace, he's going to need a little help."

"You don't have grace to give," I said, crossing my arms in an effort to steady the shake that remained in my ethereal limbs.

"No, but I do."

I glanced up at the top of the cliff. Uriel looked down at us and then hopped off, gently gliding down on wings that sparked in the sun. He landed next to me. The same righteous anger present in Michael reflected in the tense set of Uriel's jaw.

"You saw?" I whispered, blinking the sudden mist covering my eyes away.

He gave a single nod.

My gaze dropped to the sand at my feet, and I closed my eyes against the tears dripping into my lashes. I didn't have time for the devastation pummeling my heart, but it was relentless. Instead of wallowing, I focused on what was involved with taking Uriel's grace, shaking the sadness away before looking up at him.

"I don't really want to eat your heart," I said.

Uriel's face transformed, and then a chuckle erupted. Standing side by side with my father, I saw the resemblance in their smiles.

"What?" I asked, wiping at my face.

"That's the only way to steal an angel's grace," he said through his sputtering laugh. "Operative word there is 'steal'. Giving grace does not include the ingestion of an angel's heart."

I cracked a smile. "That's good to know."

Uriel put his hand over his heart and closed his eyes, letting a slow exhale out as he pulled his hand away. Inside his palm, a rainbow of moving light formed a ball like a miniature sun. He opened his eyes, holding the essence of his grace. Without it, his features aged from the vital man who looked no older than I to that of a man in his fifties, like my father.

His wings withered away and falling feathers covered the sand. Uriel gave me a soft smile and pulled me close with his free hand.

"When I'm done with it, can I give it back to you?" I asked, with my gaze locked on the swirling lights, mesmerized.

"No. The gift cannot be returned."

I looked up in surprise. "Then... why?"

"I've been granted a view of my own," he said, and his expression turned serious. "Sometimes things don't go according to plan and there is a need for extremes to set things right. This is one of those times."

Uriel pressed the light to my chest before I could push for more details and the light penetrated every cell of my spirit. Even though I'd carried the power of complete annihilation in my form all my life, it didn't compare to this, and it rendered me speechless.

The light eventually settled and then Uriel looked at my father.

"But it cannot be done without sacrifice."

Angel Heart Chapter 24

"NO!" I SLAMMED MY hand on the ancient wooden table. "I will not let you sacrifice your soul for me. Lucifer will make your time in hell unbearable."

"I can handle it," my father said.

"You can deal with it... forever?" I gawked. "For-ever," I repeated.

He shrugged and then nodded. "Yes. As long as I know he can never get to you or Tom, I'll endure."

I lifted my hands in the air and walked away. I would never win this argument with my dad. He was hell bent and hell bound.

"Please, Ty," my mother said, and he turned to her.

"Babe, you had to know this was only temporary. Forever was never in the cards for us right from the beginning." She went to argue, and he held his hand up. "I don't belong here and if my sacrifice saves our son, you damn well know I'll make that choice any day and twice on Sunday."

The room burst into arguments against the plan laid before us. Everyone from my uncle, who I was named after, to my half-sister, voiced his or her disdain with the idea. I stepped outside the little hut, unable to deal with the erupting chaos.

I closed my eyes and let my mind wander to my earlier trip that Michael had insisted upon. He took me to see the angelic ancestry traced out on the walls inside the mighty tree. The angelic lines did not cross until the last century and the irony of it all, Naomi's family tree and mine were the only ones that had more than one bloodline union out of the thousands of names carved into the wood.

The arguments raged inside the building and I focused on what we had to do. My part was set in stone now that I had Uriel's grace blazing in my blood. I had to take back my body and close every portal to Hell that existed.

Getting into my body shouldn't be hard with the power of Heaven behind me. The tough part would be getting Lucifer out and keeping him out. Otherwise, I risked infusing him with the grace Uriel gave me and that would be disastrous.

The only hiccup... neither Damian, Valerie, nor I could relinquish Lucifer's spirit to Hell from anywhere other than within Hell's portals.

It had to be someone who navigated the boundaries of the spirit world.

It had to be someone born of angel blood.

And it had to be someone who had fallen from grace.

My father was the only one in Heaven who met the criteria, and I was his motivating factor. That would haunt me each time I destroyed a portal, because every time I closed a door, my father's chances for freedom diminished.

One of the silent observers stepped out next to me and I glanced at him. It was the actor who played my father in the movie Survival Games. I remembered his death. He dove in front of a bullet meant for my mother.

"I never got the chance to thank you," I said, meeting the eyes that mirrored Tom's.

He gave me a nod. "My sacrifice didn't go to waste. Neither will your father's. I once said your dad was the most courageous man I'd ever met," he said and glanced at the landscape. "He still is."

I huffed and crossed my arms, leaning against the white wall. "But trading an eternity with my mom for unending agony..." I trailed off, just shaking my head.

"When you become a father, you'll understand why he's willing to endure an eternity at Lucifer's hands for you," he said and turned to go to wherever he called home up here.

"What about you?"

He stopped and turned. "I may have been able to circumvent the boundaries of Heaven a couple of times, but I'm not an angel descendant," he said. "And I never fell from grace." He lifted his hands in a shrug.

"Watch over my mother?" I asked, and his features softened.

"Until the end of time." He turned and disappeared around the corner.

The bickering continued, and the door opened again. A familiar face I hadn't seen earlier gave me a smile.

"Sarah." I smiled back and gave her a hug.

"Hey," she said. "Can you do me a favor when you get back?"

The fact she said when gave me an indication of the faith she had in me.

"Sure."

"Tell Steve not to sweat it," she said. "I know it probably won't make a difference, but I understand why he did what he did. I wasn't pleased, but I guess the alternative was far worse. Besides, I finally found happiness up here with my sister... and all." A glint in her eyes shimmered like there was more.

"I will," I said and followed her back inside.

Sarah stepped to Eric's side and the glance they shared told me just how good Heaven had been to them. She slid her gaze to mine and offered a smile, confirming that she and Eric both had found their happily ever-after.

"End of story!" my dad bellowed, holding his hands in the air to stop the chatter. "If I don't do this, Lucifer wins." He scanned the crowd and his gaze landed on me. "If I don't, Lucifer wins," he said directly to me.

And therein lay the crux of the situation. No matter how devastating the sacrifice was, I couldn't let Lucifer win. It was a very personal battle now. I clenched my jaw, crossed my arms and nodded assent.

He glanced at the sun's position and inhaled.

"Game on," he announced, bringing his gaze back to mine, and the hardness and resolve reflected in his eyes made me shiver. I had never seen his 'angel of death' persona, but now I understood. He pulled it off like no one I've ever seen.

He broke eye contact and crossed to my mother. Without a word, he pressed his lips to hers, lingering the way I had with Valerie. This was a true goodbye kiss, and he had to forcefully unwrap her arms from around his neck and step away.

"Love you," he whispered and turned, sending a nod to everyone else before stalking to my side.

"Dad?" my half-brother Eric said.

My father turned, meeting his gaze.

"Give 'em hell," he said, but there wasn't the usual upbeat lilt I remembered. Instead, he turned and circled his arms around my mom.

"Will do," my dad said and grabbed my arm, leading me out the door. I think he moved quickly, so he didn't change his mind, but it was enough to form a lump in my throat. He glanced down at me. "It'll be just fine," he said, and I tried on a smile to acknowledge him, but I'm sure it failed at being anything near reassuring.

Michael and Uriel stood in the inner sanctuary around the mighty tree and my father led me through the maze of fruit and flowers and stopped at the last bridge. The conflict surfaced in his hesitation and when his head shook and his jaw tightened; I pulled back.

"You don't have to do this."

He met my gaze and planted a kiss on my forehead. "Yes, I do, and so do you." He ruffled my hair. "I love you, CJ, and I'm so proud of the man you've become."

"Thanks, Dad," I said and stepped onto the bridge with him.

Fog rose from the stream, blocking out the rest of heaven, but light bathed the interior, and the ground faded, giving us a clear view of a snow-covered Paradise Cove.

Lucifer was still unconscious, but now had my open shirt draped askew over his shoulders and the jeans on, but the belt was looped around his wrists behind the chair. His feet were bare and a shade of red that wouldn't be pleasant to wake to. Valerie stood nearby, dressed in a warm down coat that must have been one of Jennifer's from the house. Tom and Damian flanked Valerie like silent guards, and Raven laid out her fortifying stones, making it safe for them to be within arm's length of Lucifer.

"He has to be awake," Michael said and leaned on the trunk of the tree.

"Can they see us?" I asked, and all three of them shook their heads.

The only one on the ground who seemed distracted when we spoke was Tom.

"Tom can hear us. Can't he," I asked.

Tom tilted his head in response, as if he was listening to a distant storm. He shook his head, and Valerie gave him a sideways glance.

"I thought I heard something," he said, and her eyes widened. She hadn't ever been to Paradise Cove, so she did not know what kind of mystical powers it contained, like the one that allowed my brother to talk.

I had to smile at the awe that lit her eyes and the real hope that sprang into her face.

Lucifer stirred, pulling his head up enough to crack an eye, before it dropped, lolling on his shoulders again.

"The belt will not be enough to hold him," I said and again Tom perked up.

A low rumble skittered across the sky, and everyone looked up at the storm clouds gathering overhead. I never recalled seeing an electrical storm over the Cove in the winter. Plenty of snowstorms, but thunder and lightning in the dead of winter were a rare occurrence.

Lucifer's eyes blinked open in confusion. I know what he last remembered and for a second, I felt pity, but it vanished just as quickly when he licked his lips and said to Valerie, "Help me."

He was playing the game again and raw fury encompassed me when Valerie stepped forward.

"It's not me," I growled, and Tom's hand reached out, grabbing her arm, stopping her from stepping into the circle and outside of their protection.

The way Lucifer's gaze transitioned from helpless beggar to wrathful archangel was enough to make everyone step back.

"You ungrateful bitch," he snarled.

I glanced at Michael and Uriel, receiving a nod. My dad gave me a quick hug and then the power of Heaven gathered around me, forming a powerful lightning bolt. My father winked and growled, "Game on!"

Lightning filled the sky, sending a spear straight toward Lucifer's heart.

Angel Heart Chapter 25

MY TEETH CLINKED TOGETHER as a shiver took hold and I blinked my eyes open, trying to pull my arms around me for warmth, but I couldn't. Bright light blinded me as I cracked my eyes open. Everything was white, and it took a moment to figure out the white landscape wasn't heavenly clouds, but a snow-covered glen.

I tried to speak, but my throat was too raw to form words and my tongue felt like sandpaper on my cracked lips. I tried again, this time a dry rasp formed the word 'help' but it was so soft, not even the small field mouse by the edge of the forest budged.

Turning my head brought forth a wave of dizziness and nausea, along with a stabbing pain behind my eye. I think I groaned. A shuffle behind me caught my attention, and I turned my head enough to see a snow filled path that was vaguely familiar.

"It could be another trick." a soft Irish brogue fell over the snow and a striking redhead came into view.

"I highly doubt it," a male voice blanketed the area, and I turned, meeting a pair of bright blue eyes that were wide enough to tell me he had just witnessed something unthinkable.

I licked my lips again and tried to articulate.

"Help," I hissed and met the redhead's gaze.

Her stoic features hardened for a moment as she studied me, and then her entire face softened, and she fell to her knees in front of me. "Oh, blessed be, it's finally you!"

I shrugged and glanced around the cove.

"Par…a…dise Cove?" I asked, still foggy as to why I was there and why there was snow on the ground.

The girl climbed to her feet.

"Rav…ven?" I asked. The name came from somewhere in the mud of my brain.

She beamed; her smile as bright as the sun-drenched snow. "Yes!"

"Why am I tied to a chair in the snow?" I looked down at my bare feet. "Without shoes."

Her smile faded, and she regarded me with skepticism. Before she could answer, a stunning brunette stepped in front of me, and my breath locked in my chest. I could neither pull air in nor exhale while this beauty filled my vision. It took a few beats of my heart before my body decided to function again and two words tumbled from my lips.

"Mind fuck."

Tears formed in her eyes, and she covered her mouth. There was a fear in her gaze mixed with longing and hope that made my eyes mist as well.

"Chris?" she whispered.

"Yeah, who else…" I trailed off and the chilly air couldn't penetrate the ice that layered over my entire form. My shivers stilled, and I slumped in the chair before glancing around at the cove. "Jesus," I whispered and met her gaze. "I dropped him into a seizure in Au…gust."

She uttered a high-pitched laugh and stepped closer, but she still didn't dare touch me.

"Didn't I?" I asked, searching her features and then Raven's.

She kept laughing, but she was now crying as well.

"Valerie," I said with more force, and she met my gaze, winding down and wiping her face.

"Yes. But that was almost six months ago."

"You've had me tied here for six months?" I couldn't help the incredulous tone in my voice and her chin trembled.

She slowly shook her head. "No."

My face fell, and I stared into her sad calico eyes. "What did I do?"

"You didn't do anything. But he did," she said and reached up, unbuttoning the collar of her coat and the raw bruises on her throat clenched my chest. But that wasn't the clincher; the crescent scars over her heart tore a gasp from my dry mouth.

She slowly buttoned the shirt and wouldn't look at me.

"What else?" I asked, reading her as if I had been with her all my life.

She lifted her gaze. "Let's just say he fooled all of us."

I hung my head. I knew the things Lucifer promised he would do if he ever got a hold of her. My last mortal memory was the exorcism, and then everything went white. It wasn't like the dark abyss of the coma; this was pure and white and warm.

"Where the fuck was I?" I whispered and glanced up at her.

Tears filled her eyes, and she shook her head with a shrug. "I don't know," she said. "I wasn't sure it was you, but he somehow convinced me, and I wanted to believe it so badly, even though I knew there was something missing, something that wasn't there when he looked at me. He almost broke me, Chris. He almost crushed me beyond recognition, and when I realized it wasn't you..."

I stared at her, knowing just how devastating that must have been, and a justified anger filled me. I should have been there to protect her, but I wasn't in a position to intervene.

The full return of memories left me hollow, because I shouldn't be sitting here, either.

She gave me a slow nod and looked around. "This was our last try. Tom suggested we bring him here. He said it might be the one place that would allow you to come back and claim your body." She wiped her face. "If this didn't work..." She pressed her lips together and turned toward the frozen lake. "I would have let Damian kill him."

"I wouldn't have blamed you if you had."

She turned. "Letting go would have destroyed me," she said.

Heat filled my eyes, pooling and distorting my vision. I blinked and hot tracks warmed my cheeks. "I'm sorry." My whisper came out wrapped in agony.

"Just don't ever leave me again," she said.

I let my lips curve a little. "Okay." That was a statement I could agree to a thousand times over, and she leaned in and pressed her lips to mine. The satin of her skin warmed me from the core outwards and when she parted her lips, our tongues mingled, and all thought ceased. Time stopped with this kiss, and she settled on my lap, wrapping her arms around my neck.

When she broke the kiss, she met my gaze, and I inhaled like I came up from too long underwater. A slow smile formed, and the sparkle returned to her eyes.

"It really is you," she whispered, and this time the kiss was filled with promises of things to come. The balance of power shifted, filling every fiber of my body, making me grin despite her lips still plastered on mine.

She pulled away, and I glanced at Raven, Tom, and Damian standing a few feet away.

"Thank you," I said, and the bonds holding me in place disintegrated. I wrapped my arms around Valerie, picking her up and setting her on her feet as I stood next to her. My legs cramped up, and I flinched, but Valerie grabbed me around the waist to steady me.

"Go easy."

I raised my eyebrows. "Go easy? I've been chilling in Heaven while all this shit went down. I can't go easy until we close every possible way that bastard can escape."

"You said you wouldn't leave me," she said with a defiant pout.

"Baby, I don't plan on ever leaving you again," I said, meeting her perplexed gaze. "Wherever I go, you will be by my side."

"But..." she started and stepped away.

I grabbed the back of the chair for support, shifting my weight against the pins and needles tingling in both my legs. Coming back to life was just as uncomfortable as this conversation.

I glanced at Tom.

"Dad got him, right?"

"I think so. I wasn't sure what the hell I was seeing, especially after I heard him say 'game on'." He paused and swallowed before going on. "That lightning bolt scared the shit out of us," he said and pointed at my chest.

I glanced down at the burn mark where the lightning seared my skin, pushing me back into my body and knocking Lucifer out. A scar in the shape of a fiery sun graced the space over my heart, and I looked back at my brother. "I think that may be Uriel's sign," I said and glanced at Valerie. "We need to have a long talk, but the bottom line is I made a deal and part of that deal was the promise to close all existing portals."

"Where did Dad take him?" Tom asked. The concern in his voice was enough; I didn't need to read his mind in order to know where he was going.

"Dad made me promise. He can only hold the devil at bay for so long," I said. "I have to live up to my end of the deal."

"He sacrificed Heaven?"

I nodded. "For you and me," I said, locking my gaze with his. "I didn't want him to, but he was the only one who could make this possible." I waved at my shivering form and turned back to Valerie. "You'll just have to get used to traveling with me when the need strikes." I shrugged.

Her expression hardened. "Like going to New York?"

My eyebrows scrunched for a moment and then everything clicked into place. "No. Not like New York," I said in a soft voice. "What he did to you..." I trailed off and looked at the ground, shivering at both the cold encompassing me and the anger surfacing. "I will end him if he ever cros...ses my path again." I raised my gaze meeting hers. My stutter accompanied my fury.

She stared me down and I opened my mind, letting down every conceivable wall, including the one holding the secrets of Heaven under wraps. Valerie blinked as she soaked in my memories from the destruction of the first portal that landed me in the coma to the existence of Heaven and the conversation with my father. Her eyes widened.

"You're a trinity?" she gasped, and I nodded, sliding my gaze to Tom.

"As I said before, we're going to need to have a conversation because what I learned in Heaven affects you, too."

He pointed to his chest, and I nodded. "Not a trinity, though. But Naomi, you and I have some things in common."

"You remember everything?" Valerie said, after things started settling in the whirlwind of her mind.

"Yes. On both sides of the grave."

Silence settled over the small group, and all shades of doubt evaporated.

"Do you mind if we go somewhere where I can get warm?" I asked as the chill threaded through my cells, setting my teeth in a constant clatter. "I can't feel my feet and I'd rather not have to deal with frostbite."

All eyes dropped to my bare feet, and I stepped toward the path, aware that they followed like a band of fanatical disciples.

Angel Heart Chapter 26

THE FIRE CRACKLED AND I shivered under the metric ton of blankets they draped over me. The hot cocoa in my hands was warm and sweet, but nothing compared to the feel of Valerie's arms wrapped around me. We overtook Steve and Jennifer's cottage, waiting for the rest of the family to arrive.

I hadn't launched into all I learned while on the other side. I just wanted to have to lay it out once and be done with it. The one thing I probably should have asked before I left was for a map showing where all the portals were, but then again, maybe it was by design that Michael and Uriel didn't enlighten me. Maybe they wanted some time to devise a plan to save my father before I closed off any chance of that ever happening. Maybe they just didn't know where all the gates to hell resided.

I could only speculate, and I sighed, sliding my gaze to Valerie's profile. She stared into the fire, reconciling the facts fed to her in the space of a few minutes, when I opened my mind. She had opened her mouth with several questions since, and I just shook my head, softly whispering for her to wait.

By the time the crew arrived, I had warmed up to the point I felt human again, and God bless them, they brought food and warmer clothes for me. Steve pulled me into a hug after he set the pizzas down on the table.

"I thought we lost you for good this time," he said.

"You won't get rid of me that easily," I said, and he pulled back with a grin. "By the way, I have a message for you."

The relief in his eyes tempered with a mixture of dread and he nodded, waiting for whatever words of wisdom I had to impart.

"Sarah asked me to tell you not to sweat it. She understands why you did what you did." I shifted and leaned closer. "It looks like she hooked up with Eric."

His eyebrows arched. "No shit?" he slipped and then pressed his mouth closed as his gaze drifted to the kids filtering into the cottage.

"Yeah. I don't think I've seen either of them so happy."

He grinned. "Damn," he said, and the guilt in his heart lifted a fraction.

The kids immediately started running through the cottage in a whirlwind and I stepped away from Steve, grabbing the offering of clothes and opting for a quick shower before I ate. I wasn't quite ready to outline the facts, either.

The shower was warm, and I could hear the happy chaos through the door. I didn't linger like I wanted, not with the building tension, as they all started speculating. After I dressed, I wiped a clear spot in the mirror and stared at the sigil on my chest, gently tracing it with my finger. It didn't hurt, but it was a reminder of the grace infused with my powers and I met my gaze before I buttoned up the shirt the rest of the way.

"Thank you," I whispered, hoping like hell my father could hear.

Before the emotions ran amok, I stepped out into the living room. The sudden silence made me falter, and I stopped, scanning the collective group that made up my family.

"Want some pizza?" Valerie asked.

I nodded and crossed to the table, sliding into the free chair next to her. She put a couple of slices on my plate and my gaze locked with Grace's. The child just grinned at me, and I couldn't help but smile back.

"I told you it would become clear," she said in that mini-adult voice before she blinked and was my three-year-old niece again.

"Yes, you did." I took a bite of my pizza and scanned the multiple pairs of eyes locked on me. "After we finish here, okay?" I said through my mouthful. I knew the anticipation was killing them, but I needed food just as badly as I needed to clean up earlier. "I promise," I added after I swallowed, and then dug into the pizza as if I hadn't eaten in months.

With my belly full and my family gathered in the family room, I moved one of the folding chairs to the side of the fireplace, where I could still feel the heat of the fire. I didn't want Valerie in my arms for this conversation and I leaned forward, balancing my elbows on my knees and clasping my hands, taking a moment to figure out where to begin.

"I died," I said and sat up. "Taking on Lucifer without the benefit of angel grace was a stupid move on my part." I let that sit out there. "Even at Black Cove, I wouldn't have survived if Damian hadn't come. It's a lesson that cost many people a great deal." I glanced at Valerie. My recklessness almost cost her her life.

My gaze moved to Damian. "You didn't beat Lucifer until you had Michael's grace and the infusion of power you stole from me."

"I didn't..."

I put my hand up, stopping him. "It's okay. I get it wasn't intentional, but the combination of those two items is needed to have a fighting chance."

"What about me?" Naomi said, and I glanced at her.

"You were a vampire in the form of a tiger. That's a bit different and yeah, you almost ended him."

"Momma, you were a vampire?" Grace asked, looking up from her coloring.

"Yes, honey, but I got better," Naomi answered and then glanced back at me.

I offered a shrug. The conversation was going to get much darker and my gaze traveled to the kids and back to Naomi and Damian. "Maybe it's time for a nap," I said.

All three children looked up at me.

"We already napped in the car," Michael said, taking the lead. His gaze penetrated in a way that I had only seen from Grace. Maybe the trinity connection was much greater than I thought and when he glanced back at the coloring book in front of him, the child was back and concentrating on coloring within the lines.

I now understood the need I had to protect the children. Raphael's bloodline ran in both of us, and that compelled me more than I cared to admit. I moved my gaze to Tom.

"You and I share Raphael's bloodline, so we are actually related to Naomi. That was one of Mom's angelic blood lines." I unbuttoned my shirt enough to show the scar turned tattoo on my chest. "I'm pretty sure this is Uriel's symbol. Uriel is one of Dad's angelic bloodlines. He and Dad helped to get me back home." I pressed my lips together and my head dipped. "Uriel gave me his grace and Dad..." I couldn't finish.

"Dad gave up Heaven," Tom signed, his words echoing in my head, and I looked up at him through a sheen of tears and nodded.

"Yeah. He was the only one who could drag that bastard back to Hell." I blinked the mist away and ran a hand down my face.

"Valerie said you are a trinity?" Damian asked. I hadn't opened my mind to share the details with him.

"Both Mom and Dad shared another angelic bloodline, which, when added to Raphael's and Uriel's, makes me a trinity," I said and scanned the room, sighing. "It's the reason being near Dad jump started her talents." I locked eyes with Tom. "We carry Lucifer's bloodline."

No one moved. No one spoke. They all just stared at me until Tom sat back in his seat and ran his hands through his hair. His face paled and his head slowly shook, trying to deny the reality that devil's blood flowed through our veins.

"Pisser, ain't it?" I asked, and he barked a laugh, nodding. "Imagine how I felt, finding out I'm a f..." I stopped before I dropped the f-word in front of the children. "A dark trinity," I finished with a softer tone.

"You aren't a dark trinity," Grace said from her place at the table, pulling everyone's attention in her direction. "Dark trinities are bad."

The simple statement and the way her eyes flitted from the coloring book to mine sent a rash of gooseflesh up my arms. A quick scan told me I wasn't the only one who reacted the same way.

"She's right," Damian said, turning back to me.

"Oh, and thanks for telling me you didn't have to eat an angel's heart to be given their grace," I said directly to Damian. "I made an ass out of myself when Uriel offered up his. I told him I didn't really want to eat his heart."

Damian's eyebrows rose, and then the group collectively chuckled.

"I apparently am not immune to making a fool out of myself in Heaven." I leaned back and crossed my arms, feeling the hint of a smile finally appearing on my lips. Valerie covered her snicker, but I saw the humor return to her eyes.

When the laughter at my expense wound down, Tom signed, "Did you see anyone else up there?"

I nodded. "Mom, Emily, Eric, and your father were all there, too, along with Dad's brother and Sarah. They had just as hard of a time accepting the plan, but it was either this, or Lucifer would win, and I couldn't live with that. Neither could Dad."

"So, your father is in Hell?" Steve asked. His complexion paled with the thought of his guardian angel burning in the pit.

"Yes," I replied. "And I have to close all the existing portals."

"Does Lucifer know?" Valerie asked.

"I'm sure he knows I'm going to try; especially given the things he did to you." My gaze dropped to the bruises still on her neck. She had yet to use the healing power to fix her wounds.

"That's not what I'm asking," she clarified. "I'm asking if he knows you are one of his descendants."

I shook my head. "He doesn't know. But he saw the resemblance to Uriel in my father." I shrugged and dropped my gaze to my hands. "I doubt that will make a difference in how Dad will be treated down there." I chose my words carefully, cognizant of the children's ears. As it was, I had already dropped a few inappropriate words that were bound to be repeated.

Oh well, what was an uncle for if not to add colorful words to a child's vocabulary?

"Are you going to follow through on closing the portals?" Damian asked with a voice as hard as the bricks behind me.

I met his uncompromising stare with my own.

"Yes."

"What about Dad?" Tom signed, his eyes reflecting the pain I held close in my heart.

"He made me promise. I'm closing the gates, even if it means his sacrifice is permanent."

Angel Heart Chapter 27

VALERIE AND I WALKED into the empty house in York after saying our goodnights to the rest of the family.

I stopped her in the middle of the room and just wrapped my arms around her, pulling her close to my chest. The only thing I hadn't dealt with since I woke was what Lucifer had done to her in the warehouse. I hadn't seen the lion's share of what was done, but I could only imagine. While I shared everything with her, she had kept her own barricades up.

"I'm so sorry," I whispered into her ear and gently kissed her forehead.

The trembling started all at once; it wasn't a slow progression but a tornado that shook her entire form. My arms held her on her feet, and she clung to me, despite the conflict brewing inside her. I was inhabiting the form that brutalized her. The soft tones of my voice were the same as the ones whispered throughout her torture.

"I love you," I said and tightened my grip, trying to enforce the fact it was me and not Lucifer. Each painful sob sent a spindle of rage through me. "He will never touch you again," I added. "I promise."

She pushed out of my grip. Her tear-stained face transformed into the same level of fury. "He used you." She waved her hand at my form. "You were the one I saw coming after me, not some random stranger. When he finished, he let the demons nearly fuck the life out of me. It was your eyes that watched. Your smile of satisfaction every time a scream peeled from my throat…" Her voice hitched and she dropped to the couch, covering her face.

I slowly lowered into the chair, afraid to ask the question that surfaced.

"How do we get past this?" I whispered after her renewed sobs dissipated.

"He knew what he was doing." She wiped her face and moved her eyes to me. "He was ruining me from the inside out, on the off chance I got away. The bastard hedged his bets, and I'm not sure what he left behind is salvageable."

I moved next to her, and she flinched. "If it's any consolation, I went ballistic," I said. "My father pulled me away, so I didn't see everything, but I saw enough for me to make a scene that all of Heaven will never forget."

"It's not a consolation." She glared at me. "Don't you get it?"

I reached out and cupped her cheek. "I get it. He fucked both of us. But he wins if we don't get past it." I pulled her onto my lap despite her tensing up and I just held her against me until she relaxed.

"I hate him," she muttered, and she turned my head towards hers so our eyes met. "But I don't know how to win this one."

"Tell me if you know the difference," I said and leaned in, kissing her lips, tentatively. The worry that she wouldn't be able to evaporate on contact, my mind went numb, lost in the silky feel of her and I swiped my tongue against her closed mouth, hoping for access. She granted it and our tongues mingled in a sensual dance that drew my breath and locked it in place. Heaven was dismal compared to kissing Valerie, and the world around me ceased to exist.

She pulled away, slapping me back to reality, and I opened my eyes, meeting her stormy irises and noting the heightened color in her cheeks.

"Can you?" I asked, praying she could.

Her hand caressed my cheek, and she broke eye contact without answering. Her hand fluttered to her throat and then she climbed off my lap, turning her back to me.

"I can tell the difference in your kiss," she said, her voice hesitant and shaking. "But I need to find out if I can tell the difference..." she trailed off, keeping her back to me.

I knew where she was going, and I stepped behind her. "You're still hurt," I said, moving her hair from her neck. I kissed the offending bruise, wishing it away. A layer of sparkles cascaded down her body and she gasped in pain.

"Why do I have that?" I asked, stepping away. It came out in more of a snap than I meant it to, and she glanced over her shoulder at me.

"You have everything."

"Why?"

She shrugged and turned forward again.

"You're the doctor. You should have the healing power." I scanned the tension present in her back. She didn't want to discuss the lack of division of the power, and I sighed, stepping forward again, placing my hands on her arms. "You're more a part of Heaven than I am," I said, and she turned her head, meeting my gaze. "You should have that side of the equation."

"You're the one who sucked everything from me," she said and shrugged.

Instead of engaging in this seduction from the back, I turned her towards me and stepped in, so her chin tilted up to meet my gaze. "You shouldn't ever be powerless," I whispered and covered my heart, wondering if I had the power to split grace. I concentrated, watching her irises swirl in response to being near me.

My teeth clenched, and I closed my eyes, concentrating on that glowing orb inside me. The effort to split the sucker made me break out in sweat. Valerie was speaking to me, but I shook my head and said, "Shush."

I rolled up a piece of healing power and the darker power into the small piece of grace that broke off and opened my eyes. The glow in my hand radiated, and I glanced up at her. She had taken a step back, and I reached out, pulling her close as I pushed the grace into her chest. I held her to me, keeping my hand over her heart and her back arched in response as the magic infused with her cells.

The pieces I pulled together were small, but enough to give her a fighting chance if we ever ran across Lucifer. "Now you won't be helpless, even on his turf."

I dropped my hands and stepped back. Her breath still hitched in her chest and her irises did the storm dance I loved. Colors shifted like rolling clouds of blue, purple, and gray. When they settled, she exhaled.

"Holy shit," she said, and her gaze dropped to my shirt. "You're going to need a new shirt," she said, and I glanced down.

The fabric over my tattoo was charred and tattered, but the skin underneath was fine. I glanced at her shirt and smiled, lifting my gaze to hers. The power of transferring grace carved the same symbol into her skin as well. "You do, too."

This time, she closed the distance and the kiss she delivered wasn't even in the realm of tender. It was frantic and demanding and consumed every inch of my soul.

Angel Heart Chapter 28

I STOOD AT THE sliders, watching the fresh snowfall. In the distance, the Nubble Light, outlined with Christmas lights, stood out amidst the white flakes. Dawn broke over the horizon, warming the cloud cover with a rainbow of colors. It had been almost a year since I got my life back, and Valerie and I eventually found our way home to that place where she didn't flinch when I went to touch her.

That battle was long and hard on both of us. There were many nights I sat on the family room couch with a bottle of scotch that did nothing to quench my bitterness. The moments where we both wondered if we would ever get through the damage Lucifer rained on us were the hardest. During those times, even the love we had for each other didn't seem like it would be enough, but it was the thing we both clung to. And it was what got us through.

That and the time we spent with Steve and Jennifer. Their history of overcoming a similar battle helped guide us. Jennifer patiently coached Valerie. Her wisdom and shoulder helped with the healing process and Steve; he took me out of the house, a lot. Giving the girls the space to work through it.

When they moved to New York City, it hit both Valerie and me harder than I expected. I missed them and understood their decision to give us space, but it was weird without them here, and moving into the master bedroom just felt wrong. It'd always been my parent's room. Whether that was Mom and Dad or Steve and Jen, it belonged to the head of the household.

We fell into that category now, and I glanced at the small box in my hand. My stomach fluttered. I didn't understand the sudden case of nerves that made my skin tingle and I turned, making sure I had set things up just right.

The shower went off upstairs and I grabbed the rest of the rose petals, extending the path that led from the stairwell out into the backyard. I waited, shifting nervously as each second ticked by.

My mind shuffled again while I waited for her.

Damian and Tom searched for portals while I worked on my relationship, and they found a few locations. Ones that we would have to check out once I got my shit together. Neither Valerie nor I were ready to face that yet. Instead, she focused on finishing her residency and she took a job in York instead of Boston. She'd learned to love this small ocean-side community just as much as I did, and I've learned to relax and breathe when she was out of my sight. Besides, the cafeteria at the York Hospital has some awesome food.

My paranoia manifested whenever I performed, and I'd gotten damn fussy about my schedule and the venues where I'd sing. I wanted places where Valerie was less than a few strides away; I couldn't seem to shake that insecurity.

It was the one place I knew I was vulnerable. The limelight overwhelmed and distracted me at the same time. I soaked it in, and everything disappeared but the music and the crowd. It was a lot like Valerie's kiss in that manner, and as much as I try to keep part of my focus on her, it didn't work, so I don't perform that often.

She approached the sliders, pulling me out of my thoughts and I met her questioning stare. I shivered with my hands in my pocket and sent a smile in her direction. The door opened, and she crossed, stopping right in front of me. Her purple scrubs and white hospital shoes poked out under the long wool coat. I knew she had to get to work, but tonight was going to be a late night for her and I couldn't wait any longer.

"You know what today is?" I asked, handing her a single rose, and she bit her lip, shaking her head.

I rolled my eyes and cocked my head. She shrugged in response. This wasn't going the way I had planned it in my head, but I plunged forward. "We met exactly four years ago today."

Her cheeks bloomed with color. "Really?"

"Yes. Really." I smiled, taking a knee in front of her, and pulled out the box from my pocket. I opened it, revealing the stunning diamond my father had given my mother in this same spot.

"Mar...ry me," I said, annoyed that the stutter crept into this perfect moment. Then again, it still showed up any time my nerves did. Instead of harping on my imperfections, I took the diamond from the satin pillow interior and waited for her to react.

My proposal wasn't a question, either. It was a statement that hung on the snowy air between us.

Valerie stared at me, her eyes widening just before her right hand fluttered over her mouth. My answer came when her left hand extended in silent acceptance, and I smiled, sliding the ring on. The fact it fit just solidified the rightness of this moment and I stood.

"I'll take that as a yes," I said, pleased that I had rendered her speechless.

"Yes. Yes. I'll marry you. Oh my God, yes!"

She nearly knocked me over with the excited hug and our lips locked in a kiss that blew me away.

The End

Continue CJ's story with Angel Wrath on the next page.

Angel Wrath Chapter 1

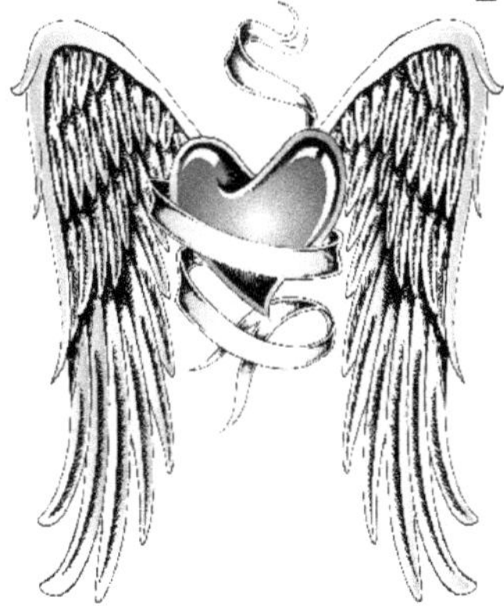

I SHIFTED MY WEIGHT, doing my best to conceal the nerves biting at my skin. The warm fall day didn't help with the light sweat seeping through my shirt and into the black fabric of the tuxedo. I scanned the small crowd settling into the chairs arranged overlooking York Harbor and smiled at the familiar faces.

I would have only recognized a handful of these people last year, but after my adventure to heaven and back, my memories returned along with the truth of what I really was. A trinity, infused with angel grace.

I glanced at my watch. The ceremony was supposed to have started five minutes ago.

Tom's hand landed on my shoulder, and I met his gaze.

"Raven was a little late to our wedding, too. Remember?"

I nodded, but it didn't really settle me. I wouldn't relax until Valerie was in my sights. It wasn't so much wedding jitters as that old paranoia that accosted me any time she wasn't with me. I'd learned to deal with it, just like I'd learned to deal with my asinine stutter. At least it wasn't as prevalent as it was when I came out of the coma, but it remained like an unwelcome reminder that I was still vulnerable to human frailty.

The violins started the wedding march, and people stood, blocking my view. I held my breath, waiting for her to appear at the end of the makeshift aisle. When she stepped into view, the familiar tingle that locked my chest took over and I had to force myself to breathe. She was beyond stunning.

"Wow," I whispered, and she lit up. Even at a distance, she knew my thoughts stalled, and I knew she had the same reaction seeing me in the finely tailored Armani.

She glanced at Damian, his arm ensnaring hers as he walked her down the aisle. He stopped in front of me, leveling the look I knew came with a warning. If I ever hurt her, I'd have to answer to him.

I gave him a slight nod of thanks and he passed her hand into mine.

My gaze locked with hers and I didn't even hear the preacher's opening greeting; I was so focused on the slow storm swirl in her lightly frosted eyes. This was the first time I ever remember seeing her with makeup and it was subtle enough to draw out the vibrancy within her irises, completely mesmerizing me to the point nothing else made a difference. I wanted to pull her into my arms and kiss her glossy lips, wondering if that shine had a sweet taste to go along with it.

Her dimples appeared, and she broke eye contact, bringing me back into the here and now.

The preacher looked at me, raising his eyebrow expectantly.

"Hmm?" I hadn't heard a word since she stepped into view.

"Are you ready to proceed?"

My cheeks heated, and I slid my glance to her. "Yes, sir."

She pressed her lips together in a smirk. *You didn't hear a thing he said, did you?* Her thought crept into my head.

Not a fucking thing. I sent the thought back and grinned, looking out over the ocean for a minute before focusing on the minister. *You are that stunning.* I glanced at her and the rose hue in her cheeks was more than just powdered blush. Her sweet dimples appeared, and I had to take a deep breath.

"If anyone here can show just cause why these two should not be joined in holy matrimony, speak now or forever hold your peace."

Silence settled, and I squeezed her hand. She squeezed back, and the minister waited another ten seconds before he glanced at the two of us.

"Please, join hands," he said.

I turned toward Valerie, taking both her hands in mine, painfully aware that I had to focus, and not zone out on the thoughts parading through my head of what I wanted to do with her on our wedding night.

"Christopher James Ryan, do you intend to take this woman, whose hands you hold, to be your lawfully wedded wife? And do you pledge before God and man to love, honor, and protect her through sunshine and shadow alike, keeping yourself unto her alone until death shall separate you?"

"I do," I said without prompting.

"Valerie Elizabeth Denongalis, do you intend to take this man, whose hands you hold, to be your lawfully wedded husband? and do you pledge before God and man to be to him a loving and true wife, through sunshine and shadow alike, keeping yourself unto him alone, until death shall separate you?"

"I do," she answered, and her eyes sparkled like a rainbow.

"Christopher and Valerie have written their vows," he said, and gave me a nod.

I licked my lips and took a breath, praying my stutter wouldn't ruin the moment. My gaze met hers and she squeezed my hands, making me smile.

"Valerie, you know me better than anyone else in this world, and somehow you still manage to love me. You are my best friend and one true love. Getting to this point hasn't been easy for either of us, but all the trials were worth it to be standing here today. I'd gladly walk through the fires of hell for you." I unclasped my hand and cupped her cheek, wiping the single tear with my thumb. "You are more precious than anything the kingdom of heaven has to offer," I said and paused with my gaze locked on hers. "I love you with my whole heart and beyond the depths of my soul, and I promise with everything I am, to love and honor you, faith…fully, for all time."

Her lips twitched into a smile at my stutter. I resisted the urge to pull her closer and deliver the kiss I'd been itching to give her since she took the spot next to me.

"Chris," she began, and her voice cracked. She cleared her throat and lick her lips. "I never used to believe soul mates existed, and then I met you. The feeling hit me the moment we made eye contact. It was so immediate and powerful—far deeper and inexplicably beyond any calculation of time and place. You described it perfectly that night with two words that I won't repeat here." Her cheeks turned crimson, and I knew exactly what two words she meant.

"You completely stole my heart with your awkward attempt at wooing me."

God bless her, she even added the right Irish inflection as she mimicked the way Raven first said those words and it earned her a soft chuckle from most of the guests. She grinned and glanced over her shoulder at Raven before meeting my gaze again.

"You're right, we've encountered a lot of bumps in the road to get to today, but there isn't anyone I'd rather take this journey with. I promise to stand by you through hellfire and brimstone, to soar with you on life's highs. I promise to help shoulder our challenges because I believe there is nothing we cannot face if we stand together. And above all else, I promise you my love, through all eternity, because one lifetime with you could never be enough."

My eyes misted, and I blinked back the tears that had blurred my vision at the bull's-eye of her words. I mouthed the words 'I love you' before I focused back on the minister and the ring ceremony.

I slid the ring on her finger, reciting the words the minister prompted, and she did the same.

"Ladies and gentlemen, I give you Mr. and Mrs. Christopher Ryan. You may kiss your bride," the minister said.

I pulled her into my arms, kissing her like it was our first kiss. Soft at first, but the strawberry wine gloss on her lips fueled my desire, and I ran my hand into her finely coifed hair, dipping her as the kiss deepened. The guests started whooping, and I stood her back up, releasing the kiss and turning toward the audience that I had momentarily forgotten existed.

"Party time, Mrs. Ryan," I whispered with a grin, and we headed toward the Reading Room where we were planning on drinking, dining and dancing the night away.

I glanced at Valerie as we organized into a reception line.

"How the hell did I get so lucky?" I whispered, and she beamed. "If I forget to tell you later, you look beautiful tonight."

"So do you," she whispered.

We strolled down the curved stairwell onto the outside deck overlooking York Harbor. The sunset painted the sky a rainbow of colors that blended with the autumn leaves and I couldn't have envisioned a more perfect evening.

We stood in the reception line greeting guests. The first one through was my grandfather. I hadn't seen him since before my accident and he looked even frailer than when we buried my grandmother five years before.

"Papa, this is Valerie. Valerie, this is my grandfather, Russ Campbell," I said, and she extended her hand, unsure of whether a hug was appropriate, especially since the man was in a wheelchair. He waved her hand away and pushed himself to his feet, offering her a hug instead.

"Pleased to meet you," he said, and lowered back into the chair, bringing his gaze to mine. "Your mother would be so proud of you," he added, and patted my hand before the nurse wheeled him into the reception hall.

"How old is he," Valerie whispered, and I shrugged, trying to calculate his age in my head.

"Close to one hundred," I said, still watching my grandfather as he directed his nurse to the bar. I smiled and turned my gaze to the next guest, and my smile froze.

Sandy's hazel eyes met mine. I had sent the invite to Dan and LeAnn as a courtesy, but I never thought they'd show, never mind bring Sandy along.

I recovered and turned toward Valerie, suddenly uncomfortable with the less than thrilled expression on her face. It took her a moment longer to replace the shock with a smile.

"It's good to see you again," Valerie said, in that fake saccharine voice that pulled a smirk to my lips.

"Likewise," Sandy said, but the flare of jealousy that tightened the corners of her lips betrayed her actual feelings on the matter. She gave me a peck on the cheek. "I'm glad you're happy," she whispered, and wandered away.

I turned to the next person in line and met Dan's hard gaze. LeAnn stood next to him, and her features were more genuine.

"Dan and LeAnn Connor," I said to Valerie, and she nodded, flashing her winning smile in their direction.

"It's a pleasure meeting you," she said.

"The pleasure's ours," Daniel replied and placed a kiss on the back of her hand. "This is my wife, LeAnn," he added, as they moved down the line.

Tom met my gaze as soon as they passed him, and his eyebrow rose.

I didn't think they'd actually show. I sent the thought and his smirk appeared.

"You really sent her an invitation?" Valerie whispered in my ear as soon as they stepped out of hearing range.

I met her glare and gave a single shoulder shrug before focusing on the next guest. I knew I'd pay for that later, but for now, she put the dazzling smile back in place and we both turned to another blast from my past.

"Ted, how the hell are you?" I grinned.

"I'm good. You remember Heather," he said, motioning to his wife.

"I certainly do. This is my bride, Valerie. Val, this is Ted and Heather Beaumont, good friends of Steve and Jen's."

"Nice to meet you," she said, and opted for hugs instead of the overly formal handshake. She had our memories, so she knew they went way back with Steve. They were one of the few real friends Steve had. They'd come by with their kids almost every summer since Steve took us in, and I smiled beyond Heather at Sydney and Andrew Beaumont who had accompanied their parents, with dates of their own.

A group of Valerie's friends approached us after the Beaumont's cleared out and she was kind enough to do introductions.

"So, this is coma-boy," said one of the women with whom Valerie did her first- and second-year residency. Her gaze slid up and down my form, and then returned to Valerie with a nod of approval.

"Nice to meet you, too," I said, and unfortunately, my sarcasm bled through in my tone.

"I'm sorry, but the last time I saw you, you were covered with tubes and wires." She offered a wry smile and extended her hand. "I'm Claire," she added.

I shook her hand and gave Valerie a raised eyebrow as Claire continued into the reception.

"She's a neurosurgeon," Valerie said, like that explained the weird, direct, non-personality.

The next two people in line brought a smile. "Mrs. Kincaid," I said.

"I've told you a million times, please call me Carolyn," she said, and pulled me into a hug. "Congratulations!" she added, and then focused on Valerie with a grin.

"Valerie, this is Carolyn Kincaid and her husband Randy," I did introductions and then added, "Randy manages our portfolio."

Randy took her hand and kissed it in the same manner as Daniel had, but his was more sincere. "Pleasure to meet the woman who finally pinned this guy down," he said, hooking his thumb in my direction.

"Nice to meet you," Valerie said, grinning.

The next few folks to pass through the reception line included our lawyer, Lynn Trueman, and Steve's old boss, Ron Cleary. Beyond them stood Captain O'Keefe, of the York Police Department.

Captain O'Keefe stepped up and offered his hand. "Congratulations, kid."

"Thanks, Captain," I said. "I'd like you to meet my wife, Valerie. Val, this is the captain of the York Police Department. He hauled my ass in so many times when I was younger, it wasn't funny."

He chuckled. "Your husband and his brother were a little wild in their youth."

Valerie grinned. "I'll bet," she said and added, "Thank you for sharing this day with us."

He wandered off and a few other stragglers from my high school days came through the line. And then it was time for the rest of us to head in and grab something to eat before the real festivities began.

"You invited Sandy," Valerie said, when we were the last two on the terrace.

I met her sharp stare. "I invited the family. I never in my wildest dreams thought she'd show up with them."

"Jesus, Chris," she said, and turned away from the building. "It's supposed to be our day," she added, crossing her arms.

I glanced up at the windows and there was the subject of our conversation just staring at the two of us. Her expression was one of longing and I turned away, irritated that my ex had the audacity to show up at my wedding. I invited her parents because of the family history and their connection with Steve. He had asked if I minded, and honestly, they were a big part of our lives for many years, so I didn't think it through.

"It is our day." I focused back on Valerie, stepping beside her and slinging my arm over her shoulder. My motive was two-fold: one to comfort my wife, and the other to bring home to my ex that there was absolutely nothing there. "I'm married to the most wonderful woman in the world, and I couldn't care less about who else is here, beyond the wedding party."

Her gaze slid to mine. "Liar," she breathed, and I rolled my eyes.

"Okay, I'm not thrilled, either," I admitted and a smirk appeared. "But here's the deal. I just promised my heart to you, in front of everyone. I meant every word of my vows. You're it, whether or not you believe me."

While my biggest insecurity was having Valerie out of my sight, hers was my ex and the fifteen-year history we had shared before it fell to pieces. I had valid concerns, but hers were just asinine.

"Why would you even send them an invitation?" she pushed.

"Because Eric was Steve's partner and Dan is his father," I said, even though she knew that. "Steve asked me if I minded having them on the list." I took her hand. "Eric is the reason I exist," I added, and she softened. "So..." I trailed off and shrugged.

"I get it." She sighed and squeezed my hand. "But you'd better not dance with her," she muttered and started in, dragging me with her.

Angel Wrath Chapter 2

THE DINNER AT THE reception hall was to die for, and everyone raved about it. I led Valerie out onto the floor and the band began the haunting melody she loved so much. Granted, Hallelujah wasn't exactly a love song, but it had meaning for both of us, and she wanted to hear me sing on her wedding day.

I crooned as I spun her around, my voice lifting over the instruments and caressing the crowd as much as it did Valerie. She just stared at me with rapture, and I grinned as the last note trailed away.

"How's that Mrs. Ryan?" I whispered in her ear.

"Perfect," she grinned, and nibbled on my neck. She led me off the floor and pecked me on the lips. "I'll be right back," she said, and pointed toward the bathroom. Raven followed her to help with the dress and I sighed when she stepped out of view.

"Care to dance?"

I turned, meeting Sandy's gaze, and shifted. Valerie's warning had been clear. She didn't want me touching Sandy tonight in any manner. But now that I was cornered, I traded a glance with Tom and he nodded to the dance floor, knowing I couldn't gracefully decline the offer without offending her. Besides, it was a dance beat and not a slow song.

"Sure," I said and as we stepped onto the dance floor, the fast beat transitioned to a slow song and I paused, glancing toward the restrooms.

"She isn't jealous of me. Is she?" Sandy asked, drawing my attention.

I sighed. "Just a little," I said. "Can you blame her?"

Sandy raised an eyebrow. "Does she have something to be jealous about?" She wrapped her arms around my neck, tilting her head and licking her lips in that come-hither way that used to get me, but it only irritated me now. She stepped close, swaying her hips against me with the slow cadence of the music.

I unwrapped her arms from my neck and took her hand in mine, opting for a more formal position with my hand at her waist and space between us. If I was going to dance with the girl, I'd damned well make sure only a limited portion of our bodies touched. I didn't want her getting the wrong idea, especially since this really was a bid to get under my skin.

"No, she doesn't," I said, answering her question. "She's just always been intimidated by the fact we were together for so long." I shrugged and glanced beyond her. Valerie hadn't come out yet and my nerves bundled in my stomach. I bit my lip, contemplating the time that had gone by since she disappeared into the ladies' room.

"What's wrong?" Sandy asked, pulling my gaze back to her. She knew my tells, and I debated just keeping quiet, but her eyebrows arched, prompting me silently.

"I don't like it when Val is out of my sight," I said.

"Why?" she asked, her voice filled with coy reserve.

"Demons," I said and her face blanched, bringing back unwanted memories. "They haven't hit in a while, and I wouldn't put it past the devil to fuck up my wedding day."

"You know, I had years of therapy for what you did to Josh," she said, and I couldn't help but laugh.

"I know," I said, still smiling. "I'm sorry for leaving such a mess."

"You killed my boyfriend," she said, and her features hardened.

"I killed a demon that was trying to kill you," I replied, meeting her gaze. "Unfortunately, that demon was wearing your boyfriend."

"You did that two places at one-time thing, too. When the hell did you start that?"

"When Valerie and I traded memories," I said. "She got the healing mojo, and I got everything else."

Sandy's gaze jumped to Steve and then back to me. "I thought Steve had that."

"A lot of shit went down after I walked in on you, but the bottom line is really simple. Val and I have everything, just like my mom and dad did."

She slowed to a stop and just stared at me. She knew the story of my parents from Eric, our half-brother. Eric had said a million times my parents were meant to be together. That they balanced each other out. That it was written in the stars.

Sadness engulfed me because now they weren't together. Mom was in Heaven and my father was in hell, and there wasn't a damned thing I could do about it.

"We were never meant to be, Sandy."

Hurt flared in her eyes, and she stepped back just as Valerie came into view. I didn't look up at my wife. Instead, I kept Sandy's gaze.

"You kept me sane at a time in my life when things could have pushed me over the edge, and I'm grateful to you for that, but Valerie is the one I was always meant to be with," I added, and shrugged. "I have a feeling if she had come along when we were together, it wouldn't have made a difference. I'd still be standing here today with her... not you."

Tears filled Sandy's eyes, and she spun away, bolting off the dance floor and passing where Valerie stood without a glance.

I met my wife's gaze as she crossed to me. She stepped into my waiting arms.

"I thought..." she started, her breath tickling my ear.

"She asked me to dance," I said, stopping the rest of her admonishment.

She pulled away and met my gaze. "You didn't need to make her cry," she said, and for the first time since we met, there was pity reflected in her eyes where Sandy was concerned.

"I told her the truth. In the nicest possible way I know how."

"It was still a crushing blow," she said, but her eyes softened.

"Not insecure anymore?" I asked, tilting my head.

She slowly shook her head. I had left my mind open to her during the entire conversation and she was privy to the sincerity of the words I spoke.

"It's about damned time," I smiled and caught a gentle kiss.

"Now we just need to work on you," she said, when our lips parted.

I let out a small laugh. "That will not be as easy. Not until we close every portal and I know that bastard can't get topside," I said. I glanced around at the people dancing and mingling in the other room, and then back at her. "I'm actually surprised he didn't somehow crash this event," I added, and met her gaze.

The mere mention of Lucifer, even if I didn't use his name, brought a shadow to her eyes. She still battled the image of me hurting her and I knew if I ever got the drop on him, I'd pummel his ass until he was worse than I was the first time we squared off.

Angel Wrath Chapter 3

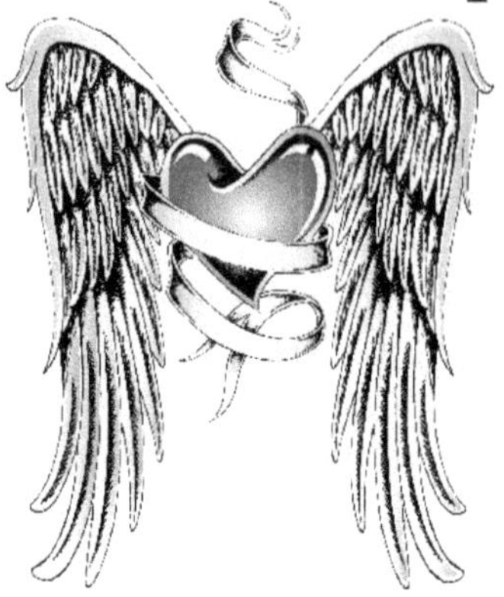

THE HOTEL DOOR CLOSED, and I turned, staring at my bride. I stepped toward her, licking my lips with anticipation. I'm not sure whether it was the hungry look in my eyes or the way I stalked toward her, but her face paled and I stopped. My eyes widened at the hints of the fear triggered in her. It had been almost a year since I saw her flinch at my approach, and it was not welcome on our wedding night.

I pressed my lips against the curses that wanted to spill forth, and she gave me a strained smile. The fact Lucifer cast a gray net over this day pissed me off to no end, but I attempted to shelve that anger and focus on Valerie.

"I'm sorry," I said.

She laughed, but her eyes sparkled with a layer of tears. "You just..."

"Reminded you of him." I tore off the cummerbund I was wearing, turning toward the bathroom before I lashed out in some other way.

"Chris," she whispered.

I came to a halt at the doorway. A deep cleansing breath and a slow count to three loosened the tension in my shoulders and I turned toward her. "You just look so goddamned beautiful tonight." I tried to explain the appearance of the hungry animal in me. The one Lucifer had used to poison her memories.

Every time I lapsed into that mindset, she freaked out and tonight I had to swallow the budding fury and forget about it. If I didn't, he'd drive a wedge between us again.

"Come, take a bath with me." I pointed at the huge whirlpool tub in the bathroom suite.

She crossed to my side and her eyebrows arched at the bathroom accommodations we had and the large tub that looked out on our private balcony and the ocean view beyond.

"A bubble bath?"

I smiled at the intrigue in her voice and nodded. "Anything you want."

The darkness between us passed, and I saw the Valerie I dearly loved in the smile forming on her lips. Her eyes danced with renewed mischief, and I grinned, waving her into the room ahead of me.

She stopped in front of me and pulled her hair to the side, revealing the intricate lace buttons lining the back. "Do you mind?"

I debated on just pulling it apart and letting the buttons sail everywhere, but she sent a cocked eyebrow in my direction.

"There's a zipper," she said and smirked.

"Oh." That sucker was hidden behind the lace, and as soon as I unclasped the top hooks, the zipper was easily accessed. I pulled it down slowly, each tooth clicking, and I smiled at her beautiful honey-tanned back. The view pulled me in, and I planted kisses along the pathway my hands took to peel the wedding dress from her shoulders.

She shivered under each swipe of my tongue, and I circled around to the front, pulling her to me in a kiss that swept us both away. When her dress dropped to the ground, she pulled away from my mouth and gingerly stepped out of the silky fabric.

"What are you doing?" I asked when she leaned down and picked up the dress.

"I'm not leaving this on the bathroom floor. Are you nuts?"

I guess a man really doesn't get the attachment a woman has to her wedding dress. She was handling it as gently as one would handle a china doll and all I could do was think of the ways to get her beautiful body out of the dress. She glanced over her shoulder at my train of thought.

"It's a five-thousand-dollar dress," she said like that explained it.

"And?"

She rolled her eyes at me. "It's my wedding dress. I'm never going to wear it again," she stressed the word wedding, and I gave her a smirk. "But if we ever have a little girl, she might want to wear it."

"We can afford for our daughter to get whatever she wants. Even a diamond studded dress."

She carefully laid the dress over the chair and returned to my side. "You mean I could have had a dress designed with diamonds instead of Swarovski crystals?"

I chuckled. "Yep. But I doubt it would have outshone you."

Dimples appeared. "That was pretty corny," she giggled, and unbuttoned my shirt. I went to help her, and she knocked my hands away. "I got this."

"By all means." I let her undress me. Each stitch of clothing dropped to the floor, and she stepped back, studying me. She still had her undergarments on, and I stood with just the black dress socks still adorning my feet.

I lifted my hands to the silky fabric of her corset, and she stopped me with a shake of her head. Again, I had to control my reaction until I met her gaze. The grin on her face told me this was her game tonight. Her tease; and it would put me into orbit.

When she stepped out of the floor length slip, I scanned her, my gaze locking on the hints of blue steel connecting her garter belt to her stockings. Handcuffs. Blue steel handcuffs. My gaze jumped back to hers and I laughed.

"Something blue?"

"Yes," she replied, and unhooked the first pair, dangling it from her finger.

I reached down to strip my socks, and she shook her head.

"Get into the tub," she added, the commanding tone of her voice arched my eyebrow.

This was her way of dealing with the atrocities Lucifer rained on her.

Control.

Without it, she flinched, and I had long since given up in that department. It was the only way we were able to get past what he did; the only way she trusted me in the bedroom. Since Lucifer defiled her, she had gone farther into the kink zone, insisting on all the control. I knew the drill well enough by now, but I had hoped tonight would be different.

Sighing, I stepped into the tub, and took a seat with the ocean view greeting me. Warm steel clasped around my wrist with a bite, and I glance up at her. She pulled my hand toward the fixed handrails on the tile outside the tub. The click of the other end split the silence and along with it came that seductive dominatrix smile that always worried me.

I dropped my gaze to the other pair on her hip and noticed the engraved sigils. In the back of my mind, I cursed Lucifer for the damage he had done to her, and when my gaze traveled back to hers, I saw the hardness move in.

She snapped the other cuff on my free wrist, pulling it to the opposite handrail. The position I was left in wasn't all that comfortable, but that was part of her game. Secretly, whether or not I wanted to admit it, the juxtaposition of the pain and pleasure was hotter than hell.

The smile returned as she stepped into the dry tub and pulled my covered foot to her stomach. The slow peel of my sock and the way she was standing stirred the heat in my stomach and I smiled back at her. She did the same with my other sock, sending it into the same careless arc that the first had taken.

I was naked and at her mercy, just the way she liked me. I hadn't tied her down since after Tom killed Raven's father, and right now, the memory of our bondage escapades ran through my head. I could have easily broken the cuffs, but I knew the power it instilled, and Valerie needed that more than I did.

To my surprise, she stepped out of the tub, cranking the hot water on full blast. The heat was immediate, unlike our slow furnace at home, and when she leaned down and closed the drain, my gaze jumped to hers.

"Are you trying to scald me?" I asked, pulling my feet away from the water.

Her reaction was almost enough for me to unclasp the handcuffs. She just smiled. Her gaze traveled to the shelf lining the wall where an ice bucket holding a chilled bottle of champagne sat, along with a plate of strawberries and cream. Her silence and the creeping water made me shift. I could easily break free any time I wanted or add the cold water to the river of heat filling the tub, but if I intervened with her private fantasy, it would end up in an argument.

I didn't want an argument tonight. I just wanted to make love to my wife.

The heightened color in her cheeks told me she was enjoying my discomfort and if I played along, I would be rewarded. I turned away and closed my eyes, gritting my teeth against the burn as the water climbed onto my toes. Valerie sprinkled an elixir in the water and the soft scent of lavender filled the room, along with the steam.

"Fuck. That's hot," I whispered through clenched teeth and opened my eyes. Bubbles had grown from the concoction she poured in the water, and I glanced at her. "Too hot," I said and willed the cold dial to turn, diluting the heat from scalding to something manageable.

Her pouty lips thinned with aggravation.

"It's not like the water at home," I said, glaring at her. "This is near boiling."

"Wus," she muttered, but she stepped closer, dipping her finger in the brew surrounding me. She yanked it back and her eyes widened. "Oh, shit, babe, I am so sorry," she said and reached for the cold water.

"I already adjusted it a little," I said, and her hand stopped, testing the water under the cooler spout.

"Really, I didn't mean to burn your ass," she said, sliding her gaze toward me and I grinned.

"No?"

She huffed a small laugh and shook her head.

"Ah. You just meant to ride me until I drown in these bubbles?" I cocked my eyebrow as the suds rose to my chin. The water had already risen above my lap and was approaching the halfway-full mark.

Her laughter rang out, and she stripped the rest of her clothing, turned the faucet off, and stepped into the water with me. I got a quick view of her slender form before she kneeled into the suds, straddling me. She leaned in, planting her palms on my chest and caught a soft kiss before she flipped the whirlpool jets on.

The results were hilarious.

Bubbles expanded at a rate neither of us was prepared for, spilling over the sides of the tub and onto the tile floor. Her eyes went wide, and she started giggling as the soft lavender-scented spheres overcame both of us. I just leaned my head back and laughed while she fumbled with the controls. Her first attempt to turn it off did the opposite; it turned the jets on full blast. They felt good against my back, but they reproduced bubbles faster than an atomic blast. By the time she found the off button, we were both laughing so hard the water was already sloshing under the thick bubble layer.

Valerie cleared a path from her to me, and still laughing, she kissed me. The kiss lingered under the laugh and then it transformed time and space, sucking the air from my lungs as our tongues intertwined. Even the soft crinkle of popping bubbles dulled to a distant white noise, and I longed to wrap my arms around her.

When she pulled back, I opened my eyes and met her gaze.

"I want to hold you," I said, diverting from her usual game.

A shadow passed over her features. "Chris," she sighed. Her fingers lightly traced the tattoo on my chest. Uriel's mark. My reminder of my time in heaven. Her gaze lifted to mine.

"I need to hold you," I whispered, breaking the rules she dictated. I still hadn't willed my wrists free, so she knew I was asking her permission. It was a psychological game, a step toward further healing, and I knew I might tip the balance, but I really didn't care.

"I want to hold my wife tonight, while we make love," I said, this time with more strength behind it. "Please," I added, and for the first time in years, I saw the same need in her. When she nodded, the double click of the cuffs releasing drifted through the bubbles.

I resisted the urge to wrap my arms around her and pull her to my lips; instead, I cupped her cheeks and met her halfway. This kiss was filled with her hesitations and fueled by her passions; it was just as polar as the pleasure-pain realm of being locked in chains while she toyed with me.

My hands drifted. One slid around her waist and the other caressed her breast. She stiffened, and I realized my hand covered her heart. Instead of reacting, I continued my gentle kneading, rolling her nipple between my fingers while our tongues danced.

She pulled away.

"It's okay. I will not hurt you," I said, meeting her gaze. She had that deer in the headlights look like she expected my hand to form a claw and tear through her skin. I kept on playing with her breast, offering her what I hoped was a reassuring smile until the tension in her face relaxed a fraction.

I licked my lips and pulled on her lower back, bringing her wet nipple to my mouth. Tasting her on my terms was better than stepping into the soothing, warm sea in heaven and her hands laced through my hair.

She sighed my name, and I moved to her other breast, alternating between gently sucking and rolling my tongue over the hard nipple. I took advantage of her bliss and moved my hand between her thighs.

Again, she stiffened and pulled away. I remained quiet, just staring into her eyes while I circled her clit with my thumb. I had won two psychological wars tonight, and I was going for the trifecta.

"I love you, Mrs. Ryan," I whispered, and tears sprang to her eyes.

The battle between fear and pleasure raged within her, and she kept my gaze. I made no other moves, but I also didn't stop my gentle fondling. I wanted her. All of her, not just the wild control monger. I needed to break down Lucifer's last strangle hold.

The soft purr that came from her throat took her by surprise and I couldn't help but lick my lips and send her a small smile. I tried not to grin. That would send her running for the cuffs, but the sparkle in her eyes set me on fire. I closed my eyes and sighed, forcing control over the wants flitting through my head.

"God, Valerie," I whispered and opened my eyes, meeting her stormy irises. I wanted to ask her to just let go and let me love her, but I left the thoughts behind the blockade I'd built in my mind. Most of the bubbles had fizzled and the effect she had on me was now obvious.

I don't think she realized it, but her hips were moving in slow circles, heightening the color in her cheeks and the hardness of her nipples. Her breath rasped in her throat as her body began accepting the pleasure and rejecting the fear.

She grabbed my hand, grinding into me, and her eyes squeezed closed. I understood and slid my finger inside her with care, despite her frantic efforts. My thumb still worked her the way she liked, and she clenched around my fingers, her moan filling the caverns of my soul as she came for me, spouting my name to the heavens.

The moment my hand pulled away, my cock filled her, and I pulled her close, crushing her lips. Her legs wrapped around me, and our sinuous motion rocked warm waves against us. Her hands threaded through my hair, and she moaned in my mouth, her body shaking with another orgasm.

I wrapped my arms around her and climbed to my feet. The kiss didn't stop when I stepped from the tub, nor did it while I crossed to the bed with her. When we were laid out on the soft linens and I was circling my hips with hers, I broke the kiss and stared down into her eyes, pushing the strands of wet hair away from her face.

"God, how I love you," I whispered, searching her soul for any shred of fear.

She smiled and pulled me back to her lips. I hadn't indulged in this bliss in over two years, and I lost track of time, moving slowly with her, letting my climax build until it burned, while she jumped hurdles like a champion show horse.

When I finally let go, I swear my heart stopped with the force of it.

I propped myself on my elbows and nuzzled my head on her shoulder. "I love you, lady," I whispered, my voice shaky with exertion.

"I love you, Christopher James Ryan," she said and planted a kiss on my shoulder.

I forced myself up from her soft shoulder and stared down into her stormy eyes. "I think the bath is probably cold."

"I'm not sure there's any water left in the bathtub."

I chuckled. "Would you like to resume that bath now?" I asked, rephrasing the question.

"Handcuffs and all?" she asked, and her eyebrow rose with the question.

"If that's what m'lady wants," I said, grinning.

"M'lady wants you at her mercy now," she said, and I rolled off her and headed into the bathroom. I stopped at the door, and she came up behind me, peeking over my shoulder.

A little giggle erupted, and I glanced over my shoulder at her. "Remind me to leave a hell of a tip for the maid before we leave, okay?"

"Okay," she swatted my bare behind and without direction, I stepped into the lukewarm water that barely covered my ankles.

I offered her my wrists and this time, there wasn't the angry flare in her eyes as she bound me in place, and the water she added wasn't enough to scald. This time, she also didn't add bubble bath, instead she engaged the jets and began her quest to slowly drive me insane with her hands and mouth and body.

After she had her way with me, we snuggled in the warm jets with glasses of champagne, and I fed her strawberries as we watched the moon's progress over the water.

"I think we finally beat him," she said, after the comfortable silence settled between us.

My heart soared.

Angel Wrath Chapter 4

WE WALKED PAST THE security lines and Valerie cocked her head at me.

"Private jet," I said, and winked. I had been successful at keeping the honeymoon destination a secret and with the private plane; it would remain so until we landed, unless she took a peek in the pilot's mind. I had packed for the two of us and figured if I missed anything, we could pick it up in Honolulu before we headed out to Turtle Bay.

I navigated her through the terminal into the VIP lounge where we waited for Ted Beaumont to arrive. His family was staying with Steve and Jen down at the lake while Ted flew us to Hawaii. His sleekest private jet sat on the tarmac, and I couldn't wait for Valerie to see the flight accommodations we had. I knew the flight plan and the stop in San Diego was only for gassing the plane up for the last leg of the trip.

I arranged for a limo to drive us to the resort, and from there we'd have two weeks of honeymoon bliss in an ocean-side cottage.

I would have opted for longer, but I had already committed to a show at Carnegie Hall the week after we returned. I almost canceled my singing gig after Damian sprang an unwanted surprise on me at my bachelor party. He didn't know if the portal at the warehouse in New York was actually closed. I almost clocked him when he sprang that doozie on me, and it was enough to want to extend our island adventure just to avoid that fresh hell, but Valerie didn't want to leave her patients for more than two weeks.

Damian had pulled me aside and wanted me to make a side trip while I was in the city. I balked and asked what the hell he actually did that day besides making the building a pile of rubble. He mumbled something about angel fire and said I was the only one who seemed to have that talent down.

That was another piece of information I have successfully kept from Valerie. I wasn't sure I was going to share that planned adventure with her or not. I would rather have her safe in Maine than standing by my side at the place that nearly destroyed both of us. Besides, if it wasn't closed, I knew shutting the portal would tear my insides to shreds. Guilt was a funny thing, even with the promises I'd made in heaven. The fact my father was rotting in hell conflicted with the desire to close the devil's topside access because that meant one less avenue my father could use to escape.

"Are you okay?" Valerie asked, catching a whiff of the sadness that had crept into my heart.

"Yeah. I just wish my parents had been there to see us get married." I pulled her hand to my lips. "I'm sure you feel the same," I added, knowing her family had been snuffed by Lucifer, as well.

She pressed her lips together, offering a tight smile of agreement. "Where are we going?" she asked after a few beats of silence.

I opened my mouth and then closed it, narrowing my eyes at her. "Oh, no you don't." She'd almost tricked me into spilling the surprise, and I shook my head. "Are you coming down to the Carnegie Hall show?" I asked, switching topics on her.

She chewed on her lip, moving her gaze away, toward the window. "I'm not sure. It depends what Martha puts on my schedule," she replied. "I'd like to, but it's usually my on-call day and I don't think it's fair if I bag out after taking almost three weeks off."

I gave her a small nod. She had taken the week before the wedding off, as well, and I saw her point. In some ways, it was a relief, but not having her with me would really up the ante where my anxiety was concerned. "Would you mind staying with Damian and Naomi while I'm gone?"

"Not at all. It'll give me a chance to share the wedding pictures with Naomi, as well as whatever we take on our honeymoon. Plus, I always love spending time with the kids."

I exhaled, relaxing a fraction. I would miss her in New York, but at least I could make sure she was safe, and she didn't question my motives. She knew how unhinged I got when she's out of sight.

"Are you staying with Steve and Jen?"

"Yes. Jen is excited about singing with me again." I stretched, yawning, and she chuckled.

"Aw, did I tire you out last night?"

I laughed and nodded, draping my arm over her shoulder. "You completely crushed any hope of me having energy this morning," I answered. "And I couldn't be happier." I planted a kiss on her cheek.

"Hey there, Mr. and Mrs. Ryan," Ted said, as he approached in his formal pilot uniform.

I grinned and stood, taking his outstretched hand. "Hi, Ted. You didn't have to get all formal on us," I said, waving to his get up.

"It's part of the job." He winked and grabbed one of our rolling suitcases, leading us out on the tarmac.

"Valerie has been trying to get me to slip on our destination for weeks." I said as we climbed the stairs into the plane.

Ted glanced over his shoulder, raising a brow at her. "Sneaky guy, isn't he?"

"Yes." Valerie laughed, and her eyes narrowed in concentration.

"Don't even think about it," I whispered in her ear, already knowing she was trying to pick his brain.

All attempts at getting the information from Ted stopped the minute we stepped inside the jet's cabin. I vaguely remember the last trip to Atlanta when I was eight and I thought that plane was posh, but this one took the cake. There was a giant screen television on the wall that separated the cabin from the captain's deck. A couch and two captain's chairs were situated mid-cabin, then there was a round dining table with two chairs that was set with a magnificent breakfast. A small kitchenette stood opposite the table and the cabinets were stocked with snacks. The refrigerator held both wine and sodas, as well.

"There's more beyond that door," Ted said, and turned toward the cockpit. He stashed our luggage in the closet as we started toward the door beyond the kitchenette.

I opened the door and stopped. I'm sure my jaw hung open, but beyond the cozy living room area sat a plush bedroom.

"Chris?" Valerie asked from behind me, and I opened the door all the way, standing to the side so she could see the private jet bedroom.

I was impressed, but she, she was floored. "This is more beautiful than the hotel room," she said, stepping inside. Her eyes didn't know where to go to first.

I smiled and crossed to the doorway beyond the bed, assuming it was the bathroom. I was right, but it wasn't like any plane bathroom I ever saw. The only thing missing was a whirlpool tub, and it would have been just as nice as our bridal suite room last night.

"I trust this is acceptable?" Ted asked from the doorway.

I laughed and nodded. "Way more than just acceptable. This is superb. When did you get this?"

Ted grinned. "I acquired this puppy about six months ago. Business has been good, so, when this was listed, I looked into it." He shrugged. "It was too good to pass up."

"This must have set you back a bit," I said. Just on the first survey of the interior, I would have guessed this ran near twenty to thirty million.

"It'll pay for itself within a few years," he said with a smile.

"Business is that good?" I asked, shocked at the cost of recovery time.

His smile deepened. "Yep. Especially with clients like your family." He pointed at me and headed back toward the cockpit. "We'll be up in a few minutes, so settle in up in the front and I'll let you know when you can indulge."

This was the one thing Steve always splurged on, and I think Tom and I were just so used to the convenience that it never occurred to us to take a commercial flight. Besides, commercial airlines were just so crowded and unreliable these days and Ted's company was always available, even at the drop of a hat.

I escorted Valerie to the captain's chairs, grabbing a piece of fruit from the table as we passed. She did the same, and we hooked the lap belts in place, waiting for our flight to be given the go ahead. I wondered if the cockpit was as nice as the rest of this plane. The last one was comfortable, but then again, I was eight.

"You've been in the cockpit?" Valerie asked, and I smiled, waiting for her to find the memory. When she did, she cocked her head and glanced around. "This plane is a lot nicer," she commented and met my glance.

"Yes, it is." I threaded my fingers through hers, and she brought my hand to her lips.

Instead of just kissing the back of my hand, like I assumed she would, she sucked my finger, pulling it out slowly in an insinuation of what she wanted to do once we were at cruising altitude.

"You don't want to see the cockpit?" I couldn't keep a straight face.

"Do we have time?" she asked, and I looked up at the ceiling, calculating the time to destination.

"I think so," I said, bringing my gaze back to her with a grin.

"Where are we going?" she asked as the plane taxied.

"Somewhere over the rainbow," I sang, and she yanked her hand from mine, swatting my arm in frustration.

"You're an ass," she muttered and crossed her arms.

"You like my fine ass," I said, and stretched my legs out in the open space, snuggling into the seat.

"Yeah, well, just because I married your fine ass doesn't mean I like it at the moment," she said, smirking.

The light-hearted spirit remained as the engines increased and the plane took off in an arc into the sky. As soon as we smoothed out, I unbuckled and took a seat at the table. Valerie spun the chair toward me with a creased brow.

"It's a private jet. They don't have a seatbelt sign," I said. "Come have breakfast." I pointed to the opposite chair and lifted the glass cover from the small grooves holding the plate in place. The berry filled crepes tasted like a small slice of heaven and I had to give it to Ted. He sure knew how to pamper his clientele.

"Oh, my god, these are fantastic," Valerie said around her first bite.

Neither of us had eaten breakfast this morning. We woke up later than either of us had wanted, and I had to push the speed limit to get to Logan on time, so this gourmet meal was well received by both of us, and we devoured the food.

I folded my napkin and regarded the sprinkle of confectionary sugar on Valerie's lips. I leaned over the table and licked the sweet confection before I trapped her in a soft kiss. I pulled away and planted my butt back in the seat, just taking all this in.

Through her eyes, this was quite the extravagance, but for me, it was just another plane ride. I guess this was one of the spoils of the rich that I took for granted.

"You aren't taking me to a deserted island that you happen to own, right?" she asked, prying again.

I chuckled. "I don't own an island," I said. "But Tom and I do have a place on the French Riviera and a cottage in the Caribbean."

"Really?"

"Yep, but we aren't going to either of those places," I replied.

"Did you grab my passport?" she asked, and I smiled.

"Of course," I said, and although I really didn't need it, having it threw her off the mark.

She chewed on her lip. "The French Riviera?"

"Yes. It's actually a rental property now. Same with the cottage on Grand Cayman."

"So, you have to rent it?"

I chuckled and raised an eyebrow. "You want to become a jet-setter?"

Blush bloomed in her cheeks, and she wiped her mouth, placing the napkin over her empty plate. "No," she said, but her statement lacked conviction.

Before I could razz her on her newfound travel bug, the cockpit door opened. Ted smiled as he stepped through the door.

"I see you didn't waste any time on those," he said, nodding toward our empty plates.

"They were fantastic," Valerie said, as she swiveled in her seat.

"Heather made them," he said, beaming. "We figured you two were the best guinea pigs to try her recipes."

"Do you mind if I look at the setup up there?" I asked, pointing toward the cockpit.

"Not at all," he said and cleared the plates.

"You're our steward?" I asked, a little surprised. Usually, we had a perky stewardess besides the pilot on board.

"Doing double duty. I could only shuffle a co-pilot for this jaunt," he said and shrugged. "Thus, the pre-set meal." He stowed the plates in a dish rack under the counter. "And the opportunity to make use of Heather's culinary talents."

"Thanks," I said, suddenly uncomfortable that I put him in the tight scheduling spot.

"Don't sweat it, CJ," he said, as he ran a cloth over the table and smiled at the two of us. "I would expect from this point forward, if you need something, you'll give us a buzz," he said, and sent a wink in my direction.

My cheeks heated, and I glanced at Valerie before I nodded. He fully expected us to make use of the bedroom during the flight.

"We will stop to refuel in about four hours," he said, glancing at his watch and then at the two of us. "Is there anything else I can get you?"

"I'm sure we can figure things out," I said and stood. "But first, I want to see the cockpit."

Valerie's surprised expression caught the corner of my eye as I passed, and I stopped. "Do you want to see?"

She scrambled out of the seat, her face lighting up at the unique opportunity and we followed Ted beyond the living space into the extra-large cockpit. Besides the comfortable leather seats and modern flight panel, they had their own bathroom, which looked more like the bathrooms on commercial flights than the extravagant bathroom we had at our disposal. They also had a small fridge, microwave and coffeemaker, so they didn't have to invade the customer space to hydrate or relieve themselves.

It was just as sweet as the rest of the plane. "Nice," I said scanning the room one more time. "Hey, Jeff," I said to the familiar co-pilot.

"Hello, Mr. Ryan," he said, in that formal way that always made me uncomfortable.

"This is my wife, Valerie. Val, this is Jeff, one of Ted's pilots."

"It is a pleasure to meet you, Mrs. Ryan," he said, and gave her a nod.

"Nice to meet you, too," Valerie said. She was still in awe of the expanse of sky surrounding them, but she offered a glance and a smile before her eyes drifted back to the spectacular scene.

With that, I wrapped my arm around her waist and escorted her back to our oasis in the sky. I gave Ted a nod, and he shut the door behind us, getting back to the business of flying the plane.

"I hate to admit it, but I could get used to this," Valerie said, as we crossed into the bedroom quarters.

I closed the door and turned toward her, aware that I held the hungry look that triggered her fear, but this time, I figured we'd already pushed the boundaries and succeeded. I wanted to dominate today, but without the bonds. There was one more memory that I needed to cleanse and now was the perfect opportunity.

I stalked towards her and this time when she stiffened; I didn't stop until my arms captured her, pulling her against my body. Her breath caught in her throat and her panicked eyes widened. Without words, I crushed her lips under mine, taking control for the first time since before I returned from the dead.

"I'm going to take you to heaven," I whispered against her lips.

I'm not sure if it was my words, or the insistence in my mind that made her mouth part, giving my tongue access to intertwine with hers. The kiss, as always, stopped time and space and when we broke free from each other, she just stared into my eyes.

"Chris," she started, and I shook my head, stopping her.

"Today is my day," I said, staring her down in an attempt to break that last barrier. Her hesitation burned, but this time, I wasn't backing down. Instead, I dipped my mouth to her neck, taking the time to nip the skin before I traced a line with my tongue from her collarbone to behind her ear. Her skin broke out in gooseflesh when I nipped at her earlobe. "I want to make you wetter than Niagara Falls before I make love to you."

Her skin paled, and I grinned, slowly untying the ties that held her pretty sundress in place. The dress fell to the ground around her feet, and she still hadn't moved. I stripped my shirt, tossing it over my shoulders in a grand spectacle.

"Baby, get ready to join the mile high club," I added, and dropped my shorts.

She blinked at me as I stepped close, staring down at her upturned face.

"It's time for me to kill the last strangle hold he has on you."

She stepped away from me, right onto the mattress, and I followed, knowing I held that predatory demeanor that scared the shit out of her. She scrambled backwards, farther onto the bed, and I crawled over her, keeping up with her mad dash before she hit the headboard with nowhere else to go.

Color bloomed in her cheeks, and before she could do any damage, I dropped my weight on her, pinning her to the bed, and I kissed her again. She resisted at first and then her arms wrapped around me, pulling the kiss from feral to burning hot.

Her chest heaved under me, and I broke away from her grasp, reversing my path, using my mouth to heighten her pleasure. It seemed like forever since I'd explored her with my mouth and my hands together. Despite the tension in her muscles, I continued my southerly route, taking my time on her breasts and her stomach, meeting her gaze every now and then and flashing a smile of satisfaction at the fact the conflict in her eyes was transitioning to the deep want I felt every time we touched.

The moment my mouth settled between her legs, her entire body stiffened, and the fear flared in her eyes. I slowly licked her and met her gaze. "Complete mind fuck," I whispered and something about that phrase settled her fear. She actually smiled at me and the triumph that ripped through me was surreal. Almost as surreal as the orgasm I brought her to moments later.

Niagara Falls. Yep, I achieved my goal and when I finally slid inside her writhing form; it was better than anything I'd imagined over the past two years. Making love to my wife and seeing her find her sense of abandon again was soul affirming.

Angel Wrath Chapter 5

"YOU WEREN'T A MEMBER of the mile high club before this, right?" she asked, turning her head toward me as we lay side by side, spent, on the lush satin fabric.

I grinned and slid my gaze to hers. She already knew the answer, but I still shook my head. "No. You're it, babe."

She let out a soft chuckle. "I really want to tie you up now," she said, and I sent her a raised eyebrow.

"I don't know if I have the energy for that," I said, and she rolled on top of me, grabbed my wrists, and pinned them next to my head.

"Well, find some," she whispered, and nipped at my throat. I smiled up at her. "Where are we going?" she asked.

"You'll love it," I said.

"How do you know?"

"Because it's on your list of things to see before you die."

She let go of my wrists and sat up, her mind wrestling with all the places she wanted to go. There were at least a dozen options, and she puckered her lips in that way that made me want to crush them under mine.

I ran my hands over the smooth skin of her thighs while she ticked off the locations in her mind.

"New Zealand?" she asked first.

"You really think we'd only take two weeks to go halfway around the world?"

She bit her lip, staring into my eyes, and I couldn't help the smirk that surfaced. Her dimples appeared briefly, and then she cocked her head to the side. Without asking another question, she leaned down and trailed kisses from my throat to my cock.

The tease was on, and I grinned, putting my hands behind my head as she slid her lips over my tip. I came to life in her mouth, and with her slow stroke, my eyes rolled back. After a while, I had to restrain myself from grabbing hold of her head and moving at the pace I wanted. The slow burn she was producing catapulted me into the realm of insanity.

"Shit, Val." I squeezed a handful of the back of my hair to keep my hands in place.

"Tell me where we're going and I'll go faster," she whispered. Her hot breath sent a shiver through me.

I met her gaze and clenched both my teeth, and my mind, not allowing our destination to slip past either. With a shake of my head, she went back to her little game.

"You know, I'm not tied up," I said to her in a low, gruff tone that made her smile.

She didn't miss a beat either. Just kept doing that slow swallow that brought me to the edge. She stopped and blew a stream of air on my wet skin, setting me back a few notches.

"If you move, I'll bite," she whispered, and I stared at her.

I dropped my head back on the pillow, wondering just how long I was going to hold out. If I told her where we were going, I'd get a hell of a reward, but it would spoil the surprise. If I moved to speed this up, she'd bite, and that thought sent a shiver through me, chilling the need to take over.

Her mouth started the slow, insane pace all over again.

"Holy fuck, girl," I breathed out the words, forcing my arms to stay in place, wishing I was tied up because it would be easier fighting the bindings than my own internal fire.

My eyes rolled, and every cell clenched. My head tilted back, and I groaned. Every inch of my body ached for release, and she knew it.

"Where?"

"To the fucking moon and back," I whispered, and I didn't give a damn anymore. My hands moved into her hair, and I held her in place, willing her to finish what she started.

It only took three more strokes before I exploded like Mount Vesuvius, and Valerie swallowed every drop. When I finally released her, she sent the most infuriating glare in my direction.

I sat up, despite my trembling muscles, and took her face between my palms. "You know I love you."

She rolled her eyes. "You're not going to tell me where we are going, are you?"

I couldn't help but laugh. "No. I'm not."

"Royal pain in my ass." She climbed out of the bed, heading into the bathroom to freshen up. I glanced at the clock, calculating the time, before following her into the shower.

Warm water cascaded over us, and we washed without toying around. I was exhausted and needed either a nap or some more food and I could tell from the sluggish movements of my wife, she was in the same boat as I was.

I stepped out of the shower first and wrapped one of the plush towels around my waist before starting the search for our clothing. The clothes were flung in different directions, and I gathered all of them, dumping the pile on the chair before pulling my boxers on. With her underwear in hand, I stepped to the bathroom door just in time to see a towel wrap around her gorgeous body, blocking my interested view.

Dangling her undergarment on my index finger, I smiled. "Sustenance or sleep?" I asked. I knew which one took priority in my mind and I yawned, voicing my preference by my actions alone.

"Sleep." She slid her underwear on before towel drying her hair.

We fell into bed, and I pulled her into me. I don't even remember my eyes closing.

My father's scream of pain ripped through me, and I sat up, panting. My eyes darted around the unfamiliar space and my heart clamored in my chest. It took me a few moments to get my bearings.

The roar of the engines broke through the cobwebs, and I closed my eyes, forcing my breath to slow down. Valerie remained softly snoring by my side. "Plane," I whispered and rubbed my face, blinking at the surroundings again.

I wondered if I'd actually heard my father, or if it was just a nightmare. Either way, the guilt crept in, biting and relentless. Instead of lying back down, I slid out of bed and headed into the bathroom to wash the bitterness out of my mouth. I ran wet hands through my hair, trying to tame the wild bedhead I sported before I slipped on my clothing and headed to the front of the plane to find out where we were.

I slowed to a stop at the new food spread on the table. Ted had already set our lunches, and I crossed to the window. Nothing but blue sea met my gaze and my eyebrows rose. We must have slept through the landing, refueling, and take-off in San Diego.

Tearing my gaze away from what I assumed was the vast Pacific, I knocked on the cockpit door.

The door opened and Ted tried to suppress a knowing grin, but he didn't do a very good job of it. His silent assumptions were pretty much on target, and I shifted under a wave of discomfort. Even though Ted had known me since I was a little kid, his silent high five still made me feel like I had done something sneaky. Heat filled my cheeks, and I dropped my gaze.

"Where are we?" I asked, doing my best to ignore the urge to apologize for my behavior.

Ted gave my shoulder a pat, and I met his amused gaze.

"You're married now, son. It's okay," he said, addressing my discomfort before he cleared his throat and adopted a more professional demeanor. "We are a couple of hours out from our destination. I set up your lunch a little while ago, so relax and enjoy the rest of the flight."

"Thank you," I said, and he gave me a nod before his gaze moved toward the bedroom. I turned and Valerie stood in the entry. Her hand combed hair and rosy cheeks made me smile.

"I'll let you know when we're on our landing approach." Ted closed the door, leaving me with my curious wife.

"Where are we?" she asked, rubbing her eyes and covering a yawn.

"Over an ocean," I said, being cryptically generic on purpose.

Her lips thinned, and she crossed her arms. "Which ocean?"

"A big one." I grinned and walked to her, planting a kiss that lingered. "Come on, let's eat," I said, and pulled her towards the table.

The minute her gaze landed on the food, her mind switched gears, focusing on staunching her sudden hunger pangs. She took a seat and lifted the glass cover, revealing the succulent steak salad presented below. I grabbed a couple of waters from the refrigerator and followed her lead. Within minutes, both our plates were picked clean.

Valerie snickered as she opened her water. "I guess we both worked up an appetite."

"No kidding," I said, and chugged my water. "Want to watch a movie?" I asked once I finished draining the water bottle.

"We have time?"

"Yep," I answered and stood, stretching my tired muscles.

"How long were we asleep?"

She was fishing, and I shrugged. If my math was correct, we had to have been asleep for close to four hours, which equated to a little more than half the trip. Our sexual romp was a solid hour and a half, if not longer, so we had just enough time to fit in a two-hour movie before we landed in paradise.

"What if I want to watch War and Peace?" She slung her arm over the back of the chair, cocking her head in that challenging way.

"Then you'd be shit out of luck," I said.

"So, we aren't traveling to the other side of the globe," she said, and the slow grin spread.

"You have no clue how long we slept," I pointed out, and replaced the glass cover so it wouldn't fall if we hit turbulence or when we landed. She did the same, and we moved to the captain's chairs facing the television screen.

"What about Lord of the Rings Trilogy?" she asked, and I rolled my eyes, turning my gaze towards her.

"How about something a little lighter?" I wasn't in the mood for battles between good and evil. We already lived that on a daily basis.

"Like what?"

"I don't know," I shrugged. "Something funny?" I handed her the remote when the movie choices appeared.

She scrolled down the list, landing on *The Avengers* and shot me an arched brow. She knew the Marvel franchise had some of my favorites, but I was looking for more of a comedy, even though this one supplied some decent laughs.

"Lighter," I said, and she continued scrolling.

She leaned forward and pressed play before I could see what she landed on. When the opening credits rolled, I glanced at her.

"Reese Witherspoon?" I asked, and she nodded. "You picked a chick flick?"

"It's funny. You'll see," she said, and I settled into the chair, crossing my arms.

Even though my skeptical radar was pinging, I tried not to pass judgment too fast. "What is it?" I sighed.

"This Means War," she answered at the same moment the title appeared on screen.

The opening scene showed promise and I uncrossed my arms, taking her hand in mine. When the final credits rolled, I pulled her closer, planting a kiss. "That wasn't bad," I said when our lips parted. "But I'd still categorize it as a chick flick," I added with a smile.

"You wanted light and funny." She shrugged.

"And you delivered."

She grinned. I didn't have time to explore the spark behind that grin because Ted poked his head out from the cockpit.

"We're beginning our descent," he said, and Valerie's gaze jumped to the windows before the door even closed.

She started to get up, and I clamped down on her hand.

"Seatbelt," I said and tried not to smile at the aggravation etched in the creases around her mouth. "You only have a couple of more minutes, and then you will know our honeymoon destination."

She rolled her eyes and sighed, clasping the belt together, succumbing to the reality that I was able to keep this a secret right to the last second.

I didn't offer the promise that she'll love it. Instead, I just glanced out the windows as the scenery changed from the ocean to lush greens, and as we descended, the cityscape of Honolulu filled the windows.

Of course, Valerie didn't recognize the city, but she had enough of a view to know it fell into the tropical category. The bump of the landing gear followed, and before we came to a full stop, she was out of the chair and leaning on the couch overlooking the airport.

Her building excitement made me smile, and she turned towards me.

"Hawaii?"

I smiled and raised my eyebrows, cocking my head. "It is on your list, right?"

She actually squealed and my grin widened.

"Waikiki?"

I shook my head and her smile faded as she bit her lip, trying to guess where I would hole us up for two weeks.

"So, what do you have planned? Two weeks in a beach bungalow?"

I grinned. "While I would love exploring—you, for two weeks—I thought we'd like to do a little exploring outside of the bedroom," I said, and sent a wink in her direction. "I scheduled a few... excursions."

"Why is it you can make anything sound dirty?" she asked, putting her hands on her hips.

I chuckled and rolled my eyes. "Because I've mastered the art of making a stutter sound cool."

She burst out laughing.

The engines powered down and Ted opened the door, collecting our baggage from the closet. When we climbed down the stairs to the tarmac, a Bentley limousine waited along with a driver. Ted handed the driver our bags and turned to me, extending his hand.

"Two weeks?"

"Ayup." I smiled. "Thanks for the smooth flight and stellar accommodations," I said and shook his hand. "See you in two weeks."

I helped Valerie into the back of the Bentley, and she grinned at the single rose laid across the seat and the bottle of champagne chilling next to two crystal flutes.

"Nice touch," she smiled up at me and slid to the other side of the car while our luggage was stowed in the trunk.

I took a seat next to her and gave her a peck on the cheek before pouring her a glass of champagne. The driver gave me a nod and closed the door, encasing us in a luxurious wrapper for the hour-long scenic ride up Oahu's eastern shore.

I tapped my glass against hers. "Welcome to paradise, Mrs. Ryan."

"Hopeless," she whispered, and I grinned.

"I told you; I wanted the fairy tale."

"You are so much sappier than I am." Her light laugh filled the car, and she sipped the bubbly before focusing on the world around us. The lush green mountainside swallowed us before relinquishing the car to the populated center of Kaneohe. The driver took us up the coast highways, giving us breathtaking views of the Pacific and the pristine shoreline beaches.

Her eyebrows rose as we pulled off the highway and followed the signs toward Turtle Bay; the excitement in her eyes sparked.

"The north shore?"

I grinned. "Killer surfing." The waves that I saw rolling in on the eastern shore put the ones I rode on York Beach to shame, and I couldn't wait to give these a go.

Concern passed her features, and I rolled my eyes.

"I want to take on Waimea Bay, even though it's a little early for the big winter waves."

Her lower lip disappeared between her teeth.

"Honey, I'll be fine. Besides, it's only one day. I have us booked for horseback riding, snorkeling, helicopter tours, dinner cruises and a couple of spa days, too."

"Spa days?"

"Yes. I figure after a day of activity; we might want a massage."

"I really thought you'd just want to hang out in bed for two weeks."

I chuckled and rolled the glass stem between my fingers. The car slowed to a stop next to one of the luxury cabanas and I met her gaze. "Hold that thought," I said as the driver stepped out and opened my door. I peeled off a couple of one-hundred-dollar bills and handed them to the driver before helping Valerie out of the car.

A bellhop took our bags and handed me the keys after opening the door. The suite was perfect; with a king-sized bed, a small sitting area that lead right out to the small patio, and the beach beyond the small grass yard. I had made sure we were in the most remote of the cottage clusters and that the other three rooms were unoccupied for the duration of our stay. We could even cottage hop between the four rooms if we so chose, but I didn't want to bring that up just yet. Not with her wide-eyed stare at the nicest of the four rooms laid out in front of her.

A candlelight dinner waited for us on the terrace just like I had planned, and Valerie turned towards me, waving her hand at the butler waiting for us to take a seat.

"Wow. You pulled out all the stops," she said, and leaned up to give me a kiss. "I'll be right out." Valerie disappeared into the bathroom, and I handed the bellhop a one-hundred-dollar bill.

He stared at it for a moment, and then his gaze jumped to mine. "I'm sorry, sir, but I don't have change," he said, his cheeks filling with blush while his mind categorized the tip as a mistake and not intentional.

"That's for you," I said with a smile, closely watching his eyes blink rapidly and his jaw pop open for a moment.

"You realize this is a one-hundred-dollar bill," he said, just to make sure I knew.

"Yes. I'm well aware," I answered. He blinked and then pressed his lips together against a grin.

"Thank you, sir," he said and slipped out the front door, closing it behind him.

I chuckled at his reaction, enjoying the shock as well as the conflict of emotions the bellhop displayed. In that respect, I was a lot like my father. My smile faded as my dad crossed my mind. A weight pressed on my chest, and I turned my gaze to the glorious sunset, wishing he wasn't in a place where he'd never see beauty like this again.

Valerie stepped out of the bathroom, her face newly washed and her hair combed back into place. Her gentle kiss on my cheek reminded me of everything he sacrificed. Sensing my melancholy, she wrapped her arms around me in that way that made me forget where I was, and my hands found her waist. Her stormy eyes drew me in, and I smiled.

"Thank you," I whispered, and she turned her head toward the waiting meal. Mai Tais and Mahi Mahi graced the table, and I pulled out her chair for her, giving her the full ocean view.

The butler filled each water glass and then disappeared, leaving us to dine in peace.

"You were going to tell me why we aren't spending two weeks in this room?" she asked, her lips toying with a smile.

I laughed and heat filled my cheeks. "Honestly?"

She nodded and dug into the meal.

"I didn't want to be tied to a bed for two weeks," I muttered under my breath, focusing on my food instead of her reaction. When I booked the trip, she hadn't gotten over her need to dominate and I was dead set against living that way for the duration of our honeymoon.

Her hands froze in place, and I chanced raising my eyes. I expected a glare, but not the cautious study she was performing on my profile.

"I, uh, I thought you liked that," she said, and I sighed.

"Yes, and no." I focused on my meal while I tried to put the conflict into words. She waited a moment before resuming eating.

The silent clank of silverware against china filled the space between us and I looked out at the water before setting my fork and knife down.

"It was exciting when we first tried it out, but after I came back..." I trailed off at the hurt blooming in her eyes. "It was the only way to get past our, um, issues." I shrugged. "And I loved you enough to suck it up until you got past it."

She just stared, her mind reeling from the revelation.

"Come on, you knew it wasn't comfortable for me," I said, leaning back in the chair. "A couple of times you purposely hurt me, like your subconscious was acting out against my image."

"I most certainly did not," she muttered, and wiped her mouth.

"Uh, yeah, you did." I picked up my drink and drained it, thinking back to the time she dislocated my shoulder and another time when she tried metal wire. My pain seemed to fuel her, giving her some underlying sense of satisfaction that was far more visceral than the sexual release.

Valerie met my gaze, and she bit her lip. "I'm sorry," she said, and hung her head.

I set my glass on the table and reached for her, cupping her chin in my hand and tilting her head towards me. I waited until she met my stare.

"No apologies nec…essary," I pushed out the words, annoyed the stutter showed up now. "You did what you had to do to get past it." I caressed her cheek with my thumb before I dropped my hand back on the table.

"I just…" she trailed off and glanced at the beauty surrounding us.

"I know," I said, pulling her gaze back. "And I'll still let you from time to time, but it won't be the norm, okay?"

"I'm not sure I could reciprocate," she mumbled.

"We pushed some boundaries already. We could try that out, as well," I asked and cursed the hopeful lilt of my voice. The time I tied her to my bedposts was still fresh in my mind, even though it was over two years ago. The power trip was just as satisfying as the sex.

Of course, Lucifer used that to his advantage when he stole my form, and the damage he did was so deep in Valerie that I think if I tried tying her in place, I might end up pushing us back to square one.

Her sharp laugh cut the conversation off just as much as her glare.

"It was worth a try," I said, and the inappropriate grin surfaced. "Besides, I like the feel of your hands on me." I backtracked, trying to bring us back from the darkness of our past.

"I forgot how good yours felt on me," she said, and the grays and blues in her eyes swirled. Her cheeks reddened at the thoughts streaming through her head of last night and today.

I pulled her to my lips, tasting her and letting our tongues intertwine in the slow dance of seduction. A throat cleared, and we jerked away from each other, our gazes jumping to the butler who had returned with dessert.

He cleared our plates and set down the crème brûlée encased in an almond brittle cup in front of each of us.

The bed of fresh berries under it made for just the right color palette. Before he left, he handed me the room charge, and I scribbled my name and room number and handed it back along with another one-hundred-dollar tip.

"Thank you, sir, madam, have a nice evening." And with that, he disappeared with dinner dishes balanced on a tray.

"If you plan on eating like this every day, I'm going to be eight hundred pounds by the time we get home," Valerie said. When she took the first bite of the dessert, she closed her eyes. "My god, this is delicious."

I couldn't have said it any better and focused on inhaling every bite.

"Want to go for a walk on the beach or..." I glanced over at the bed before returning my gaze to hers.

I thought, by the soft smile that appeared, she was going to say we needed to break in the bed. "Walk," she replied, and a mischievous light danced in her eyes.

Disappointment flushed through me, and she grinned.

"We have all the time in the world for that," she whispered and kissed my cheek as she stood. Valerie walked down the steps onto the grass and crossed to the small incline leading to the sand.

"God, I hope so," I said but a nagging feeling disrupted the peaceful setting. My fun and games would end the moment I stepped back in York and started closing the portals in earnest. I stood and crossed to her, trying to shed my sense of foreboding.

Angel Wrath Chapter 6

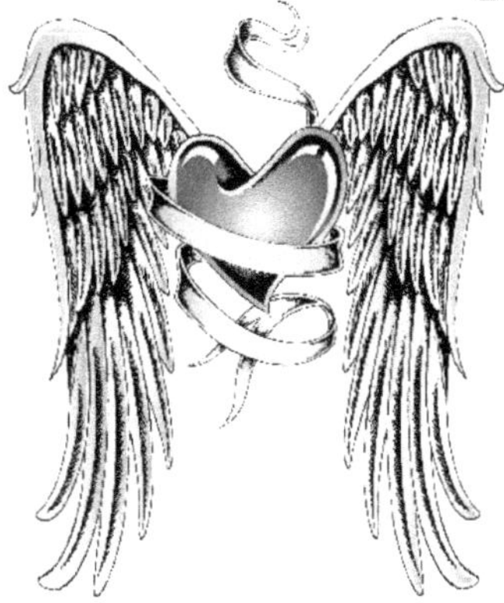

I SAT ON THE beach in awe of the ocean's power. The cadence of the waves lulled me into a state of relaxation that even the massage we had couldn't give me. Valerie lay on her stomach next to me, reading a book on her kindle. The surfboard I rented sat unused on the sand. I grabbed the ankle tie and clasped the Velcro together on my leg before leaning over and kissing Valerie's shoulder.

"It's time for me to tackle that," I said, nodding toward the ocean.

She glanced at the fifteen-foot waves and then at me. "You're crazy, you know that?"

I grinned and hopped to my feet. "I've only seen this kind of surf during a hurricane in York, and these aren't even as big as they get." I tried to convey the excitement zinging through my muscles, but she had never surfed and didn't know the feeling of flirting with the ocean the way a surfer does. It's an extension of our soul, and there was no way to describe that to her.

"Be careful," she called after me, and I glanced back with a shrug.

Respectful of the forces of nature in play was a more appropriate mind set. The volume of each crashing wave was ten times that of what we had in Southern Maine, and it pounded along with my heart. Man, did I feel alive.

The rush was more of a buildup than the zip-line we had done earlier in the week and the water here didn't numb on contact like Maine. It was more like bathwater, and I waded in and climbed onto my board, paddling out beyond the breakers. The idea of sharks never phased me like it did some people, and perhaps that's because I could project a protective net predators couldn't penetrate.

The freedom I felt when I hopped up on the board and rode that wave, cresting and cutting through the water, made me forget all the shit I had been through. The only other time I lost myself like this was when Valerie and I kissed.

I even caught the smile on Valerie's lips after the first few sets and when I finally cruised into shore and walked up to her, she stood on her tiptoes and planted a kiss.

"You're amazing," she whispered in my ear.

I grinned. "I'll show you amazing when we get back."

She bit her lip, sucking it in her mouth in that way that made me want to strip her right now. "I think I've had a little too much sun today," she said and smiled. "And I'd like to see your definition of amazing."

"You'll have to hold that thought a little longer. We've got a sunset horseback ride tonight."

"Really?" She perked up, and I laughed.

"Yeah. I thought it would be kind of cool," I said and kissed her cheek. "I'll be right back; I need to return this." I tapped the board and headed toward the surf shop on the edge of the beach.

By the time I finished settling up with the rental shop, Valerie was waiting by the door with all our stuff. We took a seat on one of the benches in the parking lot, waiting for the car service I contracted to take us wherever we wanted during the two weeks. I had texted when I returned the surfboard, knowing it would be a little while for the driver to get from Turtle Bay down to Waimea Bay.

"Do we have to go back home?" Valerie asked, and I glanced at her with a smile.

"We could always stay here. Live a simple island life," I said. Of course, my idea of simple would be an ocean view paradise with a private beach and she knew it. It wouldn't be a little shack by any means.

I saw the draw in her eyes, the possibilities and then her thoughts went to her patients, and she sighed. People counted on her, and to just up and disappear wasn't in her nature.

"You'd miss your family," she said.

"Yeah. So would you," I added and got a nod of affirmation. She had gotten very close with Raven. Closer than she was with Naomi, and I think it had to do with the abuse Raven encountered at her father's hands. Between Raven and Jennifer, it was clear you can shed your past if you put your mind to it.

The car drove to a stop in front of us and the driver stepped out, opening the back door for us with flair.

"Enough sun today, Mr. Ryan?"

"Yes, Akamu. My wife has more of a tendency to burn than I do." I smiled, peeking at the hint of pink cropping up on her shoulders. "Thank you for getting here so quickly."

He gave me a nod, and I slid into the car before he closed the door. The sun danced on the water as we rode east, and I couldn't help the thought creep. All that talk about family as we were leaving made my mind wander.

"What if I can save him?" I glanced at Valerie.

She met my gaze and said nothing. This was a conversation we'd visited a couple of times since my father's sacrifice and she was dead set against me going up against Lucifer, and even more leery of me trying to put together a rescue mission.

"You know how I feel."

"I know. But the question still stands. What if I can?"

"What if you try and end up getting killed?"

It was her normal argument. The one that always burned, because if I failed and died, my father would be pissed. I had to live with the guilt of his sacrifice, and the knowledge that if I disappoint him or screw up, his sacrifice was for nothing. It sucked.

I hung my head a moment, resting my elbows on my knees in the spacious limousine. Her hand landed on my back and her gentle scratching was meant to console, but it didn't. There wasn't anything anyone could do to take this away. The only thing that would clear my conscience was saving him from hell.

Angel Wrath Chapter 7

A KAMU HELD THE DOOR to our cottage open while we carted our beach crap inside. The sun was still high enough in the sky to create odd shadows on the walls, and Valerie dumped her stuff on a chair near the sliding screens before pushing them all the way open.

"Will you need me again this evening?" Akamu asked, and I focused on him.

"No, I think..."

His face turned pale and his eyes nearly bugged out of his head. The saliva in my mouth dried and my head whipped in Valerie's direction in time to see a clawed hand swinging toward her back.

With no thought, I stuck my hand out like I was stopping traffic and sent a blast of power at the thing. It flew into the far wall with a yelp. I held it still.

Valerie spun at the sound, and she stumbled backwards, away from the thing. Neither of us had any words to describe this thing, but Akamu did.

"Kupua," he gasped, and my head turned back in his direction while I held the thing in place.

"What?" I snapped, and his gaze jumped to mine. Akamu's audible gulp might have been funny if the thing wasn't pressing against my invisible hold.

He waved his hand nervously at the thing snarling against the wall. "Kupua... monster," he said, his voice shaking just as much as the rest of him.

I gave a nod and focused back on the thing that would have sliced Valerie if his claws ever reached her. I crossed, putting myself between it and her, studying the Kapua. Its pale features reminded me of a vampire, but it had an elongated snout with what looked like shark's teeth. Multiple rows of razor-sharp teeth snarled in my direction and my gaze dropped to the clawed hands.

"You certainly are an ugly motherfucker," I said and met its hollow-eyed gaze.

Akamu still stood plastered to the wall by the door. His broken thought process almost pulled a chuckle from me. He was terrified beyond the ability to move, but I couldn't worry about him at the moment.

"What the hell is it?" Valerie said from behind me, as she peeked over my shoulder.

"Akamu says it's a Kapua."

"What the fuck?" she asked, and I couldn't help the bark of a laugh that escaped.

"Lucifer has plans for you," it breathed, filling the room with the rank stench of the dead.

"Tell me some...thing I don't know."

"Your father broke much faster than Lucifer expected," he snarled. "And now he is coming for you," he added with a grin.

Movement flashed in the corner of my eye and before I could react, I was tackled onto my side. Whatever hit me was up on their feet faster than my blink and my concentration broke, releasing the other snarling beast I held to the wall. The one that attacked me had now cornered Valerie.

This time I didn't fuck around. The pulse of power escaped, toasting the one attacking my wife and I turned toward the other in time to see its pre-launch. Silver flashed through the air, and I blinked as a knife embedded in its throat.

The roar shook the walls, and the thing stumbled toward me. Another power burst turned the beast into dust and the blade clattered to the ground. I glanced toward the door as the first tingle of shock bit through me. Akamu stood with his pant leg pulled up to reveal an empty leather ankle holster.

He met my gaze before his wide eyes glanced at Valerie.

"Are you okay, Mrs. Ryan?" he asked. This time his voice was surer than before.

"Yeah," she said.

I climbed to my feet and hot liquid drizzled down my leg. For a minute I thought I had lost control of my bladder, which, considering the quick turn of events, wouldn't be that farfetched. However, that thought vanished the minute I looked down.

Red saturated my shorts, and shreds of skin hung from my side. The fucker cut me.

"God damn it. I just bought these swim trunks," I muttered and looked at Valerie. My eyebrows arched when she didn't immediately step to my side. Her gaze bounced to our chauffer, and I laughed. "He saw me turn those things to dust. I think we're past the 'shit, we can't show what we've got' stage."

She let out a nervous laugh and stepped to my side, planting the healing kiss. I clenched my teeth against the onslaught of pain as Akamu crossed to his knife. He picked it up, pointing it at us as my side healed from the inside out.

"Fuck, that hurts," I growled, and my fists curled in response. Closing my eyes, the sting of skin thatching together filled my senses, fusing until there was no evidence of having been nearly skewered. When I opened my eyes, I addressed the elephant in the room.

"We're human," I hissed out, meeting his frightened stare.

"No human can do what you two can," he said, his tone just as accusing as I expected.

I sighed and nodded toward the knife. "Where'd you learn to throw like that?"

"What are you?" he said, his voice growing to the pitch of panic.

I grabbed the towel off the chair, wiped the blood off my side, and held the stained cloth out to him. "Have it tested if you want."

The knife dropped a few centimeters, and he stared at the bloody towel, his face a mask of mistrust.

"Real...ly, we're just flesh and blood like you," I said, putting my hand up as the stutter arbitrarily hijacked my speech pattern.

"Who are you?" he asked, his inflection incredulous, but he lowered the knife.

"CJ Ryan," I said, using the name splashed over every news station on the east coast, but I highly doubted my rise to stardom in the singing realm made it this far west.

He shrugged, but my name tickled something in his brain, and he looked at the ground, at the blood drying on the tiles in the bright sunshine. His brow creased, and he looked up.

"The singer? The one who was in a coma for a couple of years?"

I nodded. I guess my story really did go national.

The knife arm lowered to his side and his mind started racing with questions. "I, I didn't put it together," he mumbled and shifted his weight. "Did the coma..." he trailed off and waved the knife at me.

I laughed. "Uh, no. I was born with this, whatever." I waved at the dusty air.

The events of the past few minutes hit him all at once, and his arms shook. When the knife clattered to the ground, I reached to steady him, but his eyes had already rolled into that of a faint. I stopped him before he face planted the floor. After getting his limp body into the chair, I turned toward Valerie.

"The barrier's up. Don't let him leave or he'll fry. I'm taking a quick shower, then I'll clean up that." I pointed to the bloody floor, and she nodded, still looking like the last few minutes hadn't settled in yet.

I needed a moment because the words that shit said had already embedded themselves under my skin and the drying blood started itching. The trail of red blended with the dark stone in the shower stall, and for the first time since I came back from the dead, my demons overwhelmed me.

Breathing became difficult against the imaginary strap tightening across my chest. Tears burned, and I squeezed my eyes closed against the onslaught, letting the shower spray mix with the hot saline leaking from the corner of my eyes. My ragged breath trembled with each silent sob. I couldn't seem to find a voice for the pain.

The bathroom door opened, and I shook the devastation away, sniffling and washing my face under the water.

"You okay?" Valerie's soft voice rose above the steam, and I glanced back at her, meeting her inquisitive gaze.

I thought I had blocked her from my thoughts, but the concern in her was as palpable as my pain. I nodded anyway, and shot her a smile, or at least what I hoped was a smile. I wasn't sure I pulled it off when her gaze lingered.

"Akamu is awake," she said. "And I wiped up the mess as best I could with our beach towels."

"You didn't have to do that," I said and shut the valve off. I wrapped a bath towel around my waist and sighed. "Grab me a pair of shorts?" I asked.

She disappeared, and I ran a comb through my wet hair. Going through the motions brought some sanity back and the strap around my chest released, allowing me to draw in a breath without force. I moved my gaze from my reflection to the door when she stepped in and handed me my clothes.

"He's getting antsy."

"I'll be right out," I snapped, and nearly tore the clothes from her grip.

Her sudden flinch and step back told me just how harshly my spoken response had been. Before I could say I was sorry, her jaw tightened, and she spun away, slamming the door on my attempt to get her attention.

I gathered the bloody swim trunks and deposited it in the garbage before stepping into the main room. "Val, why don't you go clean up while Akamu and I talk," I said, forcing my voice to come out soft and calm.

I waited while she gathered her things, and the moment she closed the bathroom door; I turned to Akamu. His complexion was near green, and I crossed to the refrigerator, pulling out a ginger ale. He pressed himself farther into the chair as I approached.

I offered the soda to him, and his gaze bounced between the cool can and me until he finally snatched it from my hand. His dagger sat on his lap, and I studied the ornate carvings on the handle and the more subtle designs on the blade.

"Can I see?" I pointed to the knife and his eyebrows rose.

I think he forgot he had his talisman, but when his gaze dropped, some of the fear radiating from him also dropped a notch. In the few seconds he stared at the blade, the true nature of the knife transferred.

"If I wasn't human, I wouldn't be able to hold it?" I asked, and his eyes moved to mine.

"No," he said with more confidence than he felt, and he stared at me when I put my hand out. "It will kill you."

I laughed. "You think?"

My sarcasm didn't impress him, and he shrugged. "It's your funeral," he said and offered the knife to me hilt first. He fully expected something to happen when my skin touched the knife because he flinched and moved back in the seat.

I wrapped my hand around the silver, studying the swirls carved into the blade before I inspected the handle. "What do these mean?" I asked, curious by the artifact I held.

"They are sigils," he muttered, clearly confused. "Symbols meant to protect the holder and destroy the monster."

"I know what sigils are," I said, raising my gaze to his.

"What are you?" he asked again, and awe bled through in his tone.

"I'm just a man," I said, not really interested in explaining the complexity of my heritage and the reason I'm special. It's not something I took pride in, not since I found out some of it came from my connection to Lucifer.

"Right," he said, drawing out the word, and I looked up from my study of the knife.

"I just happen to have a few... gifts that are a bit... abnormal," I said, choosing my words carefully. "And it's obviously not common knowledge," I added, handing the knife back to him before I crossed to the stocked bar and pulled out the whiskey. I needed a shot of something to calm my raw nerves and after I poured a glass for myself, I held up the bottle, extending a silent offer.

He shook his head. "I'm supposed to be driving, remember?"

I smiled. "We're booked on the sunset horseback ride." I wasn't willing to let these fuckers ruin the last half of my honeymoon. "If you want to crash in one of the bungalows, you can. I have all four of them and we won't need you until tomorrow, anyway."

"Are you out of your fucking mind?" His hand flew to his mouth, covering the words as soon as they escaped, and his cheeks bloomed red at the less than professional slip.

I chuckled and raised an eyebrow. "There are a few people who would agree that I was," I said, and a smile appeared as soon as his hand dropped away from his face.

"I meant going out," he clarified. "With those things hunting you." His hand fluttered toward the ocean.

"Did you want a drink?" I asked, and he shifted, looking at the floor before he sighed.

"I'm not old enough," he muttered. I knew he was younger, but I didn't realize he was underage.

"Okay." I threw back the shot, relishing the burn as it slid down my throat and my teeth clenched at the explosion the alcohol created in my stomach before it settled, sending warmth radiating out through to my fingertips. "Yes, we're going out," I said after the last shudder and crossed to the chair facing Akamu. "You have questions."

He laughed and put the knife on the table next to him before running both hands through his hair. "Questions. Okay. How come they are after you?" he asked, meeting my gaze.

"It's complicated." He didn't like my answer and his lips pressed together, stifling the rude remark filtering in his head. "How do you know about these things?" I asked.

"Hawaiian traditions. Myths. Word of mouth." He crossed his arms and leaned back. The mental commentary clued me in to more than just his words. His family had some history, thus the knife was handed down for generations.

"What about the knife?" I asked, prying in a way I really shouldn't have. The kid wasn't aware I could read minds, and in that respect, he had a hell of a disadvantage.

"My grandfather gave it to me when he told me the story of the different Kupua." He traded the soda can with the knife, twirling it slowly in his hand. "It protects its owner." The way his gaze drifted from the blade to me sent a shiver down my spine.

"And kills inhuman things," I added.

"Usually," he said and huffed a laugh. He still didn't believe I was a mere mortal.

"Can it hurt angels?" I asked, garnishing arched brows and a shrug from Akamu. I fell back to a conversation I had with Valerie about how clueless the general population was to the beings sharing our planet. "Never mind the angel question." I waved it away. "Have you ever seen those things before?"

"No. But my grandfather has," he said. "But I really thought he was wacked when he told me about them."

I couldn't help the chuckle. "When I was twenty, I had my first experience with true monsters, and it freaked the living shit out of me." I glanced at the bathroom door and then back to Akamu. "She doesn't even know how much finding out these things exist fucked me up." I said, just above a whisper.

Akamu chuckled and glanced around the room. "I can identify with that." His gaze landed back on me. "Really? What are you?"

"Flesh and blood, just like you. As you saw, I can bleed. If Val wasn't around, I probably would have bled out on the floor." I shrugged. "While I can destroy things, she can heal things."

"Like yin and yang?" he asked.

"Pretty much. But she..." I searched for the right word. "...inherited her gift from me."

He shifted in the chair with skepticism written on his scowl.

"I guess maybe we were meant to be," I shrugged. "When I met her, the powers shifted to what they are today. Split kind of like yin and yang."

"You never answered why they are after you," he said staring me down.

"Why do you think?" I asked and leaned back, crossing my arms.

After a moment, his cocky expression turned serious. His mind putting together the pieces with the limited knowledge he held. "They want to control you?"

I nodded. "The same way governments and crazy terrorist organizations would want to control me if they knew what I could do. That's why they went after my wife. They know without her, I'd be more likely to bend to their will."

"Shit," he whispered. "I don't envy you."

I laughed and sighed. "There're only a handful of people who know what we can do." I pointed between the bathroom door and myself and let the statement hang on the air. Threatening someone to remain silent wasn't in my makeup. If he chose to go announce what he saw to the world, I wouldn't stop him, but I didn't get that vibe from him, especially after the litany of things his grandfather recounted. All of which he had originally discounted, but now he wondered how much of it was real.

Akamu glanced at the knife, studying it for a moment before picking it up again. "You might need this," he said, offering the talisman to me.

"Give it to my wife," I said as the shower silenced. "She is the one who needs protection."

"But..."

"Besides the freaky power, I've also got a black belt, so I'm better prepared to fend off an attack. She doesn't have that advantage."

Akamu bit his lower lip.

"She's been hurt more than once," I said, soft enough so my words wouldn't reach her ears. "If that thing works..."

"It does," he interrupted, assuring me of its mythical nature with an emphatic nod.

"Okay." My gaze moved to the bathroom door as it opened and Valerie stepped out in jeans and a halter-top, her hair in a single braid and her lips shining with a gloss that set the heat level switch inside me to the on position.

"Has anything?" Trailing off, she twirled her finger, and I shook my head.

"No, nothing else has happened," I said. "Akamu and I have just been shooting the breeze."

The twitch of her lips was her attempt at a smile.

"Akamu has something for you," I said.

Our chauffer stood, crossing to her. "I present you with my grandfather's talisman. It will now serve to protect you." He held the knife out in his hands as he bowed his head. The presentation of the weapon seemed overly formal to me, but it was necessary for the blade to know who it needed to protect from darkness.

It almost drew a laugh from me. I hadn't realized I had walked into a bad horror movie until just this moment, and I turned away, choosing to look at the beauty of the Hawaiian landscape to ground myself in some level of reality.

"I trust this entire ordeal will remain between us?" I said without turning.

"Yes, sir," Akamu said. "What time should I pick you up tomorrow?"

I glanced over my shoulder, relieved he wasn't going to bolt in the opposite direction as soon as he was out of here. "If you can be here by eight, that would be appreciated. We have a Safari Catamaran tour in Haleiwa setting sail at nine."

"Will do, sir." He gave me a slight bow, and I dropped the shield I had put around the cottages. As soon as he pulled out, I moved my gaze to Valerie.

"This is beautiful," she said, studying the knife before sheathing it and clasping the sheath on the inside of the cowboy boots she unpacked.

"It's supposed to kill anything inhuman," I said, even though I knew she had been privy to Akamu's side of the conversation.

"Maybe it'll kill Lucifer," she said, and a wicked gleam danced in her eyes. One I had never seen in her before. I knew she hated him, but that gleam promised payback in ways I didn't even want to consider.

"You're not wearing that on the ride, are you?" She waved at my shorts.

"You don't think this would work?" I asked, opting for humor instead of where the conversation had veered.

A more genuine smile appeared, and she rolled her eyes, crossing until she stood in front of me. The light caress of her fingertips sent a thrill through me, along with a shudder of goose flesh.

"The lack of a shirt is okay, but I think you'll get saddle sores if you wear the shorts."

"You can fix them." I smiled.

"Go change," she said and swatted my ass.

I leaned down and kissed her gently. The taste of berries came with the kiss, and I licked my lips as I pulled away, enjoying the sweet taste of her gloss. A quick glance at the clock told me I didn't have time to explore that taste and I turned, bending to her sensibility.

Angel Wrath Chapter 8

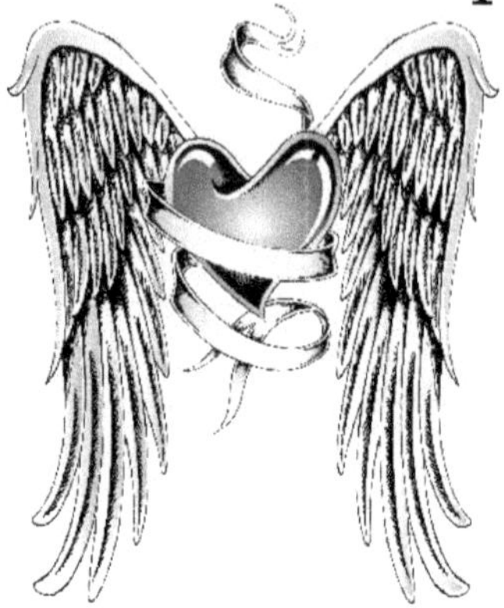

THE IDEA OF BEING on a secluded trail was not as comforting as I thought it would be when I booked the excursion. Both Valerie and I had a healthy dose of apprehension accosting us. I didn't realize the level of our unease until the moment we strolled into the stables and every last horse whinnied. Basically, we spooked a barn full of horses and their wild-eyed reaction took the stable hands by surprise. Even the three horses in the center, being prepped with saddles, pranced around in an agitated fashion.

I traded a glance with Valerie and took a deep breath, forcing my raw nerves into a lockbox at the pit of my stomach for the benefit of the now skittish animals. Valerie did the same, and our conscious effort to quiet our internal turmoil seemed to work its magic. The horses calmed, and I inspected the ones being groomed for the ride.

A gray speckled appaloosa and two chestnut quarter horses had saddles already placed and the stable hands were making sure everything was in order. Valerie and I approached the three horses, and a petite Hawaiian woman stepped out from behind the brood.

"Mr. and Mrs. Ryan?" she asked.

"Yes, ma'am," I said, giving her a nod.

"We have Koa," she said, patting the appaloosa, "and Mahina and Lanikai," she finished waving toward the two quarter horses. "You may take your pick," she added with a smile.

"You first," I said to Valerie, and her gaze moved from one horse to the other before she stepped closer. It wasn't so much she picking the horse, but the other way around when one of the quarter horses stepped forward and nuzzled her.

"Lanikai likes you," the little woman said, and she turned her gaze in my direction.

I stepped forward, focused on Koa. She threw her head back in defiance and met my blatant stare. The horse moved with grace and placed her head on my shoulder. It was the damnedest thing, and I could tell from the woman's expression that she hadn't seen anything like it either.

"I guess I get Koa." I smiled and got a nuzzle in response that knocked me back a step. I scratched the white patch between her dark eyes. After the horse settled down, I focused on the little woman and the other stable boys who fit the last horse with a saddle that came equipped with a large picnic basket. "What's your name?" I asked her.

"Jenna," she said and gave us a nod. "Once we get to our destination, dinner will be served and when you are done, we can head back."

"Or we can send you back with the basket and return when we're ready?" I asked, raising a hopeful eyebrow.

She laughed politely. "I'm sorry, but that is not our policy."

I glanced at Valerie and ran my hand down Koa's neck, waiting for our guide to instruct us to mount. Something about animals always calmed me. It had been years since my father's guide dog died; Sam hadn't crossed my mind in the last few years. He was the best damn dog in the world and I couldn't believe it had been so long since I thought of him.

"Have you ever ridden before?" Jenna asked, stepping in front of the two of us and our chosen rides.

"Yes," we both said at the same moment.

"But it's been years," I added after we exchanged grins.

"Would you categorize your skills as closer to a novice or to an expert?"

"Expert," Valerie replied. "In middle school, I used to ride on the equestrian team."

"Novice," I said when Jenna looked my way. "I'm not nearly as experienced as my wife," I added. Her history was the reason I booked this excursion.

Jenna gave a nod to Valerie, indicating she could mount. The grace with which she climbed onto the horse made my breath stick in my chest. Some of the simplest things she did could leave me breathless, and this was no exception. I smiled when my brain-stall kicked back in gear, pulling air back into my lungs.

"Do you remember how to get up into the saddle?" Jenna asked me.

I refrained from rolling my eyes. "Yes, ma'am," I answered and reached for the horn on the saddle. When my fingers brushed the horse's mane, I glanced where I thought the thing was supposed to be. There was no horn.

Jenna suppressed a grin. "It's an English saddle."

Heat filled my cheeks. That was one thing I had requested because Valerie competed with an English saddle. I just never considered what style I should choose. "I know," I muttered. Before I made a complete fool of myself, I slid my left foot into the stirrup and gripped the lip of the saddle where the horn would have been had this been western style. I swung my leg over and took the reins after I got situated in both stirrups. I was much less graceful than Valerie, and I caught her smirk when I finally looked up.

"You sure you don't want a western saddle?" Valerie asked, as Jenna mounted her horse.

Jenna's horse was the only one of the three with a western saddle. I could have easily switched with her, but now my ego was a bit bruised, and my pride wouldn't let me back down, no matter how unsteady I felt.

"I'm good," I said.

Jenna made that familiar clicking noise and her horse took the lead. Koa and Lanikai followed. Riding in an English saddle took some getting used to, and thank god Koa and I seemed to be on the same wavelength. All I needed to do was adjust the tension on one side of the reins or the other and she went the way I wanted her to.

"Do you want horses?" I asked when we trotted onto a private stretch of beach. The flash of interest in Valerie's eyes came and went like a firefly in the dead of night.

"Horses are a lot of work. I'm not sure I'd have the time."

"I'm not doing much," I shrugged. The idea of having such a majestic creature really piqued my interest.

"We're traveling enough to make having any sort of pet difficult."

She had a point, but I had unlimited resources. "I could hire a caretaker," I said.

Jenna had stopped a few feet away, meeting our gaze, and I got the silent message even before she spoke. "I believe you wanted to gallop?" She waved her hand at the open stretch before us.

Valerie nearly salivated at the thought.

"Beach or surf?" I asked, and she grinned at me, taking control of her horse.

"Yahh!" she yelled and headed straight for the water. Her form was impeccable, and I traded a shrug with Jenna before I followed suit.

Koa reacted, taking off like a bolt. I nearly fell out of the saddle before I regained my balance and figured out the natural rhythm. Water splashed under her hooves, and I caught up to Valerie easily. Koa was faster than her horse, and I held both reins and a handful of her mane to help with the balancing act.

This was as close to the feeling of pure freedom as surfing was for me, and I grinned like a drunken fool as we galloped side by side in the shallow surf. Valerie's laugh filled the small beach, and I couldn't tell you how much sheer joy pulsed through me in that moment.

It nearly wiped out the darkness that hung on at the back of my mind. The sunset shimmered on the ocean, and as we reversed course, the click of the camera caught my attention. Jenna had unpacked her Nikkon and was snapping away per the package specifications. Not only did I contract a three-hour horseback ride, but I had a candlelight dinner and picture package included.

We pulled to a stop at the shoreline, and I leaned toward Valerie to catch a kiss in the trail of the sunset on the water. Jenna snapped a few more pictures before making that clicking noise that called the horses back to the normal trail ride pace.

We climbed out of the thick canopy at the edge of a steep incline. Our dinner destination was the plateau above and the ride up the hill was unnerving for me. I had to focus my concentration on staying in sync with the horse's movement, otherwise I would have ended up on my back on the ground.

Surveying our surroundings every few minutes was also wearing my nerves thin, and I hoped my exhaustion wouldn't interfere with this dinner date. I also prayed we wouldn't be attacked by anymore of Lucifer's henchmen.

Jenna arranged the picnic on the smooth rocks near the bluff and I sat down, looking at the spread of cheese and crackers, roast beef sandwiches, and fresh fruit decorating the disposable paper plates.

It was simple, and the wine bottle sitting in the travel ice bucket made me smile. As simple as the meal was, it was incredibly satisfying to my growling stomach. After we wolfed down the food, I settled on the rocky ledge. Valerie took a seat next to me and intertwined her fingers through mine.

"Are you okay?" she asked softly while Jenna cleaned up what was left of the meal.

I glanced away, ignoring her question now that the silence surrounded us; a twinge started in my gut, like we were being watched by monsters just out of sight. Instead of answering Valerie, I turned, addressing Jenna. "I really would like to stay for a while. However, you can start back if you want," I said.

"Rules..." she started.

"Fuck the rules," I said, and her hesitant gaze hardened.

"It's…"

"A liability," I finished. "What if I granted you a waiver against all liability?"

"I still can't," she said.

"Do the horses know the way back?"

She nodded, but wasn't budging on her stance.

"Leave without us. We'll be fine," I commanded, and she blinked with surprise as her body did what I ordered, despite her emphatic desire not to leave us to our own devices. "I promise we will be okay, and we'll see that the horses are taken care of properly before we leave," I added with an apologetic smile as she mounted her horse and started the trek back without us. Granted, she had no choice in the matter.

"You really didn't have to do that," Valerie scolded me. "And you never answered my question."

"Am I okay?" I said and scanned the darkening horizon. "I honestly don't know." I turned, meeting her gaze. "What that thing said earlier…" I trailed off and looked out at the rainbow of colors painting the islands. "It twisted my insides."

"I'm sorry," she whispered and turned my face towards her. Our lips met and the soft kiss became much more insistent. Where we were was as secluded as you could get, so when I pulled her away from the edge onto the grassy knoll, she didn't stop me.

Just as I was pushing her shirt up to kiss her sexy belly, something spooked the horses. They didn't take off, but they whinnied and pranced closer to where we had stretched out. Their senses were much more in tune with nature than mine, so I paid attention and pulled away from Valerie, scanning the woods beyond their restless nickers.

"I think we should head back and resume this at the cottage," I said, moving my gaze to hers, but her eyes were scanning the dense brush just as quickly as mine had.

Valerie reached down to her ankle and pulled out the knife. "I think that might be a really good idea."

The sigils on the blade let off an eerie glow, and I hopped to my feet, pulling her up with me.

"Do you know how to get back?"

"The horses know the way," I said, and we wasted no more time. We mounted the horses, and I took the lead. I closed my eyes, willing a protective cocoon around us as we descended the hill, praying whatever was stalking us wouldn't spook the horses enough to throw one of us. Once we hit the beach, we took off at a gallop.

A shadow that reminded me of a dog slunk just inside the woods, and I caught the red glow of eyes tracking us.

"Fuck," I whispered, and Koa whinnied like she agreed, yet she pushed faster, leaving the sand behind in favor of the beaten path through the tropical forest. It was almost as if she knew nothing would get to her as long as she had me on her back.

Valerie's horse was on our heels and one glance over my shoulder told me her mare wasn't as sure as mine. The shadow darted forward and the sudden appearance of a hellhound in the path made Koa slam on the brakes. I, on the other hand, kept going.

Thank God for years of break falls in karate class. I tucked, somersaulting as I hit the ground and rolled to my feet, into karate form. The impact knocked the wind out of me, and I think it may have cracked a couple of ribs. Each breath brought forth a wave of pain. However, I didn't have time to noodle on the damage to my body. I was face to face with a snarling demon dog and still had the protection wrapped around the horses and Valerie a few yards back.

I inhaled and yelled, "Get!" waving my arms like a lunatic.

The hound's growl faded, and it cocked its head for enough of a pause to let me catch my breath. The inhuman snarl filled the space, and the thing launched at me. A flash of silver shot by me, and Valerie's blade caught the creature between its eyes, just as its paws hit my chest.

I went down, half expecting its powerful jaws to snap my neck; instead, I was slammed to the ground by dead weight. An audible "Oof" escaped as I hit. I blinked at the night sky and Koa's snout leaning down to inspect whether or not I was all right.

My already damaged ribs were singing a hellish tune at the weight of the dead dog, and I attempted to push it off, but it wouldn't budge. My gaze met Koa's intelligent eyes. "A little help," I hissed from my compressed lungs. I had never seen a horse carry an expression of disgust, but Koa's face displayed just that. Yet she leaned down with her lips pulled back and clasped her teeth on the dog's ragged ear, pulling it to my right as I tried to roll out from underneath.

As soon as I was clear, Valerie was by my side, and she planted her healing kiss before moving on to the dead hellhound. With her foot on its jaw, she clasped the knife and pulled it out. The air sizzled around us and the dog disintegrated into a dust swirl.

"Damn," I whispered and just lay on the ground, staring at the canopy of stars and palms overhead. Koa nuzzled me and I glanced at her, reaching out to rub her nose before I finally climbed to my feet. "You certainly lived up to your name," I said, taking her reins before turning to Valerie.

My entire body tingled as the last of the healing mojo faded. I debated on walking the rest of the way because I really didn't want to take another turn at flying, but I also didn't want to linger in the tropical forest for longer than we needed to.

Valerie's complexion was waxier than I cared to see, and I pulled her into a hug before we both mounted the horses. Instead of leading, the horses trotted side by side and I got the sense they were just as freaked out by the experience as we were.

I stroked Koa's neck as we rode, trying to loosen the tension I could feel in her taut muscles. "I got you covered," I said and gave her a pat before trading a glance with Valerie.

"I think they understand you," she said with a tremor in her voice.

I smiled and shrugged. "I've always been real good with animals."

"Being good and being on the same wavelength is different," Valerie muttered. "I bet you could let go of the reins and just think the commands and she would follow your directions," she added in that moody way that told me she had a bit of envy flowing through her.

"Are you upset with me?"

Her gaze snapped in my direction. She shook her head, but the way her lips pressed together told me she wasn't pleased about something.

"What's eating you then?"

"It took me years to ride with such ease. You've been on that horse for maybe a total of an hour, and it's like you've been riding all your life."

I laughed. "Babe, you weren't thrown from your horse. I was."

She chewed her lip and then sighed. "Okay, maybe not all your life," she conceded.

The path opened up to the far edge of the hotel grounds and the stable was within view, creating another notch of relaxation in both the horses and us. Once we delivered the mares to the stable hands waiting for us, we headed back to our room.

The quiet walk ate at my nerves. I could see the things that attacked us at the cottage being native to the area, but a hellhound? That meant a portal had to be on the island. I sighed, glancing at Valerie before I pulled my cell out of my pocket. I stared at the cracked screen and irritation flashed.

"That fucker cracked my phone," I muttered. It was always a royal pain in the ass to replace an iPhone. I powered it up and blew out my breath as the display came to life. It still worked, so that was a plus. I took a seat on the knee wall near the edge of the grass in front of our cottage and stared at the display, scrolling through the numbers before I settled on one.

I met Valerie's stare, as she stood a few feet away with her arms crossed and her features tense.

"Hi, Tom," I said to the mechanical voice that answered.

"Are you okay?" he asked.

"Yeah, but I think we might have a problem."

"What kind of problem?"

"I think there might be a portal on the island."

"Excuse me?"

"Today, we've been attacked twice by hell's agents."

Silence filtered through the line. "Shit," his automation program replied.

"Yeah, that was close to my first reaction."

"What do you need from me?"

"I need you and Damian to pinpoint it for me and let me know the coordinates so I can close it."

Valerie's arms dropped, as well as her jaw, and then she spun, stomping back into the cottage, leaving me with the ruined night and Tom telling me he's on it.

After ending the call and pocketing my phone, I stayed in place, unable to face Valerie's aggravation. The thing she didn't understand was now that they had waged war against us, I had no choice in the matter.

"IT'S OUR HONEYMOON!"

"Would you prefer it to be our funeral?" I countered, knowing it was low, but with the history we'd had with Lucifer, it was a distinct possibility.

"Fuck you, Chris," she snarled and turned to stomp off.

I grabbed her arm, pulling her to me. I stared down into her wild eyes; the heat in me wasn't fueled by sexual tension this time. I was bordering on furious.

"They started this. I'm just ending it before we go home," I snapped. "Otherwise, they'll send more and more until they overpower us, and I'm not about to let them tear us apart."

"They already have," she said, her eyes glistening with unshed tears.

"No. They haven't." I softened and inhaled, closing my eyes and doing that silent countdown to calm my nerves. "If there's a portal here, I have to close it." I gave no leeway for argument, and I didn't let her go.

She struggled in my grasp, and finally, she stopped and met my glare.

"By the way, I never thanked you for saving my ass. Your aim was impeccable," I said, changing the subject. Her glare warmed and she let out a nervous laugh.

"I'm not sure I can miss with that thing."

Her statement shed the last traces of irritation, and the colors in her eyes swirled slowly. I glanced up at the open deck, willing the screens closed, followed by the curtain. The concept of only a locked screen and fabric curtains between us and whatever attacked us left me skittish. I unwrapped my arms from around Valerie and crossed to our stowed carryon suitcase. When I pulled out the container of Morton's salt, Valerie let out a chuckle.

"It'll keep out the demons and hellhounds," I said and laid a line across the floor, thankful that the salt blended with the grout as I followed the groove from one side to the other. I did the same with the front door and put the container back in our bag. "And maybe I'll get a little sleep," I said, turning towards her.

She yawned, mirroring the sudden layer of exhaustion pummeling my muscles. I walked to her and delivered a sweet kiss. The thought of making love to her crossed my mind, but I was actually too tired to follow through. Instead, I led her to the bed, undressed and crawled under the covers, with her in my arms.

"I love you," I whispered and kissed the side of her throat.

She shivered in my grasp and pulled me tighter around her. "I love you, too."

Angel Wrath Chapter 9

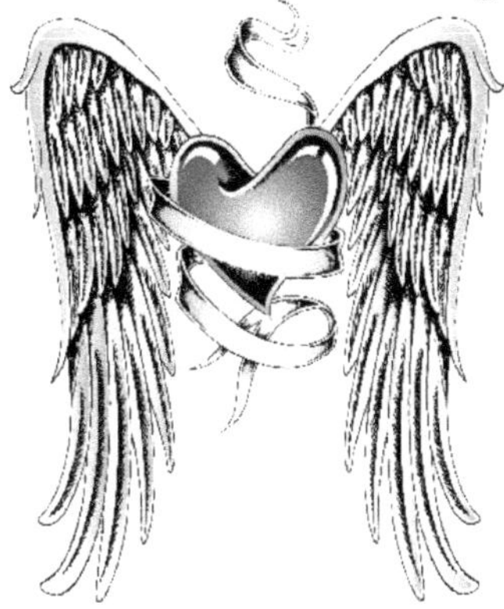

THE BUZZ OF MY phone on the nightstand interrupted my sleep, and I glanced at the display, wondering who the hell was calling in the middle of the night.

Tom's name flashed, and I picked up the phone.

"Hey," I whispered, my voice thick with sleep.

"We didn't wake you, did we?" Raven's amused accent filled the line.

The clock on the table blinked at four-fifteen and I rubbed my eyes, calculating the hour at home. "What do you think?" I muttered and her laugh filled the line.

"We're even then," she said.

"Sorry about that," I whispered. I knew it had been late when I called, but the circumstances warranted it. "Did Tom stay up?"

"Yes," she said, and her tone was less than amicable.

I slid out of bed and slipped out onto the patio, taking a seat in the pre-dawn darkness. "Did he find what I asked him to look for?"

Silence came over the line, and I looked at the phone just to make sure I hadn't lost the call.

"Raven?"

"Right between Laie and Pupukea. If you draw a line between the two, it's right smack in the middle. In the mountain range."

I remained quiet for a moment. "How far south from Turtle Bay?"

She sighed. "Five or six miles due south. It's almost as if you are the median between the two points."

"How the hell am I supposed to get there?" I muttered. I didn't mean to speak out loud, and Raven's sigh didn't help.

"I think you have to hit it from the air."

"That's fucking insane," I said.

"What's insane?" Valerie's voice pulled my attention to the cottage, and I turned, glancing at her rumpled hair and sleepy eyes.

I almost forgot what she asked as I stared at her.

"What's insane?" she said again, and I shook the cobwebs from my head.

"That I have to get to the portal by air."

She blinked at me, and her sleepy features sharpened to irritation. She spun on her heel and disappeared back inside.

"She can't be happy," Raven said on the other end of the line, and I couldn't help the laugh that cropped up.

"She's pissed."

"Can you blame her?"

My laughter subsided. "No. But if I do nothing, they'll keep coming until we leave, and people could get hurt. Hell, I've already had my guts shredded and my ribs broken," I said. "We might not be as lucky next time."

Raven blew into the phone. "Tell her I'm around if she needs to talk."

"Will do. Text the exact location and give everyone back home our best." I didn't wait for a response. I ended the call and ran a hand down my face before going back inside to my bride. Valerie was on her stomach with her face turned away, and I bit down on my aggravation.

"At least they didn't crash the wedding," I said, crossing the dark room.

She turned her head, meeting my gaze as I slid under the sheet next to her.

"By air?"

"I'm as excited about it as you are," I said, staring at the curtains moving in the light pre-dawn breeze. I really should have been sleeping, but I was wracking my brain to figure out a way to get into hell's domain and then out again as soon as I cleansed the area.

"Isn't there another way in?"

I pulled up my phone and clicked on the location they sent and stared at it on the map. "It's a little over five miles due south from here."

"That's shorter than the walk to the lighthouse and back from our house at home."

"True, but there aren't any roads through the area."

"What about ATVs or even the horses?"

I turned to her. "You're not going with me."

"The hell I'm not," she said.

Every muscle in my body tensed at the thought of walking into danger with her at my side. "Val," I started.

"Don't Val, me. I'm not letting you walk into a trap alone."

"It's not a trap, and I'm not putting you in a position to get hurt again."

"Then you're not going." She crossed her arms and pouted, setting me on edge.

"Valerie." I waited until she turned towards me and when she did, the resolve in her eyes pulled a sigh. "I can't do this with your there."

"Didn't you listen to my vows?"

I closed my eyes and covered my face. "I did," I whispered. I listened, and I thought they were perfect, but I didn't translate the stronger together part into going after Lucifer. Any other situation rang true, but not this. "But I'm not stronger with you in the mix. If anything, I'm vulnerable because he knows how much I love you. He knows how to completely fuck me up."

"Chris," she said, and I glared at her. Her mouth popped closed in response.

"He will kill you," I said. "And if he does, you know damned well what that will do to me."

She bit her lip and rolled onto her back, staring at the ceiling. "If he kills you, it will destroy me," she said.

I didn't speak, instead I reached for her hand and threaded my fingers through hers.

"So, we're at a stalemate," she said.

"No. We aren't. You are not going." I stared at the ceiling, and when she tried to pry her hand from mine, I clamped down. "You are going to stay here and wait for me to return." It wasn't a request, it was an order, and the filth that came out of her mouth when I got out of bed could have curled my mother's toes. She continued her angry rant while I pulled my jeans on. I had to give her props on the horse idea, and I knew I could get into the stables and hijack Koa. I glanced at her from the doorway. "I love you. I promise I will be the one to come back."

"You son of a bitch, let me go!"

I glanced at the clock. "I'll be back before the car gets here to take us to the marina." I stopped and turned back. "You can get ready, but you can't leave the cottage."

"Fuck you!" she screamed.

I knew there was going to be hell to pay when I got back, probably more than at hell's gate. I took off at a jog toward the stables. The gate was locked, but locks don't mean shit to me. A flick of my wrist opened the doors, and I stepped inside the dark barn.

As I walked down the center of the barn, I realized I had never saddled a horse before, never mind put a bit in. I stopped at Koa's stall, and she stood facing her door, like she had been waiting for me. I stared at her a moment and flipped the door lock, freeing her from the stall.

"I really have no clue what I'm doing," I said. Koa nudged me and walked toward the equipment wall. I followed like an inept child. The horse was smarter than I was at the moment, and I nearly laughed when she shook her head at a particular bridle.

"You understand we're going somewhere dangerous," I said as I pulled the bridle off the wall, inspecting it before I turned toward her. Koa dipped her head for me and willingly opened her mouth for the bit. I fit the bridle over her head and then turned toward the array of saddles, quickly zeroing in on the one that had been on her last evening.

I draped the soft blanket over her back and fit the saddle, buckling it as tightly as I dared and tested the stability. It slid a little, and I repositioned, tightening it a couple of notches. "Is that too tight?"

Koa just turned and looked at me. I tested the stability again and it didn't budge.

"Are we good?"

The horse actually nodded, pulling a laugh from me. I gave her a pat on the neck and mounted her. "You ready to run?"

Another nod of her head and I clicked my tongue. Koa trotted out of the barn, and she started in the direction of the path we took last night, but that wasn't where I was taking her. With a new direction, we trotted across the deserted freeway and disappeared into the tropical forest. I checked the direction on my phone as we cantered.

"I'm not sure how bad the terrain is," I said softly and gave her another gentle pat. "I figure we've got a little time, so you don't need to barrel ass across the landscape. Okay?"

Koa slowed to a trot.

Twenty minutes in, we hit our first steep grade, and according to the beeping light on the map in my hand, we had to crest this peak, and then the spot we were looking for was less than a mile down the other side. However, this hill was treacherous for Koa. Every step was a struggle, and the ground shifted under her.

"I might have to do this alone," I whispered as she slid a few feet before pushing on again. The concentration in Koa's stance told me she wasn't giving up and neither should I. What should have taken a few minutes took us a hell of a lot longer than I anticipated, but when we reached the crest, I gave her a gentle pat as I scanned the majestic vista. To the east, the sun had just crested the horizon, and I snapped a few pictures before turning to the south. The vista dipped into another section of dense vegetation and I sighed, glancing at the directions again.

"We need to go down there." I pointed to what looked like a small clearing to the right of where we stood.

"When we get close, I'll let you take a rest while I take care of business, okay?"

She turned her head, leveling a look that I could almost read. It matched Valerie's this morning when she insisted on coming with me, and I raised my eyebrow.

"Don't tell me you want to barrel into danger with me.

Koa nodded her head, and I had to laugh. This was by far the weirdest experience I'd ever had and the fact that this horse was given a Hawaiian name that translated to fearless wasn't lost on me.

I scanned the forest below.

"Well, then. Game on, Koa," I said and clicked my tongue. She obeyed, keeping the pace at a light trot. Once the thick canopy swallowed us, I glanced at my phone and slowed Koa to a stop. We were almost on top of the dot, and I sighed.

"I really don't want to put you in a position to get hurt," I said, but she was already sniffing the air and shaking her head in derision. Her small huff and agitated prancing told me more than the dot on my phone, and I slid the electronics back into my pocket.

I took a minute to gather my strength at the same time the wind shifted and the burning smell that had spooked Koa hit us full force. We were in the portal's circumference and my heart thundered at the realization.

I didn't know how big this was, and I hoped like hell there was no one out here right now, because my only goal today was to shut this down. I wasn't up for a confrontation and the shifting of light through the forest, freaked me out as much as Koa.

"Fuck," I stuttered as a pair of red eyes appeared and then another and another until we were surrounded by hell's hounds. Koa didn't like this either, and her wild-eyes caught mine for a minute. Concentrating, I wrapped us in a protective bubble and let go of the reins. I spread my arms wide, sending white light over the landscape and obliterating everything in our path.

The ground rumbled under our feet and Koa pranced. "My angel rain won't hurt you," I whispered and grabbed hold of the reins. "Yah!" I yelled and Koa darted in the direction we came, jumping over the deep crevices that now carved the landscape until we hit solid ground.

I turned in time to see the caverns close and the light fade, leaving a weird round crop circle marking the cleansed land.

"That was entirely too easy," I whispered, and Koa whinnied her agreement.

Shadows pulled at our attention, shifting under the sporadic cloud cover, and I shivered in the morning heat.

"I think I'll just leave the barrier up for a little longer," I whispered, and we continued back towards Turtle Bay. I didn't take a full breath until we were at the crest of the mountain slope. I stopped Koa and stared at the steep grade down, and glanced around us at the bright morning sun now above the horizon. I pulled my phone out and glanced at the time. I had a little over an hour left and I sent a text to Valerie, telling her the portal was closed and we were on our way back.

I swung my leg over Koa's head and slid off the saddle, onto the ground next to her. "It might be wise for us to go down together," I said, taking the reins. "Just don't drag me, okay?" I said, trading a glance with the horse. My first step sent me sliding, and I let go of the reins, falling on my ass for a good thirty yards before my boots dug into the muck. My heart clamored in my chest, and I sat, catching my breath before looking up the hill.

Koa still stood in place, waiting for my command. I still had three quarters of the mountain to scale down and if I slid, I was sure Koa would, as well. With trepidation, I made the clicking sound to call her down, and I didn't wait for her to barrel into me. I got back on my feet and started my descent again. The slide, stop, catch my breath, and slide some more continued. Except at the halfway point, Koa passed by me, her steps more cautious, and her ass nearly in the dirt like mine. She didn't slide nearly as much as I did and God bless the mare; she stopped at the bottom and waited for me.

The last few feet were easier as the base of the hill leveled out. My entire backside was covered in wet mud and greenery, and I crossed to Koa.

"You should have told me I'd be okay on your back," I muttered and climbed back in the saddle, gritting my teeth at the soggy squelch of mud on the fine leather. I wiped my hands on the front of my shirt and pulled out my phone to check the time. My little excursion down the hill took longer than expected and I sighed, pocketing the phone again before I picked up the reins.

"Let's see if we can make it back in twenty minutes," I said, and patted the side of her neck. Before I settled into the seat, it was like a gun went off. Koa launched forward and nearly unseated me. It took me a minute to find my balance, and I put most of my weight on the stirrups, riding like a jockey would. I cleared the path in front of us so she wasn't running through brush and by the time we reached the highway, I had to stop traffic in place as we flew across the four lanes and back into the forest, coming out of the woods onto the grass field that separated the resort from the stables at a gallop and I'm sure my face reflected the sheer joy of speed just as much as Koa's.

When Koa slowed down to a trot, I saw the guide who took us the night before and she did not look happy. Both Koa and I were filthy, and Koa was huffing pretty hard after the workout.

"What the hell do you think you're doing?" Jenna snapped when we came to a stop in front of the barn.

"I took Koa for a ride this morning." I dismounted and ran my hand down Koa's neck. She nudged me like she didn't want me to leave, but I had to go clean up and head out on a sailboat today.

"You can't do that," she said.

"I'm sorry, but I needed to borrow her for a bit. Trust me when I tell you it was important," I said and wiped the sweat off my brow. "I'll pay to have her rest for the remainder of the day. Koa deserves it."

"I can't do that," she said, and I raised an eyebrow.

"Yes, you can. And you will. Koa needs a bath and some TLC today."

"You don't own her. You cannot dictate her schedule."

I glared at Jenna. "Who owns her?" I asked.

Jenna pointed towards a man with a clipboard and I crossed to him.

"I'm CJ Ryan and I'd like to buy Koa," I said, hooking my thumb over my shoulder at the magnificent, mud-covered mare.

"She's not for sale," he said without looking up from his clipboard.

"I'll give you one hundred thousand for her."

His head snapped up and his jaw tightened. "I don't have time for your games, kid," he said.

"It's not a game. I want to buy that horse and I am offering you one hundred grand. Do we have a deal?"

His gaze narrowed. "Do you even have that kind of money?"

I grinned. "Yes. I do. So, is Koa mine?"

He looked beyond me at the mare being rinsed off by the staff and then at me. "Are you for real?" he asked, his face registering more hope than irritation.

"Yes," I said and pulled out my phone dialing. "Hey, Randy, it's CJ, can you assure this man that I have one hundred thousand to spare," I said and when Randy Kincaid said sure, I handed the man the phone.

After a couple of moments, the man rattled off a number and slowly handed the phone back to me.

"Are we all set?" I asked Randy.

"Yes, I'm faxing documentation to him and once he signs and faxes it back, I'll transfer the money."

"Thanks, Randy." I hung up the phone and met the man's stare. "I don't want Koa going out on trail rides today. She needs some rest after our morning ride," I said, and he gave me a nod. "I'll be back later to make arrangements for her."

I walked off, leaving him with his jaw hanging open.

I jogged back to the cottage and collected myself before stepping inside. What greeted me chilled whatever heat I had built on the run. Valerie stood in the center of a pile of bodies, her breath hitching as she brandished the knife at the last of her attackers.

The ease of my mission was explained in that nanosecond. Lucifer had sent his minions after us. He hadn't planned on me taking action so quickly, but he knew I would eventually, and by the looks of things, this was an attack meant to kill, not capture.

Fury overrode my senses, and I roared, pulling both their attention to the door. I let loose; the anger rolled across the room and incinerated the dead bodies and the last Kapua still on the attack.

Valerie's chin quivered as her gaze landed on me. "They told me you were dead," she said, and the gore-covered knife dropped to the floor. "Your text couldn't have come at a better time." She sniffled and stood her ground, glancing at the massacre surrounding her. "I started fighting the moment it blinked on the screen, otherwise..." She trailed off and met my gaze with a shrug.

The way she trailed off sent my heart to the floor, and I crossed, pulling her into my trembling arms. When the shakes subsided, I whispered, "I bought Koa."

She pulled back, meeting my gaze. I shrugged and offered my best conciliatory smile. I knew it wasn't really the right thing to say at this moment, but it was what popped out of my mouth from the shuffle of information going through my head.

"You what?" she asked, and unwrapped her arms, staring at the muck covering them before she turned me around so she could see what I was covered in. Her initial thoughts centered on blood, and I could see her point based on the tacky wetness saturating my clothing.

"I'm fine. It's mud," I said, and she met my gaze.

"You fell off the horse again?"

I let out a shaky laugh. "No, I didn't want to ride her down the hill we climbed, but I really should have. She did fine. As you can see, I didn't fare as well." I leaned forward and planted a kiss, but she stiffened in my arms. "We need to get cleaned up. Akamu will be here any minute."

"I'm still pissed at you for making me stay here," she said and peeled out of my grasp. She headed into the bathroom without another word.

I glanced at the dust-ridden room and willed it clean, rolling the gray cloud out of the sliding screens and onto the lawn where it settled into the damp grass. The grimy knife lay at my feet and I picked it up and headed into the bathroom. The warm water in the sink washed away most of the blood and gore from the blade and when I was done wiping it with a cloth, the shine from the overhead light sent a reflection of my dirty face back at me.

I glanced in the mirror, and my eyebrows rose at the mud streaking my face. I knew my back was covered, but I didn't think my face was as smeared as it really was. No wonder Koa's owner gave me shit. I would have, too, if someone looking like I did offered me one hundred grand for a horse.

Stripping, I tossed the ruined clothing into the garbage pail and opened the frosted shower door. Valerie stiffened, wrapping her arms around her chest in a protective reflex, and the glare she sent over her shoulder almost made me step back out and wait my turn. Unfortunately, we were due to leave in less than five minutes.

"Sorry," I said, and reached for her, but she swatted my hand away. I stared at her, at her complete unease at my close proximity. The tightness in her features made me sigh. I hadn't even thought about her state of mind when I returned.

She was unhinged, and it had nothing to do with killing Kapua. It had to do with her doubts that I was me.

"Complete mind fuck, huh?" I said and her tense features relaxed a fraction, but her lips pressed together and her chin quivered. This time when I reached for her, she came to me.

"You can't ever do that to me again," she said into my chest.

New York came to the forefront of my mind, and I clamped down on the thought before she could get a hint.

"I'm sorry." There wasn't much more I could say. "It was easier than I thought it would be," I added and pulled away, reaching for the soap. It took a scrubbing to get the muck off both of us and I washed her hair twice under the warm spray.

"Where are we going today?" she asked as we wrapped the towels around our bodies and headed to the main room to dress.

"Sailing and snorkeling," I said. "It's a private charter, so they'll wait for us." My phone buzzed, and I picked it up, sending a return text to Akamu telling him we would be out in five minutes.

"The car is here, so..." I said, trailing off as I filtered through the suitcase looking for my backup swim trunks. They weren't in the suitcase, and I looked at Valerie. "We did pack my other swimsuit, right?"

Valerie rolled her eyes and pointed at the beach bag that sat in the corner.

I shuffled the extra beach towels and yanked the swim trunks from under the tanning lotions and sunglasses, pulling it on under the bath towel. By the time I turned, Valerie had her bikini on and was pulling a sheer cover over her head. I never understood the use of a sheer beach cover. It didn't block out the sun the way a t-shirt did, but I have to say, it was incredibly sexy on her. Much more than an oversized t-shirt would have been.

With a few strokes of a brush and an elastic band, her hair was transformed to a tight ponytail, and she tossed me the brush. My hair took less time than hers and we slid on our beach shoes and I grabbed a clean v-neck t-shirt for the ride. With our wallets and phones stowed in the beach bag, we headed out to meet Akamu by the limousine for what I hoped was a relaxing day on the ocean.

Angel Wrath Chapter 10

THE CATAMARAN CRUISED ACROSS the water and I sat with my arm draped over Valerie's shoulder. She sipped champagne between snapping pictures. The dolphins jumped in time with our boat, and she put the camera down, giving me the widest grin I had ever seen.

After all that had happened over the past twenty-four hours, I really needed to unwind, and this was the perfect environment. The blow of a whale to our starboard side jarred me out of relaxation, and when the creature jumped out of the water, it sent a splash onto the deck, rocking the catamaran. Valerie had her camera back in hand, and was snapping pictures like a pro.

"Oh, my god, did you see that," she asked, and I chuckled, pulling the wet t-shirt away from my chest.

"I not only saw, but I think I wore most of that splash."

She turned toward me, taking in my waterlogged state and pointed the camera in my direction, snapping off pictures until I wrestled the camera from her. Her laughter rang out over the boat, bringing a genuine smile to both our faces and that of the crew. It was a rare state for us, but the total release of stress, and childish antics, really made my day.

I captured her laughter in at least a dozen snapshots and then looked up at the crew trying not to join in with us.

"It's okay to laugh," I said to the captain. He tipped his hat and grinned.

"We're almost to the reef and you have your choice of lunch then snorkeling or snorkeling first," he said.

Valerie and I traded a glance. "Snorkeling," we said at the same moment.

I grinned and sat back, watching the wonder etched into her features as she caught sight of the vibrant sea life surrounding us. I couldn't imagine giving up forever with her for anything, and my smile faded. What we had was complex and drove us at the cellular level. I would gladly lay down my life for her, and couldn't imagine a future where she didn't exist.

She glanced at me, and her smile faltered a notch.

"You okay?" she whispered in my ear and then planted a kiss on my cheek.

"I'm perfect," I said, meeting her gaze.

"Liar," she said, and sat back.

Heat pooled in my cheeks, and I allowed the smile to form, but I didn't argue with her. I knew at some level I was lying to myself. This perfection we found here would be tested when we got back to Maine. At home, I wouldn't be able to get away from my father's memory or the knowledge that I was the one who sentenced him to eternity in hell. The responsibility of closing the portals was mine, but so was trying to figure out some sort of rescue mission.

If I didn't try, I wouldn't be able to live with myself, and Valerie was going to fight me every step of the way because it meant I'd be putting my life on the line.

The boat slowed to a stop, and the captain dropped anchor. I could see the multiple colors of the coral a few feet away when the first mate approached us.

"The snorkel equipment is aft," he said, pointing towards the back of the ship.

I stripped my t-shirt, dropping it on the seat in the back where we had stowed our bag. Valerie peeled off her sheer cover and turned to the captain. She glanced at his name tag again, and I had to smirk because I couldn't bring myself to refer to him as Captain Jack.

Every time his name ran through my head, so did the Billy Joel song.

"Captain, um, you said you had underwater cameras available?" she asked.

Apparently, Valerie couldn't call him Captain Jack, either. She sent a sideways gaze my way, picking up on my benign narration.

"At least his name isn't Jack Sparrow," she whispered to me when he stepped out of sight.

I actually snorted and had to turn away.

"And you need to stop with the song, unless you're going to belt it out," she added.

I glanced over my shoulder with a grin.

"Maybe on the way back, after I've hit the bar," I said, nodding toward the interior cabin and the spread they were just setting up.

Captain Jack stepped back outside, along with his first mate, whose name I couldn't remember. There were three crew members, and you would think I'd be sharp enough to remember all their names, but I couldn't concentrate after the captain introduced himself and the song started looping in my head.

Valerie shot me a smirk. She knew me well enough to know I was embarrassed by my inability to address the first mate by name.

"Thank you, Tom," she said as the first mate handed her the camera.

Now I got her smirk. Of all the names in the universe, I should have been able to remember the name Tom. I shifted and offered a nod of thanks just as the captain handed out the equipment and instructed us on what to do in the event of an emergency.

"What constitutes an emergency?" I asked as I pulled on the flippers.

He leveled a heavy stare in my directions. "There are predators in the water and while we have been lucky, there have been shark attacks in the area." He looked out over the horizon. "But with the whale and dolphin traffic that we've seen today, I highly doubt sharks are nearby," he said, sending an unsettling smile in my direction.

"When was the last attack?" I asked, cursing the nervous lilt in my voice. While I had set a pretty decent barrier around me when I went surfing, I really wasn't sure I could put protection around us without toasting the fish and ruining the entire snorkeling experience for Valerie.

"A week ago, but it was a few miles south of here," he said.

"Okay, I'll keep an eye out," I said, and Valerie rolled her eyes. She wasn't the least bit nervous, but then again, she had the human shield at her side.

"You two have an hour. Enjoy."

"Thanks, Captain Jack," I said and clamped down on the need to break out in song. Valerie bit her lip and jumped into the water without waiting for me. She adjusted her mask and inspected the camera while I eased into the water from the stairs.

"You're on lookout duty," she said, meeting my gaze as she held up the camera. "I'm the appointed photographer." She winked at me and pushed off.

When we were far enough away to not be heard, she surfaced and whispered, "You are so bad."

I grinned and winked, and we continued over and around the reef, diving to inspect the bright sea anemone living on the reef. Bold colored fish swam in small schools around us and in the distance, we saw a large turtle heading in our direction. It was an amazing adventure, and we had close to one hundred snapshots on the digital underwater camera they provided. I couldn't wait to see them.

Valerie aimed the camera in my direction and her eyes widened behind the mask.

I turned in time to see teeth. Water pulsed and all I could do was blink as my heart thundered in my ears and the shark went flying, tumbling away from me along with anything else caught in my sudden burst.

When I turned back, Valerie wasn't there and panic bit at my skin. I shot to the surface, taking a breath. What the hell had I done? The boat rocked on the waves, but it was farther out than when we jumped in. The captain pointed beyond me and I turned back towards the reef, scanning the water until our eyes met.

Panic filled Valerie's eyes, and I swam towards her, aware that the top of the reef wasn't that far under the surface. The boat's engine seemed to get louder, and I chanced a glance back. It was approaching as close as it dared to the reef, and both the captain and the first mate were motioning for us to get back.

As I got closer, the water turned pink in places, and shock skittered through me. My gaze jumped to Valerie, and her strained smile told me more than I wanted to know. The coral had ripped her up, but by the time I got to her, there wasn't a mark and somehow, she had kept hold of the camera.

I helped her swim toward the boat, and I didn't give a damn. I set a protective barrier around us with enough juice to stun anything that hit it, knowing full well the presence of blood would draw the sharks. When we got beyond the reef, I wasn't disappointed. We were met by three agitated tiger sharks, and I could see at least two more coming from the deeper waters.

The boat was twenty feet away, and they were calling us in. We didn't hesitate; we kept swimming. One shark went on the attack, and Valerie's fingernails bit into my arm as we watched it coming. When it just grazed off the bottom of the barrier and started sinking to the ocean floor, she glanced at me. It recovered just as we reached the boat.

I let her go up first and the minute I was out of the water; we backed onto the floor of the boat and both of us let out shaky laughs.

"Holy shit," I breathed, as the captain checked Valerie for damage and came up empty.

His brow creased, and he turned his attention to me. "I thought I saw blood in the water," he said, and sat back on his haunches.

I exchanged a glance with Valerie and sat up, peeling the flippers off before I met his gaze.

He reached forward, grabbing my shoulder and turning my back towards him. "Tom, can you get the first aid kit?"

I blinked and my gaze shot to Valerie before I glanced at the gash in the back of my shoulder and the red spreading on the deck below me. "I guess it got me," I said.

Valerie peeled off her flippers and stepped to my side, inspecting the wound. "This looks more like its tail cut you and not its teeth," she said, and took the first aid kit from the captain.

"I would agree. It seems like that seismic anomaly may have saved your life, son." Captain Jack took off his hat and ran a hand through his hair as he scanned the area. "Damnedest thing I've ever experienced."

"Seismic anomaly?" I asked, as Valerie ran a wipe across the cut. I winced and pulled away from her, meeting her gaze now that the pain made itself known. She paused, raising an eyebrow. I couldn't help the sudden shakes that gripped me as the entire ordeal sank in. I could have killed her, and that realization made me physically ill.

I scrambled to my feet and leaned over the railing, hurling my breakfast all over the pristine water.

"Chris," Valerie said, and I spit before I glanced at her.

"What?"

"You're going to need stitches," she said, pointing to my shoulder.

I looked at Captain Jack. "Do you have what she needs to stitch me up?" When his jaw dropped a fraction, I added, "She's a doctor."

"All we have is that kit," he pointed to the kit on the seat and Valerie sighed.

"Okay," she said, and moved the contents around. "I think I can get him patched up with what you have here. Do you mind if I bring him into the head to do this?"

The captain hesitated.

"I'd rather have her patch me up than either of you," I said, and the captain nodded, pointing us below deck.

As soon as the door closed, Valerie wiped the cut again before placing the healing kiss on my shoulder. I sucked air through my teeth at the gnawing pain of the healing process. She quickly rinsed the blood and attached a large bandage over the spot before it completely healed.

"I could have killed you," I said in only a whisper.

She palmed my cheek. "You didn't."

"But I hurt you," I said, and she met my gaze without responding. The water had washed away all evidence, but I knew better. "I'm sorry. I just... reacted, and you got torn up in the process."

She let out a little laugh and sighed. "If you hadn't reacted, I think you would have lost your arm, or worse," she shivered, thinking about the alternatives.

"A seismic anomaly," I said, and pressed my lips together against the grin that wanted to surface.

"Yeah. How fucked up is that?" She winked at me and patted my bandaged shoulder, dropping the bloody gauze in the garbage before leading me up to the interior deck and the lunch spread that had been put out for us.

"I'll get us underway now that you're all patched up," Captain Jack said.

"I'm fine to finish lunch and the rest of the boat tour," I said, meeting his gaze. "All I need is a stiff drink."

"But, sir," he started, thinking of the liability.

"I'm fine. You warned us about sharks, and we went into the water of our own accord. I believe the waiver we signed absolves you of any liability in this matter."

"But you're injured," he said.

"It's just a flesh wound," I said, adopting an English accent and the line directly out of Monty Python. I pressed my lips together, trying not to laugh at the captain's sudden smirk. "Honestly, I've had worse," I said, after I got control over the need to burst into laughter.

"There was only one small section that was deep enough for a stitch or two, but I was able to close it up with a couple of butterfly bandages. If it opens up again, we'll see the signs through the bandage and can head back, if that happens, okay?" Valerie asked, as she handed the captain the first aid kit.

His gaze traveled between us, and he handed the kit to the man behind the bar.

It disappeared under the counter, and the Jack Daniels appeared on the bar top.

I actually laughed and then sang the chorus to the song stuck in my head. When I finished, all eyes were glued on me, and I shifted. "Sorry, but ever since you told us your name, that song has been stuck in my head."

The captain snapped his fingers. "You're that singer," he said with a grin.

"Ayup," I said, and reached for the jack and coke on the rocks that the bartender had already poured for me. "And I have to apologize. I don't remember your name," I said, when the glass passed hands.

"Howey," he said, and flashed a smile of impeccably white teeth.

I pounded the glass back and let the alcohol warm the chill that remained, and I focused on having a good time despite the close brush with death.

Angel Wrath Chapter 11

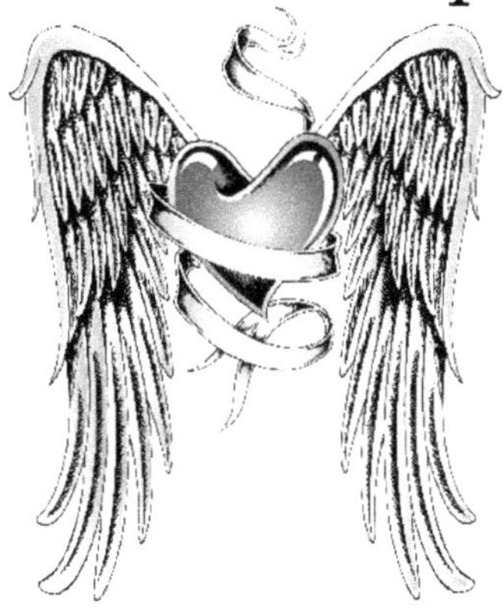

"MMMM," HER PURR SATURATED my bliss, and I turned my head towards the other massage table.

I decided our last day on the island needed to be a complete pamper session for both of us. The last few days of activity had taken its toll. Mentally, we were both trashed, more from the constant tension of wondering what horrors would crop up next, but luckily, the shark fiasco was the last of the attacks.

We expected to fall out of the sky on the helicopter tour, or have the lines snap while parasailing, or the wheels blow on the mountain bikes as we sped down the lush mountain terrain, but nothing happened on any of the other excursions. The rest of the honeymoon left us with a slew of exceptional photographs, satiated by wonderfully romantic settings in private coves along the shoreline, and some outstanding dinners while we did some island hopping.

And now, the massages. A little slice of heaven to end our honeymoon, before we stepped back into reality.

"You enjoying that?" I asked, and she peeked at me with a smile.

"Mhm," she mumbled, and we both settled back onto the table for the remainder of this part of our spa package.

With my body still tingling from the massage, the small rotations in the back of the pedicure chair seemed to enhance my relaxation. I had never experienced a pedicure in my life, so I had no idea what to expect, but the chair left me feeling like a piece of silly putty and the warm water bubbling around my feet felt incredible.

"I can't believe we have to go home tomorrow," she said.

It was my turn to grunt a response and her hand covered mine. I opened my eyes and met her smile with one of my own. "We could always stay," I said.

"You have a show next week," she said. "And I have my patients."

"Yeah, yeah," I muttered, a crust of annoyance grew over me at the unwelcome thoughts of going home. I had gotten used to the pampering and royalty treatment. Back home, I'd have to do things for myself again.

"What time is Ted picking us up?"

"We need to be at the airport at eight."

"In the morning?"

I nodded. "That will get us into Boston around ten tomorrow night and home by midnight."

"Midnight?"

"It's going to be a long day," I said with the same amount of enthusiasm as she displayed. "That's why I had this day planned. At least we'll be relaxed for it."

She let out a musical laugh and squeezed my hand.

"Where you from?" the petite Asian pedicurist at my feet asked.

"Maine," I said.

"Wow, that is far."

I smiled and shrugged. It was the farthest state from Hawaii, but it wasn't like we were halfway across the globe. "The water here is a little warmer than at home," I said and sent a wink in her direction.

The woman blushed and focused on scrubbing the dead skin off my heels.

The rest of our last day was uneventful, and as we sat on the beach watching the sun dip on the horizon, Valerie leaned over and planted a kiss on my cheek.

"I love you," she whispered.

I brought her hand to my lips. "Love you, too."

Quiet settled.

"You're going after the portals when we get back, aren't you?"

It wasn't a question, and it really wasn't a conversation I wanted to have right now when my body was so relaxed. Just the thought of what I had to do created tension in my core, and I met her gaze, keeping my mouth shut.

"Chris," she whispered, her eyes begging for some denial. Anything to appease her.

"You already know the answer."

"You know how I feel." She pulled her hand out of mine and her arms crossed across her chest.

"And you know I have to try to get my dad out." I stared at the darkening ocean.

This time, she didn't argue like she had every other time. "How?" she asked, after I thought the conversation was over, but the way she said it made me glance at her. It wasn't a facetious tone or condescending in any manner. It was a valid question, and it wasn't meant to shut me down.

"I don't know," I said. "I haven't quite figured that out." I would not put myself in the same situation I had with her. There would be no trade, no negotiation. I'd have to steal my father from Lucifer, and I was sorely lacking in the criminal mastermind department.

"I need to be there if you try," she said, and as much as I wanted to argue the point, I just focused on the water and gave her a single nod.

"Then we have to figure out a way to keep you safe, even on his turf."

Her eyebrows rose at the fact I didn't argue.

"I have a feeling I'm going to need all the help I can get," I said, to the visible surprise in her features.

"Wow. I think I need to make sure you get a massage and pedicure every week," she said with a laugh.

It was my turn to raise an eyebrow. "I think you need to bring me here every month." I pointed to the sand and flashed the smile I knew revved her engine.

Our attention diverted to the noise at the far side of the beach. The next sunset horseback ride was just beginning and this time there was a group going on the adventure. I sure hoped like hell they didn't encounter some of the less than friendly wildlife like we had. I was pleased to see the guide riding Koa and not any of the guests. I had an agreement drawn up that stated only guides could ride her and only one excursion a day, not multiple. I wanted her to have exercise, but I didn't want her ridden into the ground.

"Should we bring Koa back home with us?" I asked, turning back to Valerie.

"On the plane?"

I laughed. "No, we'd have to ship her separately. Or we can buy a cottage around here and come out a couple of times a year. It's up to you."

She chewed her lip, debating. Her mind jumping around at the possibilities and when the idea of kids cropped up, I raised an eyebrow. Granted, I loved my niece and Damian's kids, but I wasn't ready for kids. Hell, I was second guessing bringing a child into this world, especially with a fourth angelic bloodline in the mix.

Valerie's soft features hardened. "You don't want kids?"

"I never said I didn't want kids," I said. "I'm just not quite ready for them right now." I knew it was selfish, but I wanted my time with just her and no distractions, at least for a little longer.

She sucked on her bottom lip as she considered my words. Now that she was done with medical school and residencies, she was feeling more settled into a life in Maine. We had roots now, and she wanted children before she was thirty.

"I eventually want a couple of kids," I said, so she could hear the words from my mouth. "A boy and a girl." I shrugged and glanced at the painted sky. "Preferably not at the same time," I added with a grin. I saw just how ragged Damian was with triplets. Of course, he was twenty-five-hundred years old, but who was counting?

Valerie's lips curved into a smile. "You don't want twins?"

I shook my head. I had a feeling one at a time was going to be enough of a handful. Besides, being a twin had its downside. Sharing everything from birthdays to parent's attention was not always the easiest, no matter how close the twins.

"You regret being a twin?" she asked, surprised by my open train of thought.

I weighed my response, thinking about the benefit of always having Tom around and the pain I felt when he shut me out. It was a double-edged sword, but I guess that was true of any sibling relationship. "No," I said, and glanced at her. "But before I even entertain bringing a kid into the world, I need to close every last gate to hell."

Angel Wrath Chapter 12

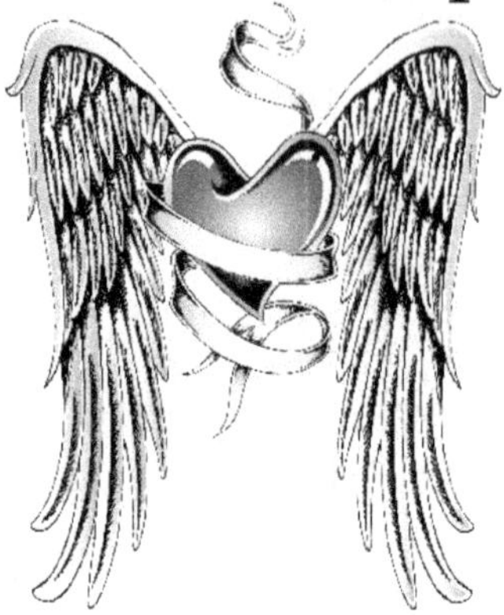

TED STOOD AS WE entered the private flight waiting area. This time he listened to me and was wearing a Hawaiian print shirt with Bermuda shorts and beach sandals. He looked as comfortable as you can get, and his wife, Heather, stood next to him, looking just as comfortable in a long sundress.

They looked as thoroughly relaxed as we felt, and I shot out a hand to go along with my welcome smile.

"You finally listened," I said, and he let out a laugh.

"We decided to take a bit of a vacation ourselves. We've been in Waikiki for the last week," Ted said. "I hope you don't mind, but Heather's my co-pilot for the trip home."

"I don't mind at all," I said, as he walked us into the adjoining hangar where they were prepping the plane.

"Is that the plane we flew out in?" Valerie asked, as I hauled both our bags across the length of the hangar.

"No," I said, studying the familiar jet. This was the one I had ridden on at least a dozen times over the years and while it was comfortable for long flights, it wasn't the luxury we had been spoiled with on the way out.

"Sorry. I couldn't take our flagship plane off the market for a week," Ted said.

I gave him a nod. "I wouldn't expect you to. Hell, I didn't even expect the accommodations we had on the flight here."

"Well, it was our little wedding gift upgrade," Heather said, and handed Ted her bag before she took the stairs up to the smaller aircraft.

Valerie climbed up after Heather, and Ted let me lead the way onto the plane. Our bags went into the closet between the passenger space and the cockpit, and Ted closed the door after the ground crew pulled the stairs away.

With everything buttoned up, I stepped into the passenger section, where Valerie had already taken a seat in one of the swiveling captain's chairs by the window. A leather couch lined the opposite side of the plane, along with a little kitchenette, and the bathroom lay in the back section beyond the kitchen area. The television screen was in the same general area as it had been in the prior plane, but it wasn't as big.

"This one doesn't have a bedroom, but if you need to rest, the couch pulls out and those chairs also recline, so you have either option." He rubbed his hands together and then pointed to the small hallway in the back. "Bathrooms are back there, along with blankets and pillows, if you need them. Drinks are in here, as well as a couple of frozen meals Heather cooked for the trip."

"Thanks," I said.

"Feel free to come up front if you want," he added, and then gave us a nod, disappearing into the cockpit to do his last preflight check before we got underway.

"So, no mile high this time?" Valerie whispered to me, and I grinned.

"I don't believe he said that wasn't allowed." I reached for her and pulled her to me, planting a lingering kiss before she pushed me away with an eye roll.

"We had private quarters before," she whispered and took her seat again, pointing for me to take the adjoining chair.

"I can make this private," I grinned.

"You can't make it soundproof," she said.

The girl had a point, and I shrugged. "You know where to find me if you change your mind." I stretched out in the recliner and yawned. Getting up early this morning wasn't really what I'd wanted to do. I would have rather just slept in and forgotten about going home.

We didn't make any decisions last night regarding Koa, kids, or my father and I put up the barrier in my mind that rendered my thoughts unattainable, and Valerie cocked her head at me. I didn't acknowledge it, instead I closed my eyes and focused on trying to come up with a viable plan. New York wouldn't be the venue and I wasn't bringing Valerie anywhere near that landmark. Not with what Lucifer did to her in that space. I'm sure a crop circle in New York would draw a great deal of attention, and she'd probably see it on the news, but it had to be done. That property needed to be sanitized; scrubbed clean of the evil it bred.

I debated on doing it before the concert, but I knew revisiting the location where Lucifer almost destroyed us would fuck me up big time. Especially if the bastard made an appearance. If that happened, the likelihood that I'd be in shape to perform would be iffy, at best. Even if there wasn't any physical damage, my mental state would be challenged. Hell, it would already be challenged, knowing I have to go take care of business as soon as the curtain falls.

"What are you thinking about?" she asked, as the plane started rolling from the hangar.

"How to keep you safe," I said, opening my eyes.

"I might have an idea that could work," she said, and I sat up, interested in what she had to say. "Well, you know how you can project that barrier?"

"Yeah," I said.

"I know you can do it on a large scale, but how targeted can you get it?"

I shrugged. I was always worried about protecting a group of people, so I never really focused on harnessing it into a small scale. "What'd you have in mind?"

She inhaled and blew a stream of air out. "I'd be willing to bet wherever we go, he will have his henchmen surrounding the area."

I thought about the hellhounds in Hawaii and nodded.

"And if I'm with you, even if I'm not within the perimeter, he'll make sure I'm captured and dragged back into the mix," she said, studying her hands before her gaze met mine.

I shook my head. "I'd never let that happen."

She crossed her arms. "You know it's going to happen. Even if he has to kidnap me before you get there. We both know I'm his bargaining chip. He already knows your willingness to trade for me. But this time, he will not let me get away. At least, not alive."

I shivered at the thought, knowing she was right, and I thought I understood where she was going with this. "What if I don't have any power on his turf? I wasn't able to protect myself last time, or you, for that matter." I bit my lip, watching the land speed by as the plane sped up for takeoff. "You didn't have the power in the warehouse, either," I added, thinking of the view I had of everything Lucifer did to her while I watched helplessly on the shores of Heaven.

"Why do you think Damian has his powers on Lucifer's turf?"

I shrugged. I had no fucking clue why Damian could use what I gave him while I was useless in the same position.

"He's infused with angel grace."

Her comment tore my gaze away from the window.

"And now you are, too."

Her statement hung on the air between us while I combed through Damian's history. He didn't beat Lucifer until he was infused with angel grace. It wasn't that he went on the offensive, like I originally thought, and my gaze moved back to Valerie. She was nodding her head in agreement before I even spoke. "So are you," I said and smiled. I had given her a piece of Uriel's grace after I came back from the dead, along with the healing powers and a small strand of what ran through my blood.

Her eyebrows rose at my silent revelation. I guess she hadn't realized the dark nature that lay dormant within her, along with the grace and healing power I infused her with.

"I told you I never wanted you to be vulnerable again," I said.

"Yeah, but I just thought you gave me back the healing mojo along with a piece of angel grace. I didn't know you gave me..." she waved her hand at me.

There really wasn't a specific word for the powers that ran through my blood, and I smiled.

"So, I could hold you down if I wanted to?" she asked, and her voice carried that coy quality that matched the mischievous sparkle in her eye.

"Oh, I don't know about that," I said, toying with her. "I think you might need to practice when we get home."

Her grin was my answer, and she glanced away as clouds filled the window and the plane leveled out. "I'll have to take you up on that," she mumbled, and then refocused from the sexual innuendo. "Anyway..."

"Back to what we were talking about," I finished, and she nodded, her humor drying up at the sobering conversation.

"If you can target your shield, we might have the element of surprise."

"How?"

"Around me."

"That's easy..."

"Let me clarify," she said, holding up her hand. "Around me so they can grab me and maybe even break skin, but nothing more."

"You w...want me to put a bar...rier in...side your skin?" The surprise her statement hit me with brought forth the full force of my stutter.

"Yes."

I leaned back in my seat and ran my hands down my face, looking at her over my fingertips. "I don't know if I can do that," I said through my fingers. The only time I may have come close to her concept was when I tapped the power within me in order to remain standing after Lucifer's henchmen nearly beat me to death. I had never tried putting a protective barrier below the surface of my skin, let alone someone else's.

"Try," she said, like it was simple, and all I could envision was making a mistake.

My mistakes weren't little, either. I shook my head, and she rolled her eyes.

"Just try."

"Not in a plane," I replied. I knew my limitations and if I screwed up, we could be free-falling to the earth in a matter of seconds. "Maybe when we get home," I said, waiting for the argument, but it never came. Instead, she nodded and unhooked her seatbelt, crossing to the refrigerator to see what sort of refreshments we had at our disposal.

"Want anything?" she asked, glancing over her shoulder.

"What are the choices?"

"Soda, orange juice, cranberry juice, water," she rattled off the listing of beverages waiting for me to make a decision.

"I'll take water for now," I said, stopping her from continuing to read off the alcoholic choices. Valerie tossed me a bottle on her way back to the chair.

I drained my water and smiled at her as she sucked down hers. The way her lips wrapped around the neck of the bottle stirred the heat inside me. As soon as she finished, I grabbed her hand and dragged her down to the restroom at the back of the plane. It was larger than your average plane restroom, but nowhere near as big as what we had coming out. Either way, it would do for the things I had in mind.

She protested, and I pushed her against the door, drowning her voice with a kiss. Time stopped and my hands explored her curves through the silky fabric of her sundress. The smoothness of the fabric from her back all the way down to her thighs pulled me away from her lips.

"You're not wearing any underwear," I whispered, my voice husky with the need riding through my bloodstream.

Her devious chuckle was my only answer before her mouth crushed over mine. I pulled at her skirt until my fingers found her skin and I shifted to get a better angle to the wet satin of her pussy. She breathed a soft moan as I started the soft rub that always made her squirm. I smiled, breaking the kiss and pulling far enough away to see the bliss in her eyes.

Her hands slid under my shirt and she ran her palms down my chest until she found the button on my shorts. She navigated the button and zipper quickly and her gentle stroke sent a shiver through me.

"Do you want to fuck me or my mouth?"

It wasn't an easy choice, and it stalled my mind for a minute. "Both," I finally said, and she smiled, lowering to her knees. Thought stopped the moment her lips swallowed me, and I closed my eyes, leaning my hands against the door, enjoying her seductive technique.

When I couldn't hold out anymore, I reached down, pulled her to her feet, and yanked her dress up at the same moment she wrapped her legs around my waist. I forced myself to hold on, to not come until she had. Luckily, I didn't have to wait long. Her pussy contracted, pulling a groan from my lips as I lost control, slamming my hips to hers until the heat exploded from my core.

"Holy shit," she whispered against my neck.

"That's the right way to do the mile high club," I whispered in her ear and then nibbled her earlobe. She squirmed in my grip, letting out a high-pitched squeal. I laughed and continued nibbling while she continued to squirm and giggle.

I pulled away and met her gaze.

"I love you, Mrs. Ryan."

She grinned. "I love you more than I thought I ever could love someone."

I slid out of her and placed her on the floor before tucking my junk back in my pants and zipping myself up. My muscles started that tired throb that always accompanied a good round of sex, and I grabbed a kiss before heading back to the comfortable leather seats. The recliner felt good, and I considered another drink, but my eyelids weren't cooperating, and the last thing I remember was the creak of the bathroom door.

Angel Wrath Chapter 13

I SHIFTED AND MY eyes blinked open. The chair next to me was empty, and I rubbed my eyes before glancing at the light blanket draped over me.

"Val?" I asked and tried to swallow, but the dryness in my mouth made my tongue feel like sandpaper against the roof of my mouth. There was an unopened water bottle sitting in the cup holder next to me and I took a drink before looking around. My brain was slow to recognize where I was, and it took the purr of the engines to snap it all together. The plane.

I had no idea how long I had been out, and I headed for the bathroom, thinking maybe she was there, but it was empty, and I did my business before heading toward the only other place she could be. The cockpit.

As I got closer, I heard her laugh through the cracked door and I pulled it open. Heather and Valerie looked up at me.

"Sleeping beauty arises," Valerie said with a laugh.

"Where are we?" I asked, glancing out at the green mountains spread out in the distance and the solid land mass under us along with the darkly painted sky.

"Over Indiana."

"Indiana?" I asked with the water bottle halfway to my mouth.

"Yes," Ted said.

"You slept through most of the trip," Heather added, stating the obvious.

"I guess so." My stomach growled and Valerie stood.

"Come on. Let's get some food into you." She linked her elbow in mine and gave Heather and Ted a finger wave as she led me from the cockpit. "They have some very amusing stories about you and Tom growing up," she said, when she deposited me in the seat and crossed to the refrigerator.

"Like what?" I was still foggy-brained, and my focus landed on the sandwich she pulled out. "Bring me one of those Coronas, too, okay?" I asked, before she had stepped away from the serving area.

"You sure?"

I nodded. A cold beer and the roast beef sandwich sounded like a perfect combination and the bag of chips she brought just added to the noise my stomach made. I practically inhaled the food and followed it with cold beer. It wasn't the nice Polynesian food from Hawaii, this was the type of roast beef sandwich you'd get from a deli in New York.

I let out a ripping burp, and Valerie's eyebrows rose. I'm usually not that uncivilized in the presence of a lady, but I was too content to really care. I offered a shrug and got to my feet, depositing the empty bottle in the trash along with the paper.

"You want one?" I asked, holding up another beer.

"Nah," she said and stretched. "I'm good."

"That you are," I said under my breath.

"What was that?"

I brought the bottle to my mouth, choosing to take a sip of beer instead of repeating what I had said. Besides, the smirk on her face told me she heard me perfectly and just wanted the ego boost.

"Assuming I can target my power, what then?" I asked, bringing us back to the original conversation from earlier this morning. "How is that going to help get my father out of hell?"

She bit her lip and shrugged. "It might give us the distraction to be able to snatch your father, but that assumes he's there at the same time."

I let out a huff. "That's one hell of an assumption."

"I never said it was a perfect solution," she muttered.

I reached out and took her hand. "At least you have something close to a plan," I said. "I've drawn a blank beyond knowing I have to do something."

I may be a genius on paper, but in situations where a devious mind was needed, I was clueless. I had snowed the devil once. I doubted he'd be dumb enough to let me do it again. But I also knew Lucifer was a bit of a megalomaniac and he would want to show off just how broken my father was, so, she might just have something that I could work from, even though I wasn't at all comfortable with the risk.

"Maybe Damian and Tom will have some ideas," she said.

"Maybe, and Steve might have some decent advice, too," I said. After all, he's the one with the closest association with criminals. His undercover career was legendary for someone so young, so he might have a few tricks up his sleeve that he could coach me on. "In the meantime, I'd rather just table this for the next hour or so until we get back to the real world."

She smiled her agreement, and we turned towards the television, electing to watch a few sit-coms for the rest of the plane ride.

Angel Wrath Chapter 14

HOME.

I dropped our bags on the floor and fell back on our bed. Valerie was downstairs sorting through the mail before we focused on the wedding gifts piled on the kitchen table.

"Chris?" she called up the stairs.

"I'm coming," I mumbled. I shouldn't be as tired as I was, especially since I had slept for a solid four or five hours on the plane. Jetlag whipped my ass, but I forced myself up and trudged down the stairs, putting a halfway interested expression on my face. The couch hugged me as I took a seat, tempting me to close my eyes, but I knew I'd get a swat from Valerie.

She had moved the pile from the kitchen onto the coffee table. With enthusiasm that reminded me of a kid at Christmas, she handed me the basket of cards and started ripping wrapping paper.

I shuffled through the envelopes. All but one was addressed to either Mr. and Mrs. Ryan or CJ and Valerie. The single envelope had my full name scrawled across the front and I stared at it as a sudden chill hit, making my stomach roll. Valerie gasped, and my gaze bounced to her.

She pulled a beautiful embroidered throw blanket out of a box and held it up. Our names and the date were imprinted, and I gave her a smile before focusing back on the letter in my hand.

Valerie continued with the next box, and I slid my finger under the tab, ripping the top of the envelope.

I pulled the card from the sheath and stared at the front. My smile faded. The perfectly appropriate wedding card was splattered with something rusty. I glanced up as Valerie displayed a silver frame; her smile was still as bright as before. I pressed my lips together in a tight smile and glanced back at the ruined card. Dread I couldn't quantify licked my soul, and I bit my lower lip, opening the card. I swallowed hard at the picture enclosed. The words were even worse.

Paper had stopped being crumpled, and I tore my gaze away from the promises listed in the card, and met Valerie's gaze. She was staring at me, and the paper slipped from my fingers. I sprang to my feet, bolting to the phone.

My heart thundered in my chest as I dialed.

"Connor residence," the familiar voice muttered.

"Dan?" I asked, unsure if it was actually Dan or someone else who answered.

Silence met my question and I glanced at the clock. It was way too late to be calling under normal circumstances, but this was far from normal.

"CJ?"

"Yes."

"You heard?"

Heard. I wish it had been a verbal announcement and not a picture with her blood splattered all over it.

"What happened?" I asked and turned in time to see the horror form in Valerie's features as she stared between the picture and the words scribed in the card.

"They say she slit her own throat," Dan said, his voice just a ghost of what it used to be. The last of his children was dead and buried and I couldn't blame him for the defeat in his tone.

Lucifer waged war by killing someone who had a line to my heart, but not enough strings to devastate. Killing Sandy was a warmup. A kind end to life compared to what he promised to do to those closest to me, and he wouldn't stop until I was dead or agreed to let him take control. He promised I would watch every depraved act.

Every drop of blood and every scream of pain would be on my soul.

"Why?" I heard myself say, and the growl that came over the line told me enough.

"Because of you," he said in that accusatory tone that made my knees weak.

He didn't know just how true that statement was, and I hung up the receiver, numbed by the confirmation that the picture was real, and that Sandy was truly dead.

"Holy Jesus," I whispered, and lowered into the chair. I stared at the phone in my hand for a moment and then started dialing. My family was spread out too thin. Steve and Jen were in New York, and Tom and Raven were on the other side of town. They both might as well be on the other side of the globe, and panic started like a bulldozer.

"Steve?" I said, as he picked up the phone.

"Did you just get back?" he asked.

"A little while ago." I glanced at the clock and closed my eyes at the late hour. I never even considered the time when I called the Connors. "Sorry for calling so late, but we got a detailed threat from Lucifer, and it covers everyone."

"Shit," Steve muttered.

"He killed Sandy," I whispered and put my head in my hand.

"What?"

"Yeah. I guess you could say that was his final warning and a warmup to what he has in mind for all of you."

"Are you sure it's not just a trick?" Steve asked.

"Lucifer sent a fucking picture, and I already talked to Dan. He thinks she killed herself. Because of me."

"Jesus," he whispered.

"Her death is on me," I said meeting Valerie's gaze. She was shaking her head, mimicking Steve's sentiments that it wasn't my fault, but it was. I was a walking death magnet and whether I was with those I loved, or halfway across the globe, Lucifer would still use my family to get to me, and he wasn't above killing them. In fact, I think he fancied the idea of slowly driving me insane.

Angel Wrath Chapter 15

I SAT ON THE couch, staring at the drawer where I had tucked the wedding card from Lucifer. Sandy's picture was no longer in view either, and my entire family argued behind me as to what needed to be done to stop this lunatic.

I hadn't slept.

Neither had Valerie, and I raised my gaze to her on the adjoining couch. She looked as haggard as I felt, and the knife Akamu gave her twirling idly in her hands told me enough about her state of mind without taking a peek myself.

Her eyes rose from the blade to mine, and she offered a shrug.

I needed to take control of the situation before the whole purpose of having my family close derailed. "How many portals have you identified?" I asked, interrupting the chaos.

Damian pressed his lips together, trading a glance with Tom.

"Sixteen," he said, after Tom waved toward me, giving him a glare fueled with annoyance.

"Is that all of them?" I asked, and silence settled over the room.

"It's all we've found on this side of the globe," Tom signed, and his gaze dropped. "We haven't looked on the other side yet."

"I need to know where every one of them is." I stared them down, appalled that they hadn't broadened their search in all this time. "Think you can handle that?" I asked, and Tom's jaw tightened. He gave me a curt nod.

"We know the signature, but we don't have unlimited access to satellites on the other side of the world," Damian said, trying to diffuse the aggravation building between my brother and me.

"You've had two years. What the fuck?"

I was waiting for you to come up with a plan to save Dad. Tom's accusatory tone accosted my brain, and I met his glare.

I checked my frustration. It wasn't aimed at him, anyway, and I stood up facing him.

"You want a shot at me?" I asked, spreading my arms wide, sensing more than just frustration with the situation in my brother.

He pressed his lips, and the muscles in his jaw jumped. The shake of his head didn't come right away, either.

I waved to the backyard, opening the silent invitation. His forms were nearly as perfect as mine and his anger wasn't unwarranted. It had been two years, and I didn't have a plan. He wasn't the only one frustrated by that, and if he kicked my ass, maybe I'd feel a little better.

Tom didn't hesitate. He stormed outside, and I followed. When he turned, throwing the first punch, I didn't block. I let his fist connect with my eye socket. It was hard enough to knock me on my ass. I climbed to my feet as his chest huffed and his hand clenched and unclenched against the sting.

"I don't have the foggiest clue of how to get Dad," I said, shaking the stars from my head. "And I was a little busy trying to put Valerie back together," I added.

His hands curled into fists again, but now a glaze covered his eyes. His fingers uncurled. "We can't leave him there," he signed, and I looked at the ground.

"I know. But the things Lucifer will do to you and Raven..." I trailed off, leaving out Lucifer's horrific detail about their daughter. "I have to close the portals." I met his stare.

"You have to get Dad," he signed, and then his fists clenched. He hadn't read the threats. I only let Damian see what Lucifer had actually written.

I stepped closer. "I don't know how, and if I don't start closing portals, he's going to get loose. When he does, do you want to know what he has in store for Raven?" I couldn't help the growl in my tone, and Tom blinked and stepped back.

"But what about Dad?" he signed, and I shook my head.

"Lucifer said he was going to stuff her so full of blood stones that her intestines would burst and then he'd set her on fire inch by inch until she choked on her own screams."

The description was less eloquent than Lucifer's, but it summed up the gist, and my brother turned the color of waxed paper.

"Is that what you want?" I snarled, stepping so close that I crowded him.

He stood his ground, searching my gaze for any hint of exaggeration, and then he slowly shook his head, taking a step back.

"No," he signed.

"That's the decision I have to make. Dad or everyone else and it fucking sucks," I whispered, with a voice filled with unbearable bitterness. "My death won't save anyone, either. I considered that option."

His eyes widened a fraction and then the pain appeared in his irises.

"If I thought that would work, I would have swallowed a bullet last night. Just like that." I snapped my fingers. "But it would only fuel that bastard's fury and leave you all at his mercy." The admission of the darker thoughts that played through my mind last night brought forth a fresh layer of tears that I blinked away.

I turned away from my brother and crossed to the rock wall, to the spot that seemed to be my go to place when the world dished out too much shit. His shadow followed, and he took a seat, facing the house.

"I have to close the portals," I said. "There isn't any other choice."

His head dipped in a nod, and he studied his hands.

"If we can figure out a way to get Dad out before I close the last one, I'd be willing to try, but it's not something that will stop me if it doesn't work." I dropped my gaze from the ocean view to his. "And I'm scared shitless it's going to kill everything good in me."

I moved my gaze away and took a deep breath, exhaling and steeling my emotions behind the iron curtain in my heart. Until this was all over, I couldn't feel, and I certainly couldn't allow myself to second guess my mission.

If I did, people would die.

It was a sobering thought, and I gave Tom a forced smile and turned, heading back inside to find a map. It took me a while to find a large map of the world in my old closet and I brought it downstairs, where everyone was quietly discussing what to do. I knew what I had to do and now time had run out.

I spread the map out on the table and handed Damian a marker. "Show me where they all are."

My brain was too foggy to follow the number of dots, but when he stopped, I counted sixteen marks. New York wasn't one of them, and my gaze moved from the map to his. He moved his hand toward that last spot, hesitating before I grabbed his wrist.

He and I exchanged a look, and I shook my head. I didn't want Valerie to know that portal was still open, and he nodded, understanding even without words. I scanned the marks and pointed to the one in Hawaii.

"That one's closed." I tapped, and he crossed it off.

"That leaves fifteen," he said, and my gaze moved back to New England.

Beyond the one in New York City, the closest mark was in Canada, just north of Quebec, and the farthest was down in Argentina. I figured anything east of the Rockies in the U.S. and Canada was the biggest threat.

"We need to hit this first." I tapped the one in eastern Canada. "And it will need to wait until after my concert next week," I said, meeting Damian's gaze. "In the meantime, I need you to figure out where the portals are on the other side of the world. Okay?"

"I'll do my best," he said, and scanned the map before exhaling.

"I'm surprised to see the lack of clusters," I said, scanning the map. "New England had three portals within a few hours of each other, but there isn't anything like that in the rest of the states." I met his gaze, and he nodded.

"I had the same impression as well, but I've got no real explanation. The closest cluster is in the southwest." He waved toward four dots between Nevada, Southern California, Arizona and New Mexico. "But even those aren't as close as the ones here were." He sighed and glanced back at me. "Why don't you get some sleep," he added. "And then you and I should have a conversation regarding options."

"Options?"

"Rescue options," he clarified. "After you get sleep. You're exhausted and you and I will need both our minds sharp to figure something out, now that you're closing these things in earnest. The more we close, the more relentless Lucifer will be."

His statement just turned the knife inside me, and I bit my lip to control the reaction. "I'm fine. What did you have in mind?" I really wanted to hear his ideas, especially after the bloom of pain in my core at his comment. Basically, the more portals I closed, the harder Lucifer would be on my father. The fact that Damian had some ideas on how to get my father out of hell shined a little hope into my foggy brain.

He laughed at me. "You and Valerie haven't slept for what... something like thirty hours now?"

"I slept on the plane," I said, but he was right. My mind wasn't working very well, and as much as I wanted to focus, my eyes kept drifting to the map and my thoughts followed. I needed at least a few hours of sleep in order to focus on any one thing. I glanced at the crew gathered in the family room and then back at Damian, suddenly worried about a surprise attack.

"I promise to keep everyone safe. Go sleep." He pointed to the stairs, and this time it wasn't a request.

I sighed and nodded before I crossed to Valerie. Grabbing her hand, I pulled her away from the family with a one-word explanation. "Sleep."

She came without question and neither of us spoke while we undressed, and I moved the suitcases off the bed. We slipped under the sheets, and I just kissed her cheek, pulling her into the spoon position. She wrapped her arms around mine and squeezed, reminding me without words that she loved me, and I squeezed back.

Lucifer's hideous promises kept looping in our heads like a nightmare we couldn't wake from. No matter how hard I tried to push back, the fear of what the future held kept coming, hitting me with the full force of a runaway train.

Angel Wrath Chapter 16

THE HEAT OF THE sun woke me, and I squinted at the blue sky outside the window, wondering when the hell sleep finally grabbed hold of me. It took a few minutes to realize it was morning, and I yawned, rolling on my back and stretching without taking my arm out from underneath Valerie.

I rolled back, molding into her, and squeezed her close. "Babe, we need to get up," I whispered in her ear, and she whined, burying her face in the pillow.

If I could hole up in the room all week, I would, but I needed to have a talk with Damian and hear what his grand rescue plans were. I'd also need to start practicing what Valerie had mentioned on the plane because I knew damned well she wouldn't let me go off on my own to destroy the portals.

New York would be my last solo act.

Her eyes blinked open, and she turned towards me. "I thought you were singing with Jen?" she asked, and I strapped down on my thoughts, admonishing myself for not being more careful.

"I'll be in the city without you," I said, quickly enough to cover up my mistake.

Her eyes softened, and she kissed my cheek before rolling out of bed and heading towards the bathroom.

I stared at the ceiling and then rubbed my face, forcing myself out of the warm bed. "I want to go back to Hawaii," I muttered, and started making the bed.

Valerie stuck her head out of the bathroom. "You and me both," she said, and I uttered a soft laugh, meeting her gaze. "I have to go into work in an hour," she added.

I turned and stared at the clock. Crap. It was Monday, and that unsettled nervous energy started in. I'd have to weather eight hours with her out of sight, and that didn't sit well.

"Val," I started, and she glared in my direction.

"I'm not putting my life on hold," she snapped, and disappeared into the bathroom.

I finished making the bed and crossed, ripping the door open and leveling a glare in her direction. "After what he promised?"

Her eyes shifted from her own reflection to mine. "I've been running from Lucifer for ten years. I'm not running anymore," she said around a toothbrush, and then she spit in the sink.

"I can make you..." I started, and she spun on me, the storm brewing in her irises.

"Chris, I swear, I'll rip your heart out myself if you even think about issuing a command for me to stay put." She stomped past me into the bedroom.

I brushed my teeth trying to justify all the reasons to keep her here, but the look in her eyes told me not to fuck with her. Not today. Especially not after what happened in Hawaii, and after I rinsed the paste from my mouth, I leaned on the counter, hanging my head while I tried to figure out the best course of action.

"He's not going to strike today," she said from the doorway, and I turned to face her.

"How do you know?"

She bit her lip and shrugged. "It doesn't feel right. It's not happening. Not today."

I didn't have the same conviction. At least not on the surface, but deep down, I knew she was right. My nerves had to do with my insecurity, not the sense of a pending disaster, and she raised an eyebrow.

"I..." I stopped myself from admitting I was scared. She already knew the turmoil wringing my stomach into knots. Voicing it wouldn't make it go away.

"I know," she said, and sighed before slipping behind the half-open door. Drawers opened and the soft whisper of fabric reached my ears.

I dragged the brush through my hair and grabbed a pair of sweatpants, pulling them on while Valerie pinned her hair up. She chose a turquoise pair of scrubs from the drawer and the color reminded me of the ocean we had left behind.

"We never settled on what to do with Koa," I said and slipped a t-shirt over my head.

She paused at the door. "Koa's used to the warmth of Hawaii. It might be a hell of a shock for her to come here."

She had a good point.

"Then maybe we need to get a couple of dogs," I said.

She smiled. "If that makes you feel better, go for it."

"I'm thinking more for you than me," I said, and her hands dropped from taming the last of the stray hairs.

"Why?"

I shoved my hands into the pockets of my sweats and looked at the ground. My justifications for a guard dog had everything to do with going out on my own to stop Lucifer and not having her along. I knew it was in contrast to what I said in Hawaii, and when I looked up, Valerie's features hardened.

"No." She turned and stomped out of the room.

"But Val," I followed her, catching up to her on the stairs.

"We already had this discussion," she said, glaring up at me. "You need to figure out how to do what we talked about. I'm going to work." She tore out of my grip and, as soon as we turned on the landing, we both stopped.

We stared at the group sitting around the table. I think we just assumed everyone had gone home. If they had, they certainly came back bright and early.

"I have to get to work," Valerie said, and turned to me. "We will talk when I get home," she added, pointing at my chest.

I nodded and gave her a soft kiss. "Have a good day, and if something happens…"

"I'll call," she said and patted my cheek. "I love you."

"I love you, too."

She stepped out of the house, and I watched her until her car turned the corner, disappearing from sight. My stomach tightened with irrational fear, and I closed the door. My back burned from the singular focus of everyone in the room, and I turned to face my family.

"Have you guys been up all night?" I asked.

"Not everyone," Steve said and leaned back in the chair. "Tom, Damian, and I have been tossing ideas around all night, but the girls got some sleep." As if on cue, he yawned. "I'm too old for this shit," he muttered, turning back to the map and the steaming carafe of coffee.

I crossed to the cabinets and pulled out a coffee cup, helping myself to the fresh brew before I slid into the empty seat. "Did you figure out anything that you think is viable?" I asked, searching their features.

"Why don't we bring the kids over to our house," Naomi said, and stood. Raven and Jennifer followed suit, collecting the kids from the family room where they were happily coloring. As soon as they left, everyone turned to me.

Steve ran a hand down his face. "We have a few options, but honestly, they're all wild cards." He met my gaze.

"Valerie isn't going to let me go alone," I said and traded a glance with Damian. *These guys have no clue about New York, do they?*

Damian's slight shake of his head confirmed my thought, and I wanted to keep it that way. I could see Steve insisting on coming, and without power, he'd be just another one of Lucifer's pawns. I couldn't walk him into that, not after all he'd done for us.

"Are you serious?" Tom signed.

"Yeah. She has the crazy idea that I can focus my power and store it under her skin so they'll think she's defenseless." I stared into my coffee and the silence pulled my gaze up.

Steve bit his lip like he was seriously contemplating that option, and then he met my gaze. "That actually could work."

"Excuse me?" My eyebrows rose.

"Look, one scenario we came up with was Damian grabbing your father. We all think the next time you go up against Lucifer, he will flaunt what's left of your dad in order to knock you down a peg or two," he said, and my jaw tightened at the thought.

"But if it's just you and me..." Damian trailed off and inhaled. "If it's just you and me, this could backfire."

"It could backfire anyway," I said, meeting their gaze. "If Valerie is there and I can't protect her, I'm as fucked as they get." I paused, focusing on Damian. "You've been there. You know what kind of sick bastard he is. If he gets a hold of Valerie..." I couldn't finish. Instead, I closed my eyes and bowed my head.

"She could distract him long enough for me to grab your father," Damian said. "I know using her as bait isn't what you want to do, but it may be the only shot we have. We both know Lucifer has her on the top of his hit list. If you can do what she proposed, it could be a more palatable risk."

I stared at him and exhaled. "Would you put Naomi in that position?"

Damian struggled with the answer and finally lowered his gaze and shook his head. I moved my sharp stare toward Tom and Steve.

"Would you gamble with Raven's life?"

Tom shook his head and when I moved along to Steve, he sat back with his arms crossed. I just raised an eyebrow.

"I used Jen as bait on more than one occasion, and every time I put her at risk, something bad happened. She was gang raped because I was a jackass and didn't listen to my gut. I didn't make her leave New York when every instinct I had told me to get her out. She nearly died because of my miscalculations. My daughter died because I underestimated the criminals hunting us. I've never gotten over that. It haunts me every day, but Jennifer is alive, and God bless her, she's still with me."

He kept my gaze. "You know the mistakes I've made, and do you know the shit thing of it all?"

I shook my head.

"If I had to do it all over again, I would probably make the same fucking mistakes." He let that sit for a moment while he leaned forward and took a sip of coffee. "I've lived my life on the borderline of reckless and left a hell of a bloody trail behind me because of it, but I did my job and caught the bad guys."

I gave him a nod and studied my coffee for a minute.

"Sometimes, you have to take that risk. The bigger the bad, the bigger the gamble in order to stop them," he added, and I looked back at him. "But there's a world of difference between this situation and everything I've lived through. I'm not you. I'm not standing in your shoes."

"I'm scared," I admitted directly to Steve.

The tension in his features loosened. "I would have you committed if you weren't."

I cracked a smile.

"Look, CJ, you know I love you like my own, and I do not want you walking into a trap," he said and paused, focusing on the table in front of him as he drew a breath. "But we all know every portal you step into is a trap. It's just how we approach it. If it was me, I don't know if I would follow through on the promises you made in heaven. Not when it puts everyone you love at risk, but at least the powers you possess give you an edge here."

"I don't have a choice. If I walk away from my responsibility, everyone is already at risk and my father's sacrifice was wasted. The more portals I close, the more desperate he'll get. Either way, no one is safe, and I'm totally screwed."

"And you don't want to use Val as bait," Steve said.

"No. But she will not let me go alone, so I have to figure out how to make this work. Hell, I already ordered her to stay behind in Hawaii, and she said she'd cut my heart out herself if I ever pulled that shit on her again."

Damian pressed his lips together, trying to shut down the smirk that appeared.

"Yeah, it nearly ruined the honeymoon," I replied, and now all three of them wore the same smirk. They didn't say a word, and I appreciated it. I was sure at some future date they'd use that information to needle me, but today, it wasn't something to screw around with.

"Besides the outstanding questions of whether I can protect Valerie, or whether I even have any of my mojo on Lucifer's turf, I'm not comfortable leaving the rest of you vulnerable while we're off trying to rescue my father. He's already dead. You aren't." I pointed between Tom and Steve. "I don't want to leave you and your families unprotected." My gaze landed on Damian.

"What if we stayed at our cottage?" Steve asked.

"I'd have to bring your father to Paradise Cove in order to get him beyond Lucifer's reach and it's the only way back to Heaven that I know of," Damian said.

I scanned the map, focusing on the dot near Quebec in Canada. "I know it's five hours to Quebec, and it looks like at least a couple of more from there."

"That's if you can drive right to the spot."

I hadn't considered alternate transportation, and I ran my hand over my face. "Do we have access to a helicopter?"

My question surprised everyone, and I focused on Steve, not Damian or Tom. He chewed his lip and nodded.

"I can call in a favor, but it won't get you in the middle of that reserve. Maybe we could get you into here." He tapped a township at the southern tip of the reserve. "And then use snowmobiles for the rest of the trek," he added with a shrug. "I'm not sure if I have the kind of clout that's needed to pull that off, but I certainly can try."

"Does Ted have one?" I asked.

Steve shook his head. "At least I don't think so. I know the FBI does, but I'm sure there will be a thousand and one questions that neither of us is prepared to answer. I know a slew of people who still haven't gotten over what happened in court. There are those with significant reservations about not having me under their thumb, and you are a wild card in their minds. I don't think opening that door is wise."

I huffed a laugh. "You think?"

He grinned. "Yeah. I think."

"So, who owes you a favor?"

He glanced at his hands. "O'Keefe."

"The York Police Department? They don't have a chopper."

"They don't, but O'Keefe's brother does some of the shoreline tours over the summer."

I leaned back in the seat and bit the inside of my lip. "Well, that would cut the trip by at least a couple of hours," I said.

"I've had helicopters land in my yard during the summer, but not the winter, so I'm not sure what options we have. In the meantime, we should figure a backup plan in case this falls through."

"Seems like the snowmobile options are pretty sound for getting in and out of the reservoir," I said and received nods from everyone. I leaned back in the chair. "But what if the bastard doesn't show off the hell he's rained on Dad? What then?"

"You really think he's going to pass up the opportunity to rub your face in the sacrifice you made?" Damian asked with an incredulous laugh. "After twenty-five hundred years of experience with the lunatic, I say he won't pass up on the chance to push your buttons."

I traded a glance with my brother, waiting for him to weigh in. He gave me a nod.

"Okay. We have half a plan," I said, but something didn't sit right. It just seemed too easy, just like Hawaii. "What happens if he sends his army after you?" I asked, looking directly at Steve before moving my gaze to Damian and Tom. "There's no one here to protect you."

Steve slowly leaned back in the chair. "You once loaned your father a slice of your power," he started and I nodded, but it wasn't Steve that my gaze slid to.

"Think you could handle it?" I asked Tom.

He pointed at his chest and his mouth popped open before his gaze bounced to Steve.

"You're the one with angel blood, not Steve," I said, and glanced at Steve. "I know you meant for you, but he's my blood and I know he's got my back along with the same impulse to protect Grace that I have." Steve opened his mouth to argue, but I put up my hand. "I know you were an FBI agent and have that ingrained in your blood, but you are also an expert shot. He isn't." I pointed at Tom. "If I'm going to leave you vulnerable, I need you to be protected on multiple fronts. I figure a tiger, a marksman, a psychic freak, and a Wiccan should do the trick."

"Fee?" Tom articulated.

"Yeah, you're a fucking freak, just like me," I said, and couldn't quite keep a straight face.

He pressed his lips together against the smile, but the small creases at the corner of his eyes told me he found the grain of humor I tried to pass. Tom nodded and signed, "I appreciate the offer, but do you think you can teach me how to use it in the time we've got?"

I shrugged. "I don't know. I also don't know if I can do what Valerie suggested, but it's worth a try. If it doesn't work, Steve can be the fall back, okay?"

Everyone exchanged glances and then nodded.

I stood up and pointed my chin toward the sliders. Tom got up and followed me outside. I took a seat on the cold rock wall, patting the spot next to me.

"You sure I can handle this?" Tom signed, and the worry in his eyes echoed the hesitation I saw in his hands.

"Yes. The only warning I have for you is to watch your temper. That's when it can do damage if it gets away from you. You remember learning to call for Steve and me?"

He nodded.

"That level of concentration is needed to shut off the surrounding noise. We're all pretty good at blocking our thoughts, but regular folks have no clue and if you're in a public place, the noise is hell unless you learn to block it. You ready?"

He scanned the house and then met my gaze with a nod.

"It's going to feel kind of weird, like something wild is filling your skin. It will settle after a few minutes, so just breathe through it." I closed my eyes, concentrating on tearing a piece of my power off. Like ripping fabric, I felt the tug and the shredding from my core until I mentally held a small extract. I opened my eyes and stared at the glow in my palm. Tom was staring at it, at well, and I turned, slamming it into his chest while I held onto him, so he didn't topple off the rock wall into the ocean.

Tom's eyes went wide, and his breath hitched in his chest as the power transferred along with my memories. Every muscle in his body contracted, and I whispered, "Breathe."

It took him a few seconds, and then he sucked in a large wheezing breath, forcing air in and then out again. His wild-eyed gaze locked with mine and I smiled at him as his memories settled in my head along with the rest.

"Kind of a rush, huh?"

He nodded as his breath returned to normal and his shaking hands ran through his hair. "Holy shit," he whispered and then blinked, his gaze shooting to mine while his fingers verified his tongue was still missing. What came out of his mouth wasn't articulate. It was his thought that was loud and clear and overrode his senses.

"You still can't speak clearly," I said.

"But..." he started and stopped, blinking again.

"Welcome to the world of the genuine freaks," I said, and he burst out laughing.

"As if being an ancestor of Lucifer isn't freaky enough," he said, and traded a glance with me. His hands remained still on his thighs, and it was good to hear him clearly over the bastardization of speech.

"I don't stutter in my head," I said and sent a grin his way.

"Yeah, well, it doesn't come out as smoothly as what you hear in your head."

"Ditto."

He smiled and flexed his hands. "So, you're hitting the warehouse in New York without telling anyone," he said, sliding his gaze to me.

"I forgot to lock that shit up," I muttered, and met his gaze.

"And damn, Jenna really turned out to be a fucking freak," he said. The smile that played on his lips made me want to smack him.

"You want me shuffling through your memories?" I asked and stood, turning to face the water before looking down and meeting his gaze. "I haven't yet, but I'd be happy to play this game."

His smile toned down a notch, and he dropped his eyes, staring at the ground for a minute before he shook his head. He glanced at the house, turning serious. "You've got a lot of shit in your head," he said, looking up at me.

"Ayup." I sighed and nodded. "And you have to lock down the information about New York, otherwise Val will skin me alive."

Tom huffed and climbed to his feet. "So, how does this work?"

"Think you can move the picnic table?"

"How?"

"Just focus and envision it moving to a different spot."

His eyes narrowed as he looked at the table and then at a location a few feet away. When the table moved precisely where his gaze landed, his eyes widened, and his head whipped in my direction.

"I felt it go," he said, and his voice filled with awe.

"Now put the table back."

He did, and he slowly lowered to the rock wall. I took a seat next to him again.

"So, anything I wish..." he trailed off and met my gaze.

"You can move things and even destroy things with a thought. Understand there are limitations and things can go wrong," I said, my mind drifting back to my snorkeling adventure with Valerie and I looked at my hands, picking a hangnail before I continued. "Most people you can hear, but true psychopaths actually create static the way we've learned to do. And you can't hear a demon or a vampire. I'm not sure why, but it could be because they're dead and you just can't get a bead on their frequency."

"But I will still be able to see ghosts, right?"

"Yes. Your inherent gifts don't go away.

"I gather you gave me a small amount?"

I nodded. "Relatively speaking," I said and smiled. "But I gave you more than I gave Dad when we were four."

"Really?"

I nodded. "When Damian and I go do this thing, you need to stand watch over everyone at the cottage. I wanted you to have enough mojo to kill whatever comes after you."

"You think he'll send an army?"

I shrugged. "Even if he does, you are now more deadly than an army of demons."

I stood and left him to noodle on the amount of responsibility he had while he shuffled through the memories emblazoned in his mind. As for me, I escaped to my room before anyone intercepted, overwhelmed by exactly what my little brother's memories revealed.

I had seen a couple of Jennifer's visions when Tom was in Georgia, but I didn't have the full scope of what happened until now. The fact he didn't die of shock, and kept a level head, even when that asshole starting cutting him, amazed me. I wondered how in the hell he made it through that without losing his mind, especially when that bastard placed our mother's head on the end of the table he was strapped to.

Nothing I had survived compared to what he'd endured, and his misguided awe of me was humbling. There wasn't much I kept from him, but the battles he had to keep his sanity intact were brutal. I gained a new appreciation for my brother and knew I'd made the right decision. He would operate with the same moral compass that guided my mother and me, and probably do it with a lot more grace than I could ever muster.

Angel Wrath Chapter 17

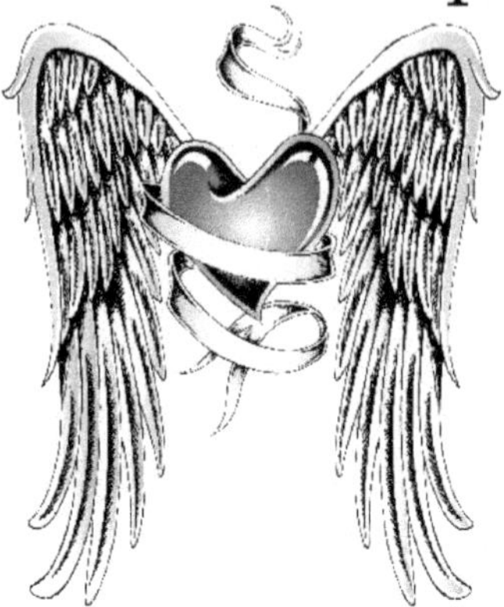

"TRY AGAIN." VALERIE SAID through clenched teeth as the wound on her side healed.

I dropped the bloody knife on the table and walked away. "I can't do this," I muttered and headed for the six-pack in the refrigerator. Over a dozen tries, and each time the knife went too deep before hitting the barrier. If I had been aiming for her heart, she would have died.

I popped the top off using the edge of the counter and drained the bottle in one long chug. I never thought I'd ever plant a knife in my wife's form, so doing it over a dozen times in the last hour was wearing thin.

"Chris," she snapped, and I turned with a second beer in my hand.

"I can't." This time, the words came out with the same force as my hand squeezing the bottle. The glass shattered, sending a spray of beer over the kitchen floor and I snapped my hand, dislodging a few of the bigger glass shards. "Fuck!"

"Jesus, let me look at your hand." Valerie marched over and peeled my fingers back to inspect the array of cuts. She pulled out a couple of smaller shards before leaning in and delivering the healing kiss, bringing with it the sting.

"I can't do this, Val," I said softly, and I looked down at the bloody tatters of her shirt. "I can't keep cutting you." She had no clue how much these practice sessions killed me. Either my protective barrier was too shallow or too deep. I couldn't seem to find the balance and if she didn't have access to her healing mojo on Lucifer's turf and the barrier was too deep, she would die. I had to operate on the worst-case scenario. If I didn't, it would bite me in the ass.

"Then I'll do the knife," she said and walked away.

I grabbed her arm. "No. Give it a rest. I need to prep for the concert tomorrow, anyway."

"Chris, you need to have this down cold," she said.

"I know." She didn't need to remind me. I hadn't put a concrete plan in place for heading north, and I knew on some level I was stalling. I needed to get through the concert and closing off the portal in New York before I thought about the one in Canada. Steve called in that favor and was waiting to hear whether or not it was a go. The timing depended on the weather, and I was all set to focus on that adventure the moment I got back home from my concert.

"Have you figured out when we are going?" she asked, pulling me back to the present.

I grabbed the paper towels and cleaned up the beer and glass from the floor. "No. Not yet. We need to wait for a decent stretch of weather." I glanced outside at the icy winter rain. "We can't fly in this," I waved towards the window as I stood and dumped the wet rag into the garbage. With a glance, whatever shards were left, levitated, and landed in the pail at my direction.

"I know, I'm just worried," she said, her quiet voice pulling my attention back to her.

"Well, at least we've gotten to the point I can put the barrier inside you," I said, giving her a shrug. The first few tries sent her flying across the room and into the wall when the power connected. I had to set it to a low-level stun to accomplish it, and pulling it out of her was easy, even to a ten-foot radius around her. We got that part down and it was kind of fun setting up a circle of blocks and water bottles to knock over. However, moving things was a far cry from toasting demons, and we both knew it.

"How's Tom doing?" she asked, giving me a blessed break from this insanity.

"He's still getting used to everything, but at least he can vaporize on demand." I started laughing and got a cross glare from Valerie. "Come on, you don't think this entire conversation is bizarre?"

She pressed her lips together against the smile. "I need to change, since we're done for the day," she said and left me laughing in the kitchen. However normal this was for me, it still had such a strange ring to it when I said everything out loud.

As soon as my laughter eased, I moved to the piano in the living room and started tinkering. It had been a while since I sat down and played and I closed my eyes, letting the notes flow. The tune was familiar now and came as easily as breathing.

When the last note faded, I opened my eyes. Valerie stood leaning on the door frame with that hungry look, and my eyebrows rose. She grinned and blushed, her gaze dropping to the ground and back to me in that coy manner that lit the fire in my core.

I stood and crossed until I was within arm's length of her and stopped, cocking my head. I licked my lips and delivered my famous grin. "You like what you hear?"

She rolled her eyes at me and turned to leave the room. My arm snaked out, encircling her waist and drawing her to me.

"You dare roll your eyes at me?" I whispered and bit her earlobe gently but firmly enough for her to gasp. She squirmed in my grasp, and I pushed her forward, holding her against the wall while my hands wandered.

"Chris!" Her voice carried both humor and now a hint of panic as my lips ran down the side of her neck.

"Yeah, baby," I whispered against her skin. My hands were split, one on her breasts and the other between her legs. Something about her tone almost made me dial back, but she had started this with that hungry tiger look. I was just taking her up on the silent thoughts running through her head while I sang.

"Stop," she whispered.

"Do you really want me to?" I continued to caress her and nibble on her neck.

She hesitated for a minute and then she pushed against the wall. The claustrophobia of being pinned finally winning out over my advances. Without her uttering the word yes, I stepped away with my hands in the air.

"Sorry," I said, but there was no sincerity in my apology, and she turned toward me with reddened cheeks.

"You know I can't..." Her fists clenched, and she stared at the floor, gaining control of the fear that had flashed over.

"I thought we got past this?" Anger now burned just below the surface.

She looked around at everything but me, and her head shook.

"What the fuck?"

Her gaze jumped to mine at the anger in my tone. "I... I don't know," she stumbled over the words. She attempted to wave toward the kitchen, and without words, her eyes expressed her confusion.

"Are you telling me our practicing fucked you back up?" My voice rose, carrying the incredulous tone of the shock skittering through me. "If I had known this would happen..." I stepped back, turning and crossing to the piano. I no longer wanted to screw around, and when I took a seat, my fingers flew over the keys, plucking the chorus of the Bon Jovi tune 'Blaze of Glory' and the words came out in such an angry growl that she backed out of the room in tears.

I slammed my hands on the keys and bellowed in frustration. My anger got the best of me, and I closed my eyes, grinding my teeth as I tried to count myself into a calmer zone. It wasn't until I got to thirty that the shakes gripping me loosened. I blinked my eyes open and forced my breathing into slow, long inhales and exhales until I had complete control.

When I finally stood, the remorse had settled in, and I went searching for her. I found her in our bedroom, face down on the bed.

I crossed and took a seat next to her, but I didn't reach for her or touch her in any manner. "I'm sorry," I whispered. This time I meant it.

She sniffled and turned her head towards me. Her bloodshot eyes met mine and I offered a hint of a shrug.

"I guess I got a little carried away."

She shook her head. "I'm sorry, too. I really thought between our wedding night and the honeymoon we had broken his hold on me."

I moved my hand to her and slowly scratched her back in silence.

"I want to tear him apart limb from limb," she said after a while.

"You're not alone," I said and met her gaze. "Just the fact I had to hurt you once, never mind over a dozen times today, upped the ante for me. I want to feel bones crush under my fist until he can't fucking move."

The venom flowing through my blood was just as potent as the powers lacing my muscles, and I inhaled, moving to leave her alone until she was ready.

Her hand caught mine and the spark lit in her eyes.

I shook my head. "I can't cope with being tied up today," I said, and her hand dropped.

"Why would you assume that?"

"You're going to tell me that wasn't crossing your mind?"

She opened her mouth and then popped it closed. Valerie shook her head and then buried it back in the pillow, looking away from me. I knew I probably should have let her. We had been home for almost a week and hadn't screwed around. We hadn't broken our home in.

I glanced around and grabbed her hand. "Come with me," I said, and pulled her through the house, out the door and onto the front stoop.

"What are you doing?" she asked.

I scooped her up in my arms. "I never carried you over the threshold."

She smiled. "You're such a sap."

"Yeah, but it's tradition for the groom to carry the bride over the threshold. It's a symbol of the start of a new life."

Her hand covered her mouth and her eyes welled up with tears. As soon as we were inside, she pulled my lips to hers. The kiss was soft and sweet. I carried her upstairs and closed the bedroom door with a sweep of my foot.

When I laid her on the bed, she kept her arms around my neck, pulling me on top of her. I pulled away from her lips and met her gaze. "You sure about this?" I asked, before I got too far down the road. I didn't want to be shot down when my libido was in overdrive.

"Yes," she whispered, and I went all in.

I took my time making love to Valerie. My slow progression drove her crazy, and she writhed under my hands, under my mouth, begging me like she hadn't in years. I wanted her to keep repeating my name in that breathless quality she had right before she came. I wanted her wet and ready for me. Hell, I wanted her crying to the gods.

I wanted this bliss to last because I had a feeling I would need all the sweet memories I could pile up before I faced the shit storm waiting for me in New York.

Angel Wrath Chapter 18

DAMIAN ANSWERED THE DOOR, and I sent a strained smile at him. Beyond him, the noise reached new levels. Grace came running by, laughing as her brothers chased her and Hannah around the first floor.

I let out a small laugh and turned to Valerie, giving her a quick kiss. "I'll call you when I get there," I said. "Enjoy the family," I added, and she chuckled at the chaos.

Tom stepped into view. "Did you want me to come down to New York with you?" he signed, but the words were clear in my head.

"Nah, I'll be okay." I appreciated the offer and gave him a nod of thanks. "How are you doing with everything?"

"He's doing great," Damian interjected. "I think he actually got it faster than I did."

Tom's cheeks transitioned to that rosy color of embarrassment, and he shrugged. "I'm adjusting," he signed, and his words echoed. "It's a pretty heady experience," he added.

"I know." I'd had a small period with nothing, and even though it coincided with Lucifer inhabiting my body, it still was weird not to wield the power of the angels, so I could only imagine what the other way around felt like.

"If you need anything..." He trailed off and looked over his shoulder at the house before focusing back on me. "Let me know."

"I will. Let me know if something happens here, okay?"

"I know how to yell for you," Tom said and tapped his temple.

That maneuver he had down to a science. He could reach me half-way around the world at this point, so I wasn't worried. With both Damian and Tom watching the brood, I was sure nothing would get to them, and if something slipped through, they always had Valerie. She was in good hands tonight. I just hoped like hell I didn't miscalculate the danger on the home front, and I prayed Steve and Jennifer wouldn't be the vulnerable ones. With a nod, I turned and climbed into my car, driving away without a glance back.

It had been a while since I had been in New York and the drive down wasn't bad for a Friday afternoon. I had expected to get to the apartment building with enough time to spare for dinner before we had to leave for Carnegie Hall, but I pulled in a little after three, a good hour and a half before I had planned.

I rolled the window down when the attendant strolled up to the car.

"I haven't seen this corvette in years," the attendant said, appraising it with envy.

"Jason, right?" I asked and my gaze dropped to his name tag.

He smiled and nodded. "You're Chris Ryan's son, right?"

"You remember my dad?" I asked, a little surprised. It had been close to twenty years since my father died, and this was the first time I had driven down on my own. Usually, I was crammed in the back of the truck with Tom and Raven.

"Sure do. He was one of the nicest residents here." Jason sighed as his gaze moved towards the ramp and his memories circled around one of his most horrifying experiences with my father.

"I guess," I mumbled, uncomfortable with the attendant's train of thought.

"He ended up paying for my college education," Jason said, and pulled his attention back to me.

His admission surprised me. I did not know my father did stuff like that. "Really?"

Jason smiled. "Yes. He took good care of a lot of people here," he said, nodding toward the building.

"I never knew that," I whispered, and sighed.

"Your father was a good man," he said. "I'm sorry he's gone," he added, and cleared his throat, adopting more of a professional manner. "Mr. Williams told me you were coming. Did you want me to park the car for you, or do you remember where the penthouse entrance is?"

"I remember," I said and reached for my wallet.

"Mr. Williams already took care of that, sir," he said, and I hesitated, glancing at the older gentleman.

"Can I ask you a personal question?" I asked and fished out my wallet anyway.

"Sure," he said.

"Didn't you get your masters in finance?"

He nodded.

"So, why are you moonlighting here?"

He offered a smile and a shrug. "Times are tough," he said.

I got a glimpse of the hardships he'd been handed and felt the first jab of guilt for having all the money I had when hard-working people like Jason got the raw end of the stick.

I pulled out a few bills and handed them to him. He stared at the cash and shook his head.

"I told you, Mr. Williams covered it."

"I know, but you told me some...thing I never knew about my dad. And frank...ly, it's something I needed to hear. So, this is my way of saying thank you." I stuttered through the awkward moment and pushed the cash into his hand before driving away.

Jennifer and Steve were lounging on the living room couch when I opened the door.

"Did you know my dad paid for Jason's college bills?" I asked when the door closed behind me.

Steve nodded. "He also put the doorman's kids through college."

"No shit?"

"Your dad had more money than he knew what to do with, and I guess those folks that showed genuine interest and kindness benefitted." He shrugged. "Why?"

"I just never knew about stuff like that." I took a seat on the chair facing the balcony. "So, you ready for tonight?" I asked Jennifer, changing the subject before it crawled under my skin.

"Absolutely." She beamed.

I tried to tap into that enthusiasm, but the information Jason gave me weighed heavy on my heart. I put on a fake smile and glanced outside.

Steve put down the paper and stared at me, pulling my attention from the skyline to him.

"What's eating you?"

My smile faded, and I shrugged, opting to keep quiet instead of bringing everyone else down with me. "Nothing," I said.

"Bullshit." He crossed his arms, waiting.

I closed my eyes and dropped my chin to my chest, allowing the turmoil inside to surface for the briefest of instances, and then I inhaled and met Steve's gaze. "My father." That's really all I had to say. Jennifer moved closer and covered my hand with hers.

"He loves you, CJ, and he made the sacrifice because he loves you. That was his choice, honey, not yours. Someday you'll understand."

"I know, but it still doesn't make me feel better."

Silence settled, and she gave my hand a small pat before standing and starting toward the kitchen. She paused at the door. "So, are you changing anything up tonight?" she asked.

"I hadn't really thought about it much," I said and she gave me a nod, disappearing into the kitchen and I glanced at Steve. "Been too busy trying to figure out how to embed my protective wall under Valerie's skin." The moment the words came out, I started laughing. I couldn't help it. We somehow walked into this god forsaken nightmare, and none of us could break the spell. I leaned forward and put my head in my hands. "In your worst nightmares, did you ever think we'd be chasing the devil?"

Steve burst out laughing, too. "Fuck no," he said, and I glanced up at him. "It's kind of a sick joke. Isn't it?"

"Yeah," I said, still huffing. Steve rarely swore around us, so hearing the expletive tickled the laughter out of me.

"Jesus, if I had only known..." Steve trailed off and his laughter faded.

My laughter faded as well. "No kidding, you would have run like hell the moment they introduced you to Eric," I said.

Steve's smile slowly disappeared, and he leaned forward. "The only thing I would have changed, in all this time, was bringing you to Georgia. That's my biggest regret where your family is concerned," he said. "Everything else just enriched our lives."

I looked around the penthouse and back at him.

His eyes narrowed. "That's not what I meant," he said, crossing his arms.

I smiled. "I know. I just wanted to get a rise out of you."

"Jennifer wanted to cook tonight," he said, glancing towards the kitchen.

"Really?" I didn't mean for the disappointment to bleed into my voice, but his smirk and raised eyebrows told me I failed.

"Yeah, really. But I have Chinese delivery scheduled to arrive about a half hour before we have to leave."

My lips spread into a grin, which I suppressed the moment Jennifer poked her head out the door.

"Can I get you something to drink?"

"You have a coke or something?" I asked, turning her way. I could use something a little harder, but I never drank before a performance. She nodded, and I focused on Steve after the door closed. "Does she know you ordered food?" I whispered.

He just smirked and picked up the paper.

"That would be a no," I mumbled, and he lifted his eyes for a second. Just enough to confirm my statement.

Jennifer stepped back in the living room with a tray of drinks and some chips.

"Thank you," I said when she handed me the coke, and I waited for her to take a seat before I asked,. "Did you want to change things up?"

"I kind of like having the last song with you. It gives me the opportunity to be onstage for the encore."

"Okay, then I won't change the order."

She smiled. "We never really had a chance to ask, how was the honeymoon?"

The darkness hanging over me lifted a fraction. "Did you know Ted has a new plane?"

Steve nodded. "Sweet, isn't it?"

"Holy cow, it's beyond sweet. It was nicer than our wedding suite," I said and the heat rose in my cheeks. "It was a great way to start the honeymoon." I grinned. "I bought a horse," I added.

"Really?" both of them said in unison.

"Yes. Koa. She's as bright as they get, and she's the one I rode to the portal."

"Where is she now?"

"Still in Hawaii. I figured it gives us a reason to get over there a couple of times a year."

"Ah, ulterior motives," Jennifer said and leaned back in the seat.

I chuckled. "Not really. It was more of a spur-of-the-moment thing. I didn't want them riding her into the ground, especially after the morning we'd had. I just had a contract drawn up that said the guides could ride her, but only one trip per day." I opened the soda and took a sip. "I need to look into buying some horses, though. Valerie grew up riding."

"Did you do anything else on the island or were you locked up in the bedroom the rest of the time?"

I laughed. Steve and Jennifer had no clue just what had gone on in our bedroom for the last few years, and I wasn't about to divulge that to them. "I had a lot of stuff already planned. I knew how much Valerie wanted to see the islands, so we did a helicopter tour and a couple of island-hopping day trips, as well as an all-day snorkel-sailing cruise. I also treated us to a couple of spa days, too."

"Wow," Jennifer said and sent a glare in Steve's direction. "We didn't do anything nearly as spectacular for our honeymoon."

"Weren't you still in a wheelchair?" I asked.

"Yeah, but a spa day would have been heaven. It certainly would have dulled the pain of physical therapy."

"By the time you were better, I was already undercover. I couldn't exactly take off on a honeymoon when my target didn't even know I was married." Steve reached for a chip and gave Jennifer that annoyed look we both were familiar with. "If you want a spa day, go for it," he said, and she rolled her eyes. "What?"

"I'd like a spa day with you."

"I don't want anyone touching me," he said, looking at her like she was just shy of a deck.

"Seriously, it's worth it," I piped in, and his eyebrows arched. "I wasn't too keen on the idea either, but after the experience in Hawaii, my entire viewpoint changed. I just need to find a decent place around us and go with Valerie at least once a month."

"You're kidding?"

I laughed and shook my head. "No, and if you go, get the deep tissue massage. You can always have them adjust to a lighter touch if you want, but you feel like a slab of putty when you leave and that lasts for a few days. Blew my mind completely."

He traded a glance with Jennifer, but his features still held his skepticism. "I think I'll pass," he mumbled. "On a different note, how is Tom doing?"

"He's doing pretty well," I said. "I'm not as much of a basket case as I thought I'd be, so that's a plus." I grabbed a handful of chips and sat back in the chair. "Is there anything on television?" I pointed to the dark screen. I wanted to keep the conversation as far from closing portals as I could, and I just wanted some down time to gather my wits.

Steve tossed me the remote. "Be my guest," he said. He knew a little of my ritual of unwinding before a show. I wasn't one of those who obsessed about my voice, or planned each step of what I was going to say, but I did do the order of songs in my head. It was my only prep, and since *The Story* was the last one that I did whenever Jennifer was available, I had an idea for the first song that varied from all of my other concerts.

I cruised through the channels, stopping on some mindless HGTV show, rolling my eyes at the false drama. "I'm opening with *New York State of Mind*," I said and glanced at Jennifer.

"That is a perfect way to open a show here," she grinned.

"I thought so, too."

"How many songs did they ask you to do?"

"Just three this time, but I'm the last one on the bill, so I'm not counting any encore in that number." I winked and smiled.

"So, *New York State of Mind, Hallelujah,* and *The Story?*"

"No. *New York State of Mind, I Don't Want to Miss a Thing* and then *The Story.* Our encore will be *Hallelujah.*"

"You got permission to use the songs this time?" Steve asked.

"Yes." We had been slammed for not getting permission the last time. As soon as I knew my song choices, I had my agent get permission to sing them. I had permission for most of Billy Joel's songs as well as Bon Jovi, Aerosmith, and now we had the written permission for both *The Story* and *Hallelujah,* as well. "We tried to get Billy Joel to join me, but he's actually out of town this weekend."

"Have you ever thought about writing your own stuff?" Jennifer asked.

"No, not really. Singing covers for charity keeps me in the shadows, you know?"

Jennifer laughed at me. "CJ, you are kidding yourself."

"I don't see paparazzi chasing me down, do you?"

"No, but you have to admit, the more you perform, the more visible you become. They even did that segment on E about you."

I couldn't help but laugh. The fluff piece they did certainly would have gotten me the sympathy vote had I been running for office, but it just annoyed the shit out of me. They hadn't interviewed any of us, but they had enough surface facts and photos to chronicle the major horrors rained on my family. "You know how I feel about that," I said, sliding my gaze away from her, back to the television.

"They somehow got photos of your wedding."

I blinked at the revelation and bit the inside of my lip. "I got married in a public space. Anyone around the harbor could have easily snapped off pictures, or even up by the road."

"True, but they got on Entertainment Tonight."

"Maybe that's why some folks in Hawaii recognized me," I muttered and sighed. I wasn't interested in any more publicity.

"There was a time I'd kill for the kind of coverage the media is giving you," Jennifer said. Her tone was offhanded, but the underlying disappointment pulled my attention to her. She gave me a smile and glanced at the clock. "I need to start dinner." Without any other conversation, she left for the kitchen.

Steve chuckled the moment she was out of hearing range.

"The media attention bothers her?" I whispered, hooking my thumb toward the kitchen.

Steve's smirk confirmed my question. "She's been working all her life to get the kind of attention you got like that." He snapped his fingers. "And she found out earlier today that she didn't get that lead on Broadway she auditioned for, so she's a little sensitive."

"She really wanted that, didn't she?" Now, I felt like shit. Here I was, blowing off all the attention I was getting like it was a nuisance, when she would have loved every second of the spotlight. "Damn, I'm sorry," I added, meeting Steve's gaze.

He shrugged. "Don't sweat it. She'll get over it the minute she walks on stage with you."

Both of us got quiet and turned our attention to the whiny couple on television looking for the perfect home. I closed my eyes and leaned back in the chair, letting my mind drift to the music. Melodies filled my head and my fingers silently tapped the notes I'd be playing later that night.

Burning bread tickled my nose and I opened my eyes, bringing my gaze to Steve. "Are you really going to let her ruin the kitchen here?" I asked.

Steve chuckled. "I guess not," he said and headed into the kitchen to salvage whatever Jennifer was burning before the fire alarms started. I started flipping through the channels again. The news was on a majority of the broadcast channels and everything coming out was depressing. There was so much darkness in the world already, and with each news story, the hope in my heart fell a notch. I watched politicians lie, intolerance, prejudice, and the complete disregard for human life. I finally turned off the television, throwing the remote on the table in disgust.

I stepped out on the balcony, scanning the city below, my heart heavy with all the evil mankind exhibited. The door behind me opened and Steve stepped to my side.

"What are we fighting for?" I finally asked, meeting his gaze.

"You watched the news, didn't you?"

I nodded and leaned on the rail. "The devil's winning," I said, and sighed.

"That's not true. You know the news focuses on things that boost ratings. Horror and scandal glue people to the television. It's a sick fascination, but that doesn't mean everyone out there condones what is going on."

What he said made sense, but in my current state of mind, it was nice to be reminded why going up against the devil mattered. The fundraisers I did usually lifted my spirits and faith in people, and I hoped tonight would do the same.

"So, did you salvage dinner?" I asked, changing the subject.

"Eh." He shrugged. "The delivery might be the best choice," he whispered, and glanced over his shoulder.

"Gotcha," I said, and we headed inside.

Jennifer stood by the door with the take-out bag in her hand and her hand on her hip. "You did this?" She pointed at Steve.

"I figured edible food was probably necessary," he said, and shuffled his feet, looking at the floor before he gave her a sideways glance.

It was like watching a puppy that had destroyed a pair of your favorite shoes being scolded. Jennifer tried to look annoyed, but Steve's endearing mannerism made it difficult. And when he gave her that half smile, half smirk, and a muttered apology, I covered my smile and turned my back on the two of them. But I couldn't quite stifle my snort of a laugh.

"Really?"

I caught Jennifer's gaze in the window reflection and turned back.

"Was it necessary?" I asked, trying to quell my laugh, but I failed miserably. She pursed her lips, but the dimples in her cheeks deepened.

"Well, I guess I should be thankful you had a backup plan," she said, and lost the battle against her smile.

"I love you, honey," Steve said, and crossed, taking the bag from her.

"Yeah, yeah," she muttered and accepted a quick kiss before he nodded toward the kitchen.

"Dinner's on," he said, holding up the bag, and we followed him into the kitchen.

THE ELECTRICITY IN THE air backstage at Carnegie Hall buzzed in my ears as I waited for my introduction. The pre-performance jitters still gripped me, and I sent a nervous smile at Jennifer. She shined as she waited. If she had any last-minute nerves, I never saw them; it was like the spotlight energized her.

"Go get 'em, tiger," she said when they announced my name.

With a quick inhale, I stepped out on the stage, flashing my brightest smile and letting the applause do its magic. The elation of being on stage grabbed hold, and I crossed to the MC, shaking his hand before the microphone was handed to me.

"Hello, New York!" I said without a hint of a stutter, which made me grin even wider. "You ready for something special?" I asked, as they rolled my piano out and the crowd went nuts. "Before I start, I wanted to thank you all for digging deep to help fight cancer! Rock on!" I sat on the bench and took a deep breath. Closing my eyes, the music took hold.

After the first three notes, the crowd went fucking nuts, and I smiled, sliding my gaze toward the camera with the most playful look I could muster. By the time I got through the opening of *New York State of Mind*, the screaming audience nearly took the roof off.

When my voice was added to the mix, they got even louder. After the first portion, a saxophone joined the arrangement, and I glanced behind me and gave the musician a nod of thanks, letting him have the solo while I continued the soft tune on the keyboard. I started the next stanza, and I wasn't alone. I'm sure my face showed the extent of my surprise when Billy Joel walked out with a microphone and leaned on the other side of the piano.

"Ladies and gentleman, the one and only, Billy Joel," I announced, and we finished the song together, our voices blending in perfectly paired octaves.

The last note faded, and I could almost feel the light dancing in my eyes as I grinned. I stood, taking his hand in mine, and pulled him close enough to whisper. "Shocked the shit out of me."

He pat my back and grinned. "You didn't miss a beat."

"Thanks, man," I said, and pulled away, waving my hand as he took another bow before walking off. I caught Jennifer's grin behind the spotlights, and she pointed her finger at me. Her silent 'Gotcha' made me smile.

"I totally didn't expect that," I said to the audience. "You have no idea how much that made my night," I added and took a seat at the piano again. "I hope it gave you folks as much of a thrill as it gave me." My answer came in the loud clapping response.

"You think Steven Tyler is backstage, too?" I asked, and the noise increased as I started playing the next song on my playlist. Unfortunately, he wasn't in the house, but that didn't seem to matter to the audience. By the time I was done with *I Don't Want to Miss A Thing*, they were in that frenzied state.

"I do happen to have Jennifer Williams in the house for this next song," I said and waved toward her as she crossed the stage. Her dress glittered, and I glanced at the VIP section where Steve stood. His entire body reacted to seeing her in the sequined gown, and I couldn't help but smile. The man loved his wife, and it showed.

I really enjoyed singing with Jennifer. She has always been a quiet strength, the support beam that held the family together, and to share the spotlight with her just felt right. The last note filtered to the rafters, and we stood, taking a bow.

Together, we soaked up the applause, and I grinned at Jennifer. "Do you think we have time for one more?" I asked, and the noise level rose. I sent a raised an eyebrow toward the MC and he gave me a nod.

Instead of sitting down on the piano bench, I took the microphone in my hand and led Jennifer to the edge of the stage, where I took a seat. It was completely unscripted, and we were less than an arm's reach from the audience.

"So, what do you want to hear?" I asked the closest patron, and pointed the microphone in her direction. It was a given, since I was now known as the new face of *Hallelujah* and her voice echoed the same song the rest of the audience cried out. I traded a glance with Jennifer and gave her a shrug. "Do you mind singing along with me?"

"Not at all."

We'd never rehearsed this one together. Hell, I had never sung without instruments of some sort, but I wanted this to be memorable and personal, not me and the piano like usual. I glanced at the audience and took a breath.

The audience stilled when the first words rolled over them, and from my new vantage point on the stage, I could see their faces as they swayed and sang along with me. Jennifer waited until the second verse to join in. I had never seen rapture etched on so many faces before, and I finally understood the power of my voice.

Raven had once said I had the voice of the angels. I think she might have been right. Coupled with Jennifer, we rivaled the heavenly host, and when the last note drifted off, silence filled the auditorium as people's eyes blinked open and fell on me.

"Thank you," I said, and the first sets of hands to clap were Steve's. The rest followed, and we got a standing ovation.

I climbed to my feet and helped Jennifer up before we took a quick bow and headed off stage.

"That was..." Jennifer trailed off, sliding her awed gaze in my direction.

"Fucking awesome," I finished. It was the boost of confidence I needed to tackle the darkness of Lucifer's portal. Now, I just needed an excuse to slip away for a while.

"Mr. Ryan," one of the stagehands approached me. "Some of the other performers and crew are going down to P.J. Carneys for drinks. Do you want to join us?"

"Sounds great," I said and glanced at Jennifer.

"You're invited, too, Mrs. Williams," he said, and I silently wished for her to decline.

"Thank you, but I think my husband and I will head home, instead," she said and glanced at me with a wink.

I immediately got the gist. She wanted some alone time with Steve, and I couldn't blame her. Something about performing made me want to take advantage of Valerie when we got home, and I imagined she was the same with Steve. The rise of blush in her cheeks when he walked in the room confirmed my thoughts and I leaned in.

"I'll take my time," I said, and straightened up in time for Steve to give me a pat on the back.

"That was the best yet. You sure you don't want to record your own stuff?" he asked, and I laughed, rolling my eyes.

"That's all I need," I said, and Jennifer led him away, leaving me to follow the crowd down to the bar. I took a seat at the bar and the group congregated around me. I raised my hand for the bartender, and he stepped over as I pulled out my money clip. I peeled off fifteen hundred dollars and put it on the bar.

"Make sure this group gets anything they need." I said, as we took over the area around the bar. "If that runs out, then someone will have to start a tab, otherwise whatever's left is yours," I said, and the bartender blinked at the amount for a moment and then pocketed the money with a nod. I turned back to the group. "First round is on me," I said with a smile, and everyone started shouting their drink orders. I offered my seat to one of the girls and made my way to the door.

"Kind of chaotic, isn't it?"

I looked up into the dark eyes of Billy Joel and laughed. "Yeah, just a little."

"That was nice of you." He pointed his drink toward the crew.

"It was nothing," I said, and took another step towards the door.

"Bailing so soon?" he asked, and I stopped, meeting his gaze.

"I have something I need to do, and if things go well, I'll be back." I glanced at the people talking and laughing and clinking their glasses to another successful event. "If not, it was a pleasure singing with you." I extended my hand.

He shook it and smiled. "Pleasure was mine. You've got one hell of a voice."

"Thanks, Mr. Joel, I appreciate it."

Before anyone else could intervene, I slipped out of the bar into the chilly October evening. I found the nearest subway terminal and took the 7th Avenue Express to Brooklyn. I made my way down to the river by foot and found the area I was looking for. The euphoria of the show had long vanished, and I crossed to the string of deserted and crumbling warehouses. I walked to the last lot, expecting it to be clear, but I found the remnants of walls still standing with only one wall gone, like someone had taken a rusty hacksaw to the structure. Damian hadn't cleared the footprint at all. He only blew the roof off its rafters.

The stench of evil permeated the small road, and I gathered my wits, focusing my power. I nearly unleashed the cleansing angel fire when an echo of sobs reached my ears. The place wasn't empty, and my gaze bounced to the other buildings. Shadows moved in the abandoned shells, and I realized this was a place the homeless congregated.

"Shit," I whispered, less than thrilled that there would be witnesses to my destruction and I suddenly wished I was wearing my baseball cap and a less high-end coat. The city lights in the distance cast long shadows on the pavement, upping the creepy factor, and I wondered if this was a trick.

Regardless, I couldn't just level the place. I had to make sure innocents were clear. Which meant I had to get a closer look. This certainly wasn't what I had planned. My get in, destroy, and get out scenario like we did in Hawaii wasn't going to happen, and I made my feet move forward against every nerve begging for me to run.

My heart hammered in my chest, making my skin pulse as I stalked closer to the opening. The blubbering got louder as I approached, and I backed against the wall, listening to the plea of whoever was inside.

The rattle of chains caught my attention and pulled me forward until I stood in the opening, looking into the belly of the decayed warehouse. The sight before me nearly took me out at the knees, and I had to blink a few times before I understood just what I was seeing.

Chains, meant to destroy, pulled my father in multiple directions. Bloody welts covered his body, and the image of my mother in the death chair from that movie turned my stomach. Except, instead of Frank Aris slicing her skin, it was my image.

I knew this display was meant for me to see, and the words flowing from my doppelgänger's mouth crushed my father's spirit to nothing. I had never seen my father blubber or beg, and hearing the pain in his voice as Lucifer sliced another piece of my mother was unbearable.

I stepped farther into the warehouse, and Lucifer's insane smile knotted my stomach just as the knife sliced through the throat of my mother's image. My father's wail set my fury switch on high, pulling the angel fire from deep within me, but before it covered the perimeter of the portal, Lucifer's gaze met mine, and then the image of both him and my father were gone.

I roared in anger, letting the fire burn and the ground crumble around me. I hesitated, almost following the debris into hell just to stop my father's torment, but I knew if I did that, I might be stuck under Lucifer's thumb forever.

I jumped back onto solid ground just in time, and the slamming of Earth's plates filled the purified circle. I stumbled away, numbed by the images presented. Halfway down the alley, I leaned over and hurled. The acid burned me back to life, and I gagged and spit, wishing I hadn't come, and hadn't seen the diabolical way Lucifer stripped my father's sanity.

Lucifer was using my image.

My fucking image was doing the damage.

Angel Wrath Chapter 19

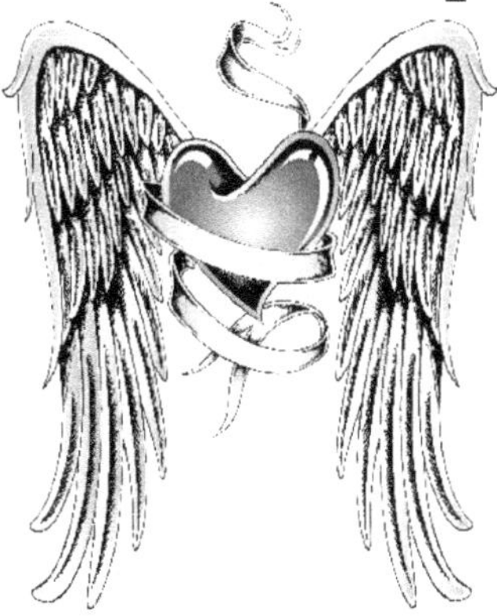

THE MINUTE I STEPPED into the quiet house, I headed for the bar by the sliders and pulled out whatever my hand landed on first. I unscrewed the cap and guzzled, hoping the alcohol would wipe away the images and the pain crushing my chest.

Even when my throat constricted against more, I forced the burning liquid down until the bottle was empty.

"Chris?"

I stiffened, but didn't turn around. I hadn't realized Valerie was in the house. I thought she was with Damian and Naomi tonight.

"Steve called when you didn't show up," she said, her voice closer. "Why didn't you pick up your phone?"

Instead of acknowledging her, I put the empty bottle of whiskey on the countertop and reached for another bottle. Grey Goose spilled into my mouth next, but this was harder to swallow past each hitching breath gripping me.

Valerie grabbed the bottle from my hand, pulling it away, saturating my shirt with vodka before she got the bottle upright. I still didn't turn and meet her gaze. I was too busy pressing my lips together against the turmoil in my stomach.

It only took a moment for the burn to explode and then I sprinted, making it to the kitchen sink as the entire lot poured out, splattering the stainless steel in a fiery storm of acid and alcohol. My knees gave, and I sank to the floor, pressing my forehead against the cabinets.

"Chris, what happened?" her soft voice caressed my ear. The arm she slung over my shoulders warmed the chill in my bones, but it didn't wipe out the images playing against my closed eyelids.

I had wandered around the city, stunned, until I finally hailed a cab to the apartment. I couldn't bring myself to go upstairs and face Steve and Jen, not with so much shit pelting me from all sides. Lucifer had promised blood and pain from this moment on. It was only a matter of time before he slaughtered everyone I cared about, and this little personal viewing was just the beginning of my hell on earth.

"I drove home." Even my voice sounded harsh and raw, and the effort to say those three words rattled my frame.

Valerie tried to pull me so I would look at her, and all I could do was shake my head. There was no chance of a verbal explanation, not with the anguish squeezing my chest. I knew on some level she would be pissed that I didn't have her with me when I closed the portal, but I knew she wouldn't be able to handle seeing the place that nearly tore her to pieces.

"Chris," she said a little more forcefully, and I ground my teeth together against the need to lash out.

"I can't. Not right now," I finally said.

The squeak of the front door followed by footsteps turned every muscle in my body into a tight coil.

"Damian, take her to your house please," Tom's voice echoed in my head, and his inarticulate speech filled my ears.

"I want to stay," Valerie said, and I turned, meeting her gaze.

"Go," I whispered.

"Chris?" she asked, and her lips pressed together.

"Not now, just... later." Talking was difficult, especially since my throat kept squeezing against turbulent acid eruptions in my stomach and the hurt in her eyes was like a knife to my heart. "Please," I forced out, and she stood, walking away. A part of me wanted to wrap my arms around her and never let go, but I couldn't right now. My need for drowning all thought still overrode everything else, and after the door closed, a chair scraped on the kitchen floor.

I looked over my shoulder at Tom.

He didn't speak, but he had a bottle and two shot glasses on the table.

I pushed to my feet and took the seat across from him, staring at the alcohol. Without a word, he poured two shots. I reached for one and he took the other, clicking my glass before downing the drink.

I followed suit and the burn nearly sent another plume of vomit out of my mouth, but I swallowed and closed my eyes, forcing the liquid to stay down.

"Are you going to show me, or what?" Tom asked, his voice soft in my head.

I opened my eyes and my vision blurred through a layer of tears. I just stared at him.

He cocked his head. "Or would you prefer to talk about your wife's bedroom fetishes?" This time he signed instead of speaking in my head and his lips pressed together against a smirk.

I didn't know whether to laugh or punch him, and my hands curled into fists. "Fuck you," I whispered, and reached for the bottle. It moved beyond my reach, and I shot my glare back at Tom.

"Seriously, talk to me," he said, and this time he meant it. He wasn't just poking the bear for fun. He knew that comment would slap me back into control and, damn him, it worked.

"He's using my image to destroy Dad," I said, as the anger overshadowed everything and I opened my mind, giving Tom exactly what he asked for. I watched as his face turned the color of waxed paper. He reached for the bottle, poured two shots with a shaking hand, and downed his before I even got mine to my mouth.

"We have to get him out of there," he said, and I couldn't agree more.

"I'm fucking ruined," I said, folded my arms and laid my head in the crook of my elbow. Hot tears burned my eyes; a few leaked onto my forearm before Tom's hand reached out and gave my arm a squeeze.

"Come on, man. You're stronger than that," he said.

I lifted my head. "No, I'm really not. Getting Valerie to the point she trusted me again was a hellish ride, and she was only under Lucifer's thumb for what, a day or two? Dad's been tortured for over two years. He's going to want to roast me alive on sight," I said. "And I wouldn't blame him one bit. You saw. You know the bullshit Lucifer is feeding him. Jesus, he's not going to believe either of us exists when Lucifer is done with him."

Tom was quiet for a minute, and he studied his still hands before looking up at me. "Doesn't matter." He shrugged. "We still gotta walk that line."

Angel Wrath Chapter 20

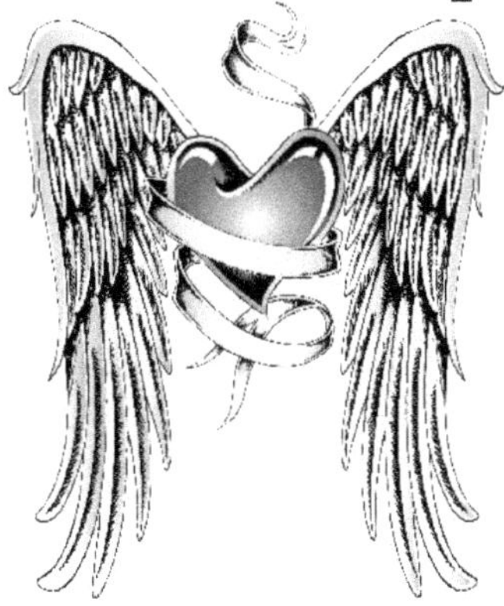

I BRUSHED THE BITTER taste out of my mouth and stepped into the bedroom. My gaze snapped to the door, and Valerie standing with her arms crossed.

"Are you ready to talk?"

"Did you call Steve and let him know I'm home?" I asked.

"Yes. I didn't know what to tell him, so I said you weren't feeling well and decided to come home instead of stay in the city." She stepped inside the room and closed the door. "You want to tell me what happened?"

"No." I huffed and took a seat on the bed with my back to her. "The warehouse portal wasn't closed," I said after a moment of silence wedged between us. I glanced over my shoulder. "It is now."

Her arms slowly lowered and the sudden mistrust in her eyes stung just as bad as everything else I saw tonight.

"It was a colossal mind fuck," I said, and blinked the burn of tears away; however, I didn't open the memory to her like I had my brother. Some things are better left unsaid.

She crossed to me and cupped my face in her hands. "Why did you go without me?"

I kept her gaze without speaking. I didn't need to say the words. Not this time, and her chin dipped in a slow nod of understanding.

"What did he do?" she asked, and her mind swirled over her hellish time in that facility.

I let a sarcastic smile surface. "He didn't give me a look at what he did to you," I started, and her exhale clued me in as to the extent of her relief. "He showed me what he's doing to my father."

She blinked and bit her lip. She couldn't comprehend what I was shown that would lead me to the near psychotic state she found me in, and I sighed. Articulating what I saw wasn't easy, and I chose my words as carefully as I dared.

"He's using my image," I said, knowing the effect that would have on her, and I was right. She recoiled. When her hands pulled away from my skin, a chill was left behind and I shivered. "And he's replaying the final scene from Survival Games, except I'm the one killing my mom while he watches, just before the chains pull him apart." My fists clenched. "At this point, my father associates my image with death."

I met Valerie's horrified stare.

"So, you can understand just how fucking off the wall I was earlier."

"Oh, baby," she whispered, and tears formed in her eyes.

She wrapped her arms around me and my arms found their way around her waist. I pressed my forehead to her chest, clenching my teeth against the tears that threatened. I hated that I couldn't push the devastation away and replace it with the raw anger that shared the same space. Her hands threaded into my hair and she pushed me away from her chest, forcing me to meet her gaze.

When her lips crushed mine, I couldn't help it. I pulled her down on the bed with me and rolled so I was on top. I needed to feel a sense of control right now. I think Valerie understood exactly what I needed. She let me exercise some aggression with her, and our love-making session was fraught with ripping fabric and kisses that plundered as hard as my hip thrusts.

She met every move with her own growling satisfaction until we lay spent, side by side.

"This is the last time you'll go it alone, right?" she asked, turning her flushed features in my direction.

I rolled onto my side and pushed a few sweat laced strands of hair out of her face. "Yeah," I agreed. "But I have to have what we practiced down to a science."

She pressed her lips together. "Um, about that," she said and shifted, sucking her lip in between her teeth before she exhaled. "We have to be really careful where we put the knife." Her eyes jumped around my face before settling on mine.

"Okay," I drew out the word because my sixth sense tickled, telling me there was more.

"It just wouldn't be a good idea to cut my lower belly," she said and her hand slid down her stomach, stopping below her belly button.

I stared at the placement, and then my gaze bounced to hers. "You're shitting me," I gasped. Her lips twitched to a nervous smile, and I looked back at where her hand was. Without thought, my hand covered hers and I stared, speechless, as a whirlwind of emotions slammed me from all sides—wonder, hesitation, joy, but the most prevalent emotion dried the saliva in my mouth.

Fear.

Fear of taking the next step.

Fear of whether or not I would be a good father.

Fear that Lucifer would kill my child.

Soul crushing fear.

"How far along are you?" I asked.

"Maybe a month at best, but I think this child was conceived on our honeymoon." Her sigh filled the space. "I'm as regular as clockwork and when I missed my period last week, I knew something was up." She shrugged. "I had Raven pick up a pregnancy test, and it turned out positive."

"And you still let me..." I dragged my hand away. Our last training session crossed my mind. I would have never stuck her with a blade if I had known.

"I had you attack me from the side on purpose."

I pushed into a sitting position and pulled on what was left of my underwear. A new irritation scratched my skin, and I glared over my shoulder at her. "I could have killed our kid," I snapped, and she rolled out of bed, pulling on her nightgown before she approached me.

"I wasn't sure," she started.

"Bullshit!"

"I had an idea, but I thought maybe the jet lag screwed up my cycle."

I bit down on the budding anger and crossed my legs Indian style, letting the information truly sink in. She climbed back into the bed next to me, adopting the same pose while her hand gently scratched my back.

"You should have told me you suspected you might be pregnant before we started practicing," I said softly and slid my gaze to her.

"You should have told me you were closing a portal tonight."

I nodded. "I should have," I said, and stretched out again, running my hands down my face. "Would you have come?" I asked, as she shifted onto her side.

She didn't answer right away, chewing her bottom lip while she debated her answer. She finally sighed and shook her head. "I had afternoon patients, and even if they weren't scheduled, I wouldn't have gone near that warehouse," she said. "But I would have gone to the show," she added.

I rolled towards her and covered her hand. "I thought as much," I said. "That's why I didn't mention it. No sense in you being a basket case all day." Her lips thinned for a minute and she closed her eyes. When they opened again, the storm colors in her irises were slowly rolling.

"How was the show?"

I smiled, due more to the subtle change in subject rather than the actual question. "It went well. I sang *New York State of Mind* with Billy Joel."

Her eyebrows arched. "No shit?"

"Yeah, I'll have to call Jo tomorrow and see if she arranged that one or not. Either way, I was shocked as hell and a little humbled." I let out a small laugh. "It was pretty cool."

Her palm caressed my cheek. "Never take on Lucifer without telling me, okay?"

I didn't agree at first. Instead, I traced her bottom lip with my fingers before moving my gaze back to hers. "You know this changes things, right?"

Her features hardened and lightning flashed in her eyes. "It doesn't change a goddamned thing," she snapped and went to roll away.

I clamped her wrist, holding her in place. "You're not going with me to Canada."

She yanked her wrist out of my grip and rolled away from me, giving me her back. Her back moved with each huff of breath and I waited for the backlash. I didn't have to wait long. She rolled back with a glare.

"I'm going." She turned away again, as if giving me her back ended the argument.

"Not when you're carrying my child," I said, and she slowly turned towards me.

"It's my child, too."

"I'm not having this argument, Val. It's not just your life on the line."

"And I don't want to raise this child alone," she threw the words back at me. This time, she rolled away from me and punched her pillow before snuggling into it. "Stupid ass," she whispered under her breath. Aggravation came off her in waves that her mutter just punctuated.

The ball of tension in my chest expanded. "I will not do this." The growl was back in my voice. "I will not let that monster come between us," I said, through clenched teeth and the muscles in her shoulder tensed.

She sighed and rolled onto her back, staring at the ceiling before she finally looked at me. "Can we meet in the middle on this?"

My gut was saying no, but my head and heart just wanted us on the same page. "How?"

She chewed on her lip and looked back at the ceiling. "What if I just went to the area with you and waited outside the portal for you?"

"He'll have demons or other things around the portal. I don't want you in danger."

Her brow scrunched. "Well, if I'm not near the portal, don't you think he'd send his goons after me, anyway?

Especially since you've already started the campaign to close the portals?"

The detailed descriptions of Lucifer's horrific promises drifted to the forefront of my mind, and I rolled onto my back. He promised to finish what Tom and Damian interrupted at the warehouse, whether I agreed to give him what he wanted or not. Valerie was at risk no matter what happened and while I trusted my brother with my life, I wasn't sure if I trusted him with Valerie's if Lucifer truly waged war.

Her vows echoed in my ears, and I closed my eyes, covering them with my arm.

"Chris?"

I lifted my arm and looked at her. "It might be better if you're somewhere that I can get to quickly," I said. "But only if I can work out the kinks. You know damned well even if you're hiding beyond the portal, they'll grab you so he can use you as a bargaining chip." The original idea had been hers, so she was aware of how that would play out.

"If I find I'm powerless on his turf, I will have Damian take you out of there. Understand?"

"But..."

"The entire mission will be aborted." I interrupted. "Because the guilt of knowing what's happening to my dad is nothing compared to what will happen if I lose you."

"And if he gets hold of you? What am I supposed to do then?"

"As soon as you're clear, I'll let the angel fire rip, like I did in Hawaii."

"And what are you planning on doing if you have your powers on his turf?"

I met her gaze and allowed the fury buried inside me to growl out the answer. "I'm going to beat him to a fucking pulp before I send him back to hell."

Angel Wrath Chapter 21

VALERIE PLANTED HER TALISMAN into the center of the kitchen table. The anger radiated off her like I had never seen, combined with her pale cheeks and the dark circles under her eyes. I knew she was just as exhausted as I was. The only difference between us was that her hormones were playing hell with her, just as much as continuously having to put the healing power into practice.

It was almost Thanksgiving, and we were no closer to getting this down.

I crossed to her, towering over her with the same ferocity coming off her tense form. Instead of doing this the same way we had countless times, I yanked her into my arms and kissed her. With our bodies touching and our tongues dancing in frenetic circles, I willed the barrier under the surface of her skin far enough for me not to feel the repelling power against my hands firmly planted on her back.

Both our chests heaved as I stepped away and I stretched my hand out for the knife. I didn't take my gaze from hers; instead, I willed the blade into my palm and then grit my teeth as I slice into her side. Her flesh gave, and she cried out in pain. This was always the part that crushed a piece of my soul every time we did this. The pain in her eyes gouged through me as much as the knife sliced through her. I kept going by sheer force of will and a little farther in; I hit the barrier. It was like hitting a live electrical current and my hand jerked away; the knife went tumbling from my grip and I was thrown across the room.

I landed on my ass a few feet away and my gaze dropped to the cut. It was deep enough to draw blood, but not deep enough to do any actual damage.

Valerie inspected the wound, wincing, but then her gaze moved from the gash to mine, and I yanked the power outwards. The furniture within a few feet of her went sliding, banging into the wall, and the recliner toppled over.

I blinked and so did she. Her jaw tightened, and the cut healed, leaving another smear of blood on her skin. She was getting faster at patching herself up. All the practice we were doing was honing her skills as much as mine. She cracked a tired smile.

"Well, shit. If I had known kissing was the fucking key, practice for the last couple of months would have been a hell of a lot more fun," I said from my vantage point on the floor.

She started giggling, to the point her hands covered her mouth, leaving bloody fingerprints on her cheeks. She was a mess, and when I stood, I got a good look at myself, as well. We both looked like rejects from a horror movie, and I started laughing too. I could have easily passed for a scientist gone mad.

I met her giggling gaze and crossed the distance on shaky legs. Running my fingers over the tacky blood covering her side, I sighed and met her gaze.

"We must be completely insane," I whispered and took her face in my hands, planting another kiss before she could answer. "I'm ready for a shower and a nap," I said.

"One more time just to make sure that wasn't a fluke," she said.

"After we get some rest. You look like you're going to drop."

She started giggling again and instead of waiting for her to stop; I scooped her up in my arms and crossed to the stars. I tapped into my inner reserves and climbed to our bedroom and the bathroom beyond. Without putting her down, I willed the shower on and stepped inside with both of us fully clothed. Only then did I set her on her feet.

Tenderly, I peeled off her clothing and tossed it over the top rail before cleaning the blood away. Once her skin was clean, I dropped to my knees and kissed the spot I'd sliced over and over, until I thought I'd scream. Knowing it was a necessary evil didn't alleviate the nightmares I'd had since we started this madness. In them, I slip, and the blade kills our child. I have woken screaming more times than I can count, and so has Valerie.

My lips moved from that area over to the front of her stomach. We hadn't told anyone the results of the test; not with all this other shit going on, and I kissed the almost imperceptible bump, looking up at Valerie.

She ran her hands through my hair and I stood, peeling my clothing off. She ran the soap over my body as we stared at each other.

"What if this doesn't work?" I asked, and the progression of soap on my skin stopped.

"Then you might as well burn both of us up in the angel fire."

Her words silenced me, and I held her face, touching her lips with mine. "We already know we'd die for each other," I whispered against her. "But can you promise me something?" I pulled away.

She put the soap back in the holder and her hands found my chest. "What?"

"That no matter what happens, you will live? Not for me, but for our child?"

She blinked and pressed her lips together. Her tears mixed with the mist from the water, and she gave me a nod.

"Thank you," I said and turned the water off.

I barely remember pulling the covers over us.

Angel Wrath Chapter 22

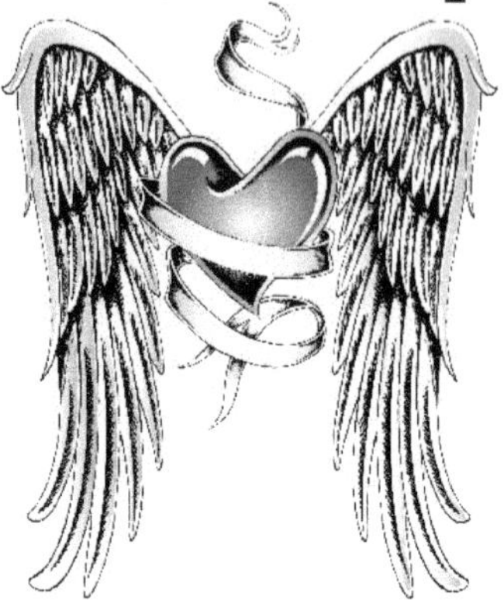

A SLIVER OF LIGHT stabbed my eyes and I rolled away, pulling my arm out from under Valerie. I hugged my pillow, turned my head toward the wall, and drifted off again. My leg jerked from that annoying half-dream misstep, and I opened my eyes, glancing at the clock.

The numbers blinked nine and my brain was still somewhere in sleep land. My lids drifted closed before the fog had the chance to clear. When I blinked my eyes back open, another twenty minutes had sailed by and the bright patterns on the wall caught my attention. My eyes widened and darted back to the clock.

Shit!

"Val, you're late for work." I rolled towards her. I shook her shoulder. "Val!"

She mirrored my initial reaction to the sunshine and rolled into her pillow, whining her discontent.

"It's after nine. In the morning." I shook her again.

Her eyes cracked open, meeting mine, and then they dropped beyond me to the clock. A few quick blinks and then her gaze came back to mine, widening. "Shit! We slept close to twenty hours?"

I nodded, and the covers sailed off her.

"Shit, I'm so late!" She nearly bounced off the bed.

Her mad dash through her bureau drawers would have produced a laugh had I been fully awake, but I was still in that foggy 'holy shit, we slept that long' phase.

Valerie was in the bathroom before my feet reached the floor and by the time I entered, she was already dressed and whipping a brush through her hair, collecting it into a ponytail before she wound it into a messy bun.

I stepped to the sink and brushed the cotton from my mouth. Before I finished, Val was already heading back into the bedroom.

"When's your next day off?" I asked, and she glanced at me, the crease between her eyes conveying her disdain at my ill-timed question. Her eyes jumped from mine to my bare chest and back before her brain caught up with the question. "Friday. And I have the weekend off, as well," she said and started for the hallway. "Why?"

"We'll close the portal in Canada on Friday."

My words stopped her dead in the doorway, and she glanced back at me. "We have to make sure last night wasn't a fluke before you set that in stone." Worry lines appeared around her eyes when I shook my head.

"I'm closing it Friday. If it was a fluke–we'll have to figure out a new plan of attack."

She gave me a tight nod and headed out of the room. I pulled on my sweats and followed her down the stairs. When she sat on the bench near the garage door, I crossed to the kitchen, swiping her pocketbook off the counter. I made a stop at the refrigerator and grabbed a juice for her. When I handed both items to her, she sighed and nodded toward the kitchen.

"Do you mind grabbing my vitamins?" she asked and started digging in her purse for the keys.

I retraced my steps and collected the prenatal vitamins for her, along with a granola bar. If she didn't eat when she took these things, her stomach would give her trouble. She dumped them in her pocketbook, offering me a grateful smile as she climbed to her feet.

"Thank you, sweetheart," she said, and stood on her tiptoes for a kiss. It certainly wasn't our normal lingering good morning kiss, but it was still sweet.

"Call if you need anything," I said as she shot out the garage door. I stepped into the opening, crossing my arms over my bare chest to ward off the November chill.

When she drove out the gate, I pressed the button to close the garage and stepped back into the warm house.

My stomach protested its empty state and sent a rumbling growl through my abdomen. "Yeah, yeah," I mumbled, but instead of heading to the kitchen to feed the beast, I went upstairs to straighten the bedroom and get dressed.

With a clean pair of jeans and a sweater on, and my hair in some semblance of order, I headed down to the kitchen in search of food. As I passed the phone, it rang, intercepting my trek for sustenance. I considered letting it roll to voicemail, but Tom's name blinked on the display, and I picked up the receiver.

"Good morning, Ryan residence," I said out of habit.

"You're finally awake?" Tom's automated voice asked.

I glanced at the call counter, but this was the first call of the day.

"Yeah, why?"

"We need to talk. Can you come up?"

I paused and the absence of noise in the background prickled my senses. I almost always could hear Hannah in the background whenever I talked to Tom. It was like she was programmed to pitch a fit whenever her parents were on the phone. "Sure, is Raven there with you?"

"No. She's on her way to Damian's. Hannah and Grace have a play date today."

"Let me grab something to eat and I'll head up after."

"I'll cook you something here."

Even though I was listening to an automated voice based on Tom's typed response, I got the feeling there was some emotion behind the request. His offer to cook me breakfast threw me.

"Are you okay?"

"Yes. We'll talk when you get here."

"Okay. I'm on my way now."

I hung up the receiver and slid on my sneakers before grabbing my coat and keys for the short drive. The sunlight dance on the water, giving the illusion of a warm fall day, but I knew better. Winter was only a stone's throw away, and the air this morning had the old man's bite to it.

Tom opened the door the minute I pulled into the driveway, and his haggard appearance sent a shockwave through me. He looked worse than both Valerie and I had yesterday. I stepped out of the car and crossed the distance. Tom just stepped aside, opening the door all the way to let me pass.

"What the hell happened to you?" I asked, as he passed me and took a seat on the couch.

His head dropped into his hands, and he let out an audible sigh. "I had the unpleasant experience of being two places at once last night." His bastardized words were overlayed in my head by his perfect enunciation, and he looked up at me. "Twice," he added, and a chill skittered up my spine.

"Who?" I said and my voice cracked.

"Steve and Jen were attacked last night. He was able to hold them off, but you were... un-fucking-reachable, so he called me."

His glare said more than I wanted to hear, and I slowly lowered onto the couch across from him, dreading whatever he was going to say next. "Are they..." I trailed off when he shook his head.

"They're fine. I vaporized those motherfuckers."

His gaze still held anger, and I didn't understand why, but the relief in knowing they were okay drew an exhale, releasing the tension in my body a fraction.

"If I had been any longer, I would have been a widower," he said. "Or a fucking soul without a body. Either way, that little jump left me open to attack. Raven was able to hold them off, but it scared the living shit out of her."

"I'll bet," I said, raking my hand through my hair.

"Right before I turned them into dust, they told me they already got to you." His mind didn't echo the bastardized words, but his momentary expression of crushed hope and his slow signing hands got the message through. "I panicked and bam..." He snapped his fingers. "...I was standing in your fucking bedroom while both you and Valerie snored up a storm."

My eyebrows rose.

"You didn't hear a thing. Did you even notice the new salt lines blocking your bedroom door and the windowsills?"

I shook my head.

"You have never slept that soundly. What the hell?"

I blinked and shrugged. "Valerie and I were… practicing, and I guess that wiped us out." To the tune of twenty hours, I thought, still stunned by that basic fact.

"Practicing? What the fuck were you practicing?"

I opened my mouth to explain, but sometimes it's better to just show. My mind opened, and Tom's eyes slowly widened in horror. Slash, bleed, heal, rinse, repeat. The insanity that we'd engaged in over the past month rolled in his head, and Tom's disgust carved a grimace in his face.

"Yesterday was the worst. It was fucking grueling, and I was mentally shot by the time we figured it out." Silence fell between us, and Tom rubbed his face. "I don't remember ever being that tired, and Val must have been ten times worse than I was."

His jaw tightened. "If I didn't have a piece of your mojo, we would all be dead," Tom said and stood, heading into the kitchen. I followed. "I thought you were," he muttered and started slamming pans around.

"You want me to cook?" I asked, and guilt gnawed at my stomach along with my hunger pangs.

"No, I got it."

He cooked in silence, his aggravation building, and I couldn't blame him. I hadn't heard Steve's call and I wouldn't have heard my brother's either. I pulled my shoulders back, cracking my spine and shook off the shiver that wanted to take hold.

Tom set an omelet before me and took the seat on the opposite side of the table. I wolfed down my meal in a matter of seconds, and my stomach growled its contentment.

"That was good," I said, and Tom met my gaze.

"I don't think I want it anymore," his thought echoed in my head.

"If you're not going to have it, I'll eat the rest," I said, eyeing his half-eaten omelet.

His eyes narrowed and his lips thinned. "I was talking about the power." He shoved his plate in my direction.

I took the offering and scarfed it down while I formulated a response. Last night was exactly the reason I gave him a touch of my power. I didn't want him vulnerable in the war I was waging.

"You don't have a choice," I said, after I swallowed the last bite. I cleared the plates and tucked them into Tom's dishwasher before I continued. "You're stuck with it until the powers that be decide to transfer it to someone else."

"Can't you take it back?"

I suppose I could have if I wanted to, but that would leave him and his family at Lucifer's mercy.

"No," I said, and his teeth clenched, making the muscles in his jaws tighten. He knew damned well I was lying.

His fists clenched, and he closed the distance, throwing a punch. Instead of parrying, I stopped his hand less than an inch from my face, without the use of my hands. His face scrunched with the fury filling him, and he pushed with more than just his fist, trying to breach my hold.

"You really don't want to tango with me like this, Tom," I said softly, and attempted to convey a silent warning with my eyes. "I get why you're angry. I fucked up, but you were there to save the day, so chill," I added. "That's exactly why I chose you."

He stopped trying to force my hand, and his fist loosened just before his arm dropped to his side. Tom stepped back, putting distance between us. Aggravation carved his features into a tight muscled relief map. "Why now?" his voice barreled into my head, making me wince. "You had twenty-six years to share. Why the fuck did you choose to do it now?"

This wasn't about my sleeping like the dead last night. I looked closer, taking a step toward him. "What the hell is eating you?"

His glare nearly sent me back a step, and he ripped a note card out of his shirt pocket. "This was on my door this morning." He flung the paper at me.

I caught it out of the air, but I didn't need to read the fine script signature to know who it was from. The same looping cursive on the inside of his note was written on the wedding card Lucifer sent to us and the words on this one were just as harsh as on mine.

"I'm on his acquisition list," Tom spat out.

"Well, that's better than being gutted," I said, thinking about Lucifer's threats outlined in my note. Lucifer outlined a pretty sweet deal for Tom. In the event I refused the devil, Lucifer offered to spare Tom's family if he said yes. If Tom stood with me, he outlined in detail his plans for Raven and Hannah.

"Did you see what he wrote about Hannah?" Tom waved at the note and I nodded.

"These... plans, for lack of a better word... are identical to what he wrote in our card." I held up the note before tossing it on the table.

"What the fuck am I supposed to do?" Tom asked, running his hands through his hair. The dark circles under his eyes seemed to grow by the second. The lack of sleep, along with the physical backlash of exercising the power, was draining his strength.

"I'm closing the portal in Canada on Friday," I snarled, feeling the first hint of anger, and his gaze snapped to mine. "And if you say yes to him..." I couldn't contemplate that option. If Tom said yes, then I'd have to destroy him. I wasn't sure that was something I was capable of following through with.

"Don't worry. I'm not thinking about saying yes," Tom said, but the sarcasm in his voice laced my anger even more. "Besides, the bastard is a lying shit. He'll still kill Raven and Hannah, even if I say yes."

We stared at each other as silence filtered through the anger, diffusing it, and I finally looked at the ground. "I doubt it," I said, and brought my gaze back to his. "If you said yes, he might be inclined to keep his word, especially if you give him a super powered vessel."

Tom blinked at me and then turned, storming into the living room, his fury too big to be contained in the small kitchen without striking out at me.

I didn't follow him right away. I let him siphon through the memories of Lucifer. The one thing I found when I examined the memories of our ancestor was that while Lucifer was vile, controlling, devious, and downright cruel, technically, he never lied.

Neither had I, but I played his own game of deception, deceiving him into thinking he was getting something he wasn't.

That's why he took it out on Valerie. If I had given him the vessel he coveted, my family, Valerie included, would have been spared. However, the rest of the world would have burned.

I sighed and entered Tom's living room, meeting his gaze.

"So, my soul for my family?" he asked, and I nodded.

"Your soul for a temporary stay of execution," I clarified. "I'd still have to destroy Lucifer, regardless of whether you were still hanging in there with him or not. So, the promises he made me would still be in play, creating the loophole in your deal."

Tom covered his eyes. "Basically, I'm screwed either way," he said and dropped his hand. "Unless you take this shit back."

I laughed. I didn't mean to. It just came out at the idiotic conclusion. "You're even more screwed without that power." I slid into the seat next to him and patted him on the back. "Welcome to my world."

"Fuck you," he replied, sliding his gaze to mine, but it had less of a bite of anger than before. "You just didn't want to deal with this alone anymore."

He had a point, and I shrugged. "Damian's been living it for twenty-five hundred years."

"What a pisser," he said and for the first time today, he actually cracked a smile.

"No shit," I sighed. "I'm sorry, man. But I couldn't leave you vulnerable. Not after the threats he left me."

"What about Steve?"

I glanced out the window, swallowing the lump that had formed in my throat. I loved the man almost as much as my father and the thought of him dying, whether by Lucifer's hand or not, left an empty spot in my heart. I turned back to Tom.

"He's not my blood," I finally said, admitting the truth to myself as much as to Tom. "I'm not sure how much I can spare before I become..." I paused, searching for the right word. "...in...e...ffective on Lucifer's turf." The stutter interrupted the flow of words, and I pressed my lips together for a moment before continuing. "I made a choice," I said softly. "One I pray doesn't backfire."

Angel Wrath Chapter 23

I HUNG OUT AT Tom's while he took a much-needed nap, and I headed home in time to finish dinner before Valerie arrived. When Valerie came in from work, I put a salad on the table and met her gaze.

"Hey," she said and hung her coat before taking a seat on the bench by the garage door, stripping off her shoes.

"Hi," I said, doing my best to send a smile in her direction, despite the conversation I'd had with Tom today.

She paused with the shoe still in her hand. "Are you okay?"

"They struck last night," I said, and her eyebrows arched.

"Where?"

"New York."

The shoe tumbled from her fingers and her hand covered her mouth as the same shock I first experienced.

"Tom took care of it," I said, and she closed her eyes, leaning against the wall. Relief swept over her features. When she opened her eyes, she still had a layer of tears making her stormy eyes shine.

"We need to stop this madness," she said, and walked to the table.

"We do." I reached out and pulled the bobby pins from her hair. I liked it down, and today I really needed to understand why we were fighting such a losing battle. I knew deep down Tom wouldn't take the deal, but I had to give Lucifer props. He pulled all the right strings.

"We have to make sure last night wasn't a fluke," she said, and I closed the distance between us.

"Later," I whispered, and leaned down, planting a kiss on her lips. I stripped the hair tie and dropped the bundle on the table along with the bobby pins. The kiss deepened when I ran my hands into her hair. Every movement of her tongue with mine sent tingles through my form, and I willed the barrier into her without her knowledge. As I ran my hands down her back, I tested the depth until the tingle in my fingertips dulled to nothing more than the heat from her skin.

When I pulled away, I met her gaze.

"I needed that." I said and stepped away, waving to the dinner table and locking my mind. If I'd miscalculated, she'd be able to heal quickly enough, but I had a feeling I'd end up in the backyard from the charge I set. It still wasn't the max load, but enough to do damage to a normal person.

I pulled out the chair for her and lifted the plate warmer. The waft of aroma from the steak smelled wonderful, and even though I was hungry, my stomach knotted with the tension now filling me. I had positioned her so her back was facing the sliders, and I reached for the steak knife and whispered in her ear.

"I love you, babe," I said and stuck the blade in her side. The blast lifted me off my feet and I snapped a protective bubble around me, at least one strong enough so my neck wouldn't snap on impact. As I flew through the air, I closed my eyes and yanked outwards and then I hit the pavers along with enough debris to make my heart slam in my chest.

A buzzing sound filled my world, and I stared up at the star filled night, blinking until she stepped into my view.

"Chris, what the fuck was that?" she snapped, holding the bloody knife in her hand.

"A test," I whispered, coughing at the pain in my back. I glanced at the knife and closed my eyes with satisfaction. An inch. The bloodline on the blade only covered an inch.

"You fucking demolished the kitchen." She pointed toward the house. Her anger was warranted, but I had to make sure I could do it before I made the call to Steve to set things up for Friday.

"Are you okay?" I asked from my vantage point.

"I'm fine," she said, and looked at the steak knife a little closer.

Silence fell with only the sound of buzzing electricity, and I propped up on my elbows, scanning the damage.

"Holy shit," I whispered. "Well, let's see if I can at least fix the wall," I said. Closing my eyes, I willed the house back to its original state. The creak of glass and metal and wood filled the backyard and the power flare in my chest grew until I didn't think I could contain it anymore.

When my eyes opened, the solid face of the back of the house was intact, and Valerie was on her knees next to me with her mouth hanging open in awe. My head dropped to the pavers as exhaustion played havoc with my muscles.

"Shit," I whispered, and before I could say anything else, her lips were on mine. I groaned, wincing at the pain filtering through me like an electrical fire. "Damn," I finally hissed, and the colors swirled in her eyes as she grinned at me.

"I don't know if I put it all back together," I said as the healing tingle faded. "And I'm not sure the steak survived."

She let out a nearly hysterical laugh as I slowly sat up next to her. "Don't ever do that to me again," she said and swatted my chest with the back of her hand.

"The next time I do that, it will annihilate a horde of demons." My gaze shifted from the house to the pathway leading to Naomi and Damian's house.

Damian stood staring at us with wide, wild eyes. "I heard an explosion."

"Yeah. I got it covered," I said and climbed to my feet, helping Valerie up, as well. We were both a little unsteady, and I wrapped my arm around her waist, guiding her toward the house.

"What happened?" he asked, as we got closer.

"I tried to cook," I said, unwilling to share our practice sessions with Damian like I had with Tom. If Damian knew, I'd get a beating from here to hell and back.

"Bullshit," he snapped, and both of us turned to him.

"We're heading to Canada on Friday."

His features tightened.

"So, we had to make sure everything we have planned would work."

His eyes traveled between us.

"I'm okay. He's okay. It's fine," Valerie said, but his gaze had already dropped to the knife in her hand.

"You can't be doing this type of shit right now, CJ," he said. "Not with the stuff that went down last night."

"Okay. We'll stop blowing things up," I said. Damian gave me a nod, and we entered the house, stopping as the slider closed behind us.

Valerie scanned the demolished kitchen table and dusty surroundings. The wall, counter, and sink were all pieced together again by my sheer will, but the table was in ruins, along with our dinner. I'd have to run out and pick up something, but I needed to make a phone call first.

"You're one fucking amazing man," she said, and I cleared off a chair for her.

"We can go out to eat tonight," I said, scanning the destruction. "After I call Steve." The wall phone wasn't an option anymore, so I pulled my cell out of my pocket and dialed the familiar number.

"Hi, Steve," I said, with my back to Valerie. "It's time to call in that favor."

"Are you okay?" he asked, ignoring my statement.

"I'm fine. I was exhausted yesterday. I'm sorry I didn't..." I trailed off, running my hand through my hair. Shards of glass made tinkling sounds as they hit the floor around me, and I stared at the dust that littered my hand. "Are you and Jennifer okay?"

"We're fine. A little shaken that they so easily got into the building, but we're fine now that we're in New Hampshire."

"I'm glad you're okay," I said. I really would never forgive myself if anything happened to either of them, but I took a gamble with Tom that I believed would pay off. I sat on the couch. The leg gave way and the side I was on dropped a foot. Valerie let out a giggle.

"About that favor?" I said again, pressing my lips together against the smirk when Valerie and I traded a glance.

"When?"

"Friday."

Silence filled the line.

"This Friday?" he asked

"Yes."

More silence, and I glanced at Valerie with a shrug.

"You realize what day that is, right?"

I blinked and tried to figure out the significance of the date and when I didn't answer him within a few beats, he filled me in.

"It's black Friday. The day after Thanksgiving."

My head whipped to Valerie, and I mouthed 'Oh Shit!' before glancing at the nearly unusable kitchen. Both of us had completely forgotten about the holiday. We hadn't gotten a goddamned thing to prepare for the feast we were supposed to host in a couple of days.

"What?" she whispered.

"Thanksgiving," I said, and her eyes did the same frantic bounce as mine.

"You are still hosting, right?" Steve asked on the other end.

"Um, about that..."

"We could have it here at the lake if that's easier."

Valerie nodded.

"That probably makes more sense. Valerie has to work that morning, but we could be there by two," I said. "Just as long as you don't let Jennifer cook."

The hearty laugh came over the line. "You forgot, didn't you?"

"Yes. Totally." I gave Valerie a shrug, and she nodded her silent thank you for deferring the holiday dinner somewhere else. "Do you think we'll be able to get a chopper out on Friday morning, with the holiday weekend?"

"I'll check when we are off this call. And CJ?"

"Yeah?"

"The next time I call you, you better wake the fuck up," he said.

"Yes, sir." I hung my head in shame.

"I'll let you know what I find out, and look forward to seeing everyone on Thursday."

"Thanks."

"I love you, kiddo," he said.

"Love you, too," I replied, and hung up the phone, meeting Valerie's gaze.

"I forgot this week was Thanksgiving," she said.

"You're not alone." I stared at the mess I made. "I'm officially an idiot," I added, and she started chuckling. "Come on, let's go clean up and I'll take you to dinner."

As we climbed the stairs, I couldn't help but be thankful. If I was going up against the devil, a family gathering the day before sounded like the perfect thing to remind both Tom and me what we were fighting for.

Angel Wrath Chapter 24

I SWIRLED MY WINE, staring at the way it clung to the glass. My mind was a thousand miles away from the cheerful banter of my family. Instead, my thoughts focused on the things I might encounter in the confines of Lucifer's portal.

I played every conceivable scenario I could think of, borrowing from past experiences where Lucifer aimed to rattle his foe. I kept jumping to the first time he faced off with my father, and how he capitalized on bringing my uncle into the mix.

What would I do if my father was the one being torn to pieces by a hellhound?

Valerie elbowed me, and I glanced at her, raising an eyebrow. She leaned towards me. "Let it go for a little while," she said, in a scolding tone that pulled me out of my reverie.

I blinked, remembering where I was. "Sorry," I said, and refocused on the conversation.

Tom's gaze pulled to mine, and we both sighed. Since I had supercharged him, every time we were together in a crowd, it was like the connection we'd had when we were younger was back online. The connection that had been broken the minute the psycho in Georgia grabbed him.

We spoke without words or thoughts in this case. We had an underlying communication that hummed between us. An understanding. A kinship I was thankful for.

I raised my glass to him, and he followed in kind.

"Thank you," I said aloud, pulling everyone's attention to me and silencing conversations. I shifted under the sudden quiet and cleared my throat, praying my stutter wouldn't tie my tongue. "I wanted to say thank you for a superb dinner." I raised my glass in Steve's direction. "Especially for not letting Jennifer into the kitchen," I added and everyone but Jennifer chuckled. "Sorry, but you and I both know, had he let you in there, this feast would have ended up a charcoal fest."

Jennifer pressed her lips against the smile.

"Thank you for the best singing partner I could ever ask for."

"You're welcome," she said. "Thank you..."

"I'm not done saying my peace," I said, interrupting her. "And I want to say what I need to before I have any more wine," I clarified. I had already downed three bottles myself. "And before my stutter slices up my speech."

Everyone gave a slow nod, exchanging wary glances.

"Thanks for giving us a loving home, a great meal and the sense to know what path to take when given choices." I turned my attention to Damian and Naomi. "I know you feel responsible for all the shi..." I closed my eyes for a second and restarted with a PG version, cognizant of the kids at the table. "Stuff that has happened to all of us, but I wouldn't have met Valerie if you hadn't shown up in York. Despite our rocky start, you two ended up becoming pretty decent friends, even if it's only a ruse, so you can be close enough to protect Valerie." I sent them a wink and moved my gaze to Tom and Raven.

There really were no words to describe how thankful I was Tom was alive. He'd cheated death a few times, and I'm not sure I'd be who I am if he wasn't around. "You have no idea how thankful I am that you're my brother..." I pressed my lips against the sudden swell of emotion and his eyebrows rose.

"Someone take the wine away from him before he gets all sappy and shit," he signed, and Raven smacked him.

"And that he met you," I said to Raven.

"Oh, no. We're too late," she chided, and her dimples made an appearance. "Maybe the wine does have to go," she said. Her Irish lilt made it sound so much more formal than she's ever been and the group laughed at my expense.

I slid my gaze to Valerie, and with a smirk, she reached for my wineglass.

"I love you, but you cannot have my wine." I lifted the glass so she couldn't reach it.

"Tom's right, you're getting sappy," she laughed.

"Yeah, well, I'm facing Lucifer tomorrow and we all know what happened the last couple of times I decided to battle the devil."

Her smile faded, and she sat back in the seat. Silence settled like a wet blanket.

"I'm just saying my peace," I said, scanning the now melancholy crowd. "I love every one of you," I shrugged, and toasted from my little soap box. I downed the rest of the glass and reached for the bottle.

Steve looked at Valerie. "He's cut off."

His statement made me pause with my hand halfway to the bottle. The silence hung on the air until Tom snorted laughter.

"You're toasted, aren't you?" he signed, and the words echoed in my head.

A smile played on my lips, and I reached the rest of the distance, grabbing the bottle and emptying the contents into my glass. "Maybe a little," I allowed.

"Don't get shitfaced," Steve said, despite the young ones gathered around the table. "Save that for tomorrow night, okay?" This request was serious, and I hesitated with the glass in hand.

With a nod, I set the glass on the table and slid it back, trading the alcohol for a glass of water.

"Thank you," he said.

"I may be a little, um, off, but I meant what I said."

"We know, and we love you, too," Jennifer said. "Now, who wants dessert?"

"Who made it?" I asked when no one's hand shot up. She sent a glare in my direction and hooked her thumb in Steve's direction.

"He did."

Everyone's hand shot up.

"You all suck," she said, standing and grabbing the dishes.

Steve stood, and I shook my head. "You cooked," I said, and stood, collecting my empty plate along with Valerie's. Tom and Damian followed suit, leaving the women and kids at the table with Steve while we cleared.

I stepped into the kitchen and Jennifer had three pies sitting on the island.

"You know I'm just yanking your chain, right?" I said, as I passed her and started rinsing the dishes.

"Yes," she said and waited until Tom and Damian had left to get the rest of the dishes. "Want to know a secret," she said, and I met her gaze. "I probably wouldn't eat it if I had baked it," she admitted with a smile.

"Want to know one of my secrets?" I chuckled.

Jennifer nodded, glancing towards the other room before bringing her gaze back to mine.

"Sam wouldn't eat your cooking, either," I whispered.

"Get out. Sam ate everything that fell on the floor."

I laughed as Tom stepped into the room and placed another pile of dishes next to me. "Anything you didn't cook, he scarfed up. But your cooking? Sam just pushed that around with his nose until he found a suitable hiding place. You had to know it wasn't either of us who hid food in the couch," I said, glancing at her. She had started that giggling that would overflow to hysterics any moment, and I traded a glance with Tom. "I even remember one time when I tried to pass something to Sam under the table when you and Steve weren't looking. He covered his nose with his paw and whined. It was the damnedest thing I've ever seen."

She went into the land of the guffaw until tears leaked from her eyes. "You're kidding?"

"No, I'm not," I said, grinning while I finished loading the dishwasher. I glanced behind me at Tom. "Right?"

He nodded. "You always blamed one of us for the hidden food," he signed. "But it was the dog."

"No way," she gasped, through the laughter.

"Yes, way," I laughed. "Your culinary skills are pretty damned sad."

"And you get way too honest when you've had too much to drink." She grinned at me as her laughter wound down.

"Yeah, he becomes one of those bad beer commercials when he drinks too much," Damian said, placing another pile of dishes on the side of the sink.

"Come on, I'm not that bad," I said, tucking the last plate in the washer and closing it. I grabbed a dishcloth and wiped my hands. "Someone else can get the pots. I want pie."

We each grabbed one of the professional-looking apple, pumpkin, and chocolate cream pies and carried them into the dining room. Jennifer followed with the dessert dishes and silverware.

By the time we were done, there were only scraps left and, collectively, we leaned back in the chairs. I glanced at my watch. "The Dallas game is probably still on," I said and chairs scrapped as we all got up, clearing the table on our way to the large family room overlooking the lake. I took a spot on the window seat, leaving the couches for the rest of the family. Valerie sat between my legs, and I split my attention between the sunset painting the sky and Dallas schooling the Eagles.

At seven, both Damian and Naomi, and Tom and Raven took their kids upstairs to the guest rooms to get them settled down. My hands caressed Valerie's stomach, and she glanced back at me with a ghost of a smile.

That was one thing I was thankful for that I kept to myself. Tom knew, and I suspected Raven did, as well, but we hadn't announced it to anyone yet, and Valerie asked me to wait until after tomorrow before sharing our news.

Jennifer crossed to us and took a seat at the window.

"When are you due?" she asked, her voice just a whisper under the sounds of the television.

We both just stared at her. I bit my lower lip and scrunched my eyebrows, pretending not to know what she was talking about.

"Due?" Valerie asked, pushing off the inevitable.

"You didn't have any wine with dinner and you're a little pale," she said. "Either you're coming down with something, or you're pregnant."

"I'm not feeling very well," Valerie said, and that probably was the truth. The morning sickness didn't seem to be confined to mornings.

Jennifer's brow drew together, and her gaze moved from Valerie's to mine, searching. I just shrugged and a bite of guilt bloomed inside me. I hated lying, but neither of us was ready to share.

Damian came down a few minutes later. "What's the plan for tomorrow?" he asked, taking a seat on the couch.

"I couldn't get a helicopter," Steve said. "But Ted is sending one of his smaller, faster planes. You need to be at the airstrip in Wolfeboro at seven in the morning, and make sure you have your passports." He looked at the three of us. "He's taking you to a smaller airport northwest of Quebec and I told Ted that if you aren't back by ten tomorrow night, to leave without you." He paused and took a sip of a beer he had cracked open after the kids went upstairs.

"I rented a truck with a couple of snowmobiles and it will be waiting at the airport."

"How far do we have to drive?"

Steve crossed to a desk in the corner and picked up a piece of paper. "It looks like the drive is a couple of hours to a public park. The snowmobile trails nearest the spot Damian marked look like another hour from where you're parked. And from there, it's about a mile. I'm not sure if you'll be able to get through with the snowmobiles, so I also have a couple of pairs of snowshoes waiting for you as well."

"What time are we landing?" I asked when he handed me the paper.

"Nine. So, you have thirteen hours to get in, close the portal and get back, otherwise you're driving home. If you don't fuck around, it should only take you six hours at the most."

Damian and I nodded, and then his gaze pierced Valerie. "Are you sure you want to come with us?" he asked, but his tone carried a warning.

"Yes," she said, stiffening in my arms, preparing for a battle of words, but Damian just blew out a stream of air and gave her a curt nod.

Tom came downstairs and glanced at us gathered by the window.

"Go over the plan again," he signed, and I met his gaze as the words echoed in my head.

"The plan for you is to stay put and protect this house until I tell you it's okay."

He nodded.

"Not Damian. Just me. When I either show up or…" I trailed off as Valerie stiffened in my arms. "Or you see my ghost," I finished, and his gaze moved beyond me to the lake, but he gave me the nod I was looking for.

"Chris," Valerie started.

"We know it's a possibility," I said. "And if things go south and I'm without power on his turf, you'd better get her the hell out of there," I said to Damian.

"And if I already have your father?" Damian asked, and it was a good question.

My arms tightened around Valerie and I met Tom's gaze. "You have to let him go and get Valerie out of there." I put my forehead to the back of Valerie's head. "And if things don't go as planned, Val, you have to run. Understand?"

She didn't move or speak, and I caught her reflection in the window. Instead of arguing with her in front of the family, I lifted my gaze to Damian.

Can you hear me? I sent the thought out wrapped in a bubble and he nodded, but neither Tom nor Valerie gave any indication of hearing my targeted thought.

"I'll keep my mind open. You'll know if there is any problem, okay?"

"If your mind is open, won't Lucifer be able to glimpse your thoughts, too?"

"I'm pretty sure I can target it." I glanced at Tom. "I'm going to try something and I need you and Valerie to tell me if you can get whatever I'm transmitting to Damian. Damian, make sure you block your thoughts." I concentrated on putting a barrier around my thought while leaving an open channel to Damian. "You ready?"

Everyone nodded.

I stared out the window. *Do not react beyond a nod, but Valerie is pregnant.* I glanced at his wider than normal eyes and got a small nod. *She doesn't want to make the announcement until after... you know... so keep it under wraps. Okay?*

I got another nod. If Valerie had heard the message, she would have sent her elbow into my stomach along with shooting me a nasty glare.

I think we can safely say this channeling thing works.

"But can you do it while keeping the barrier inside Valerie intact and juggling whatever Lucifer is throwing at you?" Damian asked.

I shrugged. "We'll see."

"I heard nothing," Valerie said, and her gaze bounced between Damian and me.

"Neither did I," Tom signed.

"Good." I shifted Valerie so I could stand, and I disappeared into the kitchen, finding a soda in the refrigerator. What I really wanted was a beer, but Steve had a point earlier. If I got drunk and ended up with a hangover, I'd be in trouble tomorrow.

"You okay, babe?"

"What if he shows me the same shit he did in New York?" I asked, turning to Valerie and voicing one of the many things eating away the lining of my stomach.

"Then you'll deal with it. If he's chained, you'll have to break them for Damian to carry him out, though."

558

I hadn't thought about the condition or placement of my father, and I met Valerie's gaze. The tiny details beyond just having Damian grab him needed to be fleshed out, and I wondered if I'd get any sleep tonight.

"I think we should probably call it a night."

Valerie's gaze shot to the clock beyond me and her brow creased. "It's still early," she said, returning her stormy eyes to mine.

"I know," I muttered and walked past her. Not only did I need to think these things through, I wanted some alone time with my wife.

She grabbed my arm as I went to pass. "What are you doing?"

I sighed and glanced at the family now gathered around the television, watching the evening game. When I brought my gaze back to her, I smiled and gave her a lingering kiss. "Hoping for the best, but preparing for the worst."

Angel Wrath Chapter 25

FIVE-THIRTY ROLLED AROUND MUCH too fast, and I banged the alarm with my palm, shutting off the annoying buzz. Yawning, I stretched; amazed I got any shut eye at all. I shook Valerie, and she lifted her head, meeting my gaze and letting off a soft groan of discontent.

"I know." I kissed her forehead. "But you can choose to stay in bed."

"No. I can't." She rolled off the side, heading into the guest bathroom ahead of me. I closed the door behind her while she rummaged through our overnight bag.

When she pulled out an antacid, I raised a brow.

"Are you sure?"

For a moment, doubt passed her features, but after popping a Tums, she met my gaze and nodded. "I didn't think I'd ever get to sleep," she said, reaching for the toothbrush next to mine on the counter.

"Neither did I."

She let out a light laugh. "You were snoring before I got settled back in bed," she said after she spit.

"I don't think so."

"Ya-huh," she said. "I thought having to keep quiet wore me out, but apparently it sucked the energy right out of you instead."

I smiled. Making love to her last night was far from the wild romp we usually got into at home. It was subdued and slow, and I loved every second of seeing her struggle with keeping quiet. It was the perfect ending to the perfect night, and just what I needed to fortify my inner strength.

"I hope you packed the long johns," I said, and she pulled them out of the bag like a magician.

We dressed in layers. Light thermal underwear underneath jeans with a fleece lining. I opted for my work boots instead of the bulky snow boots. I could stuff foot warmers in if I needed to, but the steel toe gave me a little more protection in case it came down to another fist fight. My leather jacket fit snugly over the sweater, and this time, I remembered my ski hat and a scarf. It wasn't frigid, but it was below freezing, according to the weather maps, and I didn't want to be frozen solid by the time we got there.

Valerie had the same idea of layers, but instead of a leather bomber jacket like mine, she wore her down coat that almost reached to her knees. The last thing she pulled out of our bag was the knife from Hawaii. I stared at it and then traded a glance with her. She gave me a nervous smile and strapped the sheath to her belt. It couldn't hurt having something like that, and maybe it could destroy an angel. We would certainly find out.

I tapped lightly on Damian's door, letting him know we were ready to go.

Downstairs, I grabbed a juice out of the refrigerator and tossed it to Valerie just as Damian climbed down the stairs. He was equally bundled up as we were.

"Passports?" he asked, holding up his.

"Yes. In my wallet." I tapped my jacket to make sure I had my wallet and phone in place. "Good to go?" I asked, glancing at the two of them. The creak on the stairs pulled my attention.

Tom rubbed his eye with one hand. "Be careful," he said. I wasn't the only one who heard the words perfectly in my head.

I crossed. "You, too," I said and gave him a quick hug. With no more words, I turned and stepped outside with Valerie and Damian, heading towards our car. The morning was bright, but the pending stand-off weighed heavily on me as I drove the short distance to the airstrip in Wolfeboro.

Ted was already standing at the counter as we walked in. I gave him a strained smile and shook his hand.

"I didn't think you were going to be our pilot today," I said.

He gave me a shrug, but didn't say anything until we were safely tucked in the plane. "I got the distinct impression this wasn't a joy ride," he said, meeting my gaze.

I didn't want to drag Ted into this. He was not, in any way, equipped to deal with monsters, but he had a right to know. "No. It's not. And if none of us are back by ten tonight, it's wheels up for you, okay?"

His lips pressed tight, and his gaze traveled over the three of us.

"You aren't doing anything illegal, are you?"

The three of us let out a laugh. "No. We aren't," I said. "All you need to know is we're going after the bad guy and when I pour a line of salt across the entry before I leave, know I'm not insane, and as crazy as it sounds, that line will protect you from what we're hunting."

His rapid blink put me on edge and then he turned, closing the hatchway.

"Steve once dragged me on one of his vigilante quests, and I always had a grain of regret about asking so many questions, especially when he gave me answers," he looked between all of us again. "And I know I'm going to regret this, too, but what the hell are you hunting?"

Damian reached into his pocket and pulled out another blood stone necklace. "Raven asked me to bring this for the pilot," he said and held it out towards Ted.

I took it from his hand and crossed to Ted. "You really don't want to know," I said and handed him the necklace. "But this will also offer you some protection."

He stared at the necklace and then met my gaze. "Are you packing?"

I shook my head. "A gun wouldn't do any good."

He swallowed and took the necklace, slipping it over his head. "Then why isn't Steve here with you?" he asked. He had seen enough of the things Steve was capable of over the years, but I wasn't sure he knew about me.

"I'm better suited for this trip than he is," I said, and Ted's gaze narrowed.

"You sure about that, son?"

I smiled. "Yes." *I'm the one who supercharged Steve.* I sent the thought into Ted's mind and his eyebrows rose. "Well, technically, it was my father, but I was the one who originally gave him the juice," I said aloud.

Ted uttered a laugh. "Steve never let on about you," he said and gave my shoulder a soft pat.

"Can you blame him?"

"No, can't say that I can. And I've gladly kept his secret all these years. Yours is safe with me, as well," he added before turning and marching into the cockpit.

The fact he didn't press for more answers was a relief, because if I had to burst Ted's bubble with what really existed out there in the world, it would have put a target on his back.

I bit the inside of my cheek as the realization set in. Ted was already a target, at least as much of a target as Sandy had been. His longstanding friendship with Steve made him vulnerable, and I wondered just how thin I could spread myself today.

I took a seat next to Valerie, and she covered my hand.

"You can't protect the plane."

Damian's statement pulled my gaze to his. "Why not?"

"Because you're right, that would spread you too thin," he said, throwing my train of thought back at me. "You need everything you have, and you're already splitting it, so don't even think about safeguarding the plane while we're gone."

I glared at him, but he was right. I needed everything I had. Instead of dwelling on what was coming, I pulled up the table between the four seats and opened the compartment near the window, pulling out a deck of cards.

"Five-card stud?" I asked, and both Valerie and Damian's eyebrows rose. "It will pass the time," I added as I shuffled the deck.

"What are we playing for?" Damian asked, leaning forward.

I bit my lip and glanced at Valerie. "Babysitting hours," I said, and Damian grinned.

"You're on," he said.

Valerie leaned forward, her gaze jumping between us. "You told him?"

I nodded, dealing the first five cards. "Can you grab the pen and pad in there and keep track? I have a feeling this might be a very valuable game." I winked at her, knowing she was irritated with me, but something else danced in her eyes.

I think this is the first time I have looked beyond today, and it filled both of us with hope.

By the time we landed, the damage was done; whatever hope we had in the future included owing Damian forty-five hours of babysitting. He just grinned while I muttered under my breath, sliding the cards into the box and stowing them away.

My luck was equally tested when we arrived at the car rental place to find the truck we rented. It was old enough to make me doubt it would make the trip, and the single snowmobile in the back added to the frustration. At least the thing was long enough for the three of us, so that was a plus.

Damian pulled me aside once we got the snowmobile down from the truck bed. "You need to get into the right frame of mind before we get there," he said, and I crossed my arms. "I know you're irritated with how the cards fell on the plane, the condition of the truck, and even the single snowmobile, but you ever think that maybe your luck was reserved for a reason?"

I blinked and my arms dropped, the shock stilling me for a moment, and then I let out a little laugh. "God, I hope to hell you're right," I said. "I was thinking we should just turn around and do this another day."

Damian let out a chuckle. "I hear you, but that's three things that haven't gone as planned." He pulled up his coat sleeve, showing me his watch. "But if you hadn't noticed, we're ahead of schedule," he said.

I hadn't noticed, and I offered him a nod of thanks.

Valerie stood by the snowmobile waiting for us, and I caught a quick kiss before we piled on the contraption. I took comfort in the thought that Valerie would benefit from our warmth as we squished together on the seat. I took a moment to pull out my phone and turned the snowmobile toward the blinking dot. I tucked the phone away and took off in a straight line toward whatever waited for us in the deep Canadian woods.

The snowmobile may have been big, but it certainly hauled ass.

Angel Wrath Chapter 26

THE THREE OF US stood outside the perimeter of Hell's portal. Evil spilled over like a nasty oil slick sliding over the water, destroying everything in its path. You could almost smell the foulness.

I glanced at Damian. "When my dad appears, you know what to do," I said, ignoring the plumes of white our breath created in the frigid Canadian air.

Damian gave me a nod. "Get him the hell out of dodge."

My lips curved at the cliché. I'm sure my dimple made a brief appearance, too. "Yeah, but wait until I give you the signal."

"Got it. Be careful. I will not be here to bail you out this time."

"I will. I think I'll be good, and if not, we'll have to table the rescue mission." I glanced at Valerie. "If my powers are blocked, you'd better run like the place is on fire. Understand?"

She hesitated and traded a glance with Damian before bringing her gaze to mine. I pulled her close.

"We talked about this," I said, and she nodded, but the set of her jaw and the tight line of her lips told me she wasn't leaving no matter what. "If this goes to shit, promise me you'll get out of here," I said, unwilling to move forward with the plan without her concession. My hand drifted lower to her belly and the reason for my hesitation. We had more to lose than just our lives.

Her gaze dropped to my hand. I knew she didn't want to raise our child alone, but she also knew if Lucifer got hold of her, I wouldn't be able to say no. Not with my child's life in the mix. When her gaze came back to mine, she nodded.

"Okay. I promise," she said.

"I love you," I whispered, and planted a kiss, taking a moment to let our tongues intertwine. The heavy winter attire made the transfer a little more difficult, so I dropped my gloves and unzipped her coat, wrapping my arms around her waist until the tingle dulled in my fingertips. I pulled away from her lips and pressed my forehead on hers, closing my eyes and willing the full force of my power into the barrier I layered inside her.

Damian cleared his throat, and I glanced at him, slipping my hands out from under Valerie's coat, and zipping it up before I stepped away. I gathered my wits and focused my energies on the pending battle. "Stay out of sight," I said to Damian, just before he transformed and took flight. The human-to-hawk thing still startled me, and I watched his graceful ascent until he ducked out of view, hoping like hell Lucifer didn't catch sight of him.

"You, too," I said to Valerie, and she slid farther back into the woods, using the big pines like shields.

Nerves bit at my stomach, and I closed my eyes, steadying my breathing and centering my power. I didn't know how much Lucifer knew, now that he had my father under his domain. All I could do was hope Heaven's secrets were still under wraps.

"Game on," I whispered, adopting my dad's favorite battle line and moved forward, breeching the portal boundaries. Brimstone hung on the air, and I rubbed my nose, suppressing the tickle that wanted to turn into a sneeze. I still had one hundred yards of dodging trees and thick shrubs before I got to the epicenter. The place where Lucifer would be waiting for me.

I found it odd that no demons approached, and tension filled my muscles, turning me into a coil waiting for the surprise attack. I had the benefit of Uriel's grace, in addition to my self-defense skills I hadn't had with my last encounter with Lucifer, and I was confident that the little extra juice I received in heaven would push the advantage to my side of the chessboard this time around.

I cleared the woods line, stepping into the confines of the small glen, and stopped.

The form leaning against the rock at the opposite side of the clearing set my heart banging on my ribcage. I swear my shirt vibrated in time with the beat.

The familiar face smiled, but it wasn't the warm smile I would have expected from my father. Instead, it held the promise of pain.

I took a tentative step forward, unsure of myself.

"You like the new digs?" He spread his arms out, and I recoiled.

Lucifer's curve ball hit with the level of devastation he probably expected. My chest ached like I had been sucker punched, and I steadied myself, focusing on the power swirling in my abdomen.

"Where's my father?" I asked, when I was sure my voice wouldn't shake. Everything about this was wrong.

Lucifer snapped his fingers and the meanest, ugliest hellhound I had ever seen appeared by his side. The beast snarled, pulling at the restraints holding him in place. He wasn't the only rabid dog in the vicinity, either. Shapes dotted the woods line, blocking my exit from the clearing. There must have been one hundred hellhounds all gunning for their chance to tear my flesh from the bone.

It wasn't until I took a closer look at the dog next to Lucifer that understanding overtook me. The hellhound's vibrant blue eyes followed me, and despite the violence reflected in his irises, I would have recognized those eyes anywhere.

"You turned my dad into a hellhound?" I asked. Both anger and anxiety filled my voice, and I met Lucifer's gaze.

His lips spread into an evil grin.

"And you figured I wouldn't have the heart to kill the likeness of my father?" I added, taking a step forward.

"I like this look." Lucifer waved at the fine physique. His smug smile set my fury level to almost unbearable. "And whatever was left of your father when I was through with him has turned into the most viscous hound I've ever had."

Lucifer unclasped the chain holding the hound in place and, like an obedient dog, he stayed next to Lucifer's side, waiting for the command to attack. I dropped my gaze to the ground, praying the abort information was relayed, because if Damian swooped in and grabbed the image of my father, he'd be carrying the devil out of danger.

I took a deep breath, exhaled, looked back at the bastard, and straightened my back in defiance. "You played this kind of sick mind game with Val, and it fucked her up. But I'm a different beast all together." I said, and my fists clenched as I imagined a protective shield surrounding me. "I don't give a shit what form you take. I am going to end you."

His smile faltered just before he gave the attack command. My gaze dropped to the blue eyes of the lead hound as he bounded toward me. His snarl carried on the air like a rifle report, and all I could do was prepare for the impact.

When the hound launched, my muscles clenched.

The beat of wings sent a whirlwind around us, and the yelp of a dog punctuated it. Before my brain could process any sort of response to Damian snatching the hellhound out of the air, he cleared the trees, heading south, and disappearing from sight with the hound still in his talons. I had time to blink before the rest of the hellhounds attacked.

None of them reached me, and the stench of burned fur mingled with brimstone. If Damian hadn't snatched my father from the air, he would have had the same fate as the rest of Lucifer's canine army.

I smiled, relieved that I had my mojo on the devil's turf. If not, I was certain I'd be near death right now. His smug grin faded and his eyes narrowed.

"You little shit," he said.

"Me?" I pointed to my chest. "You're the one who turned your kin into a fucking dog."

He chuckled. "I ripped my brother's head off. What'd you expect? That I'd treat Uriel's blood line any differently?"

"I didn't expect that, but I would think you might feel a little differently about your own bloodline." I dropped the bomb and from the rapid blink and loose jaw, he had no fucking clue. I crossed my arms and squared my feet. "And you know what that makes me, right?"

His jaw tightened. "With your little slut, that gives you the possibility of siring a dark trinity." His eyes danced at the prospect, and I leveled a smile.

"My mother has two angel bloodlines, as well," I said, springing these additional facts on him with a bit of glee.

His smile disappeared. "You're a... trinity?"

"Ayup," I said and tilted my head. "Funny that you never picked up on that. But I guess it was masked by the double dose of your blood."

He actually stepped backwards.

"That, along with a little infusion of angel grace, and I'm your worst fucking nightmare," I said, dropping my hands to my side where they balled into fists. "This time, I'm ready to tango, gramps." I allowed the sarcastic overtone to bleed through.

He seemed to recover much quicker than I imagined, and he squared off, crossing his arms as a little smile spread on his lips.

The bushes to my right rattled and in stepped a group of demons, all holding weapons from guns to knives, and in the center of the group stood Valerie with her arms bound behind her back.

She met my gaze and lifted one of her shoulders. The minute she had stepped in the confines of the portal, her powers were useless. I guess the trinity piece was the important one and not the angel grace. My heart pounded as I made a small calculation, wondering if what we practiced would work.

"You won't be able to save her," Lucifer said, reading my intentions, and I moved my glare to him.

What he didn't know is I had already done it before I left her in the woods. I knew an ambush was possible, and so did she. She even accurately guessed the pricks would puncture her skin just to make a point. I just hoped they didn't go too deeply because then the element of surprise would be ruined, and I prayed she still had the knife.

When she gave me a slight nod, I exhaled. She still had the knife, and that gave us more of an edge. We both wanted to reduce Lucifer to a trembling mass of flesh before I closed off this portal.

"You really are an asshole," I said, and mentally yanked outwards. The power crackled in the air, annihilating everything in its path. Guns, knives, demons. They all fell to the sharp blast before the creatures used their weapons.

"My, my, aren't you just full of surprises today," Lucifer said, and despite the jovial tone, the hesitation in his eyes gave me some level of satisfaction.

"Looks like your bag of tricks is nearly empty," I said, trying not to gloat at the small win. I needed to remember not to get cocky. Even with the advantages I had, I knew he was just as dangerous.

Valerie went to move, and an invisible hand clamped around her throat. She clawed at her neck, her panicked gaze locking with mine.

"I never got to finish what I started in the warehouse," he said, and the slow, salacious smile appeared. The buttons on her jeans undid and a pitiful whine escaped her lips.

"No fucking way," I growled and sent a mental shove.

Lucifer stumbled back, landing on his ass. The initial shock that I had enough power to derail him on his own turf gave me the window I needed to get Valerie behind me and away from his direct control.

She stumbled in my direction as her breath wheezed. I didn't move, but I made damned sure she was insulated behind me before I cocked my head at Lucifer.

"That's the last mistake you'll ever make," I snarled, letting a bomb launch from my chest. My power expanded and rolled forward, killing whatever monsters there may have been lurking in the woods. I toppled trees and turned the mighty oaks into fire tinder in one fell swoop. The portal lay barren, with only Lucifer and us standing.

"Go," I said to Valerie, and this time, she didn't hesitate. She ran in a straight line, using me to block Lucifer's access. The moment she stepped beyond the portal, she sent me the all clear.

"No display of white light or heavenly fire?" he asked.

"Not yet," I said and took a step closer. "That will come, but first I'm going to kick your ass."

He took the same form I was familiar with and then he snarled, "Game on."

It was enough to make me hesitate. I stared at the likeness of my father, knowing damned well it wasn't him inhabiting his form, but it still played with my head, whether or not I wanted to admit it.

Instead of acknowledging the bloom of fear that formed in my throat, I waved him in.

"Let's see what you can do when we are on a level playing field."

He charged, taking me by surprise, but it was sloppy enough for me to parry and send him tumbling to the ground. He glared at me and scrambled to his feet. I inhaled, finding my center and waiting for him to try something as inept.

"You would kill your own blood?" he asked, as he wiped off the dust.

I considered the question. "What do you think?"

"I think you don't have the stomach for it," he said. "You aren't like your father."

I smiled. In that respect, he was absolutely right, and that was the one thing that differentiated us. The one thing that made me forsake the dark side of my heritage. "No, I'm not."

He took a step closer, and his right hand formed the deadly claw I was familiar with, but I didn't move. I kept my hands loose and my ready stance intact.

He launched again and this time I spun away from his claw, and he roared in anger when my elbow caught his jaw, knocking him to the ground a few feet away.

"I'm not like my father. I've never killed for sport." I refrained from adding 'until now' because this really wasn't for sport. It was filled with liquid revenge.

"You're playing with me just like your father did at first, but I broke him, just like I'll break you, boy."

I laughed. "I've got trinity wrath in my blood. Bring it on," I said, and took my form again. This time, when he came in for the kill, I landed a punch, crushing his nose with a little extra juice behind my fist. Lucifer was tossed like a rag doll and hit the ground hard. His head bounced, and I couldn't help the smile that plastered on my face. My hand didn't even hurt from the effort.

Kill him. Valerie's voice invaded my mind, but I ignored her. I was enjoying the game.

He shook his head and glanced up at me.

"CJ?" the bastard asked, like he was just waking from a long nightmare. I knew damned well it was a ruse. My father was headed to Paradise Cove, regardless of his less than desirable form.

"I'm not buying it," I said, and sent a mental punch right into the bastard's balls. He made an 'oof' sound and curled into a fetal position. "That was for Valerie."

His bloody nostrils flared with anger, and he rolled onto his hands and knees. I took advantage of the situation and stepped in, setting up for a kick. Unfortunately, my foot never connected. Lucifer rolled and swept my leg out from under me. I landed on my back, and he was on me before the daze cleared.

His snarling growl caught me off guard, and his fingers pierced the skin over my heart.

"If I can't control you, I'm going to kill you and eat your fucking heart," he said, pushing farther into my skin.

I bellowed at the burning pain and threw a punch right at the bastard's throat. It knocked him back far enough that his hand was dislodged, and I threw him off me. I rolled clear and hopped to my feet, now leery.

Warm blood dripped down my chest, and the welts stung. The fact his fingers punctured through my leather coat and my thick flannel shirt sent a shiver up my back. As much as I wanted to pummel him, I started to doubt that strategy, but I knew if I sent him back under with no damage, he'd be back much sooner than if I decimated him.

"Is that all you got?" I said, egging him on.

His gaze shifted, and a flash of silver caught my eye. Lucifer caught the blade in his hand, hissing in pain as he threw it toward me. It dropped at my feet, slicing into the ground. Blood dripped from his hand and the smell of fried flesh hit me. It took me a second to understand what had just happened, and then I looked at the knife at my feet.

Valerie's talisman.

Valerie's knife had the power to damage angels.

Valerie. Shit.

The thought produced the metallic taste of fear, and my heart plummeted when Lucifer let out a growl of anger. I forgot my cardinal rule and glanced over my shoulder.

Valerie was within the perimeter, but she wasn't on the ground. Horror filled every fiber of my body, freezing me in place. She was elevated above the earth with her head bent so far back I didn't know how her neck hadn't snapped. The arch of her spine was equally alarming, as some unearthly force tried to break her in two. The scream that finally escaped from her tore at my soul.

"Say yes," Lucifer said, his voice close enough to pull my attention back to him.

The snap and sudden silence that filled the space broke through me like nothing I've ever experienced. I completely lost control.

"No!" my voice barreled out along with the lion's share of power, sweeping Lucifer into a ball of fire. I swept the knife off the ground and turned, running toward Valerie, willing whatever the hell was holding her in place to disintegrate as the ground rumbled around me.

Panic layered over me and shot out in waves. She tumbled from the sky and I caught her limp form in my arms. Without slowing down, I sprinted for the safety line, dodging the breaks in the ground as Hell's gate crumbled from my building wrath. I dove the last few feet, rolling with her in my arms.

When I glanced back, white fire rained on the portal, sending everything down into the canyon I had created. The flurry quieted as the earth fused and the righteous light faded. It wasn't until the dust settled that I glanced down at Valerie.

Her gaze looked through me like I wasn't even there, and I leaned down, putting my ear to her chest. Her heart wasn't beating.

"No!" This time my cry echoed to the heaven's. I refused to let her die, and I focused, forcing her heart to beat while I administered CPR. "You can't die. You hear me!" I bellowed, willing her body to keep functioning. "Breathe, goddamn it!"

When nothing happened, I split my focus, concentrating on keeping her heart beating and her lungs filling with oxygen while I forced Uriel's grace out of my body and into the tight, brilliant ball in my hand. I opened my eyes to prisms dancing around us and without hesitation; I plunged it into Valerie, praying angel grace held the miracle that the fraction of healing power I held couldn't.

Light filled her and healing sparks danced over her form. Valerie's breath sucked in, and then her scream filled the silent forest. Her back arched and the crunch of bones realigning made me grit my teeth, but whatever magic the grace held seemed to work. I knew better than anyone what kind of hell the healing mojo created, but it was temporary and her scream softened to a shaking whine before it stopped all together.

Her chest moved up and down as her breathing steadied into the normal cadence of life. When she opened her eyes and met my gaze, I bit my lower lip, willing the tears to remain locked away.

Valerie blinked at me with wide eyes, and then her head turned toward the clearing. "Mind fuck," she whispered and looked back at me.

Our little secret phrase brought a relieved smile to my lips, and I pulled her into my arms.

"I thought..." I couldn't finish and buried my face in her hair.

"Me, too." Her hand ran over her belly. "I don't know if the baby survived," she said, and I glanced down at her stomach.

My hand covered hers and we sat in silence, holding on to the dream that was our child just a little longer.

Angel Wrath Chapter 27

AFTER THE LONG TRIP down to Brooksfield, New Hampshire, I left Valerie in the care of Jennifer and Steve at the cabin and trudged to Paradise Cove. Damian sat on a rock watching the mad hellhound trying to get out of the salt barrier he was placed in. The beast snarled at the sight of me.

"Chill," I said, and put my hand up.

"What the hell are we going to do with him?" Damian asked, standing.

"I don't know, but it was worth a try," I said, meeting his gaze. "I'm just glad you got the message."

"This is royally fucked up." He ran a hand through his hair, and I couldn't agree more.

"Sit," I commanded, and despite the divisive snarl, the beast sat on his haunches.

I went to step inside the salt ring, and Damian grabbed my arm.

"I'm his son. He won't hurt me," I said, meeting Damian's gaze.

"That isn't your father anymore." He held fast, his gaze hard and unyielding. "And after what you told me Lucifer was doing to break him, I doubt he knows who you are."

"I gotta try, man," I whispered, and his hand dropped.

"If he attacks, he's toast," Damian promised, and I sighed.

Footsteps pulled our attention to the path and Tom stepped onto the moss.

"Holy fuck," he said, and I laughed as his eyes widened at the rabid beast.

"Yeah, Lucifer is more of an asshole than I gave him credit for." I crossed to my brother. "He turned Dad into that." I pointed, and the thing growled, its eyes bouncing between the two of us as saliva dripped from its sharp teeth.

I glanced at the sky and sighed. "I was going to step in the ring, but I have a feeling he's too far gone and would try to kill me," I said, and Tom nodded in agreement. "But there is one person he wouldn't attack." I met Tom's wide eyes.

"Mom," we both said at the same time.

Mist rose off the frozen water and the shift in air pulled our attention to the cove. My mother stood a few paces away from the wild dog. Her gaze locked on the beast and his snarling subsided. It was as if no amount of torture could erase her power over him.

His snout rose in the air, and he sniffed, and then a pitiful whine escaped, and he stretched on the ground, crawling forward until his paws stopped at the salt barrier. He laid his head on his paws. For the first time since I saw him, I got a good look at his pelt. The damage to his form was substantial. Evidence of torture laid waste in the scarring crisscrossed over his exposed flesh.

My mother saw it too, and her eyes welled with tears. "Jesus, Ty," she whispered and kneeled on the other side of the salt barrier. His head lifted parallel to hers and he whined.

Her hands moved, breaching the barrier, and cupped his massive jaws.

Damian laid a salt ring around my mother to protect us and she glanced at me before she wiped away the barrier keeping the hound from her. He crawled forward and laid his muzzle in her lap.

A lump formed in my throat, and tears burned. I had annihilated his human form, and all that was left was a beaten and butt ugly hellhound. My chin dropped to my chest, and Tom put his hand on my shoulder.

Wonder filled his eyes. "Look," he whispered.

My mother's tears fell on my father and the light that filled each prism wiped out the blackened form, replacing it with human skin, until it was actually my father's beaten and scarred form lying on the ground with his head in my mother's lap. Tattered clothing covered his body, and he lifted his head, pushing himself to his hands and knees and just stared at her.

His hand rose to her cheek, but his eyes didn't believe she was actually there.

"Baby, I'm here," my mother whispered.

His forehead dropped to her knees, and he crawled closer, wrapping his arms around her waist. His form shook.

"If this is another game, just kill me," he whispered, his voice hoarse and filled with agony.

"It's not, Dad," I said, and his body stiffened like he expected more horrors. His head turned and the glare he sent in my direction turned my blood to ice. The scene I witnessed in New York crawled back into my mind, and I understood exactly what Lucifer had done to him. He'd fucked with my father's mind just as completely as he had done to Valerie.

"Dad?" Tom stepped closer, blocking his glare, and he blinked, his eyes refocusing on Tom as my brother crouched lower just outside the salt ring.

My father's gaze moved between my brother and my mother, trying to reconcile what his eyes were seeing against the hell he endured for the last two years. I had heard Lucifer. I had heard the lies he told my father. That we never existed. That we were as much a figment of his imagination as marrying my mother had been. Lucifer promised him he died in that hellhole, that there had been no miracle.

When his gaze landed on me, his jaw clenched and the pain in his eyes shot through me. I took a step closer, and he flinched, his grip on my mother tightening.

My father never flinched. Ever. And seeing it was like a punch in the gut. The profound effect made me step forward. I had to break whatever Lucifer had done. I had to let him know he wasn't insane, that we weren't figments of his imagination.

I crossed the salt line between Tom, and my mother, and my father shot to his feet. His hand flashed out, grabbing my throat as the fury overrode every sense he had. I didn't stop him.

"I wasn't going to leave you there for...ever," I squeaked out as both my mother and brother tried to break his grasp on my throat.

Tears made my vision wobble, and I blinked. Heat squeezed out of the corners of my eyes and rolled down my cheeks. My father snarled fowl curses, promises to make me pay for what I had done to Jessica.

"Ty!" my mother yelled, pulling his gaze from my face to hers. "Let go of our son!"

The order she issued didn't compute at first and his incessant blinking announced his confusion. His grip loosened but remained clasped on my throat and my chin trembled.

"Dad," I whispered, trying to pull air into my starved lungs.

His gaze dropped to my chest and the ruined jacket before popping back to mine. After a moment, he looked around at where he was and his hand dropped from the grip on my throat to press against my chest like he was testing the boundaries of his sanity.

He glanced at my mother again. "Is..." He stopped and licked his lips with another scan of his surroundings. "Is this real?"

"Yes. Our boy decided a rescue mission was in order," she said and glanced at me. "Despite the waves it caused upstairs."

He stepped back and stared at the ground. Each time he began to speak, he rethought his statements and closed his mouth. Finally, he said, "Paradise Cove?" and looked up at me.

I gave a weak laugh and nodded.

He was slow to respond, but his gaze traveled upward and all around at each one of us before landing on Damian. "I... I think I remember..."

I knew that feeling and when his gaze landed back on me, he bit his lip and covered his mouth. "He really fucked with me," he whispered, and tears shined in his eyes.

"Yeah. Just like he screwed with Valerie," I said, and he blinked as that memory came back to him.

His gaze moved from me to Tom and then to my mother and in the next instance, his arms squeezed all of us together in a tight hug.

"He told me I died in the complex. That everything else was my mind's last-ditch fantasy to deal with Jessie's death. He made me watch her die before the chains tore me to pieces. It never stopped... and it never changed."

His body shook and his sobs layered over us like a blanket of rain. We all held onto him just as tightly as he gripped us. When his shakes subsided, we all let go, and he wiped his face before bringing his gaze to mine.

"I'm not sure what memories are real," he sniffled, and his hands gripped my cheeks as he targeted in on our original plan to send Lucifer back to hell. He searched my eyes and then tears formed in his and he pulled me into a tight hug. "But I hope to God this means what we did worked."

"It did," I whispered.

"How long..." he started before he trailed off.

"Two years," I said and shuddered at the thought. "Lucifer turned you into a hellhound," I whispered, and he pulled away. His gaze dropped to the ground as he searched for the memory, but it didn't surface and he shook his head, trying to clear fact from fiction.

"I got married a couple of months ago," I added and lifted my hand so he could see the wedding band.

He stared at the band surrounding my left ring finger and his brow creased before he glanced at my mother.

"Yes. That's the wedding band I gave you. Valerie is wearing mine," she confirmed with a smile.

His brows arched and his head snapped back in my direction. "You and Valerie?"

I nodded. "It took a while to undo what Lucifer did to her, but yeah, we toughed it out."

He smiled for the first time since the haze cleared from his mind. "Congratulations," he said, and my mother extended her hand to him.

"Come on, babe. We have a lot of catching up to do, and we can't stay here," she said. He took her palm in his and followed as she led him toward the brightly lit water. He stopped at the edge and turned, meeting Tom's stare.

"I'm proud of you," he said directly to my brother, and then his gaze moved to mine. "Both of you." With that, he and my mother faded, becoming one with the mist and I slowly lowered to the ground, wrapping my arms around my knees as the sobs took hold.

Tom's hand squeezed my shoulder and then both he and Damian left me alone in the confines of the cove.

I don't know how long I sat on the frozen moss, crying, but it wasn't until a hand threaded through my hair that I looked up. I expected Valerie, so the grand expanse of white wings before me shocked me into silence. He slowly crouched so our eyes were level.

"I will make sure Heaven takes good care of your father," he said. "Especially given his willingness to sacrifice himself for my children."

"Raphael?" I asked and wiped my face on my sleeve.

He smiled softly and extended his hand. "Yes. The last of the true archangels," he said, and his wings ruffled before they folded neatly on his back. I took his hand and Raphael pulled me to my feet. His dark eyes reminded me of Naomi's and there was something nurturing about him I didn't get from any of the others.

"I am the healer," he said to my train of thought. "Not a warrior unless I am pushed into a corner." He smiled, and calm settled over me. "I'm a bit more like my brother Gabriel than I am Michael." He winked, and my lips twitched into a smile of my own.

"So... not all archangels are dicks?" I asked, and his laughter floated over the cove, warming my soul.

"My heaven's, no," he said as the laughter wound down. "Some of us have softer hearts than others."

"Can you heal my father's wounds?" I asked, thinking of the scars visible under his tattered clothing.

"I can fix the scars on his skin, but your mother is the only one who can fix his fractured soul." He offered a smile and pulled me to his chest, wrapping his arms and wings around me. His warmth saturated my skin, taking the shake from my cold limbs. "As for you, I can ease your mind and prepare you for your next battle with Lucifer."

He pressed his lips to my forehead and light encompassed me, showing me a litany of visions that brought tears to my eyes and hope to my heart. I glanced into his eyes and his hand covered my heart, pushing in a ball of light. His pristine wings shriveled as his grace filled my form.

He stepped away and gave me a nod, fading the same way my parents had. I turned toward the path and stopped at Valerie's awed stare. I leaned down and picked up one of the fallen feathers, holding it in my hand as I glanced up at the sky.

When I turned my attention back to Valerie, my gaze lowered to her belly, to the tiny miracle that still existed, based on Raphael's vision. I grinned and closed the distance, wrapping my arms around her and delivering a kiss that consumed both of us.

Angel Wrath Chapter 28

THE KIDS RAN DOWN the beach, enjoying an early summer heat wave. Their little legs pumped, and their laughter floated on the breeze. Damian ran after them, pretending to be a big, bad sand monster, catching each one in his arms and rolling onto his back on the sand. Gracie jumped on his chest and her little fingers found the ticklish spots on his neck as Gabe and Michael yelled for help.

I smiled as I watched Damian. His kids were entertaining, to say the least, and I traded a glance with Valerie. The visions Raphael shared with me intertwined our families for the foreseeable future.

Valerie smiled at me like she knew what I was thinking. She ran her hand down my arm and we laced our fingers. I returned her grin before my gaze dropped to her oversized belly. An unearthly calm settled over me and I leaned forward, planting a kiss on the swollen skin under her beach dress.

"How you feeling?" I asked.

"Good, considering I'm overdue," she said. "I swear this boy just doesn't want to come out."

Tom and Raven chuckled, turning toward the squealing laugh of their three-year-old daughter. Hannah approached, her tiny hands grasping one of Steve's and one of Jennifer's. She planted her feet and then jumped, letting Steve and Jennifer swing her forward. Her giggle tickled all of us and we exchanged glances before returning our gaze to the wild redhead. She broke free and ran to Damian's three kids, sliding to a stop and dropping into the sand next to them.

Steve and Jennifer approached, taking the vacant seats nearest the kids.

"She's a handful," Steve said, lounging back in the chair.

Tom returned his smile, nodding and signing a simple, "Yes."

"Have you settled on a name yet?" Naomi asked, her eyes locked on her children building a sandcastle a few feet away.

"Ty," Valerie said, pulling everyone's gazes to her. "Ty Alexander Ryan."

Damian smiled, scanning the horizon, wondering if my father was finally at peace in heaven.

Grace stood and crossed the distance, trading a glance with me before she focused on her father.

"He is, Daddy," she said, patting his hand, leaving tiny traces of sand with each pat.

A CHILL DRIFTED OVER ALL of us. I knew her minor revelation sent a chill through Damian, and I raised my beer in response. Grace seemed to have a line straight to heaven, one that even I didn't have, and I smiled.

She was going to be a handful when she grew up. My gaze traveled to Valerie's stomach, and I sent a silent good luck wish to my son.

After all, Grace would be his handful someday.

The End

Continue The Ryan Chronicles with Tom's story on the next page.

Angel Blood Chapter 1

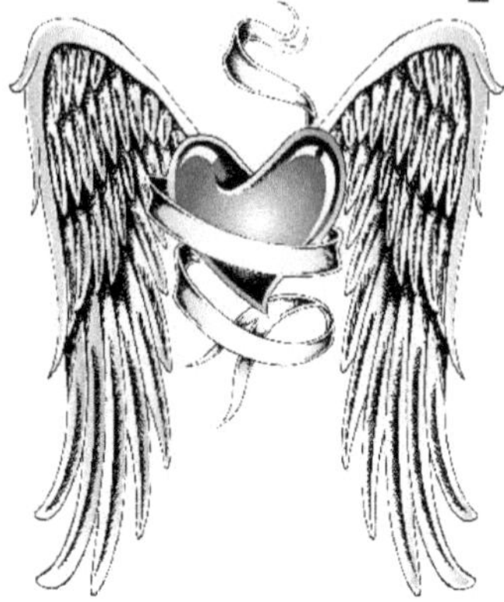

THE TELEPHONE INTERRUPTED US, and I gazed into Raven's eyes, stilling my hips. The way her hair fanned out around her made her look like she had an ornate halo made of red fire, and it fueled my slow burn. The chances we had to screw around were not as abundant as they had been when we were first married. Since Hannah was born, it was catching a quickie whenever we could, and tonight our daughter had gone to bed early after a fun day at the beach. You can bet your ass we took full advantage of the time.

Until now.

"Don't answer it," she whispered, and her legs wrapped tighter around mine, her hips circled, and that partial smile and sparkle in her eyes nearly made me reconsider.

"I have to," I said. Of course the words coming out of my mouth were garbled, despite the clarity of them in my mind. Raven understood and her sigh conveyed her disdain.

"Ya," I mumbled into the receiver.

"There's water everywhere. What do I do?" The panicked voice of my brother filled the line.

"Huh?" I pushed onto my knees, still coupled with Raven, and I put the phone on speaker.

"Water. She's like a fucking geyser," CJ said, and I locked my gaze with Raven, pressing my lips against the smile.

"Get her to the hospital, you ass," Raven said. "She's in labor."

I grinned down at her and circled my hips. My wife's Irish lilt turned me on something fierce, and even though I knew she wanted to jump out of bed and run to the hospital for our nephew's birth, I wasn't in any rush.

"Oh. Shit." CJ said with a laugh. "Okay, my brain isn't quite working right now."

"Go. We'll meet you there," Raven said, and the dial tone filled the room.

"Not 'til we finish this," I signed, and my hips started that slow grind she usually loved. However, her features turned to annoyance.

"Your brother is an idiot," she said. "Valerie needs someone who knows what they are doing."

I shook my head. "We have time," I said, and tapped my wrist so the gist of what I was trying to say would be transmitted.

Raven rolled her eyes and then her hips. "Fine, but hurry up," she whispered.

I stilled my hips and sent her a head tilt, wrinkling my brow. I wanted this to last. Besides, no one was there to hold our hands when Hannah was born. CJ was in a coma and everyone else was so preoccupied with life that we were on our own. If I got through the birth of my daughter, CJ would get through this, whether or not we were there.

"Tom," she started.

I didn't need the words. I already had a line into her thoughts ever since CJ supercharged me. My wife was torn between wanting to enjoy this and wanting to go to the hospital, which meant any chance of her enjoying this was out the window.

"Fine," I said with a sigh, and pulled out, accepting the burn of frustration that filled me as the price I had to pay for loving a woman whose heart was big enough to cover this half of the hemisphere.

I knew she loved me, but Valerie was her best friend, and she thought my brother was inept in almost every way. The truth of the matter was CJ Ryan was a Mensa-level genius with the power to destroy the universe.

"You know I love you." She grabbed my arm as I climbed off the bed.

I nodded, opting for the more simple head bob than trying to speak without a tongue or with my hands, which were now occupied with pulling on clothing.

"I promise, I'll make it up to you," she said as she shuffled through the pile of garments on the chair for something suitable to wear.

Yeah, I'd heard that before, and sent her an elevated eyebrow even as my eyes took in her incredible curves. I let my gaze linger, and the hunger I always seemed to have for her stirred.

Raven stopped with the shirt half on and blew me a kiss before she busied herself with clothing the rest of her naked form. My options were easy. Shorts, a t-shirt, and my beach sandals, considering the early heat wave.

My gaze jumped from the time blinking a few minutes before midnight to the calendar. I zeroed in on tomorrow's date. July seventh.

A chill saturated my body.

My father's birthday was July seventh, and it looked like his namesake would share that same date.

"Are you okay?" Raven's question pulled my gaze from the calendar, and I met her blue-eyed stare.

Shrugging, I pointed to the object of the goose flesh now peppering my skin.

She looked between the calendar and me. "Yeah?"

"Tomorrow is my father's birthday," I signed.

Her gaze drifted back to the calendar, her skin rippling the same way mine had. "Well, let's hope our nephew's future differs vastly from your father's," she said, pulling a laugh and a nod from me.

Ty Alexander Ryan had raised me as his own, even though I was sired by another man and shared the womb with his natural son. He had given me everything a kid could ever ask for while he was alive, from love to self-confidence, and everything in between. We lived a blessed life for many years, and then Steve Williams stepped into the picture.

My father's death rocked both CJ and me, and everything since then had been hard. At first, I blamed Steve. If he hadn't come into our lives, my father and mother would still be alive. At least, that's what I tried to convince myself for years, and I rebelled in every fashion; pushing Steve to the edge more than once while he did his best to become our default dad.

I'm not sure I would have been able to move past the blame had I not had the benefit of seeing my father on a daily basis in angel form. He stood watch over Steve for years, and while CJ could hear him talking to Steve, I could see him. His pride in us, and his disappointment when I fucked up, was as visible as Steve's was.

I shook away the wave of memories that cropped to the surface; burying them in the overwhelming flurry of Raven's thoughts already accosting my mind, and stepped into the bathroom to run a brush through my hair. My light blue eyes peered back at me, and I tried to get my black hair to look decent and not like we had been fucking around. After a few swipes of the brush I gave up and relinquished the spot to Raven. Her rush out of the house included a retouch of her makeup, and I went to collect our sleeping three-year-old.

Angel Blood Chapter 2

THEY LET RAVEN INTO the room for the birth, while I sat out in the waiting area, entertaining Hannah with *Rumble in the Jungle* on our iPad. I knew we'd pay for this interruption in her sleep schedule at some inopportune moment tomorrow, but for now, she was content.

It didn't take Hannah long to yawn, and she curled up in my lap with her thumb stuck in her mouth and her blanket wrapped around her. She finally faded into sleep around two and I set her down on one of the couches.

I sent out a couple of text messages. I knew neither Steve nor Damian would pick it up before dawn, but on the off-chance CJ hadn't notified them, at least they'd wake to some happy news. Before I could slip the phone back in my pocket, it buzzed, and I glanced down at the new text from Steve.

On our way. I sighed and glanced at Hannah, feeling that old twinge of jealousy again. I gritted my teeth, inhaled deeply, then slowly exhaled to let go of the burn. No one had immediately come when we were in the same situation. My phone buzzed again, and I glanced at the second text from Steve. *We need to talk.*

Surprise raked its nails across my chest, and my eyebrows rose.

I had just typed out the word *why* when the door to the waiting room opened. I glanced up and forgot about pressing the send button.

"Steve said I might find you here," Captain O'Keefe from the York Police Department stepped into the room looking like he hadn't slept in days. His dark eyes, as tired as they looked, sharpened as they met mine.

I stiffened. Usually, when Captain O'Keefe came looking for me, I was in a shitload of trouble. Especially in the middle of the night. However, the look in his eyes wasn't the usual confrontational scowl I was used to, and I didn't need to do a mind scan this time to get that he wasn't here to haul me in.

"What can I do for you?" I signed.

He stared at my hands and his cheeks turned red. "I still can't follow sign language."

I swiped the iPad off the table and typed my question along with a plea for him to keep his voice low, so we didn't wake Hannah. When I turned the tablet in his direction, he glanced beyond me at the couch with a small smile and a nod. Instead of talking out loud, he took the tablet from me and started typing.

I focused on him, draining the answers right out of his mind, so when he handed me the iPad, I only had to scan the text confirming what he wanted. I glanced over at him.

"You want my help?" I said. Of course, what verbally came out was a complete bastardization of the question, but Captain O'Keefe got it.

"Steve said this is the type of thing your company investigates." He handed me the file he carried.

I inhaled and glanced at him before flipping the folder open. The picture on the top of the pile chilled me to the bone, and I wished I had a blanket like Hannah, if only to hide the rash of gooseflesh now standing out on my arms and legs.

The girl in the photo was splayed out and pale to the point of being almost ashen. Even the color in her eyes had faded. I shuffled to the next picture and sat straight up. Two distinct puncture wounds, far enough apart to suggest teeth, speckled her carotid artery.

Shuffling through the dozen photos brought the same results, and I turned them over, placing them face down on the chair next to me before I leaned forward and read each of the reports. The fundamental similarity in all the cases was the bodies had been drained of blood. I closed the folder, placing it on the pile of photos before I glanced at Captain O'Keefe.

"What's your conclusion?" I tapped out on my iPad and took a moment to pull up some of Damian's memories. The bite signature was all wrong for the crazed vampires he encountered, and my limited exposure matched his, but that didn't mean it wasn't something supernatural.

Captain O'Keefe licked his lips and let out a soft laugh. "I don't know what to think," he said, and I raised an eyebrow, challenging him because his thoughts danced around the vampire lore like a moth to a forest fire. "At least nothing logical," he added, and busied himself with putting the photos back in the folder.

"What exactly do you want from us?" I asked. I also projected the words into his head, and his eyes snapped up to mine in confusion.

"I'm not sure. Steve said you investigated… paranormal activity?" His voice carried the disdain I could feel radiating from him.

I nodded. "But you don't believe in that shit," I said, again transmitting so the words would be clear over my tongue-less banter.

Again, he blinked, paling a fraction, and my lips twitched against the smirk that wanted to appear. His gaze dropped to the folder. "I don't know what to believe."

I typed out three words on my iPad and handed it to him.

Monsters are real.

He stared at the text and slowly handed the iPad back.

The Windwalker, The Slasher. The butcher in Georgia. All monsters, and all very real.

I handed him the newly typed text.

"But with all those killers, there was some sort of evidence. In these cases, there is nothing. Zero. Just bodies drained completely of blood." He strained to keep his voice from rising above a whisper, but the exasperation rang clear.

"And you think it's a vampire?" Of course, my words were more or less grunt-like without my tongue. I didn't send the thought, either.

Captain O'Keefe's brow creased. He didn't have a clue of what I said.

Instead of typing what I tried to say, I stared at him and projected my next thought loud enough to draw a wince.

"Stop beating around the bush. What exactly do you think is killing people?"

Captain O'Keefe's eyes widened before he started blinking furiously and glancing around for the source of the words in his mind.

"It's me, you dumb shit." I crossed my arms and leaned back in the chair as he paled. For a fleeting moment, I enjoyed the shock skittering over his features like an army of ants, and then I second-guessed my wisdom as he retreated into the back of his seat like I was a deadly disease.

"Look," I started, forming words with both my mouth and my mind. "I recently acquired the ability to project my thoughts. I know it's a little freaky, but it certainly helps with what I lack in diction, don't you think?" I offered a half-hearted tilt of my lips.

"I just... I just have never..." His brain was short-circuiting with this new twist and his gaze dropped to the file in his hands while he processed. He had heard a few stories about my ability to see ghosts, but he discounted those as drug-induced hallucinations or overly active imaginations. But now, with this manifestation, he started looking at all the other tall tales. His gaze slowly rose to mine.

"Is this why you opened a paranormal investigation business?"

I gave him a shrug. "Some of those stories aren't too far from the truth." I allowed, and his eyebrows arched. "I can see ghosts."

"Like the kid in *The Sixth Sense*?" he asked, his eyes as wide as Hannah's when we tell her she can pick out whatever she wants at the Goldenrod's candy counter.

I chuckled and glanced at Hannah before returning his questioning stare. "I guess, and yeah, it makes me a little bit more qualified to hunt ghosts."

"What about this?" He raised the folder. "Do you investigate things like this?"

My smile faded. "I'm not a cop, or a forensic specialist, for that matter."

"But do you look into shit like this?" he hissed, his frustration at my lack of an answer finally bubbling up.

"Captain, how many unsolved cases are there in York?"

He stared at me. There was only one I knew of. Sarah, Steve's ex-partner, had disappeared from an active crime scene at CJ's house. That one would never be solved, because Sarah had been kidnapped by Lucifer as a bargaining chip. Unfortunately, it hadn't worked out all that well for her and there was nothing left for the law to find.

"Only one," he said, and he held up the file. "But this is happening in the Portland area. Not York. They seem to think we have an inside track on catching madmen after the Windwalker case and wanted our help before they got the FBI involved." He sighed and ran his hand over his face. "So, I called your father."

"And Steve sent you to me."

Captain O'Keefe nodded.

"You remember what happened the last time I tried to intervene in an active case?" I couldn't help but ask. After all, he was the one who was positive I was the Windwalker, and he was the one who was ready to throw away the key after they arrested me. He nearly had me tried and on death row before I was even read my rights. Granted, I had been a frequent visitor to the York Police department's juvenile holding tank, but that time, he put me in with the adults and I nearly became someone's bitch.

His eyes dropped to the ground. "Yes."

"So, what exactly do you want us to do?"

He bit his lip and the flurry of thought in his mind nearly drowned out the soft, "I don't know." When he slid his gaze to mine, I got it. He couldn't wrap his mind around the existence of vampires; of a creature so cunning, that kills so completely, and leaves no trace. Captain O'Keefe was afraid of the unknown, and after all the crazy shit I've seen in the last few years, I'd say he had a damned good reason to be scared.

"What if I told you I wasn't sure what did that?" I jutted my chin towards the file. "I'm not ready to rule out a human killer. After all, the Windwalker had stumped you all on a couple of his crime scenes."

His eyelids fluttered as his mind wrapped fully around the conversations. "So, there are things out there..." He trailed off.

"You don't want to know the answer to that." I didn't give him any leeway, but his lips pressed together at my tone, even as his brain shrouded with doubt.

"I need to know."

"Trust me, you really don't. I know enough to freak you out for a fucking lifetime, and I'm not inclined to share." I pointed to the file. "We'll help you with that, but if it turns out to be something we specialize in..." I let my eyebrows rise with the lilt in my voice, trailing off in more of a question than a statement.

Captain O'Keefe didn't take the bait to complete the sentence. He just stared at me, waiting for me to finish.

"If it turns out to be our specialty, you have to let us take care of it."

"Oh, no," he started, and I put my hand up, stopping him.

"If it turns out to be your specialty, we can back you up if you need us, but if it's in our realm, you are ill suited to be anywhere near us when we take whatever it is down."

"I can't just let you put a stake through their heart," he stammered, and I burst out laughing.

"That's not how you kill a vampire," I said, thinking about the toxins in my blood. If he ever witnessed what my blood did to those parasites, he would probably check himself into the loony bin. "A platinum bullet to the brain will do it."

His incessant blink pulled a smirk to my lips.

"Sunshine will toast their ass, too."

His tense features smoothed over as the more familiar lore settled a little comfort in his bones.

"Will they... become vampires?" He held up the file.

"No."

"If I got bit..."

"You'd probably die. Vampire venom is poisonous."

"I can't believe I'm having this conversation," he muttered under his breath.

"I've known about ghosts all my life, but this shit, this fucked me up something fierce." I couldn't help the grin, or the heat in my cheeks at the admission.

He dropped the file onto the table and rubbed his face. "I must be exhausted to even entertain this crap," he said and sent a tired smile my way. "So... you're going to be an uncle?"

The change of subject brought a natural smile to my face. "Yes." I accompanied the word with the hand signal out of habit. It was one of the few sign language motions that O'Keefe knew.

He sat silent for a few minutes, his gaze drifting to my daughter. "Are you going to have more?"

Raven and I had talked about it, but so far nothing had happened in the baby-making department. However, this wasn't a subject I wanted to discuss on the heels of murder and vampires. I just gave a non-committal shrug and left it at that.

He stood to leave. "Why don't you stop in at the station when you have some time," he said and headed for the door. He paused and glanced back at me. "How does one get platinum bullets?"

The grin that surfaced held some of my good humor. "You need to make them."

"Oh." He seemed genuinely disappointed, like I should have been able to supply him with a '1-800-bullets' manufacturer. "Well, I'll see you later."

I waved, and the door closed behind him. My smile faded at the thought of another killer within a hundred miles of this place. Especially if it was of the supernatural persuasion.

Angel Blood Chapter 3

WEIGHT SHIFTED ON MY lap, pulling me out of sleep. My eyes snapped open to the unfamiliar surroundings as Hannah snuggled into me. I glanced at the clock on the wall and sat up a little straighter. It was quarter after seven and I wasn't alone in the waiting room. Steve and Jennifer sat opposite me; Steve's dark hair looked almost as disheveled as mine did last night, and his reading glasses magnified the dark circles under his eyes. For the life of me, I couldn't understand how anything he was reading could stick. Jennifer's chestnut hair fell over his shoulder as she leaned on him, her eyes at half-mast and the paperback in her hand long forgotten.

"No word?" My voice cracked as I spoke and startled both of them. I didn't bother sending the thought. Jennifer and Steve knew me well enough to understand my words, even though to most people it was just a jumble of sounds that made little sense.

Steve glanced over the top of the newspaper and shook his head.

I shifted Hannah back to the couch and slipped into the restroom attached to the waiting area. One look in the mirror told me enough about how little sleep I'd actually gotten, and I couldn't imagine Raven got any more than I did. A splash of cold water seemed to snap my senses back in order, and I dried my face before stepping back into the waiting room.

It was almost as if we had timed it. The moment I opened the door from the restroom, CJ opened the door to the waiting room with the biggest grin I've seen in years. His gaze met mine, and I smiled back. I remember that instant rush of excitement and awe the moment I became a father, and I crossed, getting to him before Steve, and giving him a hug accompanied by the usual back slap.

"Congratulations!" I broadcast, sharing his enthusiasm, and then relinquished my spot to Steve and Jennifer.

"So?" I asked after hugs were given all around.

"A healthy boy at seven pounds, seven ounces and seventeen inches long." He smiled and met my gaze.

A chill encased my spine, but I kept my smile intact.

"Born at seven-o-seven this morning."

"Kind of freaky," I mumbled, and his grin got wider and was accompanied by a mischievous sparkle in his eyes that reminded me of the mid-summer sun-drenched Atlantic.

"Yeah. Looks like sevens all around. And it was like he waited until that exact time to be born. Want to come see your nephew?" he asked, bypassing everyone else and meeting my gaze.

I turned to Jennifer.

"I'll watch Hannah, go," she said before I could ask if she would watch my daughter.

I stepped out into the hall with my brother and gave him a pat on the back. "How's Valerie?" I asked.

"Tired, but she is happier than I've ever seen her." He pushed the door open, allowing me to step inside first.

Valerie had the same radiance that Raven had after Hannah was born. Her dark hair was wet with sweat and wisps still clung to her face. Her tired eyes held the smile reflected on her lips, and I couldn't help but smile back. I still do not know how mothers can look so exhausted and radiant at the same time. I glanced down at the newest addition to our family before trading a glance with Raven, and she sent me a happy grin.

CJ stepped closer to the bed.

"Meet your nephew, Alex," he said and took the baby from Valerie.

"Alex?" I asked, meeting his gaze.

"Ty Alexander Ryan." He handed the baby to me. "We decided to call him Alex instead of Ty."

I stared down into the bright blue eyes that were a carbon copy of my father's, and I understood the aversion to calling him Ty. They wanted to give him a fighting chance and not saddle him with the stigma that came with his grandfather's name.

"Alex, meet your Uncle Tom," CJ added, stepping close and looking down into the baby's eyes.

There wasn't a thing I wouldn't do for my daughter, and that same fierce parental instinct wound its way around my heart when the child's gaze met mine. I smiled and said one of the few words I could articulate clearly. "Hi."

CJ cleared his throat, and I glanced up at him.

"We'd like you and Raven to be his godparents."

My eyebrows rose. I wasn't in any way a devout Christian, and Raven certainly wasn't, either, so why he was choosing us was beyond me. My shock must have shown because he chuckled.

"Maybe guardian is a better word?"

My brow smoothed out, and I smirked and nodded, bringing my gaze back to his son. "He's got your eyes," I said, conveying the words with my thoughts.

"Yeah," CJ said, and I turned my attention to Valerie.

"How are you doing?" I signed with one hand.

"I'm doing pretty good," she said, but it was promptly followed by a yawn, and I met Raven's gaze. She nodded toward the door.

"We should let Steve and Jen see the baby," she said, as if the head nod wasn't enough.

I relinquished the child to my brother before leaning over and planting a kiss on Valerie's cheek. "Congratulations," I said, and she smiled, hearing the thought I projected as easily as my brother. As I turned, I caught sight of the thin line of salt cutting the room in half and I brought my gaze to CJ's.

"Just covering the bases," he said softly.

My smile faded, and I nodded, making a note not to disturb the solid line when I left the room. That was another fact of our lives that I wish had remained in the darkness. We both had angel blood running through our veins and little Alex was the first of his kind, carrying the bloodlines of four archangels.

CJ's caution against a demon attack was warranted. I shivered, thinking of what Lucifer would do to that child if he ever got his greedy hands on him.

The door swung open and my partner's daughter, Grace, came running into the room, her eyes wide and her cheeks pink from breaking away from the rest of her family. She was not the typical five-year-old, by any means, and the fact she burst into the room like the place was on fire was both amusing and a little concerning. She was halfway across the room when a nurse stepped in the door.

"I'm sorry, but children are not allowed…"

Grace turned and put her hand up like a stop sign, her brow creased in irritation, but it had the desired effect. Silence overtook everyone at the child's audacity.

Damian Andreas slid next to the nurse standing in the doorway. He was as equally out of breath as his daughter, and his dark Greek features formed a mask of aggravation.

Grace turned back toward CJ, and her eyes landed on the baby in his arms. The calm that settled over the room was eerie, and I traded a glance with Raven.

The child tentatively stepped over the salt line and CJ squatted to show her his son. The silent communication between CJ and Grace had been strong since the day she was born, and today was no different. But the awe in Grace's face transformed when her gaze met the baby's.

Alex stared at her as well, and it just wasn't a normal baby stare. It reminded me of the times when Grace was his age and would look at us with such wisdom; it gave me the shivers. It was as if the child knew the secrets of the cosmos.

Grace reached for his cheek, hesitating before she touched him. Her eyes drifted to CJ's, and they were painted with such fervent adoration, I had to smile.

"Grace," Damian said as he stepped into the room, but she ignored her father.

When her fingers brushed the baby's cheek, the light I remembered Damian being bathed in the night my father died encompassed the three true trinities. Alex stared at Grace and the unyielding bond between the children formed, wrapping light strings around the two as their auras intertwined.

"Blessed be," Raven whispered, and I glanced at her. Her squinting stare told me she was seeing the same interwoven aura I was seeing.

When I glanced back, the light had already started to fade and CJ's glance met mine. He offered me a one-shouldered shrug, like he'd expected some sort of a cataclysmic event like this.

"Grace," Damian's voice rang out again, but this time, it broke the spell completely.

"What, Daddy?" Grace asked and turned, flipping her dark hair in what I could only surmise was what defiance looked like in a five-year-old.

"Only family is allowed in here," he said, reiterating what the nurse had tried to say.

Everyone's gaze drifted toward the wide-eyed nurse standing next to Damian.

"We are family," Grace said.

"Only immediate family," the nurse said, now that she regained some of her composure.

"On that note," I signed and put my hand out for Grace. She accepted my offering, but I could tell it was only because I wasn't her father, and that was further reinforced with the glare she sent in his direction, like he had initially said she couldn't go in the room.

I glanced at CJ over my shoulder before I passed through the door. He gave me his signature wave and grinned in a way I didn't quite understand, but unfortunately, I knew that look all too well. My brother had a secret. One I didn't really want to know.

Grace gave my hand a squeeze and then begrudgingly took Damian's hand, despite knowing the lecture from her dad was about to be delivered with the full force of an angry parent.

"We need to talk," I said to Damian. "Swing over when you're done here, okay?"

"Sure." he said, but both his tone and his lips were tight and the moment his gaze landed on his little girl, the tirade started.

We didn't stick around for the berating. Instead, we headed toward the waiting room to take Hannah home and give Steve and Jennifer a chance to see the new baby.

"Do you have an extra bloodstone?" I asked Raven before we entered the waiting room.

"Aye, it's woven into the small ankle bracelet I already put on the baby." She met my gaze, and I smiled, placing a kiss on her forehead as I reached for the door.

Hannah was happily playing with Damian's boys. Gabriel and Michael looked up from the coloring books and waved.

"How's Valerie?" Damian's wife, Naomi asked.

"Tired," Raven said. "It was a long night, and that boy just didn't want to come out." She covered a yawn and put her hand out for Hannah.

Hannah ignored her.

"Come on, sweetie, it's time to go," Raven said.

Jennifer stepped out of the bathroom, and I smiled in her direction.

"Your turn," I signed, and both Steve and Jennifer took off like a bolt, both of them beaming the way only grandparents can.

I focused on my daughter and crouched down next to her, hooking her chin so she had to look at me. "Time to go," I signed. She pressed her lips together and shook her head, her fiery red hair bouncing with the shake.

"Ya," I said. Lack of sleep always made her ornery, and neither of us had the tolerance this morning for a scene. I stepped away and collected our stuff, handing it all to Raven before I scooped up Hannah in my arms.

You would have thought I was murdering her with the way she was pitching a fit. I sent a shrug and uncomfortable smile in Damian's direction and carried her out into the hallway, where her shrieks echoed through the maternity ward.

By the time we got to the car, I had a scratch mark on my cheek, and I was holding my daughter in more of a bear hug than cradling her. Raven opened the back door and dumped our stuff on the floor, relinquishing the space for me to put the child in her car seat.

It's nearly impossible to bend a three-year-old who has decided she does not want to be strapped in, and finally, I let out a frustrated growl.

"Sit," I transmitted, and Hannah's eyes widened as her body behaved. The moment I had her strapped in, I closed the back door and slid into the driver's seat, more tired from the last few minutes than I was from the lack of sleep all night.

"Did you just?" Raven asked, waving her finger towards the back seat.

I rarely exercised my power over other people, but when my daughter became a devil child, I had no qualms about forcing my will upon her.

"You know that's not fair," Raven said under her breath.

"Life's not fair," I transmitted with a glare. "I can not reason with her while I'm trying to strap her into her car seat."

"I know, but there has to be a better way," she said and then chewed on her lip, signaling she had more to say, but left it alone.

I could have forced the finished thoughts from her, but I was too damned tired, and I had a case file to study. She reached for my hand, and I threaded my fingers through hers, accepting the squeeze as her way of telling me she loved me, anyway.

I pulled out, heading for home, and a nice soft mattress to catch some z's.

Angel Blood Chapter 4

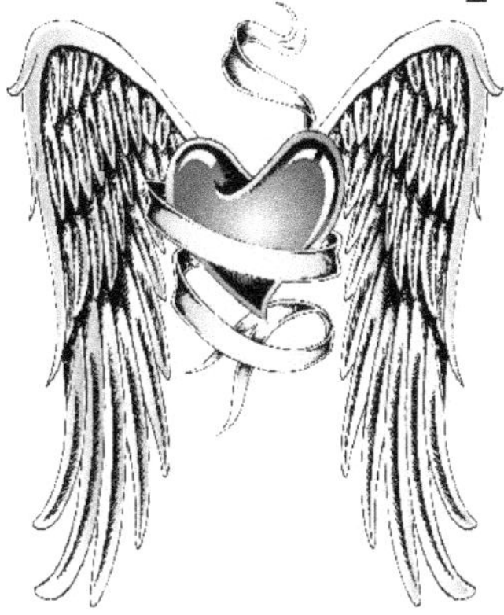

WE WALKED INTO OUR house at a little after nine; I tucked Raven and Hannah into our bed and went into the living room. Despite how tired I was, I booted up my laptop and propped it on my lap as I stretched out on the couch.

The first thing I did was pull everything I could from the media accounts relating to the murders. There wasn't as much as I would have thought, so the Portland police were really keeping the particulars under wraps. I closed the laptop and placed it on the coffee table.

My thoughts drifted to the news accounts of the Windwalker case. It wasn't until the third death that the details leaked, but in the current case, even with the speed of information, they'd kept a cap on the information.

I rubbed my face and my eyelids dropped closed. I thought, *just a few minutes.*

Shuffling papers snapped my eyes open, and I glanced at the table and the chair beyond. Damian sat sifting through the file. He glanced up at me after a few minutes, aware that I was now awake.

"I gather this is what you wanted to discuss?"

"Ya," I said and sat up, rubbing the sleep from my eyes.

"It's not a vampire." He dropped the file on the table, and I raised my eyebrows in his direction, questioning his statement.

"I know," I signed. "I'm not convinced it's anything supernatural, but I said we'd look into it."

Damian bit his lip, glancing at the photos. "Whoever, or whatever it is, is certainly trying to make it look like the old vampire lore. But as you know, vampire attacks actually look like animal attacks when the body is found, so…" He trailed off as he looked at the names of the deceased. The cock of his head pulled my attention, and when his gaze rose, I couldn't help but shiver. "I recognize one of the names," he said, and then studied the rest.

"Well?" I asked, unable to pull any information from his mind.

"It's one of Michael's descendants."

"Coincidence?" I asked, because I couldn't fathom any other rationale.

He shrugged his shoulder. "I don't recognize the rest. But then again, I was never privy to the other angel blood lines." His gaze met mine. "We might want to have CJ take a look."

"Why?" I asked, trying to hide the sudden bloom of irritation. Any time Damian asked to bring CJ into the fold, irritation raked across my back like I wasn't good enough despite the years of pulling my weight with no supernatural advantages. Now that I was infused with some of CJ's mojo, I was just as dangerous as Damian.

"Chill, I'm not trying to bring him into the business," Damian said, putting his hands up to stop my silent rant. "When he was in heaven, he saw our ancestral bloodlines mapped from the beginning. He might recognize the names if there are any other descendants here."

I rubbed my eyes and nodded. I didn't realize just how exhausted I was, but I had to be running on empty to let that ugly sibling rivalry gene come to the surface. As if my body agreed, I yawned.

"Sorry. I'm just tired," I mumbled, projecting the thought.

"You know your brother would be an asset," he started, and I glared up at him.

I wasn't stupid. What CJ brought to the table was beyond either of our arsenal, but the fact I have something of my own, apart from my fraternal twin, brought me a sense of pride. Even if I called him in, I would be the one calling the shots. That seemed different from following in his shadow, as I had done all my life.

Damian's brow creased, and he cocked his head to the side, studying me. "You don't like your brother, do you?"

I laughed at his unwelcomed assessment. "I love my brother."

"Then why don't you want him on our team?"

We'd had this argument a few times since my brother came back from the dead, but I held my ground without much of an explanation to Damian. I knew CJ would be a hell of an asset. He has been on other cases, like what happened in New York recently, but I couldn't be delegated to the bottom rung in a business I started on my own.

"CJ would want to run things," I finally signed, meeting Damian's gaze. "He isn't much of a follower."

It was Damian's turn to chuckle, and he gave me a knowing nod. "You are probably right. I don't think either of us would appreciate that."

I shared a smile, and it tuned into another yawn.

"Did you get any sleep?"

"Just whatever I had on the couch and that wasn't enough," I said.

Damian dropped his gaze to the file and chewed his bottom lip in contemplation. "Did you want to go to the station now or tomorrow after you get some sleep?"

Raven had been up all night and if Hanna woke while I was gone, my wife would probably filet my ass, especially after Hannah's hissy fit, and the morning tension my actions already caused.

"Tomorrow," I said.

"Good. I'll see if I can find any other deaths that presented similarly, in case this isn't as localized as the cops think."

My eyebrows rose. "You think there are more deaths?"

Apprehension painted his face. "I just have a bad feeling about this one."

I knew the feeling. The lack of physical evidence at the crime scenes didn't bother me as much as the method of the kill.

Angel Blood Chapter 5

A SOFT CARESS ON my cheek pulled me out of sleep and I opened my eyes to meet Raven's gaze. I glanced around at the darkened room.

"What time is it?" I asked, and as always, whenever I wake from a sound sleep, I forget my speech is limited. I forget I don't have most of my tongue. Thankfully, after over ten years together, Raven understood what I muttered.

"It's a little after eight. I thought you might like to have a little dinner and then help me tuck Hannah into bed."

"I slept all day?"

She nodded. "I had a bear of a time keeping Hannah quiet, but she was more than happy to when I said she could play beauty shop."

A smirk appeared as her gaze moved from my face to my hair and back. I reached up, running my hand over my head. The sporadic tufts of hair sticking every which way told me Hannah went to town with my longer than usual locks, and I'd be peeling little rubber bands out of my scalp for the next week. I was equally amused and astounded that I slept through it.

"Oh, the hair is just the finishing touch. You need to go look in the mirror, hon."

I got up and crossed to the half-bath off the kitchen, she followed, grabbing her phone from her pocketbook, and before I saw what kind of hellish masterpiece my daughter employed, the flash went off on her phone and Raven's thinly veiled chuckle made my lips twitch into a smile.

The minute I stepped in front of the mirror, all humor turned to mortification.

"Give me that phone," I signed and reached for it. I could just see her posting it on Facebook, or worse, sending my family the photo. I looked like a painted whore, and I would never live this down if CJ got a hold of it. The bright red lipstick matched the rose blush packed onto my cheeks, but the purple and pink eye shadow just made it all a bit over the top with the dozen or so mini ponytails.

"No way!" She laughed and dodged my attempt to grab it.

"You let her do this on purpose, didn't you?" I signed, chasing after her.

She nodded in response. "You were out cold. It's your fault for not waking," she said, with that mischievous glow dancing in her eyes.

I grinned and lunged, grabbing her around the waist. She squealed, and I rubbed my face on her cheek, smearing the makeup on her with a laugh.

"Daddy!" Hannah said from the doorway, pulling my attention away from the beginning of a moment that could have ended with us stripped down to nothing and going at it on the floor.

Still holding Raven with one arm, I glanced at my daughter and pointed at my face, raising my eyebrows.

Hannah's giggle erupted. My three-year-old could bring an entire theater to laughter with her infectious giggle. I let my wife go and ran at my little girl, swept her up in my arms, and nuzzled my face in her neck with a laughing growl, smearing the makeup on her as well.

"Well, now, I think we all need to get cleaned up," Raven said, wiping her palm along her smeared cheek.

I gave Hannah a wet kiss on the cheek and planted her on the ground.

"I can eat after we tuck her in," I signed. I wasn't hungry in the least.

Raven gave me her questioning look. I guess my perpetual lack of appetite drove her insane. She needed food regularly, even if it was just a small snack. I, on the other hand, could go all day without eating when I was at the office. However, you give me a day of surfing and I could eat us out of house and home afterwards.

I smiled and corralled Hannah toward the main bathroom to clean her up. Raven followed and after we all successfully washed the makeup off; our nightly routine took over. Finish bathing Hannah, read her a book, and then tuck her in before we retreated to either the living room or bedroom. Tonight, I changed things up by heading to the kitchen to whip up a quick meal.

Raven followed me in and sat at the table. I could see her watching me in the reflection of the windows and I glanced over my shoulder, sending a smile her way.

"I still wonder how I got so lucky," she said with a sigh, as I slid my omelet onto a plate.

Grabbing the salsa, I took a seat opposite her and signed. "I'm the lucky one," before I dug in. Just the radiance in her smile alone was enough to light my fire.

"I believe you have some making up to do," I transmitted, pointing my fork at her.

Her cheeks bloomed as red as her hair, and she smiled. "I believe you are correct," she said, and licked her lips in that way that made me want to sweep the food onto the floor and take her right there. It's funny how much she can get my libido going with one innocent, or in this case, not so innocent, motion.

I sent her a wink. "Let me at least finish my meal. I have a feeling I'm going to need it."

Her laughter rang out. "So, you're expecting a little more than a two-minute interlude?" She challenged me with a raised eyebrow.

"Hell, yeah," I signed, then popped the last bite in my mouth and put the dishes in the sink with the pan, letting it soak until the morning. I turned and leaned on the side of the counter, putting on my signature grin. It always had the same effect on Raven, and she cursed me every time I purposely delivered it.

"Damn boy, you're still as hot as you were in high school," she said in that sultry Irish tone and she stood, crossing the distance to place the gentlest of kisses on my lips.

"So are you," I whispered, transmitting just as softly. I ran my fingers through her damp hair and pressed a more insistent kiss on her lips. While I only had a stub of a tongue, she still enjoyed exploring my mouth with her tongue. Her kisses always cut me off at the knees.

Everyone else I'd dated before her made me feel like a freak, but Raven never shied away from me or my lack of being able to do certain things, like kiss properly or tongue fuck, which was the usual complaint when a girl dumped me. I learned to do a few tricks in bed that made me notorious in high school, and kept girls interested for a little longer, but it never was enough for anyone else but her.

I pulled away and stared down into her deep blue eyes. "I love you." I spoke the words, and she beamed, even though they sounded like a bunch of jumbled vowels.

"I love you, too," she said. She knew my sounds, and it always gave me a sense of humbleness when she understood what was in my heart.

The connection between us was so strong that my definition of soul mate had changed drastically from those high school days. A soul mate was much deeper than just a fuckbuddy, and Raven taught me that from the beginning.

I trusted her in ways I didn't even trust my brother, and because of that, when she asked me to show her what happened in Georgia, I didn't just shut down and walk away. She wanted to know the source that continued to haunt me in my dreams.

I didn't run, but I also didn't give in to her request right away. The last thing I wanted from my wife was the pity-look. Besides, the nightmares had changed since I became a father. Instead of me on that operating table, it was Hannah. When I had those nightmares, the fear from those dreams bled into the bedroom as she rubbed my sweat ridden back, assuring me that whatever it was, it was just a nightmare.

Showing her meant reliving the experience, and I wasn't sure I could do it again, but I eventually sucked it up and allowed her to see a glimpse of the torture I'd endured. Thankfully, it was late enough that Hannah didn't see the aftereffects. My wife vomited all over the floor and shook for another half hour afterwards. I cleaned up the mess and then held her until she stopped trembling.

That was the night I redefined soul mate. When she finally looked at me, I expected the pity-look, not one that seared her farther into my soul. Pity didn't exist in her gaze. Horror did, but it was overridden by awe along with the depth of her love, and I actually felt our connection grow.

To me, a soul mate is someone who sees your scars and doesn't run away screaming.

The two of us were damaged in inconceivable ways, but together, we made a hell of a team. And right now, all I wanted to do was make love to my wife until the sun rose. I swept her up in my arms and marched to the other side of the house, intending to make tonight last.

Angel Blood Chapter 6

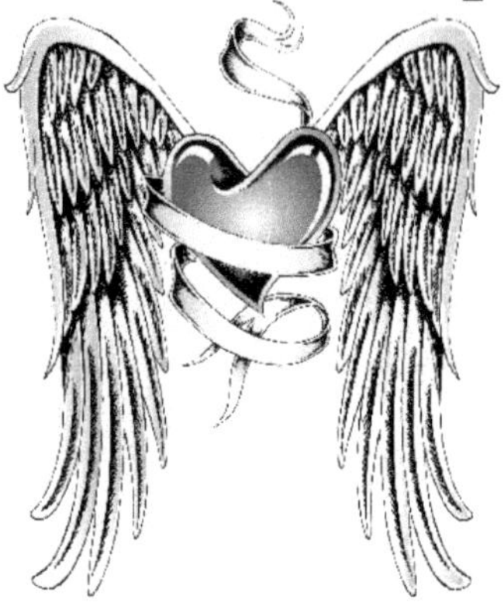

WHEN MORNING ROLLED AROUND, I was ready to focus on the case O'Keefe had handed us, and I waited on the deck with my coffee, enjoying the sunrise and the quiet of the morning before either Raven or Hannah woke.

A hand pounded on the glass behind me, and I turned, sending a smile to my daughter on the other side. I reached and slid the glass open.

"You didn't wake your mother, did you?" I signed, and she shook her head. "Good. She needs a little more rest."

"Okay," Hannah said, and hopped up in my lap. "Can you make me pancakes?"

I made the hand signal for yes and followed her into the kitchen. She sat at the table singing silly tunes while I whipped up a batch for us.

"Syrup or strawberries?" I asked, after I had a neat stack on a plate.

"Nutella," she said, and I laughed, shaking my head. I knew better. I had done that once, and it wound her up like an unstoppable mini-tornado. Pancakes were enough of a sugar fix without chocolate and hazelnut mixed in.

She pouted, and I held up her choices, putting them on the table with a bang to capture her attention.

"Which one?" I signed and pointed.

She crossed her arms and gave me the death ray look.

"I'm not giving you Nutella for breakfast," I signed, and collected three plates and silverware before sitting down next to her.

"Mommy lets me," she said, and I laughed, shaking my head.

"Oh, no she doesn't."

Hannah often tried to pit one of us against the other like this, and I could always read it. Raven sometimes doubted herself, but I had the inside track to know whether it was a fabrication done to get her way or a true statement. More often than not, it was a way for her to get exactly what she wanted, but she was learning.

I pointed at her and raised my eyebrows. No words were passed, but she dipped her head and mumbled, "Strawberries."

Raven shuffled into the kitchen and took a seat. Without a word, she grabbed for a plate, and I got up, fixing her coffee, because Raven didn't seem to speak in the morning without a little caffeine in her. It was more a series of grunts and adorable as hell.

I pushed her a coffee, and she acknowledged me with a nod and a smile, which is more than I usually get in the morning, and I smiled back, sending a wink in her direction.

That fine pink hue gathered in her cheeks at the same moment my phone buzzed. I dug it from my pocket and glanced at the text.

"Damian's on his way," I signed. "We need to head to the police station and talk with O'Keefe."

Her morning glow faded. "Why?" she asked; but it really was a 'what did you do now' question.

"He asked for some help on a case," I signed, and shrugged. I didn't want to get into it with Hannah within earshot, so I stood, clearing my plate. "I'll get this when I get home," I signed, and then waved at the mess in the sink.

With a peck on her cheek, I went out front to wait for Damian. I didn't want either Raven or Hannah overhearing the conversation, especially if Damian had

had a bad morning. The foul look on Damian's face when he pulled into the driveway confirmed my actions.

He waited until I sat and clipped the seatbelt to toss me a notebook.

I sent him a raised eyebrow in response.

"CJ wrote everything he could remember, and I've put a check next to all those who have died in the last year." He glanced in my direction. "From what I could uncover on the web, it sounds like they all died in the same manner, too."

I stared at him and then flipped open the book. Names filled half the pages, along with their location: city, and either state or country to go along with it. I couldn't help but be impressed by the magnitude of offspring. I tapped on the single letter at the end of each line.

Damian glanced at where I tapped before refocusing on the road. "Michael, Raphael, Uriel," he said. "It doesn't contain Lucifer's bloodline."

"How long did it take him to write these?" I asked, transmitting the words in my head as I flipped page after page.

"Most of the night. I felt really shitty asking him to do it when he'd had so little sleep, but he didn't seem to mind, and he didn't ask me any questions. I think the exhaustion of a newborn has him a bit overwhelmed."

I couldn't help the grin. If anyone knew more about being overwhelmed with newborns, it was Damian. After all, he had triplets, and while we were around to help in the beginning, it was still too much to take at times. I had to hand it to his wife, though; she never looked frazzled the way Damian sometimes got.

Damian raised an eyebrow in my direction. "I do not get frazzled," he said and the irritation visible in his features echoed in his terse tone.

I responded with a loud guffaw and signed, "Bullshit," calling him out on the lie.

His eyes rolled as he pulled into the York police station.

"I would leave that in the car," he said, pointing to the notebook in my hand.

I met his gaze and debated. If we had a clue of who the next victim was, we had an obligation to let the cops in on it.

"Was there anyone killed who wasn't on this list?" I asked, signing and projecting the thought at the same time.

He shook his head, and I dropped my gaze to the scribbled names, wondering if I could trust O'Keefe with this type of information. The fact he came to us for help drew my conclusion, and before Damian could snatch the notebook from my hand, I closed it and stepped out of the car with both the notebook and the folder O'Keefe had given me at the hospital in my tight grip.

"Are you insane?" Damian hissed as he got out of the car.

I glanced over the roof and closed the car door. "If we have information that could prevent the next death, I'm not keeping it under wraps."

"That list could implicate CJ."

I hesitated, torn between doing what's right and the need to keep my brother safe. He'd be pissed if he was hauled in, but if we withheld the information, we could be considered accessories to murder, or charged with obstruction of justice at the very least. I met Damian's gaze. "It also could stop the killer."

"How are you going to explain the list?"

I shrugged. I wasn't sure O'Keefe would buy any of it, but I had to try. "Call Steve," I added, before I stepped toward the station. "O'Keefe will believe him."

Damian scoffed but flipped open his phone. I didn't wait for the conversation; instead, I headed inside. At the desk, I scribbled Captain O'Keefe on a piece of paper and cleared my throat, capturing the receptionist's attention before handing my scribbled note to her.

Her brow creased, and I sent a smile meant to dazzle and disarm. When the color rose in her cheeks, I felt the smile turn into a grin.

"Who may I tell the Captain is waiting for him?" she asked in that come-hither purr I was used to from the girls in high school.

I scribbled my name and handed it to her before signing it to convey that I couldn't speak.

Her smile dropped a notch when she realized I was handicapped and that pity-look I hated crossed her face as she picked up the phone. She swiveled so I couldn't see her lips, but when the other end was picked up, she told whomever she was talking to that she needed to come pick me up, if only to see what a freaking delicious specimen I was.

I pressed my lips together against the grin that surfaced. It had been a while since I had someone drool over me, other than my wife, and as much as I was telling myself to ignore it, it was a much-needed stroke to the ego. It was good to know I still had the same charismatic effect I snagged my wife with back in high school.

She glanced back at me with a smile and told the woman on the other end to hurry.

The hinge of the front door squeaked as it opened, and I glanced over my shoulder at Damian. He accurately read the amusement in my eyes and focused his attention on the receptionist.

"You know he can hear, right?" he asked, as he hooked his thumb in my direction.

Her gaze snapped in my direction, and her mouth dropped open seconds before her entire face bloomed red. I shrugged and sent a wink in her direction.

The door shutting off the station to the public opened, and a blonde leaned against the doorjamb. She let out a bark of a laugh.

"Well, well, well, if it isn't Tommy Ryan."

I pressed my lips together, offering a ghost of a smile before I slid my gaze to Damian before returning my attention to the blonde. For the life of me, I couldn't recall her name, but I know I slept with her during my slut days in high school.

"You still shacking up with that red-headed freak?" She batted her eyes in my direction.

My smile vanished. I lifted my left hand and pointed to my wedding band. Everyone at our high school had treated Raven like a leper, and the derogatory reference was enough to set my blood on a low boil.

"Too bad," she said, looking me up and down before swinging the door wide. "Captain O'Keefe is expecting you," she added, and waved us inside.

I walked past her, ignoring the lewd memories parading through her head, and focused on the office across the floor where Captain O'Keefe stood waiting for us.

"Thank you, Bridget," he said to her, as she took a seat outside his office.

"Since when do you hire civilians?" I signed and projected the thought.

O'Keefe glanced at me. "She's my niece," he said, like that explained it all. "She needed some income, and I needed a hand." He gave me a shrug and waved towards the chairs.

"I'm Damian Andreas," Damian said, introducing himself after giving me a sideways look when he realized I had projected my thoughts. They shook hands, and I took a seat with the folder and the notebook still in my hands.

I had no idea what I was going to say, and the silence in the room weighed on me as Damian took a seat. I looked up, meeting Captain O'Keefe's gaze as he took the chair behind his desk.

"What's on your mind?" he asked, the question directed at me.

I tossed the notebook on the desk. "This may be a comprehensive hit list."

Damian sucked in his breath and glared at me.

Captain O'Keefe flipped through the pages, and when he got to the names in the file I still had in my hands, his gaze shot up to me. "Where did you get this?"

"It's not as simple as that," I said, stalling on pushing CJ under the bus.

"Then what the hell is this?" he asked, still fanning through the book.

I traded a glance with Damian, and he crossed his arms and his eyebrow rose in a silent challenge to explain.

O'Keefe stopped on a page and pointed. "Your name is in here," he said. "So are your brother and his wife."

I nodded and started the slow explanation with my hands.

"You know I can't read sign language," he snapped, leaning forward.

I closed my eyes and sighed. "It's a list of angel bloodlines." I transmitted the thought, and the absolute silence pulled my eyelids open.

He just stared at me. Damian shifted in the seat next to me and covered his smirk.

O'Keefe cleared his throat. "Where did you get this?"

"I asked CJ to write what he remembered when..." Damian started, and trailed off, unable or unwilling to express the thought.

"Are you fucking kidding me?" O'Keefe's voice cracked, and he blinked, his gaze jumping between the two of us. "Do you think I'm an idiot?"

I put my hand up, stopping his winding fury. "Regardless of where the list came from or how it was retrieved, we found more deaths that match the ones in Portland, and they're all names on this list. The next death is written in those pages," I said in both sign language and thought transmission. "And, as I said at the hospital, it's not what you're thinking this is. A vampire doesn't just have sharp canines like in the movies; their entire mouth is full of razor-sharp teeth, like a fucking shark." His face paled at my words. "I think it's a human with the same list that CJ wrote for us last night. And the killer is systematically murdering angelic bloodlines."

"What the fuck are you talking about?" O'Keefe's face reddened.

"Archangels," Damian said, pulling the captain's attention his way. "A very long time ago, they interacted with humans, and that is a list of the living descendants."

O'Keefe barked a laugh and leaned back in the chair.

A knock on the door interrupted him before he could continue.

"Come in," he snapped, and I didn't need to turn when the door opened.

"Morning, Jim," Steve said, as he stepped into the room and closed the door behind him. "Damian thought I might be of some help."

He laughed and pointed at the two of us. "Do you know what kind of bullshit they were trying to feed me?"

Steve let out a soft laugh and walked past O'Keefe to the window. "What exactly did my son tell you?" he asked, sending a sideways glance in my direction.

"He said the killer is murdering angel descendants." O'Keefe didn't mince words, going straight to the entire point of the notebook.

Steve turned towards me and raised his eyebrows. "Where did you come up with that?"

I pointed to the notebook that O'Keefe was still leafing through.

"CJ wrote what he remembered of the wall of ancestors," Damian said, and Steve's gaze moved to him. "I recognized one name, and on a hunch asked CJ to write what he could."

"And?"

"And everyone in the file the Captain gave us is on that list."

Steve sighed and turned his attention back to Captain O'Keefe.

O'Keefe met his stare and blew out an exhale before leaning back in his seat. "So, this shit is real." It wasn't phrased as a question.

"Afraid so," Steve said.

"The captain came to us because he suspected it might be a vampire," I signed, and then handed him the file. When Steve flipped it open to the first picture, he let out a small laugh and closed the file, handing it back.

"That's not what a vampire bite looks like." He rolled up his sleeve and turned his forearm in O'Keefe's direction. The scar remained from the bite he'd received while guarding Valerie. If Naomi hadn't been quick to respond, Steve would have died.

O'Keefe looked at the jagged scar and winced.

"If Damian's wife hadn't sucked the poison out, I would have died." He offered the slightest of smiles when O'Keefe slumped in the chair. "I was just as freaked out as you are to find out there are things out there that are much worse than the Windwalker."

O'Keefe stared at him for longer than he should have, his brain swirling in an almost unreadable pattern, as if the facts were short-circuiting him. He dropped his gaze to the notebook and turned page after page, scanning the names slowly before he finally looked up at me.

"Angels are real?" he asked in a small voice, like a child finding wonder.

"So are demons," I signed and transmitted at the same time.

He blinked rapidly and then stared down at the words like they would change, like this conversation was part of an elaborate dream he would wake from any minute.

"Why would someone want angel blood?" he asked, and a chill ran though me. I glanced at Steve and his face paled as much as Damian's next to me. None of us had considered that, and we all moved our gazes back to the captain at the same time.

Captain O'Keefe's mind worked the same way Steve's did, and that is why Steve had been such a great FBI agent. Although he attempted to attribute it to Jennifer's clairvoyance, it really was his base instinct to break something down to its simplest form.

"To regenerate," Damian said very softly.

O'Keefe raised his gaze. "Excuse me?"

We all remained silent as the horror of the details sank in. Not only was the assassin killing angel-kin, but he was also draining them of blood. And if this was Lucifer's hit list, it would only make sense that the killer was shipping the blood instead of doing God knows what with it.

"Holy shit," Steve finally muttered, and took a seat on the old leather couch by the door. He ran his hands through his hair and stared at the floor.

We hadn't heard from Lucifer since we rescued our father and closed the portal in Canada. The quiet had

been very nice for a change and I think we all just wrote
him off. But the fact there still were portals we hadn't
closed remained a dark stain on all our future plans. If
we were right about this, that would mean considerable
opposition. Especially if Lucifer was able to power up
before CJ took another run at him.

"Both your sons are on this list," O'Keefe added, and
Steve met his gaze with a nod.

"I'm well aware of my family's heritage," he said
softly, and glanced in my direction, meeting my
questioning stare.

Pages rustled as O'Keefe flipped back and forth,
scanning the names. His mind wrestled with the facts
we'd dumped on him, unsure of whether or not to
believe us. He wasn't as stubborn as he once had been,
and with Steve's acceptance of what had been revealed,
he was doubting his beliefs, or lack thereof.

"So, there's a heaven?" he asked timidly, and glanced
up.

I had CJ's memories, and I gave a nod, confirming
the question, and the captain's eyes narrowed.

"How the hell can you know that?" His voice carried
the incredulous expression carved into his features.

"Because CJ was there," I signed, and Steve
translated even before I finished. "It's a long story," I
added with a shrug.

"What about hell?" he asked, crossing his arms as
skepticism layered over his doubts.

I nodded again, but this time without adding any
explanation. CJ's memories of the portals made me
shiver in the seat, and our father in hellhound form
brought forth a rash of gooseflesh across my arms. My
jaw involuntarily clenched as I dropped my eyes to the
floor, studying the industrial carpeting.

"I'm not sure what to believe," O'Keefe said, and
papers shuffled again. "But let's just say I bought all
this shit you are shoveling in my direction," O'Keefe
added, focusing on me. "Who do you think is next?" He
turned the notebook back in my direction and slid it
across the desk.

"Do you have a map of Maine?" I asked, and he nodded, pulling one out of his drawer. He spread it out over his desk and Damian and I plotted the deaths on the map, starting with the ones Damian had discovered in northern Maine, using the dates and times to show the progression. Clusters of small x's showed the path of the killer from Caribou, Maine, all the way down to Portland.

He stepped around as I pulled out the notebook and marked the remaining names in the Portland area. Thankfully, there were only two left in Portland. The next cluster was in York, with only one other between our little family band and the Portland strikes.

Three more deaths before this lunatic hit us. My daughter was on this list, along with Damian's wife and kids. I traded a gaze with my business partner, and he stared at the map, formulating the same countdown in his head as I had gone through.

"Just out of curiosity, what do the single letters mean?" O'Keefe asked.

"Michael, Uriel, and Raphael," Damian said. "It denotes which bloodline the person falls under."

"What about Gabriel?" he asked mockingly.

Damian stared him down. "Gabriel only had one child."

"And how would you know that?"

The glare Damian sent in his direction chilled the room. "I know."

Captain O'Keefe chuckled like he had truly lost it. "I can't believe I haven't thrown you all in jail... or the psych ward." He kept laughing and when the door swung open with no warning, we all turned.

CJ walked in looking as ragged as I expected, but underneath the tired exterior burned an anger I recognized. My brother was pissed, and that's never a good thing. The door slammed behind him, and silence settled over the room.

"What gives you the right to share that list with anyone, let alone the cops?" he snarled at me. Captain O'Keefe stood from behind the desk, his hand automatically reaching for his sidearm in reaction to CJ's tone.

"Someone's collecting angel blood and making the cops think it's a vampire," Damian said, pulling CJ's attention. He gestured towards the map like that would explain our pulling in someone ill-equipped to tangle with the supernatural.

"I suggest you take a seat," Captain O'Keefe said, leveling a stare meant to intimidate. "Otherwise, I might be inclined to throw you in the holding tank until all this is sorted out."

CJ turned his glare in the captain's direction and his eyes narrowed in warning. "Sit your ass down," he said in that commanding tone that normal people can't resist.

O'Keefe sat, but his face registered shock at his complete inability to disregard the given order.

"That list is not for public consumption," CJ said, but his voice lost the edge it had when he first walked in.

I pointed to the map. "Look at the progression of murders. They are headed directly for us, and Valerie is on that list." I projected the thought louder than I anticipated and everyone in the room winced at the volume.

Our eyes locked and I could almost hear his thought process. If the killer found Valerie, they would also find Alex. The parental instinct kicked in and everything clicked in his overtired mind. He closed his eyes and dragged a hand down his face with a sigh. He nodded and glanced at O'Keefe.

"Captain, you are out of your element. This will put you in mortal danger."

O'Keefe actually laughed at him. "I'm a cop. This is what I signed up for."

"You're a cop in York, Maine. This isn't New York City, where you could be shot while sitting in your cruiser," CJ countered, and I covered the smirk that formed on my lips. "No disrespect," he added in a much softer voice. "But Damian and my brother are uniquely qualified to deal with this. You aren't."

"What exactly are we dealing with?" O'Keefe asked, moving his gaze from CJ to me before landing on Steve. No one spoke and O'Keefe scanned us all again.

"I have to go," CJ said, and I gave him a nod. Within a blink, the space he occupied vacated, and the sudden disappearance of my brother silenced whatever O'Keefe was about to say.

"What the fuck?"

Steve chuckled from his position on the couch. "Jim, you really don't know what you're stepping into here."

"I told you there were things much worse than vampires out there," I signed, and transmitted the thought. "I just never qualified it in a way you could understand. Think of the biggest bad and multiply it by a thousand."

He met my gaze while his brain made the connections. "If angels exist..." He trailed off and his face drained of all color. His mind combed over the entire conversation in a matter of seconds, shuffling and reshuffling all the details like a blackjack dealer. "Why would the devil need to regenerate?" he asked after a few minutes of silence.

"Because CJ nearly destroyed him," Damian said.

I guess he figured with CJ's grand exit, there was nothing left to hide.

"What?" He blinked, like someone had thrown sand in his eyes.

"There are only a few people on this earth who have danced with the devil and survived the ordeal. As circumstances would have it, they have all lived under my roof at one time or another." Steve said.

I glanced back at him, and he sat with his arms crossed, staring at O'Keefe like he'd just delivered his breakfast order instead of confirming the existence of the devil. I returned my gaze to Captain O'Keefe.

"Is he..." He pointed to where CJ had stood but I cut him off with a shake of my head.

"No. CJ isn't an angel. He's a descendant like we are." I transmitted the thought and waved my finger between Damian and me.

O'Keefe glanced at Damian and then turned the pages in the book before he glanced back up. "Any relation to Naomi, Grace, Gabriel and Michael Andreas?"

Damian nodded. "My wife and children," he said.

O'Keefe glanced at the names again. "You aren't listed in this book."

Damian huffed a laugh. "That's because I'm Gabriel's son."

O'Keefe stared at him. "You are an offspring of an archangel?" His voice cracked and his eyebrows arched. He slowly stood and turned, looking out his window, processing everything. "Then what is he. No human can just disappear like that." He snapped his fingers and turned back to us.

"He... inherited my ability to be in two places at once," Steve said from the couch.

O'Keefe pointed at him. "You never explained that shit to me."

Steve cracked a smile. "You never offered to buy me a drink."

O'Keefe muttered under his breath, but kept eye contact. "So, what are you?"

"An ex-FBI agent who inherited more than just money from Ty Ryan and his wife."

"Who, I am assuming, were also descendants?"

"Yup."

"So, does being an angel descendant warrant..." he waved towards the empty space and then pointed at me. "Or mind reading and thought projecting like him?"

Steve sighed and shrugged.

"No." Damian said. "None of the descendants I've ever come across had any discernible level of extra sensory perception like these boys do." He pointed at me. "They seem to be unique in that manner."

"And how many 'descendants' have you been in contact with," O'Keefe said, with a voice so filled with sarcasm that I let out a huff, catching it before it became an all-out laugh.

Damian leaned forward with his eyes narrowed. "Twenty-five-hundred-year's worth." He settled back in the seat. "More or less," he added with a smugness that would have made me grit my teeth had I not been so stunned by his honesty.

Oh fuck. The thought slammed home and my jaw loosened as I stared at Damian, wondering what the hell he was thinking. He sent a glare in my direction and focused back on the captain.

O'Keefe's eyelids were fluttering like hummingbird wings while his mind short-circuited. Even Steve huffed a laugh of disbelief. Damian really shit the bed with this one and I knew what was coming before O'Keefe blew sky high.

"What. The. Fuck." O'Keefe's baritone voice blared at us. If this had been a cartoon, it would have tipped us all over like a gale force wind.

The door opened and what's her name poked her head inside. "Is everything all right?"

O'Keefe recovered faster than I expected, and his gaze snapped to hers. "Yes. Now close the damned door."

Her eyes widened just before the door clicked shut, and I glanced back at O'Keefe.

"I think it's time for you to leave," O'Keefe growled low, and I sighed, standing up with no intention of leaving. I made the come here gesture, and he glared at me.

"Just come here," I said in my head and he paused but stepped closer.

I had never shared anyone's memories but my own before, and I wasn't sure how this worked, but I inhaled and concentrated on locking the power behind the door so none of it leaked out. It was hard enough for me to deal with; I'm not sure what it would do to O'Keefe if he got some residual supercharge. Once I was sure I wouldn't transfer any of CJ's mojo, I focused on only Damian's memories and reached out, placing the palm of my hand on his forehead. I held his gaze and sent as much of the memories swarming in my head as I dared.

His breathing became ragged, and his eyes glossed over. Sweat broke out under my palm and when he blinked and his eyes refocused on mine, I pulled my hand away and took a seat. Captain O'Keefe slowly dropped into his chair.

His pallid color told me enough, but then his gaze moved beyond me to Steve, and finally settled on Damian. He blinked a few times and licked his lips.

"You were a... a..." He cleared his throat again. "A vampire?"

"Yes."

O'Keefe wiped his face. "And Lucifer?" he asked without finishing, shuddering at the vision of Lucifer destroying all Damian held dear.

"He's a joy, isn't he?"

O'Keefe let out a high-pitched laugh and his gaze landed on Steve again.

"Mind. Blown," he said, staring behind me.

Steve chuckled. "Yeah, I went the denial route at first, myself. But then, seeing the bloodsuckers firsthand, well, that seemed to change my entire perspective. And Lucifer is the most terrifying thing I've ever come up against."

His eyes widened.

"Show him, Tom," Steve said, and I glanced behind me, shaking my head.

O'Keefe saved me the pain by clearing his throat. "I've seen enough," he whispered.

Steve let out a laugh and met his gaze. "Do you want to solve the only open case this town has?"

O'Keefe's incessant blinking was back, and his jaw slowly dropped so that his mouth formed a small 'o'.

"Of course, you wouldn't be able to formally close the case," he added and crossed his arms. "But at least you'd know what happened."

"Are you trying to get arrested?" I signed in his direction, and he glared at me for a moment before nodding his head toward the captain.

"Show him what happened the day Damian's triplets were born," he ordered.

Angel Blood Chapter 7

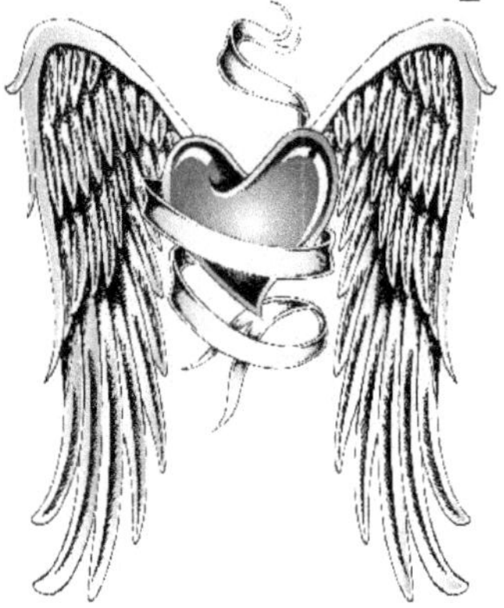

I GROUND MY JAW tight, turning back to Captain O'Keefe. The blinking had stopped, and he moved his gaze to mine with a quick nod.

I knew better. Nothing could prepare him for the hell he was about to see.

I wondered how wise this was as I zeroed in on that night. The horror of it all, from the battle in the cove to the bloodshed over the snow-covered lawn.

Damian wouldn't look at me. Instead, his eyes remained glued to something beyond the window. That night signaled a change for all of us. It opened the doors to where we were now, and he blamed himself for bringing all this shit on us.

I sighed and stood.

Captain O'Keefe leaned forward in the chair, and I had a moment to be thankful he was sitting because this vision was my viewpoint, not Damian's, and it would come with the raw emotion surrounding the entire event.

I knew where to start and I knew where to end, but that didn't make it any easier to pull the memory out of the box.

"I can handle it," O'Keefe said, and I met his gaze.

"Yeah, but I'm not sure I can," I transmitted, and steadied my breathing.

When my palm touched his forehead, the entire ordeal roared back.

STEVE GUIDED US ACROSS the snow-covered lawn toward Paradise cove. CJ and I followed the group, and every muscle in my body wound tight. This was as bad as the anticipation of the psycho's knife. I wasn't sure if we would walk out of this, even with my brother's incredible power, and all I wanted to do was hold Raven tight and protect her from harm. CJ glanced at me, and I gave him a slight nod. He could feel my apprehension as we crossed onto the narrow path leading to the cove.

"This is the perfect place for an ambush," Damian muttered while glancing at the proximity of the tree lines on both sides. My eyes darted to the dark woods as well.

"You'll be okay," CJ said, his voice soft, falling with the wind surrounding us as he traded a glance with me. I noticed the lack of the usual 'I promise', which was my first sign that my brother was just as freaked out as I was.

We made it to the glen without incident and Steve threw Damian a canister of salt.

"Make yourself useful," he said, and Damian raised an eyebrow.

"Salt?"

"Yes, make a barrier at the wood line."

"I'm not sure this is going to work," he said, but stepped to the path we'd just crossed over. He poured a thick line across the snow-covered ground, continuing onto the frozen water of the cove.

"Now what?" he asked.

Steve traded a glance with Jennifer and then started clearing a space with his feet. "Now we make a fire and wait," Steve said. CJ and I helped clear the snow off with our feet, revealing the deep green moss covering the land mass.

"You know, for such a brilliant investigator, you can be a complete idiot," Damian said, and Steve looked up at him with a crease of confusion between his eyes. "Step aside."

Damian crossed to a spot just inside the salt line. It took a moment, and then the snow rolled away like an old carpet clearing the moss and the ice all the way to the far edge of the cove where the lake began in earnest.

I was impressed and CJ rolled his eyes, but Steve was pissed, and he just crossed his arms, sending a glare at Damian in that way that made me uncomfortable. CJ smirked and turned away, like a laugh would just cause more tension.

"What? You've got the power to do this. Why the hell would you do it manually?"

"Because it reminds me I'm human, and not some all-powerful god," Steve answered, his tone as sharp as his gaze. I stepped closer to Raven in response, our hands intertwining, and she gave me a quick squeeze.

"You really know how to get under his skin," I said, and Damian's head snapped in my direction. My voice was completely restored, as it always was when I stepped into this cove. I sent a sliver of a smile at his wide-eyed stare.

Before he commented, he was yanked into the darkness, and just like that, Naomi snapped into tiger form. Instinct took over, and I let go of Raven's hand, pushing both her and Jennifer behind me. I know I wasn't super charged like CJ, Steve, and Damian, but I could put up a hell of a fight. I pulled the gun out of my pocket, but before I could level it at the ruckus coming towards us, CJ grabbed my arm.

"It's Damian," he said, and as soon as the words fell from his lips along with a plume of white air, Damian stepped back into the cove, visibly shaken with blood dripping from his arm.

Raven's grip on my shoulder tightened, and I looked back at her wide eyes.

"It'll be okay," I said, and her gaze moved to mine but no matter how much I wanted to promise her we'd walk out of this, I really didn't know if that was true or not. Her physical touch gave me an ounce of courage to believe in something more and I turned back towards the surrounding woods.

Light illuminated the cove, telling me enough. I knew if I turned, our father would be there. He always made the dark shine, ever since he died and took the position of Steve's guardian angel.

I kept my focus, and the barrel of the gun pointed towards the perimeter that I was covering. The woods shifted and my breath caught in my throat. Ice filled my veins at the sight of at least a dozen vampires stepping into view. The salt would do nothing to stop them and from the sudden loss of color in Damian's face, I gathered this was not a good thing.

"Jesus," Steve muttered.

The blood suckers stopped, collectively smiling, with their gazes locked on Damian.

"The great Damian Andreas," one of them growled. His voice settled over the cove like a form of Black Death, and I swallowed my fear, focusing my sights between the eyes of the nearest bastard.

"I'll give you to the count of three to leave; otherwise, you'll be burning in hell before you can blink." Damian raised his gun, pointing it towards the idiot who spoke. Naomi growled, and we all clicked off our safety, making sure we were locked and loaded and ready to spray bullets.

"Don't shoot. We're going to fry their asses," CJ's thought filled my brain, and I traded a quick glance and a nod, telling him I heard him.

"One," Damian said. The vampires laughed.

"You're going to shoot us?" the lead asshole said and chuckled. "You should know better."

Damian smiled, looking over the gun. "Two, and yes, I know better," he said, and the vampire's cocky stance waned.

"Platinum?" he gasped, and took a step back, fear transitioning his features from shadow back to pale white.

"And we're all expert shots," Damian said and didn't wait for them to attack or retreat. Instead, he yelled, "Three!"

A wave of heat rolled across the moss, rippling the air as it fanned out to encompass the mass of vampires. The stench of burned flesh filled the air, along with the dust of decimated vampires.

A shift in the wind blew the dust into the woods. When Damian turned towards the lake, his mouth dropped open. We all turned to see what had shocked him so visibly.

My father stood on the ice surrounded by a host of angels. A fucking army of angels, and I stared, dumbfounded. The only two without wings stepped forward and Damian uttered something in a foreign language I didn't know.

When he transitioned back to English, his words sent a shiver through me.

"Papa, is that really you?"

"Damian," he whispered. "My son," he added.

If I recall the bits of conversation from the house correctly, his father was the archangel Gabriel. I glanced at CJ, and his eyes turned to mine, like they always did when I needed clarification.

He nodded. "He hasn't seen his father since he was really little," CJ said. "His father is the Archangel Gabriel, and that's Michael standing next to him."

"No shit," I said, glancing back at the pair. Michael didn't look as formidable as our father did, and perhaps that's because he no longer had wings.

"Damian has their grace. That's why they don't have wings." CJ's narrative filled me in, and I sighed, once again the last to get all the pieces of the puzzle.

"How?" Damian asked, scanning the white-winged beings in our midst.

"The cove," I said aloud, and Damian's head snapped towards me. "It's kind of a magical place in case you haven't noticed." I gave him a shrug and Steve cleared his throat, pulling our attention to him.

"I promised you an army," Steve said, and waved his hand at the heavenly host, grinning like he knew a particularly intriguing secret.

Movement pulled my attention back to the woods, and a chill swept the area, pressing down on all of us. We moved tighter together in response to the solid line of demons that stepped into view.

The next wave of assailants took up their posts, side by side with a legion of hellhounds. Naomi actually stepped back at the numbers, and our fear blended together, leaving a metallic taste in my mouth.

Terror gripped every one of us, and we spread out on the shoreline far enough away from the woods to be safe for the moment. Steve took the left side, and Damian took the right. CJ stood dead center. Jennifer, Raven, and I stood a step behind, relying on the power centers to provide a solid wall of defense.

However, my gun was now trained on the closest demon. Steve had taught me how to shoot, and between that and my martial arts training, I was sure I could take down a few of them before they tore me to shreds. I'd kill as many as I could to protect my wife and Jennifer, and I steeled myself for battle.

The angels filtered between us, providing a protective barrier around me and the girls, and I clenched my teeth in frustration, turning towards the one that probably ordered the extra defense. My father gave me a shrug. One that said he wasn't there before, but this time, he'd make damned sure I walked out of this unharmed.

My heart scrambled in my chest, pumping a beat that nearly seized my lungs, and I traded a glance with CJ. He swallowed and curled his hands around his revolver, aiming it at the closest demon.

The air sparked with tension, and when the demons blocking the path parted, all hope for winning this battle faded. Lucifer stepped inside the ring, swiping a clean path through the salt Damian had lain down, and he wasn't alone.

He dragged Steve's partner, Sarah, forward, tossing her at his feet in front of him. When she raised her bruised face, Steve cursed under his breath and the gun moved from the line of demons to Lucifer.

Lucifer just grinned at the assembly and his black wings fluttered as he cracked his knuckles. His gazed moved over the crowd of angels. "What have we here?" he asked, scanning the line until his gaze landed on Gabriel and Michael. He tilted his head in contemplation, and then his gaze moved back to Steve.

"This lovely police officer was particularly useful," he said, meeting Steve's glare and waving his hand in Sarah's direction.

Her gaze bounced from the demons surrounding us to the angels in line, landing on the tiger pacing in front of me. Then they jumped back to Steve.

"What the fuck?" she whispered, and Steve offered her a half laugh.

"I told you not to go to the house," he said, and I recognized the regret in his voice. "You should have listened this time."

Lucifer grabbed a handful of her hair.

"Let go of me, asshole," Sarah snapped, swatting at his hand. While her voice was defiant and full of moxie, her eyes held a soul-crushing fear that I knew all too well. I had felt the same fear when I was strapped to the table in Georgia; knowing death is beating down your door and there isn't a damned thing you can do about it.

He pulled her to her feet, bringing her close to him. Her elbow connected with his stomach, and he chuckled in her ear.

"I like my women feisty," he purred in her ear, keeping his gaze locked on Steve's. This was just the beginning of his dance, and we all knew Sarah was doomed.

We were all doomed.

"I'll tell you what," he said, running a sharp nail lightly down her arm. "I'll let you and your family go, along with this lovely officer, if you leave us to settle our differences." He nodded toward Naomi and Damian, negotiating a deal that would seal Damian in his grave.

I knew a lie when I heard one and that one was a doozie. One glance at his arsenal and I knew if we stepped out of the cove, we were all dead. I didn't need the infusion of Damian's memories, like Steve and CJ had, to feel the evil radiating from this bastard.

"That includes leaving the angel and his son," Lucifer clarified, his gaze landing on my father, narrowing into a hateful expression.

What the fuck does this bastard want with my brother? The thought barreled through my mind and I saw CJ tense, and he glanced over his shoulder at me. Just the look alone was enough. I didn't need his added 'Just chill,' but it pinged in my mind just the same.

Steve's jaw clenched, and his gaze dropped to Sarah.

"Do your magic and get me out of this," Sarah said. The panic reached her voice as Steve's head shook back and forth.

His entire being shook, and the frustration and anger pulsing in his veins drifted over me.

"You bastard," Damian whispered, and Lucifer sent a chilling smile in his direction.

"I can't do that," Steve said, and Damian glanced at him. Jennifer breeched the line of angels and laid her hand on his shoulder in a show of solidarity. She gave him strength to do what was necessary, even with the silent sobs shaking her form.

Lucifer's hand ripped Sarah's shirt open, revealing a modest sports bra, and he tilted his head, smiling as his fingernails dimpled the skin over her heart. "Last chance," he said.

"I'm sorry, Sarah," Steve said, his eyes filled with tears and his lips pressed together.

Sarah's scream shattered the night, followed by the report of a gun. A ringing silence encompassed us. Smoke drifted from the end of Steve's revolver, and I stared at where his bullet landed.

Lucifer's fingers were buried knuckle deep in Sarah's chest, but that's not what silenced her scream. The neat bullet hole between her eyes had sent her to heaven before Lucifer could rip her heart out.

I knew what that shot would do to Steve. But he chose a more humane death for his partner; though his logical mind wouldn't be able to bury the guilt, despite being the right move. If he hadn't ended her life, Lucifer would have made her suffering last as long as possible.

He lowered his arms, and his chin dropped to his chest. His breath hitched once. With a violent shake of his head, his tear-stained glare landed on Lucifer and the gun rose back in place.

"Get the fuck off my property," he said with a growl.

"As soon as I have my whore," he said.

Steve pulled the trigger again, but this time nothing happened until he moved the aim to the demon closest to Lucifer and then the gun jumped to life, expelling another round. The shot was as true as the one that took Sarah's life, and the first demon fell.

Lucifer yanked his hand from Sarah's flesh and tossed her next to the dead demon. He licked his fingers and scowled, glaring at Steve. The minute he stepped forward, my father interceded, blocking the devil's path.

That hateful glare reappeared and Lucifer snapped his fingers, Christopher Ryan appeared in the center of the clearing, bleeding and on his knees, his screams filling the silent woods, echoing on the dark lake as the hellhounds tasked with ripping him to shreds continued their attack.

This time, my father moved; his face filled with a wrath I had never seen before, and CJ took a step toward him. Before I could stop him, both Steve and Damian took hold of his arms, keeping him from entering the violent scene in front of us. This was just a primer to the bigger war, one meant as an appetizer to drive the hounds in line into a frenzy, preparing them for attack.

"You can't stop it," Damian said when CJ tried to rip out of his grasp.

He turned a pleading gaze in his direction when the first hellhound turned on our dad.

A flare of satisfaction bloomed in me when my father ripped the hellhound in two with his bare hands, and from the expression on Lucifer's face, he didn't expect that at all.

My dad kicked ass.

My father grabbed Chris around the waist and launched toward the heavens, pulling his brother out of range of the hellhounds into the single beacon of light, disappearing from view before Lucifer could yank him back to the earth.

Lucifer's furious gaze dropped from the sky to Damian, then moved to CJ. His face crinkled and he roared his aggravation, squeezing a fist in front of him. Damian stepped into Lucifer's line of sight, and nothing happened at first. Then, out of nowhere, three of the *demons next to Lucifer burst, exploding into neat balls of flame.*

The surprise of the back-to-back events stunned everyone, and nothing moved until a streak of lightning flared and my father landed on one knee in the center of the clearing like Thor arriving for battle. His wings smoldered, sending tendrils of smoke into the air, but when he lifted his head, his fury filled the space and he stood, shifting into a battle stance.

"You've cheated me for the last time," Lucifer growled and pointed at my dad.

"Game on, you bastard," he said, and leveled the glare I had seen when I was little. The one that dubbed the man the Angel of Death while he was alive. And it evoked a tremor, a chill that bit at my heels and spread like a four-alarm fire. As much as I loved my father, he could scare the living crap out of me with that look.

Naomi hissed behind me, and the spell that held us in place broke. Damian aimed his gun at the closest hellhound and squeezed the trigger. The report of gunfire shattered the stillness, breaking the stalemate between good and evil.

Thirty demons went down in the span of the ten seconds it took the four of us to empty our clips and the only one who took the time to re-load was me. The angels charged forward, meeting the advancing demons in the center, but Steve, CJ, and Damian stayed put, protecting us.

When I stepped between CJ and Damian, leveling the gun at the melee, Damian pushed my hand down and shook his head.

"Hold on to those. We might need them," he said, meeting my gaze and pushing me back into the safety of the cocoon they'd created. I felt completely useless and frustrated, and Raven gripped my arm, her attention focused on the bloodbath in front of us.

"On three," CJ said. "One," he breathed low, his voice almost lost over the bellows of fighting angels and demons.

The charge built in the air, and I pulled Jennifer and Raven closer to me, taking a step back to give the three of them more room to execute whatever they were planning.

"Two," Damian said.

"Three!" Steve yelled.

The air rippled like a wave rolling across the field, leaving only a bloody mist in its wake, along with four stunned angels.

My father glanced at us with a maniacal grin.

Lucifer stood at the edge of the field, scanning the gory remains of his army.

Michael and Gabriel stared at the mess with open mouths.

Only the sound of blood rain filled the space, and I realize the three of them had annihilated demons and angels alike. Only archangels remained, and my gaze landed on my father. A shiver caught my soul, turning my blood as cold as the frigid water behind me.

We moved closer to my dad. Michael and Gabriel squared up to Lucifer, but he wasn't done with his arsenal of tricks.

Naomi howled, and I blinked down at the writhing cat before my gaze jumped back to Lucifer.

Damian charged without thought, and got one hit in before Lucifer's backhand hit him, spinning him onto the ground. The howl turned into an ear-piercing scream, snapping my gaze to Naomi. She lay in a ball, in human form, holding her stomach, screaming in pain.

The black power moved from Naomi to CJ, dropping him to his knees as he held his chest. His head dipped and his hands balled into fists. I went to take a step to help him, but both Jennifer and Raven held onto me, their fright keeping me in place. CJ was in pain and my stomach writhed. The muscles in his arms stood out under the coat, tensing against whatever assault Lucifer was sending his way. When he snapped his gaze from the ground back at Lucifer, the devil stumbled back, nearly falling on his ass.

CJ stood, with his breath coming in shallow bursts from the exertion, and he ignored everyone, focusing his attention on the devil, now engaged in a fight to the death with both Michael and Gabriel.

Damian scrambled to Naomi, and his frantic eyes searched her face before looking up at Raven and me. He glanced to where Steve stood, splitting his attention between the fight and us. Naomi's paleness caught his attention, and he stepped closer just as Damian whispered, "Can you fix her?"

Steve bent down and delivered a kiss to Naomi's forehead and light danced over her form, rejuvenating her body, filling her hollow cheeks with a healthy glow. She blinked at him and then her eyes rolled back and she went limp.

"What did you do?" Damian asked, alarmed by her slip into unconsciousness.

"She'll be fine," Raven said, "But we need to get her out of here," she added, watching the movement of the three archangels. "The path isn't blocked anymore," she said, pointing.

Damian didn't hesitate. He picked Naomi up and headed for the open escape, and we followed him at an all-out sprint. We burst into the house and Damian placed Naomi on the couch, pushing her hair away from her face.

"Come on, baby," he whispered, pressing his lips to hers. She didn't respond, and he turned toward us, his eyes begging for help. We all knew the healing power tends to knock people out, but he didn't. Even so, the lack of concern on our parts seemed to calm him.

Raven stepped forward, her gaze averted, but she forced eye contact. "She'll be okay; her life force is still strong." She touched his cheek. "Your babies shine just like you."

"Jesus," Steve's mutter called our attention away from Naomi and out the window. Lucifer stalked onto the property. The severed heads of Gabriel and Michael dangled from each of his hands, and he held them up for us to see. His roar of triumph left me shaking, and I gulped down the fear.

"Shit," my father's voice rang out behind us, and we turned, staring down the only other angel standing.

Damian pointed to Naomi. "Keep her safe. That's all I ask," he said, moving his gaze across our faces, and then he turned and crossed to the door.

"What do you think you're doing?" Steve asked.

"Ending this," Damian said and stepped outside.

My father sighed and glanced at us, his gaze moving from mine to CJ's, and then he glanced at Steve. "You know I can't just let him go after the devil alone," he said.

We all nodded, and he paused, giving us a nod before turning and following Damian out into the battle zone.

I stared out the window with CJ by my side. Words passed and then Lucifer belted out a laugh that rattled the windowpane. He leaned back, cackling at the sky. My father launched, leaving Damian standing in place like a shocked little kid.

The battle between my father and Lucifer raged, dredging up a white flurry around the two angels. My heartbeat rammed my throat, drawing my breath in fast pants of anxiety that matched CJ's. Raven slid a swaddled baby into my arms without so much as a glance outside and I held the infant tight, mindful of not crushing him.

Red splattered white, and CJ bellowed at the vision of our father's head in the demon's grip. His palms banged against the cold windowpane as blood rained down on my father's wings. My mind flashed back to my mother's head propped up on the end of the surgical table, her dead eyes staring at me the way my father's were now.

I glanced down at the small package in my arms, looking for something to erase the visions assaulting me; the boy momentarily distracted me from the darkness bathing my heart. When I returned my gaze out the window, the scene swarmed through a mist of tears. My heart squeezed against the devastation.

The baby in my arms represented hope, but how could a mere mortal take on the devil and win when archangels fell? When my father fell? I hitched a breath, pressing my lips together.

The child tempered my reaction and the cry of disdain coming from the baby's lips pulled both our eyes to the swaddled bundle; Damian's firstborn, and I propped him up on my shoulder, gently bouncing to ease his pain.

When I returned my gaze outside, Damian's hand shot toward Lucifer's chest. I had no clue what to expect, but when Damian's hand came into view, holding a beating heart, my eyes widened in shock.

And then Damian did the unthinkable: he took a bite of the bloody muscle.

I shivered with disgust; it burned through the horror of all the destruction that occurred tonight, and I covered my mouth with my free hand. One look at CJ told me he felt the same burn roiling in my stomach.

The moment the last piece of Lucifer's heart disappeared into Damian's mouth, the heavens opened, and a blinding light encompassed him, dropping Damian to his knees. I stared at the man in the midst of the heavenly glow, wondering if the angel grace effect would last. CJ and I traded a glance before refocusing on the bloodied winter scene. The glow faded, and Damian climbed to his feet. The fury etched into his features made me want to shrink away from the glass. I've only seen that kind of wrath once, and it was painted on my father's face.

A blast leaped from Damian, enveloping Lucifer, leaving only torched earth where the devil had stood. I gaped, blinking rapidly, trying to make sense of what had just happened.

Damian took an unsteady step backwards, reaching for the gazebo post for support as he stared at the same blackened spot we all were staring at. When Damian finally started toward the house, his gait was steady and he ignored the severed heads sprinkling his path.

As the former vampire passed by my father's head, my gaze locked on the vacant eyes staring at the sky. Anguish encompassed me, numbing my body, and taking me back to the ordeal in Georgia. Nothing I could do would erase the horror of what I just saw, and I knew without a doubt, this would haunt my dreams for the foreseeable future.

I PULLED MY HAND away from Captain O'Keefe's forehead and took a seat. The lump in my throat matched the wobbly vision, and I blinked, sending hot paths down my cheeks. I had buried that scene away since it happened, and reliving it was just as painful as it had been that night. I stared at the ground, feeling more like the scared seventeen-year-old the captain hauled into the police station years ago, as opposed to the man I was today.

A hand landed on my shoulder, and I glanced back at Steve as he gave me a squeeze of support. I didn't want to glare, but it was already forming. Reliving that shit opened wounds that had partially healed. Now they were raw enough to evoke the emotions again.

I turned towards the captain, trying to scrape off the horror tightening my throat, and what met my gaze softened the swirl in my stomach and made me press my lips together against a smirk.

The man trembled in the chair, just staring at a spot on his desk. Blotchy red stained his cheeks, standing out in stark relief against the pasty white of his skin. He finally raised his gaze to mine and opened his mouth to speak, but only a wheeze came out.

"Breathe, Captain," I whispered in my mind, giving him a nod of encouragement.

He took a large inhale through his nose and let it out of his mouth, repeating until it didn't sound like the startup of a motorcycle.

"Holy shit," he finally muttered. He blinked a few more times and let out a shaky laugh. "I take it back. I don't want to know this shit exists," he said, drawing smiles to all our faces. His expression sobered as his gaze landed on Steve. "I don't know if I could have made the same call," he said, his voice a fraction stronger.

Steve remained quiet, and I didn't need to turn and look to know he was staring at his hands. His mind was already reviewing that same night, looking for an alternative that wouldn't have left Sarah dead, and he couldn't find a palatable solution beyond what he did. His sigh signaled the end of his memory inspection.

"I couldn't..." he started and stopped.

Captain O'Keefe raised his hand to stop Steve. "Just tell me where her remains are," he said a little more forcefully.

I glanced back at Steve as he finished his shrug in response.

O'Keefe raised his eyebrows. "Cat got your tongue?"

"The place was clean when we went back after taking Naomi to the hospital. No evidence that there had been a bloodbath exists. The only sign that any of it really happened was the scorched grass. Everything else was as pristine as when we arrived."

"You have got to be joking," O'Keefe said. "How do you even know she's dead?"

I didn't wait for prompting; I reached out and slammed my palm on his forehead, transmitting one of CJ's memories. The one that not only proved Sarah was dead but also proved there was indeed a heaven, and it really wasn't anything we envisioned.

It only took seconds and then I leaned back, crossing my arms, waiting for him to draw the conclusion. His gaze snapped to the empty space where CJ had stood earlier and then back to me as he muddled through the memory.

"He... died?"

"Not exactly," I signed and both Damian and Steve translated aloud. "But that's not my story to tell," I added, this time following it with the mind transmission.

O'Keefe's gaze moved from mine to Damian's as the memory transfer fully hit. "Your wife turns into a tiger?" he asked, blinking again at the delayed reaction of all the facts.

Damian let out a huff of a laugh. "Yes. She does that whenever demons are near."

O'Keefe studied us and then turned to me.

"Is that what attacked Raven's father?"

I nodded, keeping his gaze.

"Jesus," he whispered and rubbed his face. The ramifications of all we could do swirled in his mind, jumping from awe to anger and back. He shook his head, focusing on the map in front of us.

I glanced down at the map, studying the small, almost overlapping cluster in Portland, and tapped. "This is where we need to be," I said and raised my gaze. "And by we, I mean Damian and me. Not you, just in case."

Captain O'Keefe's lips thinned as he debated, and then he slowly shook his head. "I need to be there as well. I want to nail this fucker just as much as I wanted to nail the Windwalker."

I raised an eyebrow in a silent challenge.

"Yeah, I fucked up with you, but can you blame me?" He crossed his arms, almost daring me to contradict him. "Besides, I need to sleep on this shit." He tapped his temple. "Because I really don't know how much was pure bullshit and how much was real."

"Look, I went the denial route as well, but the more we pussy-foot around, the more people will die," Steve said. "And honestly, it would be nice to have someone besides my wife to talk to about all this crap."

O'Keefe let out a laugh. "I'm never speaking of this. Not unless I want them to lock my ass up in a padded room," he said, waving towards the door and the station beyond it. "But I'm also not going to let you two screw up an investigation," he added, directing his sharp glance in my direction.

"Fine," I said aloud, although it came out just as just 'fi', but he got the gist.

"I don't know how I'm going to explain you two, though," he muttered under his breath.

"You can tell them the truth. We run a paranormal investigation firm," Damian said. "And due to the nature of the deaths, you felt a need to rule out anything... supernatural."

O'Keefe laughed. "That's as bad as enlisting a gypsy who reads tarot cards," he said when he wound down. "But with how desperate they are, maybe they'll understand."

"Is there a way to put these folks under protective custody?" I asked pointing to the three dots.

O'Keefe inhaled and shook his head. "Not without hard evidence and I certainly can't go to them with this."

He held up the notebook, handing it back to me. He rubbed his face and glanced at Steve. "I could just deputize you two," he muttered under his breath.

"We hold certain abilities that can aid in the investigation," Damian said.

"It would only hold until this case is solved," O'Keefe said.

"Works for me," I signed and transmitted.

"And it does not, I repeat, it does not authorize you to kill."

He pointed at the two of us and I nodded assent. I wasn't that hyped up to kill again. The only man I ever killed was Raven's father, and while it was ruled self-defense, however justified his death was taking a life still haunted my nightmares.

Angel Blood Chapter 8

NAOMI'S CAR WAS IN the driveway, and both Damian and I sighed. I felt the smirk before I realized it even landed on my lips and we traded a glance. Our hope for a peaceful afternoon in my study, doing further research, was dashed by the reality of four toddlers running amok.

When we stepped through the door, the chaos we envisioned was real. Gabe and Michael were chasing Hannah and Grace around the house with light sabers, and the girls were shrieking in that 'I'm having so much fun' way that was ear splitting.

Raven and Naomi sat on the couch with coffee and a plate of fruit on the coffee table in front of them. I wasn't sure if the food was for them or the kids. They both looked up from their conversation when we stepped into the room.

After the last couple of hours, I really wasn't prepared for the chaos, and it set my instant irritation switch to the on position. Raven homed in on my aura before she met my gaze.

"You know what might be fun for the kids?" she asked and then turned to Naomi.

"What's that?" Naomi said, sipping her coffee.

"The playground."

At that moment, I could have given my wife a long, lingering kiss. I swear sometimes she's the one with the mind-reading abilities.

Naomi smiled and turned to Damian. "Do you mind?"

"Not at all," he said. "Do you mind if I tag along?" he asked, surprising all of us, but the sideways glance he gave me told me enough. He was not comfortable leaving his wife and kids to chance. He gave me a nod, confirming my thoughts, and his eyes wandered to Raven and Hannah, including them under his protective net.

"I think I'm just going to hang out here. Okay?" I signed and Raven crossed and planted a kiss on my cheek.

"You look like you need some rest," she whispered. "We can talk later if you'd like."

I met her gaze and gave her a smile and a nod of thanks. It took a few minutes to corral the kids and then an eerie silence settled on the house. I crossed to our bedroom and lay down on the bed. No matter what position I chose, sleep was not in the cards.

After tossing on the bed for a good hour, I decided a drink on the deck was a better idea and grabbed myself a beer from the refrigerator. I collapsed into the chase lounge and stared out at the ocean, trying to figure out all that had happened today.

While I knew there were three people on the descendant list between the latest kill and York, I couldn't help but feel uneasy, like I was sitting on a prequel to disaster. Nothing settled well, not even the beer, and I ended up trading the alcohol for a ginger ale and some fish crackers.

When Raven came home, I opted to remain outside watching the sun dance on the summer waves while she cleaned the sand off of Hannah. When the television turned on to some PBS show and the door opened, I glanced over my shoulder at Raven.

She offered me that supportive smile, and I sighed.

"What happened at the police station?" she asked.

I didn't know where to start, so I just cut to the part I knew she would balk at. "He knows what CJ and I can do."

"Why in the name of all that is sacred..."

I held my hand up to stop the rant. "He came to me for help with a case that, on the surface, looked like something supernatural, but it's another serial killer that is making the deaths look like a fictional vampire. Of course, O'Keefe had no idea what an actual vampire looked like. At least not until I shared what happened at Paradise Cove the night the triplets were born." I signed and transmitted at the same time, staring out at the ocean instead of looking at her.

"Why would you show him that?" she gasped.

"Because Steve ordered me to. The killer we are dealing with may be in league with Lucifer."

Silence filled the space between us, and I finally glanced in her direction. Her lips were pressed tight in the familiar posture of anger, but her eyes held fear and I reached over, taking her hand in mine.

"It's not here in York," I transmitted, watching the tightness around her lips and eyes relax a fraction.

"Then why is the captain asking for your help?"

"Steve sent him to us. The Portland police asked for his help, considering he got the credit for busting the Windwalker."

Raven rolled her eyes. "Steve caught my father, not the York Police."

I nodded. If Steve hadn't done that two places in one shit, Jennifer and I would have died, and who knows what that prick would have done to Raven. "But the world doesn't know that," I signed.

"Do you trust O'Keefe to keep his mouth shut?"

I let out a laugh. "He said, and I quote, if I ever say any of this out loud, I'll end up in the loony bin." I signed and transmitted. That brought a much-needed smile to Raven's face.

"Aye, I sometimes wonder if that's where we all should be."

Her lovely smile caught on and I returned it before hers faded away.

"You aren't thinking of going after Lucifer, are you?" she asked.

I turned away from her and stared out at the ocean. My brother was a trinity, I wasn't. He was nearly killed by Lucifer before he was infused with angel grace. If he couldn't kick Lucifer's ass, I certainly couldn't. I didn't respond at first.

"Tom?"

I turned towards her. "As long as he leaves us alone, I won't go on any sort of hunting trip."

She blinked in response to the words I transmitted in her head. "You need to leave that to CJ." She crossed her arms and leaned back in the seat.

Her moody stare drilled through me, and I looked away. I wasn't about to promise her I wouldn't go after the bastard if he made good on his horrific promises. I had been through enough in my life to know that would push me over the edge for good.

"Can we not talk about this right now?" I finally asked.

The sharpness in Raven's glare softened as she studied me.

"Reliving that again rattled you, didn't it?"

I huffed and looked away. "I would expect more nightmares," I signed without looking her way. Her shift pulled my gaze back to her. Raven stood and swung a leg over my chair, taking a seat on my lap. Her arms wrapped around my neck, pulling me to her. I accepted the hug, ensnaring her just as tightly as she held me. Having her in my arms erased the horrors I'd had to recall this morning, and I couldn't help but be thankful for just how well she read my needs.

I pressed my lips to the soft nape of her neck and whispered, "I love you," in my broken tongue.

"I love you, too," she whispered back.

Instead of letting her go, I took her earlobe between my teeth and nibbled. She immediately squirmed in my arms, letting out a surprised squeal. A soft chuckle escaped from between my lips, but I didn't stop right away. I nuzzled her more, nibbling and sucking to my heart's content while her laughter rang out over the ocean.

I finally let go of her when Hannah banged on the glass door, yelling for Daddy to stop.

We both looked at our daughter with the same wide grin plastered on our faces. The worry carved in her young features transformed, and she smiled back at us before turning back to the television.

"I should spank you," Raven whispered in admonishment.

I raised an eyebrow. "Please do," I signed.

Her eyes narrowed, and she pointed at me. "Be good."

"Aren't I always?"

Blush heightened in her cheeks, and she pressed her lips against a smile. "Bad," she said and shook her head, getting off my lap.

I grinned up at her. "See what happens to me when I have a wild night with you? I just want more."

Before she turned away to head inside, I caught the smile and the silent promise to perhaps sneak another wild night in, depending on how well Hannah went down. I thought about using my unique talents to put her to sleep, but Raven would have my ass if I did that.

I closed my eyes, trying to enjoy the afternoon sun, but the moment my lids closed, my father's severed head and bloodstained wings painted the back of my eyelids. And just like that, all the heat of the day vanished, and my eyes jumped open.

I wondered what sort of manifestation the nightmares would take this time. Would it be my head tossed onto the pristine snow, or a far worse scenario?

I shivered and climbed out of the chair, heading inside to help my wife with dinner.

"What can I do?" I signed when she turned from the stove.

She pointed towards the cutting board, and the array of vegetables waiting to be chopped into a salad, without questioning why I was in the kitchen on her night. We usually trade off cooking duties while the other person is working with Hannah on reading or something equally stimulating, but Hannah was glued to the television program and I had no inclination to tear her from that to do some A-B-C's with her, or continue getting her acclimated to sign language.

I concentrated on chopping the array in front of me: Lettuce, tomatoes, cucumbers, peppers, carrots and mushrooms, throwing all the ingredients into a salad bowl and tossing before I cleaned up the cutting board and counter.

"Thank you," Raven said as she brought the pot of spaghetti to the table. "Hannah, dinner!"

Hannah came running in and neatly slid into the kitchen chair like a seasoned stuntman. She wiped the hair out of her face and then grinned at the two of us. The light in her eyes danced as she waited for us to serve her.

"What was your favorite thing that you did today?" I asked while Raven piled spaghetti with sauce on our plates and filled our salad bowls.

Hannah looked up at the ceiling; tapping her fork on her lips gently while her mind went through all the things she'd had fun doing. I was privy to the entire thought process, but I always waited until she articulated her favorite moment.

"Seeing you and mommy playing on the porch," she said, completely surprising me.

I glanced at Raven and her eyes were as wide as I imagined mine were.

"You didn't have fun with Grace, Gabe and Michael?" Raven asked.

"Yes, but Daddy asked what my favorite moment was, and it was hearing you two laugh."

I stared at my little girl, wondering when the last time I truly laughed in her presence was. I couldn't recall and Raven and I traded a glance.

When the hell had I gotten so serious?

She gave me a shoulder shrug wondering the same things I was, and at that moment, I made myself a promise. I would try harder to show my daughter that life is to be enjoyed, not overshadowed by darkness.

Angel Blood Chapter 9

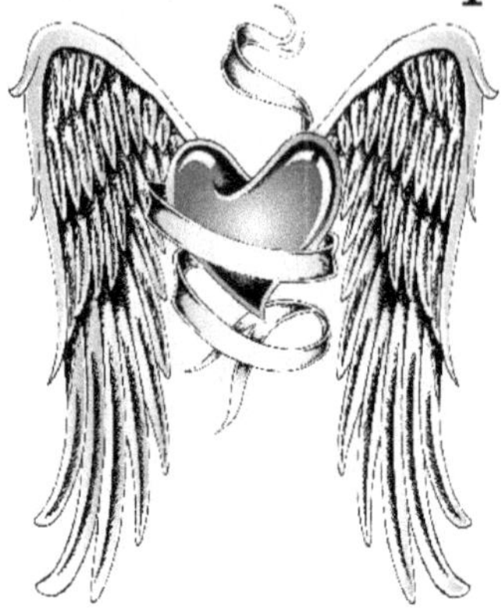

"PLEASE DON'T," RAVEN BEGGED as I approached her. She guarded Hannah, backing up with every step I took. Fear painted her features along with splattered blood.

The walls surrounding us were streaked with gore and the axe I carried dripped blood. I could feel the maniac inside advancing, but I had no control over my body and my mind screamed and pleaded for this madness to end. That I'd do anything they wanted if they would just spare my wife and child.

The floor was speckled with body parts. Arms, legs, torsos and heads of the ones I already slaughtered and all their vacant eyes were glued to my form. Devastation squeezed my insides as my gaze traveled over the familiar faces. CJ, Valerie, Alex, Steve, Jennifer and even Damian, Naomi and their children lay slain at my feet. All that was left was my wife and my child.

A maniacal laugh filled the small room as the axe came down again, slicing through Raven's delicate skin. Her blood was hot as it splashed me and the creature controlling my actions reveled in it.

Hannah's wail echoed off the walls, and I swung again, silencing the last scream.

I stood alone in a river of my family's blood and the vacant eyes of everyone I ever loved stared back.

A raspy scream shattered the silence, and I sat up in bed only to realize it was my scream. The nightmare still captured my mind, creating a terror so great I had a hard time drawing a breath.

The light brush of a hand ran across my back, and I jumped, turning towards the figure next to me. I almost struck the shape, but pulled my fist back before I smashed the face close to my shoulder.

"It's okay, it's only a nightmare," Raven said, her groggy voice cut through the fog, and I willed the lights on.

Blinking against the sudden brightness, I stared at her, horrified at the depravity of the nightmare. I shook for a good five minutes as she rubbed my back. I couldn't articulate more than a labored breath, and when my heart rate landed back in the realm of normal, I turned and wrapped my arms around her, pulling her to me so I could make sure she was really all right.

"You're crushing me," she mumbled against my chest, and I loosened my grip.

"Sorry," I whispered but still kept her in my arms to avoid the questions I knew were coming. They were already swarming in her head, and I had no words to tell my wife I dreamed of murdering her and my daughter. There was nothing remotely endearing about ending a night of passionate lovemaking with a bloodthirsty nightmare.

She squirmed, pushing back enough so she could look at my face. "Talk to me," she said, like it should be easy to share what had me so completely rattled that I didn't have the will to speak of it.

I slowly shook my head.

"Your parent's heads again?"

A near hysterical laugh escaped, and I looked at the ceiling, avoiding her gaze as I shook my head. If only it was that nightmare. As horrible as that one was, it paled compared to this violent monstrosity. This new manifestation was worse than all of my nightmares rolled into one horror fest, including the ones where Hannah was the one being carved up in Georgia.

As I stared at the swirl pattern on the drywall above me, I wondered what the hell the psychology of this dream was. They say nightmares manifest your deepest fears and this truly was the king of all nightmares.

When I brought my gaze back to hers, I drew in a deep breath, letting her out of my arms so I could sign.

"Everyone died," I started, and balled my hands into fists, clamping my eyes shut for a second. The whistle of the axe in my head made them spring back open, and I met Raven's gaze. "I killed everyone," I signed after a few minutes. "Including you and Hannah. I couldn't stop... killing."

The admission swelled in my chest, hurting the muscles in my back with the force of the breath I took. It was bad enough that I had the dream to begin with, but sharing the level of darkness that encompassed it was worse.

"I couldn't... control it."

Her palm cupped my cheek. "Do you know why you had the dream?"

I shrugged one shoulder.

"Was it the case you are working on with the police?"

"No." I was able to articulate the word, and I stared into her eyes, trying to analyze what could have triggered this. I expected a nightmare with severed heads; I just didn't expect to be the one responsible for the slaughtering.

I blinked and slipped out of bed, crossing to the sliding glass doors and staring out at the star filled sky. Was that the rationale? I felt responsible for the trail of deaths in some way?

She came up behind me and wrapped her arms around my waist, pressing gentle kisses on my slick back.

"You would never do anything like that," she said, staring over my shoulder at my reflection. I met her gaze.

I might not, but Lucifer would do it in a second, especially if he had what he wanted.

What I denied him.

Access to a body infused with the kind of magic mine had. If he had that, he could easily take out Damian. He could easily control Naomi to do his bidding and create an army of dark trinities to enslave the world. And if he ever got hold of Grace, who knows what the hell he could create.

Maybe it was all his heinous promises when I told him to go pound sand that made me feel responsible for the darkness overshadowing my family.

Maybe it was the fact that bastard's blood ran through my veins.

Maybe I was darker than I cared to admit.

I sighed and turned in her grasp, looking down into her beautiful, upturned face.

I knew I had the capacity to kill. I killed her father with no second thoughts, and I was never sure if it really was self-defense or not. Sure, he was coming at us intending to kill, but I could have disarmed him. I could have just incapacitated him, but I chose to end him with a punch to the throat.

"I don't think I'm as good as you seem to think I am," I signed.

"Bullshit, Tom. You have the heart of an angel." She swatted my chest with her hand.

I laughed. "That's what I'm afraid of."

"I'm not talking about Lucifer, you ass. I can see your aura. You can't hide your innate goodness from me, and if you had darkness inside you, I would have seen it a mile away and we would not be where we are right now."

I took a long inhalation and exhaled.

"I think I killed your father on purpose," I signed, finally admitting to something that hung heavy on my heart.

"That doesn't make you evil. That makes you human," she said. Her blue eyes were convincing enough, even without the conviction in her tone.

My lips twitched into a smile. This is why I loved this woman with every fiber of my being. She made me stronger than I really was. I pulled her into a hug.

"Come on, let's go back to bed," she said and peeled out of my arms, taking my hand in hers.

I let her lead me back to the bed, and I wrapped my arms around her, molding my body to hers. She fell asleep long before I did. While I appreciated her faith in me, I never told her I didn't immediately turn Lucifer down. I actually considered the offer, especially since it came with a promise to keep my wife and daughter safe.

It wasn't until I realized Raven would never forgive me if I sold the rest of my family out that I said no. That reason was more powerful than the possibility of having to kill my own brother and I felt like a shit heel for even considering the idea.

You see, Raven would rather die a thousand deaths than make a deal with the devil. I, on the other hand, would sell my soul to keep my family safe.

Angel Blood Chapter 10

THE PHONE RANG AT a little after eight and I grabbed it off the bedside table, yawning as I said, "Hey."

"Tom?" O'Keefe's voice sounded on the other end of the line.

"Ya," I said into the receiver.

"I need you and Mr. Andreas at the station in ten minutes. I think we might have another situation," He cleared his throat. "I would like you to come for a ride-along, just in case this is more than I can take on myself."

I had to force the smile onto my face as Raven rolled over and looked at me with those inquisitive eyes so full of concern. "O'a," I said, transmitting the full 'okay' so O'Keefe would know what the hell I was saying.

Ten minutes. It would take Damian that long to get halfway across York in the summer traffic. I sent him a text and then gave Raven a quick kiss before jumping out of bed for a record-breaking shower. All I smelled was sex and sweat. I didn't need to walk into the station reeking of Raven's sweet sensual perfume mixed with nightmare sweats.

The night left me feeling sluggish, seriously compromising my ability to rush. But I took the time to cross back to the bed and sit on the edge while I laced my sneakers. Flip-flops and shorts probably wouldn't have gone over well on a ride-along, so I donned a decent pair of jeans and a short-sleeved button-up shirt.

Raved kept her sleepy eyes on me and I turned my attention to her, wiping the stray wisps out of her face before I planted a kiss on her forehead and then lips.

"We're heading to Portland to investigate another missing person." I signed and caressed her cheek. "I'll be back as soon as I can."

"Just promise you'll be careful," she said.

I gave her a nod. "Love you," I signed and stood, heading out of the bedroom to her soft response.

When I pulled into the station, both Damian and O'Keefe stood outside, leaning on one of the police cruisers with their arms crossed. I gave them a half shrug as I crossed the distance.

"I said ten minutes," O'Keefe snapped.

"Sorry," I muttered and transmitted, blocking all of my rationale from Damian's probing stare.

"Just get in the damned car," he said, and stepped to the driver's side.

"I can't believe I got here before you did," Damian muttered and handed me a coffee after he slid into the front seat.

I grunted my thanks and sent the sign for sorry, again.

I spent the rest of the ride letting the caffeine do its thing and wake me up. The closer we got, the more on edge I got. It didn't stop, even when we pulled into the driveway. We got out of the cruiser at the house and every nerve in my body thrummed. My stomach dropped and I couldn't pinpoint what the issue was, but things were not right.

And then I saw the shimmering shadow, and I sighed, even before O'Keefe could knock on the door. Damian came up short as well and his gaze shot to mine like he was seeing what I was seeing. The ghost of the latest victim looked out the window at us as we approached.

"We are already too late," I transmitted, and O'Keefe looked over his shoulder at me, his finger poised over the doorbell.

His eyes followed mine, and he huffed at the empty window. He didn't see the ghost that stared at me, and his finger stabbed the doorbell.

I traded a glance with the ghost of Mrs. Freeman, trying to convey just how sorry I was.

The door opened seconds later, and a frantic Mr. Freeman stared at us. O'Keefe pulled out his badge and Mr. Freeman's gaze hardened.

"It's about time they sent someone over. I've been calling you people since last night. There is no way Ellie would have just run off."

O'Keefe glanced at us, but I was too preoccupied with the ghost that now stood in the entryway behind Mr. Freeman.

"Where?" I signed, like the ghost could relay the information, but she just stared with wide eyes and a gaping maw. The holes in her neck were bruised, almost as if a machine was used to suck out every drop of blood from her body.

"When did you last see her?" O'Keefe asked.

"She went out to pick up some milk at the store around eight, and that was the last time I saw her. When she wasn't home by nine, I knew something wasn't right. She didn't answer her cell phone either, and that is not like my wife." His eyes darted between Damian and O'Keefe before falling on me. "What's wrong with him?"

My gaze shifted from the ghost of his wife to him.

"He's a psychic that we employ for missing person cases," O'Keefe explained.

The man's eyebrows arched in response.

"Especially where finding the missing person quickly is paramount to their survival."

I ignored the blatant stare, moved my gaze back to Mrs. Freeman, and signed. "I am going to need your help to bring you home."

She just shrugged her shoulders. "I don't know where he has me."

"Can you give me anything to go on?"

She looked up at the ceiling and tapped her lips. "When I got back into my car, I felt a sting on my neck and I saw a shadow in the backseat, but before I could turn, I lost control of all my muscles."

I raised an eyebrow. The only time I can recall something acting that fast had to be in Steve's memory banks when the Slasher drugged him. He was aware, but couldn't control his muscles.

"I couldn't feel a thing," she added softly.

That differed from Steve's ordeal. He felt every horror that man rained on him.

"But you were awake?"

"Yes."

"Did you see who or what was responsible?"

She shook her head.

"He blindfolded me and moved me into the passenger seat. I couldn't speak and I couldn't move, but I could hear." She swallowed. "I could hear his plans for me," she added, in only a whisper.

I waited as her image shimmered in and out; her hold waning, repelled by fear. Fear made ghosts disappear, and I didn't push because I needed her to remain tangible, to remain talking.

After a few moments, she solidified again, and I asked, "Was it a big space or small space?"

She cocked her head, thinking. "There was an echo, so I think it might have been big, and it smelled like mold."

"A basement?" I signed, transmitting to the ghost.

She shrugged. "Now all I smell is seaweed."

I exhaled and closed my eyes, hanging my head. If she smelled the ocean, that meant the killer had already dumped the body and was targeting the next victim. I opened my eyes and moved my glance to Damian. He held the same stoic expression, except I recognized the building alarm in his eyes.

"We will do everything we can to bring your wife home to you, but I'm afraid we may already be too late," I signed, and Damian translated for me.

Mr. Freeman's expression slowly fell, and tears filled his eyes. I purposely did not listen to his morbid thoughts; instead, I gave him a nod and turned, heading back to the car. I slid into the passenger seat and waited for Damian and O'Keefe to return to the car.

Angel Blood Chapter 11

"WHAT THE HELL WAS that all about?" O'Keefe asked, after he closed the driver's door, sending a glare my way.

"She's already dead," I signed, without the additional transmission. "We need to go to where the others were found." I added, and Damian was kind enough to translate.

O'Keefe glanced at me. "Are you sure?"

"He was talking to her ghost," Damian said.

O'Keefe glanced at Damian in the rearview mirror before sending his sharp stare in my direction. "Did you ask if she could identify the killer?" His tone was as condescending as I remembered when I was seventeen.

I glared at him and crossed my arms. "I'm a damned good investigator, Captain." The thought barreled out, and he winced.

"Did you ask?" he said through clenched teeth.

"You really think I'm an idiot, don't you?" It was my turn to snap, and I transmitted at full volume just out of aggravation. The physical discomfort written on his scrunched features made me soften my tone. I needed him functional and not blinded by a migraine from my recklessness. "Of course, I asked. And no, she didn't see her attacker, but she said she felt something like a bite on her neck and within seconds, she couldn't move. She was blindfolded and brought to a damp and dark area that echoed. I'm guessing a large basement or even an abandoned mill of some sort."

O'Keefe started the car and headed towards Wright's Warf. There was already a circus of police lights when we pulled in. The three of us got out.

"Stay here until I find out what is going on," O'Keefe ordered, and Damian and I exchanged a glance, but we stayed put.

O'Keefe stepped into the chaos, leaving Damian and me standing next to the car like a pair of junior detectives not cleared for a homicide case. I closed my eyes, choosing to infringe upon the conversation he was having with the lead officer.

Get out of my head. O'Keefe's thought overshadowed the conversation, and I opened my eyes, catching his glare. I sent a smirk in response, but it quickly faded with the next set of facts.

Two people were found in the same condition, both bled dry and tossed out like a sack of garbage.

My gaze snapped to Damian, but he had already pulled his phone from his pocket and was busy dialing home. His warning was simple. Get to my brother's house with the family.

I followed suit, texting Raven to do the same and then followed with a warning to CJ. His response came before my wife's and I felt a moment of relief until Raven's text popped up.

I'll head over as soon as Hannah wakes from her nap.

My gut clenched. Our house was the farthest north and the first this psycho would hit if he continued his systematic elimination of angel blood. I didn't want to alarm her, but I also didn't want her vulnerable and every nerve in my body shouted to get her out of the house.

There was only one person left between Portland and York, and she was in Ogunquit. Just a fifteen-minute ride from our place. I took a seat in the car and gave Damian a quick glance before I bowed my head and did the one thing I vowed I'd never do again. I projected myself into my house.

Raven glanced up at my image and her eyebrows formed that surprised arc that always made me smile, but it fell short this time. I didn't have time to enjoy her cuteness and my lack of a smile formed a frown on her face.

"I need you to wake her and go now," I signed.

Her features transformed, and she crossed her arms. "I most certainly will not," she said in that stubborn Irish brogue.

I inhaled, trying to calm the building annoyance. "Hannah is in danger," I signed slowly, watching her turn from that stubborn jut of her chin to wide-eyed panic.

Her gaze locked with mine and there were no more questions. She gave a nod, and I felt the pull back to the car an hour away from my daughter. When I opened my eyes, O'Keefe was sitting in the driver's seat, just staring at me.

Damian was already seated in the back as the car idled.

"What?" I transmitted.

"Damian said, uh, he said you stepped out for a minute."

I nodded and pointed for us to get moving.

"The names match the list," Damian said quietly as O'Keefe pulled back on the road.

I already knew that. I also had a sneaking suspicion that all this was staged in some way, and I glanced in the mirror at Damian. He sent me an imperceptible nod, telling me we were both on the same page.

"Is that what your brother looked like at the other end?" O'Keefe asked.

"Ya," I said.

"It never ceases to freak me the fuck out," Damian said from the back seat, pulling a chuckle from O'Keefe.

"Imagine actually doing it," I transmitted, keeping my eyes on the passing scenery.

"I can't," O'Keefe mumbled under his breath.

Neither one of them could grasp the feeling. CJ and I share the same distaste for astral projection. I'm not sure my mother ever got used to it either, but both my father and Steve used it as a weapon. To them, it offered a profound sense of security, but to me, it just magnified what kind of an inhuman freak I had become.

Angel Blood Chapter 12

O'KEEFE'S PHONE RANG JUST as we crossed through the tolls back into York. He listened, sighed, and hung up. Without enlightening us to the content of the call, he swung off the southbound side of the highway and immediately re-entered on the northbound side, heading back the way we came, except instead of the long drive back to Portland, he took the first exit for Wells, turning south on Route 1 and backtracking to the Ogunquit town line.

My heart rammed against my ribcage as we pulled to a stop over the Ogunquit River. The latest body was dumped over the side of Route 1 into the river. When I saw the arm hanging out of the body bag, my throat closed. This body had been there for a while, certainly longer than the bodies dumped in Portland this morning, and that scared the hell out of me.

"We have to get home," I signed to Damian. It had only been a couple of hours since we'd left Portland, but with every second that passed, the alarms inside my head clamored louder.

He exhaled and glanced at O'Keefe talking with the Ogunquit police.

I shot off a text to Raven, telling her where I was and that I'd be a little longer, and then refocused on O'Keefe. When the name of the victim surfaced, I glanced at Damian. His reaction confirmed it. He wiped his face and leaned against the car, defeat written into the lines surrounding his eyes.

Whoever this killer was, he was operating with a playbook that was several steps ahead of us. I glanced at my phone, expecting the usual 'k' from Raven, but nothing had been returned. The unease increased to a silent tension that wrapped around my midsection like a python squeezing the life out of me.

I sent a text off to CJ asking if Raven had gotten there. His response took me out at the knees and I grabbed for the hood of the car to steady myself. My mind clouded over at the morbid possibility and my feet moved of their own accord. Before I was even aware of what I was doing, I was in the driver's seat, turning the ignition key.

Damian slid into the front passenger seat. "You can't steal O'Keefe's car," he said. "Give him a second."

I stared at him like he had lost his mind, and then the driver's door opened.

"Get in back," O'Keefe said.

I clenched my teeth, but something told me I shouldn't be the one driving right now and I relinquished the seat. Before I closed the back door, O'Keefe hit the gas. He went full board with lights and sirens, and the way he drove earned him an ounce of respect.

"The last time you saw her was when we were in Portland, correct?" he asked without taking his eyes from the road.

"Yes," I transmitted. "She agreed to go to my brother's house, but she hasn't gotten there yet," I added. "And she didn't answer my text."

O'Keefe's eyes moved to mine in the rearview mirror. "You have the ability to check the house. Do it."

I blinked, feeling foolish for not thinking of it myself, but I nodded and closed my eyes, concentrating on home. The pull started in the center of my chest, and I opened my eyes to my empty living room. All the rooms were empty, and her day-trip bag was gone as well. She always took that whenever she was going to be anywhere for a period. I crossed and opened the front door. The car was gone.

I closed it and crossed to the garage entrance just to make sure and the garage was equally empty as everything else. My heart pounded in my throat and my breathing started that short rasp of panic. The pull yanked me back to the car and my wild eyes met O'Keefe's in the rearview mirror.

"She's not there. Neither is her car."

"Color, make, model, and license plate," O'Keefe barked at me.

"Blue Ford Explorer, RAVEN."

O'Keefe nodded and picked up his radio microphone. "I have a report of a stolen vehicle. Blue Ford Explorer, Maine, Romeo, Alpha, Victor, Echo, November. I need this to go out on an APB right now."

The dispatcher on the other end repeated the information back and assured O'Keefe that the bulletin would go out immediately. He replaced the microphone in the holder and glanced at me.

"Thank you," I said with my mind and the proper sign language gesture.

He gave a curt nod and focused. Twenty minutes later, we pulled into my still empty driveway, and I headed inside, hoping things had changed since I projected into the house less than a half hour before.

"Is she there yet?" I texted to CJ.

The phone rang, and I snatched it off the wall.

"No, but everyone else is. What do you need from me?" CJ asked.

I scanned the house with my heart pounding in my throat, unsure of how to answer him. I needed my wife and daughter and an icy fear spilled into my body, freezing me in place.

"Tom, it will be okay," he said softly, but he stopped short of adding a promise. "Steve's already out looking for her."

I traded a glance with Damian and O'Keefe standing in the entryway.

"Thanks," I transmitted and hung up and closed my eyes wondering why my wife wouldn't call me if she was in danger.

The harsh truth bit at every centimeter of my skin. She was dead, or the madman threatened Hannah. Raven would do anything for our daughter, even if it put herself in harm's way.

Angel Blood Chapter 13

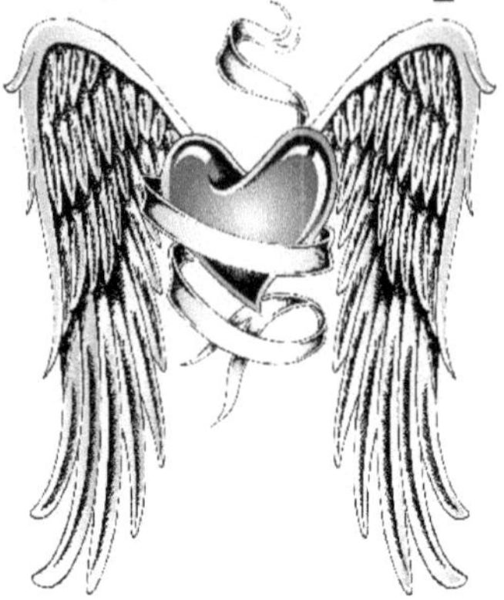

I GLANCED AT THE house as we pulled into the driveway. CJ stood in the open doorway, looking more tired than I've ever seen him. He knew something of the panic assaulting me, so did Damian. I had already decided. As soon as Damian was with his family, I was going hunting for this bastard.

I didn't plan on going inside, and from the way O'Keefe lingered by the car, I got the same sense of urgency from him. He had had enough exposure to my wife in the aftermath of the Windwalker case to have a small soft spot for her, and he was damned if he'd let this killer terrorize his town.

"Take a fly by later," I sent to Damian as he stepped next to my brother. He sent a nod. Once it was dark, he'd transform into a giant hawk and take a once over. From an aerial vantage point, he might see something those of us on the ground would miss.

The radio squawked in the car as I slid into the passenger seat, but O'Keefe didn't bother answering right away. Instead, he glanced at me. "You sure you don't want to stay with your family?"

"I can't just sit still," I transmitted. "And you know damned well that if I'm not with you, I'd end up hunting on my own. Then you'd probably throw my ass in jail."

He sent a half smile in my direction with a nod. "You're probably right," he said, and picked up the radio microphone. "O'Keefe here."

"We found the car in Hannaford's parking lot, sir," the dispatcher said.

"I'm on my way," he replied and spun the car around, heading out without any further delay.

When we got to Hannaford's, the police had sectioned off the farthest corner and our SUV sat in the second to last space. The forensics team was already combing through the vehicle for evidence.

Steve stood by the crew, scanning computer results; he looked over the roof of the car, directly at me, as I got out of the car. The concern in his eyes made me pause. He gave a nod to the officer and stepped around to meet me before I got close.

"You shouldn't be here," he said and sent a glare towards O'Keefe.

I pulled out the deputy shield O'Keefe had given me and raised an eyebrow.

"You are too close to the case," Steve said in response.

"Tell us what you found," O'Keefe said to the approaching detective.

The detective raised an evidence bag containing a needle. "This contains traces of etorphine," he said in a tone that I didn't understand. O'Keefe sucked air through his teeth, and I glanced at him.

"What the hell is etorphine?" I signed and transmitted, and Steve grabbed my arm, leading me away as O'Keefe conferred with the rest of the forensic team.

"It's used by veterinarians to knock out big animals."

I stared at him, waiting for the rest.

"It knocks out humans like that," he snapped his fingers. "And can be fatal if the antidote isn't given within a matter of hours." He shoved his hands in his pocket and dropped his gaze to the ground. "We think he must have had a van because no one in the parking lot noticed him transferring Raven or Hannah from the car."

Before I could ask anything else, a sound echoed, like someone had set off a firework display. Over the trees toward York Harbor, a black plume of smoke rolled into the sky. All activity in the parking lot stopped for a second, and then the chatter started on all the radios. O'Keefe moved away, pointing for the team to continue what they were doing, and he waved for both Steve and me. The address of the explosion rang through the scanners and before I knew it, both Steve and I were in a dead run.

The address was my brother's house. Where most of the angel blood congregated. Shit.

Steve didn't bother with O'Keefe's car; he was in his little BMW flying out of the parking lot before we even backed out of our spot. A second explosion rocked the road as we turned the corner onto Roaring Rock. I stared at the two towers of smoke so closely aligned and let out my breath.

As we turned the bend, approaching the iron gates that once held my family's home, smoldering rubble met my gaze. The house next door was in the same condition and the fire trucks had beaten us to the location.

Steve's car was stopped in the middle of the road and empty. The door hung open as he stood on the lawn with his hands threaded through his hair.

"We're in back," CJ's thought crept into my mind, and I exhaled, leaning back in the passenger seat while a wave of relief swept through me. O'Keefe pulled to a stop, and I got out, crossing to Steve and signing their location. He didn't wait for me; instead, he bolted around the cleared side of the house. I followed, with O'Keefe on my heels.

As we passed onto the back lawn, CJ had Alex in his arms and Valerie stood by his side. Both of them just stared at what remained of their house. Damian and his family stood close by and Jennifer sat on the rock wall, just as stunned as the rest of them.

The debris field was more to the front than the backyard and I stared at the untouched pool and the expanse of green lawn before turning and looking at the rubble of the home I grew up in.

"What happened?" Steve asked, as he skidded to a stop in front of Jennifer.

She just shrugged.

"I had less than a minute to get everyone out of the house, between Jennifer's vision and the explosion," CJ said, still staring at the house.

I started toward CJ and when I was halfway across the lawn, a third explosion in the distance pulled all our gazes to the left. Across town, on the bluff, another plume of smoke colored the sky. My stomach dropped as I watched smoke billow from the exact location of our home.

All our memories reduced to rubble, and my gaze bounced back to CJ's. The war had started in earnest, and we knew who was directing the troops against us. Just the thought of Lucifer calling the shots burned through my shock and I clenched my fists.

The promises he'd made to both CJ and me regarding my family shook me to the core, and the urgency to find my wife overrode all the destruction around me. They had to be in town still.

I just had to figure out where.

Angel Blood Chapter 14

O'KEEFE ASSEMBLED US IN one of the larger meeting rooms at the station, leaving us to our own devices while he sent his deputies out to get us something to eat and drink.

"What are you doing about all this?" I signed, as O'Keefe entered the room with a stack of pizza boxes. He was followed in by another officer with a tray of drinks. He placed the boxes on the table.

"We're taking a closer look at the veterinarians in the area that have access to etorphine."

"And how many have access?" Steve asked as he opened the nearest box and dug into the pizza.

O'Keefe looked away and cleared his throat. "There are only two on record between here and Portland. York Wild Kingdom and the first victim up in Portland." He returned his gaze to mine. "They think some of the drug is missing from the victim's office."

Shit. I pressed my lips together, trying to clear my mind of all thoughts. I stood and crossed to the window, glancing out at the dwindling light. It had been six hours since I saw Raven in our house. A body could be drained of blood in six hours, and yet if she was dead, I was certain her ghost would have found me by now.

There were precious few large remote areas around here and even fewer abandoned ones. With the way this guy was killing, the outdoors wasn't the place to do this, especially during the summer when the risk of hikers and trail riders was high. Which led me back to abandoned buildings.

"Eat something," Steve said as he stepped next to me, handing me a plate with a couple of slices of pizza.

The last thing I wanted to do was feed the acid burn in my stomach, but I took the plate, anyway. I kept silent and took a few bites before Steve put his hand on my shoulder. His silent support didn't help.

"I need to find them," I projected.

He nodded, but before he could speak, Jennifer gasped behind us. We spun, and I had just a moment to view her eyes—the milky eyes of precognition—before her vision assaulted me.

"WHAT HAVE YOU DONE with my daughter?" Raven's soft Irish lilt fell in the low light as the bonds holding her in place tightened. She shifted and tried to twist her wrists against the bindings, but she had no wiggle room. Her knees were bound to handles on the table at her sides. Her ankles were tethered as well and her range of motion for her lower legs was perhaps a couple of inches. The way this madman bound her left her exposed.

The chill caressing her bare skin gave her an indication of either air conditioning or being in a basement. The space wasn't huge, but it was bigger than the average cellar. A hint of ammonia filled the air, along with an underlying smell of feces, even though what she could see was clean.

"Don't worry your pretty head about that right now, sweetheart," he said, pushing her hair away from her face with a gloved hand. The lamp on his hardhat only gave her a sense of a figure, and he wasn't a small man by any means.

She caught a hint of a tattoo on his forearm before he pulled his hand away. But she couldn't identify it; just a blur of color, and then it was gone.

"Let her go," Raven begged. "You can do anything you want to me, but please don't hurt my little girl."

"Sorry, princess, she's on the list," the killer said, his voice flat with no discernible accent.

"What list?" Raven asked, trying to keep him talking. If he was talking, maybe that would buy Hannah some time.

"The same one that dictates exactly what has to be done with you."

"And what is that?"

The rolling of an industrial sized barrel crossed the smooth floor into her line of sight. He righted it, peeled the cover off, shining his headlamp into the container as he reached in and took a handful. When he lifted it into view and let the sharp red and black stones filter through his fingers, she knew exactly what the barrel held.

"Blood stone?" she asked, as confusion clouded her mind.

The light flashed in her direction, blinding her. "Yes, ma'am," he replied, and reached down, picking up a package from the floor, and put it on a small table near her. When the box opened, he huffed a laugh. "My boss has a really twisted sense of humor," he said and pulled one item out to show her. The smooth shaft caught the light and Raven gasped.

"That's apparently the last item I get to use," he said with a chuckle, shifting the paper next to the box before returning the obscene dildo to the table. The next item he picked up looked like an industrial-powered calking gun. He unthreaded the cap from the tube, twisting it off and scooped some rocks from the barrel in his hand, dropping them into the cap. She watched as they easily fell through the hole.

"That'll do." He crossed to the table and put the cap next to her head. A ripping sound followed, and duct tape covered her mouth.

"I can't have you screaming to wake the dead while I stuff you with rocks, now can I?"

Terror passed over her features when he picked up the cap and stepped between her bound legs.

"JENNIFER," STEVE'S VOICE CUT through the vision.

The plate fell from my hand, and I bolted. I had no idea where I was going, but I needed air. I needed not to hurl what little I ate, and I didn't stop running until I was standing knee deep in the water at Short Sands.

My breath hitched harshly in my chest as the horror of what was happening to my wife settled into every fiber of my body. Lucifer had threatened to stuff her with bloodstone until her intestines burst and that was exactly the intent in Jennifer's vision.

The cold water bit at my legs, reminding me of where I was. I turned to head back to the police station and take this investigation to the next level. I couldn't let that vision happen.

CJ stood in the water behind me, his face as ashen as mine must have been.

"Jesus. I am so sorry," he started, and I shoved him with everything I had.

He went down with a splash.

"She isn't dead, yet!" I screamed in my inarticulate tongue. My face heated with the building fury. "Don't fucking talk like she is dead!"

CJ climbed to his feet and put his hands out. "Calm down."

"Calm down?" I snapped with a glare.

He let out a nervous laugh. "Not the best choice of words, but I need your head clear. I'm too fucking exhausted to see straight, never mind analyze what was in that vision. I need you to put aside your panic and everything else assaulting you and get your fucking head clear."

"Why?" I couldn't help but growl.

"You need to look at what we just saw with as much objectivity as you can muster," he said, pointing at me. "Because there has to be some kind of clue as to where she is. We need to figure that out before he gets that god awful machine going."

I blinked at him, trying to shed my wife's palpable fear. She had no idea what he meant by Hannah being on the list, but I did, and it chilled me to the core. My horror was nearly as debilitating as hers, and I didn't even know if my daughter was still alive.

"We need to walk through everything, Tom," CJ said as he wrung the hem of his shirt out.

I stared at him for a few minutes before I started walking up the shore. "I don't know if I can." Tears blurred the Goldenrod sign, and I hung my head. "She was terrified."

His hand landed on my neck, and he pulled me into a hug. "I know, but she needs us to figure out the clues she fed to us. You know damned well she's operating under the assumption that we're going to see what's happening at some point. She knew Jennifer and Steve were in town."

I stepped out of his awkward embrace and stared at him. Getting hold of the beast raging inside me was easier in theory than reality, but he was right. I had to put my shit-show aside and focus.

I took a seat in the sand, shuffling it through my fingers as I went through the vision in slow motion. CJ sat next to me, filtering through what Jennifer fed us in the same way, keeping his mind open to me as to his observations. I did the same.

"Did you see... fencing?" I asked as I scanned the room through Raven's eyes.

"Chain link?"

"Yeah, on the perimeter of one side."

CJ glanced at me biting his lower lip with a nod.

"What the fuck?" I asked and then shook my head to clear it again. The clock was not our friend, and the longer it took us to pinpoint her surroundings, the longer it would take to get her out of there, before catastrophic damage was done.

"Does it seem familiar to you?" CJ asked.

I shook my head, but something at the back of my mind tickled. I did another slow scan of the memory and then sat up straight up, like the lights suddenly flipped on.

"It's a kennel." I signed and snapped my head in CJ's direction. His eyes widened.

"But it's not a normal one. The kennels on the inside are limited, almost like a temporary shelter," he added. His gaze dropped to the sand, and the crease between his eyes deepened.

"Either way, we need to let O'Keefe know," I said, getting to my feet. I offered my hand to CJ and helped him up.

We jogged back to the station and entered through the same door I'd left. The family looked up at us as I glanced around for O'Keefe, but he wasn't in the room.

"I told him I thought the killer had her in a kennel or some kind of animal shelter, and they are out looking right now," Jennifer said. Her eyes were bloodshot, like she had been crying.

Valerie crossed and deposited Alex in CJ's arms before she turned to me. "When you go, you have to take me. I can fix whatever damage they've done."

I stared into my sister-in-law's sincere eyes and slowly nodded. As much as I didn't want to put her in harm's way, she had the God-given gift of healing. And my wife and daughter may need that miracle edge to survive.

"Val," CJ interrupted, but her warning glare shut him down.

"She's my best friend," she said. That's all she needed to say.

The bond between Raven and Valerie was stronger than blood, and had been since Valerie walked into our house. They'd clicked in a way that Naomi and Valerie never had, and now she shared my panic. I felt it radiating off her, and I'm sure she felt mine just as acutely.

Angel Blood Chapter 15

"HOW LONG AGO DID they leave?" I signed, meeting Steve's gaze. I had been pacing enough so that the wet fabric of my jeans had started to chafe. I thought about getting a change of clothes and then remembered that I had nothing left to change into. At least not in York and a slow burning anger surfaced.

Steve glanced at his watch and stood, disappearing into the heart of the station, leaving us without much of an answer. Time wasn't something I was accustomed to measuring and right now, a second felt like an eternity. I had no idea what qualified as a minute or an hour. Either way, the longer I paced, the more unsettled I became.

I finally ripped open the door to the station and scanned the group; zeroing in on Steve at the far side of the room. I crossed and took the space next to him, looking down at the map spread on the desk.

"I got it. It looks like you've covered all the kennels in the area," he said into the phone. "Did you check the zoo?" He nodded and sighed, rubbing his face for a minute. "Thanks for the update," he added and hung up the phone before he corralled me back into the room.

"They've been to every kennel and vet office in town, including the zoo. Nothing," he said, looking between Jennifer and I. "Are you sure it was a kennel?"

I exchanged a glance with her and CJ and then closed my eyes, willing my brain to search the scene for more clues. My eyes snapped open.

"Maybe the fencing we saw was more for a storage area?" I signed but CJ was shaking his head.

"It was familiar to both of us, Tom," he said, staring at me like he was missing something, too. "Where else did we take Sam?" he asked and just the reference to my father's dog opened the floodgates of memories.

I turned to Steve. "I doubt it would be Petsmart."

He huffed a small laugh.

The one place Sam became completely disobedient was that store. I remember being pulled down aisle after aisle until Sam found what he wanted. The memory brought a smile to my lips, but the reality of our situation made it fleeting.

"The only other place we brought him was the groomers," I said, looking up.

CJ and I locked eyes, and ours both widened, before we could say anything, Steve spun on his heel and marched back to the desk he was at before. The officer overseeing the coordination effort looked up at him as he relayed the information. There were three groomers that we took Sam to over the years we had him, and I tried to remember where they were in town.

"They'll look into it," Steve said when he stepped back in the room.

"I can't just sit around and wait," I signed.

"You can, and you will," Steve said, pointing at me.

The last time I intervened in a case, I ended up in jail as a suspect.

"Fine, but if we hear nothing in the next half hour, I'm going to start looking myself."

"You can't go off half-cocked," Steve said, staring me down.

He didn't need to remind me of the last time I took matters into my own hands. I was already painfully aware of that mistake.

"The hell I can't." I returned his hard glare.

"With what?" Steve asked.

I pressed my lips together and pulled my car keys out of my pocket. "I drove here this morning." I signed and shoved them back in my pocket.

"Then I'm going with you," he said.

At least if I was with him, my affinity for getting into trouble might be tempered. The same thought paraded through his mind, and I nodded. "Okay," I signed, and this time I actually glanced at a clock in order to get a beat on the passage of time.

I slowly paced the room, trying not to disturb the baby sleeping on Valerie's chest on the couch in the corner. Her eyes drooped as well, and I traded a glance with CJ, cocking my head in their direction. He nodded in response. The collective communication between the two of us could be summed up by head shakes and shoulder shrugs, but we both knew what was going on in each other's heads.

The fact neither he nor Steve promised things would be okay was an indication of how grave this was. I couldn't face the possibility that I might lose my wife and child today. Every time that thought surfaced, panic overrode my bloodstream, and I focused on something else.

Damian's kids were all quietly coloring at the table. It was as if they knew this wasn't the place to run around like the wild children they usually were. Grace looked up and gave me a strained smile. I wanted to ask her why she smiled at me like that, but Steve tapped my shoulder and then his wrist.

Time was up and we both slid out into the heart of the station, leaving the rest of them in the quiet calm that pervaded the room. We stopped at the desk.

"Any word?" Steve asked.

"Not yet," the young officer answered.

"We're stepping out for a few," Steve said and got a nod in response. As soon as we cleared the door, he looked at me and said, "I'm driving." He didn't say anything more until we were seated in the car. "Where to?"

I pulled out my phone and searched dog groomer. There was one right down the street from the police station, one right near Hanniford's, and one on Woodbridge. I showed the three to Steve.

"We can hit the closest one and then go to the one near Hanniford's." He glanced at me, and I nodded. After all, Raven's car was found at the Hanniford's lot. I almost asked him to forego the closest place, but I saw the benefit of being systematic.

We slowed down at the sight of the police car in the driveway, but the officers were talking to the owner at the door.

"They've already done a walk-through of the place," I said, catching pieces of their thoughts. "It's clear."

Steve nodded and headed out to Route 1. The second shop was dark, and the parking lot was empty. Even though this was the closest one to where Raven was last seen, it didn't have the right vibe. We pulled into the lot behind the building and got out of the car.

"They share the building with other businesses," I signed and transmitted, and glanced at Steve. He nodded.

"We should still have a look, just in case," he said, approaching the door. He turned towards me. "Can you do the honors?" he asked, pointing at the locked door.

I closed my eyes, concentrating on unlocking the door. It was an easy lock to mentally pick, and the door popped open. The moment we stepped inside, I knew this was not the place. It was far too small to house the kill room I saw in Jennifer's vision.

"This isn't it," I said, transmitting the words, but Steve still did a quick walk-through.

"That leaves the one on Woodbridge," he said as he locked the door and closed it behind him.

The stress had my muscles knotted. If the one on Woodbridge wasn't it, I was all out of ideas and I didn't think there was much time left. Too many minutes had passed since Jennifer's vision and if that marked when the bastard started his torture, he would have long finished by now and that thought scared the living daylights out of me.

Steve gave my shoulder a pat as he navigated back toward York Harbor and Woodbridge Street.

The only thought looping through my head was that we were out of time.

Angel Blood Chapter 16

O'KEEFE'S TRUCK SAT IN the small parking lot in front of the last dog-grooming place and we pulled into the parking lot next to his cruiser. We got out, and I put my hand on the hood. The vehicle was cold, and I shot Steve a glance.

"It's cold." We both looked at the building on high alert. The front door of the dog grooming shop hung ajar and as we approached, Steve pulled out his service revolver and put his hand out for me to cover the rear.

"I'll go first, just back me up if the shit hits the fan, okay?" Steve whispered, and clicked off his safety.

While I had the power to level the building, he had the skill and experience to clear each room without potential harm to either himself or any innocent in the building. I was so wound up that if I went first, I might toast the first person I stumbled on. I gave him a nod and reeled my nerves in as I followed him through the door.

The front waiting room and reception desk met our slow scan as our eyes adjusted to the dark. The usually brightly lit entry was eerily dressed in shadows and Steve quickly covered the space, making sure he targeted corners and under the counters. It took him seconds to clear the room, and he ended his sweep at the side of the door leading to the grooming area and the kennels beyond.

"Clear," he whispered, and both our gazes landed on the adjoining door. The small window was shrouded in darkness and didn't give us any indication of activity. Steve took a glance through the glass, but he shook his head, counting on his fingers to three before moving into the space.

The door was spring-loaded and swung closed before I could get through the space and by the time I pushed the door open again, Steve was writhing in the center of the room, hissing and spouting foul curses. With the racket he was making, I figured whatever stealth approach we were attempting was already foiled, and I willed all the lights in the place to turn on.

Bright lights momentarily blinded me, but when my vision cleared, my gaze locked on the writhing mass in the center of the room and it took a moment to figure out what was all over Steve. A trap door in the ceiling had opened and dropped a shitload of snakes on him. And they were in full attack mode, biting like there was no tomorrow. Shock turned into a burning panic because I had no idea how to pinpoint the power I held. If I tried to annihilate the snakes, I could very well take Steve right along with them.

Instead of attacking all at once, I focused on each creature, one at a time, flinging them into the wall with deadly force. I stopped counting after twenty, and while freeing him from the attacking reptiles only took five minutes, Steve dropped to his knees, unable to make it as far as any of the others. His breath wheezed, and the gun dropped from his grip. I looked at the other bodies. Two officers lay still, and closer to the other door lay Captain O'Keefe, just as still as the others, and I gulped down the burn of bile.

Steve interrupted my blatant stare with a raspy, "Go." He heaved the word out just before he collapsed, but his eyes moved from me to the door and back.

The horror of seeing Steve incapacitated raked through me, and a sliver of guilt rammed my chest as I stepped beyond him, picking up his gun. I crossed to the door. When I glanced back in his direction, his eyes were still tracking me and his mind echoed his last order.

I nodded and closed my eyes, sending out an SOS to Valerie. We had left the station without her, but I knew she would be on high alert, just as much as I was right now. I owed Steve a fighting chance.

"Help is on the way," I transmitted to him.

"Go. Now," his voice reprimanded me, and I turned back to the door, showing the same care he had when he entered the building. "Be careful," his whisper caught me before I pushed through the door and I glanced back at him with a nod.

I would not take any chances. Not after the trap I'd just navigated. I took a second to gather my strength and imagined building a force field around me that would protect me from falling snakes or any other booby traps that may be set between me and my family.

When I was sure I had enough of a shield in place, I swung the door open and stepped through with the gun at the ready. The overhead lights showed me the situation in prime detail and I had to concentrate to keep from dropping to my knees.

Raven was tied to a metal table that looked like the one I had been strapped to in Georgia, but it was tipped at a forty-five degree angle. The duct tape remained across her mouth, keeping her whimpers almost silent. Her arms were stretched over her head and her legs were hip distance apart and tied to the edge of the table. Her abdomen looked like someone had taken a baseball bat to it and drops of blood ran in slow paths down the insides of her legs.

Pain filled her eyes, and her voice echoed in my head. "Trap."

I took a step forward, right into a wire, and the bastard had the audacity to smile before a wall of fire and debris filled my vision. The roar that followed almost drowned Raven's wail of anguish. Heat wrapped around me, but retreated just as quickly. Shrapnel hovered, impaled in my invisible shield, blocking my view, and I snarled; turning what should have ripped me to shreds into a dust cloud.

My wife's captor was no longer smiling. Instead, his jaw hung open and his dark eyes widened. He looked like every cliché mercenary I had ever seen in the movies. Built like a two-ton truck, and I hoped he was just as dumb.

I stepped farther into the room, refocusing the gun on the bastard. That seemed to unlock his paralysis, and he stepped closer to Raven, putting a blade across her throat.

I took a quick glance to my left, validating there was no other trap, and my gaze locked on my little girl. Hannah hung by her feet with her arms bound at her side. Her face was almost purple from the blood pooling in her head. A tube ran from her throat, emptying into a gallon sized milk jug. What alarmed me the most was that the container was almost half-full, and my gaze snapped back to the madman.

"Mother fucker," I said, but my inability to articulate just made it sound like an animal's feral growl. I gathered the fury into a tight ball in my chest, focusing.

Raven gave a slight shake of her head. "Save Hannah," she whispered, but I ignored her, willing the knife pressed into her throat to move away from her skin.

Despite the killer's taut muscles, the knife pulled away, and I had a moment where I believed saving them both was possible.

"My boss said you were a force to be reckoned with," he said, and before I could react, he raised his free hand, pushing the button on the remote detonator in his hand.

Movement to my left pulled my attention before I could harness the power into something that would save us all. Instead, I reacted, sending a force field around Hannah just in time to stop a pendulum blade from slicing her in half. It stilled an inch from her face and kept the heinous instrument of death in place and Hannah from any further harm.

I turned back, and the moment my gaze landed on the table, my breath hitched in my chest. The blade of a spear punctured Raven's chest running straight through her from behind. The tip glistened with the blood from her overtaxed heart. The light in her eyes faded and within a blink, her spirit peeled away from her dead form and stood, turning toward me with both sorrow and relief painted on her beautiful features.

I couldn't hold the fury that overtook me. The power let loose, rolling across the room like a bulldozer bent on destruction. I'm not sure if the man knew what hit him, because one second he was standing next to the table with a smug smile, and the next he was flying through the air. With murderous intent, I yanked the pendulum blade from its housing and sent it spinning in the same direction.

With a sickening thud, it split the bastard right in half.

I didn't know if there were other vehicles of torture or booby traps left to trip, but I didn't care. I ran towards my daughter, willing the chains holding her in place to unlatch and I was there to catch her falling form.

My thoughts were jumbled with the shock of Raven's death, but I was with it enough to grip the tube in my fist, intending to rip it out of my daughter. At the last minute, I paused, taking a second to collect my wits. This tube was embedded in her carotid artery. If I yanked it out, she would bleed out in minutes.

"Fuck," I whispered, knowing just how screwed I was. The flow had slowed, but now I had air bubbles in the tube and the change in position made the danger of an air bubble getting into her veins just as horrifying as her bleeding out.

"Don't pull it out," Raven's ghost said as she crouched next to me. "She'll bleed to death."

I stared at her and then dropped my gaze to Hannah, searching for life in her limp form. Her chest rose and fell in shallow breaths, and I closed my eyes, bowing my head in a little prayer to spare her.

When I raised my head, I asked Raven, "Are there any other traps?"

Her eyebrows arched in that cute way I loved, and the sharp pain of loss hit, tightening my chest. "You're a ghost, hon, you can hear my voice like when we go to

Paradise Cove," I added, forcing my lips to twist into a small smile. "Traps?" I asked again, twirling my finger indicating the room, reminding her of my original question.

She shook her head. "Not that I know of."

I had no idea how to ensure there were no more boxes of snakes waiting to fall from the ceiling, or another Claymore Mine waiting to detonate.

She glanced over her shoulder, and I followed her gaze to the other ghost now occupying the room. He backed away from his impaled dead body and spun like he was going to run, but something near the door stopped him. The panicked deer-in-the-headlights look on his face pushed my attention to the doorway.

My stomach dropped at the sight of Steve standing there. My breath locked in my chest, and I closed my eyes against the sudden swell of tears. I lost two people I loved today and the child in my arms just couldn't die. Not now.

A hand landed on my shoulder. The physical weight of it pulled my eyes up, and they met Steve's pained gaze. Before the words could come out, Valerie slid to her knees next to me and reached for Hannah. It took my brain a few seconds to catch up, and then I willingly released my daughter into her care.

I stood, staring at Steve. "You're okay?" I asked, and it came out bastardized as usual, but Steve's gaze was locked on the table displaying Raven's dead form.

"Jesus," he whispered before looking back at me with a nod. "Yes. Valerie got there just in time."

As if on cue, CJ stepped into the room, his gaze surveying the damage before landing on Valerie. Seeing her work on my daughter smoothed some of the worry lines on his forehead before his gaze raised to mine. Sadness and fury lived in his irises when they met mine. We both knew who orchestrated this, and I turned towards the ghost on the other side of the room.

"How many of you does Lucifer have working for him?" I snarled.

His gaze snapped to mine, scrunching in fear and anger.

"Fuck you," he said.

I didn't know how to hurt a ghost, but CJ did, and a stream of angel fire crossed the expanse, wrapping around the ghost like a lasso. He screamed as CJ controlled the burn of it.

"He's going to keep crossing off names until there's nothing left. There are plenty of mercenaries willing to take the job with what he's paying."

CJ stepped closer and twisted his fist. The ghost screamed.

"What is he doing with the blood?" I asked.

He laughed. "I have no idea what he's doing with it. He just said to make the deaths look like vampires, and to send him the blood." He waved at the room. "This town was the only one that had different instructions. It was supposed to be last, but I like to be systematic..." He trailed off, his glance bouncing between CJ and me.

"You killed my wife," I said, trying to keep the crushing truth from knocking me to my knees.

He grinned like a true psycho. "I've never stuffed someone with rocks before. It was actually fun."

Before I could react, the angel fire spread, consuming the spiteful bastard. I couldn't help the momentary satisfaction that crept into me. His agonizing screams quenched the vengeance thrumming in my soul, but deep down, I knew it wasn't enough.

Lucifer had to pay for this, one way or another.

When there was nothing left of the ghost, I glanced at my wife.

Heaven was waiting for her, but I didn't want to let her go. I wanted her to stay with me until Hannah was all grown up and I was ready to join her. I wanted a lifetime with her, not a meager blink in time.

Hannah's whine of pain whipped my head in her direction. All the muscles in her small form stood out in stark relief against the light that traveled over every inch of her. Valerie had removed the tube and the gaping wound in her throat stitched up in seconds, leaving only a smear of blood against her perfect skin where the slash had been.

She remained pale, but her breathing steadied, and Valerie looked up at me.

"She may need a transfusion, even with the healing mojo," she said, eyeing the jug of blood.

Unable to trust my voice, I signed, "Thank you."

She sent me a nod, and I met Steve's sad expression. He pulled me into a hug, and I couldn't speak. The last time he hugged me like this was in high school, and I didn't want my mind to go there. That entire nightmare brought Raven into my life.

I broke free and turned, crossing to Raven's body even as her ghost trailed next to me. I felt the cool warmth of her hand on my arm, but I ignored the ghost for a moment. Instead, I focused on the woman who had shared my life for the past eleven years. Tears blurred my vision, and I blinked them away. Gently, I pushed her hair out of her face, and pulled the tape off her mouth before I leaned over and pressed my lips to her cold ones. My hand landed on her abdomen, and I froze at the hard relief map under my palm. Rocks jutted into her skin from the inside and I turned to her ghost, searching her pained expression.

"I'm so sorry, sweetheart," I whispered, and she shook her head.

"I don't want you to remember me like this," she said, and tried to pull me away from her stuffed form.

I sent her a sad smile and blinked away the layer of tears that had formed. "It's a little too late for that, babe."

She knew enough about my nightmares. She knew it was the vision of my parents' death that haunted my thoughts, and not all the happy memories before those horrifying moments. This was just one more that would overshadow all the good we had shared.

I closed my eyes and turned from her body, letting the hands that wrapped around me lead me out of the death room and into the dark night. Strobes of red and blue descended as I sat on the curb with what was left of my family.

Angel Blood Chapter 17

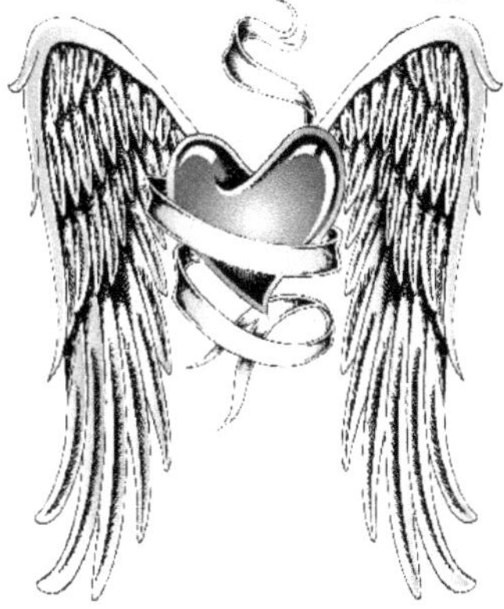

THE CHIEF OF THE York Police department, Duke Gallagher, corralled both Steve and me in an empty waiting room as soon as my daughter was settled in the ICU.

"What the hell did you think you were doing?" he barked pointing at me.

"We..." Steve began, and Chief Gallagher glared, silencing him.

I pulled out the deputy papers that O'Keefe had instituted and handed them to him. He glanced at the orders and then back at me. "He had my wife and daughter. I wasn't going to stop until I found them," I signed. He followed my hand signals and then met my gaze.

"When you became personally involved in the case, you should have stepped down." He shook the papers at me. "The perp had your family, and while I get it, you still should have let us do our job."

My jaw tightened. "O'Keefe and those two rookies were dead when we got there, and that psycho had the place wired with traps," I signed, my hands moving faster as the frustration built. "If I had left it to the police, more people would be dead, including my daughter."

"You don't know that," he growled, and I stepped closer to him.

Steve grabbed my arm, holding me back and the warning in his gaze came through. This wasn't O'Keefe, and revealing what our family could do was not a wise move.

I let my tightly coiled muscles relax and dropped my gaze to the ground.

"What the hell happened?" he asked, but this time it was softer.

"He had a claymore mine set up for anyone who came in the second door."

Chief Gallagher's eyebrows rose.

"I guess it backfired." I knew how unlikely that scenario was, but the force that I used to launch him into the wall was consistent with a bomb of some sort.

"What about the snakes?"

I huffed a laugh. "I hate snakes," I signed.

"So, they were alive?"

I traded a glance with Steve and shrugged.

"Neither of you were bitten, right?"

We both shook our heads.

"Do you know what those were?"

I shook my head.

"Those were death adders, one of the deadliest snakes in the fucking world, and there were at least twenty of them. How the hell did you not get bitten?"

"Just lucky, I guess," I signed.

His lips thinned, and he glanced at the preliminary reports coming in on his blackberry. The crease between his eyes deepened, and he glanced at me as the words on his screen echoed in his head.

"He videotaped it?" I said and signed at the same time.

The chief's gaze narrowed as much as my eyes had widened.

"How did you know that?"

"I can read upside down," I signed, hoping to appease his curiosity. "He videotaped the whole thing?" I asked, paling at the thought.

The Chief didn't answer, but the suspicion in his gaze chilled me. "I expect you to stay in town until this case is closed." He pointed at me and headed towards the door.

I glanced at Steve, but he was staring after Chief Gallagher. When I started towards the door intending to check on Hannah, Steve's hand landed on my arm, and I stopped.

"Why would he tape it?" He turned his gaze to mine.

I shrugged. I had no fucking idea.

"I'm serious."

"I don't have a clue. I need to go see my daughter," I signed, and didn't wait for him to continue, instead, I crossed from the waiting room to the nurse's desk. Steve followed.

He cleared his throat. "Can you tell us which room Hannah Ryan is in?" he asked.

"Only family is allowed in the ICU," the nurse said without looking up.

I banged my palm on the counter and when she looked up, I signed, "I am her father."

"He is Hannah's father," Steve translated, and I flipped open my wallet, showing her my driver's license.

"Oh, I'm sorry, she's in Room 57. Down the hall that way," she said, pointing to her left, after she studied the picture on the license.

"Thank you," I signed and headed down the hall.

Hannah looked so small in the hospital bed, and I slid into the seat next to her, taking her tiny hand in mine.

"She's going to be okay," Steve said and gave my shoulder a pat.

I glanced up at him with a nod. I knew from all my experiences with the healing mojo that she would be okay, but it might take some time. After all, Jennifer had taken over a week from the time my mother infused her to when she woke up.

The machines continued to monitor her vitals, and I scanned all the equipment in the room wondering why she was in intensive care. I glanced at Steve like he could enlighten me, but he was studying the equipment with the same puzzlement I had.

The doctor stepped into the room.

"Mr. Ryan, how are you holding up?"

"Okay, considering," I signed, keeping it as simple as possible.

He pulled up a chair at the foot of the bed and looked at the notes on his tablet. "Your daughter is in a coma, and we aren't sure why. We couldn't find any sign of injury; however her blood count is dangerously low." He glanced up at me. "We are concerned she may have internal bleeding and want to do a CT scan to pinpoint any issue."

I signed yes, with a nod of my fist and followed it with a simple, "Ya."

"If we don't find the cause with the CT scan, we would like your permission to do emergency exploratory surgery," he added.

"No," I articulated, with an emphatic shake of my head. A CT scan was not invasive, and I'd allow that just to appease the doctors. But surgery was out of the question.

"Sir," he started, and I could feel the hardness returning to my muscles. I slowed the shake of my head, stopping him.

"The CT scan is okay, but I will not give you authorization to cut her open," I signed, and Steve translated.

"My son said no," Steve added, when the doctor argued again.

The doctor turned towards him, thinking he was a fountain of reason that could sway me.

"I don't think your son understands the critical nature of the problem."

"He understands better than most what's at stake, and if the CT scan shows internal bleeding, we can revisit this conversation."

The doctor sighed and nodded. "A nurse will be in to bring her down in a few minutes."

"Thank you," I signed.

"Do you need me to stay?" Steve asked after the doctor left.

I didn't know how to answer him. I was still numb from the night's events. Our home was destroyed, as was CJ's and Damian's. Captain O'Keefe was dead. My wife was dead. And my daughter was in a coma. The facts of what had happened in the last few days layered on me like a ton of bricks dropped from a bulldozer.

He offered me a smile of commiseration. He knew what it was like to be in my shoes, except he had sat next to Jennifer's battered body trying to make sense of it all. At least I knew my daughter would wake. Eventually.

"Let me ask you an easier question," he said, pausing in order for me to focus on him. "Can I get you some clothes?"

I huffed a laugh. "From where?" I signed.

"I can take a run down to Kittery and get you a couple of things to tide you and Hannah over," he said.

I gave a nod. Having clean clothing on would be a start. Then maybe I'd be able to feel something other than this complete numbness of mind and emotion.

"Jennifer should be here in a little bit. She's helping CJ and Valerie to find temporary housing. We found a place for you and Hannah to stay until you have time to rebuild."

I hadn't been by my house, but I had seen the rubble at CJ's. "Did they ever figure out what caused the explosions?"

He gave me a long look. "They think it was ship to shore missiles," he finally said.

My eyes widened. "Missiles? What the fuck? Does that mean there was more than one person?" My mind went back to the things the assassin's ghost rattled about. They would never stop until all the angel descendants were dead, including us. The way he glanced over my head and out the window unnerved my already frazzled psyche.

"I honestly don't know. Based on the timing of Jennifer's vision and the hardware he had in his van, he had the means and the time to get a boat out there and back. People on the beach said they saw the heat trails but couldn't identify the boat they came from. The Coast Guard found no trace of whoever had done it, either."

I digested the information and gave him a nod. "Just make sure everyone is close together. We are stronger that way," I added as he stood to leave.

"Jeans or shorts?" he asked at the door.

"Both." York could get chilly at night even with the hot days and I wasn't sure how long I'd be sitting at Hannah's bedside in the chill of the hospital room.

He gave me a nod and disappeared through the door.

I focused on the figure I had been ignoring since I walked into the room and offered Raven's ghost a brief semblance of a smile. She stood on the opposite side of the bed with Hannah's hand in hers.

I think the fact I could still see my wife kept the soul-crushing pain at bay.

Angel Blood Chapter 18

I WASN'T VERY GOOD at praying, but I closed my eyes and bowed my head. Before I could form any words, the door swung open. I glanced up at a face I hadn't seen before, and behind him stood Valerie.

"What's up?" I signed, looking at my sister-in-law and not the doctor who had preceded her into the room.

"Dr. Phillips has a proposal for you," she said. Her mind was projecting static, so I didn't really know what was coming.

"As you know, your wife was listed as an organ donor. Unfortunately, most of her organs were damaged beyond use; however, there were a few parts that were salvageable."

I crossed my arms, pressing my lips together at the way he referred to my wife, as if she were a used car.

He cleared his throat and offered me a nervous smile. "We would like your permission to send her eyes to John's Hopkins for a transplant."

I glanced at Raven's ghost and she smiled, nodding. If her death could result in someone else living a better life, she was all for it, and my skeptical irritation eased. I turned my gaze back to Dr. Phillips and gave him a nod.

"She would want that," I signed. Valerie translated.

He handed me one of the two papers in his hand, and I signed on the dotted line where he indicated.

When I handed that back, he licked his lips and glanced at Valerie.

"Did you know Raven's blood type matches yours?" Valerie asked, and I gave her a nod. That I knew, but I had no idea where they were going with the question.

"Were you aware that Mr. Williams had you on a transplant list?"

My eyebrows rose, and I glanced between Valerie and Dr. Phillips. "That was a long time ago, and they said it wasn't possible," I signed, as Valerie translated.

Dr. Phillips offered me a soft smile. "There have been significant advances in this area, and I'd like to offer you the option, especially since we have a viable tongue that matches your blood type."

I blinked at the statement and when the facts came together all at once, I balked.

"Are you asking me if I want my wife's tongue transplanted into my mouth?" The shock of his offer left me stunned, and when he nodded, I looked at Valerie. "And you're on board with this?"

"You know she would have done anything to make you whole again," Valerie said.

I gave a sarcastic laugh and sat back in the chair, staring at the two of them, unsure of how to react. "I'll never be whole again," I finally signed, irritated at the suggestion.

"Tom," Raven's ghost interrupted, and I looked square at her. "Let me do this for you. Please," she whispered.

"Why should I?" I asked the ghost.

"If you do this, I will always be a part of you."

"You already are."

She cocked her head and leveled her 'don't be an ass' look.

I closed my eyes and laid my forehead on the side of the bed; taking a few breaths so the burning tears would stay at the back of my throat and not cascade down my face. Raven's rationale hit home, and my heart ached for her.

Valerie came closer and crouched down so I could see her. "Tom, this is an opportunity to actually speak to your daughter."

I turned my head and stared at her. "I speak to her now," I said aloud. She heard the thought, and the bastardized sounds. "What makes you think she doesn't understand me?" I added, trying to keep the irritation from overwhelming me.

"She's going to need you, Tom," she whispered. "And if you don't take this opportunity, they will give it to someone else. I have a feeling Raven would rather have you find some benefit from her loss than some stranger." She looked directly at the spot where Raven stood, and I followed her glance.

Raven was nodding.

I sat up and sniffled, still not sure I should accept the offer. "How long is the procedure?"

"The surgery takes between four and six hours, depending on factors such as how damaged the nerve and muscles are in your mouth," Dr. Phillips answered. "And the hospital stay afterwards can range between seven to ten days, depending on how you react to the transplant."

"Could I stay in here with Hannah?" I asked, looking between the doctor and Valerie.

"Unfortunately, that is not an option," Dr. Phillips said. "This is the children's wing. Adult patients are not allowed to stay here," he added, clarifying the rules.

"Then, no." It was a simple choice for me. I had to be here when my daughter woke, even if it meant giving up the possibility of normal speech.

"We will take turns watching over Hannah for you, and once you are out of danger of infection, we can make sure you can spend your days here instead of in a hospital room in the adult wing. If Hannah wakes up, we can take her home with us until you are released. Would that change your mind?" Valerie said. I knew she wanted this for me, the same way Raven did, but I couldn't leave Hannah unattended even for a minute.

"You and CJ have a newborn. You can't be here twenty-four-seven," I signed, digging in on my argument.

"True, but it isn't just the two of us. We have Steve and Jennifer and Damian and Naomi, so between the six of us, we have this covered. She will not be left alone at all."

"Tom," Raven's ghost interjected, pulling my attention to her. "Don't be such a stubborn ass. Take the opportunity," she added, and her hands found her hips. Even in ghostly form, she knew how to project her irritation.

You really want me to do this? I silently asked, and she nodded. *Then you have to stay by Hannah's side and let me know when she wakes up, otherwise, I'm not doing it.*

"I promise I will stay by her side," Raven said. "Please take this gift. It's all I have to offer you now," she added, her voice softening just as her eyes pleaded with me. It was a look I could never say no to when she was alive, and as a ghost, the effect magnified.

I looked down at the floor, weighing my options. Leaving Hannah didn't sit well with me at all, but neither did disappointing Raven.

"You promise she won't ever be alone," I signed, looking up at Valerie.

"Yes. I promise. Someone will always be by her side, keeping her safe while you are in surgery and recovering." She spelled it out for me, so nothing was left to chance, and I sighed.

"If she wakes up, you have to let me know immediately, and I need to be brought here to her side, so she knows I'm okay. All right?"

Valerie translated for the doctor and they both nodded ascent.

"Absolutely," Valerie said.

I leaned over and whispered in Hannah's ear. "I promise I'll be back." My words were a jumble of sounds, and I kissed her slack cheek before following the doctor out of the children's ICU and into the pre-surgical unit for a quick physical and blood work.

Two hours later, I was being prepped for surgery and Valerie came into the room.

"I have a feeling your recovery will be faster than normal," she said and sent me a wink, which meant I'd have to endure the pain that came with her healing mojo once the operation was finished.

"Am I doing the right thing?" I signed, meeting her gaze as the nerves started in earnest.

Valerie nodded. "You heard what she said. She wants this, and deep down, so do you." She gave my arm a squeeze and left just as the anesthesiologist stepped into the room to administer the anesthesia into my intravenous line.

I was told to count backwards from one hundred. I think I got to ninety-seven before everything went black.

Angel Blood Chapter 19

I SHIVERED AND TRIED to swallow, but my mouth was so pasty it just produced a dry hack instead. Someone was talking to me, and I attempted to lift my eyelids, but they were so heavy that all I got was a dose of light and then I let them drop again.

The world sounded like I was underwater, and I drifted, letting the flow take me down.

Again, I tried to swallow, and something stuck to the roof of my mouth. I opened my jaws to dislodge whatever it was, and something cold ran over my lips. I forced my eyes open and looked into a nurse's hazel eyes.

Her mouth was moving, but I was still underwater, so it was all garbled. Until the thing stuck to the roof of my mouth moved and something scraped my lips. I blinked, and her words came into clear focus.

"Mr. Ryan, can you hear me?"

I nodded, distracted by the colored hue surrounding her. The flow of the pinks, greens and oranges mesmerized me as much as her calm voice did .

"You are in the recovery room and as soon as the doctor comes in to check on you, we will move you to the intensive care unit for the night."

"Intensive care?" My hoarse whisper was more pronounced than I remembered, and the nurse put her finger on my lips.

"Don't try to talk. It will aggravate the swelling in your tongue." She rubbed another ice chip on my lips.

"From what I heard, you did really well," she added with a smile.

I was still foggy on where I was, so I just let it go and enjoyed the cool wetness of the ice chips being rubbed on my lips.

When the doctor entered the room, the light surrounding him pulsed with yellow, red, and silver strands. He scanned the tablet in his hands and then met my gaze.

"The surgery was quicker than I anticipated, and the blood flow into the new tongue seemed adequate in the operating room. I will just want to check it again to validate it is still circulating. We will have to monitor the swelling through the night, and if all goes well, we can take the oxygen tubes out tomorrow."

I reached up, feeling the tube under my nose with my finger before signing, "Do you know if my daughter has woken yet?"

He offered me a wry smile, and the red bloomed around him. "Your sister-in-law said that would be the first thing you asked, and no, she is still in a coma."

The colors surrounding both him and the nurse distracted me, and I blinked, trying to focus on the people, not the surrounding flares. "I think I'm still out of it," I signed. "I'm seeing a lot of colors."

"Well, you are on some hefty pain medicine and some people have mild hallucinations from the anesthesia. It is nothing to worry about." He put the tablet down and leaned closer, pulling what looked like a popsicle stick from his pocket. "Can you open your mouth wide for me?" he asked.

I did as he said, but then Valerie stepped into the room and the white light radiating from her was blinding and I squinted, trying to avert my gaze. She stopped short and through the light surrounding her; I saw her wide-eyed surprise.

"Things look good," Dr. Phillips stood and gave me a nod. He turned to the nurse. "He can be moved as soon as his vision clears." He turned and gave Valerie an encouraging nod. "I don't think there is anything more for me to do here. I'll write up the instructions for the

ICU and the daily checks after. If signs of rejection present, call me." He shook her hand and left the little fabric enclosed room.

Valerie approached, and the nurse excused herself. When they were out of earshot, Valerie leaned over and placed a kiss on my forehead, and my mouth immediately felt like it was on fire. I clamped my eyes shut against the knitting agony. Instead, I focused on taking long, slow breaths while the pain eclipsed everything else.

When it finally receded into that annoying pins and needles sensation, I opened my eyes and stared at Valerie. The silver-white surrounding her now flowed with all the colors of the rainbow. It was beautiful. She smiled at me.

"You can see auras now?"

My gaze snapped away from the colors surrounding her to her eyes.

"Is that what they are?" I asked in a nearly perfect diction. The clarity made my chest draw tight. The only time I spoke clearly was when someone was a ghost.

"I'm not dead, Tom," she said, reading my mind as easily as CJ did.

I reached up and tentatively touched the muscle in my mouth. The sensation was odd after not having most of my tongue for twenty years. I felt the pressure of my fingers and then swiped the back of my teeth, feeling the smooth enamel for the first time since I was nine years old.

"Holy shit," I said, my voice raspy from surgery, but intact except for a slight lisp with the letter 's'.

"You have a lovely voice," she said and offered me a smile. "But you have to play along." She twirled her finger around and I got her reference, nodding.

"Your aura is stunning," I said, and pressed my lips together against a smirk at the 'th' sound instead of 's' when I said stunning. CJ and I would make a fine pair. His stutter and my newly formed lisp would be the center of fun at our next Thanksgiving feast.

Valerie allowed a smirk in response. "I promise not to make fun of you," she said, but I could tell it was total bullshit. Especially since I gave CJ such a hard time with his stutter. "Wait 'til you see your aura. Raven said yours was the most beautiful one she had ever seen."

Just the reference to my wife carved a pain in my chest and I pressed my lips together, closing my eyes against the sudden wetness that blurred my vision. I turned my head away so Valerie wouldn't see the tears, but the chair scraped against the floor anyway, and her hand squeezed my shoulder.

I preferred to be numb than the emotional rollercoaster the medicine seemed to brush me with. I took a breath and turned back to Valerie.

"Thank you," I signed, blinking the wetness from my eyes.

She pressed her lips together. "If I had my choice, she would have made it and you'd still be mute." Her eyes swelled with tears, and I took her hand, squeezing.

"Me, too." I whispered and pulled my hand away. "How's Alex?" I asked, hoping for some sort of distraction from the pain wrapping around Valerie. Otherwise, I'd drown in it.

She wiped her cheeks. "He seems like such a happy baby," she said. "Kind of like the way Grace was, you know?"

I nodded. Grace was a joy. Even as a newborn she exhibited awareness of her surroundings and she rarely fussed unless she was wet or hungry. The rest of the time, she had been content just to observe.

"And Grace doesn't want to leave him alone. Talk about a mother hen," she said and rolled her eyes.

I couldn't help but smile. The interaction in the hospital room gave me a hint of what she was talking about. If Hannah had been awake, I am sure she would dote on the newborn as well. She loved playing mommy with her dolls, so I'd imagine Grace would have some competition there.

"As tiring as it is, she has been quite the little helper," she said, and my smile faded.

I glanced at her, all of her, and then returned my gaze to her face. She gave birth three days ago, and she didn't look like it at all. "How are you holding up with all this?"

Valerie gave me a shrug. "I am still pretty numb. Giving birth and then all this, it's been quite taxing." She offered me a small smile. "Truth is, the only thing keeping me together is Alex." She looked down at her hands before she returned my gaze. "CJ wants to start closing portals again."

I nodded. If I had my druthers, I'd be out doing that right now, but I also knew Hannah was still on Lucifer's hit list and I wasn't leaving that to chance. I'm sure the devil was livid with how his hired hand screwed up the grand plan by being systematic instead of following orders.

I wondered what kind of torture chamber that bastard was in right now.

I fancied one where he was continuously stuffed with bloodstone until he split wide open.

The chair scraped again, and I glanced at Valerie. The agitation in her aura told me more than her wide eyes and I toned down my thoughts, signing the symbol for sorry.

"Is it bad that I hope he suffers her pain a thousandfold?"

I reached for her hand, cradling it, letting her express her feelings instead of focusing on my misery and I shook my head because I wished the same, but magnified by a million. She'd lost her closest friend, and her hurt wavered between manageable and overwhelming; as long as I focused on her feelings, I could pretend mine didn't exist.

"Was this your idea?" I whispered and pointed at my mouth. York Hospital was not known for their revolutionary technology, but Valerie had contacts from her days at medical school at Harvard.

She nodded. "When they told me they were harvesting her eyes for a donor down at John's Hopkins, I asked if her tongue was viable for a transplant. When they said yes, I called Dr. Phillips. He's done this a couple of times down in Boston, so I thought it would be worth his while to take a trip up here." She kept eye contact with me while she explained. "Raven and I talked about it. She said if she died before you, she wanted me to make sure you got the voice you were meant to have," she said and huffed a little laugh. "The conversation went totally off track when she mentioned her tongue, but in the end, she said she was serious, and I agreed."

I just stared at her wondering how that conversation really went. How would Raven even know how to approach the subject?

"Raven was direct when a thought entered her head, you know that," she said, reading my thoughts again.

I gave her a huff of a laugh in response, nodding. "That she was," I signed to save my voice.

"And you were still on that list, so it lifted a lot of red tape," she added with a smile.

The curtain shuffled, and the nurse peeked her head in. "How are we doing?"

I gave her a thumbs up and she smiled through her now yellow-orange glow. I was going to have to get used to ignoring the colors and seeing the people inside the aura.

"Actually, you should pay attention to them, at least on a cursory glance," Valerie said, pulling my gaze to her. "Raven gave me a sheet of what the colors mean and while I used to think it was hogwash, I eventually came around when I saw her father's aura through her eyes."

She shivered in the seat, and I raised my eyebrows, waiting for her to continue.

"I'd give it to you, but it's under all that rubble," she continued. "I'm sure we can look it up online, but she told me to watch out for anyone showing predominately dark brown or black auras. Those are trouble," she said. "The color rationale is quite intriguing, and she said it was pretty accurate."

"Good to know," I said aloud.

She glanced at her watch. "I need to get back. Steve is with Hannah while I came here. I still have an hour before CJ brings Alex in."

"Thank you," I whispered, and she gave me a pat on the shoulder, leaving me to the mercy of the happy nursing staff. I focused on faces while letting the colors swirl in my peripheral vision.

The swelling in my tongue had reduced significantly, and the ICU staff wasn't sure what to make of me, but when I was safely tucked into the bed, they gave me another dose of pain medicine. I didn't make a fuss, even though I didn't need any medication after Valerie's visit. I figured it would dope me up enough to allow me to get some much-needed sleep.

Angel Blood Chapter 20

I STUMPED THE DOCTORS the next day when they examined me. The lack of swelling and the range of movement I had amazed them, and the healing around the stitches was more advanced than they'd expected.

Dr. Phillips left a detailed set of instructions that outlined the conditions for release. I met every one, and they removed the oxygen tubes, which burned all the way up my throat and through my nose. Once they were out, I was able to breathe through my mouth and my nose with no issue.

They let me have a smoothie to gauge how well I could swallow food, and I let the cold drink drench my tongue, fully tasting a meal for the first time in twenty years. It was exhilarating, and I wanted more.

"Can I have pancakes?" I asked as the ICU doctor reread the notes left behind.

He looked up at me. "I'm not sure," he said, and the confusion clouding his aura pulsed. "According to the notes, you are presenting better than day seven, but if I'm reading this right, you're only on day one, right?"

"I've always been a fast healer," I said softly and shrugged, trying to pass this off as normal, but he didn't take the bait.

"I think I should give Dr. Phillips a call to confirm, because according to his list, you are ready for a full release."

"Maybe you should touch base with Dr. Ryan first. Wasn't she the one who brought him in for the surgery?" I asked, trying to lead him down the right path for subterfuge.

He gave me a nod and started out of the room.

"Pancakes?" I asked before he was out of earshot. He turned, contemplating, before he gave me a single nod.

I lifted the phone and put in an order for pancakes with syrup. I almost asked for Nutella because I always wondered what that tasted like. It wasn't something I had when I was young, so I really had no clue.

I stretched out on the bed, flipping through the television channels waiting for either my meal or the doctor to come back. As luck would have it, my meal came first, and I didn't wait for permission. I drenched the short stack in syrup and took a bite.

The sugary substance tasted glorious, and I was so preoccupied with enjoying the full taste of food, I didn't even notice the visitor in the doorway.

"Feeling better I see," Gallagher's rough voice pulled my attention from my food and I met his blatant stare. His aura pulsed a dark blue and deep green and I wished like hell I had that guide, because his eyes were piercing.

"Is Hannah awake?" I said around the mouthful of food.

"Talking already?" he asked, raising an eyebrow.

I nodded and wiped my mouth. "Faster than anyone expected," I said, and his lips pursed.

"Well, I just came by to see for myself. I'll be on my way," he said, and turned before I could say anything more.

The doctor scooted by him in the doorway, giving the chief a smile before focusing on me. "With how well you're doing, we can let you get out of here." He grinned. "I've taken the liberty to schedule a couple of outpatient appointments for you. We want to touch base daily to make sure your body continues to accept the transplant. Here's a list of things to look out for; if you experience any of those, immediately return." He handed me a list and a prescription bottle. "Antibiotics," he said to my raised eyebrow. "Twice a day until they are gone to prevent infection."

"Okay," I said and took the last bite of pancakes, soaking up the rest of the syrup before I stuffed it in my mouth.

"Your clothing is hanging on the back of the door over there and there are towels in the cabinet if you want to take a quick shower. Otherwise, you are officially released."

"I think I'll take you up on that shower," I said. I felt utterly grimy from the surgery.

"I'll send the nurse to get you in…" He looked at his watch. "Twenty minutes."

I gave him a nod and climbed out of the bed, heading for that shower. My clothes felt fresh compared to the hospital gown and when I wiped away the steam to get a clue as to what my hair looked like, my aura sparkled back at me, and I stared at the myriad of colors. Interwoven in the rich rainbow surrounding me was gold, silver and pure white, like an intricate braid. It certainly was unique from the other auras I had seen since I woke from surgery, and there wasn't a hint of brown or black to be found.

My gaze shifted to my eyes, and my wonder sobered. The only reason I was seeing auras was because a part of my wife's tongue was sewn into my mouth. The joy of speaking and tasting fell flat with the surfacing of the only reason I was enjoying myself.

My heart twisted in my chest, and I ran my hands through my hair, making it presentable before I stepped back into the room.

A young nurse waited with a wheelchair.

"Really?" I gestured towards the chair.

"Standard protocol," she said with a sweet smile.

"I would rather not," I said, my voice much smoother than it had been when I left the recovery room yesterday. "Besides, I'm going to the children's ICU where my daughter is. She's in a coma."

Her gaze softened. "I can bring you there," she said, still quoting procedure in her head.

I knew it wasn't a battle that I would win, and arguing would only waste time, so I deposited my ass in the chair and let her roll me to Hannah's room.

At the door, I stood and turned. "Thanks for the ride," I said, and she gave me a nod. Across the hall, an officer lingered at the nursing station, his aura predominately red with fleeting strands of blue slowly twisting with red strands. I turned back to the cracked door, pushing it open.

Naomi glanced up from the book she held and smiled. Her aura was intriguing, it held gold and silver along with strands of blue and yellow and a very light braided strand of gray and white. I imagine that might be the tiger strand. I wondered if this was what her aura looked like when she was a vampire.

I shook the thought from my head and glanced at Hannah. Her aura was like mine, except it was absent the gold and silver braid. Hers was just a sparkling rainbow, exactly what I envisioned for my three-year-old princess.

"That was fast," she said, and I glanced at the clock. It was just about thirty hours from when I had been escorted to surgery and I shrugged.

"I owe that to Valerie," I said. My gaze traveled across the space to where Raven's ghost sat. "And my wife," I added, giving her a nod of acknowledgement. "Any change?"

"No," she said while shaking her head. "They've been pressuring us to get permission to do exploratory surgery, but we've all held them at bay. The CT scan showed nothing."

"Thank you for keeping watch," I said, and she stood, crossing and giving me a quick hug.

"You know, it wasn't a problem. You've been there for all of us so many times. It was refreshing to be the one to help," she said as she pulled away. "I have to admit, it is strange hearing you talk. I've only heard you when we were at Paradise Cove."

"Trust me, it is just as strange being able to talk." The lisp presented itself and I felt the heat in my cheeks, but today it was a lot less prevalent than yesterday, so maybe there was hope.

"I'm going to get going. Damian and CJ are sifting through the rubble, trying to see if there's anything to salvage. I think Steve and Jennifer are doing the same at your place. If you need us, just yell."

I would have to remember to thank them. I would have let the pile sit until Hannah woke up, and who knows how many more days that would be. "Thanks. I'll be here if anyone wants a break," I said, and she nodded, heading out of the room.

I took a seat next to my daughter and looked at Raven's ghost. She had a hint of an aura, but it was faded. The colors muted in a way that tightened my throat.

"Did you know I'd be able to see auras?" I asked. I was amused by this new manifestation, and I wondered what other surprises I'd have to deal with because of this lovely transplant.

The right side of Raven's lips tilted into a half smile. "I had hoped," she said.

I let a small chuckle out. "Does this mean you'll be with me from now on?" I asked. A sliver of hope bloomed in my heart, but it quickly disappeared, along with Raven's smile.

She slowly shook her head. My heart squeezed, and I leaned back in the chair, sobering at the thought of not seeing her again.

"I'm waiting to say goodbye to Hannah." Her eyes held the depth of her sorrow. "You know I can't stay."

As much as I wanted her to, I knew what happened to ghosts who overstayed their welcome. Any goodness they possessed faded until they were bitter, angry entities bent on destroying everything around them.

My father was the exception.

He called it penance, but I'm not so sure. I think he just returned to his true self.

A guardian angel of sorts, albeit a kick-ass guardian angel, and he'd be there to welcome Raven into heaven.

Angel Blood Chapter 21

THE NEXT MORNING, CHIEF Gallagher stepped into the room with an armed officer and his aura pulsed erratically with an array of color, including a light brown, which made me pay attention based on what Valerie had said.

"Tom, I'm going to need you to come down to the station with us," he said with such caution that I stiffened in the seat.

"Why?" I said, wishing Steve hadn't gone to the hotel to catch some sleep after his quick visit last night.

He cleared his throat, studying me for a moment, especially with how clear my voice was today. "We have some questions, and I don't think this is the right environment for us to ask them."

I leaned back in the seat, staring at him, trying to pull information from his mind, but all I kept getting from him was raw anger, and I was too damned tired to push. The antibiotics had given me a bout of heartburn and I hadn't slept much because of that.

"If I refuse?" I waited to see what would come next.

He shifted and reached into his jacket, pulling out a sheet of paper. "We don't want to cause a scene here," he said, and handed me the paper.

I opened it and stared at the first line. It was a warrant for my arrest, and I glanced up at him in complete confusion.

"I don't understand?" I said, and the lisp presented like it had yesterday. I was dumbfounded enough to sign as well.

"We can discuss this down at the station," he said, and his hand fell onto his service revolver.

I glanced at Raven's ghost and then at my daughter. From everything Steve told me, a warrant for arrest meant they had enough evidence for probable cause, and I just nodded and stood.

When he pulled the handcuffs out of his pocket, I gave him a look and said, "Really?"

"Standard procedure," he said.

I put the arrest warrant on the table and put my hands out in front of me so he could cuff me. "I have a post-surgical appointment at noon. Is that going to be a problem?" I asked, glancing at the clock. It was barely seven.

"I'm afraid you will have to turn around," he said, eyeing me and ignoring my question. I closed my eyes against the irritation, turning without anymore protest. "You might want to cancel that appointment," he added as he clamped the cuffs tighter than necessary.

I sent the current situation out to CJ, Damian, and Steve while the Chief read me my rights. When he asked if I understood them, I nodded. Being paraded through the hospital in police custody made the day that much worse. The glares I received from the nursing staff were enough to ruffle my feathers, but I had been through worse, and I kept my eyes straight ahead, with my head up.

By the time we got to the police station, CJ, Damian, and Steve were leaning on the back of my SUV, waiting for me.

"Who's with Hannah?" I asked, my gaze traveling over the three of them.

"Jennifer is," Steve said, and straightened along with CJ and Damian.

Chief Gallagher held up his hand, as they approached. "Go home boys, the only one that I'll allow in the interrogation room is his lawyer."

"That would be me," Steve said, following us into the station. CJ and Damian paused, unsure of whether or not to follow, and Steve stopped at the door. "Go back and make sure the family is looked after."

CJ and I exchanged a glance, and I just shrugged. I didn't know much of anything right now, but I knew the interrogation room was where I'd find out much more than I probably wanted.

They took the cuffs off and pointed at the farthest chair, and Chief Gallagher took a seat across from me, with a folder in front of him. He stared at me, sizing me up—waiting. A couple of minutes passed, and I never broke his inquisitive stare until the door opened and a deputy stepped in with a laptop encased in a plastic bag. I blinked a couple of times and then turned to Steve.

"What are they doing with my laptop?" I asked, and I received a glare in response. Steve wanted me to shut my mouth, but I couldn't help the flurry of questions fighting to spill all over the table. Instead, I pressed my lips together and remained quiet.

Gallagher let a smirk appear. "You thought since you destroyed your own house, we wouldn't bother looking at your office?"

"What the hell are you talking about?" I snapped, mystified at the accusation.

"The feed went from the kill room to your laptop." He spun it around so I could see the screen and I shrank back in the chair at the view of Raven hogtied. The noise of the air gun pumping bloodstone into her couldn't drown her muffled screams. "You're a sick fuck. Recording this shit for posterity?"

"Turn it off," I hissed. I couldn't tear my eyes from the agony reflected in my wife's eyes. My stomach clenched, and I pressed farther back in the chair, fully aware of the last thing I ate now rolling in my stomach, getting ready for a mass exodus.

Steve leaned forward and shut the laptop, glaring at Gallagher.

My chest hurt and my entire form shook. I couldn't shake the imprint that video left on my brain. I stared at the laptop like it was one of the snakes that attacked Steve. I had seen enough horrific things in my life, but that took the prize, and I finally raised my gaze, still unable to draw a sufficient breath.

Gallagher sat with his arms crossed, studying me closely.

"Breathe," Steve said softly, pulling my attention to him. I stared into his sea-blue eyes as the panic started shutting down my lungs. "Breathe," he said again. Slowly, he inhaled and exhaled. "Slow and easy," he said, repeating until I found I was following his breathing pattern and able to draw enough air.

My eyes misted, and I closed them, concentrating on the hot paths that cut across my cheeks. One tear found the corner of my lips and I swiped my tongue out, capturing the salty bead. I drew another slow breath and when I thought I had control; I opened my eyes and met Gallagher's gaze.

"Sorry," I said, but my voice vibrated with the shakes still present in my form.

He didn't seem fazed by my display, but his thoughts centered on wondering if I was genuine or just a phenomenal actor like my father.

He opened the folder, turning a photo around so I could see it. "Is this your boat?"

I looked at the name—Celtic Princess—and nodded. "Yes. Why?"

"It was found on the rocks over at Lobster Cove with this inside." He turned the next photograph my way, and I stared at a long gray cylinder with what looked like a gun trigger on it.

"What the hell is that?" I asked before I picked up the picture.

"A rocket launcher."

My gaze snapped to his, and my jaw dropped open. I turned to Steve, and he took a cursory glance at the photo before returning his sharp gaze to Chief Gallagher.

"Were my client's fingerprints found on it?"

"No." Chief Gallagher said and leaned forward. "But who else could have orchestrated such an elaborate plot to get rid of his wife?"

I stared at him. "You are out of your fucking mind," I said, and then leaned back in my chair, running my hands through my hair. "I can't believe you think I would do that to my wife." I pointed at the computer, utterly disgusted. "Or to my daughter. What do you think I am?"

I was on my feet, staring down at the Chief.

"I think you're every bit as evil as Ty Ryan was."

"Sit down, Tom," Steve barked, and I glanced at him and pointed at the Chief.

"He thinks I orchestrated all this?"

"Sit down," he said again, and the hardness in his eyes gave me pause. I lowered into the chair slowly. Then he turned that glare in the Chief's direction. "I'll give you props for the theatrics, but you do not have evidence that my son was in cahoots with the killer." His emphasis on the words my son did not go unnoticed by the Chief. "All you have is an elaborate setup designed to make him look guilty."

"Are you in here as his lawyer or his surrogate father?" the Chief asked.

"I'm here because you are as wrong about this as you were about the Windwalker," Steve said. "What's his motive?" Steve asked after a few moments.

The chief looked down at the file like the evidence would manufacture some sort of concrete motive. "A viable tongue," he said and glanced up from the file.

His tone chilled me, and my mouth dropped open. "I would rather have my wife than be able to talk. What the fuck?" I couldn't help the outburst and Steve shook his head, silencing any further rant.

"Maybe she was going to leave you and take half your fortune. Maybe you were having an affair and wanted her gone, or you found out she was screwing around." He knew he was reaching, but his mind wasn't willing to latch on to any other logical explanation, not without exhausting this one.

"What about blowing up the houses? If what you are insinuating is true, why would he do that to his brother and his business partner? Why would he blow up his own house?" Steve pushed.

"A diversion. And maybe he hates his brother and business partner."

"You are out of your goddamned mind," I said, and received a glare from Steve.

Steve leaned back in the chair. "Chief, Jim was the one who got Tom and his partner messed up in this case. How does that play into your outlandish scenario?"

Gallagher collected the pictures and dropped them on top of the folder, closing it. "Jim mentioned he spoke with Tom and said there was a lot he had to think about. He wanted to keep an eye on him but wouldn't give me any details," he said to Steve, and then looked at me. "Why would my best detective want to keep an eye on you?"

I kept my mouth shut and crossed my arms, shrugging.

"None of this makes sense," Steve said. "You have seen Tom and Raven together, Chief."

"Appearances can be deceiving." Chief Gallagher leveled a glare at Steve and then it turned on me. "What are you hiding?"

"Nothing," I said. "I was working with Captain O'Keefe to help catch this psycho before the bastard got to our town." That earned a glare from Steve. Keeping silent was nearly impossible now that I could speak, especially with such bullshit being thrown in my direction.

Gallagher stopped pussyfooting around and went the direct route. "Were you involved in the abduction and murder of your wife?" he asked.

"No." I shook my head and out of habit, added the hand sign for no.

"Were you involved in blowing up your brother's home?"

"No."

"Were you involved in blowing up your partner's house?"

"No."

"Were you involved in blowing up your own home?"

"No."

The Chief's aura calmed from violent pulsing to a slower calmer flow, and he rubbed his face before he pushed the off button on the recording.

"Whose blood is in the snake room?" he asked looking between Steve and me.

I pointed at Steve before he could stop me.

Gallagher sighed. "I thought you said neither of you got bit?" Instead of waiting for an answer, he barreled ahead. "How did half a gallon of blood that matches your daughter's get into that jug? And how the hell can you talk so fluidly the day after a fucking tongue transplant?"

Neither of those questions was easy to answer, because giving up Valerie as a miracle healer wasn't something I was willing to do. I glanced at Steve for help and all I got was a miniscule shake of his head.

"Look. Either you are the best fucking actor on the planet, or your father here is right. Someone is trying damned hard to set you up. I've got a shit ton of questions that I don't have any logical answers to, and there is zero on that video that would explain any of this." He ran his hand over the top of his buzz cut and sighed.

I glanced at the laptop. "Where does that end?" I asked and pointed.

"When you tripped the explosion." He stared at me, expecting a different answer than I gave earlier and I dropped my gaze to the table. "You are hiding something, aren't you boy? And if it isn't your involvement in this case, what the hell is it?"

"Are we being observed?" Steve asked, looking at the one-way mirror behind the Chief.

"No," both the Chief and I said at the same time and his eyebrows creased.

"How the hell do you know that?"

"Because he is psychic," Steve answered.

"Don't bullshit me."

"I'm not, Duke. Jim came to me because he knew… he knew I had some special abilities, except I don't. Not anymore. I'm the one who sent him to Tom."

"Then you know what we were originally thinking," he said, looking between Steve and me. "Unfortunately, that video changed the entire thought process," he added and laid his hand on the computer. "We now know he was using the snake venom to subdue the victims and a low suction machine to drain the bodies. But I still don't know how your daughter came out of there without a scratch."

"There is an explanation, but it's as out there as vampires," I said. "It pertains to how fast I healed as well."

Chief Gallagher let out a short laugh. "Both Jim and I were nearly convinced that vampires existed," he admitted, and I kept my expression neutral. I didn't want to burst that bubble.

"Where do you want me to start?" I transmitted without speaking.

He blinked and moved his gaze to Steve, unsure of himself. A thin thread of light brown weaved into his aura, and I had to focus on not staring at the hesitation so visible around him.

"Chief Gallagher, this is Tom, and you aren't losing it. I really am talking in your head."

Steve looked between the two of us, and I glanced over at him and shrugged.

"For the love of God, Tom," he said to me with irritation laced into every syllable and then turned to Gallagher. "He's talking to you, isn't he?"

"How?"

"I told you, he's psychic. He can read minds and transmit thoughts."

"Based on what I saw on that video, his daughter should have died. So should both of you. That bomb didn't malfunction. The debris field was in an arc around where he stood." Gallagher pointed at me, still staring at Steve. "The walls, ceiling, everything. He should have been shredded to hell and back. We should have been picking up pieces of him in the parking lot. Instead, he's sitting here without a scratch, and he's got a new tongue out of the deal." He gave me a cursory glance and continued. "According to the preliminary report, the blood on the floor matches the blood on at least a dozen of those viper's teeth. You should be as dead as O'Keefe."

"Would you believe we have a guardian angel?" Steve said, offering a hint of a smile.

"I'd believe just about anything right now," he muttered. "You and I have known each other for a long time," he said to Steve with more of a sigh than a statement. "And I know these kids gave you a run for your money at times." He waved in my direction. "But despite what the evidence suggests, I'm having a hard time putting any other logical explanation together in my mind."

"There isn't anything logical about this, Chief," I said. "Just like there is no logical explanation why I've been able to see ghosts all my life."

He took a great inhalation. "So, do you know why he was killing all these people?"

I stared at him for a few minutes and then gave a slow nod. "Yes."

"Do you know why your wife's death differed from the rest?"

I knew this question was coming, and I bit my lip as a sheen of tears blurred my eyes. I blinked away the tears, unwilling to break down any further than I already had here. "Because I got in the way of his goal."

"Who's goal?"

"Whoever orchestrated all this shit."

Gallagher's face reddened in frustration, and he pulled a couple of sheets from the file, smoothing them out before he handed them to me. "Can you tell me anything about this?"

I glanced at the list. It was similar to the one CJ wrote, except in geographical order, going from northeast to southwest. Names and towns, and it did indeed say we were to be the last of the hit, so in that respect, the ghost was telling us the truth. The instructions for how to terminate the rest of the angel kin were outlined at the top. The instructions for York, however, were annotated and on an attachment Gallagher did not have. I, on the other hand, knew exactly what was in store for us. Lucifer had sent me a litany of promises that made me shiver. If I had said yes to helping him get what he wanted, the entire world would have fallen into dark times, but my family would be left unharmed. Instead, I had stood on the side of the angels and now my wife was dead, along with a dozen angel descendants.

I scanned the list and moved to turn the page but stalled at a name I recognized in New York City. I glanced at Steve, holding the list so he could see the name, and his gaze shot to mine. We ran into that descendant by chance, and I'd have to remember to warn him if I ever got out of this jam.

The crossed off names corresponded to the deaths, and I finally glanced up at the Chief, handing the list back.

"That looks like a hit list," I said, playing the game the way Steve was silently directing me to.

"That's a pretty damned expansive list, and the only names in this town are related to you in some way. Why is York tagged as last?"

"I don't know." I really didn't understand the logic of Lucifer's logistical orders. First, last, what did it matter? Then the answer came like a sucker punch to the stomach. Any chance of another CJ or Grace was limited to right here in York. If either Valerie or Naomi had another girl, the odds of Lucifer getting his hands on a trinity to create his dark army increased.

I closed my eyes and dropped my head.

"You're lying to me again."

I glanced up at him. How could I tell this man the devil existed, and he wanted both CJ and me dead, or using one of our super-powered meat suits to get what he wanted?

"Duke, are you going to process him or not?" Steve interrupted, reading my hesitation correctly.

"Whose hit list is this?" He waved the list before slamming it back on top of the file.

"Lucifer," I said, and the space between his eyebrows creased.

"Come again?"

I kept my hands still and just stared at him. "I run a paranormal investigation agency. I was bound to piss off the wrong... entity... at some point," I finally said. I knew how flippant that sounded, but it was easier to point to my job as the culprit than the truth. The truth could get me locked up in an uncomfortably small padded cell.

His eyebrows arched in surprise. It was something he hadn't considered, especially since he thought paranormal was complete bullshit.

I shifted. "If you're not going to process me, can I please go back to the hospital? I don't want my daughter waking up without me there."

His lips thinned. "You never explained all of your miraculous recoveries."

"I stopped the debris from hitting me," I said.

"How?"

"Psychic, remember?" I tapped my temple. The exhaustion of the last few days was taking its toll, and I knew it wasn't prudent to get snarky, but at this point, I was beyond caring.

"Bullshit," he said, and his thoughts circled back to me being a part of all of it.

I had had enough and moved forward, slamming my palm to his forehead. The memory transfer took a few minutes, and I'm sure revealing everything from the point we pulled in until the point I caught Hannah in my arms was going to haunt me but it would at least shut off this circle of questions, and I really wanted to get back to my daughter.

His incessant blinking pulled a huff out of me. Served him right for pushing me, and Steve just sent me an 'are you kidding me?' stare.

Finally, Chief Gallagher's eyes focused on me. "How much of that was real?"

"Unless you are going to tell me my wife is alive, and I just hallucinated her death, it's all real."

"What the hell did you just do to me? Was that some kind of hypnosis?" Gallagher snapped.

"No. I just shared the memory. It's part of my psychic charm." I snapped and the snarky remark earned a huff from both Gallagher and Steve.

Gallagher's eyes narrowed as he glared at me. "There was no explanation in that memory as to how the hell your daughter and Steve walked out alive," he muttered.

"Look, sir, I figured it was the fastest way for you to see what went down and as far as how we are alive, chalk that up to a miracle. Now, if you don't mind, I'd really like to get back to my daughter."

"Is my client free to go?" Steve asked and Chief Gallagher glanced down at the file with the information he used to get a warrant.

"One last question. When was the last time you were in your office?"

"The end of June. We usually close the first two weeks in July for summer vacation."

"So, you haven't been on your computer since then?"

I shook my head. "I always shut it down before I leave and lock it in my drawer."

"The laptop was on your desk and in sleep mode. Are you sure you haven't used it since June?"

"I locked it in my desk drawer before I left for vacation," I reiterated and my teeth clenched at the sudden rise in anger that overcame me. "Did you check to see if there were any signs of a break in, or did you just assume it was me that did all this and to hell with due process?" I growled and glanced at Steve.

He put his hand out to calm the beginnings of my rant.

"Did you check?" Steve asked.

Gallagher shook his head. "No. But I will have them check both the office door and the desk for signs of tampering," he said, appeasing my aggravation for the time being. Even with all he had been privy to, he still carried some doubt about me.

If the table was turned, I'm not sure I could swallow this either, but I was too tired to be sympathetic to his confusion.

"Can I go back to the hospital now?"

He studied me for a few minutes and then straightened up the notes in his folder before he nodded. "I'm not going to hold you in custody. But until we come to a solid conclusion on this case, I don't want you to leave town. Got it?"

"I got it." I stood, letting Steve walk me out to his car.

"You'll get me a copy of the case file once they close the case, right?" I asked, as I slid into the passenger seat.

"Why?"

I met his gaze. He of all people should understand my need for information.

I needed to know what happened.

I needed to know how long Raven suffered while we dicked around trying to find her.

I needed to know just how deeply I had failed her.

Angel Blood Chapter 22

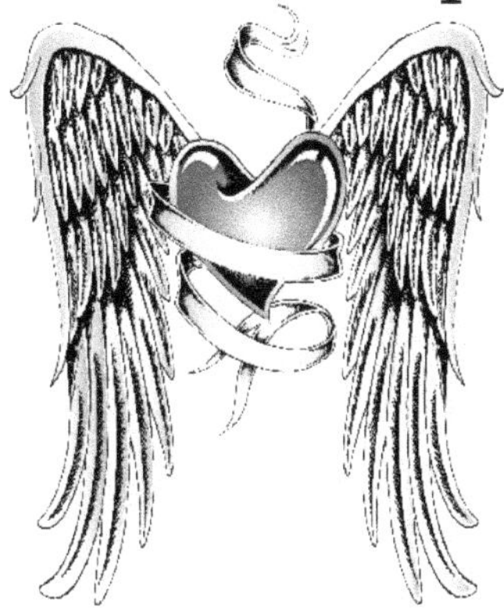

MY DAYS BLENDED TOGETHER while Hannah remained in a coma.

Gallagher had been in to talk to me a few more times since he hauled me into the station, but since they had found signs of a break in at my office, they had dropped all charges. Relief wrapped around me, easing my fear of having to leave Hannah's side for more than a few hours. She was vulnerable here and her name was still on that hit list.

Gallagher's questions now centered on the why, and if I thought there would be more deaths based on the hit list. I did not believe this was over, as a matter of fact I thought it was just the beginning, and I made my thoughts on the matter crystal-clear.

I also told him he needed to warn the others on the list because someone eventually would come for them.

They identified the killer. His name was Scout McHenry, a former Special Forces operative who was dishonorably discharged, and had a criminal record a mile long, including assault, battery, and petty larceny. He was a known mercenary, and from the little bits I was able to pull from Gallagher's mind, it seemed he had a group of friends that held themselves out in the same manner.

My mind kept returning to the ghost and what he said, and it seemed he wasn't bullshitting me in the least. There were plenty of others like him, willing to finish the job.

Gallagher stationed a plain-clothes cop outside the hospital room in response to my reasoning and I'm not entirely sure if it was for my daughter's safety or just to keep an eye on me. The glimpse he had of what happened was enough to make him wary of me, and of what I could do. He wasn't sure about Steve either, but he had the impression I held the power of the universe at my fingertips, which wasn't far from the truth.

I didn't quite understand his frequent visits. It was as if he kept having to validate the truth by seeing the results over and over again. It took a week to close the case and clear my name and my daughter still hadn't woken up.

I stared out the window, ignoring Raven's ghost when the knock came on the door. I turned, meeting Gallagher's gaze as he poked his head in once again.

"Any change?" he asked with genuine concern.

I shook my head. "Unfortunately, no."

"Do you have a second?" he asked, stepping in the room.

"Sure," I said, turning my focus towards him.

He closed the door behind him and crossed to the end of Hannah's bed. His hands fidgeted and he let out a small nervous laugh. "I've been turning over all the things you fed into my head for days now and I need to ask you a question," he started and cleared his throat.

I gave him a nod, waiting. He now had my entire attention and the flurry of thought in his mind only allowed for a few broken words to bleed through.

"Are you... from here?" he asked, and my eyebrows rose.

"You know I was born in York," I said and refrained from adding more because the words I was getting were laughable and all related to Superman or some other insane superhero reference from outer space.

He glanced at the floor and shoved his hands in his pockets. "I know, but were your parents..." He trailed off, shifting his weight and I pressed my lips against a smirk.

When I was sure I wouldn't laugh in his face, I said, "I'm human, Chief. So were my parents."

He looked up at me and his cheeks turned red with embarrassment.

"I'm just a little more supercharged than most," I added and this time I couldn't wipe the grin from my face.

He let out a nervous laugh, shuffling his feet.

"And I get the distinct impression you didn't come here just to ask me if I was from another solar system," I said, yanking his chain. It had the desired effect. This time his laughter was more natural, and he pointed his finger at me.

"You got me there, son. I came because even with the odd questions rolling around in my mind, I think you'd make a hell of an officer. We certainly could use someone with your talents on the force."

I stared at him and now that his mind had cleared, I was able to evaluate his motives and it wasn't to keep an eye on me. It was a genuine offer. One I had never in my wildest dreams considered.

"Are you seriously offering me a job?" I asked, laughing. "After all the trouble I got into when I was younger?"

He joined me, chuckling as he pulled his hands out of his pocket. "You certainly were a piece of work. And yes, I am offering you a position on the force."

I glanced at my daughter and sighed. I knew what kind of demands a cop's life entailed and while York was fairly quiet in the crime department, the hours away when things went to hell wasn't something I was willing to do. Not now that I was Hannah's only surviving parent.

"It's a quiet town," he added as if he knew my current thought process.

I turned to him. "I appreciate the offer, but I've got the paranormal investigation agency and I have the freedom of dictating my own hours. I can't give that up right now. Especially with everything that's happened. Hannah is going to need me when she wakes up."

His calm exhale and nod told me he knew it was a long shot. "I figured. But I had to give it a try. I also came by to let you know O'Keefe's memorial service is scheduled for Friday."

My smile faded. "I'll do my best to be there, but it all depends on my daughter," I said. "And I'll let Steve and CJ know. I'm sure they'll want to make an appearance."

"I appreciate that," he said and turned to leave.

"Chief?"

He half turned back, meeting my gaze.

"If you ever need help with a case in the future..."

"I know where to find you," he said with a nod.

I watched him go, and for the first time, I felt at ease with the cops in this town. We had a long adversarial history, but for some reason, this time, the hatchet was buried, and I'd earned a little respect from the top. It was a good feeling, even though I could never see myself as a small-town cop.

I glanced over at Raven and she stood with her arms crossed, looking at me through her upper lashes like I was in the doghouse.

"What?" I said to her.

"You would make a fantastic cop. You should have taken that job."

"I don't need to work at all," I said, crossing my arms in response. "Besides, I lived the life of a cop's son. I'm not doing that to Hannah."

Her arms dropped, along with her attitude and her sigh ruffled the bed covers. Both our gazes dropped to Hannah. She was more important than a job.

Besides, I now had another goal. I needed to make Lucifer pay for what he did to my family.

Angel Blood Chapter 23

I SHIFTED IN THE chair, and my back muscles clenched in response, sending a sharp pain up my spine and I sat up, glancing at the morning sunrise from the window. Hannah still slept peacefully and Raven still stood watch.

I crossed to the john to relieve my bladder and splash some water on my face. It had been over a week now, and I doubted the possibility of her waking up, even with Valerie's magic. I sported the start of a serious beard, and I glanced in the mirror at the door where Raven's ghost leaned on the doorjamb like she was waiting to impart some level of wisdom. But she remained silent.

I had prayed more in the last few days than I have since I was locked in that butcher's garage in Georgia. I begged God and the heavens to make my daughter forget the horrors she saw. I didn't want her to remember her mother that way. I knew all too well what that does to a person's head.

Steve came by for a few minutes last night to bring me another change of clothes, and he had the copy of the police report for me. I told him about the memorial service, but neglected to tell him Gallagher offered me a job on the force.

I'm not sure what his take would have been, but I knew he would understand my rationale. Besides, I didn't need the money, not with the millions already in my name.

The report still sat on the side table, unread. Every time I reached for it, Raven intervened, asking me not to. She didn't want me to know what he did to her, but I needed to know. I saw enough on the video to give me nightmares for the rest of my life, but I needed the clinical assessment.

I crossed from the bathroom and took a seat next to the bed, staring at the report once again. I moved aside the necklace and her wedding rings that Steve had delivered along with the file and reached for the folder.

"Please don't."

I glanced at Raven's ghost standing on the other side of the bed and hesitated. Her hair shimmered red, as if a band of sunshine now lived in the strands. She was beyond beautiful, and I sighed, pulling my hand back.

"Why didn't you try to contact me?" I asked. The question ate at me, and I finally found the courage to ask her. Everyone in the family knew how to send a mental SOS, but she never even made a peep.

"I was too worried about Hannah to focus enough to send a message out, and then I was in too much pain to form a thought." Her gaze dropped to the floor in shame.

I closed my eyes with a sigh and then turned, reaching for the file, despite her protests.

"Babe, I need to know," I said, meeting her gaze before I opened the file.

Just like the reports O'Keefe showed me earlier this week, the folder began with photos, and I glanced at her, turning them over to give her some level of comfort and her protests calmed. She didn't know I had seen the beginning of the video, and her rationale was focused on the images, but it was already there, just behind my eyelids. The pictures couldn't do any more damage than was already done.

I focused on the notes. Words were easier to digest and keep the reality at bay for a little longer, but the details outlined in the autopsy swept a layer of ice over my skin.

Raven had been full of bloodstone from her esophagus to her anus, so full, in fact, that her intestines perforated in multiple places and her stomach had lacerations as well. The bastard had sewn her shut so the stone would do more damage than the insertion had. The leakage of stomach acid and intestinal bacteria into her abdominal cavity had already formed infection, and she had transitioned into a state of septic shock. If the spear hadn't punctured her heart, the damage was so widespread that she would have died within hours, anyway.

Even if Valerie healed her, the stones would have continued to tear her to pieces from the inside out.

I scanned the next paragraph. Not only was her digestive track full, but her sexual organs were also filled with the sharp shards. The next sentence made my eyes dart to Raven's and the pain in the center of my chest spread.

"You were pregnant?"

She bit her lip. I didn't think ghosts could cry, but a teardrop leaked from the corner of her eye, tumbling down her cheek like a glass prism. When she nodded, I dropped the file on the floor and folded my arms on the side of Hannah's bed before I buried my face in the crook of my elbow.

My loss hit all at once and the tears came in a torrent of shaking sobs. It wasn't until a warm hand landed on the back of my neck that I realized I wasn't alone in my misery. I glanced up, right into my daughter's deep blue eyes and she smiled.

"It's going to be okay, Daddy," she said in that small and innocent voice and then she looked straight at the ghost of my wife and said, "Right, Mommy?"

My daughter carried my affinity for seeing ghosts, and I wondered if she had her mother's natural gift for witchcraft. Wiping my face on the edge of the sheet, I straightened and forced a smile to my lips, sweeping her into my arms in a big bear hug.

I glanced at Raven and she gave me a weak smile.

When I released Hannah, Raven leaned in and planted a soft kiss on her forehead. "You be good for your father."

Hannah's smile faded, and she blinked in confusion, like she recognized her mother wasn't solid. She was more like a wisp of smoke, instead.

"Mommy has to go, but your dad knows a special place where you can come visit me whenever you need me. Okay?"

Hannah glanced at me.

"Paradise Cove," I said. It was a place I wanted to make camp for the rest of my life now that it was the only way to see or feel Raven again.

Hannah stared at me, her eyes widening.

"Daddy can talk," she pointed at me and looked at Raven.

My wife smiled. "Yes. That was the last gift I could give him." Raven leaned close to Hannah. "Make sure your daddy finds another someone special. I don't want him to be alone for the rest of his life, okay?"

I sent my best 'you're out of your fucking mind' glare at the ghost and then met my daughter's wide-eyed gaze.

Raven leaned across the bed and planted a soft kiss on my cheek. "Love you, always," she whispered.

"Love you, too," I said, and Raven's solid form turned to smoke, wrapping around the two of us before dissolving to nothing. "Always."

I kept Hannah's gaze even as the emptiness swallowed my soul.

"I guess Mommy waited until you were awake to say goodbye," I said, softly.

Hannah's chin trembled, and I reached for the necklace on the table, bringing the beautiful Celtic knot into view.

"She left this for you," I said and slipped it over her head, giving her a piece of her mother's magical protection that had done nothing to prevent her demise.

Hannah pressed it to her chest and then reached for me like she understood just how much I needed a hug. At this moment, she reminded me more of Grace than

738

my little ball of unending energy, but I accepted the hug, along with the fact that perhaps the angel blood coursing through our veins made us a little stronger than we had a right to be.

The End

Continue Tom's story with Angel Fire on the next page.

Angel Fire Chapter 1

MY NAME IS THOMAS Patrick Ryan, and I have been mute since a psycho cut out part of my tongue when I was nine. For twenty-one years, I communicated differently than those around me. But now, because of my wife's death, I can speak.

All things considered, I'd rather be mute and still have her by my side.

Cold wraps around me as I stare at the urn in my hand, testing the weight of it. It seems way too light to contain my wife. Her spirit alone would not fit into such a tiny container, and I cannot fathom her remains reduced to the slip of nothing I held. This was all I had left.

Ashes.

Dust.

Tainted memories.

I can't seem to find the will to open the jar and drop what's left of her over the bluff and into the churning Atlantic. This was her wish. To be scattered in our backyard. In the sea we loved to play in. In the waves we loved to listen to every night.

The roar of the ocean did nothing to fill the void in my heart.

A gentle tug on my shorts lowers my gaze to the only reason I haven't planted a bullet in my brain. My daughter looks up at me with those wide, innocent eyes, and I remember why I am standing on the edge of our bluff.

With a silent nod, I find the strength I need to open the urn holding my wife's ashes, and without ceremony, dump it into the swirling wind. Behind me, in the small crowd of my family and friends paying tribute to my wife, my brother sings her favorite song. While Hallelujah isn't really a funeral song, it was her favorite, so we thought it was appropriate for this dismal day. The clarity of CJ's voice tickles my spine with chills.

The ashes swirl on the summer breeze, hanging in front of us as if Raven doesn't want to leave me, either. They condense into a brief image of her, and I stare, scanning her gray form. Before I can reach for her and pull her from the drop, she raises her arms and turns, executing the graceful dive I have seen her do a thousand times from the diving board of our old home. But I've never seen one like this. Never a final swan song.

I choke back the sob lodged in my throat, and just watch her ashen form fall. When she hits the surf, ashes scatter like the splash of the diver before settling on the water and disappearing with the next wave.

My daughter's hand wraps around mine, and I close my eyes with the contact. She gives me the purpose I need to not take a step and drop to the jagged rocks below. When I glance down at Hannah, her chin trembles and silent tears tumble down her cheeks. Her eyes are on the same spot where I had been staring. The spot where the ashes met the water. Her aura darkens, muting her normally bright colors, and I scoop her into my arms, feeling her sadness more acutely than I care to. The emptiness in the center of my chest threatens to take over my form, but I focus on my little girl, meeting her teary gaze.

CJ's voice cracks, and I finally turn, acknowledging that I am not the only one mourning my wife's death. I squint in the glow of CJ's aura. It's as bright and vibrant as the sun, outshining both his wife, Valerie's, and my business partner and best friend, Damian's. You see, my brother's aura is powered by trinity blood and angel grace. He is the only one of the group that has the distinction of having both riding their bloodstream.

Damian's is the next closest in brightness. I'm not sure if his is manufactured by the grace of three angels, or if it is because he is the son of the Archangel Gabriel. The rest of us are distant descendants, but we have enough angel blood in our systems to be considered a delicacy to Lucifer. Our blood apparently revives that fucker.

When we met Damian and his wife, Naomi, we had no clue of our roots, and we thought their triplets were the first true trinities ever born, having the blood of Gabriel, Michael and Raphael infused in their lineage. It wasn't until my brother ended up on the bad end of a deal with the devil that we found out we were also descendants of archangels.

Our mother came from two bloodlines, Raphael's and Lucifer's. CJ's father, Ty Ryan, also came from two archangel bloodlines and the combination created something the world has never seen. CJ is the first true trinity, with Raphael, Uriel, and a double dose of Lucifer in his blood, and he holds the power to destroy the universe.

As for me, I am not a trinity, even though I shared the womb with CJ. The man who sired me was not an angel descendant. I do, however, have a natural born ability to see ghosts. I'm not sure if that results from my mother's angel heritage or just a freak accident.

The rest of my supercharge came by way of a gift from CJ. He wanted to make sure the family was safe while he went off to shut down the closest devil's portal.

Lucifer got wind of the power transfer and offered me a deal, one I said no to because, in the end, my wife never would have forgiven me if I had said yes. It was because of that power transfer that my wife and daughter came into Lucifer's sights with a vengeance.

I try not to blame CJ for Raven's death, but it's there, just at the tip of my newly acquired tongue.

I scan my family. Steve and Jennifer Williams stand together on one side of my brother and Valerie. Jennifer's green eyes hit me like a shot to the heart. She and Steve raised me after my parents died, and she knows me as well as anyone here. She knows that under my cool exterior, I'm a fucking mess. But at least neither she nor Steve is privy to my dark thoughts.

I avoid looking at CJ. His voice cracked for a reason, and it wasn't because he was mourning Raven. He has a direct line into my head and I'm sure my suicidal thoughts, however brief, are what caused his perfect voice to waver.

I give a slight nod to Valerie. I'm pretty sure she heard my thoughts as well, but the devastation in her heart for losing her best friend was almost as crippling as mine. Damian and his wife Naomi flank CJ and Valerie, and their kids haven't made a peep the entire time I stood contemplating my wife's death.

My gaze falls on the children standing stoically in front of Damian and Naomi. Grace, their daughter, is close enough to CJ's newborn's car seat to slowly rock it, keeping little Alex quiet for the time being. Her eyes meet mine, and she offers me a sad smile before her gaze moves to Hannah's. The same silent communication follows, and Hannah struggles in my arms. I put her on the ground, and she crosses, letting Grace give her a heartfelt hug.

Five true trinities stand in our midst and the responsibility of keeping them safe from Lucifer's grasp weighs heavily on each and every one of us. Protecting the angel legacy is more critical now than it ever was before, because once the last angel descendant outside our town is slaughtered, York will become the final battleground.

Angel Fire Chapter 2

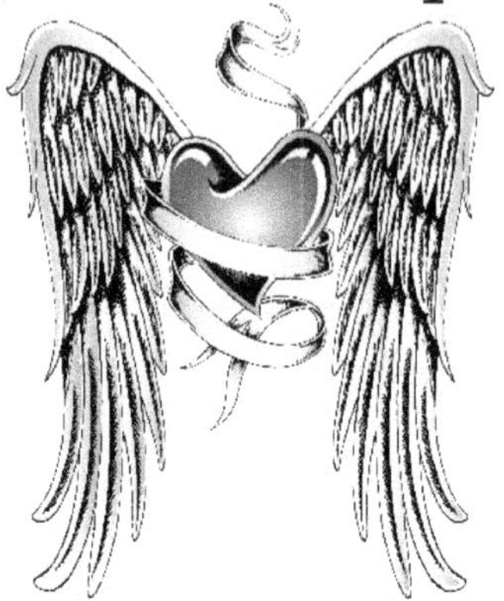

ANOTHER DAY, ANOTHER FUNERAL, and this time Hannah can't seem to keep still. She squirms in my lap like my holding her is the ultimate offense, but at least she hasn't pitched a fit. Yet.

The Star of the Sea Catholic Church is as much of an enigma to me as it is to Hannah, but I figure I owe it to Captain O'Keefe to be at his funeral, since he was the one trying to find my wife and daughter when he was killed.

While the funeral service runs on, I try to figure out the last time I set foot in a church. I think the last time was my father's funeral when I was nine, but that was at the Congregational Church in the center of town, and it was more of a memorial service than this ultra-formal funeral procession.

I feel completely out of place in my shorts and polo shirt, but I haven't had time to get down to any of the stores in Kittery to get anything beyond what Steve brought that first night at the hospital, and I figure blood-stained jeans would have been worse than what I am wearing.

The incense tickles my nose and several times over the last few minutes; I had to press my knuckle to my nostril to contain the urge to sneeze. Hannah isn't as successful and lets out three mouse-like achoos. Her sneezes always make me smile, and this time is no different.

She is so darned cute, and so the opposite of either Raven or me. We sounded like a freight train when we sneezed, and she sounded exactly what I envisioned a tiny rodent would sound like.

I set her down on the seat next to me and trade a glance with CJ. His lips are pressed against his own smirk, but the small dimples in his cheek tell me he might lose the battle and smile. He is just as amused by Hannah's sneezes as I am.

CJ at least salvaged a pair of pants and a button-down shirt for the occasion, as did Steve next to him, making me feel much more like a slacker than I was. His lighthearted smirk faded.

"You're fine," he says, nodding toward my clothes.

Hannah wore a little sundress that Raven had packed in the overnight bag she had in the car, and I'd successfully corralled her wild hair into a single braid down her back. Just that simple task had made me feel like I could do this. I could raise my daughter without my wife by my side, and as empty as I felt, at least I had our little girl.

Fortunately, Raven had packed a few of Hannah's favorite toys and the blanket she couldn't go to sleep without, so my daughter had some of her comforts. The only other bag in the car was the one with Raven's magic crystals and potions and her spell book. It also contained her polished gems, including a handful of bloodstone pendants, which we all wore for protection from the spirit world.

Unfortunately, bloodstone will always remind me of her death.

Raw bloodstone had been the tool used to rip my wife apart from the inside out, killing her and my unborn child with it.

CJ's stare pulled my attention his way. His wide eyes told me he had been in my head for my little narrative. No one knew Raven had been pregnant, and I only found out via the police report.

"She was..." he says and stops, mindful that my daughter is sitting between us. He keeps eye contact with me.

I wrap my arm around Hannah and place a small kiss on her forehead, and my gaze never leaves CJ's.

He inhales and looks forward, blowing the breath out while he digests the new fact my silence has confirmed. His lips press together, forming a frown, and his eyelids blink more rapidly than normal. When he slides his gaze back, there are unshed tears glossing his eyes. He gives me that silent nod I am used to, his way of saying he was sorry without any words, and I acknowledge it with the same.

Both of us refocus on the front of the cathedral, and what I hope is the end of the ceremony. Officers lift the casket, and the procession begins. The church empties from the front and by the time we get to the reception line, we are the last people left to give condolences.

I step in line behind Steve and CJ, with Hannah perched in my left arm. "I'm sorry for your loss," I say, and shake hands as I move down the line, repeating the words until I'm standing in front of Bridget O'Keefe, the captain's niece.

As the words flow from my mouth, her bloodshot hazel-eyes widen. Her aura flares with curiosity, but the darker colors inscribed already have me stepping away. I turn to O'Keefe's widow.

"Tom?" Bridget's voice pulls my gaze back to hers.

"Yeah," I say clearly, meeting her stark stare.

"I... I'm sorry for your loss, too," she says, and there is sincerity in her words that I had never expected.

I force a ghost of a smile to show my appreciation and give her a nod. "Thank you," I add, because there really isn't anything else to say.

I turn to Mrs. O'Keefe, and her gaze meets mine. She knows who I am from all my past scuffles with her husband when I was younger. From the sad expression donning her features, along with the parade of thoughts through her mind, she also knows about my loss.

Instead of shaking the hand I offer her, she wraps me in an awkward hug. No words are exchanged, but as she pulls away, I have to swallow the lump that formed in my throat, and blink away the sudden sheen covering my eyes.

I give her a nod and step away, holding Hannah closer as we head to my car. CJ and Steve are already waiting.

"Tom?" Bridget's voice calls and the fast click of her heels on pavement stops my progression. I put Hannah down and take her hand.

"Who is that?" Hannah asks as we watch Bridget dodge cars in a light jog to catch up with me.

"Someone I knew in high school." I glance down, meeting my daughter's gaze.

"Thank you for waiting," Bridget says as she approaches us. She gives Hannah a smile before looking back at me. "I have an odd question for you," she starts and shifts, looking away from me at the rest of the parking lot. "Um. Are you hiring?"

When she returns her gaze to me, I can tell she is trying to keep from fidgeting, but isn't doing a very good job of it.

"Excuse me?"

"Hiring. A job. You know?" She wrings her hands, and the breeze loosens a couple of her golden locks from the classy bun at the back of her head.

I couldn't help it, a small laugh comes out and her gaze snaps to mine.

"Look, I am very organized, and I could answer calls and do whatever paperwork is necessary." Her eyes plead with me, to the point I don't know exactly what to say.

"Do you even know what we do?" I finally ask.

"You hunt ghosts," she says in a way that leads me to believe everyone in town knows what we do. The only thing missing was a 'duh' and an eye roll.

Now I did laugh. Hannah looked up at me, and in all her innocence says, "Mommy always said you and Damian need a secretary."

Oh, great. Now my three-year-old is weighing in. Bridget smiles down at her before looking back at me.

"Let me talk to my partner," I say in more of a sigh than anything else and Bridget's aura responds, becoming much brighter than it had been before. I guess worrying about where your next meal is coming from puts a lot of dark ribbons in your aura.

"Thank you," she says, and rummages around in her purse. She finally pulls out a business card and scribbles her number on the back. "If you, or your partner, would like me to come in for an interview, please call me. I can start any time."

Out of politeness, I take the card and slip it into my pocket. When I cross the rest of the distance to where Steve and CJ are standing, I get a smirk in response.

"What did Bridget O'Keefe want?" CJ asks, jutting his chin in her direction. He knows the history as well as I do. In high school, I tagged her, along with almost anything in a skirt. I think I slept with most of the girls in the school, and they all seemed to blend into one big fuck-fest in my head. I stopped sleeping around when I started dating Tanya, and then the Windwalker got hold of her. Out of that horror show, I met Raven, and the rest was history.

"A job," I answer, and open the back door, depositing Hannah in her car seat. CJ snorts a laugh and I glance at him over the car.

His laugh fades and his eyebrows arch. "You're considering hiring her?"

"It would help to have someone answering the phones and screening the nut cases we get calls from." I say, after I get Hannah all hooked in her seat. I close her door and step to the driver's door. "Besides, she needs the money," I add with a shrug.

"She is perfectly capable of getting a job somewhere else."

"Don't be such a dick. She's not a gold digger, otherwise, she would have tried to seduce me instead of asking for a job," I say and slide into the driver's seat.

CJ leans down, looking at me through the window. "Are you sure about that?"

I bite my tongue before I tell him to fuck off, but based on the smirk he sends my way, he heard the thought as clearly as if I had said it aloud.

I didn't want to be arrogant, thinking the change in her aura had to do with anything other than a job prospect. I was also not naïve in any sense of the word. Because of my bank account balance alone, I'm sure the line of single women will start to form once the word gets out. It doesn't hurt that I'm not bad to look at, either, and that's what got me into a world of trouble in high school.

If I ever get past this hole in the center of my chest, I'm sure I won't be hurting for a date, but I can't even imagine that right now. I have no interest in anyone but my wife.

Angel Fire Chapter 3

THE SHRILL RING OF my alarm reminds me that vacation is over and I crawl out of bed, heading to the bathroom to clean up before I head to the office for the first time since the end of June. As the water pelts my skin, I wonder if the cops left it a mess or not.

My computer sits idle by the front door, waiting for me to open it. I haven't had the heart to look to see if Chief Gallagher actually erased the video that the killer fed to my hard drive or not. It isn't something I want to see, and I certainly don't want Hannah finding that horrifying tape by accident.

I turn off the water and dry myself, still in a stupor, like I always am in the morning. My office attire isn't much different from what I wore to the funeral, because I haven't gone shopping yet. The idea of leaving Hannah for the time necessary to pick up an entire wardrobe just didn't settle well, and bringing a three-year-old into a department store is something akin to disaster.

The bed is a mess, and I stare at it for a moment before turning away. I never saw the benefit of making a bed. Especially since I'm just going to mess it up again tonight. I turn to leave the room and pause in the doorway, glancing over my shoulder.

Raven's Irish brogue echoes in my head, "We're civilized, Tom, not some nomads that have no appreciation for what we have. You don't like garbage piled up around the house, so I make sure the house is clean. Well, *I* hate an unmade bed, so get your fine arse over here and help me make it."

I can almost see her standing by our bed at home, with her hands on her hips and that irritated glare of hers catching mine. The memory pulls a smile to my lips, and then I remember she will never scold me about an unmade bed, ever again. Emptiness threatens to overtake me, and I sigh, turn back, and abide by the wishes of the ghost in my head.

I duck into the other bedroom in this drab cottage, wishing the rebuilding of our home could be instantaneous, and not months away from being livable. Hannah is still out, and I stare at my sleeping daughter. I doubt she is going to like me today, especially since she didn't wake to the alarm or my tooling around in the bathroom. And the office isn't exactly the playscape she is used to. But I really have no choice.

I can't bring myself to leave her with anyone else. Any time I try, I am paralyzed by the same sick fear I felt when she and Raven were missing. I don't even make it to my car without a panic attack.

When we were in the hospital, it was easier. It was a containable environment. Out here in the real world, I am terrified of her going missing, and this time, ending up dead.

I know this isn't healthy for either of us, but I am not even close to being able to cope without her in my sight. So, she's coming to work with me until I can get my shit together, or she goes off to college, whichever comes first.

I sit on the edge of her bed, and run my fingers through her knotted hair. "Sweetie-pie?"

Hannah mumbles and curls into a tight ball, rolling away from my touch.

"Come on, honey. Daddy needs to get to work."

She growls at me, glaring through her red hair. If this is what she is like at three, I am going to be in for a nightmare when she starts school.

"I'll tell you what. I'll go get our lunches ready, and you can take your time thinking about what toys you want to bring with you."

"Can I bring all of them?"

I smile at her. "You can bring whatever fits in that duffel bag over there." I point to the bag in the corner, knowing she could fit all her things and then some in it right now. Her eyes light up and I push her hair out of her face and plant a gentle kiss on her cheek. "You pack your things, and when I'm done with lunches, I'll come help you with your clothes."

She climbs out of bed and starts to pack her toys even before I hit the small hallway leading to the miniscule combination living room and kitchenette. I throw together a couple of peanut butter and Nutella sandwiches, because it's Hannah's favorite and I can't say I disagree. It's my new favorite as well. I can't understand how Raven didn't like it, but then again, she was never into sweets. Give her dark chocolate and she was happy, but she stayed away from anything else full of sugar and preservatives.

By the time I finish, Hannah drags her bag into the kitchen. I glance over at her and have to press my lips together against a laugh. She attempted to dress herself and do her own hair, and it isn't pretty.

"Did you brush your teeth?" I ask, knowing that may be the only way to get her into the bathroom where I can try to salvage her hair. Her accomplished smile drops and so does the bag in her hand before she turns and runs the short distance to the bathroom.

I wipe my hands and follow.

"Let me see if I can straighten out your hair for you," I say and grab the brush off the counter, blocking her exit. She finishes with her teeth, and I nod toward the closed toilet seat.

"But, Daddy," she starts, and I reach down and lift her up so she can see the partial ponytail sticking out at an odd angle from the side of her head.

"You did a good job. I just want to make it neater, so it lasts, okay?"

She studies the job she did and then meets my gaze with a meek nod.

"Do you want me to braid it like I did the other day?"

The smile is my answer, but she says "Yes, please," just to make sure I know she wants me to.

The other day I did the braid when her hair was wet and as I try to tame the dry curls, I find it nearly impossible, but at least what I've done to her hair looks marginally better than her attempt. Next, I eye her sundress and nightgown pants. The combination is a glaring error of colors, but they rightfully mix with her vibrant aura.

"Can we do without the pajama pants?"

"What if I need to take a nap?" she asks and puts her hands up in a shrug that seems so logical I can't argue.

"Speaking of naps, do you have your blanket?"

Her eyes widen and she runs into her room, emerging a moment later with her blanket and snuggle pillow.

"I want pancakes."

I glance at the kitchenette area and sigh. "We don't have pancakes, honey. How about some cereal instead?"

She crosses her arms and I'm not sure what to do with her grumpy glare.

"We can stop at the store on the way home and I'll get us what we need for pancakes, okay?"

My attempt to appease the oncoming tantrum worked, and she breaks out in a smile. "Pancakes later?"

I grin back at her. "Absolutely. As long as you are a good girl today. And if you are extra good, maybe I'll let you have it with Nutella."

Her eyes sparkle and my heart swells. Given what has happened to us in the last month, I would say we were coping pretty well, and right now, I feel pretty good about my chances to pull off this single dad thing.

I pick up the duffel bag with her toys, and the diaper bag that doubled as our lunch sack, and take Hannah's hand. "Ready to go to work?"

"Can I answer the phone?" she asks with such enthusiasm that I laugh.

"Maybe," I say and give her hand a squeeze. I lock the little cottage behind me and dump all our things in the passenger seat before I hook Hannah into her car seat.

Thankfully, my ride is short. Damian's car is in the driveway of the house we renovated for our offices. The view of the York River is both relaxing and exhilarating, and today there seems to be a wealth of activity on the water, and cars are lining the street already, despite the early hour.

I pull next to Damian's car and unhook Hannah, taking her hand and guiding her to the passenger side, where all our crap for the day is stowed. After shouldering the bags, including my computer, I lead Hannah to the door and hold it open for her.

I'm so focused on Hannah that when I look up into our small reception area, I freeze halfway in the door. Damian's bright aura has me squinting, but that isn't what has me at a loss.

Bridget sits in the chair at our reception desk, going over something on the computer screen with Damian.

"I figured you might not say anything to your partner, so I decided to come and introduce myself."

I guess she can accurately read the shock that slackened my jaw and has my skin tingling.

Damian straightens and gives me a shrug. "He hasn't had the chance to talk to me since your uncle's funeral," he says to smooth things over. "Miss O'Keefe seems qualified to handle receptionist duties, don't you think?"

"Hi!" Hannah announces, pulling all our attention to her.

"Um, okay," I say, and head towards my office to dump the crap I'm carrying. Hannah follows, and as soon as I have her settled in the small sitting area with her toys, I turn toward the outer room.

Bridget stands in my doorway patiently waiting for me to finish with Hannah.

"I'm sorry. I just really need a job. My aunt is selling the house and moving south, so I'm kind of in a jamb."

I don't say anything at first because Hannah is still within hearing range. Instead, I study Bridget's aura before meeting her gaze. Both her aura and thoughts are nervous and I cross my arms, raising an eyebrow.

"You didn't think I'd say anything?" I ask, because, despite her doubt in my following through, it was something I had been considering.

She shifts from foot to foot, and her gaze drops to the floor before flicking towards my daughter and then back to me. "With our past?" She stops speaking and offers me a shrug. "No. I didn't think you were going to say anything."

"Well, you didn't really give me a chance."

Her face flushes and she does that single shoulder raise, but she at least keeps eye contact. "I'm kind of desperate here," she says in barely a whisper.

"I know; you had to be to approach me. That's why I had planned on talking with Damian this morning."

"My uncle was all I had left," she says, and pain flares in her eyes, sending a dark ribbon through her aura.

"What about your parents?" The words tumble out and she just shakes her head, but the thoughts swirling in her mind give me a clear picture. They died in a horrible highway crash a few years ago.

I close my eyes and sigh, feeling her pain for a moment more before I dull the sensation and meet her gaze.

"They died," she finally forces the words out.

"I'm so sorry." I lead her out of Hannah's hearing range and into the reception area.

She sniffles and shakes her head, pulling herself together in a matter of seconds. "I'm sorry if I've made you... uncomfortable." She meets my gaze.

My irritation at her bypassing me fades, and I glance over at Damian's office. "So, it looks like my partner offered you the job."

She smiles and nods. "He said the job was mine unless you had an issue."

"Did you tell him you jumped the gun a little?" I cross my arms, putting her on the spot.

She shuffles her feet and stares at the floor, shaking her head. "I kind of told him you said I had a job, as long as it was okay with him," she says, and her eyes move to mine as she lets out a nervous laugh.

The irritation scratches at my chest. "Excuse me?"

Humility passes over her features, and she drops her gaze again.

"I can't believe you lied to get a job," I say and point at Damian's office. "I'm surprised he didn't call you out on bullshitting him."

"He didn't know."

I let out a harsh laugh. "Both Damian and I know when someone is bullshitting us."

She blinks and steps back at the anger laced into my words.

"Daddy?" Hannah's meek voice pulls my attention away from Bridget.

Her wide eyes calm the aggravation, and I point toward the back of my office. "Go play with your toys. I'll be a few more minutes."

We both watch as my daughter trades glances with each of us and then disappears back to the sitting area. I refocus on Bridget.

"She is a beautiful little girl," she says, still looking at my office doorway.

"Thank you, but we aren't discussing my daughter. We are discussing the conditions of employment."

Her gaze snaps to mine. "You're still going to hire me?"

"Under two conditions." I hold up two fingers, and she stares at them before meeting my gaze again.

"What conditions?" Her voice shivers with nerves.

"One, that you never lie to me. Ever." I glare down at her, stepping closer to intimidate her. I'm a pretty big guy, and right now I'm charged with irritation, so it works.

She just nods and shuffles a step back while tilting her head farther back to keep my gaze.

"Two, whatever you hear within these walls stays within these walls."

This time she isn't as quick to nod, and her mouth drops open a fraction. The question in her mind stalls, but then she shifts and clears her throat.

"As long as it isn't illegal," she says, jutting her chin in a challenge.

I glance over her head at Damian, who is now leaning on his doorjamb with an amused smirk.

"Define illegal," he says, and she spins at his voice.

"Drugs, tax evasion, murder," she spits out, and her hands find her hips. "Child abuse," she adds after a moment. "You know, illegal activities."

I share a glance with Damian and then focus on the naïve woman in front of me.

"Do you agree?" I ask, and she glances over her shoulder at me. She hasn't agreed yet and without the promise of confidentiality, I am not inclined to hire her.

"I'm not agreeing to keep illegal activities within these walls." She crosses her arms and turns my way.

"Do you consider killing a ghost illegal?" I ask.

Her arms fall to her side. "No."

"What about demons, or vampires?"

She takes a step back and her eyes widen as she shakes her head. "No."

"Good, then I think we are on the same page. I just need you to agree to the terms."

She blinks, glancing between the two of us. "I... I," she stutters and gulps before trying again. "I'm okay with that."

"Are you okay enough to sign a confidentiality agreement?" Damian asks, drawing her attention.

She nods and stutters out a yes.

He crosses to the cabinet, pulls out our standard confidentiality agreement that we use with all our clients, and drops it on the desk. The moment she signs, he smiles.

"Welcome to R.A. Paranormal Investigation Agency," he says and puts out his hand.

Bridget shakes it timidly and turns towards me. "You were just saying those things to scare me, weren't you?"

I smile and turn toward my office, hesitating at the door. "Just one more thing." I turn back towards her in all seriousness. "If either of us ever tells you to run, you run to where we tell you to go, like the world's on fire. No deviation, no stops, just haul ass, okay?"

She just stares at me, licks her lips, and nods. I can tell without being in her head that she is now

questioning whether she really wants this job. "O...
Okay," she says and slowly sits down at the desk.

I glance at my business partner. "I'm going to need
that list," I say, and his response is a raised eyebrow. "I
think I know one of the names, and I want to make sure
my eyes weren't playing tricks on me," I add when he
doesn't move.

I disappear into my office and unpack my computer
on my desk. Hannah is busy with a couple of Barbie
dolls and her stuffed bear, having a make-believe tea
party. I can't help but smile at her innocence as she
chatters away.

The moment I have dreaded for weeks is now at
hand, and I drop my gaze to my computer.

"You want me to turn it on for you?" Damian asks as
he strides into the room. He drops the notebook on the
corner of my desk.

"Uncle Damian, do you want to join my tea party?"
Hannah asks.

"Thank you, sweetheart, but I've got some work to
do. Maybe next time." He glances at me and nods
toward Hannah.

"I can't leave her," I mumble. He gets it as much as
the rest of the family.

"Are you going to stare at a blank screen all day, or
are you going to turn that thing on?" He waves toward
the laptop, changing the subject.

He wasn't in the interrogation room when Chief
Gallagher played the video. He doesn't know the depth
of awfulness put on display for those few seconds, nor
does he know what it did inside me. I just stare at him,
keeping a lid on that memory and all the emotions that
go along with it, but they burn through anyway.

Instead of lamenting, I flip it open like it's my worst
enemy and press the on button before pushing my chair
back and stepping away. I glance at Hannah, wondering
if she can feel my anxiety. I know Damian can, because
he swivels the laptop in his direction and starts typing.

I'm not a computer genius like he is, so when he
turns it back in my direction, I'm satisfied that whatever

had been on the computer is now gone. I don't need his confirmation, but he gives it anyway.

"It's clean."

"Thanks," I mutter and take a seat. Reaching for the list he put on my desk.

"How are you doing?" he asks quietly, and I squint up at him.

"As best as one would expect. At least I have her. She keeps me going," I say, focusing my gaze on my daughter. "The nightmares suck, but I'll live," I add, with what I hope is a smile.

"Your lisp seems to be clearing up," he says, leading me away from any sort of emotional outburst that he perceives might happen any minute. And he isn't wrong. I am never sure when the impact of Raven's death will hit.

"Yes. It certainly has. Now you can't poke fun at me at Thanksgiving." I purposely make my S's into a TH sound just for comic relief.

"I wouldn't count on that," he says with a laugh. He's still chuckling as he steps out of sight, leaving me with Hannah and the list of angel descendants.

Angel Fire Chapter 4

I STARE OUT THE window, with nerves bundled in my stomach, as Bridget takes Hannah for a walk to see the lobsters on the other side of the bridge so I can make a phone call. I scan my contacts, finding the number I want before pressing the call button and refocusing on my daughter.

The phone rings in my ear and just as I am going to hang up, a breathless voice announces, "Hello," on the line.

"Hello. Is Austin Shelton available?"

"Um," the female on the line says. "He's in the shower. Can I ask who is calling?"

"It's Tom Ryan."

Silence filters over the line. "Come again?" she asks.

"Tom Ryan. We met briefly in New York," I say.

"That's what I thought you said." Her voice trails off, and I get a glimpse of her frightened thoughts.

My name brings back memories she has been trying to suppress for months. "How are you, Paige?" I ask, my gaze still locked on my daughter.

"I'm... okay," she says quietly. "What kind of software are you using to talk? It sounds amazing."

I drop my gaze and huff a laugh. "Well, that's a very long story that I'll save for another time." I glance out the window again as the panic creeps in, but a sigh escapes as my senses are filled with the vision of my daughter picking up a lobster from one of the tanks. I'm stunned into silence as Bridget leans down next to her and picks one up as well. "In the meantime, I can hang on if you want to tell him I'm on the line," I say, as I notice the quiet on the phone.

"He will be out in a minute," Paige says. "How's your wife doing?" she asks with genuine curiosity.

It was a logical question... after all, both Raven and I had a great deal to do with saving her from a possessed psychopath. But it still tightened my throat. I cough and close my eyes as the pain slams home, making my chest feel like a cannon shot through it.

"Raven died recently," I answer, and despise the shaky quality of my voice. When my eyes open again, Hannah is standing on the pier holding the lobster, but staring in my direction, as if she can feel the debilitating pain radiating through my soul. She puts the lobster back and takes Bridget's hand, leading her back in this direction.

Paige is speaking, but I hardly hear her condolences over the buzzing in my ears.

"Thank you. Your thoughts and prayers are appreciated," I say as the automatic response takes over.

Hannah breaks free of Bridget and runs. She is barreling towards the house with no consideration for traffic, and that bright light of fear nips at the fog settling over me.

"Stop," I yell, putting my hand up like a traffic cop, and Hannah stops in mid stride just before she breaches the curb onto the road.

My heart thunders in my chest, and Bridget catches up to Hannah, scooping her up in her arms. I release my hold and then my focus comes back to me.

"Are you all right?" Paige is asking.

"Yes. Sorry about that. My daughter nearly ran into the road," I answer. "She is only three," I add, feeling the need to explain.

"Oh. Well, Austin is here," she says and the phone shuffles.

"Mr. Ryan?"

"Please, call me Tom." My breath is still constricted, but my chest loosens just as Bridget and Hannah step back on the property. However, the way Bridget is staring at me tells me I might have some explaining to do.

"Tom, to what do I owe the pleasure?"

I turn away from the window with no idea how I'm going to broach the subject. "Are you and Paige still in New York?"

"No. I decided Dartmouth was a safer option," he answers, and I let a sigh of relief out.

That meant the hit list wasn't as up to date as we thought. According to what the killer had on him, Austin was in New York.

"Why?"

"Because I've got some bad news."

Hannah steps into the room and stares at me the way she had in the hospital. Just a hint of worry pulls at the corners of her mouth, and she runs across the distance, grabbing my leg in a tight hug.

"What bad news?" Austin asks, his voice guarded now and his mind swirling around Hunter Garrett, the ghost that attacked Paige. CJ annihilated him just as surely as he killed the ghost of the bastard who killed Raven, so Austin had nothing to worry about from that ghost.

"It's not Hunter," I say and hear the release of the breath he was holding. If only it were, at least a ghost can be contained. "It's much worse than Hunter," I say, as I stroke my daughter's hair. "Think you can arrange a trip to York Beach so we can talk?"

"Sure. I don't start classes for another couple of weeks," he answers.

"Let me give you to my secretary. She'll give you the address of my office and some suitable places for you and Paige to stay. Your choice, it's on me."

"Sure. We still owe you and your wife dinner," he says and again that hole in my chest widens.

I can hear Paige in the background, correcting his error.

"Shit, man, I'm sorry, I didn't know," he says after a few whispered words.

"Thanks." That's all I can get out before I hand Bridget the phone. "Please find a hotel close to the beach for them and give them our address here."

Bridget takes the phone and I lean down, scooping up Hannah in my arms and giving her a bear hug. She hugs me back just as fiercely.

When I put her back down, Bridget has already left the room, and I kneel in front of Hannah. "What got into you back there?" I jut my chin towards Off the Boat Lobster across the bridge. "You know better than to run into a busy street without looking," I scold. My heart rate finally settles into a normal rhythm.

Hannah looks at the window. "I... I remembered I was too far from you," she says, and her chin trembles. When her eyes fill up with tears, I know I have gone overboard with my over protectiveness of the past few weeks into the realm of obnoxious.

I wrap my arms around her before her tears fall in earnest. "I could still see you," I whisper.

"I could see Mommy, too," she whispers back.

That hole in my chest expands, and I bite down on my lip, blinking the wetness from my eyes. A throat clears behind me, and I turn, meeting Bridget's hesitant gaze.

"Sorry for interrupting," she says and clears her throat. "But I need a credit card for The York Harbor Inn."

I nod and reach into my back pocket, pulling out my wallet and offering it to her. Her gaze is just as pained as mine feels. She takes my wallet and hustles from the room, but not before I see a tear escape from the corner of her eye.

"Hannah, baby, how much do you remember?" I ask, even though it's not something I want to know, but her memories flood my head, and I have to suck in air and close my eyes. This is the first time the memory surfaced vividly enough for me to catch, and I pray she can stuff it back down into whatever dark, subconscious box contained it.

She remembers enough to haunt her for a lifetime. I wish I had the power to erase the memories, to wipe those horrible visions from her, and take away the fear making her little body shake in my arms.

She doesn't answer me, and when I pull her away from my shoulder, her tear-stained cheeks rip another piece of my heart. She remains silent and I wipe the tears with my thumbs, giving her a small nod.

"Can you remember Mommy's laugh?" I ask, trying to get her to focus away from the memory of the machine and my wife's muffled screams.

Hannah's chin quivers again and I put my hand over her heart. "Mommy's here, in our hearts. Can you feel her?"

When she shakes her head, I try something different.

"Close your eyes," I say softly, and close my eyes along with her, pulling Hannah's most recent favorite moment into my head, offering it to my daughter. In it, Raven is laughing with me. "Can you hear her now?"

"Yes," her little voice fills my world, and I open my eyes, meeting hers.

Her arms fly around my neck, tightening. I wrap her in my arms again, wishing I could take away her pain, her loss, and let her have the carefree life she was meant to have. When her shakes subside, I realize her body is limp.

My baby girl cried herself to sleep on my shoulder.

I move her to the couch and tuck her in with her blanket and teddy bear before I step out into the reception area, fighting my own demons. Bridget stands and crosses, handing me my wallet, and without a word, she gives me a hug.

In a way, her warmth reminds me of Jennifer, and as much as I want to man up right now, I can't contain the tears. My entire body shakes with them, but no sound escapes. I accept the hug, letting her hold me together until I can collect my wits.

I finally pull away and wipe my face. "Thank you," I say with a voice gruff from tears.

"I am so sorry about her running off like that," she says, wiping the tears from her own cheeks. "Had I known..."

I shake my head. "There's no way you could have known."

"Yeah, well, I keep forgetting how much you two have lost," she says and takes another step, distancing herself from me to gain control over her emotions.

I wish taking a step back was all it took to get control over the raging storm threatening to drown me. "I wish I had the luxury of forgetting." I can't help the bitterness, and Bridget doesn't seem to mind. I stuff my wallet back into my pocket and clear my throat. "When will Austin be in town?" I ask, because I need a change of subject.

"He said he would come this weekend," Bridget says. "I have them booked at the York Harbor Inn. I figured it was the right mix of quaint, and close enough to the beach to keep them entertained."

"So is The Union Bluff," I say, thinking they might like York Village better than York Harbor.

She shakes her head. "Trust me, York Harbor Inn is more the feel you want. Besides, it's a much easier drive here than it would be from town."

She had a point.

"Thanks." I say and start to turn.

"What happened outside?" she asks before I can escape.

"I stopped Hannah from entering the street," I say with my back to her, and then I glance over my shoulder. "Anything said within these walls..."

"Stays within these walls," she says and nods. "Kind of like Vegas," she adds with a smile, "Or being the assistant to a police detective."

I guess working in the police station had given her some idea of the need for confidentiality.

"Yes." I debate on answering, and then sigh. "I can do... things."

"Beyond seeing ghosts?"

My lips twitched into a smile. "Yeah."

She perches on the corner of the desk, her stare now intent. "Like what?"

"Like stop small children from getting hit by cars."

"How?"

I tap my temple. "Psychic crap." I don't know any other way of putting it.

"What else?" she pushes, and her hazel eyes sparkle with contained excitement.

I study the new and vibrant covers swirling in her aura, recognizing the mix as curiosity.

"I can see auras," I say when my gaze finds hers again.

"No way?" She stands up, like I've told her I know where the pot of gold at the end of the rainbow resides. Despite being almost thirty, like me, Bridget seems to have the youthful spunk of a teenager, along with the innate inquisitiveness of a child.

"That kind of came with the tongue," I say and smile, but it feels awkward, so I just huff and offer her a shrug. I'm not sure I want to go further with this conversation.

Her eyes blink a few times and she slowly lowers herself back to the corner of the desk. "Your wife's tongue, right?"

"Ay-up," I say, shoving my hands into my pockets and half turning in her direction.

"How weird is that?"

I actually laugh. "Very fucking weird."

"I still can't get over you talking. And now this, holy cow." Her mind searches for someone she could trust enough to share this new bombshell with, because she isn't sure she can keep this juicy fact locked inside.

"And you need to keep this quiet." My sternness captures her attention, and she keeps my stare. "I can also read minds. I was dead serious when I told you both Damian and I know when someone is bullshitting us."

She let out a nervous laugh. "It's a good thing my motives aren't nefarious," she says in a way that leads me to believe maybe there was a hidden agenda after all.

"I can smell a gold digger a mile away," I say with a wicked grin, narrowing my eyes at her.

"You didn't have this in high school, did you?" she says slowly, eyeing me in a way that makes me complete my turn towards her.

My smile fades and I shake my head. "Unfortunately, no."

"If you had said yes, I was going to seriously question the accuracy of your radar."

My eyebrows rise as my skin prickles in shock. "Why?"

"Oh, come on, Tanya was all over you because of your money, and then she realized she just couldn't deal with..." Bridget presses her lips together against the rest. She would be the one person to know the real reason Tanya broke up with me. After all, she had been Tanya's best friend. Her gaze drops away. "I'm sorry, I never understood her rationale..."

"It's okay. We both know why Tanya broke up with me, and to tell you the truth, it fucked me up a little. Not as much as seeing her faceless ghost did, but..."

Bridget let out a nervous laugh and met my gaze. "You saw it, too?"

"It?"

"Tanya without a face," she whispers and glances over my shoulder towards my office before meeting my gaze again.

I stare at her, unable to speak. Instead, I search her aura, her face and the depth of her eyes, pushing myself into her head just enough to retrieve the memory. "Did you know I was innocent?"

Bridget drops her gaze to the ground. "I didn't know what to think," she admits. "The last time I saw her, she was getting into your car," she adds and shrugs, forcing her gaze back to mine. "Besides, the ghost didn't speak. She just appeared the night she was killed, and it freaked the hell out of me."

I let out a harsh laugh. "Yeah, imagine what seeing her like that for real did to me." I shift because this is the last thing I want to talk about, especially since it would bring me right back around to Raven and slam the loss home again.

Bridget seems to sense I'm uncomfortable, and she slips off the corner of the desk, approaching me, only to stop a couple of steps away. "If you ever need an ear, I'm really good at listening," she offers in all sincerity.

I search her mind and aura for ulterior motives and find none. "How were you ever friends with Tanya?" The question blurts from my mouth before I can stop it.

"We basically grew up next door to each other, and I kind of rode the popularity wave on her skirts," she says and her cheeks color with embarrassment. "She wasn't a nice person either, but I didn't have a prayer on my own. I'm too... different, and would probably have been just as shunned as your wife was, had I not been a part of the 'in' crowd." She makes finger quotes when she says in, and I smile, knowing just how desperate I was to be a part of that crowd as well.

"I guess it had its benefits," I say, shifting and looking at my feet.

"I guess it would, if you were the class slut..."

I raise my gaze to hers and catch the smirk. Her thoughts drift in that direction before she scolds herself, bringing her back to the more professional office demeanor.

"If I recall correctly, you didn't seem to have an issue sampling those benefits." I can't help the velvet purr in my voice, and Bridget actually laughs aloud.

"I wouldn't trust my recollection. It's been a while, tiger," she teases, and slaps me on the chest before retreating to her desk, but her thoughts linger for longer than appropriate.

Heat fills my cheeks and I shift. "I'm sorry for being such a jackass back then," I say, and turn towards my office.

"Never said you were a jackass. I just said you were a slut," she mutters under her breath.

I stall in my doorway as a question pops into my head. "Was Tanya the only ghost you've ever seen?"

Silence answers me and I glance over my shoulder to confirm what her mind renders.

"No."

"Is that why you wanted to work here?"

She gives me a one-shoulder shrug. "It seemed like a good fit," she says after a moment.

"I'm not sure you'll feel that way in a few weeks."

She blinks at me, and her mouth drops into a little 'O'. Her mind swirls, zeroing in on my inappropriate purr before transitioning into instant dirty mode. Her lips form a secret smile and I know she's just giving me back a little of my medicine.

"Stop that," I snap and glare at her. "I'm talking about the day you find out monsters do exist."

"I'm aware they exist. One killed my best friend, and another killed my uncle," she mutters and turns toward the computer.

I refrain from correcting her, but I have a feeling I should. This was going to get complicated, and her idea of monster is going to be completely blown out of the water when she finds out Lucifer exists. But for now, I can't bring myself to burst her naïve bubble.

I glance at Damian's closed office door, wondering why he hadn't come out, and made this more awkward than it already was.

"Where's Damian?" I ask, because it is unlike him to let this kind of opportunity to yank my chain go to waste.

"He went to pick up his daughter. He said if you insist on bringing Hannah here, he'd get someone she can properly entertain herself with while you brood over the files on your desk."

"Brood?"

She smirks and nods. "He's an odd duck," she adds.

I can't help the laugh that rolls out, filling the reception area. "Oh, you have no idea," I say under my breath as I step into my office.

Angel Fire Chapter 5

THE WEEK BLURS AND when Friday rolls around, I am more than ready for a weekend on the beach. The house construction is moving along, but it's still slow, and the little cottage is wearing thin on my nerves. At least the space at the office was more expansive. The cottage living area was smaller than my single office.

I sit at my desk while Hannah and Grace color, chattering away about CJ's son. Grace oozes adoration, and I can tell there are days she would rather stay home and dote over my brother's child than play with Hannah.

Bridget knocks on the doorframe.

"Do you have a minute?" she asks.

"Sure, come on in," I say, and she glances at the kids before stepping into the room. Her fidgety demeanor is enough to give me a clue.

"What's upstairs?" she asks and takes a seat on the other side of the desk.

"A couple of conference rooms, a storage area, and a bathroom. Why?"

She glances at her hands. "My aunt's house sold."

"Oh." I must be over-tired because I don't get the connection, and then she lifts her gaze. "Oh," I say again as her thoughts comb over me. "You need a place to stay."

"Unfortunately, yes."

"And you want to stay here?" I point to the ceiling. The stairwell leads down into the kitchenette in the back and the rooms upstairs once were bedrooms, so it's not really a farfetched idea.

"I know there is a full bath up there," she says, "but the other rooms were locked, so I didn't get to explore." Her cheeks turn red.

I let a smirk form on my lips. "Searching for skeletons in our closets?"

She laughs when my eyebrow rises.

"No, just looking around before you got in this morning. My aunt sprung the sale on me last night. I need to be out by the end of the month."

"Like, two weeks end of the month?"

"Yeah. I think that must have been what I looked like last night." She lets out a nervous laugh. "I need somewhere to stay until I can find something I can afford."

"You really want to stay in this house?"

"The commute would be easy," she says, and I can't argue with that.

"I need to talk to Damian. The house is registered under the business, and I can't make the decision without his input."

The smell of pizza precedes Damian's voice. "Did I hear my name?" he asks and steps into the doorway with three pizza boxes in his hands. Without waiting for an answer, he announces, "Lunch is served. Follow me if you want to eat!" He turns, heading toward the small kitchen at the back of the house.

The two girls run after him, and I glance at Bridget. "After you," I say, as I stand and wave towards the door. I follow, mulling over the request, glancing around at the rooms as we pass through. My office used to be the formal living area and Damian's was the dining room. The reception area is the home's atrium with a hallway that leads to the back of the house, and the kitchen, half bath, and the stairwell upstairs.

It had once been a home, but we'd turned it into a business. The upstairs bedrooms were used as our conference rooms and an empty storage area. I suppose we could move some of the crap out of what once was the master suite and let Bridget stay there.

We step into the kitchen just as Damian shovels two cheese pizza slices onto paper plates in front of the girls. He glances our way.

"You need a place to stay for a spell?" he asks Bridget as he straightens, and when she nods, he shrugs my way. "We have that storage area," he adds, and I know he's been eavesdropping on my thoughts. "Besides, if she's here, there may be less chance of another break-in."

"Wo," Bridget says with her palms in front of her. "You've had break-ins?"

"Just one," I answer, staring at Damian, weighing the benefit versus the danger. The last thing either of us wants is someone else getting hurt because of us. "But staying here could be dangerous," I add, because she has a right to know before making a decision.

She glances between the two of us. "Does this mean you're considering it?"

"It means we need to have a discussion before you go out and start decorating the space."

She actually squeals and throws her arms around my neck. She releases me just as fast, and does the same to Damian.

"Thank you, thank you, you won't regret it!"

Both of us huff a laugh at her raw enthusiasm.

"Why are you not married?" Damian asks, shaking his head in amusement.

Her smile fades away, and the silence even affects the children. What rattles through her mind echoes in mine, and my smile disappears as well. Before any of us can speak, she slips away toward the offices.

I trade a glance with Damian and then turn, going after Bridget.

I catch her before she gets to the door, grabbing her arm and stopping her blind progression.

"He didn't know," I say, and she turns, facing me with tear-stained cheeks. "Neither did I."

"I lost everything in that accident," she whispers. "Everything," she repeats, meeting my gaze.

She'd lost more than I had, and all in one fell swoop. Her mother, her father, her husband and her child died in that car accident. She wasn't in the car because she was pregnant with her second child and prescribed bed rest. She got up to answer the door and had a miscarriage when her uncle told her the news.

I gain a new respect for the woman standing before me. I doubt I would have refrained from eating a bullet if I lost both Raven and Hannah, so in that respect, Bridget was a hell of a lot stronger than I was.

"I just need some air," she says, and another tear tumbles down her cheek. She looks down at my grip on her arm and I release her. "I'll be back in a few minutes, okay?"

I nod and let her go. She closes the door behind her, and I wander back to the kitchen where Damian and the girls are stuffing their face with pizza. I grab a slice and take a seat next to Hannah, sending her a reassuring smile.

"Where's Bri?" Hannah asks.

"Bri?"

She rolls her eyes at me and then says, "Bridge-et. She said I could call her Bri because I'm special."

"Well, Bri said she'd be right back, and when she gets here, we need to show her the room upstairs, because she's going to be living there."

"You think that's wise?" Damian asks, pulling my attention away from Hannah.

I certainly did not want to voice my first response out loud, and I just stare at him. "I'm sure it will be just fine," I finally say and dig into my pizza.

After we finish eating, and stow the remaining slices in the refrigerator, I corral Hannah back to my office for a nap while Damian takes Grace home for the afternoon. Hannah is snoring in a matter of minutes, and I open my computer to see if I have any emails.

I have a few inquiries and I sift through, reading each one as if it was real, but I usually could smell crazy, and a couple of these were whoppers; but even though I sensed bat-shit crazy, I still call to confirm, because you never know.

The last email includes an attachment and very little information. I glance at Hannah before I click. After the link is successfully scanned for any viruses and malware, a new window opens to a black screen. The noise in the background is muffled. It sounds like a busy industrial plant or garage. When the picture pops up, the vulgar display on the screen freezes me in place. I blink, trying to figure out what the hell I am looking at, and then the camera zooms out.

My legs act on their own, pushing me away from the desk with such force that I crash into the wall behind me. A laugh overlays the audio.

"Maybe this will be your daughter's fate as well," Lucifer's chilling voice radiates out of the speaker and my breath locks in my chest. I can't breathe, and my heart is pumping too hard, too loud in my ears. Tears blur my vision as the final insertion is completed on screen. Raven is whimpering under the duct tape as the bastard sews her up. I can't pull my gaze from the screen, even when she is untied and stretched out. The agony etched in her features drives pain through every fiber of my soul.

The laptop slams closed, and I look up, right into Bridget's eyes.

"What the hell were you watching?"

I still can't breathe. I can't move, but I am now aware that my entire form is shaking, rattling the chair that I am sitting in. My lungs are locked closed, and I can't even wheeze.

The concern in Bridget's face transforms to all out panic, and before I know it, she's twirled me around in the chair and does the fucking Heimlich maneuver. It forces all the air out of my lungs and finally I can draw some in, but it's now coupled with a nearly hysterical laugh.

I lean over with my elbows crossed on my knees and my forehead resting on my arms. I focus only on breathing. In, then out, rinse, repeat. It takes a good five minutes before I turn my head.

Bridget is there, concern filling every line in her face.

"Are you okay?"

I turn my head away, because I'm not sure what to say. My daughter is still snoring on the couch, and I nearly passed out from a horror-induced asthma attack because Lucifer threatened to kill my daughter the same way he killed my wife. How does one explain that to a perfect stranger?

"No. I don't think I'll ever be okay," I whisper.

"Ah, Tommy, I wish I could tell you the hurt goes away," she says as her hand slowly traces my back in a soothing pattern.

I look at her again. "You don't understand. My wife's death was calculated, and my daughter was supposed to die along with her. And that was another horrifying promise to do more harm." I sit up and point at my laptop. Anger has taken root and grown into an unmanageable tangle inside me.

Bridget sits back on her haunches, and a line of confusion deepens between her eyes.

"I don't think you want to be any part of this agency, never mind anywhere near me. I'm a death sentence. Don't you get that?"

"I call bullshit," she says, surprising me. "I used to think I was cursed. It's an excuse to curl up and die, instead of actually trying to live, which is damned hard when you've lost everything you've ever loved."

Coming from anyone else, I would have scoffed. But Bridget had lived through losing everything and come out okay, although her nemesis was a car accident, not the devil himself. I slowly sat up and glanced at Hannah before looking back at Bridget.

"You don't have all the facts and you need them before you decide if staying here is what you want. And by stay here, I don't just mean living here." I reach over to the closed notebook on the desk and hand it to her. "That's the same list the police have."

She opens the notebook, scanning the pages of names. When she comes to the page containing our names, she looks up at me.

"What is this?"

I give a sarcastic laugh. "It's Lucifer's hit list."

Her eyebrows arch. "Pardon?"

"It's a list of archangel descendants, and Lucifer wants every single name on that list dead."

Her gaze drops back to the list. "But both you and your brother are on the list," she says. Her brain isn't wrapping around the facts properly, and I don't want to show her the horrific events that put us front and center.

"Do you get what I'm saying, Bridget?" I say and do a quick glance towards my daughter, making sure she is still asleep. "That's the devil's hit list," I hiss. "It's a no-win situation for me. Are you sure you want to be around for the fucking fallout?"

She looks at the list in her hand and then at the computer. "What was on the computer?"

"What happened to my wife in living color, and a threat to do the same to my daughter."

Bridget paled. Her gaze drops to the list, and she blinks incessantly before looking up at me. Caution paints her features, and she slowly puts the notebook on the desk. Her mind swarms with images of straightjackets and padded rooms and my jaw tightens.

"I'm not crazy."

Skepticism forms in both her mind and the corners of her mouth.

"I don't need a straightjacket or padded room," I say, mirroring her thoughts. "I just need some way to kill the devil before he kills everyone on that list."

A knock on the door and a hearty hello, interrupt our conversation.

"If you don't believe me, you can ask Austin about us. He's seen both CJ and me in action." I stand up, shaking off the horror and anger biting every inch of my skin, and step towards the reception area.

Bridget moves into the space I was about to occupy, a friendly smile plastered on her lips, belying the volatility in her aura.

"Hello, welcome to the Ryan-Andreas Paranormal Investigation Agency. I'm Bri," she sticks her hand out. "What can I do for you?" She cocks her head, studying our guests that are just a step out of sight.

A hand envelopes hers.

"Austin Shelton," he introduces. "And this is my girlfriend, Paige. We're here to see Tom Ryan. I believe we spoke on the phone," he added as his grip released hers.

I step into the doorway, sending what I hope looks like a smile, and I recognize the angelic strand weaving through Austin's aura. I'm surprised Raven never said anything about it to me, because it's clear he has angel blood coursing through his veins. Paige's aura mutates into darker shades, like this entire trip has dredged up all her horrifying memories.

"Austin, good to see you," I say, and both he and Paige jerk in place at the sound of my voice. "Transplant," I add, pointing to my mouth. "Come on in." I wave to my office space.

Their unified hesitation is warranted, and I'm glad they are cautious enough to question whether or not I am really me, because it means they will apply those same hesitations to everything around them once I explain what they are up against.

"I know this is... unusual. Just imagine how strange it feels to me."

Paige huffs a laugh and glances at Bridget. "Sorry, I hadn't heard him speak before."

Bridget sends a smile her way. "I've known him since middle school, and I never thought his voice would be so..." She trails off and I catch the blush rising in her cheeks.

So does Paige, and it seems to break the ice enough so Paige and Austin step into my office. I glance back at Bridget, and she sends a wink in my direction, coupled with a light laugh just soft enough for no one but me to catch.

"Who are you?" Hannah's sleepy voice interrupts my momentary loss of focus.

"Hannah, this is Austin Shelton and Paige Turner. Your uncle CJ and I met them when we were in New York for CJ's concert a while back. Austin, Paige, this is my daughter, Hannah."

"Hello, Hannah," Paige smiles and crosses, crouching down in front of my daughter on the couch.

Hannah glances in my direction for assurances that it's okay to talk to a stranger. I give her a nod and the worry on her face transitions into a smile.

"Hi," she says and sits up, hugging her blanket.

"Did you know your daddy saved my life?" Paige asks.

"He saved mine, too," Hannah whispers. The two of them turn their gazes in my direction.

"He's a very special man, so you need to take good care of him now that your mommy's gone. Okay?"

"Okay," Hannah replies.

The smile on my face now feels foreign and I'm not sure how to broach the subject of angel descendants and the danger they are in, with Hannah awake. I glance towards Bridget and shift under her scrutinizing stare.

The creak of the front door draws her attention and an eyebrow arches.

CJ steps into view, meeting my gaze like it's the most natural thing in the world for him to waltz into our agency. I think he's only been here twice since he came out of the coma, so I'm just as surprised as Bridget.

"Miss O'Keefe," he says, giving her a cool nod.

"CJ," she says, opting for the less formal salutation just to be contrary.

He ignores her now that the formalities are out of the way and turns in my direction.

"Damian thought Hannah might want to come over to help Valerie with the baby for a bit," he says as he approaches the door.

"Paige, Austin, you remember my brother, don't you?" I wave towards the door and Paige flushes to the point her face turns red. Her eyes drop to the ground, and then she offers a hesitant smile. It really is amusing to see how tongue-tied people get around my brother.

"Hey," Austin says, and gives a nod, but he keeps his distance, like the affiliation with someone who can wield angel fire might toast him on the spot.

CJ gives a polite smile and returns the salutation before his gaze falls on Hannah.

"What do you say, peanut? You want to come help us out with Alex for a spell?"

I know Hannah wants to, but she looks at me with the same panicked gaze she had the other day.

"It's okay, honey. I will come get you once my meeting is over and you can choose the restaurant we go to tonight."

Her eyes light up at the bribe, and she looks at her scattered toys. Before she even asks about whether or not to pack her toys, CJ crosses and helps her put her things in the duffel bag.

I wait until she's all packed up before I step in and give her a tight hug.

"You be good for your aunt and uncle."

"I will," she says, but is still holding on like letting go would be a disaster.

"I will be fine," I whisper, and she finally loosens her grip. "And you'll be with Uncle CJ." I meet her pleading eyes, and offer the sure smile that knocks her fear down a couple of notches. She knows her uncle is unstoppable.

I hesitate before I pass her into CJ's arms, silently transmitting the latest threat from Lucifer. The tightening around his mouth and the glare that forms in his eyes is enough to settle my nerves. He gives me a reassuring nod.

"Thanks," I mutter, matching his stare and knowing nod. I don't need to tell him to keep her safe. With him, it's a given, so when they step out of sight, the panic that takes hold is tempered enough for me to breathe.

Austin watches the car pull out before turning to me.

"What happened?" he asks.

"Lucifer sent an assassin, and he followed through on an old promise."

Both their eyes widen at the drop of one of the devil's known names. Until we entered their lives, they didn't know angels existed, and now I was dropping the king of hell on them.

"And this is his global hit list," I add, and toss the notebook to him. I don't mince words, and I'm sure on some level Austin would be more prepared had I sugar coated this or danced around the entire issue. I wait while he flips through the pages and he gets to the one with his name; his gaze snaps to mine.

"What does the R stand for, next to my name?"

"Raphael."

"Raphael..." he twirls his wrist, prompting me for more.

"The archangel Raphael. The letters represent which angel blood line the person falls under."

"Your brother wasn't shitting when he said he recognized angel blood," Austin's wide eyes locked with mine. "But I still have no fucking clue what it means."

"It means you are a delicacy to the devil. Historically, he's eaten the heart of descendants just for giggles, but now he's harvesting their blood to rejuvenate himself to his former glory."

Both Paige and Austin wear a horrified stare I can relate to.

"Can I get anyone a drink?" Bridget asks from the doorway, jolting both Paige and Austin out of their shock.

"I'm fine," Austin says with little more than a glance in her direction. His gaze drops back to the pages, flipping them one by one until he comes to our page. "Damn," he mutters and glances up at me. "So, this is why you called me? To tell me I'm on the devil's hit list?"

He tosses the notebook back to me, and turns away, crossing to the window while Paige just stares at me.

"He didn't tell you?" I ask at the blatant confusion in her gaze.

"I'm not sure I follow any of this. Are you telling me Austin is a distant relative of an archangel?" Her voice rises to almost a squeak.

"Yes."

"A fucking archangel?" she asks, and her eyes widen.

Bridget is still in the doorway, and the pale shock in her features as she scans the three of us is humorous, but I can't focus on her right at the moment.

"Yes. And so are my brother and me."

She blinks and slowly sits on the couch. "That would totally explain what I saw the night you two killed Hunter's ghost."

Austin glances over his shoulder at her and then turns towards me. "So, outside of being a blood bank for Lucifer, what does having angel blood running through me do?"

"Not a whole hell of a lot," I say. "I was useless until CJ gave me a dash of his mojo."

"What makes CJ so special?" Bridget asks from the doorway, like I had been unjustly slighted in some fashion.

"He's a trinity."

Her eyes widen and her arms drop to her side. Her expression reminds me of that little meer cat in Lion King, after Simba recognizes Nala. It draws a brief smile to my lips and some much-needed humor into the conversation.

"Like... Father, Son, and Holy Ghost trinity?"

I laugh. "No. He's not a holy trinity," I say, although sometimes I wonder how deep the blood goes in him. "He's a product of three archangel bloodlines. His son, though, that's another story. Alex is something no one has ever seen. That child hosts four angel bloodlines, and if he and Grace ever hookup..." I trail off because I don't have a clue what the combination of all five archangel bloodlines would bring to the table.

Bridget jumps way ahead of me. "Revelations," she whispers reverently.

I am already shaking my head and ignoring the questions popping up in Paige and Austin's heads.

"No. Revelations will only occur if Lucifer gets hold of either Naomi or Grace. If that ever happens, then we are looking at total annihilation." I answer, and turn back to my guests. "Which is why he is systematically wiping out descendants. So, he can get back to the strength he was before Damian stole his grace."

"Who's Damian?" Austin asks.

"My business partner. Naomi and Grace are his wife and daughter, and they are on this list, too." I drop the notebook on the desk.

"So, this shit is actually real?" Bridget asks looking between me and Austin. She doesn't realize she has just voiced the common thought filling all their heads.

"Yes." I take a moment to meet each one of their questioning glares. "And both CJ and I have been..." I look up at the ceiling, trying to formulate Lucifer's proposals. "...propositioned, by Lucifer. He wants the power we wield in order to defeat Damian. We have both told him to go pound sand. So, we are at the top of his hit list."

I bite my lip for a moment.

"Raven died because I told Lucifer to fuck off."

"You can't blame yourself," Paige says from her position on the couch.

"Yes. I can. I can also blame my brother for putting us in this position. I could blame Damian for seeking us out after Lucifer tried to frame him." Hostility rises in me, coloring the edges of my vision. "I could blame a whole host of things on this moment, but it would be futile because everything is predestined."

"Bullshit." Paige stands and Austin steps closer to her. "If you believed that, why bother calling us to come here so you can give us a heads up?"

"Because I'm naïve enough to think maybe there is a way to save you." I glare at her as the words spit out.

"You know the only way to stop this," Damian interrupts, making us all jump.

I hadn't heard him come in, but I was wound up too tight to hear much of anything beyond my pounding heart.

"We need CJ to close all the fucking portals," I say.

"Yes. And Lucifer knows that's our end game. These murders... it's all a diversion. A distraction from our real purpose."

I gawk at him. "Raven wasn't just a diversion."

"No, she was payback. She was a means to tear you down to nothing, so you'd eventually say yes to his proposal." Damian glances around the room and his gaze lands on Austin. "Your evil spirit was like a child compared to Lucifer. He has an unlimited supply of things that he can send to do his dirty work. This time, it was a human assassin. Next time, it might not be human at all.”

Damian’s response draws a cold shiver up my spine. He turns his hard stare in my direction.

“And you are going to have to get your shit together,” he says, pointing at me. Anger burns in his eyes. “You’ve got that little girl so freaked out that when she’s away from you for more than five minutes, she has a meltdown.”

Whatever fight I had in my sails dies with his admonishment. “Is Hannah okay?”

He just stares me down and then sighs. “Now she is, but it took all ten of us to calm her down. I don’t have any idea how he did it, but Gabe finally got her calm. I think he might have bribed her with offering to let her choose whatever movie she wanted to watch. Christ almighty, you have got to stop this. Now.”

Everyone’s eyes are now on me, and I shift under the weight of Damian’s words. I knew my reactions weren’t healthy, but I didn’t realize they were poisoning my daughter’s mind as well.

My gaze falls on Bridget, and her eyes are not judgmental like the other three pairs. She witnessed Hannah’s freak out first-hand earlier in the week. Bridget turns toward Damian.

“How do you know so much about this situation?” she asks, waving at me and Austin.

“Because the archangel Gabriel is my father. I’m not a distant relative like these two, and I would venture to guess that is the only reason I have survived for so long.”

“I kind of feel like I stepped into a family fight where all the dirty laundry is being aired,” Austin said, breaking the mounting tension.

“Welcome to the family,” I add, and my attempt at humor works. Both Austin and Paige break out in a smile and Damian huffs, turning to leave.

“So, what do I do?” Austin asks, and Damian pauses.

“Honestly, outside of moving here, I have no idea.” Damian answers and shrugs.

"What about magic?" Paige asks, pulling the pendant Raven had given her out from under her shirt, and both Damian and I shake our head.

"That will only protect you from being possessed. And magic is only as good as its host. Raven was a tremendously powerful witch, but she still couldn't contain Lucifer or banish him from CJ's body." Damian says and then glances towards me.

"Not even a protection spell?" Paige challenges. "I would think that would deter someone from finding us, don't you?"

"Against a human, you will probably survive. So, once you get home, it would be beneficial to enact some of that practical magic to keep you hidden from prying eyes." Damian says and turns his attention to me. "I'm going home to give CJ a break from the girls," he adds and then leaves us to continue our conversation.

"Why would moving here keep us safe?" Austin ventured.

"Because Lucifer has this town tagged as the last one to hit. I'm not sure if his rationale is that he will be strong enough to take on the three of us by that time, or if he is hoping Damian and CJ will produce more trinity girls that he can enslave for his dark plan."

Quiet descends, and both Paige and Austin take a seat on the couch; unsure of what to say or do next.

"Why don't you go enjoy the rest of the afternoon," I say. "We can talk at dinner. You still have my cell number, right?"

Austin pulls the card I gave him in New York earlier this year, out of his wallet, flashing it at me. "Thanks. We've got a lot to digest."

He isn't kidding, and I'm more than aware the moment he is in a normal hotel room, all of this is going to sound insane. Hell, sometimes I question my own sanity, so I wouldn't blame him if he chalks all this up to me cracking because my wife died.

They cross and Austin offers me his hand; I shake it. Paige trades places with him and instead of shaking my hand, she wraps me in a hug. For a moment, I'm stunned by the sadness flowing from her, but I recover before she releases me, and I offer her a strained smile.

Bridget walks them out and I slump on the couch, studying my clasped hands until she steps into the office again. She approaches slowly, like I could break at any moment, and I glare up at her.

"Don't treat me like I belong in a padded room."

"Seriously? After all the shit you laid out, can you blame us?"

"Us?" I straighten.

She flicks a card at me and takes a seat on the opposite side of the couch. "It's a number for a national help line. Austin thought you might need to use it."

I let out a humorless chuckle. "Your uncle believed us," I say, keeping her gaze locked on mine.

She looks away and sighs, "Yeah, well…" She trails off and crosses to the window. Her doubts wrap around me like a hangman's noose.

"Do you need some sort of demonstration?" I ask and she turns towards me with eyebrows arched in surprise.

"That's not necessary," she says, but her curiosity is already itching to see something more than my daughter held in place by an invisible hand.

I can only think of one way to truly show her what freaks of nature we really are, and I glance at the window, willing myself to be on the other side. After a blink, the sunlight streams down, hot on my skin and I turn, glancing inside my office from the outside of the house.

Bridget is crossing the room towards my body, which is sitting in suspended animation. The glazed eyes really freak me out, but I reach up and knock on the window. When she spins toward the noise, her gaze locks with mine and she halts. Her head whips between my still form and me outside, making strands of hair fall out of her neat bun. It's quite comical, and a smirk finds my lips. That seems to jump-start her movement, and she comes to the window, opening it.

"What the fuck?"

I reach in and grab her hand, pressing it to my cheek. "I'm solid in both places." Then I step back and close my eyes, feeling the pull back into my body.

When my eyes open, her gaze locks on me, and her back presses against the window.

I lean back on the couch, taking in her horrified stare, and then look beyond her at the window. It closes at my direction. Bridget jumps away from the glass, her eyes nearly bug out of her head, and I send a cocky smile in her direction. Not only have I made her a believer without showing her the memories, I have truly freaked her out.

"So, knowing what you do now, do you really want to work here?"

Bridget takes a deep breath, quelling the fear pulsing from her, before she considers my question. My gaze never leaves hers and when she finally nods, I can't help but ask.

"Why?"

"Because my uncle told me I needed to look out for you," she says quietly.

A cold sweat passes over my skin. "Excuse me?"

"The day he died…" She stops and closes her eyes. "After he died, he came to me and said it was my job to look after you because you were going to need someone who had suffered a similar loss." Her eyes open, meeting mine. She adds a small shrug. "So, I'm kind of obligated."

Stunned doesn't describe what's happening in my mind, and my body goes numb from the shock. I take a full minute to find my voice. "So, your uncle assumed Raven and Hannah were going to die."

She lets out a little laugh. "I guess he underestimated you and your family's arsenal."

"Hannah would have died if we hadn't had some magic at our disposal," I say, but I'm not ready to disclose my sister-in-law's healing powers. I swallow and stand. "I guess you will want to see that room then."

She shifts and sighs. "If you don't mind."

Without waiting for her, I turn away and head toward the kitchen. Her footsteps follow, and I don't acknowledge her until I've unlocked the door at the end of the short upstairs hallway. The master suite is close to six hundred square feet, and as I swing the door open, to the mostly empty room, her eyes twinkle. Our storage consists of a half dozen file cabinets in the center of the room. We could easily move them to one of the conference rooms. A few empty boxes also speckled the space.

Bridget slows to a stop next to the file cabinets, her gaze locks on the river view, and then she turns back to me. "Are you serious?" she asks, waving at the ample space.

I'm not sure whether her statement is because she's upset by the accommodations or awed by it. "Um, yeah," I say, glancing around. Before I can ask if she's okay with it, she has crossed the distance and throws her arms around my neck.

"It's perfect," she says and squeezes me tighter than I think she means to.

Without thought, my hands find her waist and she pulls away, her smile fading a notch as our eyes lock. The flurry in her mind revolving around furniture and curtains, and everything else required to make the bedroom livable stalls in her mind.

I am more than aware of her heartbeat next to mine, and she licks her lips, stirring an animalistic need. I drop my hands and step back, appalled at the turn of my thoughts. Bridget is as beautiful today as she was in high school, but this is completely wrong.

Wrong time.

Wrong place.

Wrong woman.

I sidestep out of her loose grip and head to the room to our left. "There's an en suite," I say, opening the door to an ample bathroom. "I think they had just redone this before we bought the house," I add, trying to ignore the question in her gaze.

Bridget crosses and stands next to me, surveying the old claw-foot tub and the corner shower and the granite covered vanity.

"Why didn't you take this space?" she asks, glancing at me.

I look around the area and then back at her with a shrug. "It never dawned on me," I say. "And I think where we are all staying isn't a bad temporary solution. Having everyone within walking distance is good for our peace of mind right now."

She gives me a soft smile. "Are you going to move closer to your brother?" As she talks, she steps closer and I'm now aware of the attraction radiating off her. Her hand lands softly on my chest.

"What are you doing?" I ask, staring down at her.

Her eyes widen and drops to the hand pressed against my chest before she yanks it away, like I am hot enough to burn. "I... I'm sorry," she says and her cheeks bloom red. She steps away quickly.

"Just to make things perfectly clear. Nothing is going to happen here." I point between us. "You took a job with my firm, and I will *not* complicate things by sleeping with you, no matter how attractive you are. Got it?"

She crosses her arms and levels a hard glare in my direction. "Just for the record, I do not want to sleep with you."

The burn of rejection flushes my skin, and I step closer.

"Liar," I growl and march out of the room, because I know if I stay, I am going to do something I will regret.

Angel Fire Chapter 6

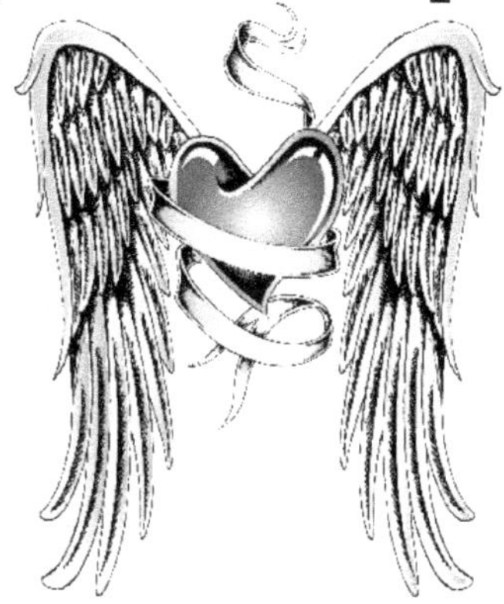

AS SOON AS I settle into my car, guilt replaces the burn of anger.

"What the hell are you doing?" I glare at my reflection in the rearview mirror. No answer comes and I close my eyes while the air conditioner kicks in, blowing marginally cooler air on my face.

Instead of further complicating matters, I slide the car into reverse and back out of the driveway, heading toward the cottage and the remainder of the afternoon on the beach. I'm tempted to leave Hannah with Damian and just surf my aggravation out, but I can't help the nervous itch in my core.

At the cottages, only CJ's car is there, and I cross to his door, knocking. It takes a few minutes and the door cracks open. Valerie's tired eyes look out at me. The rest of the cottage behind her is dark and quiet.

"I guess Damian picked up Hannah?" I say, keeping my voice quiet.

She nods. "They all went to the beach."

"And I just woke you, didn't I." My timing sucks and I mutter an apology and turn to leave.

"How are you doing?" she asks, stopping me.

I consider how to answer and turn back to her. I've been on autopilot taking care of Hannah for the past month, so much so that I really haven't had time to think. "I'm numb," I say and meet her gaze. "Just going through the motions for Hannah's sake," I add. "And when I'm not numb, the emptiness hurts so much I can't breathe."

She bites her lower lip, and her eyes fill with tears. "I miss her," she says.

"You and me both," I say and step closer, offering a hug because she looks like she needs it. Valerie steps into my arms and her tears dampen my shoulder. She stays there for a full minute before she pulls away and wipes her face.

"Thanks, I needed that," she says and tries on a smile. "I'm going to attempt to get a little more sleep before Alex wakes up," she adds and retreats into the cottage.

With surfing in mind, I change into my suit, grab a towel and my wallet, and head towards the surf shop. The missile destroyed all my boards and wetsuits, and it's time I replace some things.

Twenty minutes later, I'm suited up and standing on Long Sands beach, right in front of the bathhouse. The waves are decent for the southern Maine shore.

"Daddy!" Hannah's happy shriek pulls my attention and I smile as she breaks free of Naomi's hand and runs at full speed in my direction.

I lay the board down on the sand and scoop her up in my arms, twirling around with her the way she loves me to. "Hey, peanut! Mind if I go surfing for a little while?" I nod toward the waves and her smile falters.

I see the hesitation I'd built in her, and I silently curse my overprotective tendencies.

"Hannah, why don't you let your father catch a few waves while we finish building that sandcastle," Naomi says as she steps next to me. Grace pulls on her hand, trying to maneuver her towards the bathhouse, which I gather was their original intent before my daughter saw me standing here.

"That sounds like a great idea. Make sure you make a tower just for me," I say, trying not to cling too tightly. Now that she is in my arms, I don't want to let her go, but I force myself to put her on the sand next to Naomi. "I won't surf all afternoon, I promise," I say.

A part of me weeps when she takes Naomi's offered hand, and she turns away towards their destination. Instead of watching her until she is out of sight, I force myself to turn and study the waves, fighting the internal battle to just find where they are parked and hang out there all day. I need to feel something again, and that clinches my decision.

I pick up my board and choose not to harp on my daughter today. It would be healthier for both of us if I loosen the reins a little. Without over-thinking it, I head into the ocean, letting the cool Atlantic chill the burn from my body as much as from my mind. I focus on the waves and nothing else, riding them in and then dropping and paddling back out. I have no idea how long I surfed, but my legs ache in that worn out way when I finally walk back onto the sand.

I scan the beach slowly, unsure of how far the family is from the bathhouse. It takes two sweeps of the beach to find the crew. I let out a small laugh at the elaborate sandcastle in progress, wondering how the hell I missed it on my first scan.

I drop the board next to the chairs and peel off my wetsuit, laying it out on the board before I approach the intense construction.

"What are you building? The Taj Mahal?" I ask, and all eyes snap to mine.

"Daddy, it's our castle," Hannah says and wipes a stray hair from her cheek, leaving a sand streak instead. "Do you like it?"

Her eyes sparkle like I haven't seen since before Raven died, and I return her beaming smile. "I'm seriously impressed. What do you need me to do?"

She glances at the monstrosity surrounding her and then looks up at me. "Can you get us water for the moat?" she asks, pointing to one of the discarded buckets. I trade a glance with Damian and he nods towards the bucket.

"You heard the boss," he says.

I collect two buckets of water and cross the expanse of low tide beach.

"Where do you want these?" I ask, and both Hannah and Grace point to the deep gully surrounding their castle.

I pour the buckets in, and the water spreads before seeping into the sand. It isn't deep enough to hold the water until closer to high tide. I glance at my daughter, and she presses her lips together in contemplation.

"Maybe I should just watch you build?" I ask, hoping she lets me off the hook.

Her gaze moves to Grace's and then back to mine with a nod. I collapse in one of the chairs, hoping neither Damian nor Naomi are upset by my begging off. They seem to have the kids under control.

I close my eyes, letting the heat of the afternoon cancel the chill that settled into my bones from my time in the water. The chatter of the kids fades into the thoughts accosting me, and I focus on nothing until it all becomes a dull swirl in my head.

"Tom?" her Irish lilt caresses me and I open my eyes to Raven's auburn framed face.

"Yeah," I say and offer a smile. The closeness of her fills my world, erasing the emptiness and leaving me longing to touch her.

"Ya have to let go," she whispers, her voice rides on the gentle breeze.

"Why?"

"Because if ya don't, you will become bitter and end up doing something you will live to regret."

"Like what?" I get lost in her deep blue eyes.

"Like becoming as destructive as my father... or worse."

I sit straight up, like someone zapped me. My chest constricts with the weight of her words. I'm not sure if it was just a dream or really Raven talking to me from the great beyond, but the last thing she said strikes such fear in me that my gaze darts to Hannah.

I must not have been sleeping long because the kids are still actively discussing how to get the moat working. The only one looking directly at me is Damian, and that small crease between his eyes tells me he might have heard some of my dream, or at least feels the fear scratching every inch of my exposed skin.

I just shake my head because I really don't want to discuss this, especially not in front of my daughter. I tap my wrist and raise an eyebrow.

"It's a little after four," Damian answers my silent question.

"Thanks," I direct towards him, and then my attention shifts to Hannah. "Hey, missy, where did you want to have dinner tonight?" I ask around a yawn, and I'm really hoping it isn't McDonald's. I am in the mood for a more formal setting.

She turns and points to the Sun and Surf, which is a little over a hundred yards away. "I want to watch the castle."

"Okay. Do you mind if my friends come to dinner with us?"

Her head cocks like an intrigued puppy.

"Austin and Paige?" I clarify. "The ones who were at the office this morning?" I add when that blank look doesn't disappear.

She presses her lips together in that unhappy frown that I am getting used to.

"You can talk to Paige about her magic," I say, reaching for something to turn this around, and her head cocks farther, but interest sparks in her eyes.

"She knows magic?"

I smile and nod. "She isn't as practiced as your mother, but maybe she could teach you a few things."

The spark ignites and she grins. "Okay," she says, and goes back to carefully crafting a small path from the castle entry. "Can Bri come too?"

"She's probably busy tonight, hon," I say, avoiding saying 'hell no' out loud. I don't even want to think about how that would go down. Besides, I'm not even sure Bridget will be at the office on Monday with how we left things.

The instant scowl on Damian's face brings the guilt back full force. I should have shown more restraint with Bridget; letting her get under my skin was a mistake.

There will be no more mistakes.

Mistakes in my world mean someone dies.

Angel Fire Chapter 7

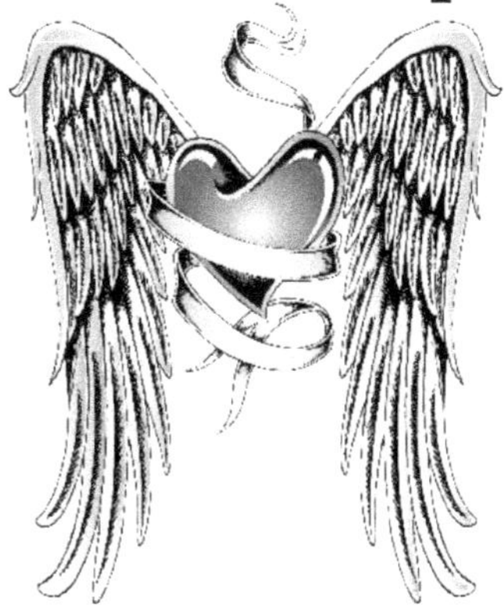

I SIT WITH MY back to the ocean, leaving the stellar view for Paige and Austin when they arrive. Hannah sits next to me on the side, where she has an unobstructed view of their delightfully elaborate sandcastle. Her legs swing on the chair, and she picks at the chips I asked the waitress to bring to the table. I sip the screwdriver I ordered, and we watch the tide creep towards her masterpiece.

"Daddy, can you keep the water away from my castle?" she asks, still staring at the approaching water.

It's close to a yard away from the moat encircling the sand art and I sigh. I could keep the water away if I wanted to, but the spectacle it would create wouldn't be worth it.

Hannah glances at me when I don't answer.

"Daddy?"

"You know I can," I say under my breath and glance down at her. "But it really isn't wise to use the power for selfish reasons."

She bites her lip and turns back towards the castle.

"We took a lot of pictures," I remind her. My cell phone has close to thirty photos of Hannah, Grace, Gabe, and Michael showing off around their mighty construction, and I stopped to get a few more of just Hannah in her cute new sundress on the way to the restaurant.

Before she gives me a major three-year-old attitude, Austin and Paige are escorted to the table. They take the seats opposite us and when their gaze drops to mine, I smile.

"I figured you'd appreciate the view. Besides, munchkin here wanted to watch her sandcastle until the tide took it." I nod towards the expanse of beach on my right.

Paige's eyebrows rise. "She made that?"

"Yes. I made that with my friends," Hannah says with such pride, it brings a smile to all our faces.

"Damian and Naomi helped, too," I add, and she nods.

The waitress interrupts, and both Paige and Austin glance in the menus while I rattle off Hannah's meal and some appetizers for the group.

"Are you ready to order or do you want her to come back after she puts in Hannah's meal and our appetizers?" I ask.

Paige looks over the edge of the menu. She's debating and Austin folds his menu, smiling up at the waitress.

"Why don't you put those in and bring us both a Corona?" He glances at Paige and gets a nod in response.

The waitress wanders off.

"My daddy says you know magic," Hannah asks, pulling Paige's attention away from the menu.

"I know a little," she says. "Why do you ask?"

"Can you create a spell to keep my castle safe?" she asks with such sincerity that an amused smile finds its way to my lips.

I trade a glance with Austin and his bemused smile says enough, and I focus elsewhere to drown out the stream of his thoughts. I don't want to eavesdrop, and sometimes I can control the stream flowing into my brain, especially in crowded places like the restaurant. I turn it all to static by not focusing on anyone in particular. At first, the din is overwhelming and I have to curb the instinct to cover my ears, but after a few deep breaths, I am able to bring it all to a low background buzz, like white noise.

The waitress steps back to our table carrying a tray of appetizers and drinks, as well as Hannah's meal.

The three of us order dinner and as soon as the waitress steps away, Paige leans over the table towards Hannah.

"Is the castle something you cherish more than anything else?"

Hannah's eyebrows arch and she glances at her work, biting her lip as she studies the sand. She slowly shakes her head, but I can tell from her melancholy expression that she is coming to terms with losing it already.

"No," she finally whispers and stares at the food on her plate.

"Then magic isn't something you want to turn to in this case. Magic, whether for good or for bad, requires sacrifice. If you aren't using it for someone you cherish, it isn't worth the price, however small it may be."

The more Paige says, the more she reminds me of my wife in her beliefs, and I turn away, scanning the rest of the patrons, letting the white noise dull the sudden ache in my chest.

"My daddy said you might be able to teach me to use magic," Hannah says, and I meet Paige's glance.

"I'd be happy to teach you the Wiccan principles," Paige smiles. "Do you know the first rule?"

Hannah glances from Paige to me, and back.

Even I know the first principle.

"Do no harm?" Hannah asks, like she isn't sure. It's something her mother would tell her from time to time.

"Yes," Paige nearly shouts, and she grins at my daughter as if she just answered the million-dollar question.

Her enthusiasm pulls a smile to my lips, and I focus on Austin while my daughter and Paige chatter about Wiccan principles.

"She's going to be a handful," he says, pointing his chin at Hannah.

"Tell me something I don't know." I can't help it. I let out a quiet laugh. "I have no idea how I'm going to pull this single dad thing off."

"Well, it certainly looks like you're pulling it off just fine."

I raise my drink, and he taps his bottle to the glass. "Thanks," I mutter, uncomfortable with compliments as a whole, but Austin has only seen a few interactions between my daughter and me, so I know he's just being kind.

I reach into my shirt pocket and drop the card he gave Bridget on the center of the table. His easy smile shifts and his shoulders tense in response. His eyes become guarded, and he can't hide his discomfort. Even if I wasn't a mind reader, all the physical cues radiating from him point to fear.

"I meant no disrespect," he says, pulling Paige's attention to ours.

I let out a little laugh. "You know, until a year ago, no one was afraid of me. Except maybe the ghosts I confronted." I keep eye contact with Austin. "I'm a third-degree black belt and no one ever batted an eye at that, but then I became supercharged and everyone becomes skittish around me, like I'm going to lash out unjustly."

"People who are unstable are unpredictable," Austin says, leaning back in his seat.

His quiet challenge starts a slow simmer inside me, but I'll be damned if I get aggravated in front of my daughter. Especially since she is now quiet and observing the tense dynamics.

"Are you mad at my daddy?" Hannah asks in a voice soft enough not to drive attention to us.

I glance down at her and she is staring at Austin with wide eyes full of surprise.

"No. I'm just worried about your father," he says, and her gaze jumps to mine.

"Austin believes in magic, but he doesn't believe in angels," I say and shrug. "He thinks I'm nuts."

Hannah looks between us and then picks at her food, unsure of what to say. The tension increases and Paige clears her throat. Hannah looks up and flips her hair over her shoulder.

"My daddy's a hero," she says with all the conviction in the world, and I huff a laugh at her sincere and stubborn set of her chin. Her glare challenges Austin to say otherwise.

Austin puts his hands up in surrender and smiles at Hannah.

"I never said he wasn't. He came to my rescue as well, so I can't argue with you there. But some things your father told me today are a little hard to believe, and it worries me."

"My daddy doesn't lie," she says, narrowing her eyes and I can't help but fill with humbleness at her defensive attitude.

"So, you grew up here?" Paige asks, trying to distract us from the tension that blankets the table.

"Yes," I answer, focusing on her, and very glad for the interruption. I really don't want to alienate the potential friendship we have. I've done enough alienating as it is today.

"It's a pretty town," she adds, and picks at the hors d'oeuvres.

"I can't imagine living anywhere else. Even though it's a summer town, busy as all get out from Memorial Day to Labor Day, the calm of the fall and winter makes it an ideal hideaway."

"What's the hospital like?" Austin asks.

I shrug. "A hospital?" I'm not sure what he's digging for. "My experiences there haven't been horrible, despite the circumstances, but if you're looking for more details of what might be available for jobs, well, I'd refer you to Valerie. She's been working there since she finished her residency and as far as I know, she loves it."

It takes me a few seconds to catch up with his thought process.

"Are you really thinking of relocating?"

He takes a breath and then scans the ocean behind me. "I could get used to a view like this."

Paige's eyebrows rise, but it's more that of hope than surprise. "Really?"

"I'd love to see what residencies they offer," he says, and smiles over at her.

"Did you want to talk to Valerie before you leave?"

Austin gives a non-committal shrug.

Hannah is quiet and staring off at the beach. I turn in time to see the first wave hit her castle, crumbling the outer wall. I lay my hand on her back and she turns to me with a sheen of tears.

"Look at it this way. It's nature's way of giving you a new canvas to work on tomorrow," I say, and she blinks as my words sink in.

"Will you help me build a sandcastle tomorrow?"

I smile at her innocence. "Of course. It's Saturday and I don't have to go to the office until Monday. So, I'm all yours for the weekend."

"Just you and me?" she asks, hope flaring in her eyes.

"If that's what you want, you've got it."

It's amazing how much both her face and her aura light up when she is happy. I nailed it this time, and I glance up at Paige and Austin. Their auras are a little more reserved, but they both held a smile.

"York is a great place to raise kids," I say, and offer a smile. "Classes are small enough, so you get the personal attention, and the town is very much engaged in the school sports."

"Really?" Austin asks.

"Yes. At least they were when I was on the football team in high school. Everyone came out of the woodwork for home games." I glance at both Paige and Austin. "Neither of you were into sports in high school, were you?"

Paige shakes her head. "Sorry, no. I was more of a bookworm," Paige says. "I went to an occasional game, but it really wasn't my scene."

"I was actually on the soccer team," Austin says. "It never drew the same crowd as the football games did."

"You played soccer?" Paige glances at him in surprise.

"In high school and college," he says with a grin.

The waitress stepped to our table, passing out plates to the three of us before retreating just as quickly.

"You two don't talk much, do you?" I ask, knowing it probably pushes the line, but it just pops out of my mouth and the light conversation goes dark as both their gazes lock on mine.

"We talk," Austin mutters, but there is something in his tone that tells me otherwise.

Paige glances toward the crumbling sandcastle.

"I'm sorry," I mumble. "Raven always said my candor was going to get me in trouble someday. I guess relying on sign language and people to translate sometimes buffered it."

"You say what's on your mind. That's refreshing," Paige says and digs into her meal.

I laugh. "Well, it all depends on what comes out of my mouth. I don't seem to have a handle on editing my words now that I can speak." I glance at Hannah, happy to see her eating her chicken tenders now. "I used to be a bit more diplomatic," I add, meeting her gaze again.

Austin quietly picks at the food on his plate. His gaze darts to Hannah before he sends a sideways glare in Paige's direction. The tension in his jaw makes his muscle twitch, and he turns back to the lobster stew in front of him, digging in without comment.

I'm not sure what to say, so I focus on the baked stuffed lobster on my plate.

The sound of silverware against china fills the void and before I know it, the plates are cleared, and the waitress is asking us for our dessert order.

"Can I have a sundae?" Hannah asks, her eyes as big as saucers.

I know I'll regret this later, but I nod. "Bring two spoons," I say, because I know my daughter will have two or three spoonfuls and be done.

The waitress smiles and turns towards Paige and Austin. They both order the New York Cheesecake, and the waitress moves away again.

"That was superb," Austin says.

"Try the Inn tomorrow night, and have them charge it to your room. Order the Colligan Filet, and then we can talk about a good meal."

Despite the underlying tension, they both relax with my offer, and the rest of the meal goes by without another incident. As we are walking out, Hannah pulls me towards the beach.

"I want to see the last of the castle disappear!"

I glance at Paige and Austin.

"I'd like to see it as well," Paige says. "Will you walk with me?" she asks Hannah and puts her hand out. With no hesitation, my daughter takes her hand and starts leading her down the beach towards the bathhouse.

Austin steps by my side and watches them for a moment before he turns to me.

"It's been tough," he says with a sigh. "And you were right. We don't really talk much, because every time we do, it circles around to what happened at that warehouse."

"That's a hard situation."

"Every time I go to touch her, she flinches," he admits, and I shift my stance, uncomfortable with where this conversation is going.

Raven never flinched with me, ever, so I could not relate. Her nightmares were another story, and they rivaled mine. Instead of drawing from my experiences, I inspected the catalog of CJ's memories that I had stored in my head.

"Do you love her?" I ask, and start a slow stroll in the direction Hannah and Paige went.

"Yeah," he answers, and shoves his hands in his pockets. "I should know how to navigate this shit. I've worked at the sanitarium for long enough to understand how to handle this, but it doesn't seem to work."

"Maybe you just need to talk and not handle it," I say, using finger quotes around the words 'handle it.' "She doesn't need another shrink."

Austin stops and levels that stare that I'm used to from CJ. The one that tells me I've said more than enough, and I need to shut up.

"Look. Have you dealt with what happened?" I ask, stopping and turning his way. "I only ask because it happened to both of you. She was fucked up on every level, but she seems to be handling it, from what I can tell. You're not. You're still stuck in that mental rut that you can't seem to get past."

"You don't know shit about me," he literally snarls at me.

"Do you approach her with kid gloves, or do you just let the moment happen?"

His jaw drops and he walks, passing me without comment, and I follow, letting him lead the way. The girls have taken a seat on the sidewalk at the point where the sandcastle still partially stands, and we are far enough away so our conversation cannot be heard.

Austin stops and turns. "What the fuck, man?"

I put my hands up. "Look, I'm just calling what I'm seeing. Did you even discuss what I talked to you about earlier with her, or did you just shut her down because you don't think she can handle it?"

"She wants to move here where it's safe," he says, and I now understand her reaction to his question about the hospital.

"And you shut her down." I glance over his shoulder, and Paige glances in our direction.

Austin's hands land on his hips, and he looks down at the sidewalk. "If..." He starts and trails off, shaking his head and turning toward Paige. "If we move here, I have a feeling I'd lose her."

"Why?"

"I think she has a thing for you." His hands slide into his pockets.

Laughter chokes from my throat and he glares over his shoulder. "You've got to be fucking kidding me."

Austin shakes his head. "She responds to you."

"It's because I don't treat her like damaged goods. No one wants to be treated that way. Trust me, I've been there and resented the hell out of it."

I step by his side and together we watch Paige and Hannah watching the ocean strip the castle of sand. They are smiling and laughing and Paige's aura flares bright, just like my daughter.

"We all are damaged in some way and none of us like to be reminded of it. Our nightmares are enough, so during the hours we are awake, we want to be treated like anyone else. Like nothing bad ever happened to us. With how you're treating her, it's a constant reminder of what she went through." I offer a shrug. "So basically, your training isn't doing shit right now."

"You really need to learn how to self-regulate your thoughts," Austin mutters and glances at me.

"Yeah, well, if I kept my mouth shut and did the polite thing, you two would drift farther apart, and then Hunter wins. Right?" I meet his stare. "So, drop the clinical attitude and treat her like the girl you are in love with."

Angel Fire Chapter 8

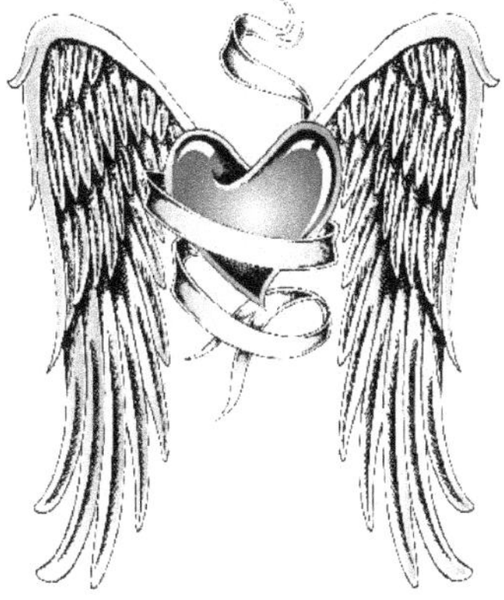

MONDAY MORNING CAME TOO fast and I glance at the clock on my nightstand. It isn't even five yet and I'm wide awake, stressing over what the hell is going to happen in the office today. I don't even know if Bridget will show up for work or not, and if she's there when I get in, I have no clue of what to say.

After a half hour of staring at the ceiling, I close my eyes and send feelers out to CJ, testing whether or not he is awake.

I'm awake. What the hell are you doing up at this hour? His voice echoes in my head and I smile. Having a newborn throws off any sort of normal sleep pattern.

Can't sleep. I am hesitant to ask him to take Hannah this early, but I had agreed to let CJ and Valerie take care of her while I went to work today. It's a step in the right direction, but dropping her at their cottage at five in the morning is pushing the envelope.

And you want to go to work instead of staring at the ceiling.

I huff a light laugh. My brother knows me too well. "Yeah," I say aloud and transmit the thought. "Hannah is still sleeping and probably will be until around eight," I add, with a yawn.

Do you want me to come over until she wakes up?

I remain quiet, debating.

Valerie doesn't mind. Alex just settled down again, so he'll be good for another couple of hours.

"Okay. Give me fifteen minutes."

Will do.

I climb out of bed and hit the shower, cleaning up and dressing before the knock on the door comes. When I swing the door open, I'm glad I opted for shorts and a t-shirt. It's already uncomfortably warm, and the sun hasn't even reached the horizon.

"Mind if I crash on the couch?" CJ asks as he steps inside.

"Go ahead," I wave him inside. "I appreciate this." That itchy anxiety of leaving Hannah sets itself in the pit of my stomach and CJ pauses halfway across the room, turning back to me.

"I promise she will be fine," he says, keeping my gaze. CJ doesn't make promises he can't keep, but even that doesn't settle these false nerves.

"I know, it's just..." I trail off, knowing he is intimately familiar with the panic biting at me. It took him more than a year not to have an anxiety attack when Valerie was out of sight. I don't want to leave, but I can't keep such a tight grip on Hannah all the time, and right now, I'm finding it nearly impossible to step out the door.

"It gets easier every time," he says in response to my hesitation. "And I know I have to get off my ass and start knocking those portals off the list," he adds as he falls onto the couch.

I say nothing, instead I just give him the usual curt nod and step outside before I lose my nerve. The farther away I go, the more my stomach knots, and by the time I pull into the office driveway, I am so tense, I'm sure if someone jumps out of the bushes, my power would go all ninja on them without my permission.

I step into my office and drop my keys on my desk before heading to start a pot of coffee. I'm so wound up that the fact the light is on doesn't register until I am standing in the doorway. Any fog in my brain clears at the sight of Bridget, in a baby doll nightgown, with her back towards me. She is already filling the coffee carafe with water.

When she turns, a startled yelp fills the room and the glass pot falls from her grip. Before the pot can hit the floor and shatter into a million shards, I will it to stop.

We stare at each other in the silence. Her wide hazel eyes and her bed-ruffled hair catch me completely off guard, and that animalistic hunger is back. My eyes slowly scan her from head to toe and back.

"I, um..." I have no idea what to say, and all I do is point at the coffee pot suspended a foot from the floor.

She drops her gaze and plucks it out of the air with a mumbled thank you, but the motion gives me a peek at her chest before she straightens. She turns away and pours the water into the coffeemaker and when she does, her nightgown rides up enough for me to see the lace panties barely covering her ass.

Her aura is as chaotic as I'm sure mine is, and after she slides the pot onto the hotplate, she flips the on switch and turns in my direction.

Crossing her arms to cover herself, she stares at me.

"What are you doing here at this hour?"

I'm too stunned to speak, so I just offer a one-shouldered shrug. Unlike her, there is no easy way to hide my reaction. When her eyes fall to my tented shorts, she raises an eyebrow and meets my gaze again.

Heat fills my face, but I'm afraid to move because I have a feeling if I do, it will to be to cross the room and fuck her right there on the kitchen counter. Instead, I utter a nervous laugh.

"I guess seven weeks is a long time," I say, and it's the truth. I don't think I've gone seven weeks without sex since I was fourteen, and seeing her in that skimpy, sexy as hell outfit isn't doing anything for my self-restraint.

"Try three years," she says and lets her arms fall to her sides. She glances towards the stairway and then back at me. Her thoughts muddled between a graceful escape and doing the same thing my mind is focused on.

"I thought you didn't want to sleep with me," I say, meeting her hungry stare.

"Yeah, well, when presented with such a sexy package, I'm not exactly sure what I want." She waves at me from the other side of the room.

I blink, and then her words penetrate my brain. "Three years?" I cock my head at her.

"I haven't been with anyone since Andy died," she says and like that, her mind is made up and she bolts for the stairs, opting for escape.

I follow, because my brain isn't the one in charge right now and that high school mentality kicks in at the unspoken challenge. She hears me and before I can grab her to stop her aggravated march, she spins in my direction.

"What?" she snaps. "Isn't it enough that you scared the hell out of me in the kitchen?"

Her glare catches me off guard and I pull my hand away. The heat that drove me up the stairs fizzles. "I didn't know you'd already moved in. I'm sorry for scaring you."

"You should be. You haven't set foot in the office before nine since I started. Why are you here at five in the morning?"

"I was hoping to avoid you." The words tumble out before I can catch them.

The tiny widening of her eyes tells me I've shocked the hell out of her, and when they narrow along with her lips, I know I'm in trouble.

"You're still an asshole," she spins and marches into the bedroom at the end of the hall and slams the door. The cabinets that had been in her room line the hallway, and I focus on those instead of the blooming aggravation in my stomach. The office doors open, and I will the cabinets one by one into the meeting space. Two in each room, and as the last two are floating at my direction, she opens the bedroom door.

Keeping my concentration on the cabinets, I look at her as the furniture completes my silent instruction. She's donned a bathrobe to hide her little negligee and a layer of disappointment crumbles my concentration and the cabinets drop in place with a unified thud.

Instead of hitting this head on, I turn to go back downstairs.

"Why?"

I stop with my back to her. "Because I miss my wife, and wanting to fuck you to ease that pain is wrong." Voicing the shit turning my stomach into a knot doesn't feel any better. As a matter of fact, it makes me feel every bit the asshole she accused me of being.

Angel Fire Chapter 9

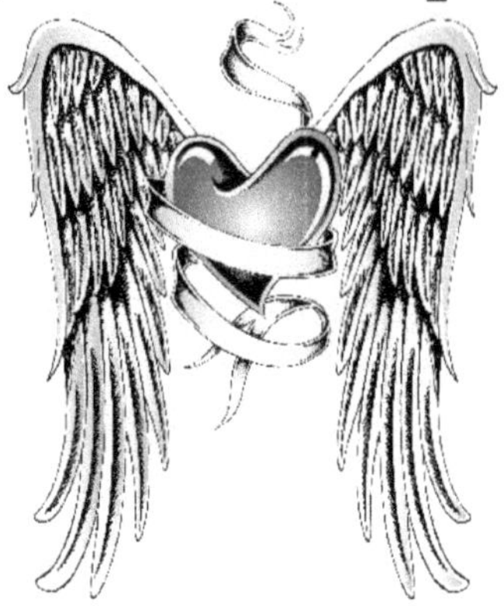

I STARE OUT THE window from my desk, ignoring the chatter coming from the outer office as I have for the past two months. Ever since I ran into her in the kitchen, Bridget and I have avoided each other the best we can.

Any interaction is cordial and brief. It's like having a stranger in the outer office. And the tension between us is almost visible when we are in the same room.

I've gotten used to not having Hannah with me during the day, but I make it a point to make a daily run home to see her at lunchtime. Sometimes I ditch the rest of the day and hang out with her at the beach, or we watch the construction on the house. It's almost completed, and I am eager to get back in a home instead of a tiny rental cottage.

CJ's house is complete, and from what he said last night, they'll have the furniture moved in by the time I pick up Hannah. The timeline given to me for my home is mid-November, which means I'm hosting Thanksgiving, according to the family.

The knock on my door interrupts my thoughts and I turn my chair, meeting Bridget's gaze. She stands uncertainly in the doorway, with a piece of paper in her hand.

"What's up?"

She glances at the paper. "I think you need to look into this one," she says and crosses, handing me the note.

The seriousness in her gaze straightens my spine, and I take the information, reading her meticulous notes. "They think their house is haunted?" I raise my gaze, and she nods. I lean back in the chair, studying her. "Where's Damian?"

"He left early to go pick out furniture."

I bite the side of my lip. I rarely go on a ghost chase without a backup.

"You want to come with?"

I've seen Bridget shocked before, but this time, the visible jaw drop, and the arched eyebrows bring some humor into the awkwardness between us.

"Really?" she asks when she finds her voice.

"It might be handy having someone else who can see ghosts." I give her a shrug. "So, are you game?"

She blinks a few times, looks around my office, and then the biggest smile I've ever seen appears on her face. It glows as much as her aura.

"Hell, yeah!"

I can't help but laugh at her enthusiasm. "It isn't that glamorous," I say and stand, gathering my keys. I pause and turn towards the closet, where I stowed Raven's bag. I cross and unzip the top, rifling through the contents before I find what I am looking for. Before the shot to my stomach can take hold, I zip up her duffle bag and close the closet. It's been close to four months since she died, and this is the first time I've opened her bag. I take a second to push the pain back down before I turn back to Bridget.

"You might need this," I say, holding out the silver chain that has a Celtic Knot made of bloodstone.

Bridget stares at it and then raises her gaze. "It's beautiful," she whispers, and takes it gingerly from my hand.

"It's bloodstone," I say, and her gaze shoots to mine.

She knows what killed Raven, so she knows how hard retrieving that from her stash is. I can hear her mind working through the facts, and thankfully, she isn't reading anything into the gesture.

"It's for protection, right?"

"Yes. If there is a ghost causing problems, the likelihood of it trying to attack us is pretty high. This protects us from possession, but not anything else."

"So, an angry ghost can hurt us?" Her enthusiasm dips a notch.

"Yes." I did not want to sugarcoat this. If she is going to accompany me, she needs all the facts.

"Have you ever gotten hurt?"

I chuckle. "No. I had Damian backing me up, but now that I'm supercharged like he and CJ, I'm the backup."

"And I'm the helpless loser?" she asks and clasps the necklace around her neck.

I smile and shrug. "You said it, not me."

"Fuck you, Ryan. Let's go get us a ghost." She turns and heads out. I grab my phone off the desk and follow.

"So, we're on a last name basis?" I ask, mocking her over the roof of the car.

"It's better than me calling you asshole, don't you think?" She slides into the passenger seat, and I take a breath. I haven't said more than two words to her since I caught her in the kitchen in her negligee.

"I guess I deserve that," I say and take the driver's seat, pushing the start button while I glance at her.

"Seriously, why are you taking me on this ghost hunt?"

"Because I've been a dick long enough." I give her a strained smile and punch in the address on my GPS system. I take a second to shoot a text to Damian and CJ, telling them I'll be later than normal tonight, before I put the car in gear. "And I thought it would be refreshing to have someone with me who can tell me when something is coming at me from the opposite direction."

"You sure this isn't some elaborate plot to get rid of me?"

I utter a laugh. "Yeah, that's my plan. Just like your plan is to seduce me and steal all my money."

She actually bursts out laughing. "I'm not after your money, Tom."

I glance at her. "I know." I note she didn't deny trying to seduce me, and that familiar stirring flutters in my stomach. I follow the GPS, letting the quiet filter between us until we are a few minutes from our destination.

"When we get there, the first thing we need to do is assess the situation. If it's as dangerous as they say, we will need the owners of the house to leave."

"Okay. And then what?"

"Well, if we can start a dialog, we might not need to call in the cavalry."

"What do you mean?"

"If the ghost can listen to reason, we can show him the way to move on. Otherwise, Raven taught me a banishment spell that traps the ghost so they can't exercise their will on the physical world."

I open the console between us and pull out a small satchel, handing it to her. "Hang onto that. It has what we need for the spell."

Bridget unzips the bag and peers inside before closing it and glancing at me. "And if this doesn't work?" She holds up the bag, shaking it to prove her point.

"Then I have to call on the only person I know who can wield angel fire."

Silence captured the car, and I glance at her as we pull onto the road. Our destination is less than a quarter mile away on the right.

"How many times have you had to do that?"

I'm glad she doesn't ask who has that power, but from the clatter in her mind, she already knows my brother is the one I'm referring to.

"Twice."

"And how many ghosts hunts have you gone on?"

As I pull into the driveway, I silently count the ghost encounters Damian and I have had over the past five years. "I don't know. Over a hundred?" I say and turn off the car.

"So, your failure rate is less than two percent."

I can't help but smile. "I guess. Let's go." I don't wait for the other swarming questions to pass her lips. Instead, I step out of the car and cross to the door, with her following behind me. Before I can knock, the door swings open and I stare into the eyes of a terrified teenage girl.

"Tammy?" Bridget says from behind me.

Her eyes dart to Bridget's and she nods. "Are you from the paranormal investigation agency?"

"Yes," both Bridget and I say in unison. The clatter in the house pulls my attention from her face and I stiffen. "Maybe you should step outside," I add.

"It's hurting my mother," she whispers, and I move her onto the front step, meeting Bridget's gaze.

"Stay with her," I order, and before I step into the house, I take the satchel from her hand. She gives me a nod and her eyes transition from me to the opening of the house like it's a portal to hell. Fortunately, she has never seen a portal. This is child's play in relation to one of those abominations.

"Tom?"

I glance back at her.

"Be careful," she says and her eyes echo her plea.

I turn away from her concern and step over the threshold. The turmoil within the walls is palpable and I resist the sudden tension clenching every muscle. A shuffle behind me turns my head in that direction and I meet Bridget's wide-eyed gaze.

"Where's the girl?" I ask, suddenly annoyed with her for not following my orders.

"Locked in the car."

Her gaze darts away from me and the front door slams closed, trapping us in the house of horrors. Muffled screams come from the room down the hall, and I take a deep breath, putting my aggravation on the shelf, and focusing on the situation at hand.

"Watch my back," I say.

"Ditto," she answers. When she pulls out a mini gun from her pocketbook, I raise my eyebrows.

"Put that thing away before you shoot someone." The admonishment in my tone is clear, and her frazzled gaze meets mine.

She presses her lips together and flips the safety back on before she stows it away at my request.

"Bullets don't hurt ghosts, but they can kill both of us," I say, and focus down the hall again. I understand her rationale. It's for her own sense of control, but a gun in the realm of the paranormal is not a smart move. Angry ghosts can and will use whatever weapon they can get their hands on. Getting bloody doesn't bother me, but I'm not ready to die just yet. I keep that tidbit to myself and proceed with caution.

I step into the entry to the family room and halt. The scene is right out of a violent movie or an x-rated porn flick. I can't decide which and the sheer number of ghosts partaking shocks me to inaction. Their auras are as black as the thick Maine woods on a moonless night.

Tammy's mother's arms are bound at the wrist and she hangs from the ceiling while the pack of ghosts accost her. Bruises line the skin that is visible through her shredded clothing, and I now understand why her screams are muffled and why Tammy was so fucking freaked out.

A silent admonishment recoils through me. I should have done some research on the address before coming here, then maybe I'd know what the hell to do. I'm actually at a loss.

"What the hell?" Bridget announced our presence, and the pack turns in our direction, stopping their assault on the homeowner. She crumples to the ground, sobbing, as their collective focus looks right through me.

The air actually makes a popping sound when they disappear, and I shiver with the shock of it. I'm not sure what the fuck we are dealing with at all, and I scan the room in front of me. It isn't until I hear a yelp and a thud behind me that my heart jumps in my throat. I spin and Bridget is pinned to the wall with a ghostly hand covering her mouth. Rope wraps around her wrists, pulling her arms overhead in the same position as the homeowner. I shiver as their filthy hands start their exploration amidst her muffled scream for help. Her wide, terrified eyes mirror that of the woman sobbing behind me.

Reality slams home. If I don't do something now, they are going to hurt her in ways she will never fully recover from. A protective wave surges through me, wrapped in anger.

"Leave her alone!" The voice bellows from my chest in an inhuman growl. The power in me blurs my vision, and heat encompasses every cell. When her shirt rips and the button on her jeans unlatch, I can't control the fury. It lashes out and the horde of ghosts is thrown in every direction. Bridget slides to the ground, her breathing raspy, and her eyes wide with fear.

I unzip the satchel and dump the contents on the ground, uttering the Latin words that comprise Raven's banishing spell. My voice is unsteady with the adrenaline and doubt rushing my system. Usually Damian reads the words, so I'm praying I have the right accent, otherwise I might just be brewing things to a different level.

The explosion of the spell knocks me on my ass and the ghostly screams of protest fill the small house. Bridget covers her ears, but my erratic heartbeat muffles the sound. I stare at the writhing mass above me as they fight against the chains I've locked them in.

Murderous promises hurl through the space between us, and I'm not sure the spell will keep. I don't want to end up being a ghost's bitch, and I can't watch them hurt Bridget.

It's time to call the cavalry before they get loose.

My thought barrels from my core loud enough to wake CJ, or at least make him bolt out of whatever seat he's parked in. A phone call in this situation isn't enough and I'm sure the panic filling me came through loud and clear.

The air ripples next to me and CJ appears. I project what I'm seeing right into his head and with a cool inhale of breath; he closes his eyes. Angel fire builds in his aura, making me squint, but I can't look away as it forms wings on his back before it fully encompasses him. When his eyelids fly open, the white fire shoots like a bolt of lightning, engulfing the raging ghosts.

It's over in seconds and CJ glances at me, and that cocky smile I want to punch appears just before he pops out of existence. I'm sure I'll hear more about how stupid I was to bring Bridget into this when I get home, but for now, I turn my attention to the conditions around me.

The quiet is deafening, and I sit on the floor, getting my bearings before I lock my gaze with Bridget. This is so much more disturbing than any of the past ghost hunts I have encountered, and I have a second to wonder if what happened earlier this summer opened up some door between our world and the next.

Angel Fire Chapter 10

AFTER GETTING TAMMY'S MOTHER to the emergency room, I drive back to the office with Bridget in the passenger seat. Neither of us speaks, and I go directly to the kitchen pantry, pulling out a bottle of whiskey, pouring two shots before I stow the bottle. I turn and offer Bridget one.

She takes it and we tap the glasses together before downing the shot. I lean against the counter with my eyes closed, letting the burn flow down my throat, the scrape of a chair opens my eyes. Bridget sits at the table with her face in her hands.

"I shouldn't have brought you," I whisper, and she turns her head towards me. The dampness on her cheeks glistens in the light, and I sigh.

"Did you know you have black wings?"

"Excuse me?" I can feel the arch of my eyebrows.

"Right before you knocked the ghosts away from me, I swear I saw black wings spread from your back. Like you're some kind of fallen angel, or something."

I laugh and run my hand through my hair. The only angel I ever saw with black wings was Lucifer, and the thought chills me.

"You really weren't kidding about being angel blood." She leans back in her seat studying me.

"No. I wasn't." I glance away, because her words are still pinging around my head. Black wings. CJ has the heavenly white wings and mine reflects the devil. Well, shit. That just ruins my night, and I turn away, staring out the window.

Her hand lands on my shoulder and I try to shrug it off, but she steps to my side, reaching out and turning my face in her direction.

"You saved that woman today. And you saved me. Thank you."

I can't help but laugh. "CJ saved everyone, like he always does," I say, and direct my gaze away from her, but I don't pull away from her lingering touch.

When her thumb caresses my bottom lip, my eyes turn back to hers.

"I haven't felt that... alive in a very long time," she says, with her gaze focused on my lips. She licks her own and her eyes dart to mine. Hunger lives there.

"I'm one of Lucifer's descendants." The words wrap in bitterness, but she doesn't shy away.

"And Raphael's if that list is correct," she says, making me feel like less of a freak. When she leans in, I let her.

The gentle press of her lips against mine opens a door I had closed tight two months ago. Logic goes by the wayside, and I wrap my arms around her, pulling her tighter against me. There is no fight this time, and when her lips part, allowing my tongue access, I'm overwhelmed with the sensation. The movement of our tongue dance captivates me, and I pull her closer, breathing in the fresh scent of her.

"Tommy, stop," she whispers under my lips and her hands push on my chest.

I take a step back and put my hands out with my palms facing her. We remain in place and I'm not sure if it is aggravation or want making my heart pulse in my ears. We are inches away from each other, and her ragged breath matches mine. I search her eyes as her aura pulses, giving away the want she is feeling just as acutely as I am.

"I haven't been with anyone for so long..." she whispers and reaches out, placing her palm on my chest. It isn't to push me away, it's to feel my heartbeat, and she stares at the contact.

"Maybe I should go," I say and utter a sigh.

Bridget turns her gaze outside, giving the slightest of nods before looking back at me. "What if I don't want you to?" She bites her lower lip now that the thoughts swarming in her mind have trickled out.

She has the good sense to take a step back, distancing herself from me. "This probably isn't a good idea," she says, but the juxtaposition of her words and her actions as she licks her lips just adds fuel to my already stoked fire.

"Why not?" I advance a step closer, letting my carnal desires out of the locked cabinet in my soul. I need the human connection. I need to let this tension between us ignite.

"Because you are not ready for this," she says, and her voice has that breathy quality that I remember from our encounter back in high school.

Memories flood my brain and I'm not sure if they are hers or mine or a potent concoction of both, but the effect has me stalking her, trying to maneuver her towards the stairwell and her bedroom on the second floor. This does not go unnoticed by that little voice in my head, but my mind is decidedly not in control at the moment.

"But you are," I whisper and close the distance, leaning in and delivering another heat filled kiss. The sensations drown out any warning my brain tries to launch. When her hands pull at the hem of my shirt, I peel it off, pulling away from her mouth for just a split second. Which gives me just enough time to see the iridescent pink of raw lust painted in her aura.

I lick a line from her clavicle to her ear, and she shivers, letting out a squeal. Her skin tastes like sweat and honey and as I nibble on her earlobe and attempt to undress her, I wonder what her pussy will taste like. I can't seem to work the buttons on her shirt and with a growl, I rip it apart, sending buttons bouncing across the kitchen tile.

"Tommy," she says in a gasp as I pick her up and set her on the kitchen counter. She wraps her legs around me, pulling me closer as our lips connect again.

The madness of this moment engulfs me and I home in on every sensation, from her tongue twirling with mine, to the hardness of her nipples under the thin fabric of her bra.

"I want to taste every fucking inch of you," I whisper, breaking the kiss. She moans when my mouth trails down to her chest. I tease her with my tongue, tracing the edge of her bra while I reach around her back and flick the clasp, freeing her from the fabric.

Bridget's breasts are beautiful, and I stare at them, rubbing her nipples with my thumbs, and meeting her gaze. The grin slowly stretches my lips and I lean in, but this time I avoid her lips and catch the underside of her jaw, trailing kisses until I have her hard nipple in my mouth.

I explore every inch of her breasts with my tongue and my hands run up her jean-clad thighs. Her hands are buried in my thick hair, and her soft purrs when I do something she likes guides me along with the hints freely accessible in her mind.

Her thoughts toggle between the pure heat and wanting to stop before we step into the land of regret, but she voices neither. Instead, her thoughts tangle in the sensation, just the way mine do.

She leans back on the counter, allowing me access to the buttons on her jeans. I explore her belly button with my tongue while tugging at the fabric. There is no easy way to take her jeans off without destroying the current mood we are both in, so I do something I've only seen in a memory. I will the fabric to shred.

Bridget gasps, and her grip on my hair tightens. I send a playful glance up at her, and then nip at her inner thigh. She sucks in her breath when I pass over her clit with only a cursory flick of my tongue. I'm too far gone to care about the ramifications of my actions. I want to taste her. I want to feel her come. I want to hear her moan my fucking name.

When I take a knee and cover her clit with my mouth, she lifts her leg onto the counter, leaning on one hand while the other has a solid grip on my hair. I roll my tongue around the nub, and she groans.

Her reaction burns just as hot as the fire raging inside me. With her hands still webbed in my hair, she moans, widening her legs, begging me with her thoughts until her mouth echoes the same sentiments.

"Oh, fuck," she whispers, and her body shudders with her first release.

Tasting her hot nectar drives me further over the edge and the salty sweetness fuels my need. I continue to drive her over the edge until she's dripping on the counter and her juices coat my lips and my fingers.

My cock is so hard I'm not sure I can get my jeans over my hips, but I manage, and in one motion, I stand and bury my cock inside her before she can catch her breath.

"Oh, my god," she whispers and wraps her legs around my waist.

Every hip thrust is met with the same bravado, and Bridget arches into me, pulling me to her lips again. I plunge my tongue into the recess of her mouth, exploring, tasting, enjoying every sensation accosting my body.

The heat pulls from my fingers and toes, pooling in my belly until it's burning for release. My body stiffens with the rocket of an orgasm, pulling a groan from my lips. The aftermath saps the strength out of me, leaving my muscles quivering, and I lean on the counter with my head resting on her shoulder, but I don't move yet. Not with my heart slamming against the walls of my chest like I just ran the thousand-yard dash.

"Holy shit."

Her breath tickles my ear, and my eyes focus on the cabinets behind her. Now that the physical sensations have abated, the reality of what I have just done seeps in, and I close my eyes.

Regret is a fucked-up thing, and it now has a tighter grip on me than Bridget. I know damned well I shouldn't have done this, and I really have no rightful excuse beyond just being a sex hound.

I push myself away from her shoulder and look at the woman I've just compromised, feeling like an absolute shit heel.

She blinks up at me and her easy smile fades. Her eyes dart to where we are still joined and they widen, meeting mine again.

"You didn't use anything."

My heart literally skips, and I think my jaw drops open. I know my eyes widen, and I pull out of her like she was a leper. "Fuck," I mutter, and pull my underwear and jeans up from around my ankles. It's been years since a condom entered my mind, never mind how long it's been since I had cause to use one.

"You're not..." I wave at her like she is supposed to finish the sentence, but my mind is so fuzzy with the ramifications that I can't even concentrate to hear her thoughts.

"I'm not what?" she says, and hops off the counter. She has no clothing left to put on, so she grabs my shirt from over the back of the chair where it had been tossed. "Diseased?" she asks after the fabric covers her.

"No. On the pill?" I ask, hoping for some way to not have another mistake in my life.

"No. I'm not on the pill," she says. "And it's a really shitty time to be this stupid," she adds before she disappears into the bathroom.

I'm not sure if the comment was aimed at me or not, and I just stand there like an incompetent fool waiting for instruction.

I lean against the counter we've just desecrated and stare at the floor.

"I'm sorry," I say when she steps back in the kitchen. "I never intended..." I trail off because I'm not sure if that's really the truth or not. The thing between us was not easy, like it had been with my wife. This was filled with fits and starts, battles of wills, and tension so palpable I thought I'd scream at times.

The intensity of it worried me, and I met her tentative stare.

"I didn't intend on this either. Otherwise, I would have been prepared," she adds with a little laugh.

My lips tilt in a half smile. "I guess ghost hunting sharpens the appetite."

Her light laugh answers my attempt at humor. "I thought you were good in bed back in high school, but damn, you've jumped into a whole new category all your own," she says and her cheeks fill with red blush.

"And what category would that be?" I ask, trying not to grin at the compliment.

"Beyond earth shattering," she answers, and takes a deep breath, trying to control the creep of blush that now has taken over her entire face. She shifts and utters another laugh, but this time, it's laced with nerves. "As much as I'm going to hate myself for allowing this to happen, I have to admit, it was worth every moment of awkward silence that will precede this."

"Awkward silence?" I straighten.

"Yes. Tomorrow, you're going to be all weird when you come in, like you don't know what to say to me. It will be frustrating and endearing all at once." She heads towards the stairwell and pauses, pointing at the shredded fabric all over the kitchen. "You are cleaning that up."

I huff a laugh and she challenges me with a raised eyebrow.

"Fine," I say, and she disappears up the stairs. Glancing around, I made a hell of a mess. "I'll buy you another pair of jeans," I yell up at the ceiling, hoping she can hear me.

"Damned straight you will!"

The answer pulls a smile and I grab the garbage pail from under the sink. Cleaning up is the easy part and I concentrate, willing every stitch of torn fabric into the receptacle before returning it to its place.

I rinse my face and hands in the sink and dry my face with paper towels before grabbing a couple of counter cleaning wipes. I scrub down the area we just christened, and my thoughts swirl between her comment about black wings and the way she tasted. The two thoughts didn't belong in the same zip code, never mind side by side, volleying for my attention.

She cleared her throat, making me jerk in surprise.

Her low chuckle told me she caught my startled jump, and I glance in her direction after throwing the nearly torn wipes in the garbage. Bridget tosses me my shirt and I slip it on. She's right. Now that the euphoria of the moment has faded, I'm not sure what to say.

"See. Awkward silence," she says with a sigh.

"Sorry." I shuffle my feet and glance at the clock. It's close to seven and I need to get home to my daughter. When I turn back to Bridget, she just smiles.

"Go. You've kept Hannah long enough," she says.

The sudden need to kiss her moves my feet in her direction, but she holds up her hand, stopping me.

"This was a onetime deal," she says, nodding toward the counter. "We both needed to blow off some steam, okay?"

It's more like a line I would have used to gloss over a good fuck back in high school, and it makes me more uncomfortable than I care to admit. "Sure," I say. "I'll catch you tomorrow," I add, and head out to my car without a glance over my shoulder.

In the confines of the car, I stare at the house, watching as the front lights turn off and then the kitchen, before she walks by her bedroom window a few minutes later. She pauses and pulls the curtain back. Our eyes meet across the distance.

My hand sits idle on the gears, and I take a deep breath, blowing air out in a slow stream before I put the car in reverse. One last glance and she's still standing there, watching me drive away, with her face framed in a thoughtful expression.

Angel Fire Chapter 11

I PULL INTO CJ's house, scanning the familiar architecture. He had the builders recreate the home we grew up in, instead of making it his own. A furniture van was in the driveway, and I parked to the side. Scooting around the truck, I cross to the front door and let myself in.

Even the layout is the same, and I step into the formal living room, complete with CJ's new baby grand piano stationed in the same spot as before. The decor is minimalist, which is a bit of a divergence from our parent's warm, cluttered environment. When I step into the kitchen, all familiarity with the house ends. The kitchen and family room is much more customized, and more of a natural fit to what I envisioned as my brother's tastes. The kitchen includes an extended counter that wraps around to form a breakfast bar, as well as a sizeable island in the center of the kitchen, which is also adorned with bar stools.

They are missing a formal dining table like we had before, but the amount of sparkling granite makes up for the lack of seating. I have to admit, I'm a little impressed with the modifications.

The television is in the same place it once was. However, it's probably the biggest one CJ could find, now that the built-in cabinets are no longer gracing the wall. Despite the overbearing size of the television, the room looks bigger without the built-ins. The very comfortable looking sectional couch seems dwarfed by the room size, and I glance towards the front of the house.

They put a new kitchen table by the windows, turning the front half of the room into the dining space. I still haven't run into anyone, and I only have one room left. The exercise room—beyond the family room. I cross by new extra wide French doors leading to the backyard, glancing at the covered pool before focusing on the door to where the exercise room used to be.

I open it and stare. The room is split in two, with a glass panel separating the far room from this one. A control panel is laid out before me, and my eyes do not know where to focus, so I step into the room, inspecting the space beyond the glass. Another piano is parked there, along with microphones and egg crate foam walls. I let out a little laugh.

CJ built himself a state-of-the-art recording studio.

This is all well and good, but where the hell is my daughter?

I spin on my heels, closing the door.

"CJ?" I call out with only my voice. When no response comes, I close my eyes and reach out with my mind. They are in the house, but not where I expect. I turn and cross the kitchen, stepping beyond the first-floor powder room and into the entry to the basement. In the old house, this space was unfinished, but I glance down a fully finished stairwell with colorful berber carpeting.

I descend, and it isn't until I reach the bottom that the noise reaches my ears. The soundproofing in this place is out of this world.

"Daddy!" Hannah's excited screech pulls my attention away from the construction and into the heart of the multi-purpose room. Various exercise equipment lines the outer wall, and in the center is the biggest indoor playscape I have had the pleasure of seeing, and another large television set is being hung on the wall by the furniture company.

CJ pokes his head out from the other side of the playscape and smiles at me just as my daughter flings herself into my arms. I cross the distance and suppress a laugh at the instruction booklet laid out on the floor, along with various pieces and parts yet to be put together.

Grace and her brothers are running around through a mini-maze of toys while Valerie nurses Alex in a comfortable-looking glider.

"The house looks great," I say and put Hannah back down so she can resume playing.

"Thanks." CJ glances at the instructions and tightens a bolt before he meets my gaze. "I've been putting this monstrosity together all day." He points his screwdriver at the playscape. "The only break I've had was when I saved your ass," he says, lowering his voice as he stares me down from his seat on the floor. "What the hell were you thinking taking her there?"

"She can see ghosts. I thought she'd be useful, but honestly, I have never seen anything like that."

He let out a laugh. "Yes, you have," he says, and I know damned well he's referring to our interception of the ghosts attacking Paige in New York.

I glance around the room again, but CJ's sharp stare pulls my gaze back to him.

"Thanks for helping me out with Hannah," I say, leaving off thanks for, yet again, saving me from myself. He's made a lifetime habit of that and right now, it irks the hell out of me.

He's still staring at me, and now his dimples appear. I realize he's trying not to smile and I form a glare. He's in my head, snooping, and now that I realize it, I can feel the alien presence.

"Really?" I say and the smile forms on his face.

"I'm the one who should be asking that," he says with a laugh.

Fuck you. I hurl the thought and he winces at the volume in his head. And he has the audacity to raise an eyebrow.

"I believe you've already done that today."

"What?" Valerie's voice yanks my attention in her direction. Unjust betrayal radiates from her, and I bite my lip as the guilt builds inside me.

"Leave the boy alone," CJ says, sending what I call the 'shut up' look.

"It's only been three months," she balks.

I shift my weight and shove my hands into my pockets. I feel like I'm being reprimanded by my mother, and I slide a sideways glance at Valerie. The verbal conversation is scarce enough that the kids don't pick up on it, but her sharp admonishment in my mind leaves me quiet. I'm damned if I am going to apologize to her for my behavior. If anyone needs an apology, it is Bridget.

"Hannah, it's time to pack up," I announce at the same time the technician announces his task is complete.

CJ climbs up from the floor and walks the workman out of the house. I follow him upstairs because I can't stand the judgment radiating from Valerie.

As soon as the front door closes, he turns to me with a grin. "You shut down those thoughts pretty damned quickly after my comment."

"It's none of your fucking business," I snap, glaring at him. "And I really don't need Valerie judging me right now. Opportunity presented itself and I took it."

He chuckled. "Once a whore, always a whore."

He's not talking about Bridget, and I'm not sure whether or not to punch him. My palms ache and I realize I've clenched my fists. I loosen my hands and stare at my brother.

"Yeah, well, at least I didn't let some random chick tie me up and show me what her strap on is used for."

CJ bursts out laughing. "Yeah. Okay. You've got me there." When he winds down, he sighs. "Still, are you sure she has your best interests at heart?"

I narrow my eyes. "What do you have against Bridget?"

CJ shifts and slides his hands in his pockets. "I don't know. I just have a feeling she has an ulterior motive for... everything."

This is one situation where I have more information than my brother, and I crack a smile. "O'Keefe asked her to look after me. I guess he figured both Raven and

Hannah were going to die, and he knew Bridget lived through something similar."

CJ's brow creased.

Usually CJ was quick to get the gist, but I guess sleep deprivation is taking its toll, because after a moment, I say, "Bridget can see ghosts and her uncle paid her a visit after he died."

CJ's eyes widen in understanding. "Oh." His exhausted mind mulls things over before he blinks and refocuses on me. "On a different note, Valerie is going back to work tomorrow."

It is my turn to be slow on the uptake, but after a moment, what he is trying to say seeps in. "I need to make alternate arrangements for Hannah," I say, and he nods.

"At least for a couple of weeks, while I get used to taking care of Alex on my own."

"No problem," I say, and Hannah comes running around the corner, her eyes a little wild like she thought I left without her. "Hey, peanut. You feel like coming to work with me in the morning?"

She beams and I have my answer. I glance at CJ again. "Thanks for helping for as long as you have."

"Give me a few weeks, and by that time, I'll probably be good to juggle a little more again." He glances at Hannah and messes up her hair before meeting my gaze.

"It might be time for me to find a more permanent solution." I'm almost as surprised by my words as CJ is, and I utter a soft laugh and a shrug. "Besides, I have to think about pre-school."

"Pre-school. I can't believe she's getting that old." He glances at my daughter and sighs.

"We're getting old," I say. Thirty is right around the corner for both of us, and the fact we are both still breathing blows me away, especially with all the shit we've lived through.

He scoffs at me. "Speak for yourself." He opens the front door, signaling the end of the conversation.

I scoop Hannah up in my arms and head out while she chatters endlessly about all the adventures she had today. By the time we reach the cottage, her continuous chatter is now the background noise to the memory of my own adventure.

Angel Fire Chapter 12

THE NEXT MORNING, I linger at the cottage, cleaning up the dishes from last night and letting Hannah wake on her own. Sleep had been restless, and now I am trying to wake from the morning stupor, and coffee isn't doing it for me.

Nightmares hit with hurricane force last night. In each one, some horrifying end came to Hannah, no matter how much I begged and pleaded. Variations put Bridget under the knife, and the resulting panic attack almost made me call her, but I had a feeling she would roast me alive if I called her at three in the morning.

The rest of the night, I rolled from side to side and finally dragged my ass into the shower at a little past five. I've been watching the morning news for a couple of hours now and restlessness has set in. I climb to my feet and head to Hannah's room to get her moving.

The door squeaks when I swing it open, and it takes me a second to digest what I'm seeing. An empty bed meets my stare, and my gut clenches like I've just been hit with a wrecking ball.

"Hannah," I yell, spinning towards the bathroom and then my bedroom. I scour every inch of the cottage before I dart outside and bellow her name. No response and fear as hot as a stove burner on high fills every fiber of my being.

I did not hear anything. I did not wake up.

I freeze in place, unsure of what to do. I don't know how long she has been gone. She was there at midnight when I got up to make sure she was okay. The panic accosting me makes it hard to think clearly, but I had enough sense to dial nine-one-one.

"York Beach Nine-one-one, what is the location of your emergency?"

"Chapman's Cottages, Unit four," I respond. "My daughter is missing. She's three, and she was in bed when I checked on her at midnight, but she is not in the cottage." My words tumble out as my chest constricts, tightening with every second. "Oh, Jesus," I whisper as my breathing becomes ragged.

"Can I have your name, sir?" she asks, still keeping that calm voice that does nothing to stop my hyperventilating.

"Tom. Tom Ryan," I say between breaths.

"Sir, I need you to sit and put your head between your legs."

Sitting wasn't going to happen. "My daughter's gone!" I yell breathlessly. "I can't sit down, not..." I stop speaking as my better sense kicks in. Babbling about Lucifer would get me checked into the psych ward, and I didn't have time for that.

"I understand that, sir, and a cruiser already is on the way, but it sounds like you are hyperventilating and if you don't sit down and do as I ask, you will pass out," she says with that calming cadence.

She has no clue just how terrified I am, and there is no way to explain that my little girl may already be dead. The thought is like a slap, and I blink as my breath finds the right rhythm again. I, of all people, would know if she were dead.

Frigid fear slowly wraps around my heart. If she isn't dead, what the hell is the game?

"That's it, sir," the dispatcher on the phone says, and I take another slow breath.

A police cruiser pulls into the lot with its lights on but the sirens off and stops in front of my cottage. A single officer climbs out and I balk at the lack of response.

"Only one officer?" I say into the phone. "My three-year-old is missing, and God knows where, and you send only one officer?"

I can't help the growl in my voice. Didn't this nitwit know anything? I disconnect the call and stare at the approaching cop. The familiar gait raises an eyebrow.

Bear Whipple, an ex-friend from high school, approaches, and he tips his hat back when he stops in front of me. I hadn't taken notice of him at O'Keefe's funeral, but then again, I hadn't been looking for any familiar faces.

"Tom," he says with a cautious nod.

"Bear," I respond, and if I wasn't so damned panicked about Hannah, his reaction would have cracked me up. He actually steps back and points, like he just witnessed a miracle. "The last gift Raven gave to me," I say and inhale. "My daughter is missing," I add, and turn towards the cottage behind me. "I checked on her before I went to bed, but she wasn't in her room when I went to wake her."

"What time did you last see her," he asks, and crosses to look at the door.

"Around midnight." My voice cracks and Bear turns his attention to me.

"She'll be all right," he says.

I let out a high-pitched laugh. "Just like my wife would be all right?"

Bear stands from his crouch, and I catch the pity in his eyes and the remorse at screwing up our friendship back in high school.

"Look, we'll find her," he says, and I know he means well, but he has no idea what I am up against. "In the meantime, I need to radio this in. It looks like your lock was tampered with and with any luck, maybe we will get a set of prints we can work with."

Last night was the first night that all three of us were not staying here. The timing really unnerves me, and I take a seat in the small living room, feeling as if I can barely draw a breath.

After Bear comes back into the cottage, and he does a sweep of each room, he comes back and clears his throat. "I need to ask. Do you have any enemies?"

A stress laugh escapes, and I glance at him. "Not since high school," I say, knowing it's a low blow, but I can't help it. He glances down at his notepad. The red hue rises in his cheeks. "Our names were on that list that was found at the groomer's in July," I add after a moment.

When his gaze finds mine, he grimaces. "I know," he says. "The chief had us on watch for a couple of months after your wife's death, just to make sure there wasn't another attempt on your family." He glances at the ground as his mind struggles to find the words to convey his sorrow for the loss of my wife. He looks up without voicing anything running through his head.

He takes a few blinks before his professional demeanor is back. "Just on the off chance the marks on the door aren't what I think they are. Is there any way she could have wandered off while you were in the shower?" he asks.

"I don't think she would. Besides, where the hell would she go?"

It takes a second and then my gaze jumps to the road and the beach beyond.

I am moving before my brain registers and Bear is scrambling to catch up. When I get to the sidewalk bordering the beach, my heart thunders and I scan the sand, praying she came to see if her sandcastle made it through the night. She isn't on the beach and my gaze darts to the retreating surf. While I know on some level, this is all futile, and my daughter is not anywhere near York at this moment, I cling to hope that my underlying intuition is dead wrong.

"We, uh, we made a sandcastle yesterday," I say, because it is all I can croak out of my tight throat. "But she'd never cross the road by herself," I add after I swallow. I had yelled at her not to go near the road alone enough times over the summer. If she was a teenager, I wouldn't put it past her to disregard whatever I say, but at three, she listens intently and follows orders where crossing the road without an adult is concerned.

My hand runs through my hair and my stomach clenches enough that I think I might vomit my morning coffee all over the sidewalk. "Jesus," I whisper, and spin around, looking back at the cluster of cottages.

Bear's hand lands on my shoulder and I stare at it before meeting his gaze. He glances at where we were staying as well. "We'll find her," he says, but his brain is already radiating the loss.

My pocket vibrates, and I pull out my phone. The office number blinks and I connect the call.

"Damian?" I ask without waiting for salutations to be passed.

"No. It's Bridget," she says, and her voice is full of hesitation. "Are you okay?" she asks after a pause.

"Hannah's missing."

The squeak of a chair sounds in the background. "I think you need to come to the office now."

I'm already crossing the street, heading towards the cottage where my car keys are. A couple of other cruisers are now in the parking lot and police are congregated outside the cottage door.

"Why?"

"A package came with a note."

"Did you open it?"

"No. It says for your eyes only, but it also says it is urgent you open right away. First thing this morning."

I slow to a stop before I enter the cottage and trade a glance with Bear. "Don't open it. Not until I get there with the police, okay?"

"Okay, and Tom?"

"Yeah?"

"Hannah's okay."

Her conviction is sweet, but she is wrong. Hannah is in Lucifer's hands, and nothing is okay about that. I end the call and nod towards his cruiser.

"A package was delivered to my office this morning. Think you can drive me there and possibly bring the bomb squad?" I ask Bear, and refrain from requesting the animal control officer as well. The last killer used snakes to poison his victims, and I could just envision a box of writhing cobras waiting to strike.

Bear's face pales, but to his credit, he nods and speaks into the microphone clipped to his shoulder. I rattle off the address to my office and he transmits the information before pointing to the passenger side of the car.

I slide into the seat, feeling a sense of déjà vu as we take off, this time with lights and sirens. When we pull into the driveway, Bridget steps out of the front door. Her face hardens when Bear steps out of the car with me.

She doesn't approach, instead she just crosses her arms and turns back into the house.

"Bridget O'Keefe works for you?" Bear asks as we are walking toward the house.

"Yes," I answer. I don't feel like explaining myself to Bear Whipple. He follows me, but waits on the front porch for the bomb squad.

I step inside and approach the desk. "Where's the package?" I ask, glancing around, looking for a box of some sort.

She picks up a small mail pouch and hands it to me.

"This is what you pulled me here for?" I ask, holding it out as the irritation burns through the terror that had gripped me since I opened Hannah's door.

"The delivery person stressed you had to open it before nine."

We both look at the clock. I have five minutes to open the envelope. Thoughts of anthrax or something equally deadly spin in my mind, but just by the feel, I highly doubt that is what this thing contains.

"You should step outside just in case," I say, looking back at her. "And you can tell Bear it isn't a bomb."

As soon as she is out the door, I tear open the package and dump the contents into my hand. A zip drive lands in my palm and I close my eyes for a second before sitting down at the desk and plugging the drive into Bridget's already booted machine. Just for good measure, I plug in her earphones so there is zero chance of either Bridget or Bear overhearing what is on the zip drive. The only other thing in the envelope is a small piece of paper with what looks like a time stamped on it.

The minute I click on the eternal drive icon, the screen goes black. I glance at the packaging again, looking for some sign of where it originated, but there are no postmarks, or anything beyond block letters spelling my name. There isn't even an address, which I find odd, but the screen flashes and a video comes up.

All logical thought ceases as I stare at my daughter's terrified face. I have to force myself to look at her surroundings, and my stomach drops. She's in a private airplane.

His low chuckle comes over the microphone, and then the likeness of Lucifer steps into view, and I recoil. He crosses and peels her arm from her body, holding it out so I can see it.

"She is delicious," he whispers and Hannah screams as he bites her arm, drawing blood. He only drinks from her arm for a second, but when he pulls his mouth from her tender skin, he grins, showing off his blood-streaked lips and teeth. Hannah pulls her arm back to her chest. Her sobs continue.

I want to tear through the screen and destroy that bastard.

"Here's the deal," he says, pulling the camera to focus on his face. "I will trade your little bundle of joy for Damian Andreas. Bring him to Athens, Greece, by nightfall. If you deliver him to me, I will deliver your daughter to you. If you fail, I'll send you a video of what I do to her, as payment for your failure." He pauses and smiles. "If he finds out about this deal before we are face to face, I will make sure she suffers for a very long time before I kill her."

The screen goes blank.

I just stare.

"Tom?" Bridget's voice cuts though my shock and I look up from the display in front of me, yanking the drive from the side of the computer and palming it.

"Yeah?" I answer.

"Is that related to Hannah's disappearance?" she asks and I shake my head.

"No. It's a job request. Damian and I are requested in Greece." I'm not sure if I'm convincing at all, but the knot in my stomach tightens.

"I can go with him. You stay here and look for Hannah."

My gaze darts from her to Bear and back. I don't know how to pull this off. I close my mouth for a moment and turn my gaze to Bear. "There's nothing here." I push the thought. "Go back to the cottage." I add with an extra push, just for good measure.

Bear blinks and turns, wandering away. The minute the car starts and pulls out, I turn to Bridget. She stands with her arms crossed.

"I have to go to Greece with Damian."

She cocks her head at me, searching my eyes with hers. "Hannah is being taken there," she says, and it isn't a question.

My brain is flying through excuses, but I just nod. "They asked for a ransom." It's the only logical thought I can produce, and it might just be one that I can convince Damian of. "And if I don't deliver it in person, they'll sell Hannah into slavery."

"You need the police," she says, and I raise my eyebrow, challenging her.

"I need Damian to come with me on this, and I need CJ hanging tight, watching over the rest of the family."

"It's not…" she trailed off.

"No. It's a goddamned kidnapper, looking to make a buck off the filthy rich," I snap. "Call Damian and tell him to meet me at Pease airfield in an hour." I don't know if I can get Ted Beaumont at this short notice, but if I go with this story, it might light a fire under everyone's ass.

I also have to lock down my thoughts, otherwise Damian will know. And I need to come up with some sort of plan. Damian stole Lucifer's grace. If Lucifer gets it back, there is little either CJ or I can do to stop him from starting Armageddon.

Angel Fire Chapter 13

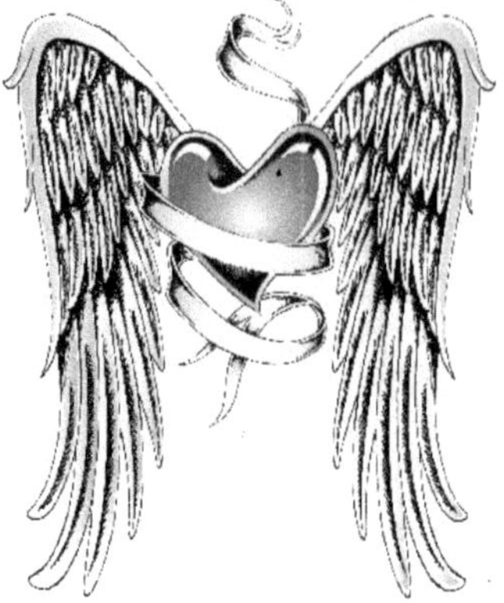

I STAND AT THE terminal, waiting for the private jet Ted promised us. I'm still planning the story in my head when Damian walks in. The duffel bag at my feet contains reams of paper cut into dollar size strips, and a couple of thousand dollars spread over the paper so it actually looks like a bag of ransom money, if someone isn't taking a close inspection of the contents. I also have my nine-millimeter in a holster under my jacket. I know it's useless against the devil, but it might help with my bogus story.

Damian steps to my side. "So, what's the plan?" he asks.

I huff a laugh. "I really have no plan. We just go in and storm the castle. I think we can handle whatever they throw at us, and get Hannah out before they have a chance to hurt her."

"Do you know where in Greece we are going?"

I shake my head. "The next contact will be on the plane." I layer the bullshit some more. I really don't know when Lucifer will contact me again, but I'm willing to bet it will be when we are in the air.

"Did you get proof of life?" Damian asks.

I'm glad I had the forethought to send a picture to my phone from the video. I saved a still of Hannah that included the date and time, and showed the interior of a private plane. Nothing else was in the video except her terrified face looking directly into the lens.

Damian whistled through his teeth. "And you're sure it isn't our mutual friend?"

I glare at him. "I doubt he'd ask for five million in cash." I jut my chin towards the bag at my feet. "Besides, do you really think Lucifer would be so fucking cryptic about it?"

Damian stares at the bag for a moment, and the crease deepens between his eyes.

"Lucifer would make me squirm," I say, because that's exactly what the bastard was doing.

Damian meets my gaze and lets out a small laugh. "Yeah, he'd do more than just send a picture of her," he says and guilt bites at the lining of my stomach.

Before either of us can say anything else, our names are called, and we cross to the sleek jet sitting on the tarmac.

"My name is Josh and I'll be your pilot today. Unfortunately, because of the short notice, we don't have a stewardess for this flight," a young pilot I've never seen says to us. "I'm told they can squeak us in for takeoff in ten minutes. We should arrive in Athens just before seven p.m. Athen's time."

"Thanks," I say and take his offered hand.

"I understand the turnaround time may be quick?"

"That's what we are hoping. We will know more once we are on the ground and get our next set of instructions."

He gives me a nod and I take a seat, stowing the duffel bag under my seat instead of in the overhead compartment.

Damian slides into the seat across from me.

"Is that really five million?" he asks, pointing at the bag.

I roll my eyes. "What do you think?"

Damian smirks. "I think it's probably the petty cash in our safe and a whole lot of shredded paper."

I keep his gaze and cannot help the smirk that surfaces. He's only known me for six years, but he probably knows me just as well as CJ. A pang of sorrow hits deep within me. This will be the last time we work as a team. If I fail, I'll be the one to die today, but if I succeed, I'll never see my friend again.

I turn my gaze out the window as we begin our taxi out on the runway and focus on something else. If I don't watch it, he will sense the lies I'm feeding him, so I go over what happened with Bridget yesterday in as much Technicolor detail as I can muster. It's my buffer, my subterfuge while I figure out just what the hell I'm going to do once we are on the ground.

"You slept with Bridget?" His tone carries the shock displayed on his features.

"Yeah," I confirm, and look back out the window as we ascend into the clouds.

"What the hell were you thinking?"

I glance at him, unsure whether to be glad he took the bait of my surface thoughts or not. The one thing CJ and Steve taught me over the years was how to hide my thoughts when I really wanted to. If I concentrated on certain memories, I could think on a deeper level that they couldn't access. "I wasn't *thinking* at all," I say. "At least not with my brain, and I don't know what the hell I'm going to say to her when I get back."

"You realize she has a thing for you," he says and crosses his arms.

"She has memories of sleeping with me in high school, and a promise to her dead uncle to look out for me. That's not a thing."

Damian laughs, long and loud. "You don't know shit about women."

"I don't know. We had just gotten back from a job…"

"Wait. You took her on a job?"

"Yes. It was a ghost thing, and she can see them, too. I thought it would be helpful, but it turned out to be a disaster." I open that part of my memory, pushing it to the forefront of my mind, allowing Damian access to that piece.

He scrutinizes it, biting his lower lip as he assesses the situation, weighing each action and reaction in his mind. The open view layers another slice of guilt. When my phone buzzes, I'm glad for the diversion from his clinical assessment of my failure.

I glance at the sender and the message preview.

Bridget.

I sigh and open the text. The time blinks at the top, showing the same number as on the piece of paper in the envelope.

We need to talk...

"Yeah, I know." I can't help the verbal response and I look out the window for a minute, sharing the information with Damian without saying a word.

"See," he says, and I don't appreciate it. "And as far as bringing her in on jobs, she might actually be an asset to the company," he adds, yanking my attention back to him. "She didn't freak out. And she can see ghosts just like you."

"Yeah, but she could have gotten hurt," I say, and his eyebrows slowly rise.

"You have a thing for her?"

"No. Of course not. I just don't want to see her get hurt." I wave it away, and glance down at the text again, scrolling to see if she had any more to say. My brain jumps to the way she tasted as I stare at the next directive from Lucifer. The fact he is using Bridget's phone number does not sit well, either. It means he knows she isn't just another fuck.

When we land, a driver will be waiting and will bring us to where he has Hannah. Once inside, I am the one to deliver Damian's beating heart to Lucifer in exchange for my daughter. My stomach rolls, and I glance at Damian.

He's studying me, still lamenting on my relationship with Bridget.

"It's too soon." The words escape, wrapped in the anguish pummeling my insides. I can't hide the surfacing of emotion, and I use Raven's death as the buffer to the pain tearing me from the inside out.

Lucifer expects *me* to kill Damian.

How the fuck can I do that?

My eyes close and my head dips in defeat.

Damian mistakes it for grief, and his hand lands on my shoulder.

"What would Raven want?"

My throat constricts, and I slowly shake my head. *Get your fucking shit together. Hannah's life depends on it.* My silent admonishment comes from deep within the barrier, blocking Damian from any of the turmoil pounding my intestines to pulp.

"She would want me to be happy," I whisper, and force myself to look up through a sheen of gloss. When I blink, a hot path traces my cheeks. "But I just can't…"

He turns to look out the window. "I'm not one to talk. It took me twenty-five hundred years to let my guard down after Athena."

"Timing is everything," I mutter. "I gotta hit the head," I say, and unhook my seatbelt. I cross to the bathroom and close the door, just in time for my stomach to shoot the meager contents into the toilet. I flush and rinse my mouth out in the sink. With my stomach empty, I pull out the phone and stare at the response.

With a few keystrokes, I send another text, this time to myself from an unassigned number with the pickup instructions only and delete the item from my sent list once it is received.

I pocket the phone and wash my hands, avoiding looking at my reflection until I have finished. Silently, I reason with myself, trying to justify the horror I'm hours away from doing. There is no justification that will wipe away the building self-hatred, and I wonder if this is another step in tearing me down.

The sick truth is, I can't gamble Hannah's life on phantom intent. I have to follow the facts. Lucifer outlined a deal and CJ once told me Lucifer would honor the deal, although if there was a loophole in that deal, the devil would exploit it.

Is there a loophole here? One that I could capitalize on?

I can't think of one that would leave both my daughter and my best friend alive.

"Fuck."

I turn away from my accusing eyes and stomp back into the cabin, dumping myself into the seat. Digging in my pocket, I pull up the text I sent as the smoke and mirrors of the deal.

"I guess a driver will be at the airport."

His eyebrows rose.

"Yeah. I was hoping for an address and not this." I run my hand through my hair, trying to think of an alternate plan that would make us arrive at the same place at the same time. "You have to figure out a way to follow us," I say when I look back at him.

He smiles. "It will be dark out, right?"

"I think it will be dusk, not quite dark," I say because I don't think seven o'clock is after dark. If it is, I've missed my first directive and Hannah will suffer.

"Shit," he mutters. "I'll figure something out."

"Cab?"

The look he delivers tells me that is highly unlikely.

"You're going to steal a car?" I ask in exasperation.

The way he huffs at me burns, because when I was in high school, I thought nothing of lifting a car for a joy ride, but the last thing we needed was him getting thrown in jail in a foreign country.

"I'm not going to get caught."

"Famous last words," I can't help the irritation. "And what happens if you do?"

He sends that smile that leaves me uncomfortable. "Then I'll take to the skies."

"If you screw this up..." I trail off and close my eyes, leaning back in the seat. Damian wasn't the screw up on the team. I am. I have always been the one who is in the wrong place at the wrong time, and I pray this time, luck turns in my favor.

"I won't screw it up. I will be there to storm the castle with you, okay?"

I give him a nod.

"One more thing. Prepare yourself to take someone out."

The intensity of his stare makes me shift in the seat. He reminds me of my father. God knows I loved the man, but his moral compass was fucked up. Taking a life was easy when he thought it was warranted, but for me, it's much more difficult, even when it is warranted.

I'm not sure my soul will survive murder, but if it means my daughter lives, I'll yank Damian's beating heart from his body without a second thought.

I stare into the eyes of the man I have to kill in less than three hours and nod.

Angel Fire Chapter 14

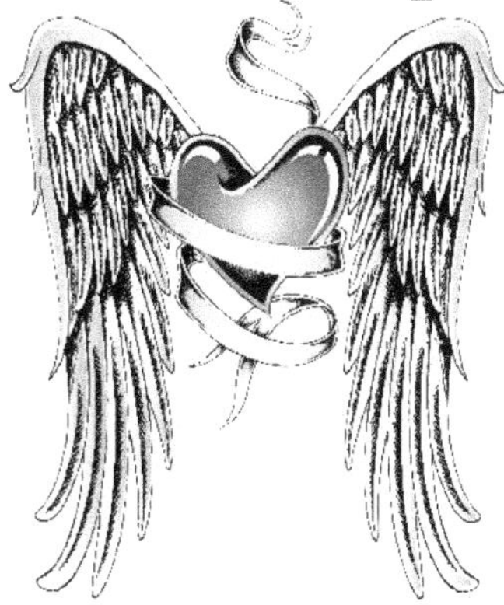

THE PLANE LANDS AND I grab the bag under the seat and take a deep breath. There is no way to be ready for this, and I send Damian a nerve-filled smile.

"If shit gets fucked up…"

"It won't. I'll be there. I promise." Damian unhooks his seatbelt. "Let me go first. That way I can scope things out and I won't lose you anywhere. Give me a five-minute lead."

I nod and remain in the seat while Damian climbs down the stairs. Josh glances in my direction.

"Sir?"

"I'm letting him scope things out." I get to my feet and cross to where he stands by the door. I glance out directly at the molasses colored sky and the sun low on the horizon, but at least it is still above the line. I made it here in time.

A measure of relief scrapes my back, but it is short-lived. Each minute that passes takes me closer to becoming a monster. I refocus on Josh. "The minute I get back, we need to haul ass home, no questions asked, okay?"

"Yes, sir. Mr. Beaumont was very specific with his directions."

"Ted's a good man." I glance at my watch. Almost five minutes have passed. "If we are not back in three hours, leave without us," I add and descend the stairs without a look back.

The walk into the hangar feels like everything is in slow motion. My examination of my surroundings doesn't reveal any danger, and I send my mental sniffer out looking for the same thing. Nothing, except Damian's cursory inspection as well.

When I step through the doors, my scan passes over Damian at the phone charging stations. To the right of the charging stations stands a cluster of chauffeurs holding signs. The third one back holds my name and I cross directly to him, meeting his gaze.

"I'm Tom Ryan," I say.

"Do you have identification?" he asks with a heavy Greek accent.

I sling the duffel bag over my shoulder and scan his mind, just as Damian is doing. This man is just a hired driver, he knows nothing, and I dig in my back pocket for my wallet while trading a glance with Damian.

The driver studies my license and then gives me a nod. Instead of my back pocket, I stow the wallet in the inside pocket of my jacket. The driver's eyes widen at the flash of black metal and I stare him down.

"Astynomia?" he asks quietly as his eyes dart around.

I offer a tilted smile and put my finger to my lips. I'd rather have him think I'm a cop of some sort than a killer, and my actions seem to settle his nerves.

He turns and I follow to a stretch limousine, and he holds the door for me. It's the only stretch limo in the vicinity. Damian will have no trouble following this. The driver climbs into the seat and closes the divider. As he moves into the line of traffic, I glance back in time to see Damian slide into the driver's seat of an idling car.

His smooth exit into traffic makes me sigh and I turn towards the front of the car.

Another text comes through, and I again focus on Bridget and our little excursion last night.

"Alone?"

"Yes. Damian is following." I hit send and the television screen turns on in front of me.

When Lucifer fills the screen, every muscle clenches, and I wonder if I can follow the connection. The thought is dashed by the reality. If I leave my body for any reason, he has an opening to take possession. From the smirk on his lips, he knows that fact as well.

"You don't want to make the jump?" the teasing tone clenches my teeth and I shake my head. "Pity."

I keep my mouth closed because if I speak, I will issue every creative death threat I can think of.

"I have to admit, I was hoping you would not make it here before nightfall. I have been refraining from taking another drink from your daughter's potent blood," he says and steps aside.

Hannah is there, but she is hanging upside down in the same position I found her in July. Although the drip from her neck does not look like anything is flowing, unlike the river of red that flowed through the crude tube stuck in her before. Her terrified eyes meet mine through the screen and tears slide up her forehead and into her hair.

"Daddy," she cries.

"You son of a bitch," I growl, turning back to Lucifer.

"I have not turned the drip on," he says. "I trust Damian is close by?"

"Yes," I say, through clenched teeth. My fists are so tight I think my skin might split.

He just smiles and gives me an encouraging nod. With a flick of his wrist, the valve opens and a slow red flow fills the tube. "Just in case you have second thoughts. You now have less than an hour before she is drained of blood. The minute I have that little shit's heart in my hand, I will stop the drain."

The screen goes black, and my heart is throbbing in my chest, fear and desperation fight in every cell, and I knock on the window.

The panel comes down.

"How long until we get to our destination?"

The driver points to his GPS. "Twenty minutes if traffic cooperates."

I can't wait twenty minutes. "Can you go faster? It's an emergency."

He waves at the thick traffic ahead of us and I press my lips together.

We need to get there within fifteen minutes, I transmit the thought to Damian. *That's when our window closes.*

So, clear the way. I'll keep up.

I concentrate and floor the gas pedal under the driver's foot. He lets out a surprised squeak and presses on the brake. Nothing happens and I innocently ask, "Is everything okay?"

"No, sir," he says and concentrates on driving, although his heart is beating hard enough that I can see his temple throbbing.

I control the car's swerve between traffic, moving drivers out of the way if they don't yield to our fast approach, and catching Damian's car hot on our trail. The GPS beeps, indicating a right turn, and we take it, cutting off the line of traffic, and I keep the path open for Damian.

We are out of the city and winding into the green country. The GPS shows us minutes away from our destination, but I don't see any buildings, only a hill to our right and nothing but rolling fields in front of us. The driver takes the right and I get a glimpse of the city, before we circle around the base and slow to a stop in the hill's shadow. The structure in front of us leaves me speechless. The driver is panting, and brakes squeal behind us, jerking his head towards the rearview mirror.

"I apologize for my erratic driving," he says and slides out of the car. A moment later, he opens the door for me, and I tentatively step out with the duffel bag on my shoulder. My brain is skipping around and I give him a nod.

"Thank you. You are welcome to leave now."

"Oh, no, sir, I am supposed to wait for my next assignment."

"Leave," I order, and his eyes widen as he obeys the direct order. I step to the side of the road and Damian parks next to me, turning the car off before stepping out.

I wait until the taillights are gone before I focus on the house in front of us. My palms sweat, and I'm having a hard time drawing air; but I force myself to appear calm, even calculated.

"Let's do this." I take a step towards the house, and he grabs my arm.

Damian is scanning the modern design of the house, along with the surrounding area like he's trying to place it.

"I have less than five minutes to show up, Damian."

"I don't think Hannah is there. I can't feel her."

"I can," I say, and I'm not lying. I feel her getting weaker, but her terror is there, like a live wire. I'm surprised he can't feel it. "She's in there. Follow me," I say, and instead of sneaking in, I walk towards the front door. After all, in my bullshit story, they are expecting me and my bag of money.

The minute we clear the door, metal drops behind us, locking us inside. When the panel at the far end rises, my heart squeezes. Hannah is in the center, the line of blood filling a jug, like in every nightmare I've had since July. Her eyes widen at the sight of me.

I concentrate and close my eyes.

"What the…"

That's the last thing Damian says before I blow a hole in his chest. I spin and stick my hand through his shattered ribs, meeting his shocked gaze. My fingers grasp his warm heart and I yank, ripping it from its place before Damian can react.

Betrayal glazes his eyes, and I think I whisper I'm sorry.

I turn back towards my daughter and the devil standing next to her. The muscle still beats in my hand, spilling blood over my arm, and it runs hot on my skin. If I give this to Lucifer, both Hannah and I are as good as dead.

"Don't," Damian's last word pierces my ears just before his body hits the ground, and tears blur my vision.

His death plea doesn't make going through with this any easier. Lucifer starts in my direction and I know what I have to do. Before I can second guess my actions, I shove the entire heart into my mouth, crushing it to a pulp with my mind before forcing it down my throat.

From the surprise written in Lucifer's features, he never thought I'd pull a double cross, especially with my daughter's life in the balance. I had a moment to revel in the sheer bliss of fucking with the devil's plans before the power hits.

A bomb goes off inside me, shattering my cells from my stomach outward. I bellow with the pain of it. Everything Damian had, from the piece of CJ's power to the grace of Gabriel and Michael, slices through me. But it's Lucifer's grace that causes the agony. His grace not only fills me, it merges with my cells until every malignant force in my blood is boiling.

Lucifer is running in my direction, wearing a mask of rage. I roar at him. By sheer force of will, I pick him up and launch him towards the opposite wall. In the same moment, I vaporize Hannah's bonds and yank her towards me.

I miscalculate the distance between Lucifer and Hannah, and before I can react, Lucifer's sharp nails shred the side of my daughter's throat as they pass in the air. Her blood sprays and I am bellowing her name and sprinting towards her. She collides with my chest and I wrap her in my arms as her blood soaks through my shirt.

My gaze rises to Lucifer, climbing to his feet. The impact with the wall left crumbling drywall in his wake. My daughter's last gurgling breath pulls my gaze down to hers. The light fades from her eyes and my head whips back with the force of the cry ripping from my throat.

It swirls and ripples from me like a tornado, flashing red and black, as I hold my dead daughter to my chest. The ground rumbles beneath me and the only thought I have is to let it swallow me.

In the back of my mind, that little voice I hate tells me to get up and run. To get out before it's too late. I'm obeying, as the ground crumbles under my feet. With Hannah's body to my chest, I dodge from one crumbling strip to another until I'm beyond the kill zone. When I turn, I see rolling fire swirling, and blackened earth crumbles into the wide hole in the ground. Rage still shakes my form, and then everything flashes white, knocking me on my ass.

When the spots clear from my vision, I'm staring at a clear circle of dirt and Hannah's ghost standing in the aftermath. I have failed both her and Damian in ways I can't fathom, and I climb to my feet, focusing on my little girl.

If I can get her back to Valerie, she can be saved.

I reach out, grabbing Hannah's ghost before she can stop me. I'm in the stolen car before she can speak and I think I make it back to the terminal in ten minutes flat. With Hannah pressed to my chest and my hand tight around her ghost's wrist, I stalk to the plane, not letting anyone or anything deter me.

"Fly," I snap as I crumble in the chair.

When Josh doesn't move, I turn and glare at him. "Fly. Now," I say, and this seems to kick his ass in gear. He closes the hatch and disappears into the cockpit. Hannah's body has no warmth to it and she is hard to hold. She's dead weight, and it feels like I'm wrestling a rag doll. Her ghost is quiet, as she looks on with such sadness in her eyes that I feel the weight of my failure pressing down on my chest. I lay her body out on the chair across from me and kneel over her, pushing her hair out of her face. Unfortunately, I leave bloody streaks across her forehead.

"Just hold on, baby. It will be okay once we get home. Valerie will fix you up."

I don't know how long I kneel, running my hand through her knotted locks with one hand and a vice grip on her ghost with the other.

"Daddy, let go," her ghost whispers, and I look up at her.

"I can fix this," I say, refusing to let her go. Refusing to accept this outcome. I have damned my soul by murdering Damian, and if she doesn't survive this, there is nothing left.

"Daddy..."

"No, you listen to me! You are not going to die! Understand?" And with that statement, I push the plane into mach-speed. The sonic boom echoes through the cabin and the fuselage shakes against the knots I am forcing it to go. If it breaks apart and drops me into the ocean, I'm strangely okay with that as well.

Dying might stop the pain filling every cell of my being.

I go back to running my fingers through her hair, streaking it with her own tacky blood, but I'm too far gone to care.

The phone in my pocket buzzes and I let it ring. I don't want to lose physical contact with my daughter and I'm not letting go of her ghost, either. I once forced my father's ghost back into his body, and I plan on doing the same once I get her to CJ's house. Valerie's healing power can fix this.

It had to.

The phone doesn't stop, and I finally untangle my fingers from Hannah's hair and pull the cell out of my pocket. Bridget's number flashes on the display and my fist clenches around the metal.

Lucifer.

I don't wait for his taunting. "I am going to kill you," I growl into the phone.

Silence.

"Tom?" Bridget's concerned voice whispers over the line.

I blink as my heart skips a beat.

"Bridget?" I'm unsure whether to believe it is her, or just another cruel joke.

"Damian's waiting at the office for you," she says in a soft whisper.

"Damian's dead," I say, and my voice cracks. Saying it aloud makes it real and my chest hitches. "I killed him, Bri," I add, using the name Hannah calls her. My head drops onto Hannah's stomach as I try to control the shaking overtaking my body.

"Yeah, I got that. He's pissed."

I huff. I can't blame him. I betrayed him on every level just to save my daughter.

"Do you have Hannah?" she asks.

I raise my head, scanning Hannah's prone form. "Yes, but I need to get to Valerie as soon as we land."

There is another pause on the line, and I hear something smash in the background.

"I think maybe I need to get out of here before he turns his anger on me," Bridget says.

"Tell him I'll be there soon enough, and instead of destroying the house you're living in, he can have a run at me."

I hear her relay the message, and the rumbling in the background continues until I hear a door slam.

"Do you need me to pick you up?" Bridget says into the phone.

I glance up at the ghost of my daughter and then her prone body. "Yes," I whisper. I can use all the help I can get right now, and I have a feeling after all this blows over, she will be the only one left still speaking to me.

That is, if Naomi doesn't tear me to pieces herself.

"Does anyone else know?" I ask.

Bridget laughs. "You and I are the only ghost whisperers in town, or haven't you figured that out yet?" The sarcasm in her voice rattles me.

I close my eyes and attempt to listen to what is going through her mind, but it's muddled. She's angry, disappointed, and hurt, but she also can't turn her back on the promise she made to her uncle.

"You should have told me," she says.

"If I told you, Damian would have known…"

She cuts me off. "You don't think he would have readily sacrificed himself for your daughter? Jesus, Tom, didn't you know how much he loved you? You were like a brother to him, and you pull this shit?"

Guilt and devastation mixes with the shakes already accosting me. I couldn't voice the remorse, it was just too big.

"I hope you know just how much you've fucked this one up," she mutters under her breath.

"I know, okay? I am painfully aware of how much I screwed this up," I yell into the phone. "Valerie can fix it. She can make things right. She has to." The rawness of my voice rings through the cabin and my vision blurs.

"Dad, you need to let go," Hannah says, and this time her voice sounds more mature.

I glance at her and shake my head. "Valerie will fix this."

We both look at her pale form that holds no hint of life, and I end the call with Bridget. I can't face more of her questions or accusations. Not when my little girl isn't breathing.

Angel Fire Chapter 15

THE MINUTE THE PLANE lands, I collect Hannah in my arms and wait until Josh comes out of the cockpit. He leaves a wide berth, but opens the hatch and folds down the stairs, letting me exit without a word.

The moon has started its slow rise and I pause, staring at the fullness before I glance at Hannah's ghost, remembering my mission. People scatter as I enter the hangar, but I don't stop, not even when the security detail tries to change my course. Nothing is going to keep me from getting my daughter's body into Valerie's healing hands.

Bridget steps inside just as I am crossing towards the door and her eyes widen at the sight of me. I get a glimpse of my reflection in the door behind her, and my forward motion stalls. I am drenched with blood. It streaks my exposed skin like some ancient Indian markings. Hannah is limp in my arms and she, too, is painted in deep red. The only clean one is the ghost whose wrist I grip with my free hand.

I resume my gait, crossing by Bridget without a word. The car waits at the curb, and I will the back door open, forcing Hannah's ghost in first before I climb in with her dead body.

It takes Bridget a minute before she slides into the driver's seat, and with shaking hands, turns the ignition. I don't speak. There isn't anything to say, but I avoid her glances in the rear-view mirror.

"Tom," she starts.

"Valerie can fix this," I say and finally meet her worried stare. "Just get me to CJ's house, okay?"

The minute we pull into the driveway, I'm out of the car, dragging Hannah's ghost along with me. I will the door open and march into the kitchen where everyone is congregating. Valerie is the first to see me and she gasps. The glass she holds tumbles to the floor, shattering.

I lay Hannah's body on the floor and slam her ghost down onto the prone form, looking up at Valerie. "Fix her," I growl.

Valerie's eyes bounce between my dead daughter and me, and then she is next to me on her knees with tears filling her eyes. Her hands float over my daughter's face and around the shredded bits that once was Hannah's throat.

"Fix her!" I yell in her face. "I have her spirit. I need you to fix her!"

When Valerie's eyes meet mine, I gulp down the fear, denying the truth in her gaze.

"Tom, I don't have the power to bring someone back to life," she says through a fog.

"Goddamnit, just fucking fix her!"

"Daddy, let me go," Hannah's ghost sobs as she struggles beneath my hand.

"Tom!" CJ yells, pulling my attention.

"Valerie can fix this," I insist and turn towards her. "Why won't you fix her?" I say, my voice filled with accusation and disbelief.

"Thomas Patrick Ryan!" a voice bellows from the family room. Her Irish brogue is unmistakable, and my gaze shoots to hers. Raven stands bathed in heavenly light, and I'm not the only one who can see her. "Let go of our daughter."

Her command falls between us and she blurs behind a flow of my tears.

"I can't," I whisper, and she moves forward, floating with grace I cherish. "You know damned well why I can't."

"I know. But you have to let her go, Tom," she says softly, her voice baptizing me in her disappointment.

"Please, fix her," I plea, turning to Valerie.

No one moves. Raven's hand reaches out and finds my cheek, turning my face to hers.

"Let me take her with me, Tom," she says ever so softly, and a sob escapes from my chest. "She deserves the peace of heaven."

I hang my head, knowing I'll never see either of them again. The peace of heaven is now beyond my reach. My punishment is just, and another sob breaks through my tightly pressed lips. I drag my hand away, releasing Hannah's spirit.

Hannah's ghost rises and places a soft kiss on my cheek before she takes her mother's hand and fades into the woodwork.

I shatter. There is nothing to hold me together anymore.

"Where's Damian?" Naomi's question breaks through my harsh sobs.

I don't look up at Naomi. I'm shaking too hard to function, but I squeeze out the words anyway because I owe it to him. I could coat it with excuses, with the promises Lucifer made, but that would cheapen it, make it less of the horrific act that it truly was.

"I killed him."

Silence surrounds me like a death march, and I slowly raise my head, meeting her horrified stare. Her mind becomes a flurry of questions, right alongside those accosting Valerie and CJ. It is only when Grace enters the room that their thoughts stop, and everyone focuses on my daughter's best friend.

She crosses the room slowly; her gaze locked on the dead body next to me. Tears brim, sliding down her cheeks as she slowly drops next to Hannah. Her little hands gently caress my daughter's cheeks and then she looks up at me with such pain that I gulp down my sobs.

"I forgive you," she says and I stumble backwards.

This child does not know what I've done.

"You stole my father's grace," she says, answering my thought. "And you did not give it to Lucifer." Her gaze drops to Hannah's dead form, and a tear slides down Grace's cheek, landing on my daughter's forehead.

I stare at the drop and then raise my gaze to Grace's.

"It still doesn't make it right," I say, despite my throat tightening. I force my gaze to the family surrounding me. Every one of them knows what stealing angel grace entails, and the disgust is written in their expression.

There is only one thing left for me to do, and I climb to my feet, navigating my way to the sliders. They open with no conscious direction and before CJ intercepts; I am sprinting towards the rock wall and the drop to the jagged boulders below.

I launch into a dive with my arms at my sides and I close my eyes, waiting for the impact. Air whistles in my ears and then a blow hits my midsection, driving me into a tumbling mass and I hit the frigid water twenty yards out from my original destination. The cold grips me and I surface, turning back towards the house. CJ stands at the wall with his fists clenched as tight as his jaw.

"You ain't dying yet," he growls low.

But this time, he has no control over me or my bleak fate. I close my eyes and stop treading water. I've never been a floater and without the motion of my arms and legs holding me up, I sink. While I want to die, it takes great effort to stop holding my breath and before I can suck in water, arms wrap around my neck, yanking me to the surface.

"Just as soon as I warm up, I'm going to kick your ass," CJ says to me.

"Just let me die," I whisper, trying to break his chokehold, but it's no use. He drags me to our dock and hauls me up onto the wood, where we both lay shivering.

I stare at the dark sky.

"I fucked up something fierce," I whisper.

He sits up and rubs his hands together, blowing on them to warm up before he looks at me. "When we fuck up, it's pretty damned colossal."

I let out a shocked laugh. Only my brother can make me laugh during the biggest tragedy of my life.

"Besides, I can't do this shit without you."

He concentrates on rubbing his hands together to warm them, and I'm still laying on the cold wood, hoping to freeze to death in the fall night air. Of course, it isn't even below freezing, so that's just wishful thinking on my part.

"I killed my family," I say and bite my lip. The fiery burn of tears blurs my vision.

"No. Lucifer killed your family."

"My actions killed them, CJ. I lost my wife because I said no to his offer, and my daughter because I didn't give him Damian's beating heart." I sit up. "I've got nothing left."

The left hook knocks me on my side and CJ glares at me. His silent rant is not so silent in my head and I rub my jaw.

"Like you wouldn't want to give up if you lost Valerie and Alex," I snarl, letting the anger overwhelm the self-pity. "Especially if it was because you fucked up."

CJ's glare remains but his rants soften.

"I murdered my best friend to save my daughter, and I couldn't even get that right." I let out a sarcastic laugh. "Lucifer is going to have an eternity with my ass. I'm sure it's going to be delightful."

CJ stares at me. "And you want to start paying right now?"

My first reaction is hell no, but that completely overshadows my will to die. I narrow my eyes at CJ. He brilliantly turned my death wish into the exact opposite, and I hate him for it.

"Fuck you," I mutter, because like it or not, while I don't feel worthy of living, I also don't want Lucifer to win at this shitty game. I climb to my feet and slick back my wet hair with my fingers.

"What would you have done?" I ask because I need to know just how off base I am.

CJ stares out at the water, weighing my question and he looks down at the wet boards beneath our feet before meeting my gaze.

"For my son," he says and presses his lips together, blinking away the sudden sheen over his eyes. "If there was a chance to save him, I would have done the same goddamned thing you did, with one exception." He looks over the water.

"What?" I can't read him at all and I'm expecting him to tell me he wouldn't kill Damian.

"I would have given Lucifer his grace," he says and turns, climbing up the stairs and leaving me with that morbid thought. He pauses and looks down. "In that way, you're a better man than I am."

His praise is unwarranted and I shake my head. "No, CJ. You've always been the better man."

He raises his gaze from mine, and he does a scan of the ocean, instead of addressing my comment.

As he turns away, I say, "I think I closed the portal." My brain is not entirely sure what the hell happened in Greece, but at some level, deep down inside where the angel grace rages, I know.

CJ's turns back towards me as he processes my words. His eyebrows rocket up and his jaw drops, making the look on his face that much more comical.

I huff a laugh. "I think I produced angel fire."

Angel Fire Chapter 16

I FINALLY CLIMB UP and make my way into CJ's back yard. Bridget is the only one outside, and she sits on one of the lawn chairs waiting for me. I can't meet her gaze. Instead, I stare at the ground as I walk. To say I'm numb is an understatement.

She stands. "The police are here." She hooks her thumb over her shoulder.

I look inside. Bear is taking a statement from CJ, and he keeps glancing in my direction. I don't have an explanation. What I have is a pilot who saw me carry my dead child onto a plane in Greece, and a hanger full of people who saw me carrying her to the car here. And, of course, my psychotic rant for Valerie to fix her, followed by my suicide attempt. I wouldn't be surprised if I find myself in the psych ward on suicide watch tonight.

"I told them Hannah was kidnapped, you attempted to rescue her, and things didn't go as planned."

My eyes shift to hers and I give her a nod. "Thanks."

Bridget stares out at the ocean, avoiding my gaze. Her mind swirls with the loss of my daughter, and I blink at the pain centered in her aura. I didn't know she cared for Hannah that deeply.

When her eyes find mine, she asks, "Can I ask why?" She waves towards the rocks.

My eyes find my dripping shoes and I shake my head.

"You just have to concentrate on breathing; the pain will fade," she says.

My hands clench and I level a glare at her. "This differs from a car accident, Bri."

I know my words are harsh, but her loss was a tragic accident that had no bearing on a decision she made. She recoils and opens her mouth to speak.

"Do not compare my colossal fuck up to a car accident." I look back in the house as they place my daughter in a body bag. Just the sight of it washes the numbness away and clenches my insides with a pain right down to the cellular level. I close my eyes and turn away, ignoring the urge to pull the soaking revolver out of my holster to see if it still works.

"I made the wrong call," I say, and my voice is raspy, as if I've swallowed a bucket of glass. "I can't live with the results." I open my eyes and meet her gaze. "However, my brother, in all his wisdom, reminded me that if I put a bullet in my brain, Lucifer gets exactly what he wants. He gets me splayed out on a carving station for eternity." Tears burn the back of my throat and I find it difficult to swallow. "Whatever I do, I can't seem to win."

"Does it always have to be about winning?" she asks.

I stare at her. I want to ask what else there is, because right now I have nothing. "It's all I've got."

A throat clears and I turn towards Bear as he steps out on the patio with CJ.

"That envelope you got at the office. Do you still have the contents?"

I dig into my pocket and pull out the zip drive, tossing it to him. If the salt water hasn't corroded the disk, I'm sure I'll have more rigorous questioning soon, that is, if the content doesn't scare the piss out of him.

"Are these the terms of the ransom?"

I inhale. "Ransom. Okay, if that's really what you want to call it, then yes."

He studies the zip drive and then plugs it into the iPad he's holding. With a couple of swipes of his fingers, the screen fills with my daughter.

Lucifer's voice drives my teeth together in a clench, and I blink the edges of rage from my vision, choosing to watch CJ's similar reaction. Bridget stands, staring at the screen, her face bathed in horror, mirroring Bear's.

Bridget's face pales, and she glances at me with haunted eyes.

Bear's gaze jumps to mine as the video fades. "What the hell is that?"

"That is the thing that ordered my wife's death, and my daughter drained of blood. That is the fucker systematically killing off anyone who doesn't do his bidding." The words come out in a feral growl that Bear shrinks from. "That is the thing that waged war on us."

Anger rises to an uncontrollable level, but I'm helpless to stop it.

"*That* is the thing that killed my daughter, and I swear, as God as my witness, I am going to hunt him down and tear him into so many tiny fucking shreds, there won't be enough angel blood to rejuvenate that fucker."

Bridget's palm lands on my chest, and I look down at it. I hadn't realized I even moved from the space where I'd started, but I am now towering over Bear like he is a subject worthy of my wrath.

Bear's shaking hand is on his service revolver, and his eyes are wide and terrified.

When my gaze moves to CJ, his equally wide eyes shock me out of the fury burning my cells. The image he projects into my brain makes me stumble backwards and I trip, landing in one of the chaise lounges.

The mask of fury on my face was terrifying, especially since my irises looked like a fully involved forest fire. There wasn't a hint of my baby-blues in them and the kicker was the fucking massive midnight black wings that appeared out of fucking nowhere. The image is nothing like what CJ looks like wielding angel fire. His wings are as pristine white as the light in his eyes.

The image yanks at a memory and my stomach rolls. Before I can stop it, vomit covers the ground at my feet.

I look exactly like Lucifer did just before he killed my father.

Angel Fire Chapter 17

I STAND UNDER THE hot spray of the shower at the cottage, trying to control the shivers knocking my teeth together. CJ took control of the situation as soon as I threw up. He palmed the drive and walked Bear around to the front of the house. I don't know if it was just CJ's influence or Bear's raw fear that concocted the lie about my daughter's death, but according to the coroner's report, as well as the news stories, Hannah died from a bear attack.

If I wasn't so fucking freaked out, I might find some irony and humor in the form of attack my ex-friend centered on.

Bridget helped me to the car and brought me here. I don't know if she is still in the living space or not. I just stand and let the burning water pelt my face and chest with no motivation to move. If I move, every horrifying thing that happened to me today will hammer my midsection like a prizefighter.

The door squeaks. I guess she didn't leave.

"Tom?"

I remain silent, but bow my head so the water flows down my back.

The shower curtain rattles enough so she can see I haven't done something drastic again. I turn my head and our eyes meet. I haven't said anything since we left the house. I have nothing to add.

When I lose my shit, I take on Lucifer's form and my angel fire is more like hell fire.

That makes me a world-class freak. Except Bridget isn't looking at me through that lens. I look away, because I can't deal with the awe living in her irises. I reach out and close the shower curtain.

She yanks it back open, this time wearing a glare, and she reaches out, turning the water off. "You're clean enough. Get out and get dressed." The bark in her voice startles me.

"Who the fuck do you think you are?"

"I'm the bitch who's going to keep you functioning until you can do it by yourself." She throws the towel at me. "Now move!"

Whether I want to, my body obeys because I'm too damned shocked at her little drill sergeant act to deny the orders. I stop at the sink to brush my teeth, because I still taste vomit and blood and need that final comfort before I can feel human again.

Clanking comes from the kitchen, and I wrap the towel around my waist, opting to see what she is up to before I head to the bedroom to find some clothes. She has the coffee pot brewing, and she catches sight of me out of the corner of her eye.

"What? You need help to dress now?"

"Cut the attitude," I snap back and her eyes narrow as her arms cross. "Fine," I mutter and turn. I avoid the second bedroom. Just passing draws a sharp breath and then I am past it and in my bedroom. I take a few minutes to pull on jeans and a sweater. I carry a pair of socks with me to the living area, dropping on the couch to slip them on.

As I sit up, she hands me a coffee. "I don't know if you need that or not, but it might help you warm up." This time, her voice is softer. "You still have a ghost to confront."

"I know."

"And you're stalling while he is probably ripping that house to shreds."

"It's all about you, isn't it?" I mutter under my breath.

"Sometimes it has to be." She turns away and collects her cup off the table.

I stare out the window, thinking about what Damian said to me on the plane.

"Bri, I'm damaged goods," I say, and I'm not sure why my throat tightens. I clear it, keeping my gaze outside, on the deep dark of the ocean.

"When did you decide to start calling me Bri?"

I shrug. "It's what Hannah said you preferred."

Silence, and then a sniffle comes from her direction and I turn. My jaw tightens as Bridget sits with her hair shrouding her face. Her shoulders shake in that all too familiar posture of sorrow. I know I should console her. Instead; I turn back to the window.

"I'm ready to go get my ass kicked." I set the coffee cup on the table and stand, crossing to the shoe rack by the door. My choices are limited to flip-flops or sneakers. "Where are my boots?"

"Everything you had on is in the dumpster." She stands and wipes at her cheeks before she meets my gaze. "I got the stuff from the pockets before I chucked it all," she says and tosses me my wallet.

Overshadowed with anger and disappointment, Bridget's soft nature is now creating hardness I never would have thought possible. She keeps my gaze as she passes me until she reaches for the doorknob.

I put my hand on her arm, because under all this badassery, she is hurting.

She stiffens at my touch and this time; she doesn't look at me, but she trembles under my fingers. I force her to turn, and then I pull her into a hug. I'm not sure why I do it, because solace is not what I want right now. I want to wallow in the pain until it swallows me and I disappear.

But she needs this.

From me.

And I can't deny her right now.

She folds into herself, and the tremors turn to sobs against my chest. I hold her, but I've got no more tears, and I've got zero in the way of reassuring words.

Angel Fire Chapter 18

WE STAND IN FRONT of the door to our office and her apartment above. Smashing glass resounds inside; I take a breath and reach for the doorknob, stepping inside. Bridget doesn't make it through the door before it slams shut. The force rattles the molding, and it shakes the floor under my feet.

Bridget pounds on the door, crying out my name, but I'm too preoccupied with the destruction spread before me. Every stitch of furniture in the entryway is destroyed to the point the wood is in splinters. Glass litters the floor, and the same destruction is happening in my office.

"Damian!" I bellow, and the air stills.

The crunch of glass under foot announces his progression into the entry, and when Damian's ghost steps through the doorway, I actually gulp at his murderous gaze. Then again, I deserve every ounce of pain he intends to dish out.

I move into the middle of the room and open my arms wide. "Do what you have to do."

He charges, knocking me off my feet and into the drywall on the far side of the room. The impact pulls all the air from my lungs and leaves my ears ringing. His fist drives what little air is left from inside me, and the pain spreads, acute and welcomed.

After a few punches, Damian's ghost steps back, glaring at me. I lean against the wall, forcing my knees to lock so I don't slide to the ground.

"Fight back," he growls.

"No," I say in barely a wheeze. His fist connects with my jaw, and I stumble a few steps to my side.

"You fucking murdered me!"

I meet his angry gaze and nod. "Yes."

"Why?" he bellows and takes another shot.

I go down to my knee. The side of my face pounds with the pain. "Because that's what I had to do to get Hannah back alive. Your heart was the ransom." I force myself to look up at him and climb to my feet.

His eyes narrow. "Did you get Hannah back alive?"

My gaze drops and I shake my head.

"Then what the fuck did you kill me for?" His voice barrels out, rattling the windowpanes.

I shrink away from his anger. "What choice did I have?" I mutter and force myself to stand up straight and own the mistakes I made. "If I didn't bring you to him, he would have killed Hannah the same way he murdered Raven."

Damian loses some of his fury and his fists drop to his sides. The rage over this entire situation surfaces and I step toe-to-toe with the ghost, leveling my glare.

"Could you sentence your daughter to that kind of death?" I scream in his face. "So, yeah, I traded your life for hers and then I made a fucking mistake and my daughter died because of it."

His expression hardens. "The mistake you made was killing me!" He roars and throws his next punch.

I parry, blocking it, but I'm not fast enough to account for his counterattack. I sail through the air and land on my back in the center of the room. Before I can get my bearings, he's on me, lifting me by the throat.

I claw at his grip, trying to break his hold, but with my feet dangling above the floor, I have no maneuverability. He means to kill me, and CJ's words from earlier light a fire under my ass. I mentally push.

Damian's ghost loses his grip and falls back a few steps, and I'm once again on my feet, drawing in air in great gulps. When his fist connects again, the bone in my cheek gives and pain wraps all the way around my head until all I see are spots.

"Stop!" Bridget's voice cuts through the haze, and my triple vision slowly rights from my position on the floor. She stands between Damian's ghost and me, blocking him from delivering any more crushing punches.

His angry mask sets my heart on overdrive. It's one thing to let him pummel the shit out of me, it's another to let him harm her, but I'm too slow. His backhand sends her tumbling towards the wall.

I'm on my feet, and the fury inside me ignites, making every agonizing bruise he delivered fade to nothing. I roar at him, sending him crashing through the wall into his office. Drywall sprinkles the space, and he steps back into view, dusting himself off.

"You do not lay a hand on her," I growl, and point towards Bridget.

His gaze transitions from me to Bridget climbing to her feet, and the violent interest in his eyes has me stepping into the path between them.

"Don't you dare." My skin burns and my fingernails dig into the palm of my hands. The shift in the air is subtle, but it's enough to identify what's happening. The same sensation filled me when I lost it in front of Bear.

Damian stumbles back a step and grabs for the wall, the fire leaving his eyes at the sight of my transformation.

"You said yes?" he whispered, his ghostly eyes going wide with fright.

"No. This is what that bastard's grace does to me," I growl and point at him. A swirl of angel fire flies from the tip of my finger and wraps around his midsection, leaving just enough of a charred burn to make my point before I close my fist, making it disappear.

It takes Damian's ghost a full minute to digest the words, and the fact I could have toasted him with angel fire had I wanted to.

"You?"

His expression turns incredulous, like, I wouldn't have the guts, or the stomach, to eat a human heart, and it just fans the flames of irritation within me.

"Yes. Me." I stare at him, taking a deep breath, calming the burn back down; and rub my sore jaw, wincing as my fingers brush my broken cheekbone. "I heard you, and for once in my life, I listened."

"Are you two done destroying the place?" Bridget says from behind me, reminding us there is someone else in the room.

I meet Damian's gaze. "I'm sorry," I say, knowing it's not enough, and the hardness returns to his glare.

His internal fight with the fury bludgeoning him is written on his features. When his hands curl into fists, Bridget has her answer. He is far from done with me.

"Go upstairs, Bri," I say over my shoulder. I don't want her in the middle of this fight. Not when things were going to get bloody.

"Bullshit," she snaps, again stepping between us, her gaze bouncing between me and the barely contained rage across the room. "I'm not letting him kill you," she adds, staring me down.

She turns to Damian. "I'm not," she says, much softer and lowers her arms, shifting her stance into a defensive form. "So, if that's what you truly want to do, then you'll have to go through me."

I've never seen a ghost blink in confusion, but Damian does. The slow shake of his head worries me.

"You really need to be careful who you side with. He'll rip your heart out," he says jutting his chin in my direction. "Literally."

Bridget's serious expression alters in slow motion. The smirk finally appears just before her snort of a laugh. "Did you really just say that?"

I glance at her before looking at Damian again. His lips twitch and one of his shoulder's rises and falls.

"Put yourself in his shoes," she adds, after her snorting laugh fades.

"I would have told him what Lucifer was demanding," he starts, but Bridget's shift and crossed arms silence him.

"And then what?"

His mouth opened and shut a couple of times before he huffed and looked at the floor. "I would have found another way, and my daughter would be alive."

"Like Athena?" I say.

"I beat Lucifer before," he growls. "And I'll beat you, too."

Before I can blink, he has me pinned on the wall to my office, one hand squeezing my throat and the other aimed at my chest. My heart.

I close my eyes, expecting ripping pain, instead, his frustrated growl yanks them open again. His hand cannot pierce my skin. It can't puncture Raven's pendant.

"If I can't have your heart, no one else can," he hisses and tosses me across the room.

I laugh, flashing back to another time, and another ghost and within a blink, I'm pinned against another wall.

"I think Tanya said those same exact words." I squeeze out between hysterical laughter.

His angry gaze meets mine and I can't stop laughing. There's no rhyme or reason to it, either. I'm not sure if I'm having a bona fide breakdown, or what, but I cannot stop.

His grip on my throat loosens, and he actually glances back at Bridget before focusing on me again. "I meant..."

The start of his clarification just pushed me into the gale realm, and my knees buckled. He releases his grip, and I drop to the floor, holding my abdomen, still in hysterics until I fold over, pressing my forehead into the debris on the floor and shake until the laughter turns into something else entirely.

Laughter, tears, screams; I have no idea how to control whatever this is that grips me.

Damian retreats a few steps.

The flurry of emotions beating me to shit turns into a tornado, decimating everything inside me.

A warm hand lands on my back and the crunch of shifting glass settles next to me. Bridget's soft coo fills my world. Tones follow, like she's dialing, but I still can't stop.

"Hello, this is Bridget O'Keefe. I need an ambulance sent to 375 River Road."

Her words compute, but I still can't stop whatever it is that is happening. My insides feel as though they are shattering, and the shards are stabbing through every organ in my body, except my heart.

My heart continues to beat, to keep me alive, despite the pain.

Angel Fire Chapter 19

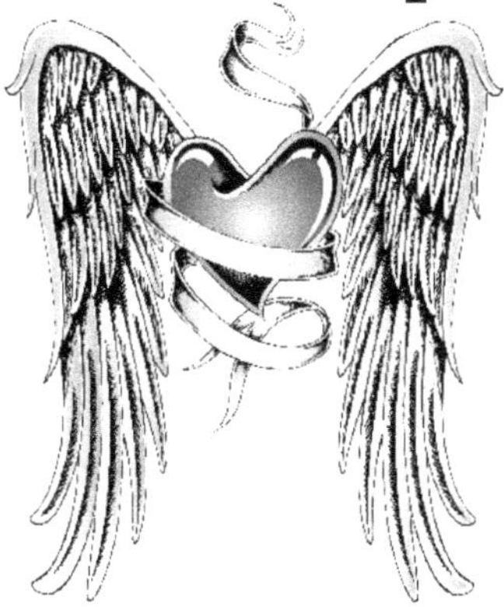

I WAKE, GROGGY, AND my hand lifts to wipe my face, but stops with a clink of metal on metal. My gaze travels above me, focusing on an intravenous bag hanging on a T hook.

Scraping pulls my attention to the left and my stomach drops. Steve takes a seat in the chair next to me. His face was haggard and his eyes streaked with red veins. I glance around the hospital room and then at the wrist restraints, and back to Steve.

"Suicide watch?" I ask, because I know where I am.

Bridget covered up the destruction of the office by telling the paramedics I was responsible. They had to give me a sedative to get me to move from my balled position. I vaguely remember someone saying I was bleeding, and then the sweet bliss of nothingness.

"Yeah. Your prognosis is a tossup between psychotic break, or just a run-of-the-mill breakdown." He lets out a tired laugh. "Valerie came in and checked your injuries at my request," he added and folded his hands together so tightly his knuckles turned white. "Which might be why you are coherent now."

"How long have I been out?"

"They brought you in last night." He stands and steps to the small window. "CJ called me after you left the house." Steve's voice cracks, and his chin drops to his chest when he looks my way. A layer of tears coat his eyes. "I know how it feels to lose a child," he says and presses his lips together. "The only thing worse is the loss of a grandchild." He turns back to the window.

My mind fills with excuse after excuse, and I know they don't amount to anything. "I fucked up."

"I'd say so."

"How's Naomi?"

He stares at me and lets out a sardonic laugh. "How the fuck do you think she is?" His anger and disappointment lace his voice.

If I could shrink to nothing, I would. It was like asking me the day after Raven died how I was doing and I close my eyes, knowing it was an asinine question, but it popped out on its own. Now I'm afraid to open my mouth for fear of what other stupid questions might make an appearance. I don't know what else to say.

Strained silence settles between us, and I shift on the bed, trying to find a comfortable position.

"Is Bridget okay?" I ask, hoping the change in subject will warm up the chill in the room.

"She's been waiting for you to wake up." He crosses to the door. "I need some air anyway," he says and steps out of the room, holding the door for her.

When the door latches, Bridget crosses soundlessly and takes a seat. She glances at the bindings strapping me to the bed.

"You know, there was a time I dreamed of a situation like this," she says and her eyes meet mine. The smile on her face is framed with sadness.

"And now?"

"Now I just want to beat the crap out of you for so many things."

"Oh." I can't say I blame her.

"But I also want to be there for you. To help you get through this."

"You should run, Bri. Run far and run fast," I say and I mean it.

She runs her finger over the back of my hand. It's such a small gesture and yet says more than her words did.

"Don't fall in love with me."

Her eyes lock with mine. "It's a little late for that."

My eyes close and my head falls back on the pillow.

"Damian warned me about you when I started working at the firm. I guess he didn't realize I was already a notch on your bedpost."

"He knew." I meet her gaze.

She inhales and crosses her arms. "Just shut up and let me get this shit out."

"Fine." I really don't want to hear her out. What I want are no complications that Lucifer can exploit.

"He warned me that falling in love with you would be easy. That you are innately good and pure, right down to your core." She lets out a small laugh. "And it would be years before you let anyone else in."

I look up at the ceiling.

"I had no intention of opening my heart again, either. And then you were such a terrific dad." A tremor shakes her voice and I clench my teeth. "Everything he said that first day before you came into the office, he reiterated last night when I was cleaning up the house."

I turn, shocked by her words.

"That's how I know he wasn't just feeding me a line that first day." She sniffles and blinks her eyes clear. Taking a deep breath, she continues. "He may have wanted to kill you for what you did, but it was because he cared so deeply for you and your family."

"I'm pretty sure he wanted to kill me because I ripped his heart out with the intention of giving it to Lucifer," I say.

She does that half shrug thing and I can't tell if there is truth to my statement or not.

"Your little reveal about what exactly was at stake sank in after you left." She glanced away from me. "He also muttered something about some twenty-five hundred odd years was long enough. What did he mean by that?"

"Damian Andreas was born in 500 BC."

She laughs and I remain stoic. When I don't change expression, her laugh fades.

"You really believe that?"

I look down at the binding holding my wrist. It unlocks, and I signal her to move closer. She gives me a skeptical look, but scootches forward in the chair. I move the wisps of her bangs to the side and place my palm on her forehead. With a breath, I transmit the total of Damian's life into her brain. Everything from his first memory to his last. I had every piece ingrained.

I knew how he felt about my brother and me. None of his thoughts, feelings, or experiences while he was breathing was a mystery, but his response as a ghost—that humbled me.

The transfer took moments, but when my hand relinquishes her forehead, I act on impulse, running my hand into her hair and I pull her to my lips, because I know after seeing my ultimate act of betrayal, she will never forgive me.

She fights against me at first, but after a whine of derision, she melts into the kiss and our tongues slowly twirl. The kiss consumes me, showing me the possibility, and with it, the need to burn this bridge before something horrifying happens to her. Finally, I release her before I end up pulling her onto the bed with me.

Bridget puts her forehead on mine for a minute, closing her eyes. "Damn you," she whispers, just before she pulls away. Pain resides in her hazel eyes, along with a thin sheen of tears.

"I'm sorry. I know I shouldn't have, but..." I quietly trail off and drop my hand into the restraint, willing it back in place.

She gives me a little smile and takes a minute to smooth her hair back and gather her wits. It was quite the opposite of her uncle's reaction when I downloaded Damian's life to him. "There was one more thing Damian wanted me to tell you." She draws a deep breath and sighs.

I wait for her to form the words, wondering just how long they'd talked.

"He said, since you seem to have such a mastery over angel fire, you need to be the one to close the portals."

"I don't even know if it is angel fire." I say, but my argument is based on self-doubt, not the facts, not the certainty present in my heart.

"He thought you might say that," she says and smiles. "But he assured me that was angel fire, and from what I saw CJ do, I would have to agree. Damian really knew you better than I think you know yourself."

I let a light laugh escape and turn my gaze to the ceiling. "Damian only saw what I wanted him to see. He never saw any of the darkness. Raven didn't see it either, but it's there, poisoning everything that once was good in me, and I'm afraid I might not be able to contain it anymore." I have no idea why I'm confessing this to Bridget, but it's tumbling out like I've been given a dose of truth serum. "And there's a part of me that doesn't want to contain it. It's like the part of me that wants you in my life, despite the odds of you becoming a target." I huff. "But I know better now."

Silence blankets us, and I keep staring, waiting for her to speak. I finally glance at her and see tears slowly tracking down her cheeks. My hands ball into fists as I resist the urge to wrap my arms around her.

"I should have said no to you when you asked for a job. That would have been the best way to protect you." I let out a sarcastic laugh. "I was so damned naïve."

"Damian said CJ would not close the portals. He won't leave his family. Not unless he is forced to." Her voice cracks as she tries to get the conversation back to what Damian wanted, and not what either of us might want. "He said that's what you needed to do to keep *his* family safe. He said you owed him that much."

I close my eyes against the burn of tears and turn my head towards the tiny window. She's right of course. I owe Damian this, even if it means I never set foot back in York, it's the only way to keep what's left of both our families alive.

I nod, with my eyes still closed.

"I'm coming with you."

My eyes fly open and my head snaps in her direction. "No fucking way."

Her low chuckle catches me off guard. "I've got nothing left here, either, Tom. At least if I'm with you, I can help. I can make a difference."

"Did you not see what I'm going up against? I'm not bringing you anywhere near that." My heart pounds against my chest at the thought, but her eyes are unyielding, taking on that drill sergeant quality again.

"Bri," I start and take a deep breath because now my chest is tightening with the start of a panic attack. "You give him leverage."

Her eyebrow rises.

"I give a damn about you, okay?" I snap.

"I give a damn about you, too." She crosses her arms and cocks her head as if to say take that. It's adorable and clouds my thinking.

I lay my head back on the pillow. "I can't take you with me." I don't leave room for negotiation in my tone. If she comes with me, it will be a disaster of epic proportion.

Angel Fire Chapter 20

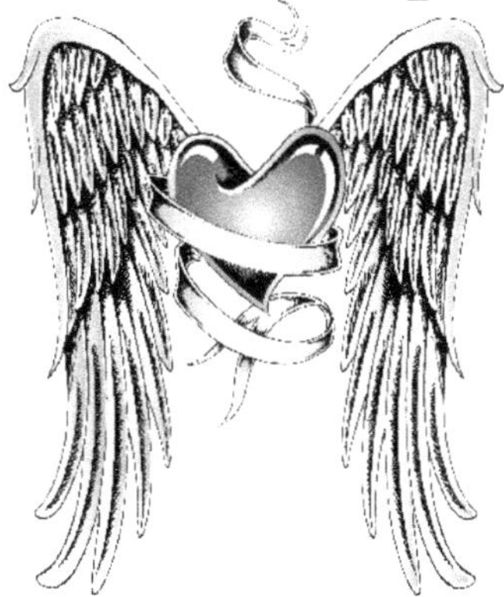

THE HOSPITAL IS VERY serious about their thirty-six hour suicide watch, but at least after the first twenty-four hours, they take off the restraints. I appeased the resident psychiatrist, and he signs my release form on the third day and hands me a counseling schedule for the next month.

I stare at the paper showing three sessions a week and balk.

"I really don't need this many sessions," I say, holding up the paper.

Dr. Minswell just raises an eyebrow.

"Fine," I answer and fold up the paper, stuffing it in the pants Bridget brought this morning. I climb down the stairs and step out into the crisp autumn air.

She pulls my car up to the curb and gets out, tossing the keys to me without a word before climbing into the passenger side. I feel as though I'm going from one psych ward to another, but I climb into the driver's seat.

"I'll drop you off at the office. I need to take a drive."

"I'm good," she says.

"I'm not going to off myself," I snap and send a glare at her.

"Fine, then you won't mind if I tag along."

"Jesus Christ, woman, can't I have a couple of hours of peace?"

"What are you doing?" she asks, challenging me.

"Planning my daughter's funeral."

Her cocky, overbearing attitude disappears. "Oh. Okay. I'm sorry."

I sigh. "I know you mean well, but you can't be my shadow. Not today. Today, I need my time with my little girl, okay?" I glance at her and she nods. "So, the office?"

She gives me a small nod.

"I'll be a couple of hours. You have my cell if you need me," I say as I pull up in front of the house.

She pauses. "Are you sure you don't need me?"

I give her a soft smile. "You'd know if I needed you." If my day goes as I expect, I might just need an ear when I get back. I made an appointment with the funeral home, but that isn't scheduled until late this afternoon.

This morning, I have a completely different destination. I was serious about time with my little girl and the only place that can happen now is Paradise Cove.

Bridget stops at the door and glances at me. I give her a half-hearted wave and back out of the driveway. I head in the opposite direction of York Village. The drive to Brooksfield is only an hour, and I have time to mull over what I'm going to say to my wife.

I cross over the frost-ridden grass to the path leading to Paradise Cove, still unsure of what I want to say. Her disappointment in me was pretty clear the night she took Hannah to heaven. I slow to a stop before I cross onto the soft moss.

The person standing with her back to me is not who I expect. The minute I step onto the moss, my mother turns towards me.

"They thought you would come sooner," she says and turns back to the sun dancing on the water.

I give a nervous laugh. "I would have, had I been able to. They had me on a thirty-six-hour lockdown."

She glances over her shoulder with a crease between her eyes.

"Suicide watch," I admit, and heated shame fills my cheeks.

"Tom," she sighs, and there is sadness in her eyes that chokes me.

"I know. I've gotten lecture after lecture about the sanctity of life, over the last three days." I can't stand having my mother look at me that way. It's almost as if I've already been lost to her. "Can I talk to my wife and daughter?"

Her gaze drops to the ground. "It's not sanctioned."

"Sanctioned? What the fuck does that mean?"

"It means you are damned," she says, turning in my direction. "And there are major... discussions going on upstairs as to what that means."

I stare at her, waiting for more, and she crosses to me.

"They can't come. If they did, it would upset things more than they already are."

"But, Mom," I start and she shakes her head.

"I may have already done irreparable harm to your case by coming." She closes her eyes. "But I couldn't leave you here thinking we all abandoned you. We are trying." Her hand caresses my cheek.

"I still don't understand." I can feel the tremble in my lips.

"The argument to set aside your damnation is raging. It's ugly and heartbreaking."

I hang my head. "I guess Damian would lead the opposition."

She hooks her finger under my chin and raises my face so I meet her gaze. "He is fighting for you. Every life you ever touched is fighting for you. Raphael is even fighting for your redemption."

"Dad was forgiven for all the shit he did. And if Damian is up there, he was forgiven for his sins, too. Why is my head on the chopping block?" Aggravation fills me.

Her fingers caress my cheek. "You betrayed and murdered someone who loved and trusted you. It's the ultimate sin."

"So, I should have let Lucifer torture Hannah? Kill her?"

"There is no justification for what you did, Tom. The ends do not justify the means."

The snap in her voice stings because I know she is right.

"So, basically heaven is closed to me, along with whatever magic this cove offers."

She bites her lip and nods.

"And there is nothing I can do to change it?" I ask, because without hope, I am lost.

She closes her eyes, and when she opens them; I have my answer. Tears brim, sliding down her cheeks.

I step back. "So, my options are close all the portals and try to stop the devil from getting hold of Naomi and Grace, in exchange for an eternity being ripped to pieces over and over again, or say yes to Lucifer and become his weapon and possibly survive eternity without torture?" My voice rises with anguish and anger.

"No. Those aren't your only choices. You can help close the portals and let us hash this out, knowing every portal you shut down is a step closer to us." Her snarling reprimand makes me feel like a little kid. "Don't you ever contemplate saying yes, do you hear me?"

She blurs through my tears and hot trails slide down my cheeks. "I won't."

"Promise me," she insists.

I look up at the sky and then out over the mountains on the other side of the lake. The need to never disappoint my mother again outweighs my hesitation. Despite that, the words stick in my throat. When I bring my gaze back to my mother, I force the words out.

"I promise," I whisper with a quivering voice.

My chest squeezes when she fades away.

With that promise, I have damned myself in other ways.

Lucifer won't ever give up his quest to tear me down, and anyone I care about will be at his disposal.

Angel Fire Chapter 21

I WENT DIRECTLY TO the funeral home after leaving Paradise Cove, instead of waiting for my original meeting time. My instructions are simple. Cremation and no service. I will handle the service myself. Hannah will get the same treatment Raven did.

"When can I have her ashes?"

"Friday. Do you have an urn picked out?"

I shake my head and he guides me to the adjoining room displaying coffins and a mantle with various urns. One has blue butterflies painted on it and I bite my lower lip, pointing at it.

"She'd love that one." My voice is raw, and he gives my shoulder a caring pat.

"I'm sure she would."

I take leave and head over to the office. I haven't been inside since the night Hannah died, and I wonder how far in the cleanup Bridget really got. When I open the door, fresh paint assaults my nose and I scan the pristine entry. Even the drywall is fixed. A radio blares from my office and I step to the doorway.

All the debris is gone, and Bridget is erasing the damage with a fresh coat of paint. With her back to me, she wiggles to the music as the roller drifts up and down the wall in a uniform strip. Her hair is piled in a mess on her head, with a random streak of paint on the side, like she swept a stray wisp away without the knowledge her hand had paint on it. The entire effect is so sexy and down to earth that the overwhelming need to strip her down and ruin her paint job takes hold.

I take a step into the room and stop. The promise I made to my mother makes this impossible, and I turn away, crossing to Damian's office instead. His office is still furnished, and everything is mostly untouched.

I take a seat in his chair and stare at the pictures on his desk. Naomi and the kids stare back at me with beaming smiles. Guilt edges in and when I turn to the other photo on the desk, my hands grip the chair arms. It's a picture of me and Damian holding up a fifty-pound striper and grinning like fools. The fact that the picture sits on his desk is like a kick in the gut.

It's funny. In all the years we've worked together, I've never noticed the pictures on his desk or the stupid little knickknacks on his shelves. Things representative of his current life. Things I'll miss like fishing with him. That damned fish fed our families for months.

The hole in the center of my chest grows with each memory. When I finally look up, Bridget is in the doorway with the paint roller dangling from her hand.

"I didn't hear you come in."

I just shake my head. "Sorry."

She disappears, but before I can get to my feet, she is back, wiping her hands on a cloth and crossing to stand at my side.

"Are you okay?"

I stare at the picture, wondering if I'll ever be okay again. I look up at her, and my need burns through every caution flag in my brain. The small shake of my head sets her in action. Bridget pulls me from the seat and into her arms in a warm hug.

My arms wrap around her, holding on as tightly as I dare. I hadn't realized I was trembling until she grounds me in place. We stay like this for a while and then she makes the mistake of looking up at me. Tears cluster on her eyelashes and sparkle in her eyes.

Her hand snakes to the back of my head, and she pulls me to her lips before I can break the hold. The moment the kiss ignites, I turn with her in my arms and press her to the wall, following my base instincts and not what my head is telling me.

At the core, I need human contact. I need to feel adored. I need heat and passion, and everything that makes life worth living. Without it, there is nothing left to fight for.

The kiss breaks, and her aura flares iridescent pink. She takes my hand and leads me up to the bedroom, and I let her, despite the objections in my head.

In the confines of her bedroom, she focuses on unbuttoning my shirt in silence. I pull the elastic from her hair, freeing her messy blonde locks. Her hair is like silk on my fingers, and I slowly comb through it with my fingers. When she winces, I meet her gaze, catching the flare of pain in her eyes as I extract my fingers from the knot. The small rush of air between her lips calls my attention and when her tongue wets them, I can't help myself.

Holding her face, I lean in, delivering a kiss along with every bit of my fractured soul. I want her to understand everything, and I pull her to me, deepening the kiss as she whines under the intensity of it. Every thought, every memory, every emotion running through my form flows into her.

Wetness flows over my nose and I don't know if it's her tears or mine. What I shared with Raven was a fraction of what I am downloading into Bridget. This hides nothing, it bares all, right down to the petty jealousy I harbor for CJ.

It isn't a matter of love or trust. This is an act of desperation. I need to know that someone is capable of loving me, even after I show my darkest secrets. When the last memory transfers, the last moment before this second, I break the kiss and step away. Her eyes slowly open and focus on me as if she's seeing me for the first time.

Her aura flares like the sun for a moment, and then threads of iridescent pink weave through it, along with deeper pink and blue.

"You really are beautiful," I whisper with a sigh and meet her gaze.

She doesn't move or respond just yet, and an icy fear grips me. It must show on my face because she quickly shakes her head and closes the gap between us, taking both my hands in hers.

"I'm not rejecting you. I'm just... processing everything." She keeps her eyes locked on mine and releases my hands. I can't see a hint of pity in her eyes, just a combination of heat and sadness. Her hands move up my chest until her palm stops right over my heart. Her lips twitch into a smile. "Your heart feels like a jackhammer."

I allow a smile. "Yeah, well, I just pretty much bared my soul. Even the shitty side of it that no one has ever gotten a glimpse into."

"You've been through a lot of dark times," she says.

I narrow my eyes at her. "You're not... freaked out?"

"No. I've skated on the dark side myself, so I'm not one to judge. Of course, I never killed my best friend..."

She pulls the hand that isn't over my heart away from my chest and shrugs with it. I can't tell if it's a dig or a half-assed attempt at a joke, and I'm not sure how to respond.

"It changes nothing." Her soft affirmation rocks me to the core.

"You still want..." I can't finish, and I press my lips together against the rest of the question and the turmoil her words cause inside me.

She doesn't answer, instead; she steps closer, pressing her lips to my chest. When her kisses trail lower, I close my eyes and tilt my head back, letting an inaudible sigh, framed with her nickname, roll from my tongue.

I remember what Bridget O'Keefe can do with her mouth, and she is just as skilled, and twice as sexy, as she ever was in high school. The low hum in the back of her throat nearly does me in and she goes deeper, swallowing me until her lips caress my balls.

"Oh. Fuck." I groan, unable to hold on any longer. I come in her mouth, and she sucks until I'm trembling. "Okay." I whisper, and she rolls her tongue around the sensitive tip before leaning back on her heels.

Her hazel eyes are almost entirely green and her aura pulses in time with my cock. I can hardly keep my balance, but I help her to her feet and lead her to the bed in the corner. This time, I'm not frantic, like I was in the kitchen. This time I linger, memorizing the sensations of my mouth on her body, her soft skin under my fingertips, every physical contact between us until she is trembling beneath me as badly as I am.

I climb back to her lips, and deliver a sensual kiss that locks a rumbling moan in both our throats, and then I pull away, searching her eyes.

"You didn't happen to pick up anything since the other night?" I ask, poised in place, aching to feel her pussy wrapped around me.

The ecstasy etched on her face fades and her eyes close. "Shit."

I roll onto my back and stare at the ceiling. Silence falls with only our labored breathing to voice our mutual frustration.

"Fuck it," she says and swings her leg over me, sliding my throbbing cock inside her before I can stop her.

The moment her hips start that slow grinding circle, my reservations fade, and I close my eyes, savoring the sensation. I make a mental note to keep my head this time, and pull out before I shoot my load.

When I open my eyes, I take her in, from her bright aura, to her messy blonde hair and hazel-green eyes. Her summer tan still hangs on and the bikini patches on her breasts show me just how skimpy her summer attire really is.

As my gaze scans her, I zero in on a small tattoo that I missed the other night, and again tonight. I'm not sure how I missed it, considering how fully I explored her, but right next to my thumb, just below her hip bone, are three small hearts and one heart is new. I run my thumb over them and glance up at her.

Her hips still and she glances at where my thumb is, and then lets out a soft sigh. "A heart for each lost child," she says, and her cheeks redden in embarrassment.

"This one is new." I lightly pass over the raised skin with my finger.

Her hips slowly twirl, and she leans forward, kissing me instead of answering. Mingled with the kiss comes her memory. My little girl captured her heart, and the tattoo was Bridget's way of dealing with her death. It's a mark to remember her by, to honor her spirit, just like the other two honor her own children.

I deepen the kiss, sliding one hand in her hair and the other cups her ass. The rawness of her emotions ensnares me, and I can't stop. I need more, more of her heart, her mind, her gentle soul.

Her hips speed up, riding hard as her teeth clink mine. We shift, deepening the kiss until I am overwhelmed with stimulus. I siphon every memory she has, collecting them, storing her lifetime alongside those that mean the world to me.

Her moan fills my mouth as her body tightens and her orgasm milks me, clenching and unclenching around my cock with such intensity it drives me right over the edge. When our lips unlock, she pulls up for breath and her bright eyes stare into mine.

Both our chests heave and she has a light layer of sweat that makes her skin glisten. I want to lick her all over again.

"I felt you," she whispers.

I let out a sharp laugh. "I would hope so," I say, because to me, my come must have felt like a fucking rocket.

Bridget rolls her eyes. "No, well, yeah, I felt that, too. But I'm talking about you being inside my head. I felt you there." She bites her lower lip as her thoughts swirl around my words more than hers, and then her head drops to my shoulder. "I meant to stop before..."

So had I, but I got so lost in the feel of her and the feed of her memories, that I just plain lost my good sense, which seems to be the pattern here. I stare at the ceiling, unmotivated to move, wondering why I keep letting this happen.

"I meant to as well," I admit with a sigh and lock eyes with her.

"We can't keep doing this," she says and rolls off, snuggling in the crook of my arm.

"No shit."

She glances up at me and concern floods her gaze.

"We need to make sure we have protection next time," I clarify, and the worry lines on her forehead smooth. She lays her head back on my shoulder.

"Nice save there," she mumbles, and I give her a soft squeeze.

I smile, but as her breathing smooths out into a light snore, my smile fades. This is all wrong, and my eyes close at my utter stupidity. I'm not sure if this is a half-assed attempt at saying goodbye or just a selfish act meant to reinforce my broken ego before I go hunting for Lucifer's portals.

Bridget's utter acceptance of me clouds my judgment. It doesn't hurt that she's sexier than hell and actually has a good heart, despite whatever misgivings I had about her in high school. She had been part of the bitch squad and I assumed she belonged there, just like I had assumed Raven was an outcast who wasn't worth the hit to my social status before I really got to know her.

I stare out at the darkening skies, wondering what would have happened if I had seen under Bridget's facade in high school. I glance down at her and shiver. An odd certainty grips me. If I had taken a deeper look, I would never have given Raven a second glance.

The ramifications of not having Raven in my life play across the shadows on the ceiling. The Windwalker might not have been caught. Steve's FBI career would not have been cut short. Valerie would have died at Damian's hands. CJ probably would have gone dark. And the most significant ramification, I would not be suffering with the loss of my wife and child. I wouldn't be fraught with fear at the very thought of trying to build something with Bridget.

Angel Fire Chapter 22

TWILIGHT MOVES INTO NIGHT and I continue to stare at the shadows, measuring my next move. Sometime over the past couple of hours, her light snore transitioned to the deep cadence of sleep, and I make a decision.

I slide my arm from under her. She rolls and curls into a ball. Before the chill wakes her, I cover her with a blanket, and climb out of bed as soundlessly as I can.

She stirs, but I will her to remain asleep.

My clothing is scattered, and I dress in pieces until I'm completely covered. I pause at the door and take one last look at her before slipping out of the room. I head down to the office where my indiscretion started, and pull a couple of pieces of paper out of the desk's top drawer, along with a pen.

The first note isn't long. It is to CJ asking him to take care of Hannah's remains, and when my house is done, to rent it out so it isn't empty for however long I'm gone. He'll understand; if not, I'm sure I'll get a flood of texts and phone calls.

The next note is harder to write, and I close my eyes, clenching the pen in my hand before I attempt to explain.

Dear Bri,

I have no excuse for what I'm about to do, at least one that you'll ever forgive me for. You really should have heeded Damian's warning. I seem to make a habit of tearing hearts out, and I'm sure you'll damn me all to hell after this, but I have to go.

I have to try to redeem myself before I have any hope of a happy ending.

For what it's worth, right now, that happy ending includes you, but I know once you read this, that will no longer be possible.

I need to close those portals. It's dangerous and I have no idea if I'll ever get back home. I don't expect someone as beautiful as you to wait around for a damned jackass like me, but if the fates see fit, maybe we'll find each other again.

Know that tonight will be a lifeline for me. The one thing that will keep me moving forward, even when I want to lie down and die. The memory is cherished enough in my heart to do that. So, yeah, I kind of give a damn about you... a lot more than I should.

Thank you for sharing your soul, and I'm sorry I have to break your heart.

Tom.

I stare at the words and leave the paper on the desk before crossing to the bookshelf. The map Damian and I made showing every conceivable portal in the world is folded neatly between Shakespeare and Stephen King, and I pull it from its place.

I hesitate at the office door and turn back, grabbing the photo of us with the fish. It's a heavy reminder of what I owe him, and I'm sure there will be days I need the reminder. I open the closet door and exhale. This space was left untouched by Damian's rage and I squat, unzipping Raven's duffel bag, and stow both the picture and map on top of her crystals and potions.

My leather jacket hangs untouched, and I slip it on, picking up the bag before I make a last sweep of the empty space. I haul it over my shoulder and head for the front door. My hand reaches for the doorknob, but I hesitate, my chin dropping to my chest as new loneliness layers over my own shattered heart.

I pull my hand back and glance at Damian's office before I cross and scribble a postscript on Bridget's note.

It isn't much, but at least she won't have to figure
out money or housing on top of losing a piece of her
heart. I walk out without another glance and climb into
my car, even as my heart and mind continue to argue
over this decision.

The lights are still off in the bedroom, and I back out
of the driveway with only my fog lights on. At the
cottage, I throw the few articles of clothing and toiletries
that I have into a bag, and I'm in the car in less than ten
minutes.

I don't have a plan beyond heading west. There are
twelve remaining portals in the western hemisphere,
stretching from Alaska to Argentina. We mapped
another twenty-five overseas, covering every continent
on the globe except for Antarctica, which seems to be
free of any portal and angel kin alike.

I glance at the European map, staring at the number
of portals in Greece. The cluster is bigger than the one
that had resided in New England and a shiver crawls
through me.

Greece is my end game. Just like York is Lucifer's.
But for now, the nearest portal is in Detroit, so that is
where my redemption starts.

The End

Continue reading Tom's story with Angel Fury, the sixth
book in The Ryan Chronicles on the next page.

Angel Fury Chapter 1

I TAKE A SEAT in the private airport in Greece and pull out the ragged map from the inside pocket of my equally worn leather jacket. Ten years ago, I set out to close all of Lucifer's portals around the world, and I've seen every corner of the planet in the process. My dog has been with me all this time, as well, and I stroke Sam's fur as she sits by my side, laying her head on my lap like she does after every long journey. It's as if she knows I'm damned tired.

I unfold the atlas, crossing off the last circle just outside of Athens and I send Sam an exhausted smile.

"It's done," I whisper and fold the remains of the map, tucking it back in my pocket. Her soft whine prompts me to rub her ears again. "Well, girl, I think it's time to go home."

Home.

The word seems foreign on my lips, especially since I really didn't think I'd live to set foot in York again. And trust me, there were times that doubt was warranted, and both Sam and I have the scars to prove it.

All told, I closed thirty-eight portals; some were easy, some not so much. I got in, scrubbed the land and got out. Most times, I didn't encounter resistance from anything, but when I did, it usually came in the form of a horde of demons or an equally undesirable foe.

But nothing was a match for my angel fire, especially when I thought Sam was in danger. Well, nothing except

Lucifer. And that bastard only showed his face once. In Death Valley, of all places. Much to my chagrin, he kicked my ass and nearly killed Sam before I got my head in the game and let the angel fire rip. I rained it down with such force I left a crater behind.

Sam had been in bad shape, bloodied and broken, but at least she was still breathing when I carried her out of that crater. I hauled her close to ten miles across the desert. A normal healthy male would have plenty of issues carrying a seventy-pound German Shepherd that distance. It nearly killed me, between my blood loss, coupled with heat exhaustion, and a busted shoulder just to top it all off. The vet said it was a miracle she survived, and my doctors proclaimed the same about me.

Seeing her limp to my side again when I picked her up at the vet was well worth the six days in the hospital, followed by four months in a cast, followed by another six months in rehab, before I was given a clean bill to move on.

It was a valuable lesson.

I hadn't used my head. Instead, I operated on fury alone and lost the calculated advantage. I swore I wouldn't let that happen again. Unfortunately, I never got to test that theory.

A glance at the clock tells me I have a solid two and a half hours before someone from Ted Beaumont's organization lands to pick me up. I lean back in the chair, tucking my chin to my chest with Sam's leash hanging on my wrist. I close my eyes, drifting back over the years to the day I found Sam.

MY PHONE BUZZED YET again, like it had been for the past six hours, and I glanced at the caller ID. Bridget O'Keefe. Again. She wasn't going to let this go. I clenched my fists, fighting every instinct to answer. Instead, I glanced out the window of the little coffee shop in some rural nowhere in Ohio. The strip mall across the street had nothing of interest on my first scan, except maybe the miniscule animal shelter housed at the end.

Needing some sort of diversion to keep me from answering her calls, I threw money on the table, took one last sip of the coffee, and stepped outside. The road wasn't busy, so I crossed, taking my time to glance at some of the window displays on the storefronts. Anything to keep my brain occupied with something other than Bridget.

Last night I'd nearly turned around a dozen times, just thinking of her soft flesh under my hands, and the taste of her. I knew that memory would both drive me and bite me in the ass, but I didn't expect the fucking turmoil accosting me with every thought.

When I stepped into the shelter, my mind totally blocked Bridget out. The sheer chaos of the open space and playtime for the dogs had my focus. I gave a nod to one of the shelter workers and she bounced over with a smile.

"Hi. My name is Nikolina. How may I help you?"

I returned her smile and just watched the dogs playing. I turned my gaze to hers, and, on impulse, asked, "You wouldn't happen to have any German Shepherd puppies, would you?"

The blues and greens in her aura flared at the question, as did the light in her eyes. "You're in luck! We had a litter delivered today. Come with me," she said, and led me to the rear section of the shelter and a smaller play area with bumbling pups.

I squatted and waited. My eyes studied each puppy until they fell on her. Sam was sitting on the opposite side, staring at me. When our eyes met, she trotted through the pack to the spot right in front of me, where she sat and waited just as patiently as I had. It was eerie and felt right as rain.

"I want this one." I pointed and looked up at the salesgirl.

Her eyebrows were already arched, and then her gaze moved from the little puppy to me.

"That's the damnedest thing I think I've ever seen." She nodded as she spoke, and I couldn't help but smile.

"Dogs choose their owners. Not the other way around," I said and scooped the puppy up into my arms, following her to the front.

She pulled out paperwork for adoption and slid it across the counter for me to fill out. I scribble the information while the puppy licked my face. I laughed and dodged her tongue, but for some reason, I didn't want to put her down, either, for fear someone else would step inside and steal her from me before I could finish the paperwork.

"You really are lucky. We don't normally get them this young. Usually the dogs are older, and the owners just don't want them anymore." She glanced over her shoulder at the dogs playing together. "At least they seem to get along, but sometimes we get one or two that have to stay in their kennels during playtime." She smiled at me. "I'm sure these puppies will go fast. It's unfortunate, but the owner passed away and their family had no idea what to do with these little rascals." She kept chattering on and I finally pushed the paper across the counter.

"I guess I need supplies as well," I said and glanced around at my limited options.

"I can hook you up with a collar and leash, but for anything else, I'd suggest Petsmart, which is only a mile down the road," she whispered over the counter.

I gave her a nod, she found a small red collar and a light leash, and I passed her the shelter fee along with another twenty-five bucks for the supplies.

With the leash on, I gently put Sam on the ground and started out of the store.

"Good luck!" Nikolina yelled after me and I gave her a wave before I walked back to the crosswalk. Instead of letting Sam cross on her own, I scooped her up and jogged to my car.

The minute I got her within the confines of the car, she sat and just stared at me as if I was supposed to impart some ancient wisdom or something.

"I hope you don't mind me calling you Sam," I said. Her tail wagged, and she stood, letting out this pitiful puppy yelp that immediately formed a grin on my face. I pulled my phone out and snapped a picture of her. "You just sit down and stay right there until we get to Petsmart. Then you can show me all the things you want. Okay, girl?"

Again, the wag of her tail and a bark followed.

I searched for the store, and just as the GPS loaded, a text flashed on my screen.

Fuck you, Ryan.

Bridget's use of my last name told me just how pissed she was, which was better than having her a crying mess. I debated on answering, but starting a dialog would only string her along and give her hope where there might be nothing but heartache for her.

The dog crawled across the console and onto my lap, as if she knew I needed reinforcement of some sort, and I glance beyond the phone in my hand at her. She lay her head on my thigh and gave the biggest sigh I've ever heard from a puppy.

I popped the phone on the console plug and moved her to the passenger seat before I put the car in gear and headed to find dog supplies.

"MR. RYAN?" A VOICE cuts through the memory, and I open my eyes, glancing at the pilot approaching me.

I stand and study him for a moment. Ten years flood back, along with the unwelcome sorrow. "Josh," I say, as his name pops into my head. I stick out my hand to the pilot who had flown me home from this precise airport the night my daughter died.

He hesitates and then clasps my hand. His memory flashes in my head and I drop my hand after a quick shake.

Sam whines at my side, as if she can feel the cracking of my reinforced heart.

"This is my dog, Sam." I lay my hand on her head, reassuring her I am okay. It has been long enough that I don't curl into a tight ball, fighting the pain through tear-stained vision anymore, but she remembers, just as well as I do.

"Ted said there will be a car for you in Wolfeboro," he says and reaches for my bag on the seat. This time, I let him carry my cargo onto the plane. "Unfortunately..."

"You don't have a flight crew," I finish his thought.

He lets out a soft chuckle. "And I'm getting near the max flying within twenty-four hours."

"I can help fly if you need a co-pilot," I say, and his eyebrows rise. "I had a bit of time to kill when I was laid up in California and figured a pilot's license might come in handy." I pull out my wallet and show him my certificate.

"I might take you up on that," he says, but his mind is shadowed with doubt, especially with the memory of my mental state being so fractured the last time he flew me home from Greece.

I don't respond. I just follow him with Sam at my heels.

The flight home takes much longer than that first trek, but I'm not using my powers to make this sucker fly at some insane mach speed like last time, either. Sam is the perfect traveling companion, calm and serene, and as always, has her head in my lap.

The hum of the airplane drops my eyelids farther and farther until the shadows mix together.

Angel Fury Chapter 2

THE BUMP OF TIRES on pavement jerks me out of sleep and I rub my eyes, pushing myself up from the arm of the chair. Sam jumps off the seat and stretches, yawning in the process, and I follow suit.

Josh comes out of the cockpit looking haggard and exhausted, and I give him a nod of thanks.

"I didn't want to wake you," he says and waves towards the seat where I fell asleep.

"I appreciate it." I am still groggy, but I don't think I've slept that soundly since I was a teenager. When Josh reaches for my bag, I say, "I've got this. You look like you need some rest."

I exchange a handshake and climb down the stairs into the cool spring New Hampshire air. Sam follows and I open the hangar door for her, letting her lead the way.

"Mr. Ryan?" a chauffeur stands, folding the paper he had been reading.

"Yes, sir," I reply, and head towards him with Sam and my light load.

"Mr. Beaumont said I should take you anywhere you want to go."

I smile my appreciation. Being as foggy as I am, I probably will make a better passenger than a driver.

"I need to make a stop in Brooksfield, and then I'll want to head to York."

"Sure thing," he says and glances at my dog. "She's a beauty," he adds.

"Thanks. I'll have to find a grassy spot for her before we go."

He opens the door for me, and I glance at the small parking area and a large grass patch on the opposite side of the asphalt. I unhook Sam and she waits.

"Go on, girl."

She takes off straight for that grass and her sniff-circle-sniff-pee routine ensues. The relief in her features is actually readable and I smile at her, waiting. As soon as she is back, we climb into the back of the town car.

From Wolfeboro, it's less than a half hour south to Brooksfield and I give him the address to Steve's cottage on Mirror Lake where Paradise Cove resides. My hand passes over the map in my breast pocket and I close my eyes, saying a brief prayer that it's enough. I'm done with being a nomad with little to no connection with those I care about. I want to plant roots and let Sam live out her days chasing balls in the surf.

When we pull into the long dirt driveway, I have a moment to wonder if Steve and Jennifer are at the cottage, but as we round the last bend, the darkened windows and empty driveway indicate no one is home. The driver pulls to a stop and puts the car in park.

"Wait here, I shouldn't be long," I say as I slip out of the back seat. Sam climbs out with me and I cross the dark lawn, smiling at the crunch of the grass under my feet. I don't hesitate, like I had that night ten years ago. Instead, I tromp through the path in the woods until I'm standing on the soft green moss underfoot.

Nothing has changed. Nothing ever changes in the cove. Even in the dead of winter, flowers poke from the edges of the snow, creating a surreal landscape. Now that the winter snows have melted, the flowers bloom vibrant, even in the dark, creating a luminous glow like that of a nightlight.

I pull out the map and clear my throat, not sure of whose name to call. Eventually, I look up.

"Mom?" My voice sounds meek, like a scolded child's voice, and Sam whines and leans her entire body against my leg. I shift, disgusted with how weak I sound.

I'm almost forty, for God's sake; I shouldn't sound like a scared little kid.

By the end of my mental rant, I realize there has been no answer.

I repeat her name a little louder and my question echoes out onto the lake.

Still no answer.

"I did what was asked." I hold up the map as if the heavens could see it.

"Mom? Dad?" I call, because the silence is deafening. Sam nudges me again, her ears falling back on her head as she reads my budding distress correctly.

"God damn it! Answer me!" This time my voice bellows with a growl.

Nothing. No ripple of the air, no smoke, no heavenly light, and I'm left in the dark.

"Raven!" I scream, the anger getting the best of me, I can feel it building under my skin, the burn of it right there in my simmering blood.

This time, the air changes and the form standing in the middle of the cove, doesn't settle my nerves. As a matter of fact, I'm much more on guard than if it was a member of my family.

The archangel Michael walks towards me, and his face is a mask of wrath.

"You dare step onto this sacred ground?"

"I closed all the goddamned portals," I wave the map at him, but take a step back, wary of the archangel. I not only harbored Lucifer's grace, but in killing Damian, I also absorbed Gabriel's and Michael's grace.

So, I am as much a target to Michael as I am to Lucifer. I shift, setting myself in a defensive position, protecting my chest at all costs.

Sam's low growl causes me to look away from the angry angel and down at her.

Her teeth are bared, and all the hair on her neck stands on end.

"Sit," I command and her growl fades as she glances up at me in confusion. "I know he's dangerous," I whisper and look up at Michael, weighing my chances. He no longer sports wings and his power is not as strong as it once was, but he could do the same type of damage that Lucifer did to Sam and me back in Death Valley, especially since this is Michael's home turf.

Paradise Cove is a portal to heaven. And based on the reception, it looks like I'm still not welcome.

"I closed the portals. Every last one of them," I say and throw the map in his direction.

"We are very well aware of what you have done."

The venom in his tone catches me off guard. I'm at a loss and I just stare.

His eyes narrow and he crosses his arms. "You really have no idea, do you?"

"Apparently not," I say. "I kind of expected a thank you," I add, pointing at the faded map lying at Michael's feet.

His sardonic laugh echoes. "You really are an inept fool." He scoops up the map and scans all my red marks for the closed portals.

"I worked my ass off to close every goddamned portal on that list!" Anger brews beyond a simmer and the heat spreads. "I spent the last ten years doing CJ's job, and this is the thanks I get?"

He glares at me and tosses the paper back.

I catch it before it hits my chest.

"You closed the portals, but you left Lucifer topside," he growls and takes a step towards me.

Like a flash, Sam is between us and her menacing growl fills the space.

My anger dulls and I blink, trying to reconcile my achievements with what he just stated.

"I closed the portals," I say again, but with less force.

"Yes, and you locked Lucifer out of hell, you stupid bastard!"

The map crumples in my hand, and I glared at Michael. "How the hell was I supposed to know that? Huh?" I step closer with purpose, crowding Sam between us. "I was told to close the portals, and I did. And now you're insulting me?"

The burn rakes my skin and from the widening of Michael's eyes, I know I've transformed. His shock is momentary, and then his growl of anger forming

Lucifer's name announces his intentions. He charges and I sidestep my dog, parrying into a block before I toss Michael over my hip and he slams into the ground on his back.

"I am not Lucifer," I yell in his face and step back, calming the burn. I know I look exactly like that murdering bastard when I lose my temper, but I am not the devil. I take another step, and another breath, putting more distance between us. "And I don't understand. I did what was asked of me. Why are you so pissed off?"

Michael sits up slowly, still staring me down. "Give me my grace," he orders.

I know from CJ how to transfer grace, but I hesitate and shake my head. I had other plans for the magic inside me, plans that would ensure the safety of my nephew and Damian's daughter. "No. I'm saving that for my nephew," I say. "I have a feeling he might need it more than either you or I."

The anger burning in Michael softens and his head cocks. "You... care about his welfare?"

"Why the fuck do you think I've been running all over the world? It certainly isn't to enjoy the perks of travel."

"I didn't think you gave a damn about anyone but yourself, especially after what you did to Damian," he snaps.

"I thought I could save my daughter." I glance out at the water for a minute before looking back at Michael. "I screwed that up royally." I step closer and offer him my hand.

Michael stares at it and then meets my gaze again. He takes my grip and the instant he is on his feet; his hand forms a claw and covers my heart, his fingers dig into my flesh with purpose.

My reaction is immediate, and the explosion moves outwards from the center of my being, knocking him back into the woods beyond the edge of the cove. I can't pull the power back in. It's already formed a life of its own and it engulfs the cove in flame, like it has every other portal on the planet, obliterating it off the map.

I turn, scooping up Sam before she is consumed, bolting towards the path. My heart thunders in my ears as the voices of my family echo in my head in one final chorus of "Don't!" Then the door slams, shutting off any further contact with the dead.

I trip on a root, and Sam goes flying. She lands on her feet, and I find myself on my hands and knees, horrified at what just transpired.

I roll and scan the crop circle that is left. All the beauty and lushness of the cove is gone and only dirt remains. Michael slowly stands in the protection of the woods a few feet beyond my destruction.

Holy fuck.

My chest clenches with the knowledge that I've just locked Michael out of heaven.

Angel Fury Chapter 3

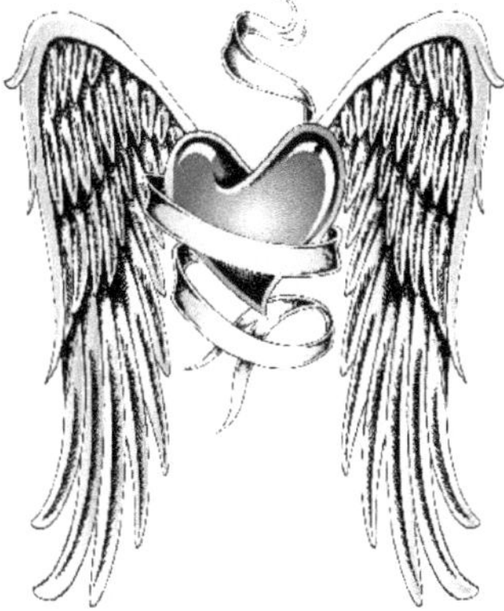

THE DRIVER KEEPS LOOKING at me in the rearview mirror, as if I've lost it completely.

I can't blame him. I came skidding back nearly throwing myself in the car yelling for him to go, to drive, to get the hell out of dodge—right now.

I think we were moving even before I got the door closed, leaving a path of dust and dirt.

Sam pants next to me and I turn just in time to catch Michael stepping on the lawn. Even with the building distance, I gulp at the glare in his eyes. He's coming after me.

In resignation, I lay my head against the seat, going over my options. I'm not sure if CJ will back me up on this. Not when I've closed his only contact with our parents. I run my hand over my face and lean forward.

"Instead of the address on Roaring Rock, please take me to 375 River Road."

"Yes, sir." He glances at me again with a nod.

I calm my raw nerves by stroking Sam's head. She huffs that heavy sigh like she did that first day, and I give her a gentle pat before continuing the calming stroke, from between her ears down to below her collar.

Lucifer's on the loose.

That thought keeps pinging into my consciousness, bringing with it a fear that my coming home might put those I love in the crosshairs between two angry angels. The dark scenery passes, and I catch my reflection in

the window every time a streetlight passes. My stubble
has transitioned to scruff over the last few days, and my
hair is almost as long as it was when I left ten years ago.
The lines at the corner of my eyes are more pronounced,
but outside of those faint crow's feet, I look the same as
I did the day I picked up Sam from that animal shelter.

When we pull into the driveway, a car is parked in
the carport, but the house is dark, like it should be at
two in the morning. The agency name catches my
attention and I pause, staring at it over the top of the
car. Ryan-O'Keefe. At least she kept my name on the
marquis.

I shook my head to focus and leaned into the car,
grabbing the end of Sam's leash along with my
backpack before handing the driver a sizeable tip for
driving me all over creation.

With Sam in tow, I cross to the front door. I no longer
have keys, so I close my eyes, disengaging the locks.
Stepping inside feels a little like I am trespassing, and
as soon as I latch and lock the door behind me, I turn
back to what used to be the reception area.

Shock fills every cell. The old entry, along with what
used to be my office, is open and decorated like a living
area and not an office. The door to Damian's office is
still intact and I debate on which direction to go.

The comfortable-looking couch won the coin toss in
my head, and I cross, setting my bag down, and fall onto
the soft fabric. Sam stretched out on the floor next to
me. She really didn't have a choice, either. I am not
going to let her snoop around the rest of the house and
scare the bejesus out of Bridget.

I close my eyes hoping to catch a few hours of sleep
before I'm thrown to the curb.

A PIERCING SCREAM SLAYS my dream, bolting me into
a sitting position. My hand instinctively tightens,
grasping the leash before Sam lunges at whatever
vibrated my eardrums to the point of pain.

A very pretty, blonde girl with wide blue eyes is frozen in place as much as I am. I expected Bridget to find me here, not a girl who could be...

My eyes widen as Bridget slides into place next to the screaming girl. A pistol is trained in my direction, in hands that shake from pure adrenaline. My gaze jumps between Bridget and the girl next to her, and the relation is clear. I am looking at Bridget's daughter.

The gun is slowly lowered as recognition sets in. "Tom?"

It's the girl's turn to level a surprised look in Bridget's direction. "You know him?" she balks and waves in my direction.

"Yes. From a long time ago," she says to her daughter. "April, this is Tom Ryan. Tom, my daughter April."

"Ryan, as in the name on the sign?"

Bridget nods. "Go. You'll be late for the bus," she says and points towards the door.

April gives me a wary look and then disappears. The door opens and closes a moment later and I stare at Bridget.

"This is Sam," I say, remembering I have a dog attached to my arm.

Bridget doesn't even look. "What the fuck are you doing in my house?" She flips the safety on her gun and crosses the room, dropping it on the coffee table as she passes by. Bridget stands with her back to me, waiting until the bus pulls away with April safely on board.

"Well?" she asks as she turns and levels a frosty glare in my direction.

"I finished closing the portals."

"Big fucking deal."

Sam whines and paws my leg, her sign that she needs to go out.

"I'll be right back," I say and get an eye roll in return. I let Sam out and stand at the door, watching while she does her business. A low whistle calls her back inside and I return to the couch, unsure if I should sit down or just go, and while it would be easy to dive into her mind to find out the answers to the questions swirling in my head, I leave well enough alone.

She would probably pop a cap in my ass if she caught me snooping in her head.

I gave her a small smile. "I'm sorry I hurt you," I say in barely a whisper.

She moves across the room and stops in front of me before she shoves me with everything she has. I stumble back a step and Sam growls. I give my dog the hand signal for stay, but that doesn't stop the menacing rumble coming from her.

"You're sorry?" Her voice is feral along with the anger boiling in her eyes. "You left and didn't even bother to answer any of my calls or texts. I didn't know if you were alive or dead."

The next time she goes to shove me I grab her wrists.

"I screwed up. With you, with everything," I say to soften her anger. Now that our skin is touching, the emotional turmoil pounding in her chest travels into me just as acutely. Her aura flares with it. "And if I picked up the phone and heard your voice, I would have turned my ass around."

She tries to break free of my grip, but I keep hold, making her meet my eyes.

"Let go," she says through clenched teeth.

I drop my hands away.

"Why are you here?" she asks again, but this time there's less bite to the question.

"I didn't know where else to go," I say and look around with a shrug. "This is the closest thing I've got to home." I look at her when I speak.

"This is my home. You need to go book a hotel, because you cannot stay here."

I give a nod and sigh. "I gather you're married now?" I hook my thumb towards the door where her daughter went.

Bridget hesitates looking beyond me and back. She shakes her head and laughs, looking at the ceiling. "No, Tom. I never got married."

I raise my eyebrows as a dawning idea blooms. "How old is she?"

"She turns ten in July."

My brain runs the calculation and I glance towards the door again. That's when it strikes me. Her daughter's aura was bright. Bright enough to indicate angel blood, and my gaze snaps to Bridget's.

I stumble into the nearest seat, just gawking at her.

"The answer to your question is yes. She's yours, but you have no right to be in our lives, not after abandoning us for so long."

I'm too stunned to speak. That familiar numbness takes over, as if all my synapses cannot handle the emotional swirl in my stomach and I run my hands into my hair, lowering my elbows to my knees.

"I fucked up again," I say quietly, and the full scope of what this means hits like a bulldozer. "Lucifer is locked topside." I look up at Bridget. "And so is Michael."

"Michael who?" Her arms cross.

I lean back. "The archangel. And both of them want to kick my ass."

"They'll have to get in line," she says.

I rise to my feet and cross, stopping in front of her. "Bri..."

"You don't get to call me that!" Her outburst is followed by the sting of her hand on my cheek. Sam growls in response, but I keep Bridget's angry gaze.

There's only one way to make her understand and I grab her face in my palms, pressing my lips to hers before she can react. She struggles, but I push the past ten years into her mind and at the same time siphon her memories. Her struggles cease and she opens her mouth to tell me to stop, but the moment our tongues intertwine, her hands slide up my chest. The warmth of her surrounds me, but it's only temporary. When I pull away, tears swim in her eyes, and she pushes off me, distancing herself.

"You can't do that," she whispers, and her voice shakes. "You can't fuck with my head like that."

"Bri," I whisper. "You kept me alive, just as much as Sam did."

"Don't," she points at me.

"I'm sorry, but I left to keep you safe."

"Bullshit! You didn't do it for me. You did it for you."

I look beyond her out the window, analyzing her accusation. "You're right. I did it so I wouldn't have to see you murdered at the hands of Lucifer."

Sam nudges my hand and whines. I point to the floor. "Lie down," I say, meeting my dog's worried stare. "I'm okay, just lie down." I clarify when she doesn't move.

She lowers to the floor, keeping her eyes on me.

"I did it so I wouldn't be put in the position of sacrificing myself for you." Admitting the selfishness of my actions is humbling, and I slide my hands in my pockets, letting out a soft laugh as I study the floor. "Because that's what I would have done if he got hold of you. I would have let him rip my heart out, because it wouldn't matter anymore."

I look up, meeting her skeptical gaze and throw a shrug her way.

"You are so full of shit." She remains planted in place.

She had my memories. She knew I wasn't bullshitting her, but I also knew the depth of how hurt she was. I'd crushed her spirit when I left. She opened up to me that night, letting me see her deepest fears, her darkest times, and I slipped away in the dead of night with only a few words scribbled on paper as an explanation. I took the coward's way out.

"I still care, Bri." She shakes her head at my admission and instead of arguing with her, I look around at the modifications to the house bathed in daylight. "I like what you've done to my office," I say, avoiding her stark stare.

"Tom, you can't stay here," she says. "I can't have you anywhere near April."

I close my eyes and nod, and the emptiness creeps back in, but I understand. Affiliating with me is a death sentence, at least while Lucifer walks the earth. "Okay."

I turn to leave, picking up my bag.

"Tom," she whispers, and I glance over my shoulder at her. "I stopped caring a while ago."

I huff a laugh. "You're as bad a liar as I am." I don't wait for a response, instead I snap my fingers and Sam is at my side. I cross the threshold into the cool morning air with no clue of where to go next.

Angel Fury Chapter 4

I STAND AT THE front door of the house I grew up in and glance down at Sam standing at my side. I have no idea how welcomed I'll be, or not, and I raise my hand to knock. The door opens before my knuckles hit the wood.

My brother, CJ Ryan, stands on the other side, with that mischievous sparkle in his eye. He hasn't changed one bit since I left, and that old flare of envy blooms.

"Val and I took bets as to how long you'd stand out here," CJ says, and he breaks into a broad smile, pulling me into a hug.

I return the welcome. "You might not be so happy to see me after we talk," I say as the hug breaks.

His smile falters, but the moment his gaze drops to my side, it's back.

"Who's this?" he asks, crouching.

"Sam. She's been with me since before I got to Detroit."

CJ looks up with a smile. "Good choice in names," he says and puts his hand out.

Sam tentatively takes a sniff and then allows CJ to pet her. Valerie stands, leaning on the doorjamb to the kitchen, and she gives me a nod of acknowledgement. But there is something just below the surface. A warning of sorts.

"He's here, isn't he?"

CJ stands and sighs. "Yes."

I close my eyes and hang my head, shaking it slowly before I meet my brother's gaze. "And you're still happy to see me?"

"Hell, yes, I'm happy to see you. You're my brother and I haven't seen you or talked to you outside a random text in ten years. I missed you, bro," he says and the sincerity in his eyes and the purity of his aura tell me all I needed to know. "Don't just stand there, get your ass in here," he says, yanking me inside.

I step inside, dropping my bag on the floor. "You have a couple of bowls so I can feed Sam?"

"Sure," Valerie says, and turns away into the kitchen.

I unzip my duffel bag and pull out the dog food, bringing it with me to the kitchen. I slow to a stop halfway to where Valerie has two bowls in her hand. Three kids sit at the breakfast nook with workbooks open in front of them. A boy and two girls. The boy is readily identifiable. He's CJ's doppelgänger, much like CJ was our father's.

The girls are a few years younger, but all three kids have the same features and the bright, almost blinding auras.

"You had twins?" My gaze snaps to CJ, and he smiles.

"Kids, say hi to your Uncle Tom," CJ says as I take the bowls from Valerie. "Tom, this is Alex, Amber and Arianna."

"Hi," I say and pour a bowl full of dog food. "This is Sam." I add water to the second bowl and set it on the floor before standing and facing them.

I get the smiles and hellos of children trying to be polite, and a pang hits. I should have been around to see them grow up. Instead, I was running around the world closing portals.

Beyond the children, sitting on the couch, is Michael and the glare he sends in my direction makes me stay close to Sam, where I feel reasonably safe.

"He will not harm you," CJ says quietly, so only I can hear.

I huff and meet my brother's gaze. "I think you might underestimate just how pissed he is at me."

"Come on," CJ says to me and heads for the door at the opposite side of the kitchen, leading to the finished basement.

I glance at the group, send a strained smile, and follow my brother downstairs. The playscape I remember gave way to a sectional and gaming controls and an arts and craft table in the corner.

CJ takes a seat, studying me, and now that we were alone, his smile has disappeared. I take the cushion opposite him.

"Before you say anything, I need to thank you. You gave up a hell of a lot to go out there and do my job for me. I can't begin to repay you."

"But I fucked it all up," I say.

He laughs, shaking his head. "No. They fucked it up by not telling us all this shit." He points at the ceiling, and I catch the burning anger underneath his calm exterior. "They told me I had to close the portals and they never once said to make sure Lucifer was there when I closed the last one. I shut Michael down on that. Yes, he's pissed, but it's not your fault."

I stare at CJ and press my lips together. "He didn't tell you he's locked here, too, did he?"

CJ blinks and leans back in the seat. The confusion written in his features tells me he does not have the full story.

I choose my words carefully. "Michael tried to... steal the grace inside me."

The clarity of what that means slams home in CJ and his jaw tightens.

"I lost control," I add with a shrug. "Paradise Cove is no more."

He's still reeling from my confession when I add. "Did you know I'm a father?"

His entire form sinks into the cushions and CJ rubs his face, collecting his thoughts.

"I didn't know about Paradise Cove," he finally says, and meets my gaze.

My muscles tighten, and I close my eyes at the burn. "And you didn't think to tell me I had another daughter?"

"Would it have made a difference?" He crosses his arms and sends me that challenging raise of his eyebrow.

I bite down on the automatic yes that wants to come out, because it's as much of a lie as Bridget telling me she no longer cares. Finally, I shake my head because if I had known, it would not have changed my course.

"I figured, why give you something else to kick yourself over."

While it irks me, I understand CJ's rationale. The jangle of Sam's collar pulls our attention to the stairwell, and she comes trotting over, settling at my feet.

CJ smiles. "What possessed you to get a dog?"

I shrug and lean down, running my hand over her soft fur. "I figured I needed something to keep me from becoming suicidal." I meet CJ's gaze. "It probably was a good call; otherwise, I would have died in Death Valley."

CJ cocked his head. "The crater?"

I chuckled. "Yeah. That was the only time Lucifer appeared. Instead of using my head, I had no strategy and no control over the emotional turmoil, and he nearly killed both of us."

Sam shifts to a sitting position and lays her head on my knee. I scratch behind her ears. Her tail slowly sways in contentment.

"I carried her ten miles to the nearest town and then spent the next year in physical therapy."

CJ's eyes widened. "And you didn't think to call us?"

"Oh, I thought of it. Every time I had to figure out how to put clothes on with my shoulder in a fucking cast, but I sucked it up. I had a lot of time to kill and some serious therapy to get back into fighting shape. Instead of just wallowing in my pain, I used the time and enrolled in a flight course."

"Really?" CJ asks, but he isn't mocking me, he's impressed.

"Yep. I earned a private pilot's license." It's something I'm proud of, and it's something my brother doesn't have.

"So, when are you buying a plane?"

I laugh. It would be like CJ to ask that question, and we both have that kind of money to spare, but I hadn't considered buying a plane, not when I have Ted Beaumont's private jet company on speed dial. "I haven't put much thought into that," I answer.

"You should. Think of all the exotic places you can take Bridget whenever you want to." He grins and sends a wink my way.

"I can go anywhere right now; all I have to do is pick up the phone. And as far as Bridget is concerned, she's still pissed at me," I say, and CJ laughs.

"Yes. I hear about how much of an asshole you are every time she's here. But don't let that discourage you. Underneath all that spitfire, she is still in love with you. The question is, do you feel the same?"

"I don't know. It's been ten years."

His eyes narrow and I feel the tickle in my mind.

"Bullshit. She's been on your mind almost the entire time you were gone."

"It's a moot point. She wants nothing to do with me and she certainly doesn't want me anywhere near April until after the threat is gone. I don't blame her, either. Seems I'm a walking death sentence, or hadn't you noticed?"

"Cut the pity party shit." CJ leans forward in the seat. "You didn't screw up by leaving to do what you needed to. That's something that, while hard to digest, is forgivable. Where you did screw up was excommunicating yourself from all of us." He takes a deep breath. "Both Valerie and I get it. We've been casualties of Lucifer's before, and know what kind of focus it takes to commit to the quest you were given by default. It should have been me out there, but I couldn't leave my family, especially after what happened to yours."

"CJ, he's coming for us. You know that, right?"

CJ nods and glances down at the floor. "Yes, I know that. I have two daughters that are on his acquisition list." He snaps his gaze to mine and there is an underlying controlled fury there. "And he's been powering up for the confrontation."

"He's been killing angel blood again?"

"Yes, and he's obliterated the list."

I can't help my jaw from falling open. There had been hundreds of names on that list, but considering I hadn't had a run in with him for almost eight years, perhaps I should have been able to make that educated guess. "Is that why Paige and Austin are here in York?"

CJ gives me a nod. "If you hadn't been such a stubborn jackass, and had returned my calls, you would know all this."

I concentrate on petting Sam for a few minutes, trying to calm the nerves bundling in my stomach. CJ's reproach is not without credence. He has every right to be as pissed as Bridget is.

"I'm not," CJ says quietly, pulling my gaze to his. "I am just glad you're back. For purely selfish reasons, of course," he smiles.

"Yeah, you don't want to be the only one tasked with everyone's safety."

His smile deepens and he shrugs. "It's been tough. There isn't anyone else who can do it besides you."

I study him, reading into his words. "None of your kids..." I can't finish the sentence. I naturally assumed they'd inherited his gifts, but the slow shake of his head unnerves me. It means that he and I are the only ones with the ability to stand up against Lucifer.

"If we fail..." He stops, keeping eye contact.

"It means the end of times." My words produce a shiver in both of us.

Angel Fury Chapter 5

"GUYS?" VALERIE'S VOICE CALLS down the stairs. I glance at my watch. CJ and I have been shooting the shit for hours.

"Yeah, hun?"

"I need you on grill duty." Valerie pokes her head around the stairwell corner.

"Sure thing," CJ says, getting to his feet.

"I naturally assumed you were staying for dinner," she says to me as we approach the stairs. "I also assumed you might need a place to stay tonight, so I made the bed in the guest room."

"Thanks," I say, and offer her a strained smile.

CJ passes her and heads upstairs, with Sam on his heels, but Valerie stops me with a hand on my arm. She glances over her shoulder to make sure CJ is out of hearing range, and then she brings her hard stare back to mine.

"You and I need to get something straight."

"What's that?" I ask, thinking she was going to tell me I was not welcome in her home after everything I have done.

"You don't ever skip town without talking with your brother, you hear me?"

I blink at her and raise my eyebrows.

"You may be fine on your own, but CJ was a fucking mess, and I'm not dealing with that again, you understand?"

I just nod.

"And you'd better get shit straightened out with Bridget." Her finger pokes my chest.

"I thought..."

Her glare shuts me up. "I was angry at first. Raven was my best friend. I shouldn't have judged you, but I did. I thought you were being a self-centered jackass." She shrugs. "But after you left, I got to know Bridget a little better, and I think Raven would approve."

"Oh." I'm not sure what else to say and her gaze softens. She pulls me into a hug.

"It's good to have you back," she whispers and steps away, heading upstairs, leaving me humbled.

Sam sticks her head around the corner and just stares at me.

"I'm coming," I mutter, and climb the stairs. I need a second to put on a smile and cheery disposition for the kids. When I step into the kitchen, I scan the family room. "Where did Michael go?"

"I asked him to go visit with Naomi," Valerie says, and CJ's dimples deepened, but he kept his mouth shut.

"Didn't want a moody archangel hanging out with the kids?" I say what CJ wouldn't, and Valerie presses her lips together against a smile.

"If that guy was an archangel, where're his wings?" Alex asks and looks up from the papers spread on the counter.

"It's a long story, Alex. Finish up your homework." Valerie taps the counter. The girls have already moved to the couch and are engaged in some kid's television program.

Valerie turns to me. "You have still not learned to self-regulate what comes out of your mouth." Valerie's tone is scolding, but she's laughing at the same time.

"Guess not," I say, and heat fills my cheeks. "Can I help with anything?" I ask, waving at the food prep on the kitchen counters, while CJ grabs the plate of burgers and heads out into the backyard.

"I'm almost done, but if you want to set the table, you can."

"Sure," I say, and cross to where the silverware drawer had been in the old house. I find a utensil drawer instead.

"Over here," she says, and points to the drawer on the inside of the breakfast bar.

"Thanks." I gather the appropriate number of forks, knives and spoons for six of us. "The dining room table?" I ask, pointing to the front portion of the family room where the table sits.

"Sure," she says and continues to build an appealing salad.

I set the table and then slide onto one of the bar stools at the breakfast nook, next to my nephew. "How's Naomi," I ask, finally voicing the question I dreaded asking.

Valerie meets my gaze and before she answers, she glances at Alex sitting next to me and I get that this conversation is best reserved for after the kids are in bed. "She's good."

I glance at the papers Alex has strewn over the counter and recognize my brother's blocked script. With just a raise of an eyebrow, Valerie answers my question with two words.

"Home schooled."

"Really?"

"That common core crap is making the kids stupid," she says, and I let out a laugh. "My kids are already reading at a high school level, and Alex is doing advanced math. They wouldn't be doing that in the public grade schools," she adds, and I catch pride radiating from her.

"Well, they are CJ's kids," I say and she gives me that look again. "No offense. I know you're smart, but he's a genius. Seems logical his kids would excel in the same way."

"Dad's a genius?" Alex asks looking between us.

"He didn't tell you that?" I meet his inquisitive stare. "Your dad qualifies as Mensa, just like your grandfather did."

Alex glances at her mother and she nods.

"CJ has a pretty tough curriculum, too," she smiles. "Naomi's kids had some… challenges with it and they went to York High last year instead of sticking with CJ."

"Huh." I can't help the grunt. It seems to me, Naomi would have a difficult time letting her kids out of her sight, but I keep my narrative quiet.

"Naomi volunteers at the school," Valerie says, catching my thoughts.

Sometimes the mind reading ability we share is a good thing and I smile at her with a nod.

"I think I'll go help your father on the grill." I slide off the chair and head out to the patio, letting Sam accompany me. The ocean breeze is more than welcome, and for the first time in over ten years, I feel like I'm home.

"You doing okay?" CJ asks as he glances at me.

I stare at the familiar rock wall and the ocean beyond, and nod. "Yeah. At least for the moment." We both watch Sam sniff the property, do her business in the far corner garden, and trot back, like she'd just delivered a package of gold.

"I'll clean that up," I nod toward the corner.

"At least she went in the garden. Remember cleaning up the landmines all over the yard with Dad's dog?"

"Yeah, and it sucked when we missed some. Inevitably, someone would land in it when we played football here."

CJ belts out a laugh. "You remember that time when Bear slid right through a patch of crap? He was covered in it."

My laughter joins him at the memory. That was long before our senior year, when everything went to hell. It's one of my fonder high school memories and the entire team had ended on the ground laughing while Bear stomped around covered in German Shepherd shit and swearing at the top of his lungs.

"He had to have been a shit magnet," I laugh, because if memory serves me correctly, he was usually the one who found the missed piles in our yard.

CJ glances at the slider, still laughing. "You gotta watch the language, okay?" he asks once he winds down.

"Sure." It's been forever since I had little ears around, and I'll have to attempt to keep my language clean.

CJ opens the grill and flips the burgers one last time, laying cheese slices on all but one. He closes the top and glances at me with a smile. A few seconds later, he opens the top and transfers the meat from the grill irons to the plate.

The minute the sliders open, the kids run to the table, where Valerie has already garnished the plates with salad and French fries. CJ flips the burgers onto the waiting rolls and we all take a seat. I don't remember the last time I had a home grilled burger, and as I sink my teeth through the juicy meat, I close my eyes.

"This is the best damned burger I think I've ever had," I mumble around the bite glancing between CJ and Valerie. They both smile at me and between both of them, I hear "language," in my head. "Pardon my language, kids, it's just I haven't had a real hamburger in years."

Their eyes grow as big as saucers.

"I've been all over the world, and I can honestly say, I missed this." I focus on eating the rest of the meal on my plate, while what I assume is normal dinner chatter resumes. It's more of a drill on what the kids learned today before the conversation transitions to tomorrow and Valerie's work schedule.

"How long are you staying?" one of the girls asks, and I can't remember which one she is.

"Just a couple of days until I can find a place," I say.

CJ's eyebrow rises. "You can stay as long as you'd like. We've got enough room."

Instead of thanking him for the offer, I turn to Valerie, because it's really in her court. My brother would offer me a place to stay if they lived in a one-room shack. I don't want to impose, but I hadn't really thought through living arrangements at all when I decided to come home.

I no longer have a house of my own in York. I never stayed around to see the final rebuild of the house on Nubble Road, and when Austin texted to ask if I knew of any decent rental properties, I offered a rent-to-own contract on the house. They are more than halfway through the contract now.

I had figured the couch in my office was my best bet for the time being, but Bridget made it perfectly clear she didn't want me under that roof. Besides, my private office is gone, and that portion of the house acts as the living area for Bridget and her daughter.

I suppose I could see if my house on Lake Wentworth could be opened, but I really don't want to be that far away from the family, with everything I learned in the last twenty-four hours. So, it is either impose on CJ, or find a hotel.

She sends a soft smile in my direction. "CJ's right. You're welcome for as long as you'd like."

I look at the child who asked the question. "Do any of you mind if I stay here for a while?"

The girls emphatically shake their heads, their auras flared with welcoming golden light, and I sigh, glancing at the only one at the table who hasn't weighed in. Alex remains quiet as he picks at his food. I wait, even though I hear his internal dialog, weighing the options.

He finally raises his eyes to mine. "It's dangerous having you here, isn't it?"

"Alex," CJ snaps, and I put my hand up, silencing him.

"I got this," I say to my brother, before turning towards Alex. "Yes. It is. The reason I left when you were a baby was to protect you and your family. I thought I was doing that, but unfortunately, I didn't have all the facts, and may have made things worse for everyone." I glance around the table. "There are two furious archangels out there. You had the pleasure of meeting one today. He was the nice one, but I still think he wants to kick my a… butt." I correct my use of words at the last moment. "Michael won't hurt any of you," I add, to calm their growing fears.

"And the other one?" Alex asks.

I trade a glance with CJ.

"The other one isn't so nice." I say, watering down the truth to a palatable child's level. "So, yes. It is dangerous having me here."

"Why do they want to hurt you?" Amber asks from the other side of the table.

I inhale and slowly exhale. "Because your uncle stole something of theirs and they want it back."

Eyes all around the table widen and I wondered just how wide they would get if the kids knew I murdered my best friend to steal that something.

"Why don't you just give it back?"

I laugh a little. "I can't. It's kind of... inside me," I say.

"You could give Michael his back." Valerie's quiet comment pulls my attention to her.

"Really, we want to talk about this now?" CJ says, but neither Valerie nor I are paying attention.

He can help. Her silent communication echoes in my head.

He'll smite me the moment he has it back. I killed his nephew, and I'd do the same damned thing if I were in his shoes. I transmit, keeping her gaze.

Her color pales a fraction, and she trades a glance with CJ before addressing the kids. "Your Uncle Tom is kind of like Flynn Rider from Tangled."

"He's Eugene?" both Amber and Arianna say at the same time.

I can't help the smile that comes to my lips. That was one of Hannah's favorite movies, and we had seen it so many times that both Raven and I could drop quotes from the movie without so much as a blink. "I've never been compared to a Disney character before," I say, and Valerie smiles as well.

Even Alex is smiling. For a kid who's almost eleven, he certainly acts a hell of a lot older.

"If you stay, Sam stays, right?" Alex asks.

"Yes. Sam goes where I go."

He glances at my dog and then the rest of the family. "Then I guess I'm okay with it," he says.

"Well, then I guess I'm staying." I give him a pat on the back and stand, collecting the now empty plates.

"You're a guest," Valerie starts.

One glare from me, and she stops. "Let me at least feel like I'm earning my keep."

The slider opens when I'm halfway to the sink and I slow to a stop.

Naomi stands in the entry, just staring at me. Her stare is anything but friendly.

"Bath time," Valerie announces and points to the stairwell. None of the children argues, as a matter of fact, they all move up the stairs as if their lives depend on it. Valerie trades a glance with CJ and follows the children upstairs.

"Naomi," I say, and give her the slightest of nods. My hands are full of dirty dishes and my heart pounds in my throat. Sam moves to my side and a low growl emanates from her, but at least her teeth aren't bared. I can't say the same for the woman across the room.

"I heard you were back," she says. Her intentions are as clear in her mind as on her face.

"Don't," both CJ and I say at the same time, but it's too late.

Naomi launches, changing from human to tiger in mid-air and there's murder in her heart.

I don't defend myself, instead I brace for impact when Sam launches, catching Naomi mid-flight and knocking her off course. She misses me and slides into the wall with Sam's mouth wrapped around her front leg.

"Sam, back off!" I yell and transfer the dishes onto the counter, moving to intercept before Naomi turns her anger on my dog.

I catch her collar and yank.

"Drop it!" My command confuses both Sam and Naomi and she drops her grip. Blood speckles the white fur and Naomi hisses at me. Sam tries to lunge again, but I have a solid grasp on her. "No, Sam. Sit!"

CJ steps in front of me, blocking Naomi from another attack, while I try to calm Sam. When I glance back up,

Naomi is back in human form, holding her bleeding arm.

Before I have a chance to speak, something connects with my back, knocking me flat on my stomach. I roll in time to see Sam getting ready to attack the other animal in the room.

"Stay," I yell, giving Sam the hand signal before I focus on the other cat on the attack. A white tiger with wings; a memory surfaces, shocking the name from my lips.

"Grace?" I say as I scramble backwards. Her paw swats towards me and I duck under it as the breeze ruffles through my hair.

"Stop this! Right now!"

Valerie's command halts everything, and we all turn our gaze toward the stairwell. Behind her stands Alex, his eyes wide and his jaw slack.

"Don't you dare step into my home with violent intent," she says, maneuvering herself between Grace and me.

"Do you know what he's done now?" Naomi asks with a hitching breath.

"I don't give a shit what you think he's done. He's family."

"So am I," Naomi growls back.

Valerie gives her a hard glare. "It's not the same."

Naomi's jaw clenched and her gaze moved to Grace pacing in front of me, her teeth on display in a feral snarl. She does one more pass in front of me before she transitions back to human form. I stare at her angry teenage features, so different from the five-year-old I left behind. All the forgiveness she had given back then is gone, replaced with a hostility that borders on hatred.

"He fucking closed Paradise Cove," Grace yelled. "Now I can never see my dad again!"

Valerie moves her gaze to mine. There is a measure of shock there, but she recovers after a moment.

"First of all, you watch your language under my roof... understand, young lady?"

Some of the fire in Grace calms, and her gaze moves to the stairwell where Alex stares at her, and then her eyes drop to the floor. Her cheeks burn red, and she gives Valerie a meek nod.

While Grace is humbled by Valerie's scolding, I climb to my feet and snap my fingers for Sam. She darts to me, positions herself just in front of my leg where she plants herself on her haunches, studying the dynamics in the room as acutely as I am.

"Did you bother to find out what happened, or are you assuming Tom just did it out of spite?"

"Val?" CJ says, calling her attention before she can get truly get wound up. "Naomi needs a little help." He points to the torn skin and the blood dripping and they trade places. It's a strategic move because the doorway behind Grace is now filled with three others. Michael and Damian's sons stand just outside the open sliders, and they all carry the same fury in their eyes as Grace.

I do not want to hurt anyone, but I'm starting to quake in that familiar way I do when I'm close to losing it. CJ glances over his shoulder at me and sends one word. *Breathe.*

I huff and give him the slightest of headshakes. He hasn't seen me in action. He doesn't know what happens when this shit inside me ignites. It's devastating, and it has a tendency to spin out of control.

Valerie gives me a quick glance as well before she delivers her healing mojo to Naomi. Naomi's audible flinch nearly echoes in the room's silence, and the broken skin mends.

"You can't keep fanning this hatred," Valerie says to Naomi. "It's poison, and it's deliberate. It's exactly what Lucifer wanted when he orchestrated Damian's death. Don't you get that? This is what he wants, for all of us to be divided."

God bless my sister-in-law. She might not be a genius, but she knows more about Lucifer's subterfuge than anyone in this room does. She knows his game plan even better than CJ, and my brother shared his body with the devil for months.

"He gave Tom no choice. Even if Damian had known what he was walking into, you really think he'd sacrifice Hannah for his own skin?"

931

Naomi lowers her eye to the floor, and she shakes her head.

"You would have done the same for any of your children," Valerie's voice softens. "Whether or not you admit it, you know in your heart what I'm saying is true."

Naomi looks over Valerie's shoulder at me, and I don't shy away from her gaze. I need her to see how much I regret my actions. I need her to understand that the moment Lucifer had Hannah, I was at his mercy.

"And I'm sure there is a damned good reason why Tom closed Paradise Cove."

"Actually," I interrupt Valerie because I don't want her to defend my actions. Not when that debacle resulted from my lack of control. "It was more of a reaction than any conscious decision." Heat fills my face and I unbutton my shirt, showing the fingernail welts on my skin over my heart. "Michael..." I start and shrug, jutting my chin towards where he stands. Every adult in the room understands what the welts mean. "At least I knocked you clear of the destruction."

Alex stood still on the steps, taking all this in, and finally others in the room besides Grace and I take notice.

"You should be upstairs," Valerie says.

He just stands, planted in place and when his eyes meet mine, he says, "You killed Grace's father?"

I nod.

"So, you're a murderer and a thief?"

I trade a glance with my brother before I look back at my nephew and nod.

"I don't want you to stay here."

"Okay," I answer, and I fully understand his aversion to having me under the same roof.

"You don't get to make that decision," CJ says, pointing at Alex. "Go upstairs and check on your sisters."

Alex spins and stomps up the stairs, leaving us in the tension layering the family room. Valerie has moved into a strategic position as well, blocking Naomi from Sam and me the way CJ is blocking Grace.

"You don't need to protect me," I finally say when I realize what they are doing. "I'm perfectly capable of destroying everything on my own."

Everyone turns towards me.

"I am a living, breathing fuck up, so just stop protecting me, okay?"

I didn't realize how much anger and hostility is brewing under the surface, or the depth of my self-loathing, until this moment when it all bubbles to the surface.

"I'm not a victim," I add, glancing between Valerie and CJ. "I made the decision. The choice to damn my soul was mine, and mine alone. God help me, if I could turn back the clock, I would do the same goddamned thing, and you know what?"

Heads slowly shake.

"Hannah would still be dead."

I point at Michael. "You want your grace?" My question is framed in a growl.

"Tom," CJ has his palms facing me and his cautious tone sets my irritation switch on high.

"Let him try to take it," I snarl, as the fury swirls inside, and the dishes on the counter rattle.

It isn't until everyone takes a step back that I realize my control is shot. Sam whines, nudging my hand. I can't stay. I spin on my heel and slip by Naomi, heading for the front door with Sam at my side.

I get halfway down the front walkway, when I run into an invisible wall. My breath turns white on the cold air and I stare in front of me, counting my breaths, trying to calm the rabid beast that has taken over my soul.

"CJ, let me go," I say, once I've gotten control.

"You really want someone to kick your ass?" he asks.

I glance over my shoulder at him. "Why? You really think you have it in you?"

He closes the distance, and I turn meeting his glare.

"I never treated you like a victim," he snaps.

I let out a laugh. "You're kidding me, right? That's all you've ever done. We've never been on equal ground, CJ. You're always the fucking white knight and I'm the poor pitiful kid who needs to be taken care of, to be watched over. I've always been the victim in your eyes."

"That's bullshit and you know it," he says, and the spark of anger in his eyes matches mine.

"The only time you didn't treat me like a child was the day you transferred this curse to me, and it wasn't because you thought I could handle it. It was just so you wouldn't be alone in this. Well, great job, big brother. You put me in Lucifer's path. This shit show is yours to bear."

"You were already on Lucifer's hit list, Tom. I just made sure you had a fighting chance."

My fist swings intending to smash that smart ass look right off his fucking face. CJ blocks my swing and launches an attack of his own. All those years of being sparring partners come back to bite me in the ass. CJ knows my thought process as well as I know his, and this battle leaves both of us frustrated and unable to get a solid shot in.

The catalog of moves shuffles through my brain, and when he charges out of pure aggravation, I pull my next move from a more unorthodox defense list. I grab his shirt and plant my right foot on his hip, dropping onto my back and launching him over my head. I roll and climb to my feet before CJ catches his breath.

I step to his side, looking down at him, my breath huffs with exertion and he just lies there, staring at the stars, puffing just as hard as I am. After a full minute, he meets my gaze.

"I'm not a little kid anymore."

CJ utters a laugh. "No shit," he says and glances at the house. "We have an audience."

This is not the first time I've bested my brother. "Yeah, well, at least I finally have witnesses this time," I say and offer him my hand.

He stares at it and then up at me. "I never meant to treat you like a victim."

"I know you never meant to, but you did, whether you realized it or not." I sigh and pocket my hands since he isn't taking the offer of help.

"I'm sorry," he says and I nod, accepting his apology.

I kick at the dirt while CJ climbs to his feet.

"Lucifer orchestrated my downfall, and I walked right into it. I've had ten years to think about that night. Ten long years to figure out where I went so wrong. I had a choice, and it isn't what you think it is." I finally meet his gaze. "It wasn't the simple choice of Damian or Hannah. It was the choice of good versus evil." I keep his stare. "I chose the wrong path and there is no way back."

I shift my weight from foot to foot, looking everywhere but at him. "It's taken me a long time to come to terms with that, along with the fact I would do it again if I was presented with the same circumstances."

"It doesn't look like you've come to terms with any of this," CJ says and his eyebrows arch. "Seems to me you're still fighting."

I laugh. "Well, I've gotten to the point that I can look at myself in the mirror. Not saying I like what I see, mind you, but at least I can now look myself in the eye."

We trade a smile, and I shrug, making a calculated decision.

"Sooner or later, I'm going to be the devil's bitch. I'd rather like that to be as far off as I can possibly make it. In the meantime..." I grab him by the back of the neck while I use my other hand to extract both Michael's and Gabriel's grace from my core. CJ struggles, but by my sheer will alone, I hold him still.

The combined grace is blinding, and with both my hand and my mind, I shove it inside my brother. The transfer takes seconds, but the effect on CJ stuns me. Every cell emits light, and his eyes roll back as it engulfs him. My mental hold is the only thing keeping him upright at this moment, and I hang on while fear tears through my insides.

The lightning display surrounding us creates a tinny taste in my mouth and I'm not sure if it's just the electricity in the air, or the combination of the current along with my building fear. Flashes illuminate wings, but not the white ones I've seen him sport in the past. No, these are golden with a shine so bright I have to look away.

I have a second to wonder if the neighbors are witnessing this spectacle, and then CJ's eyes snap back in place, meeting my gaze.

"What the hell did you do that for?" he breathes, as the light encompassing him fades.

"A true trinity, with trinity grace, makes you unstoppable. Now you have everything you need to win." I step away, letting go mentally and physically. "Especially, if I fall."

He keeps my gaze. We both know what happens if Lucifer gets hold of me, but at least now it's only his grace that's subject to being ripped out of me, and not a trinity of grace like it had been a few moments ago.

"You want to let go of that mental hold you have on my dog?"

CJ's lips twitch into a hint of a smile and he gives a nod. Sam streaks across the distance, winding around my legs in a frantic display, and just like that, the tension between my brother and me is gone.

I can't say the same for the rest of the crew.

Angel Fury Chapter 6

"WHY ARE YOU LETTING him stay here?" Alex's voice echoes through the house, and I close my eyes, rolling towards the wall and covering my head with the extra pillow.

After our little spectacle outside, I'd begged off and headed to the guest room. I'd stood in the doorway and my chest squeezed. The last time I'd slept in this location was with Raven, after her father had been caught, and the memories just magnified the nothingness gripping me.

Arguments rage until doors slam, and I lift the pillow only to find Sam's wet nose in my face.

"You need to go out now?"

She licks my face and I sigh, pulling on a pair of sweats and my zip up sweatshirt. Quietly, I climb down the stairs and open the slider to the backyard. Instead of waiting inside, I cross onto the cold patio stones in my bare feet. The chill grips my heels and I move onto the grass, but that's no better. I move towards the rock wall and take a seat, leaning against one of the posts while Sam inspects the lawn.

The sliver of a moon sends light dancing off the waves and the calm cadence of the sea keeps me in place, despite the nip in the air. After a few minutes, I know I'm not alone and I turn my head, staring into Grace's bloodshot eyes a few feet away. I'm surprised

Sam didn't approach her, but then again, she doesn't have murderous intent in her posture or her mind.

I wave towards the rock wall, silently inviting her to sit with me.

"I'm sorry," she whispers.

"Don't be. You have every right to hate me."

She let a small laugh out.

"That's the thing; I can't seem to dredge up the will to hate you."

I turn my gaze back out to the sea. "That makes one of us." I let the soothing sound of the waves come between us. Finally, I sigh and look at her. "What changed from earlier this evening?"

It was her turn to look out at the ocean. "I remembered."

"You remembered what?"

"I remembered the promise I made to Hannah."

My throat tightens and I'm almost afraid to ask, but I force myself to. "What promise was that?"

"She said I needed to promise not to be mad, because what you did, you did to save me."

I chuckle under my breath at my daughter's innocence. "Grace, I did what I did to get my daughter out alive. I knew it was wrong, and I didn't care."

"If you didn't care, why didn't you give Lucifer what he wanted?"

I chewed on the inside of my lip. Sam trotted up to us and sniffed Grace cautiously, giving me a minute to figure out how to frame the answer.

"Grace, I wasn't thinking of you or your family. I wasn't even thinking of Hannah. I was thinking of myself and no one else," I say in barely a whisper. "I'm not the flawed saint my daughter made me out to be. I'm the demon in the closet."

She blinks a few times, and her expression darkens.

"If I wasn't so goddamned self-centered, I would never have risked your father's life or brought him within a hundred miles of Lucifer, despite the consequences." I offer a shrug and cross my arms. "The truth isn't pretty, sweetheart."

Her gaze narrows and her lips thin.

938

"When did you start to turn tiger?" I ask, trying to distract her building anger.

Her lips rub together for a moment and then she answers me.

"When I started my period." Her words are clipped and short.

"That must have been a joy."

My response pulls a bark of a laugh from her. "It sucked, and until today, I had successfully hidden my affliction from Alex."

I let out a heavy sigh. "It's not an affliction. It might just save your life someday."

"I'm a fucking freak."

"We're all freaks, if you hadn't noticed." I wave towards the house.

"What do you care? I thought you said you were the bad guy?"

I keep quiet and just level a stare that communicates 'really?' She shifts in her seat and flips her hair over her shoulder, slamming home a memory of what she was like at five. I can't help the smile that finds its way to my lips.

"You are about as evil as your damned dog," she says, her words loaded with teen-age attitude.

"Sam's a pussycat." I reach out and give my dog a pat.

She stares at me for a second and then laughs. This time it starts soft but soon it's the snorting kind of laughter that's echoing off the surrounding rocks.

"Shhh. You want to wake everyone?" I scold but I smile.

"You aren't the badass you pretend to be," she finally says and gets to her feet. "And at least you own your mistakes. That's rare, you know."

"So, it seems."

She takes a couple of steps and pauses. "I still miss Hannah," she adds without turning.

"So do I."

I watch her go and embrace the familiar ache in the center of my chest. I close my eyes and memories of Hannah and Grace running around this back yard roll through my mind. Their laughter still rings in my ears, and I clench my jaw against the burn at the back of my throat.

Sam nudges me.

"You about ready to go inside and catch some sleep?" The slow sweep of her tail answers and I climb to my feet, moving across the backyard at a fast pace on feet numbed by the cold.

Angel Fury Chapter 7

SAM WAKES ME AT some ungodly hour and I brush my teeth before I head out for a morning walk with her. Long Sands beach at low tide is such a relaxing walk, especially with the sun coming up over the ocean. It's reviving, and even the cool wind whipping off the water invigorates me. I forgot the sense of peace the Atlantic Ocean brings me. It's been way too long, and I can't imagine settling down anywhere else.

It's early enough on the beach to let Sam walk without her leash and I unclasp the hook. She glances up at me as if she's unsure about leaving my side and investigating the unfamiliar surroundings.

"It's okay, girl. You can check things out."

Her tail wags and I continue walking. Sam runs ahead of me with her nose to the sand before she stops, looking over her shoulder to make sure I'm still in the area. Her concern makes me smile, but I continue my leisurely gait. She stays within twenty feet of me at all times and when other dogs approach, she does a cursory sniff and then she's on her way.

"Tom?"

My gaze snaps up from Sam. A familiar face is walking towards me, but I'm at a loss for a name. I smile anyway.

"Hi," I say.

"Austin's going to shit," she says and the name snaps in place as she stops in front of me.

"How are you, Paige?" I ask.

"Pretty good. When did you get back?"

"Two nights ago."

A large and very wet Alaskan Malamute, with one blue eye and one brown eye, trots up to Paige and drops a ball at her feet. Sam slides between us, positioning herself in front of me in that protective stance I'm used to.

I reach down, stroke her head, and she looks up at me.

"It's okay, girl," I say and glance up at Paige. She has the ball in her hand and pitches it into the water. The massive dog bounds after it and Sam just watches.

"Nice dog," I say and Paige glances at Sam.

"She's beautiful," she says and crouches down offering her hand.

"Sam, this is Paige," I introduce, and she sniffs Paige's hand.

"Wow, she's really trained well," she says, looking up at me as she pets Sam.

"I guess."

"I can't get Goliath to stay by my side like she does," she says and smiles, standing while her dog comes bounding back.

"Goliath, very appropriate name." I smile and her dog finally takes notice of Sam and the sniffing begins until Sam issues a low warning growl. "How old is he?"

"Five. And we really thought he'd calm down by now, but he really hasn't." She laughs and tosses the ball again. "He has pulled me down a couple of times, but he's been good lately."

"Sam's been with me from a puppy and she's kind of kept me alive," I say as Sam nudges my hand and I stroke her head, scratching behind her ear.

"So, I imagine you were successful?" She looks out over the ocean before bringing her gaze back to mine.

"All the portals are closed, if that's what you're asking," I say and she nods slowly. "However, there was a loophole none of us were aware of."

Her pleasant smile fades. "What loophole?"

"Our, um, enemy is locked topside, so we are all still in danger."

Her face pales. "How the hell did that happen?"

I shift and shrug. "They forgot to mention that he had to be present when the last portal was closed. He wasn't, and I shut it down without knowing."

A pained sigh escapes her. "You know we barely got away with our lives, right?"

"Yes. CJ told me what happened when he contacted me about the house." I slide my hands in my pocket. "I understand Austin's a doctor now?" I deftly change the subject.

The genuine smile forms again. "Yes, and he works here in York now."

"That's what Val was saying yesterday. What about you? What are you doing?"

"I work in the Ogunquit Museum."

"Nice." I can't think of anything else to say and I shift my weight.

"We got married a few years ago." She raises her hand showing off the gleaming diamond.

"So, he finally popped the question. I wondered if he'd ever get the nerve up."

She raises her eyebrows with a laugh. "It took him entirely too long, but yes. He finally grew a pair."

I laugh and a gust chills me to the point I shove my hands in my pockets. She shivers as well.

"Well..." I start.

"You want to see the house?" she asks, pointing her thumb over her shoulder.

I never saw the finished product before I left and I shrug, even though I'm curious as hell.

"Come on, Austin will be happy to see that you're okay."

"All right," I say and she whistles for Goliath.

He trots to within a few feet and shakes the water out of his fur, spraying Paige, Sam, and me, before going to Paige. She snaps on the leash and starts up the beach. I keep pace, with Sam between us.

"Damn, that is a really special dog," she says as we reach the stairs.

"That she is," I agree and wave her forward. We follow on the narrow sidewalk until the sidewalk disappears on Nubble Road. I stay behind Paige with Sam on my right side. She never strays and I have to smile as Goliath seems to be distracted by everything he sees.

We stop in front of the property where I spent my life with Raven, before she died. The house looks completely different from the quaint cape that sat there before, and I smile at the realization of the design I worked on with the builders. The multiple roof lines of the California Bungalow style is much more pleasing than the plain lines the house used to have.

"It looks fantastic," I say.

"It's a little weathered," she says, "but outside of replacing some shingles, it's been a great place to live."

Something in her words makes me take a closer look at her. "Paige, I don't want the house back," I say, just to settle her nerves and her creased brow smooths. "I knew I was giving it up when I signed the papers."

She looks at the ground and then up at me with a small smile. "We love it here," she says and heads into the garage. "You can bring your dog inside if you want," she adds when I pause at the entry.

She towels off her malamute. The moment Paige opens the door, the dog darts inside. Sam looks up at me and I swear her eyebrows rise at the behavior of the other dog. I press my lips against a smirk and follow Paige inside.

"Austin," Paige yells. "I found an old friend of yours on the beach!"

Austin steps out from the front of the house and his aura is as bright as the rest of the angel kin. I smile and give him a head nod.

"Holy shit! How the hell are you?" he asks, crossing to me, offering his hand and I shake it.

"I'm well, thank you." I give a glance around as we step farther into the home. The kitchen is wide open to the family room, as I had arranged. I never liked the separation between rooms, and this set up was as light and inviting as I had hoped. The back wall is almost entirely made of glass and the view is just as spectacular as I remembered.

"I'm going to clean up for work," Paige says and disappears upstairs.

"That's right, you never saw the finished product," Austin says.

"No. I never did, but I have to admit, it came out much better than I ever imagined."

"Then let me give you a tour," he says, waving me farther into the house. We walk from room to room and my mind goes from pleased to remembering every little thing I did for Hannah. The familiar sadness hits when I stand outside what was to be her room. A lump forms as I scan the mural of the Disney Castle.

"We never changed the decorations in here because someday, we'll have kids," he says.

Sam nudges my hand, picking up the melancholy that drifts over me. I scratch her ear and say, "Hopefully you have girls, because that would be a little much for a boy."

He laughs and nods, taking me back to the great room. "Can I get you something to drink?"

"Nah, I'm good."

"You sure? I just brewed a fresh pot of coffee?"

I glance at the pot of liquid energy and think about my walk back to CJ's. "Coffee might not be a bad idea," I say, and step up to the island while he fixes two cups of java.

"Cream and sugar?"

"Yes, both, please," I answer, glancing out at the backyard. Hannah and I had walked through the house a couple of times during the construction, but my last solid memory here was dumping Raven's ashes over the bluff.

"So, are you just visiting?" he asks as he passes the cup.

"No, I'm here to stay. I finished closing the portals."

He smiles and his eyes light up.

"It's not all good," I reply to his reaction. "Lucifer is stuck topside. They never mentioned he had to be there when I closed the last one." I shake my head in disgust. "So, we are pretty much in the same boat as before."

He closes his eyes and his chin dips to his chest. "I thought…"

"You thought you were free and clear the minute you saw me."

He nods and meets my gaze. "He's been powering up, too."

"So, I heard." I take a sip of the coffee.

"I held off having kids because I was betting on you closing the portals," he snaps.

"Sorry." I sigh.

"I'm not snapping at you. I'm just pissed at this whole thing. We barely made it out of Dartmouth, and I've been looking over my shoulder ever since."

"I don't have a clue how many of us are left, but I know when that source dries out, he's bringing the fight here."

"Have you talked to Naomi about who on that list is still alive?"

"No. She's tracking the list?"

He nods. "Apparently, Damian set up a program that posts an alert when someone dies. She knows the exact number of us who are left, along with where we are. You should talk to her."

"I'm not sure she's going to want to talk to me," I say.

"Why would you say that?"

I open my mouth and close it, studying him. "You don't know."

"Know what?"

I run my hand through my hair. "Shit. I would think after all this time, someone would have said more about why I took off."

"After your daughter died, CJ asked you to close the portals for him," he says with a crease between his eyes.

"No one told you what happened to Damian?"

Creases appear on his forehead and his eyebrows lower in confusion. "I know he died."

"I killed Damian."

His eyes widen and he steps back.

"Lucifer wanted his grace back in exchange for my daughter's life."

Bewilderment returns and his mind circles on how that had anything to do with me killing Damian.

"Damian harbored Lucifer's grace as well as Michael's and Gabriel's. I had to steal it for Lucifer."

Still, he did not get what that means.

"I had to rip out Damian's heart and give it to Lucifer," I finally spell it out. "Not my finest moment, but once I had it in my hand, I realized if I gave it to that bastard, we would all die. So, I ate his heart instead of handing it over."

"You're shitting me," Austin says with a laugh.

"No. That's how you steal grace."

His smile fades and the color in his face pales. "You ate his heart?"

I nod. "Hannah died anyway. And CJ didn't ask me to go. I went because it was my only chance to redeem myself, but considering I fucked up by leaving Lucifer on earth, I'm still damned."

Austin slides back until he's leaning on the counter next to the kitchen sink, putting as much distance between us as he can. His clinician's mind runs down all the psychosis' he might be dealing with and I chuckle, sipping my coffee.

"I'm not crazy. I was desperate, and a desperate man will do anything to keep his child safe."

"But in your case it backfired," he says still keeping his distance.

"Yes." I stare into my coffee and again, Sam nudges my hand and I glance down at her. "I'm okay," I say and rub her head before I meet Austin's gaze. "I should go, but thank you for the information. I did not know he set up a watch system."

I turn to leave the way I came in and stop. "If we know he's coming, I'll make sure someone calls you. It might be safer for everyone to be in one place."

"Why, so he can slaughter us all in one shot?"

I glance over my shoulder at him. "No. So he doesn't slaughter you before he comes to get his grace back."

Austin gulps and I give him a sarcastic smile.

"I'll catch you later." I take my leave before I say anything else. Sam trots next to me and I move faster on the way back. Sam's a good sport and keeps up, but by the time we walk in the door at CJ's, I can tell the old girl is tired. I give her food and water, wait until she is finished doing her business outside, and settled into a light sleep before I hear movement upstairs indicating the house is just waking up.

I slip outside and cross to Naomi's, and I stand at the back door for a moment, wondering how prudent this is. Last night she wanted nothing more than to rip me to shreds. I lift my hand and knock, hoping I'm not opening myself up for catastrophe.

She opens the door and the pleasant look on her face sours. "What do you want?"

"Austin said you had a program that's tracking how many angel decedents are still alive?"

She blinks and crosses her arms before she gives me a nod.

"And neither you nor CJ told them what I did?"

She presses her lips together and looks out over the ocean, shaking her head. "We didn't think it was his business."

I let that digest a moment. "Do you know how many descendants are left?"

She nods and waves me inside. Michael is sitting in front of the computer and the tightness of his neck and shoulders screams aggravation.

"Let Tom see," Naomi says, and Michael glances over his shoulder at me before he slides the chair away, inviting me to take a closer look.

Red dots fill the map of the world. There are a few green clusters in Central America, a few in Mexico, and then a concentrated cluster in York. The number tally at the bottom reads forty-five, and the screen refreshes. Another dot turns red, and the number decreases to forty-four.

"Jesus," I whisper.

Michael glances up at me. "Even he wouldn't be able to help us now."

My gaze snaps to his and he runs his hands through his hair.

"With the rate he's going through the list, he isn't alone. He's got his guard with him, which means we have a slim chance of winning, even with giving your brother a trinity of grace."

"We have no issues toasting demons," I say and straighten.

"They aren't like any demon you've ever encountered. They are his elite guard. The oldest and strongest demons, and if they are feasting on angel blood along with Lucifer, I'm afraid your powers might not be enough."

"How long?" I nod towards the screen, and Michael gives me a shrug.

"A week. Two weeks at the most." He looks up at me. "I honestly don't know. I have no idea how fast he's been moving, so my guess is only as good as Naomi's information."

"It would take about four days of straight driving to get from Costa Rica to Maine without stopping. So, unless he wants to give up the rest of that angel blood, it's at least four days."

"He has access to a private plane," I say.

Naomi's gaze jumps to the screen and the fact that the dots are clustered doesn't settle well with either of us. He has four plane hops to decimate the bloodline before he heads to York.

"I don't know, then," she says, less certain this time.

"Well, keep an eye out and let me know when the last one goes red. That's when we will need to warn everyone."

They nod and I head back to the house. CJ's tooling around the kitchen and I take a seat at the breakfast bar.

"Why did you tell Austin you asked me to go close the portals?"

CJ stops and faces me. "Would you rather I told the truth?"

"Actually, I would. It's the same as treating me like a victim. You're making excuses for my actions. Don't."

"I'm sorry; I was just trying to avoid the conversation." He turns back to the stove and flips the egg, letting it sizzle on the other side before sliding it off onto a plate. He turns off the burner and takes a seat.

I get his aversion. No one wants to admit their brother murdered someone. It just isn't socially acceptable. "Did you know about Damian's tracking machine?" I ask, hooking my thumb towards Naomi's house.

He nods with his mouth full and takes a sip of juice. "Yeah. I was going to suggest we look at that today to see where Lucifer is right now."

"Central America. I've been over there. There are less than fifty of us now."

His eyes widen. "He's already swept South America?"

"Yes."

"Oh, man," he whispers, and stares at his food. CJ slowly pushes the plate of half-eaten eggs away. "I'm not ready for this."

"No one ever is." I give him a tight smile and file the facts about Lucifer's guards for a conversation we need to have later.

"We have a couple of days. Let me have today to get my head clear, okay?" he asks.

"Sure, what do you need from me?"

He stares at the countertop and then looks up. "We are going to need some serious groceries if we are going to be holed up in the house for the next few days."

I smile. "I can run to the store after I clean up, as long as you have a car I can borrow. I also need to run to Kittery to get some clothes."

"Sure," he says. "I'll put together a list, and you're going to need to stop at the hardware store, too, just in case."

I cock my head at him.

"You'll understand when you see the list."

"No problem. And it's okay if I leave Sam here?" Sam's head lifts at the mention of her name.

"That is no problem at all. She's a good dog."

Sam yawns and puts her head back down and I head upstairs to shower and shave.

The warm water pounds the back of my shoulders, and I take my time washing up. My nephew is still pissed that I'm staying in the house, and I can't think of what to do to turn that around. Maybe something at the store will present itself, but I'm not sure what a ten-year-old is into these days.

I climb down the stairs, and everyone is up and sitting at the breakfast bar helping CJ with the list.

"I can also pick up some movies if you'd like." I say and get a nasty look in return from Alex.

"We've got streaming movies, so that's unnecessary," Valerie says, and glances at her watch. "I need to go. Be good for your father today." She looks straight at Alex when she says it and he drops his eyes to the paper in front of him. "Love you, hon," she adds, and catches a kiss from CJ before she waves her fingers at me and disappears out the garage door.

"Here's the list, and the keys to my truck," CJ says, swiveling on the seat and holding out both items.

A quick scan of the list tells me the kids might have gotten to CJ before Valerie did, and the list of junk food covers half the page. I glance over the edge at CJ and he shrugs. Reading down the list, I get to the rock salt, which explains the hardware store. I give him a nod and start for the door. Sam gets to her feet and I turn back.

"You're staying here," I point at her. "You've earned a day of rest."

Her ears drop and she looks totally dejected, almost to the point I give in, but with the number of stores I need to hit, it wouldn't be fair to leave her in the car.

"She'll be fine," CJ says. "We'll keep her busy." He smiles and I nod, taking my leave.

AFTER LIVING OUT OF a duffel bag for years, I'm hard pressed to buy more than what can carry me over for a few days. I chuckle as I glance at my meager pile of clothes. Just a couple of pairs of jeans and a half dozen shirts are balanced on my arm, but with the shit still hanging over my head, I don't want to stock up for nothing.

The morbid thought sours my mood and I glance around the store as I wait for the next cashier to free up. Once I have my clothing and slide into the truck, I have one detour in mind, and I swing into the toy store outlet, not sure if a gift would help, but it couldn't hurt.

I debate on what to get and I travel back and forth between the boy section and the girl section so many times that finally one of the salesclerks comes to my rescue.

"Can I help you?"

"I have no idea what to get my ten-year-old nephew." I say. "And I didn't want to show up empty-handed for my seven-year-old nieces either."

He smiles and turns, leading me down a few aisles before he stops in the section with all things nerf.

He pulls down a couple of nerf guns. "You will want to get the refills because these things get lost easily. I suggest getting them for both the kids, they will have a blast."

"Really?"

"Yes. I have two girls and a boy and they constantly ambush each other."

I look at the one he hands me and then up at the others. "How about the Zombie strike one?"

"Good choice. Two?"

"Three, my brother has twins."

He brings me up to the register and checkout, and I request gift bags to go along with them. With all three packaged up, I put them in the cab of the truck with my new clothes, and then I'm on my way to the supermarket.

My cart screams party and I huff as I toss in yet another bag of chips and as I take the turn to hit the soda aisle, I bang carts with another shopper.

"Sorry," I say and look up.

"Thankfully you don't drive as sloppily as you push a shopping cart," Bridget says and I laugh. She eyes the contents and then looks at me. "Think you have enough junk?"

I turn the list in her direction. "CJ's, not mine."

An awkward tension builds between us, and she starts to navigate around me.

"Can we talk?"

She slowly shakes her head. "I can't Tom, not with what's at stake."

Her words belie the colors swirling in her aura and my jaw tightens. "You can't just write me off," I hiss under my breath.

"I have for ten years," she says and walks away with her cart as if I'm a complete stranger.

It burns, and I turn into the soda aisle, nearly pitching the boxes of soda onto the lower shelf of the cart. Eventually, she would have to listen to reason, but with the cold shoulder, today would not be that day.

I focus on the rest of the list, but just knowing she is in the store is distracting. With my cart nearly overflowing, I step into the checkout line. Bridget just happens to be in front of me and as I stack my groceries on the belt, she gives me a dirty look.

"What?" I say in response, opening my arms wide. "This is a public place, right?"

Her lips press together and the fire of anger burns in her eyes. I continue stacking, and when the cashier states her total, Bridget reaches into her back pocket, pulling out her credit card holder. She unzips it and pulls out the few cards enclosed, shuffling through them.

Flares of panic color her aura as she shuffles again and now looks in the empty pouch.

"I, um, it seems I've left my card at home," she says, as her cheeks bloom.

"I got this," I say, and pull out my card.

"No." Her glare is enough, but I hand the card to the cashier.

"Don't be difficult. This saves you a trip back," I say and the cashier ping-pongs her gaze to Bridget.

"I'd rather have to drive across the country and back than take your money," Bridget says, and the cashier's lips form a shocked 'o' before she looks at me.

"Charge the card," I say with authority, and she swipes it through the machine without any further argument.

"Damn it, Tom," Bridget says, and her hands clench into fists.

"You're welcome," I say, and she lets out a derisive huff, stomping away from the line.

The only word I catch is 'asshole,' and I glance at the cashier and her equally wide-eyed stare.

"She's a little mad at me," I whisper and finish stacking the conveyor belt.

The cashier chuckles. "I would say so." She hands me the card back and rings up my bill. By the time I get to the parking lot, Bridget is gone, and I shake my head at her angry display. I am so tempted to swing by the house and give her hell, but I have some frozen foods sitting in the truck bed that might end up as mush if I do that, so I head to the last stop.

The hardware store.

It seems rock salt is pretty scarce in late March and all I can get is the last five-pound bag, not a twenty-pound bag CJ asked for. When I pull into the garage, the first things I pull from the cab are the gifts, along with my clothing.

I cross to the coffee table where the kids are working hard and deposit the three bags right in the center. "You can open them once we have all the groceries inside," I say, before they can grab the gifts. All three pairs of eyes look up at me and then, collectively, they get up and head out to the garage to help with the groceries.

I trade a grin with CJ, and we step out, grabbing the lion's share of bags before coming back inside with the crew.

"You can't buy me," Alex mumbles, but the minute he opens the bag and pulls out the Nerf gun, I can see some softening in his hard features. "I get to shoot you with this, right?" he asks with narrow eyes.

"If you can hit me, sure." I say, and glance down at Sam as she stretches and trots over to me. "I didn't forget you," I say, and rummage through the grocery bags for the dog bones I bought.

The girls both grin at their guns and turn their gaze on Alex. "We can play zombie wars!" Amber or Arianna exclaims.

"Dad, can we stop for the day?" Alex asks, inspecting his new toy.

"Sure. Why don't you take those downstairs, though?"

He didn't need to say things twice. They grab their gift bags and bolt to the basement.

I'm thrilled they like the gifts, and I grab my clothing bag and bring it up to the guest room before I return to help CJ put the groceries away.

"What time does Val get back?" I ask as I unload the bags onto the countertop.

"Thursday's are her late day," he says. "So, she won't be home till almost eight tonight."

I glance at the clock and it's a little after two in the afternoon. "I ran into Bridget at the store. She's still pissed off at me."

"She'll get over it." CJ grabs the soda boxes and slides them into the pantry before he takes a seat on the couch, picking up the papers and a pen, correcting his kid's work.

I slide onto the couch across from him.

"I know you said you wanted today to get your head together, but there's one other thing you need to know."

He looks up from the paper, waiting for me to finish.

"I guess Lucifer is traveling with his guards. From what Michael said, they aren't like normal demons."

"And?"

"And they can't be turned to dust as easily as normal demons."

He slowly lowers the paper.

"Especially if they are drinking angel blood along with Lucifer."

"So, things might get bloodier than we expected." He leans back in the couch cushion and closes his eyes.

"Michael's worried. So, yes. I think we're looking at a serious beating."

"That's just great," he mutters, and picks up the papers again, focusing on the kid's schoolwork instead of the inevitable.

I let him have his space, but I know what I just told him is scalding his insides as much as it is mine. I stand and cross to the kitchen to find something to munch on. Nacho chips, cheese dip and a beer sounds like a good snack, so I grab two bottles and carry my bounty to the coffee table, setting one beer in front of my brother before opening the chip bag and dip.

He sends a sideways glance at the beer and then looks at me.

"What else are we going to do?" I ask when he raises an eyebrow. "Besides, it's not like it's ten in the morning."

"I can't go and get drunk. I've got three kids to watch tonight," he says.

"Relax. It's just one beer." I kick my feet back on the table and Sam jumps up next to me, laying her head on my lap.

Begrudgingly, CJ reaches out and snatches the beer, giving me the evil eye as he takes the first sip. "You could have gotten a bowl," he nods towards the chip bag in my lap.

I offer him the open end of the bag and he grabs a handful. The cheese dip ends up on the corner of the coffee table between us.

"How's the studio working out?" I nod to the closed door to the right of the television, trying to take the edge off the swirl building in his mind.

He sighs. "Good," he says. "It gives me that needed outlet, since I haven't toured in a long time."

"I saw you on an international charity telethon about a year ago," I say. I remember that one because Sam and I had just gotten back from closing a portal and had some bruises from the beasts we encountered. We had just chilled in the hotel room with ice packs and whatever I could find of interest on television. Surprised to catch the airing in the middle of China was an understatement, but it had been one of those moments that made me glad I was the one risking my ass as opposed to my brother. The world needed him more than it needed me.

Before he can comment on the wandering narrative in my head, the air shifts and the whistle of a nerf bullet whizzes by my face and hits CJ's beer dead center as he draws a sip. I turn and the arsenal of nerf comes at a clip fast enough, so my diving roll away from the couch is speckled with foam.

I stand, assessing the damage... at least a dozen of the sticky nerf arrows are now tacked on my shirt. Alex, Amber, and Arianna stand from their hiding spot behind the couch with grins so wide I have to laugh.

"We got you!" Amber exclaims.

"That's because you ambushed me," I say, pulling the darts off and offering them to the kids. Even Sam has a few sticking to her fur. I have a moment, wishing what was coming for us was as benign as these nerf darts, but I know better than to waste a wish on a lost cause.

So, for now, I decide to embrace the lighthearted mischief blooming in the children's eyes.

"You don't happen to have any of these things hanging around that we could use," I ask CJ, and he shakes his head.

"Well, then, it's time to rectify that." I put my hand out. "Can I borrow your keys again?"

CJ tosses me the keys and Sam gets to her feet. I glance at the kids.

"Alex, you feel like coming to the store with me?" I ask and he glances at his father before looking back at me. He's torn, he still doesn't trust me. "Neither of us bite," I add as Sam stands by my side wagging her tail.

After a moment of complete indecision, he nods and puts his nerf gun on the counter before following me to the truck. I open the back door for Sam, and Alex climbs into the passenger seat.

Quiet encompasses the cab, and I glance at Alex.

"I'm sorry if I disrupted your life," I start, and he just looks out the window. "I missed out on watching you and your sisters grow up."

"Why did you even come home?" he mutters under his breath.

"Because I thought it was done and everyone was safe. Guess I blew that one."

Alex narrows his eyes at me. "My dad doesn't even have a picture of you at the house."

"That's because our homes were blown up before I left town." I say. "The only pictures I have of the family are in Wolfboro."

"Wolfeboro?"

I nod. "I still have a house there. At least I think I do," I clarify. I really don't know if that house is still standing, but I would imagine my real estate agent would have told me otherwise, and I have consistently paid the upkeep bills over the years. "Your dad never took you guys over to the lake?"

Alex shakes his head.

"Well, this summer, we will have to take a trip. If I recall correctly, I have videos of when your dad and I were kids."

"Really?" His eyes spark with interest. "I'd like to see what he was like at my age."

"Your dad was always the good kid," I say and send a wink in his direction. "I was the one that dragged him into trouble."

"So, you've always been a troublemaker?" he asks.

"Kind of. But I had some bad stuff happen when I was a little younger than you are, and it screwed me up."

"Like what?" There isn't a hint of sarcasm in his question. It was asked with all the innocence of a child, and I sigh.

"I was kidnapped by a serial killer." I glance over at him. "Obviously, I survived, but that's only because of the magic your mom now holds."

He is quiet but I can hear the questions plaguing him.

"Go ahead, ask your questions," I say and glance at him. "But you might not want the answers."

"What did he do to you?"

"He practiced surgery on his victims without knocking them out."

Alex's eyes widen and his jaw loosens as he stares at me. "What kind of surgery?" His voice is small as he whispers the question.

"He cut out my spleen, and he butchered my tongue." I say. "I had to learn sign language and used my hands to talk for twenty years until my wife died and willed her tongue to me."

His horrified glance locks on me, but I don't look his way.

"I knew real monsters existed long before we ever knew Lucifer was real."

"Why didn't my dad stop him?" he finally asks.

I glance at Alex as I pull into a parking spot. "If your father had known where to find me, none of it would have happened. I didn't have this back then." I tap my temple. "And I didn't know how to get a message to him." I turn the vehicle off and stare ahead for a moment. "Are you okay?" I ask, glancing his way.

Alex nods. "I didn't know." He gives me a forced smile.

"It's okay." I mess up his hair. "Now let's go buy out the entire stock of zombie nerf guns and whatever else you think would be fun."

True to my word, we buy the remaining guns and as many refills as they have, and we head home to take this zombie war game to the next level.

By the time Valerie rolls in, the house is littered with nerf darts, some still sticking to each of us, and we are all lounging on the couch with the remnants of homemade pizza on the counter and discarded plates on the coffee table. In short, the place is a disaster, and a twinge of guilt bites me.

I rise and gather the plates, offering her a tired smile.

"Sorry about the mess," I mumble, as she takes her coat off and crosses to grab the last few pieces of pizza that we saved for her.

"I'm not upset. I know you and CJ will clean it up," she says, smiling around the pizza. "Did you guys have a fun day today?" she asks, focusing on her kids.

"Yeah," Alex says. "Uncle Tom got us all nerf guns and we played zombie war most of the day."

She glances my way with a nod of approval and I smile. My nephew still has some reservations about me, but today did a great deal to thaw some of the frosty attitude.

Overall, it was a good day, and right now, I'll settle for as many of these as I can rack up before hell comes knocking on our door.

Angel Fury Chapter 8

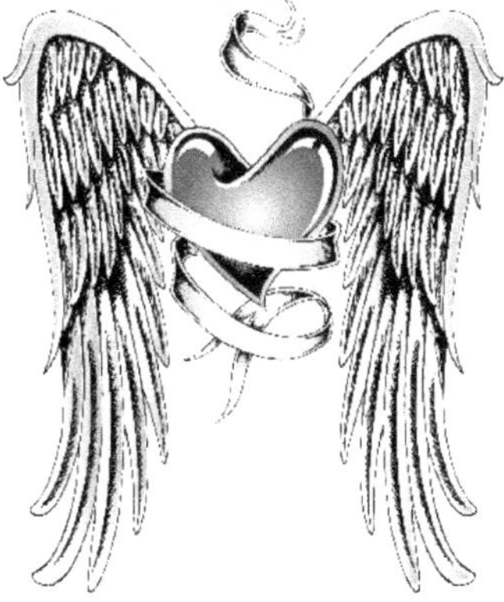

THE NEXT MORNING, I wake before anyone else and tinker in the kitchen, making a pot of coffee. The light knock on the door interrupts my morning stupor and I look around as if I expect someone else to answer it.

No one else is awake.

The second round of knocks comes, and I slide off the bar stool and cross to the door, pausing a moment to do a security scan with my mind. What I find on the other side makes me yank the door open.

Bridget meets my bewildered gaze.

"I, um, I just came by to say thank you for helping me out at the grocery store yesterday. I'm sorry I was such a bitch," she says and shifts her feet. When she tries to hand me the cash to cover the bill, I shake my head.

"Look, you don't have to pay me back and you certainly don't have to apologize to me," I say and open the door wide for her. "If you want to pay me back, why don't you just come in and have a cup of coffee with me and we can call it even."

Her eyes dart from the kitchen entry and back to me.

"No one's up yet," I answer her unspoken question. "It's just me and Sam puttering around the kitchen. How about that cup of coffee?" I wave toward the back of the house and after a moment of hesitation, she crosses the threshold.

"I just didn't expect you…" Her hands flutter towards my open shirt as she speaks and she can't seem to find the words to finish her sentence. Her entire demeanor amuses me.

"Why are you nervous?"

A high-pitched laugh escapes and I close the door behind her, placing my hand on the small of her back to guide her into the kitchen. Just the touch spreads warmth through me and she glances down at the contact, and then her gaze lands on my lips for a brief second before finding my eyes. Her aura is a chaotic mess, including flares of iridescent pink, and she just shakes her head at me.

I drop my hand and a chill builds between us.

"I shouldn't have sprung April on you like that," she says and takes a seat at the breakfast bar.

"I probably should have called first," I admit and grab a mug for her coffee. I fix it from memory and slide it across the marble to her. I figure if I keep the stone between us, I won't be tempted to screw this up by making a move that really isn't welcome.

"You should have called a long time ago."

"I walked right into that, didn't I?"

She doesn't answer. Instead, she just takes a sip of her coffee and her gaze travels down to my bare chest. I can almost feel her caress as her eyes move lower to the waistline of my low riding sweats. Suddenly, she looks away and takes a deep breath.

Now, all I can think about is that last night before I left. I'm trying like hell to concentrate on this moment, but my brain keeps going back ten years to how she tasted under my lips.

"Damn it," I mutter and shake my head, trying to drive the thoughts away, but it's difficult since that memory ran through my head at least a dozen times a day since I left. By now, it was over-glorified, embellished with enough fantasy to confuse what was real and what was my brain making up shit just to grasp onto her, and each revisiting of that night drilled feelings for Bridget farther into me, deeper than I ever anticipated.

"What?" she asks, leaning away from the counter, her eyes now guarded.

"I really want to get this countertop dirty."

Her mouth pops open and her cheeks flare pink.

Heat fills my face as well, because when I went to answer her, those were *not* the words forming in my head.

"I'm sorry. That was crass." I take a physical step back as well, trying to distance myself from the swirl building in all the wrong places. The laugh that breaks loose isn't my normal one; it's too high and shaky. "I didn't mean for that to come out..."

Now it's her turn to suppress a smile, but dimples make a brief appearance.

"I used to be so damned smooth," I say and my hand runs through my hair.

She loses the battle and a grin surfaces. "Not always, Casanova."

"Fuck you," I growl, now terse from this inability to concentrate. I had thought seven weeks was a long time without sex. Try ten, almost eleven years, and now I was acting like a complete moron.

Her smile fades as my catalog of memories sweep through her mind. She straightens in the chair and her eyes widen. "You haven't been with anyone?"

"You haven't either."

"I had a child. I was a little busy."

"I was closing portals," I shrug, knowing it's not even in the same league, but I had to throw out some kind of excuse, even though it was bogus compared to hers.

We both just stare at each other and the chaos of pinks lacing through her aura makes me want to pull her over the counter into my arms.

"So, not even a hooker?" she asks.

Now I do laugh, and glance at the ceiling, formulating my come back, but all I do is shake my head. The sad truth is I didn't want anyone else, and sometimes a hand and a memory is all you need.

"And you didn't hide... anything from me?" she balks.

"No. You have everything." I tapped my temple. *At least everything that matters.*

Her gaze drops into her coffee.

"Do I need to look a little closer at your memories?"

The speed at which her eyes jump to mine tells me maybe I do, and I cock my head, offering a smile. Her cheeks bloom and her lips part as if she is going to speak.

I circle around the counter and she turns her chair facing me. The closer I get to her, the more pronounced her breathing is, and the more pink flashes in her aura. I slow, enjoying the pursuit and the flush in her cheeks.

Her hand lands on my chest and her elbow locks, holding me at a distance, but her palm against my bare skin burns in a way I missed.

"Bri," I whisper, and the plea is clear.

"I can't," she answers, slowly shaking her head. I cover her hand with mine, holding it in place.

"I came home for you." There's nothing like laying it all on the line in one phrase, especially when it sits out there like the last over-ripe banana of the bunch.

She pulls her hand out from under mine and turns the chair towards the counter.

I'm not sure what to do with her reaction. I'm a couple of steps away from her and I close in, putting my hands on the counter on either side of her.

"I saw everything, Bri. You can't hide from me," I whisper in her ear and nuzzle her neck. "And you know damned well I'm better than any of those toys in your nightstand drawer."

Her elbow rams into my stomach so hard it knocks the air out of me, and I stumble back. She spins towards me, swinging, and I catch her arm. When she swings the other, I grab it with my free hand. Her chest rises and falls, and the fire in her eyes sparks something deep within me.

Before I know what I'm doing, I have her pinned to the wall and my mouth is on hers, our tongues dancing in all the frantic anger and frustration of the past ten years. My fingers slide from her clasped wrists down her elevated arms until I'm cupping her breast in one hand and her cheek in the other.

The kiss torches everything inside of me, disintegrating time until her teeth bite down, drawing blood. I yank back and my hand goes to my mouth, coming away with red-tinged saliva on my fingers.

"You bit me?"

Bridget wipes her mouth, staring me down. "You cannot just take what you want."

I step back; every fiber of my being still tingles with her. Distancing myself, I take a few more steps back and run my hand down my face. It takes a few moments, but I realize just how wrong that was.

"You are right. I have no idea what..." I trail off and turn away. "I'm sorry."

"Jesus, Tom. What the hell is wrong with you?"

I let out a laugh. "What is wrong with me? Where do you want me to start?" I slide into the nearest chair and reach for my forgotten coffee.

The scrape of the chair next to me pulls my attention and Bridget settles into the seat, picking up her coffee again. She doesn't look at me; instead, she just nurses the coffee.

"I can't let you in if you're going to go off on another suicide mission," she finally says.

"I'm not going anywhere."

Her gaze rises, meeting mine. "Do you know how many gallons of angel blood the devil has consumed?"

Her left field comment makes me shrug. "What does that have to do with this?" I point between us.

"You're going to make a stand with your brother, aren't you?"

I lean back in the seat, away from her. "I don't have a choice. Not if I want to have a life."

"He's powered up, Tom. More so than what you hit in Death Valley." She taps her temple and her hand lands on the shoulder that kept me in physical therapy for months on end. "And he nearly killed you; imagine what he will be like at full strength?"

"He won't be at full strength. I have his grace and this is our turf. Mine and CJ's. It isn't a devil's gate."

She sighs and her hand falls off my arm and grasps her coffee cup. "I can't let you in." She shakes her head slowly.

She's trying to convince herself more than me.

"Hope is a powerful weapon, Bri," I say, and sip my lukewarm coffee.

She huffs at me. "I lost the luxury of hope the moment I gave birth to your daughter. Now, I have to be practical and think of her safety above everything else."

"So, the way we both feel doesn't matter?"

Her eyes narrow. "What is it you think you feel, Tom?"

"Love."

"That's just priceless," she leans back in the chair, slinging her arm over the back. "If you are so in love with me, tell me one thing?"

"What?"

"Why are you still wearing your wedding band?"

I look down at my left hand, at the wedding band my dead wife, Raven, had given me. From the moment she slipped it on my finger until now, I had never removed it from my left hand. She's been dead for almost eleven years, and it never crossed my mind to take it off.

"I just..." I have no idea what to say, and I have a feeling words would mean shit to Bridget right now. Instead, I slowly work it off and place it on the counter between us.

She stares at it and then brings her gaze to mine. A measure of shock is displayed in her irises, and in the slight part of her lips. I smile at her.

"You didn't think I'd do that for you," I say, and she slowly shakes her head. "When are you going to believe in me?"

Her eyes blink rapidly. "I believe in you."

It's my turn to laugh. "Yeah, like you were so convinced I'd talk to Damian about hiring you," I say, using a name I hadn't spoken of since I left.

"Well?" She cringes and looks away.

"And you don't think we can win this battle," I add.

She bites her lip, meeting my gaze. "Even without his grace, isn't he... supercharged like you and CJ?"

I open my mouth to answer and snap it closed. When Lucifer had his grace, he was supercharged beyond our combined powers, and on his own turf, he still had that spark, but I didn't know what kind of damage he could do on our turf without it. Michael certainly was more fragile without his, and he did not exhibit any psychic ability outside of Paradise Cove.

"I don't know what he's capable of without grace and outside the confines of a portal."

"Exactly my point."

I stare out the window at the ocean, weighing her remark. I know we are in for a nasty fight and there could very well be a line of casualties before it's all over. The likelihood I would be one is pretty high, considering what I harbor. Still, I can't help but latch onto that last sliver of hope. Hope kept me breathing, kept me moving for all these years.

"Do you love me?" I blurt, because while I feel it in her mind and her memories, I need the confirmation that this battle is worth the fight.

"What *I* feel does not matter. Don't you get that?" She slams her cup down on the counter and slides off the chair heading towards the front of the house.

I jump off my seat and follow her, grabbing her arm before she reaches the door.

"Bridget," I start, and she turns towards me.

"Don't, Tom. I saw what that bastard did to Hannah, and I saw the police report after your wife died. I know enough to scare the living shit out of me. I cannot..." She shakes her head. "...I will not put April in the same kind of danger."

"Do you love me?" I ask with more force.

Tears frame her lashes, and her jaw tightens. "Yes, goddamnit. I love you, you son of a bitch." She rips her arm from my grip and stomps out of the house with the slam of the front door.

Angel Fury Chapter 9

I STEP BACK INTO the kitchen after Bridget's hasty exit.

"You don't think Lucifer already knows you have another child?" Michael's voice startles me, and my gaze snaps to him.

"Excuse me?"

"If I was aware of your spawn, you can bet Lucifer will have already been apprised of that information as well."

Even his tone is condescending, and my fists curl at the need to punch the disgusted grimace right off his face.

He steps to the breakfast bar and bends out of view. When he straightens, he has a purse in his hand and looks beyond me. I glance over my shoulder, right into Bridget's wide eyes. I hadn't heard the front door open back up.

She sidesteps by me and crosses with all the attitude she left with, including a glare that matched mine.

"I would prefer if you didn't refer to my daughter as spawn," she snaps, and plucks her pocketbook out of Michael's hand.

"Do you know who I am?" he asks, puffing out his chest like a self-absorbed jackass.

She narrows her gaze. "You're the asshole Tom locked out of heaven."

I can't help the yelp of a laugh that escapes my lips and I cover my mouth. She hauls the strap over her shoulder and juts her chin out at Michael.

"I am the archangel Michael," he growls and pumps his chest up some more. "And you had better watch your tone."

She purses her lips at him but doesn't cower in the least. "You had better watch your tone with me." She flips her hair over her shoulder in a challenge, and then both hands find her waist.

It's the damnedest thing to watch, and I didn't think I could adore the woman anymore than I did when she walked out the door a few moments ago. But now, now, I need her on my side, backing me up.

"Tell me something, almighty archangel. Is Lucifer as impotent as you are?" She wiggles her fingers at him as she asks the question.

His hand moves to clasp her throat and stops an inch from her skin. Sam's growl overshadows Michael's and my hard warning glare makes him take a step back.

"My brother does not have the same limitations as I do," he says. "Especially with the amount of angel blood fueling him."

"Just as I thought," she spins on her heels and starts to leave.

"The safest place for you and your daughter is here," Michael says before she can march by me. I meet her gaze before she turns back to Michael.

"Why? So, we can live like fugitives? Hiding away until the devil walks in to kill us all?"

Michael blinks at her brazen response, and then raises his gaze to mine.

"He has a point," I say softly and look down into her hazel eyes. "If you and April are here, we can keep you safe."

"I don't need to be protected," she says.

"Your daughter does, and so does your friend Austin. They are the last of the angel blood outside of this compound." He points to the ground in front of him.

A chill swirls in my blood and I stare at him. "Already?"

"It made the international news." He hooks his thumb towards the dark television screen. "They were slaughtered."

The hourglass just turned, and the sands are sliding through at a pace I'm not sure either CJ or I are ready for. I turn my gaze to Bridget, sending a silent plea with my eyes.

"You can't watch us twenty-four-seven," Bridget says to me, ignoring Michael.

"Please." It's all I can drum up at the moment.

"The timing could be hours or days, depending on how Lucifer is traveling." Michael's narrative is irking me, and I send him a glare to shut the hell up.

"Michael's right," CJ says from the stairwell, pulling our gazes to him. "Hi, Bridget," he adds with a hint of a smile.

"Hey," she returns the salutation.

"I think it's time to assemble everyone on this side of the fence," he says. "Because otherwise, my brother will go off and do something devastatingly stupid to save you and April." He gives us both a soft smile, cocking his eyebrow, challenging me to say differently, but he's right.

"You and April can have the guest room upstairs and I'll stay on the couch in the basement."

"What about Paige and Austin?" Bridget asks.

"I believe Naomi has an extra guest room they can use until this is over." CJ says and looks to Michael. He gives a confirming nod.

I turn to Bridget and see the skepticism layered in her gaze and the tight set of her lips.

"Bri, having you here is better than having you vulnerable across town. I promise I'll give you your space."

"I can't just pull April from school. That's insane."

"She can join my home school program," CJ answers, knocking down another one of Bridget's arguments.

"You can make the choice. But he's right. You already know what I would do if Lucifer gets his hands on either you or April."

"Don't put that on me," she snaps.

"I can't survive another slaughtering of those I love."

"And you think I can?"

I keep eye contact with her. "You are stronger than I am."

"Bullshit," she hisses and takes her leave.

I follow her out onto the front walkway, catching up with her.

"Did you orchestrate that bullshit?" She points at the house, still moving towards her car.

"No. I didn't even know you were coming by." I grab her arm before she can open her car door. "Do not go."

She hesitates and looks at me.

"I can help you grab stuff from home and we can pick up April at school and bring her here. Please, this is the least I can do for the two of you." She rolls her eyes at me, and I continue, "When this is all over, I will honor whatever decision you make about having me in your life, but until then, for the love of God, let me keep you safe." Even I can hear the desperation in my plea, and Bridget sucks in her lower lip before she takes a deep breath.

"April does not know you are her father."

"I won't say a word. We can make up some bullshit excuse about the agency being a target, and we can say I came back to warn everyone. That could explain away my sudden appearance as well."

She cocked her head, narrowing her eyes at me. "You're pretty good at that," she says.

"At what?"

"Thinking up excuses on the fly."

I laugh and cross my arms against the chill in the morning air. "Yeah, well, my brain works on overdrive when I'm desperate."

"Ah," she says, and a smirk appears. "Are you planning on wearing that?"

I look down at my open flannel shirt and sweats and then back at her. "If it means you'll stay with us, I'll wear anything you want me to."

Her eyes sparkle with mischief. And I know I will live to regret those words, but I don't care. Even if she makes me put on a dress and high heels, it's worth it if she and my daughter are safe.

"Go put some jeans on. I'll wait here for you."

I smile and turn, jogging back inside while she waits by the car. My wardrobe choices are slim, and I grab one of the new pair of jeans I bought yesterday, buttoning and tucking in the shirt I already have on. I slide my bare feet into the pair of flip-flops I have at the top of my bag, instead of trying to find a matching pair of socks for the shoes.

Sam wags her tail as I lumber down the stairs. "Stay," I say to her, and you would have thought I just took away all her toys, but I didn't stop to reassure her. I kept my course, heading back outside. I close the front door and stop short.

The driveway is empty.

Frustration burns through me, and my stomach tightens. I turn, stepping back inside and CJ is already in the living room heading towards me.

"She gave you the shaft?"

I just nod, not trusting what my response will be.

He tosses me his keys and I look at them for a second, debating. Maybe Michael was wrong, but one glance in CJ's eyes and I know I have to either convince her or kidnap her.

"Thanks," I say and turn, heading after her, praying I don't have to do anything that will put a greater wedge between us, but deep down, I know her stubbornness is going to make that impossible.

I pull into the driveway of the office behind her car and shut the truck off, blocking her in place. I find her in the bedroom, haphazardly throwing clothes in an open suitcase on the bed, and I stand in the doorway, just watching her. The flurry in her mind is enough to make me clench the keys in my hand.

She turns with a handful of clothing and yelps at the sight of me.

"You can't run."

"Watch me," she says and throws the pile in her arms into the suitcase.

"Goddamnit, Bridget," I cross and turn her towards me. "You can't run from him. He will know you aren't here and he will find you and use you against me."

"You don't know that," she snaps.

"Don't make me control you," I warn and her brow creases.

"You wouldn't dare."

"I'm not playing games with your life. Or April's for that matter and I will be a fucking bastard if I have to be." I drop my hands from her arms. "So, take all the shots you want, but I'm not letting you go on a suicide mission." I use her words against her. "Not with my daughter riding shotgun."

"Fuck you!" She turns back towards the suitcase, trying to shovel the array of clothing into the confines of the box.

"I would rather you hate me than get hurt," I say and take a deep breath. "So, pack your bags with anything you think you might need, and then we are going to pick up April at school." As I speak, I push the command into her brain, and her mouth drops as her body obeys.

The glare she gives me tells me I've gone too far, but I don't care.

"I fight dirty, remember?" I say as she crosses in front of me and disappears into the bathroom, only to come back with her toiletries a moment later.

"I am going to make your life a living hell," she mutters under her breath as she packs the rest of her things.

Once she is done in her room, she picks up the empty suitcase and disappears into April's room. I close her bag and bring it down to the truck, tossing it in the bed before I head back to collect April's possessions.

She is nearly done with April's things, and I step close enough to reach out and tilt her chin towards me.

"I'm doing this to protect you."

She yanks her chin away from my grip and nearly throws the suitcase at me.

"Hey, I could have made you repeat the last time we were in your bedroom together," I say in my defense, and her jaw tightens, her eyes flashing a warning so deep that I look away. "So, I'm not that big of a dick."

She laughs and turns, leaving me with April's packed suitcase. I follow her downstairs and she disappears into the office while I put April's bag next to hers. Inside, I hear the scrape of metal against metal along with a stream of curses that should make me uncomfortable, but they pull my lips into a smile.

I step in the doorway and my smile fades as I stare into the barrel of her gun.

"I swear, if you don't release me, I'll blow your goddamned brains out."

"Put the gun away," I say with force, and she lets out a frustrated yell when the gun drops into a bag containing several other weapons.

"I hate you, Ryan," she hisses and the dark threads weaving through her aura, overriding what is left of the pink, supports her words, but I do not want to believe what I am seeing.

I kick the bag aside and step close. "No, you don't."

"Right now, I do!" She glares at me, and I reach out, gently pushing stray strands of her hair out of her face.

My touch brightens the pink strands in her aura, giving me that grain of hope that this could all be salvaged, with a great deal of groveling on my part. Instead of acknowledging her fury, I glance at the arsenal she's accumulated.

"I'm impressed," I say and crouch down, looking through the large bag. I pull a bow out and glance up at her, cocking an eyebrow.

"It's my hunting gear," she says. "I think your ass would make a fabulous target."

Even her sarcasm is cute, and I stow away the bow and zip up the bag. "You'll need to keep this locked up so the kids don't get into it," I say and haul the weapons over my shoulder. "You ready to pick up April?"

"No, but I have no choice, do I?"

"Unfortunately, you are correct." I open the door for her and lock up the house behind us. When I open the passenger side of the truck, she glares and climbs in. She would rather have her car, but that isn't going to happen. At least not until I can ensure she will not run away, as she was planning when I got here.

I drive to the school and park at the curb, helping her out of the truck before locking it.

"How am I supposed to explain you?" she asks as we walk to the door.

"Tell them I'm your bodyguard, because as of now, that's exactly what I am."

She glances sideways at me.

"I'll kill anything that tries to hurt you," I say in my best deadpan voice, and she slows, stopping just outside the door.

"You're serious."

I meet her stare. "I've never been more serious about anything in my life."

Instead of voicing any of the stream of thoughts flowing through her mind, she turns and enters the school without a word. I follow a few steps behind and hang in the doorway to the office instead of stepping completely inside.

Bridget adopts a pleasant voice and requests that April be sent to the office, making up an excuse of a dentist appointment. I'm surprised at the ease with which she applies the snow job, and I have a second to wonder if she's blowing smoke at me as well.

She glances over her shoulder at me and gives a small laugh, sharing comments with the school secretary. That same pink flows in miniature ribbons through her aura, and then it's gone almost as quickly as it comes.

Her aura flashes at the same time April steps out of the nurse's office with an ice pack over her eye.

"What the hell happened?" Bridget asks, waving at her daughter and addressing the school secretary.

"One of the boys hit her at recess," the secretary says. "He probably likes your daughter," she adds with a small smirk.

My protective instincts kick in, but I hold back. This is not the time or the place to make an issue of it. But as soon as we were under CJ's roof, not only would April start home schooling with CJ, she would also start learning Jujitsu, so if some other little punk tries to hurt her, she can take them down.

"Excuse me?" Bridget announces, loud enough to call the attention of everyone in the office. "Are you telling me it's okay that my daughter was hit because you think the boy might like her? What the hell kind of message is that?"

The school secretary's eyes bulge at Bridget's statement, but it is more because of her language than the real meaning of Bridget's words.

"I'm sure she didn't mean it to sound that way, because it is never okay to hit a girl for any reason," I say, interjecting myself before Bridget loses it completely. I can almost see steam rising from her. "And if she was insinuating that it was okay because the boy likes her, then perhaps she should take a hard look at the message she is conveying."

The secretary's attention is now on me, and her eyes are wide enough to see her entire irises.

I step to Bridget's side and place my hand on the small of her back, guiding her out with April's hand tightly in her grasp. We make it to the car before April takes off the ice pack and stares at me.

"Why are you here?"

"Because your mother needed a ride, and we are stopping at my brother's on the way home."

Her eyes darted to her mother.

"Uncle CJ's house," Bridget says and climbs in the front of the truck.

I open the back door and step to the side, letting April get inside. Silence prevails and I can't help but listen to the swirl of thoughts in both their heads.

"How much do you know about the business?" I ask, glancing at April in the rearview mirror.

"She knows nothing," Bridget says.

"Mom hunts ghosts," April says at the same time. "She's pretty badass."

"April!" Bridget turns, staring down her daughter with eyes wider than I expect.

"Yeah, I think she is, too," I say, and glance in the rearview mirror.

"You want to tell me what happened?" Bridget asks, still looking over the seat, bringing the conversation back to what possessed that boy to hit her.

April shakes her head.

"You can talk to me," Bridget says softly, and April meets her gaze.

"I told him about my dream, that everyone in York is going to die, and he got mad at me," she whispers, and I nearly run off the road. "York is going to burn," she adds after I jerk the car back into the lane.

It wasn't her words that catch me off guard; it was the vividness of the vision of my hometown looking like a battle zone that accosts me, and when I meet her gaze in the mirror, accusation leaps from her eyes.

"You're my father, aren't you?" she asks, changing the subject. I glance at Bridget, looking for help in answering the question.

"Why would you ask that?" Bridget's voice rises into that nervous tone that even April catches.

She glares at her mother. "I'm not stupid, Mom. I see the way you look at him and I see the way he looks at you. Besides, look at him. His eyes look exactly like mine."

That's a pretty astute observation for a ten-year-old, and I'm impressed. I glance back at her just before I turn onto Roaring Rock and nod. The kid has a right to know.

"Are you the reason I have these dreams?" she asks.

"I see ghosts, so I don't know."

Her eyebrows arch. "You see ghosts?"

I let out a soft laugh. "Yes. It's the whole reason I opened a paranormal investigation agency." We pull up to the closed gate and I type in the access number instead of just willing the gates open, like I could have done.

When I finally park the truck inside the garage and close the door, shutting us in, I pull the keys from the ignition.

"Why did you leave us?" April's voice is low and quiet and I glance at Bridget.

"I left so I could keep you safe," I say, keeping Bridget's gaze. The fact I didn't know I had a daughter until yesterday is a moot point. I turn away and climb out of the truck, opening the door for April and helping her down. When I haul the luggage out of the back, she stares at it and then me before turning to her mother.

"We are apparently staying here for a while," Bridget answers the unspoken question in her daughter's eyes.

"So, CJ is really my uncle and Alex, Amber, and Arianna are really my cousins?" There's an interesting spark in her eyes that makes me smile, and she smiles back. Everything clicks into place in her mind and she turns to her mother.

Bridget is sending me the evil eye, as if this conversation is not welcome right now, not with the danger that we all face.

"Yes," I say when she doesn't answer. "This is your family and right now, we are here to keep everyone safe."

"You brought the danger, didn't you?" she asks and I look straight at her.

"It would have come whether or not I was here, but at least with me here, you all have a fighting chance of surviving."

She steps closer to her mother, seeking comfort in the proximity.

"Go on inside," I nod to the door, and the three of us enter the chaotic family room. I leave them in the midst of everyone and haul their bags up to the guest room I had stayed in last night, dumping the suitcases on the bed. The arsenal stayed on my shoulder. Finding a safe place is going to be a challenge, but when I open the closet, a logical spot presents itself. The top shelf is half-empty and I haul the bag into the space.

Sam nudges me and I smile down at my ever-present dog.

"Hey, girl," I say as I step out of the closet and close the door. Squatting, I let her lick my face, and I rub behind both ears. "I'm sorry I had to leave you here, but it wouldn't have been a very fun trip for you."

I gather my things and carry my duffel bag downstairs, crossing through the animated discussions and dump my bag on the landing of the stairwell to the basement.

Instead of engaging in the heated discussions between Naomi, Michael, CJ, and Austin, I slide into the farthest seat at the breakfast bar, with Sam at my feet, and just watch. Paige sits with the kids on the couch, just as dumbfounded as the group.

Bridget doesn't know whether or not to interject and April just stares until she finally turns and trudges over to me, squatting to address my dog. She slides onto the seat next to me, watching with the same fascination as I am.

"You're not going to say anything?" she asks and turns towards me.

"No. Do you want a soda or something?" I ask, trying to be polite. Now that we are inside the confines of the house, I'm not sure what to do or say, and I've let go of the mental hold I have had on Bridget since we left her place. She crosses her arms, glaring at me.

"I'm okay," April says.

"There are some things you are going to learn in the next few days that are going to scare you. I'm here if you need to talk, okay?"

She looks up at me, chewing on her lip, and I study the bruise around her eye.

"Do you want more ice for that?"

Her hand flutters to the bruise, and she shakes her head. "I'll be okay. I didn't mean to upset Danny today."

"He shouldn't have hit you. No matter how upset a boy gets, it is never okay to hit a girl, and if anyone tries to sweep it under the rug like the boy hit you because he likes you, you tell them to go pound sand. It's never okay." I reach over and move her hair back so I can see the mark. "It's never okay," I say again and meet her gaze.

She looks down at the ground and I reach out, hooking my finger under her chin and force her to meet my gaze.

"It's not your fault, either. Don't even go down that road. A boy needs to treat his girl with love and respect, and not make her feel guilty for speaking her mind."

Bridget steps closer with her arms crossed and her lips tight. "A boy needs to learn to grovel when he's done something wrong," she adds, looking directly at me.

"I'm not apologizing for forcing you to come here," I snap at her at the same time the room gets quiet, so only my voice is heard. Everyone turns towards us, and heat fills my face. I certainly didn't want an audience for this argument.

"You forced my mother?" April's voice rises, and I look down at her.

"Yes, I did, because she was going to run away with you, right into the danger we are trying to avoid."

"Jesus, Tom," Bridget hisses.

"Everyone in this house has a right to know what's coming." The snarl in my voice makes both April and Bridget move back.

April's face blanches. "The dream…"

I meet her gaze, holding it, but I don't confirm or deny it. The fact my daughter is clairvoyant, and none of CJ's kids exhibit any supernatural abilities, tickles me, but being a dream seer probably won't bode well for her if Lucifer finds out.

I finally raise my gaze to Bridget. "Your mom has every right to be angry with me, but not about this," I say, and scan every face in the room until my gaze lands on Michael. "If I had been given the full set of instructions when I left ten years ago, we wouldn't be facing this sh…" I stop pressing my lips together. Shit storm isn't appropriate for some of the ears in the room. "So, if we are going to point fingers, we can all look to the archangel in the room."

I lean back in the seat and cross my arms. He glares at me, and the hate radiates from him in waves.

"We can play the blame game all day long, but it won't stop the fact that Lucifer is coming." Michael says, and he scans the faces in the room, including mine. "This house contains all that is left of the angel descendants. Lucifer would like nothing more than to crush most of you into oblivion, and the rest, well; you do not want to entertain the hell he has in store for you." His gaze lands on me to make his point.

April swings her eyes from Michael to me, her mind swims with what she is being told, and Bridget reaches out, placing her hand on her shoulder to lessen the building fear.

"We are angels?" she asks, and the shock of her words draws smiles from both CJ and I.

I shake my head. "No, the only actual angel in the room is Michael," I say, trying to bring her up to speed. "We are all grandchildren and distant great-grandchildren of angels," I add, to put some kind of reference on it that she can understand.

Alex sits on the couch with his arms around his sisters. "It's his fault," he says, nodding towards me.

"No. He made a valid point," Michael says, surprising the hell out of me. "He has made some very damning mistakes in the past, but this isn't one of them." He glances at CJ. "And he made a very recent decision that we never saw coming, but it may very well be the only choice that could end up saving everyone in this room." He turns back to me. "That was a smart decision, smarter than what I expected from you."

While I know it was a compliment, it was backhanded in a way that burned, but I keep the irritation to myself and just give a nod of acknowledgement.

"I think we've probably done enough scaring the crap out of the kids for now," I say, interrupting the direction of this conversation and sparing both CJ's kids and April from more of this dark talk. Naomi's children were teens and able to handle the uncertainty of it all much better than our kids. "Why don't you guys all go down and play some video games for a bit while we hash this out, okay?"

The relief on all the children's faces as they scatter and make a beeline for the basement makes me smile.

April remains in the seat, just looking at the group before she turned to me. "What did you do that upset everyone?"

I looked up at Bridget and she shook her head, her eyes warning me not to be honest with this one. However, the moment she is downstairs and asks the same question, she will be told exactly what kind of a monster I am.

"I killed my best friend to save my first daughter's life."

Her eyes widen, and she shrinks into Bridget's side. After a few blinks, she asks, "I have a sister?"

I shake my head. "No. She died, despite all my efforts to save her."

She turns to her mother. "Is that why you had me?"

Bridget's gaze rises to mine. "His little girl was not mine," she says. "I only knew her for a little while, but I was there for Tom after she died." She bites her lower lip and blinks, not knowing how to tell her daughter that she was actually an unintended mistake. She clears her throat and lowers her gaze. "Your father didn't know about you when he left," she says.

April stares at her mother and then looks at me. "You said you left to keep me safe."

My mouth pops open, and I'm not sure what to say now that I am caught in a white lie.

"He left to keep me safe, and by default, that kept you safe." Bridget saves me the pain of having to backtrack my words, but April's gaze hardens as she studies me. She glances between the two of us and slides off the chair, heading downstairs to be with the other kids.

"Way to go, asshole," Bridget mutters, and we focus on the rest of the group staring at us.

"She asked," I say, and defensiveness creeps into my voice.

"And you don't go telling a ten-year-old that she was a mistake," she snarls.

"I never said that." I put my hands up and back into the seat, trying to distance myself from her anger.

"You two can discuss your situation later," Michael interrupts. "We have more important things to discuss."

"Like, how do we stop York from burning?"

Every eye turns towards me, and a collective chill slips into the room.

Angel Fury Chapter 10

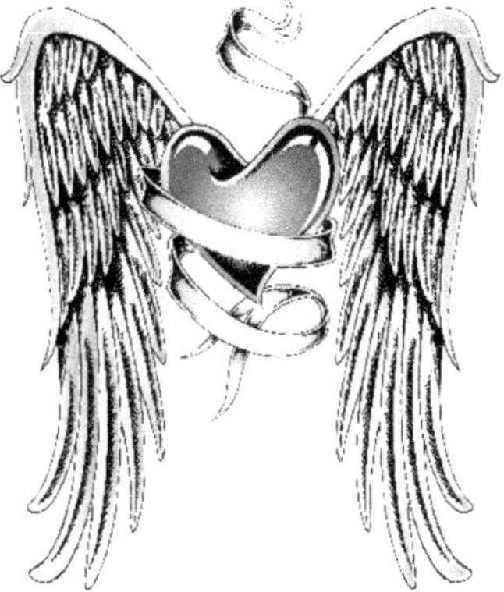

"WHEN SHIT GOES DOWN, the women and children need to get into the panic rooms we built," CJ says.

"Bullshit!" Naomi, Valerie, and Bridget say in unison.

"You built a panic room?" I ask.

CJ glances at me and nods. "Both Damian and I did, and it connects houses underground, so there is an escape route." His eyebrows stitch together. "You didn't know that?"

"No. I wasn't exactly paying attention that summer," I say and sigh.

"We did some serious revisions, like replacing the fence around both properties with bars that are a mixture of iron and platinum, and a solid salt line from rock wall to rock wall. No demons can get onto the property, and assuming there still are vampires left that Lucifer can call on, they can only access the property from the water. We basically protected this place like he had done to his property in Connecticut. Sigils, salt, platinum and anything else we could think of."

I really had been on a different planet during that time; I was more concerned with getting through the day after my wife's death than with anything else. I did nothing to protect our house, and I glanced at Paige and Austin sitting quietly on the couch, offering them a conciliatory shrug.

"We made sure the fencing around your place had the same protections," CJ says quietly. "Both Damian and I knew you weren't thinking straight that summer, and someone needed to watch out for you." His gaze moves to Bridget, and she sighs. Her hand lands on my arm.

I glance at her, but she is still holding CJ's gaze. I don't think she is fully aware that she reached out for me until my stare pulls her attention away from my brother. She glances at her hand and yanks it away, readjusting the expression on her face to annoyance.

Her aura threads with darker colors, and I can't tell if she's angry with me or herself. The silent pause directs my attention back to the family room.

"So, there's little to no weakness in the perimeter?"

CJ bites the side of his lip before he speaks. "I don't know. I only know how to defend against vampires and demons. There is no defense against crazy fuckers like the guy who killed Raven, and Lucifer can just walk onto the property, just like Michael did."

"And who knows what else Lucifer has at his disposal," I say, slumping in the seat.

CJ and Michael slowly nod at my assessment.

"This is such a fucking mess," I mumble, and swivel the chair towards the counter. Exhaustion from exercising control over Bridget, along with jet lag, seems to have caught up with me today, and I prop my head on my hand, attempting to keep my eyes open.

Bridget steps to my side and meets my gaze, with concern etched into the corners of her mouth and eyes. "Are you okay?"

"I'm tired," I admit.

"Go lay down," CJ says and I move my gaze to his without moving anything else.

"The kids are on my bed," I say.

"You look like shit," Bridget says, and I try to focus my eyes on hers, but my eyelids keep closing longer with each blink.

"This is what jet lag and exercising control over someone's will for more than a minute or two looks like,"

I mumble, and the throbbing in my temple fights to take over my entire consciousness.

"Come on," she says, and slings my arm over her shoulder.

I'm vaguely aware of her leading me through the family room, and the click of Sam's toenails as she follows us across the wood floor. Climbing the stairs taps me out, and when we get to the bedroom, she leans me against the wall while she clears the bed.

I hit the mattress and my vision fades behind the throb of a killer headache.

"Stay," I whisper, trying to focus on her.

She takes a seat on the edge of the bed and runs her fingers across my forehead and into my hair at the temple. The slow progression of her soft touch lulls my eyes closed and dulls the pounding in my head.

I open my eyes and focus on her for a moment. "I love you, Bri," I whisper. She rolls her eyes at me, but continues to rub my forehead and I let my eyes fall closed again, sinking into a migraine stupor.

"MR. RYAN?"

The soft voice reaches into the darkness, pulling me to the surface, and I shift, blinking my eyes open. April stands in the doorway with Sam licking her fingers.

"Mhm?" I mumble, and stretch. My head still has that post-migraine heaviness, but at least I don't feel like I have an axe planted in my cranium anymore.

"Mom asked me to wake you to tell you dinner's almost ready."

"Dinner?" I ask, pushing myself into a sitting position. Last I knew, it wasn't even ten in the morning.

"Yeah. You slept all day," she says.

"Holy cow," I whisper, and rub my face. "Did anyone feed Sam?" I ask, after dropping my hands to my lap.

April smiles and pats the dog on the head. "Yes. My mom did. We've been playing with her all day. She's a lot of fun."

I nod very slowly, taking care not to jolt my head. "You can call me Tom, you know," I say after getting my bearings. She just shrugs in that non-committal manner that tells me she still isn't sure about me yet. "Thanks for waking me. I'll be down in a couple of minutes."

She turns and Sam follows her downstairs. This is the first time since I bought her from that shelter that Sam has opted to follow someone other than me, and I can't help the smile that surfaces. It's as if the dog knows that April's safety is much more important to me than my own.

I head to the bathroom to relieve the pressure in my lower abdomen. After I take care of my body's needs, I brush my teeth and run my hands through my unruly hair, getting it back into some semblance of order.

It is much quieter downstairs now than when I was escorted to bed, and when I step around the corner, I see why. Only CJ's family and mine are sitting in the family room.

"Where's everyone else?" I ask, calling their collective attention to me.

"At Naomi's. We'll regroup tomorrow," CJ says.

"And Val?"

CJ's lips thin and he looks at his watch. "She should be here any minute. She had a few patients that she couldn't rearrange."

I can tell by his tone that he isn't happy that she isn't here, but I also get the sense he had no choice. Valerie was much more stubborn about her responsibilities as a pediatric surgeon than anyone else I know. That came first, even before her safety, and CJ seems to have accepted that over the years.

"Has anyone warned Steve?"

CJ stops what he is doing and looks at the phone. What color was in his face disappears, and both of us move at the same time. I get there first, pulling the receiver off the wall. I dial by memory, staring at my brother with my heart pounding in my throat.

After the third ring, the phone connects.

"I was wondering just how long it would take you."

The voice chills me to my core, and I meet CJ's gaze. Lucifer has Steve and Jennifer Williams, our adoptive parents, and I know damned well what he is going to demand for their lives. CJ's face echoes the same panic ripping through me, and I shake my head at him. We can't make the jump. If we do, we leave the possibility of Lucifer taking possession of either of us, and that would be a disaster for our family.

It's futile to beg for their lives and I squeeze the phone for a moment, gritting my teeth.

"You bastard," I whisper as I listen to the scraping of metal against stone.

"I want your brother's heart this time," he says with a laugh.

"That's never going to happen." I close my eyes, dipping my head because I know what the price for my insubordination is.

Lucifer locks onto my mind's eye, holding me hostage and giving me a full view of Steve and Jennifer in their apartment. I struggle to break free, but it is no use. And when he runs the edge of the blade down Jennifer's arm, she screams.

I bang my head against the wall, holding the ripping pain inside, helpless to look away from the unfolding massacre.

Steve bellows, struggling against the demons holding him in place. With whatever strength he has, he tosses the first demon on the ground and punches the second in the throat. His face is a mask of fury, the same type of fury pummeling every muscle in my body.

Just as he is within reach of Lucifer, that bastard snaps his head towards Steve, blasting him right off his feet. Steve sails through the sliding glass doors and right over the edge of the balcony. I can hear his cry fade and the faint sound of smashing metal, followed by the shrill sound of a car alarm.

"It seems your adopted father does not have the ability to fly," Lucifer says, and my knees buckle. The swirl of rage and remorse fills every fiber and I can't breathe. I slowly sink to the floor, still gripping the phone to my ear.

I know it's useless, but it still tumbles from my mouth anyway. "Please don't kill Jennifer."

The ghost now squatting next to my form overshadows the horrifying laugh that comes through the line. CJ throws a punch at the wall, burying his fist in the drywall.

The knife in Lucifer's hand lashes out, slicing through her abdomen. She screams as she tries to hold in her viscera. Blood spills along with her intestines and my stomach rolls.

He drills the knife into her multiple times, relishing her fading cries, and I just want the connection to end, to unsee what he is doing. The receiver drops from my hand and my breathing stalls and starts in inadequate fits until the light fades from Jennifer's eyes and the connection severs.

I can't seem to recover, to pull air into my lungs, and Steve's ghost whispers, "Breathe."

It's a mantra I've heard from his lips before, in that calming tone, that seems to loosen the tightness in my chest and give me the ability to draw sufficient air.

My gaze travels to Steve's ghost crouching next to me. "I'm so sorry," I whisper, and he pulls me into a hug.

"There was nothing either of you could do," he says, trying to wipe out the guilt embedded in my heart.

CJ is still beating the shit out of the wall because he knows as well as I do that Steve and Jennifer are dead, but at least I was able to block him from the disturbing mind-meld I had with Lucifer and the visions he fed to me. That is something I would keep on lock down until I stopped breathing.

Jennifer shimmers into view at the same time Valerie steps inside the house.

"Lucifer's in New York," I say, for the benefit of the rest of the family in the room.

Valerie looks at me, and then the spaces that the ghosts fill before her gaze darts to CJ and his bloodied fists and tear-stained face.

Tears don't come for me. They are locked with the horrors I've survived, and I stare at the ghosts in our midst. "You need to move on," I say, knowing what happens to ghosts that hang onto this life. My father was an exception and we all know it.

"Maybe I can help," Steve says, and I shake my head.

"Go see your daughters and give Hannah a kiss for me, okay?" My voice cracks and I press my lips together. My vision swims and I close my eyes. A hot path cascades down my skin and I swallow the lump in my throat.

When I open my eyes, Steve has his arm around Jennifer, and they both meet my gaze.

"We will see you again," he says, and I try to give them a smile. They don't know I've destroyed Paradise Cove and, with it, any chance of ever seeing them again.

"Go," I whisper, and they fade into nothing.

My chest squeezes and I glance at Valerie, still frozen just on this side of the garage door. Her complexion is ashen. My announcement of Lucifer and New York brings back all sorts of horrifying memories for her, and CJ's complete melt down doesn't help.

The hole in my soul widens again, and I finally turn my gaze to the family room, meeting Bridget's wide-eyed stare. The only other one staring at the spot Steve and Jennifer just vacated is my daughter, and from her expression, she knew them enough to be shattered by their death.

Valerie already has CJ in her arms, offering her warm comfort to her husband, while I shake uncontrollably on the floor a few feet away.

Sam whines, crawling across the floor. When she reaches me, she lays her head on my leg. She knows how close I am to losing my shit, and I look up at the ceiling, trying to control the whirlwind building in my chest.

It isn't until Bridget takes a knee next to me that I focus on something other than the swirl pattern on the ceiling. The words I said to her so long ago bubble up to the forefront of my mind.

"I should have let you run," I say. "You might have gotten far enough away to be safe." My voice is flat, devoid of the emotions tearing into my stomach, and I slowly stroke my dog to settle her. She's seen me like this enough to know there is a very dangerous storm brewing inside, but Bridget doesn't understand the complete absence of emotion.

"What is wrong with you?" she asks, tears flow in a steady stream down her cheeks and I stare at her.

"I'm broken," I say and find my feet. I need the chill of the evening air and the spray of the waves crashing on the rock, so I leave everyone and cross to the rock wall. I take a seat, stretching my legs out as I lean against one of the posts. Sam takes her position next to me and I continue stroking her head. The tide is rising and every now and then, a rogue wave hits the rocks and splashes up into my face, but I'm so numb that the cold does not penetrate my skin.

I don't acknowledge CJ when he takes a seat on the opposite side, adopting the same position. He is quiet, and I don't bother listening to his thoughts. I just need the nothingness right now, the numbness to remain and if I speak, the swirl inside me will crash down like a rogue wave and leave me decimated.

"I can't do this without you," he finally says, and I turn my eyes in his direction.

"I will not survive whatever goes down," I say.

"The hell you aren't!"

We both jerk at Bridget's harsh interruption. She looks at CJ. "Dinner is burned, and I think Valerie and the kids need you," she adds, and he glances at me. I nod towards the house, and he goes. I'm not ready for the turmoil inside the family room, and I look out over the ocean again.

"Sam, go inside." She points towards the house, but my dog doesn't move.

"Go take care of April," I say and she lifts her head, meeting my gaze for a moment before trotting off.

Bridget watches and then turns towards me. I turn away because I have to keep the shit locked inside right now. It's the only way I'll be able to function, and we've both seen what happens to me when I embrace the darkness. I end up under suicide watch in the hospital.

She steps closer. Her fingers touch the cheek facing the water, turning my gaze to hers. I meet her sad hazel eyes, and my teeth involuntarily clench. She keeps her hand on my cheek with her thumb caressing my skin. When the soft pad of her thumb travels over my lips, that flare of burning heat warms the chill in my bones enough for me to acknowledge her.

I shift, planting my feet on the grass, and pull her into a hug. My ear rests on her breasts and I focus on the thumping of her heart. She kisses the top of my head, wrapping me in her arms just as tightly as I hold her.

"I'm sorry for your loss," she whispers, and I pull away, meeting her gaze.

"I'm not the only one feeling the pain," I reply.

Her lip turns up on one side with acknowledgement. "I didn't think you were feeling anything."

I pull her closer, delivering a kiss. This is the only way I can show her what is brewing within my skin. It's the only way I can share my loss, and she gasps before she deepens the kiss, letting our tongues perform a slow and aching dance.

I'm the one who breaks the kiss this time, and I stare deeply into her haunted eyes. "He's just as dangerous as we are, except he has zero qualms about destroying everything in his path. CJ and I are hung up on preserving all we care about. That includes this town. The idea of innocent people dying…" I shake my head and press my forehead to her chest. "That's going to be the thing that undoes us."

Angel Fury Chapter 11

I DON'T KNOW HOW long we remain like this. All I know is the moment I let go of her, this connection will pass. Finally, I glance up. Bridget stares out at the ocean with a slow stream of tears running down her cheeks. I push her back a step and stand without losing the physical contact.

"If I come out of this alive, will you be there?"

Her gaze snaps from my chest to my eyes. Hesitation, along with a rollercoaster of emotions passes over her face.

"I might have to kick your ass first." Her voice trembles. "If you survive, will you be here?" She squeezes my arms.

"I'm not sure how much of me will be left, or if you'll even be willing to help me pick up the pieces," I say, searching her eyes and take her hand, covering my heart with it before moving mine to cover hers. "But if you are, then I'll be waiting right here."

She sucks in her lower lip and nods.

I inhale, centering myself and hardening my shell for a moment.

"Think you're ready to face everyone?" I ask and glance at the house behind her.

"I wasn't the one who ran off," she says, stepping back and wiping her face.

And like that, the connection breaks. I clear my throat. "Thank you," I say and drop my gaze to the ground.

"For what?"

"For reminding me what really matters." I step towards the house, and she follows. A new determination revives my senses and instead of the pain, I sharpen it into a boiling anger, keeping the lid on it until the right time.

"Lucifer must be stopped. No matter what." I glance at my daughter. "Even if it means the rest of this town burns." When I swing my gaze back to CJ, he stares at me with an open mouth.

"We can't..."

"We have to. That's his play. Devastate us and then strike in order to divide us. His end game still holds, CJ. He wants an army."

"You can't expect me to..."

I hold up my hand. "Do you want to win this?"

"Jesus, Tom, I can't let innocent people die!"

"Then say goodbye to your family, because that's who will suffer." I can't help the venom in my voice. CJ just blinks at me in utter incomprehension. "We have to think like Dad."

Our father was notorious for being ruthless when necessary. If his family was in danger, nothing was going to stop him from keeping them safe. Nothing. Not loss of life or limb or anything deterred the man. I never thought twice about that hard resolve of his, of that Angel of Death persona he displayed when cornered, but now I understand it more than I ever expected to.

CJ had yet to grasp it. Even though he could project the same image, he just doesn't understand the tenacity and dedication this cause requires.

His lips thin and his eyes turn icy. "I know what this requires," he starts, and I cross my arms, cocking my head in challenge. "But sacrificing innocent lives to protect our own is not okay. Ever. Just like killing your best friend to save your daughter."

He went there, and the burn starts in my core like a mini-cyclone. I cross the distance in seconds and slam him against the wall. There is nothing I can say because he's fucking right again.

"If we fuck this up..." I can't finish and he doesn't complete the sentence.

"You can't expect me to do nothing," he says.

"And you can't expect me to make those kinds of sacrifices. It's not in my DNA." We are nearly screaming at each other and the building tension between us is close to exploding. "This is a no-win situation, just like that phone call." I point to the phone. "The only way we win is if we take him on here." I point to the ground to make my point. "With all of us in the fight except those he covets most."

Horror dawns on his face.

"He's right," Valerie says from the other side of the kitchen. "We all have to be in this fight and with us here, there is no one for Lucifer to use as a pawn."

"You aren't fighting with me," CJ says, looking beyond me at Valerie.

"I will be fine."

"He snapped your fucking spine like a twig last time," he growls, and I drop my arm from across his chest, stepping back with as much surprise as that radiating from Valerie behind me. "I'm not going through that again."

His gaze narrows and jumps to mine. He turns and disappears into the living room and after a moment, the piano rings out as he smashes the keys, drilling out a tune that takes me a few seconds to get.

I step into the room and start laughing, crossing to the other side of the piano. I had never heard Highway to Hell so clearly on the ivory keys. He stops playing and just bangs his forehead on the keys.

"Raven was a pawn, CJ. So was Hannah. Lucifer tore me down to nothing and stole any hope of heaven in the process. I'm no longer pure in any sense of the word, in case you hadn't noticed, and I have that fucker's grace burning away whatever goodness is left."

He lifts his head and just stares at me.

"I don't think I could transfer the grace, even if I tried. It's bound with his blood inside me like a malignant disease." I inhale, calming the burn to a low simmer. "The risk in all this is that I fall into the same trap and have to make a choice. If that happens, you'd better be the one to rip my heart out, because if he gets his grace back, you are dead, along with Valerie and Alex."

He blinks his eyes and swallows hard. "I don't know if I can do that."

"If it comes down to it, you have to; otherwise, your daughters become the devil's concubines." Just the thought clenches my stomach, and I turn to step back in the kitchen, but Bridget's wide eyes meet mine.

I halt, meeting her glare.

"You said..."

"I said if I survive, I didn't make any promises," I whisper. "But I expect my brother to do as I ask if shit goes south. It's the only option we have, and it will save lives. Lives I give a damn about."

She studies me, and I keep her stark stare. I know it's not something either of us wants to come to fruition, but it's important to lay as much of the plan out there, so no one gets blindsided.

"How do we kill him?" she asks, looking between CJ and me.

I only have one idea of what needs to be done, and I glance at my brother before I answer. "We have to tear off his head." Visions of my father's head in Lucifer's grasp surface in an unwelcome wave, and I shiver under the thought.

"Tom? CJ?" Valerie's voice calls from the other room. We both cross and step into the kitchen.

"Where are the kids?" CJ asks looking around at the empty family room.

"I sent them downstairs when you took your argument in the other room. I'm glad I did. Look at this." She points at the breaking news tag on the television.

The screen displays the scene right out of a horror movie, and the caption reads Ex-FBI agent falls seventy stories to his death. Wife found brutally murdered in their apartment.

I glance at the clock. It had only been a little over an hour since that phone call, and the reporters were already swarming. When I glance back at the screen, my eyes widen at the image of me leaving the apartment with Sam by my side along with the tag—wanted for questioning.

"That fucker," I whisper and trade a glance with CJ. His jaw is just as tight as mine is.

"But..." Bridget starts just staring at the screen.

"He's framing me for their death," I say, pulling her attention away from the screen.

"But you were right here."

"Doesn't matter. He's hedging his bets, and after what happened to Jennifer, I'll be lucky if I ever see the light of day again."

CJ grabs my arm, turning me towards him.

"Lucifer gutted her," I say without sharing the visual.

"How do you know that?"

"He forced me to watch." I turn back to the television and the camera footage from the hallway outside the penthouse rolls across the screen again. The vision of me covered in blood is unsettling, but the additional touch of having an image of Sam next to him really burns.

I collect my thoughts and glance at CJ. "Why do you think I shut down like I did?" I ask softly.

CJ processes what I said with an open mouth, and he blinks a few times before he says, "What do you mean forced you?" He speaks slowly to control any chance of his stutter surfacing, and I let out a sarcastic laugh.

"I have his grace, CJ. We are inexplicably bound by the shit inside me."

"Damian wasn't," he points out, lifting a cocky eyebrow.

"Damian was not Lucifer's bloodline." At least that was my theory as to what was happening within me. Otherwise, I had no answer to how he could just lock me down like that, and force those images into my head.

The back door opens, and Michael and Naomi step inside. "Have you seen..." They trail off at the news report running across the television.

"What in God's name happened?" Naomi asks. Her voice, while carrying the pain of loss, also carries some accusation as well when her gaze lands on mine.

"Lucifer." CJ and I say at the same time.

"But that's you." Naomi points at the television.

"No, that's Lucifer wearing an image of me." I run my hands through my hair. "And if he continues to use my form, I am utterly screwed."

This new and morbid twist unsettles me more than the accusations being flung on the television. All I can think about is April's prediction that York will burn and if it does, that fucker will make sure everything points to me.

I turn to Michael. "He doesn't know," I say as all this processes. Lucifer wouldn't go to these kinds of lengths to set me up if he knew he had an ace right here in York.

A light of hope shines inside me, and I spin, staring at Bridget. "Lucifer does not know about April."

She glances from me to the television. "What does that have to do with him setting you up?"

"He wouldn't bother doing that if he knew he had some other leverage," I say and my heart rate increases with this new epiphany. My excitement is short-lived as the siren sounds outside the gate.

My smile fades and I move my gaze to Noami as every alarm inside me sounds.

"Panic room," I say, looking at her. "Now!"

No one moves.

"This is the beginning. Go!"

My voice barrels from my chest and seems to jumpstart the rest of the group. Both Michael and Naomi slip out the back, and I spin to Bridget and point towards the basement. "Go, keep her safe, please?" I whisper, and she gives me a shake of her head.

"Valerie, go with Bridget," CJ says, and she balks the same way Bridget does.

"No one has eaten," Valerie says.

"For Christ's sake," CJ says and turns towards the cabinet, pulling out a couple of boxes of granola bars, shoving them into her hand. "Just go."

After both of them retreat downstairs, I glance at CJ and he crosses to the call box.

"Hello?"

"Mr. Ryan? It's Duke Gallagher. Do you have a minute?"

CJ glances at me and I nod. It would make sense that the Chief of the York police department would be the one to notify next of kin.

"Sure," CJ says and opens the gate. When the police cruiser clears the iron, CJ closes it again. Duke is not alone, and neither CJ nor I recognize the deputy walking to the house with him.

Sam's low growl from behind me clues me in before CJ opens the door.

"The Chief is okay. I don't know about the other one," I say softly, and CJ nods. I pull Sam into the kitchen and give her the sign to sit. The television still drones behind me and I turn, willing it to turn off. Quiet emblazons the room and the front door creaks.

"Hi, Chief. What can I do for you?" CJ asks, with a steady and reasonable voice.

"I'm afraid we have some bad news. Do you mind if we come in?"

"Look, I don't mean to be rude, but I rarely let strangers into my house, even strangers in uniform," CJ says, in such a smooth manner I almost smile, but the fact he is leery of the other officer tells me he has no read on him, which is my problem as well.

"I'll wait by the car," the other man says. The door creaks, and footsteps enter the living room.

"I'm afraid there's been an accident in New York."

"I know," CJ says, and continues into the kitchen before turning.

"I need to ask..." Chief Gallagher stops in the doorway when his gaze lands on me. "...if you've seen your brother," he finishes with hardness in his voice that spells trouble. Just to prove he is in control, his hand lands on his revolver.

"Tom has been here for the last couple of days, sir."

"I came in three days ago and slept in what used to be my office that first night before I came here. I can get you my flight records and the name of the driver who dropped me off," I say to calm his wind up, but Chief Gallagher is still trying to reconcile the video he was shown with the current situation. His gaze narrows, especially when Sam whines at my side. I drop my hand to her head, calming her as best I can.

Gallagher glances at the clock and then back at me as a crease forms between his eyes. His time calculations of travel between New York City and York Beach, Maine, is the only reason he hasn't un-holstered his weapon.

"You also might want to pull my phone records. We called Steve's penthouse..." CJ's voice cracks, and he presses his lips together as his eyes close. He takes a moment to gather himself again. "We were on the line." He brings his glossy gaze back to the Chief's. "We heard firsthand."

"You'd better start explaining," he growls.

"The same... thing... that ordered my wife's death killed Steve and Jennifer." I cannot help the hostility in my voice, and his grip on the handle of his gun tightens.

"Son, I know you can do some hocus pocus magical stuff, but if you don't start explaining, I'm going to have to haul you down to the station until we sort out all of this shit."

"Will you trust me enough to step closer?" I ask, because if I cross right now, I'm likely to be shot and that would put as much of a crimp in our battle plans as me being hauled down to the station.

His lips pinch together and then he nods, crossing to within a few feet of me.

"You might want to be sitting for this," I say and irritation blooms in his eyes.

"Is everything okay, sir?" His radio squawks and he rolls his eyes.

"Yes. I'm just waiting for Mr. Ryan to get the last known address for us," he says, and it's my turn to cock my head. As soon as he finishes the transmission, he glares my way. "This better be good."

Relief floods through me for a second and I reach for his forehead. "Just don't shoot me, okay?" I ask, and he lets out a laugh.

"You would already have had lead in your ass if I was going to shoot," he explains.

"You might want to when you see everything," I say, and before CJ can stop me, my palm presses to his forehead. In order to show him enough for him to understand the danger we face, I have to go back fifteen years to the moment Damian and Naomi entered our lives. The flood I transmit includes both my thoughts and feelings along with CJ's. To understand, Gallagher needs to see heaven and hell, and everything in between, including what I did to Damian ten years ago.

As the last trauma of Steve's death passes through to Gallagher, his eyes clear and I remove my hand, stepping back, waiting for him to process.

Suddenly, he turns to CJ with his eyes blinking rapidly. "What. The. Hell?"

The scuffle near the back door pulls all our attention and Gallagher draws his weapon. The door slides open and Michael steps inside with the barrel of a gun pressed to his temple. The officer that had been with Gallagher follows him in the door with eyes blazing red.

Sam growls low. The deep sound rumbles across the room and I don't even look. I know she has her teeth bared and all the fur on the back of her neck is standing on end.

"Curt?" Gallagher asks, his voice full of doubt, even with the catalog of memories I shared.

"Curt's not home anymore," the demon says and his breath smells of brimstone.

"Well, shit," Gallagher breathes and takes careful aim.

CJ swats as if he's batting at a fly and the gun in the demon's hand goes flying right into my grip. Michael's roar jolts me and I am thankful I don't have a finger on the trigger and equally surprised that Gallagher has not taken a shot.

The crunching of bones echoes and Michael snaps the fool's neck, nearly severing the head from the demon's body. I guess he isn't as useless as I thought.

"Freeze," Gallagher announces, and Michael glares his way.

"Chief, that's the archangel Michael," I say under my breath, and he snaps his gaze to mine for a moment, but his aim doesn't move.

"I don't give a shit if he is God Almighty himself. He just killed a man."

"I killed a demon," Michael says with a mix of pride and wrath. His chest puffs in that way that I find condescending. "Would you have preferred I let him kill you instead?"

Finally, Gallagher lowers his gun a fraction and looks at me. "All that shit you fed me was real?"

I nod and the gun moves in my direction. Slowly, I place the service revolver I am holding onto the counter. "You get what's at stake, right?" I ask as I raise my palms to face him, but his mind was already flooding with my sins.

"You murdered Damian Andreas."

I bite my lower lip and nod. "Not my finest moment," I whisper after a beat of strained silence.

The gun never wavers. Neither does the hardness in Gallagher's eyes.

"You can arrest me after," I add, when he doesn't yield.

"After what?"

I glance up at the clock, calculating in the same manner as he had. We have a little over two hours before Lucifer sets foot in York and all hell breaks loose.

"After we send the devil back to where he belongs."

Angel Fury Chapter 12

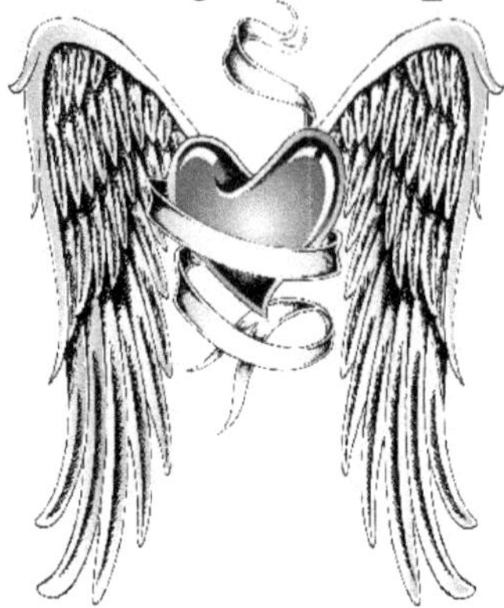

IT TAKES CHIEF GALLAGHER a lot of convincing before he agrees not to arrest me on the spot. The fact that Michael adds to the conversation as a proponent of having me on the battlefield with him helps more than my brother's rationale.

When Chief Gallagher finally lays his pistol on the counter, he rubs his face. "You really know how to screw up someone's night."

I let out a sharp laugh. "Yeah, well, it's only going to get worse," I say, and glance at his hands. The wedding ring sobers me up. "Do you need to call anyone to tell them to get out of town before hellfire rains on us?"

He glances up at me and sighs, shaking his head before his gaze lands the same place I am looking. "Cancer got her," he says, and both CJ and I trade a glance. "How safe is that bunker of yours?" he asks CJ.

"As safe as we could make it. In layman's terms, it could withstand a missile," he answers, and Gallagher gives him a slow nod, both recalling vividly what a missile did to this very same property over a decade ago.

Chief Gallagher slips out his cell phone and climbs to his feet. "I need to let the police in New York know you have a concrete alibi, and we believe the video was tampered with."

I give him a nod of thanks and he steps into the family room with the phone to his ear.

"Are you serious about the panic room?" I ask, because I remember the amount of rubble that missile made.

He meets my gaze. "I think the only thing that could destroy it is angel fire." There is a clear warning in his tone that makes me inhale.

"Good to know," I say because who the hell knows what will happen when I confront Lucifer.

"You cannot lose control like you did at Paradise Cove," Michael says from his perch on the breakfast bar. He is nursing a black coffee like it's liquid gold.

"I'll do my best."

The cup slams onto the counter and his glare follows. "You will have to do better than that, because lately your best has been sorely lacking."

"Give him a break. He didn't have to go off and close the portals, but he did," CJ says coming to my defense.

Michael shoots him an equally damning stare. "I'm just laying it out for you. You've done some marginally redeeming things since your downfall, but I'm afraid it isn't enough."

"You know, I really don't give a shit whether or not I get into heaven. All I care about is making sure the rest of my family remains untouched. If I make it through the night, you and I can figure out a way to settle up." I stare Michael down, tired of his condescendence.

"Are you challenging me, boy?"

"You bet your ass," I reply, and he is on his feet in a blink.

CJ blocks him from coming around the island.

"Chill, okay? I've got bigger things to worry about than playing referee." The edge in his voice catches both of us and I put my hands up.

"Sorry, that was out of line," I say, trying to drop the tension a notch or two.

Michael's shoulders relax and his hands unclench before he gives me a curt nod.

"Can you bring some drinks and snacks downstairs?" CJ asks as he reaches for a tray over the refrigerator. "The natives are getting restless."

"Sure." I keep my initial response to myself. "Do they have facilities behind the vault door?" I'm half kidding, but when CJ nods, I raise a brow.

"They even have a mini-refrigerator and a microwave. We also put in a television and DVD player."

"And the only way in or out is through the house?"

When he hesitates, a chill tickles my neck. He opens his mouth and I shake my head, focusing on the Chief's thoughts as opposed to CJ's. If I have that kind of information and Lucifer somehow gets hold of me, the entire plan to protect CJ's girls will fail.

"I don't want to know. Lock it down."

Instead of responding, CJ busies himself with preparing a tray of goodies for everyone. When he is done, he hands me the overflowing tray and sends me downstairs. Sam follows and bounds forward with her tail wagging at the sight of Bridget and Valerie standing by the couch.

"Is everything okay?" Bridget asks.

I look between the two of them and take a long, slow breath.

"Yeah. Chief Gallagher has agreed to not haul my ass in until after the shit goes down with Lucifer." I place the tray on the coffee table.

"Why would he take you in? You have an alibi for what happened earlier."

"I have an alibi for that, but not for what happened to Damian."

Bridget's brow creased.

"I showed him everything that's happened since we met Damian and Naomi." I shrug. "So, I might not be locked up for what happened in New York, but what I showed him might be used as a full confession, and if he puts me in front of a microphone and asks the right questions, I could be looking at life in prison."

"You were not of sound mind," Bridget says softly.

I sigh and meet her gaze. "We'll cross that bridge if we get through tonight, okay?"

Valerie does not weigh in, and I glance in her direction. She drops her gaze, keeping her mind closed to me.

"Thanks for bringing the snacks," she says, and picks up the tray.

I glance around and can't recognize where the door to the bunker is, but neither Valerie nor Bridget go to leave.

"Where did you put my bag?" Bridget asks.

"It's up in the bedroom closet. Why?" I already know the answer. Her thoughts magnify the helplessness she feels, and that bag would give her a sense of security that playing a sitting duck doesn't.

"I want it," she says, and heads towards the stairs.

I give Valerie a tight smile and turn to follow Bridget.

"Stay safe, Tom," Valerie says.

I pause at the wall. "I'll keep CJ safe," I reply, glancing over my shoulder. "I promise," I add, and some of the worry lines carved in her face soften.

By the time I reach the guest bedroom, Bridget is at the opening to the closet. I reach past her and grab the duffel bag.

"I'm sorry," I whisper, and she turns towards me.

"Are you trying to sabotage any future we might have?"

I stare into her angry features, not knowing how to respond. Anything I say right now will set her off, and I am holding a bag full of weapons that could be used to make me regret the day I gave her a job.

When her lips thin, and her hands find her waist, I shake my head.

"No, but the Chief needed to know what is coming. Otherwise, he would have hauled me down to the station for who knows how long, which would have left everyone here vulnerable."

"Stop being so fucking honest, will you?"

Laughter chokes me, and she smiles at my snort.

"I'm serious."

"You want me to lie?"

"Yes. Well. No. You know what I mean," she says, and reaches for the bag.

As painfully aware as I am of time passing, I can't help but pursue this line of thought.

"I have no clue what you mean," I say, holding the bag just outside of her reach.

"Being honest is one thing, but baring your soul is another. Stop doing that with strangers."

I raise my eyebrows, surprised at the outburst. "You're upset because I shared my memories?"

She chews on her lip, staring at me, and finally nods. "Why?"

"Because I thought I was special, but I guess I'm not." She glances at the floor.

I sigh, tilting my head to the side to capture her gaze. When she looks up at me, I say, "You are special."

She waves at the door with a huff.

"Memories and the emotional punch that goes with them are two separate things. You've seen both, even the deeper baggage that comes along with all the shit I've experienced. I have ever only shared that piece of me with you. Raven never saw that part of me, and neither has CJ. So, you'd better believe you're special."

The way her shoulders fall from the tight set of tension to almost relaxed releases some of the tightness in my stomach. Her cheeks flush and she starts that nervous shuffle of weight from one side to the other and back. When she reaches for the bag again, I pull it out of reach because I am enjoying seeing her humbled.

"Give me that," she hisses, and stomps her foot.

A genuine smile forms on my lips at her mini-hissy fit. Her hazel eyes flash with aggravation and an underlying humor that tugs at the edges of her frown.

"Give me a kiss and I'll give you the bag."

She balks, and I cock my head, challenging her. I know it's childish, but right now, I need as much to lighten the knot in the center of my chest as I can get, and teasing Bridget is providing me with a few moments of comic relief.

"Thomas Patrick!" she says, in nothing more than a whisper.

"Bridget Elizabeth!" I use the same exasperated tones she used.

Her fight not to smile fails and she pushes me against the wall, still trying to snag the handle of the bag. With a frustrated growl, she plants her lips on mine. It was meant to be a quick bribe to get the bag, but the spark between us ignites. My mouth opens, as does hers, and I thread my free hand into her hair, cradling her in place as the kiss sweetens with our leisurely tongue dance. My arm holding the bag lowers and Bridget's hand lands on mine and she deepens the kiss, increasing the intensity.

A loud bang separates us. I stare at her with my heart pounding in my throat and I am sure my eyes are just as wide as hers. Outside the front window, smoke rises into view and I hand her the bag.

"Go," I say, and she doesn't hesitate until we are at the top of the stairs.

"You'd better not get yourself killed," she says.

I give her a strained smile. "I love you, too. Now go."

I slide to a stop in the family room, making sure Bridget has safely disappeared down the basement steps before I turn to CJ, Michael, and Chief Gallagher, looking out the front window.

"We can't do this inside," I say as a certainty grips me. The entire house will implode if we choose this as our battleground. I can see enough damage outside already. The gate hangs open, adorned with twisted metal from whatever was used to blow it up.

I spin and tear outside with Sam at my heels and the first thing I notice is the stench of burning propane. I step far enough into the yard to see the Long Sands shoreline, and my eyes close against the bright flickering of flame peppered throughout the horizon.

April's precognition of York burning was as accurate as it gets, and I shiver, glancing at the house just as a flow of demons come from both sides of the yard. Behind them saunters Lucifer, still wearing my image, including that cocky smile that usually melts women's hearts.

Sam positions herself right in front of me and every hair on her body stands, making her look just as vicious as her growl.

CJ and Michael step out of the house and stop. Their gaze jumps from me to Lucifer and back. I clench my teeth at Lucifer's perfect mimicry of my shaking fear. He is convincing enough that even CJ has a moment of pause. The hellhound adopting Sam's exact posture does not help.

Before I can signal CJ in some way, the demon horde Lucifer brought launches their attack. It isn't until I step into the fight that Michael heads for Lucifer, letting CJ and me take care of the demons.

Out of the corner of my eye, I catch a blur heading for Sam. I don't have a chance to react and her yelp as the hellhound's teeth dig in drives home desperation. My attempt at annihilating the demons with my mind only serves to push them off balance instead of turning them into dust.

When the first demon hits, I'm slammed into the ground with the force of his tackle. Air explodes from my lungs and I roll, falling back on my Jujitsu skills to throw the demon off. I no sooner get to my feet than two more attack, but this time I am ready, using everything our father and Steve taught us in self-defense.

The growling yanks my attention to the dogfight between us and I freeze at the image of the hellhound's jaws around Sam's throat. Her frantic eyes find mine as she tries to break the grip. Her paws rip at the hound's chest, but it's no use.

"No!" my cry sends a rumble through the ground like an earthquake, but I hold on to the angel fire burning my muscles. It's too raw and powerful, and uncontrollable for me to let it loose.

The hellhound shakes Sam like a rag doll and the sharp crack comes at the same moment I'm blindsided. From my stunned position on the ground, I see my loving, and ever faithful companion go limp. The loss hits like a lead weight, especially when her spirit peels from her dead body.

I break free from the demon pounding on me, and charge, diving and tackling the hellhound. A force I can't control races through my blood, painting my vision red. I wrap my arm around the beast's throat and squeeze, pulling its muzzle into the air. It drops Sam, but the damned thing keeps struggling, trying to break my hold. I pull with everything I have, bending its head back and twisting until its neck snaps, but that isn't good enough to satisfy the building rage. I keep twisting until the head tears clean off.

Hot hellhound blood saturates my shirt and jeans and I turn, pitching the head at Lucifer with a guttural roar. Instead of falling into defense mode, I go on the attack, pulling a demon out of the circle attacking CJ. Every muscle in my body is charged with fury and I spin, throwing the bastard into the two others charging towards me.

Again, I try to snuff them out with my mind, but all it does is make them stumble back a few steps.

The report of a gun makes me jump and I glance over my shoulder at the house. Butch Gallagher stands with his legs a little wider than hip distance apart and his gun trained on the surrounding melee. The second report echoes and another demon attacking CJ falls.

Before I can turn back towards those advancing on me, the Chief is launched backwards into the house by an invisible force. The crashing of furniture gives me a hint at the strength with which he was thrown, and I snap my gaze towards Lucifer. He has Michael in a mugger's hold, but before I can help, a couple of demons hit at once.

I glimpse CJ's split lip and bruised cheek as I break free and roll away from the demons. My roll isn't fast enough, and a boot connects with my lower back. Pain radiates from my kidney, but I force it out of my mind, climbing to my feet and throwing a punch of my own.

Air whistles and a breeze caresses my cheek. I spin in time to see an arrow embedded through the eye of the demon behind me, and he falls. Surprise rakes its nails down my back, and I turn towards the house as another arrow sails true, taking down one of the demons attacking my brother.

Bridget looks like a warrior princess in her tank top and jeans, with her hair pulled back. The rage in her features matches what pounds my insides, and when her aim turns towards Lucifer, the arrow falters at the image of me grappling with Michael. At that moment, a demon attacks her, and I sprint, avoiding another hit.

Bridget is driven through the open door and I can feel the angel fire surfacing along with the unbridled rage. A flash of metal flies through the air inside the house and the demon falls. I glimpse Valerie crawling from behind the counter and she gives me a thumbs up to tell me Bridget will be okay.

An arm wraps around my neck, pulling me away from the house and spinning me in front of another demon. The bastard smiles and his fist connects with my stomach, driving all the air out. I reach up and grab the arm holding me in place before the second hit lands. With a twist of my body and a hip roll, the demon holding me in place lands between us. I grab his head and twist with all the viciousness I can muster, and his neck snaps.

That leaves one demon between me and the group attacking CJ. Michael and Lucifer are still sparring, as if this is a demonstration instead of a fight to the death. Irritation burns and I refocus on the circling demon.

"Why the hell can't I just toast your ass?" I hiss through clenched teeth.

The demon smiles. "Angel blood," he says with a mouth full of crooked teeth. His voice reminds me of twisting metal and a chill slides down my spine. If angel blood hypes them up like a group of druggies on PCP, then I can't imagine how strong Lucifer is.

I draw in a breath, trying to center myself.

"Duck," Valerie's voice rings out.

I follow her order, expecting her knife to sail over me, but I'm not the only one who ducks, and when the shot rings over the backyard, I follow it, watching as it slices through CJ's shoulder, catapulting him over the rock wall.

Valerie's wail and two more rounds echo before metal clatters on concrete. Stunned into inaction, I glance over my shoulder in time to see her hair streaming out of sight towards the basement. I have a second to wonder where that extra escape route is before I am tackled by the remaining three demons.

Dozens of punches land before I can break free. I hold my arm against my pounding ribcage and cautiously move away towards the rock wall. The fact I can't feel CJ in my head brings a newly formed panic to my bones, and I glance toward Lucifer and Michael in time to see the final struggle.

Michael sways on his feet, hardly able to lift his arms in defense. Lucifer's next punch spins Michael, and he lands on his hands and knees, facing me.

Lucifer steps behind him and grabs a handful of his hair, pulling him back so I can see Michael's bruised face. His eyes lock on mine. Horror and defeat echo in his irises as Lucifer pulls out a knife. Lucifer waits with the blade on Michael's throat until I look up at his maniacal grin.

His eyes sparkle with bloodlust as the knife rakes across Michael's throat, slicing deep enough for blood to fly across the lawn in pulsing spurts. My stomach rolls as Lucifer grips his brother's head and twists it, decapitating Michael in one swift motion.

He rolls the head in my direction and points at me.

"Your turn," he growls as two of the demons grab my arms.

I spin, wrenching my wrist out of one demon's grip and land a throat punch with the momentum on the other. I mimic Lucifer and twist the fucker's head, snapping his neck before the two remaining demons attack.

An itch tickles my mind and I tap into my energy reserves, fending off as many punches as I can until I spin right into Lucifer's reach. His punch lifts me right off the ground, and the pain flares in my rib cage. I land on my knees and roll away before he can do the same thing he did to Michael.

CJ, if you're out there, I need you! I send the thought along with every ounce of panic pulsing in my veins.

I climb to my feet, taking stock as to where my attackers are. Keeping Lucifer in front of me, I slowly limp to my right, trying to keep my distance. I need to win. If I don't, my family will be tortured and killed until all that is left are the ones who can provide Lucifer with his army of dark trinities.

I need my odds to increase, and I sense one of the demons approaching behind me. I still have reserves left and when the crunch of the grass is close enough, I jump into a spin kick. My foot catches his jaw with enough force to snap his head almost all the way around, and the satisfying crunch of bone follows. I land, wincing as pain radiates from my ankle all the way up my leg. Not only did I kill the demon, but I broke my ankle in the process.

Fucking fantastic. I take a limping step and almost crumble, catching myself before I fall. The other demon drives in and the bottom of his boot slams into the calf of my good leg, just below the knee.

Ripping pain follows me to the ground and I roll, grabbing my knee as the howl escapes my lips. Awareness of a follow up kick coming in my direction splits through the pain and I roll out of the way, sweeping my leg, and dropping him to the ground. I'm not sure how I pull it off, but as the demon falls, he clocks his head on the edge of one of the rock pillars.

He doesn't get up and I force myself onto my feet because I am dead if I remain on the ground. My torn knee barely holds me, and I stumble closer to the house.

"Where do you think you're going?" Lucifer's growl precedes the yank of my hair and I fall backwards into him. His hand wraps around my neck, tightening enough for the airflow to shut down to a small wheeze.

"I promised you pain," he hisses in my ear.

I don't see it coming, but the searing pain across my abdomen reminds me of what that killer in Georgia used to do. My hands drop from the arm holding my throat to the hot pain gripping my stomach. Blood and entrails spill over my fingers and I gasp, trying to stuff my insides back where they belong. With his hand still clasped around my neck, holding me upright, he steps in front of me.

"That is only the beginning. I have a very special place for you in hell, and my staff has instructions to make your suffering more horrific than anything ever seen before." He smiles and his hand forms that familiar claw. "Now give me my fucking grace," he snarls.

His fingernails pierce my chest and I bellow in pain, even with the tight grip he has on my throat.

I'm coming, hold on! CJ's groggy and pain-filled voice fills my head.

I reach up, grabbing Lucifer's wrist, trying to stop his progression, but the blood makes my grip slick, and I cannot stop him. My heart squeezes under the pressure.

The whistle of air breaks my pain and an arrow pierces Lucifer's throat, shocking him enough to twist towards the house. His grip on my throat loosens and gravity does the rest. His claw dislodges from my chest as the second arrow pierces his chest and I land on the lawn on my back.

My gaze drops to the house as well, and Bridget sets up another arrow. Lucifer swats his hand as if he is knocking a gnat out of his face and Bridget flies backwards, right through the sliding glass door. The shattering glass cracks through the silence, and I grasp onto that last straw of anger.

I pool the power and shoot out what little angel fire I have left. All it does is pitch Lucifer ten feet onto his back. My failure magnifies as he rises to his feet, yanks the arrows out of his skin and then wipes himself off as if all he did was fall into a pile of dirt.

I shiver at the cold settling over me. My heart hurts, as does every other inch of my body. Heat fills my eyes and I say a small prayer asking God to deliver whatever CJ needs to beat this bastard. A buzz fills my ears, and the soft lick of Sam's tongue bathes my face. I look into her soft brown eyes and reach to pet her silky fur. My bloody hand touches air and falls back over my chest. Over my heart in the last protective action I can muster.

Lucifer is now in a dark haze, and he steps in my direction, but his head snaps to the right. White heat singes the lawn around me, and my battered brother launches at Lucifer. His golden wings are in full view, along with his blindingly scorching aura. The righteous fury emanating from him gives me a sliver of hope.

My body numbs and the thump of my heart slows as I watch the last battle unfold.

He has a knife. I send the thought just as Lucifer swipes it at CJ, but my brother parries like a pro, and with a quick maneuver, he disarms Lucifer. CJ controls his anger, using every bit to fuel his defense. When he turns the table and goes on the offence, his blows crack bone and split skin, until Lucifer falls to a knee.

That is the opening CJ has been waiting for and he grabs Lucifer's head, twisting with all the power of heaven behind him. Not only does angel fire add to his strength, it serves as purification, rolling across the blood drenched yard in a blinding light the moment he severs Lucifer's head.

The heat engulfs me, drowning out the screams of Bridget and my brother. My body feels light, as if it is rising off the ground, but my upward trajectory halts as Bridget reaches out, grabbing a handful of my shirt.

I meet her gaze and she yanks me down, trying to press me back inside my broken body.

"You are not dying on me," she says and Valerie blocks my view of her.

Warm lips touch my forehead and agony sears my soul. Blinding pain, flashes of light, and then it is all extinguished into the black.

Darkness drags me down, whether or not I want it to.

Angel Fury Chapter 13

THE BUZZING IN MY ears continue and I'm afraid to open my eyes, afraid of facing Lucifer in his domain. His promises were not lost in the transition, and cold bites into every layer of my soul.

The steady cadence of waves breaks through the buzz, along with the distinct sound of sobbing. I blink my eyelids open and my vision clouds. It takes me a minute to understand I'm not looking at fog, but drifts of smoke, and as the light wind shifts, stars peek out of the haze. The wind deepens the chill in my bones.

My focus shifts to the whispered prayers falling from Bridget's lips. Kneeling next to me, her hands are clasped in prayer, and her bow and arrows lay discarded to the side. A steady stream of tears flows down her cheeks from behind closed eyelids. I try to move my arm to wipe them, but it's just too heavy to budge, so I stare, helpless to offer any comfort.

My gaze moves a few paces beyond her to CJ and Valerie in a tight hug. My brother's back faces me, but his shoulders shake in the clear posture of grief. Chief Gallagher is on the phone asking the forensics staff to come along with the medical examiner.

A dull ache forms in my chest and within every inch of my body, and my lungs clench as if I have been underwater for far too long. That familiar burn grips me and I force an inhalation. The cold air tingles as it fills my oxygen-starved lungs.

My first attempt at speech is only a soft wheeze, and I close my eyes, gathering my strength.

"Who died?" I say loud enough to draw attention, but my voice sounds like I swallowed a shovel full of gravel.

Bridget's eyes snap wide enough for me to think they might just shoot right out of her head. CJ spins out of Valerie's arms, facing me with tear-soaked cheeks. His eyes are just as wide as Bridget's.

"And send an ambulance," Chief Gallagher says into the phone before he ends the call.

They all gather around me as if they are witnessing a miracle.

"You did," CJ says, and his voice is raw from the kind of crying tied to grief. I should know. I'm the king of emotional disasters.

I turn my head, look at the bodies still strewn across the lawn, and then turn back to Bridget, Valerie, and CJ. Valerie squats and takes my wrist, with lips pressed together in doubt. After a minute, her eyes widen, and she glances up at CJ.

"He has a pulse, but it's weak," she says and then drops her gaze to me.

"I was dead?" I'm still trying to catch up with the conversation.

Bridget still hasn't moved, and her face is now paler than it was before. Her gaze drifts down my body and back, as if she does not trust what she is seeing and hearing.

"My healing mojo didn't fix everything," she says. "You had lost too much blood..." She trails off and closes her eyes, putting the back of her wrist to her forehead. Her hand is covered in blood. "I tried CPR, but..." She blinks her eyes and a tear rolls down her cheek.

I move my gaze to the starry heavens above and then turn to Bridget as a memory surfaces. "You were the one who caught my spirit," I say.

She finally nods, but it is very slow, cautious, and her gaze jumps to my dead doppelganger a few feet away.

"How are you alive?" she asks, and she is the only one who has fear quaking her voice. "You were dead, like, no pulse, no breathing, dead. For at least five full minutes before Valerie stopped trying to revive you, dead."

I really want to say 'sometimes we come back', but the fear radiating from her is enough to chill out my warped sense of humor. CJ's smirk tells me he's in my head, but he has the courtesy of not repeating my thoughts. That familiar connection settles my nerves.

My fingers tingle and I wiggle them back to life, focusing on Bridget and her nearly hysterical question. She's on the edge and I want to reach out to her, but I have a feeling she would freak out more than she already is. I move my shoulders in a shrug because I have no explanation, especially since Valerie said her healing powers were useless.

"It might have been Raphael's grace," CJ says and I meet his gaze. "I had to try something. I wasn't ready to let you go." He looks up at the sky, blinking. When he seems to have his shit together, he continues. "Uriel's grace brought Valerie back, so I figured my best bet was giving you the grace of your great grandfather." He presses his lips together. "It didn't take right away, either," he adds, swiping at his eyes as he glances out over the ocean. "Needless to say, I didn't take it too well, so... you might have a broken rib or two." He gives me that cockeyed smile and I let out a soft laugh.

"I can deal with broken ribs," I say to the clouds above me.

"You are still in rough shape," Valerie says.

I turn to her before following her gaze to my chest. It's covered with thick, tacky blood, imprinted with her palm print where she tried chest compressions to revive me. Blood oozes from the welts where Lucifer's nails had sunk into my skin. I look beyond my chest, expecting to see my abdomen sliced open, but no scar remains where Lucifer gutted me.

I push up on my elbows and wince with pain as my midsection screams at me. My muscles still feel like they had been run through a woodchipper, but I force myself to focus and rotate my right ankle, bracing for pain that never comes. I lower my head back to the ground and pull my feet in, raising my knees, thankful that the last of the damage from what the demons did no longer exist. I sigh, thankful for small victories, but based on how I feel now that the numbness is receding, I have a feeling I might be in for more than just outpatient services.

"You are probably going to need a transfusion," Valerie says.

I nod and refocus on Bridget. Now that I can move, I reach out and take her hand, studying her. "Valerie fixed you up, too?"

She gives a little laugh and a nod. "The glass cut me up pretty badly."

Chief Gallagher steps into view and squats, running a hand down his face. "I have no idea how I am going to explain all this." He glances around at the carnage and shakes his head. "But I'll figure out a way."

I give him a small nod. Any more than that makes my stomach clench and the world spin. My eyes slip closed and Bridget's grip on my hand tightens, snapping my lids back open. I look at the fear carved in her face.

"I'm not dying again," I whisper. "I'm just in a hell of a lot of pain." I squeeze her hand gently, and her lips stretch into what she hopes is a smile, but all I see is a grimace. I try on a smile of my own. "I promise."

"Mom!" April's shrill cry rings from the house.

"She shouldn't see this," I say, but the girl is already running across the yard, dodging the dead bodies, followed by CJ's kids.

She skids to a stop next to Bridget at the same time CJ's kids fall into Valerie's and CJ's arms. Behind them, Naomi and her children follow slower, scanning the carnage as their faces go pale, and in the rear come Austin and Paige, looking as shell-shocked as I am sure everyone else is.

The slow realization that the people we have been tasked with protecting for the past fifteen years would never need our services again crawls into my mind, and I trade a glance with CJ. He presses his lips together

and nods. While we both mourn the loss of Steve and
Jennifer, and a hole in my chest remains for Sam, I
can't help but embrace the hope filling my senses.

Angel Fury Chapter 14

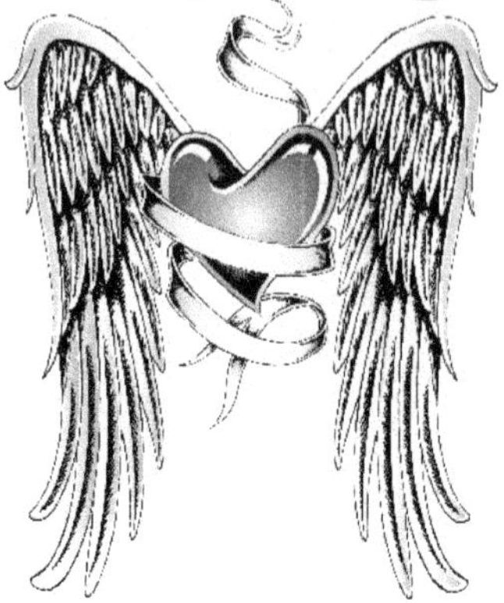

HOSPITAL FOOD SUCKS AND I pick at the green gelatin as the electrocardiogram beeps in a semi-steady rhythm. My diagnosis is six cracked ribs, along with myocardial contusion. A bruised heart, which means I am sequestered in a hospital bed until my heart rhythm returns to normal.

My red cell count is low as well, but I can't exactly tell them I already bled out on my brother's backyard, so I succumb to a transfusion along with a healthy dose of pain medicine and every conceivable test known to man. I have been poked and prodded, stuck and scanned for the last few hours, and they finally left me hooked to the ECG and two separate intravenous bags, one with blood, the other with saline and those horribly mind-bending pain meds.

Valerie and CJ step into the room once the doctor steps out. I glance up from the tray, rolling my eyes. Both of them are clean, and that old twinge of jealousy hits. While they cleaned most of the blood and gore from me prior to patching up my chest, I still had streaks of it on my skin.

"At least twenty-four hours on this monitor?" I say, hooking my thumb at the beeping machine. My voice sounds distorted in my ears and annoyance blooms at the medicine impeding my speech.

Valerie steps closer and leans in, pressing her lips to my cheek. A tingle starts in my ribs and then the blinding pain grips me, making my heart, and the monitor, beat more erratically.

"Shit, woman, a little warning," I hiss as my ribs mend under her healing magic. At least the pain is dulled by the medicine they are pumping into me, but it is still bad enough to register in my fog-filled brain.

"I doubt it will fix your heart, but it should fix the damage CJ and I did to your ribs."

"You mean *you* crushed my ribs?" I ask, because I saw the x-ray and it wasn't pretty, but at least they didn't need to crack me open to fix the damage.

She gives me a tilted smile. "I'm responsible for the crack in your sternum."

A nurse comes darting in before I can say something rude to Valerie about finally doling out a little justice of her own. Her tilted smile grows, and she sends me a wink while the nurse dotes on me.

Concern presses the nurse's lips in a straight line, and her gaze bounces from the monitor to me.

"I'm fine, I just shifted my weight," I say, trying to give a logical explanation, but she comes to the side of the bed, crowding Valerie and CJ out of the way.

"Perhaps you should rest," she says and picks up my wrist.

"What I'd really like is a shower and something clean to wear," I mumble, and she gives me the same look she did when they first rolled me into this room.

"Tomorrow, Mr. Ryan," she reminds me, and I nod. She turns to CJ and Valerie. "Perhaps you should let your brother get some rest."

"I said I am fine."

CJ and Valerie exchange a glance before they look at me. "Get some rest. We'll bring you some clean clothes in the morning," CJ says and leads Valerie out the door.

The nurse follows them out and lowers the lights, drenching me in darkness.

I lie back on the bed and my gaze travels to the window and the night beyond. As much as I'd like to rest, I'm not sure what form of nightmare will grip me as soon as I fall asleep.

The door squeaks, and I turn my head. The soundless movement across the dark room gives me a start, but the moment the weight gathers on the edge of the bed, I stiffen.

"Bri?" It's the only logical explanation.

"Yeah," she whispers and I shift, giving her more room than just the half inch between the edge and me.

"Come here," I say in a low whisper, and she doesn't hesitate. She slides to my side, stretching out next to me, and her head finds my shoulder. My arms wrap around her as best as I can, but I'm limited with all the wires and tubes. Still, having her against me strengthens my heartbeat, steadying me. I press my lips to her forehead. "Where's April?"

"She's having a girl's night with Grace at Naomi's."

"And you didn't want some of that fun?"

She laughs softly. "No. I needed… this." She gives me a gentle squeeze.

It isn't until the bed shakes that I realize she's crying. I can't see her face in the dark, but the damp heat where her cheek rests on my shoulder is enough.

"Babe, please don't cry," I whisper, and gently run my fingers through her hair.

"You were…" Her voice chokes on the sob and I pull her to my lips, quieting her and trading memories, so she doesn't have to tell me how much my death crushed her.

When the kiss breaks, my eyes burn with unshed tears. The turmoil still present within her tempers my horror at what I saw through her eyes. I knew I had been bad off, but I had no idea just how close Lucifer had been to getting his grace and damning my soul to hell forever.

"I'm so sorry," I whisper in her ear.

"I haven't prayed that hard for a miracle in years," she sniffles.

"I'm glad someone upstairs heard you," I say, and she squeezes me tighter. I let out a soft laugh. "I'm afraid to go to sleep," I admit, and her head lifts off my shoulder.

"Why?"

The burn in my eyes increases and I blink, trying to soothe it. Hot paths trace down into my ears and the memory of my father's disorientation when we pulled him out of hell lingers. "What if this isn't real? What if I wake up to find I have utterly failed, and I'm in the pit?"

Her hand finds my cheek and her gentle caress grounds me, but that nagging fear keeps me on edge.

"What if I can't ever get rid of this fear?" I ask, but it isn't for Bridget to answer. It's for me to deal with, and I squeeze her tighter to me. If this is a dream and I'm indeed in hell, I'm holding onto this vision as long as I can.

Angel Fury Chapter 15

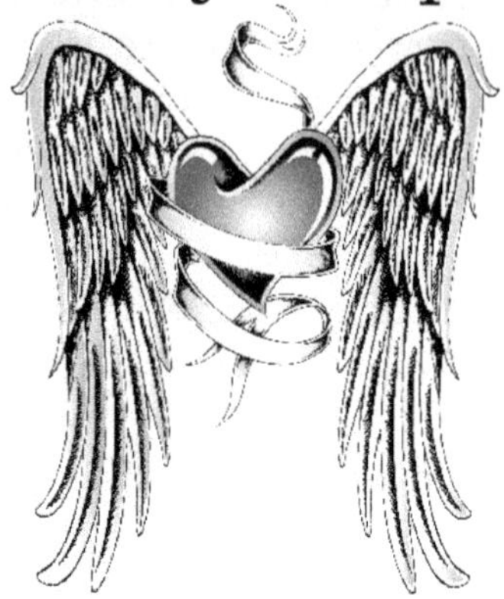

AT SOME POINT DURING the early hours of the morning, the medicine and exhaustion won out. I slept dreamlessly and soundly, with Bridget tucked by my side. My eyes blink open to the bright sunshine filtering into the room and I turn my head, expecting Bridget still to be next to me, but the bed is empty. My heart trips and the monitor echoes the change in adrenaline.

A light sweat breaks out on my exposed skin, and my breathing picks up as well. My eyes dart from corner to corner, looking for signs I might be missing. When my heart rate pulses in my temple, the door opens, and a nurse rushes in.

"Where is she?" I ask, my voice hoarse from sleep.

"Mr. Ryan, I suggest you calm down," she says softly, her wide eyes dart to the display and then back to mine.

"She was here when I went to sleep," I say as I try to calm my breathing, but my pulse continues to race.

"Who?" the nurse asks and checks my IV line. After a moment, the burn of medicine filters into my vein, and I glare at her.

"I don't need drugs," I say, even as the edge seems to come off the panic gripping me.

She pats my hand. "You've been through quite the trauma, sir. It's normal to have some disorientation." She glances at the chart and then up at the nearly empty bags of blood. She smiles and leans over, unplugging the drip from my hand before pulling the empty bags from the post. She drops them in the hazard box and returns to my side.

The anxiety still resides at my core, but my attention focuses on the nurse removing the blood transfusion tube from my hand. "But Bridget was here with me last night. Where is she?" I ask again after she presses a band-aid over the entry point.

Before she can answer, the door opens and all the tension releases at the sight of Bridget carrying two Dunkin Donuts coffee cups. Her smile fades and a crease appears between her eyes as she meets my gaze.

The nurse turns. "Visiting hours aren't for another hour."

"She can stay," I say and the nurse glances at me, raising an eyebrow in a challenge.

My gaze hardens. "Bridget can stay," I insist, pushing the command and the nurse purses her lips, but doesn't contradict the command. She gives Bridget a glare as she leaves the room.

"I thought you might need some coffee today," she says and puts the cup on the table next to me.

I glance at it. "I'm not sure I'm allowed yet," I say and give her a smile. I don't want her to know how panicked I got when I woke up and she wasn't here, but I guess I don't do a very good job of it.

"You were freaked out," she says and leans back in the chair.

I let a little laugh escape. "No," I add, but she knows. In the light of day, all my fears seem to be unwarranted, and I grab the coffee off the table. Rules be damned.

"How are you feeling?"

I take a sip of the coffee and close my eyes, debating on how to answer. My chest still aches, as does every muscle in my body, but there is no pain. "I'm not bad," I say after my self-assessment. "Considering I still smell like death," I add, and open my eyes.

"Well, now you smell like death and coffee," she smiles and glances at her phone. "CJ said the cops were still trying to figure out what in the hell happened and what those things were in the yard." She glances up at me. "Apparently, neither Michael nor Lucifer had a heart. It has completely freaked out the medical examiner. And no one can identify what kind of animal attacked your dog."

My smile fades at the mention of Sam. I'm not sure the mystery of the hellhound will be solved, but the ache in my chest gets worse. "She was such a great dog," I say and glance out the window.

Her hand touches mine, and I glance at the contact.

"What happened to keeping your distance?" I ask and thread my fingers through hers.

Her cheeks flush and she looks at the ground. "You came back," she whispers and shrugs.

"I'm still damaged," I gently remind her, but keep her hand in mine.

"I'm not exactly a pillar of strength, either," she says, and I laugh.

"You could have fooled me. You were fearless and pretty damned accurate with those arrows."

She meets my gaze, but there is no smile. "I knew what was at stake if we lost."

That nonchalant shoulder shrug appears, minimizing her contribution to the fight, and I was having none of it. "You were the one who saved us. If you hadn't created a diversion..." I close my eyes and take a deep inhalation, trying to loosen the knot that built as we discussed what could have happened. "You saved all our asses."

"CJ did that."

I shake my head and meet her unsure stare. "CJ ended the threat, but you gave him the time he needed to get it done." I took another sip of coffee and sighed, running my hand down my face. "He got shot, and I never asked him how he was doing." I exhale.

"I'm fine, but for a while there, I wasn't so sure. It's a miracle I didn't bash my head on any of those rocks. As it was, I broke my hip when I fell, and halfway to the dock, I blacked out. That's why it took me so goddamned long to get my ass up the ladder and back in the game," CJ says, stepping into the room. "I guess we are both damned lucky it was high tide."

I had no idea how bad off he had been, but it explains the lack of mental connection for part of the time I fought those bastards. I give him a nod of acknowledgement.

He smiles at me. "The yard is a fucking mess. I didn't realize demon blood was black and as hard to get rid of as melted tar."

"What are you talking about?" I clearly remember him blowing up a couple of demons and what went splat was red.

"None of the demons we ever fought before this were Lucifer's guards," he says softly. "And I think we're going to have to dig up the entire backyard and reseed."

Such mundane and utterly normal stuff to worry about pulls a smile to my face. "It's nice for that to be your biggest worry," I say and he huffs a laugh.

"Yeah, well, I'm sure when my daughters start dating, I'll be a fucking basket case, especially knowing there are guys like you out there."

Bridget chuckles and glances at him. I press my lips together against the smile gaining traction, but both CJ's etched dimples and Bridget's laugh make me lose the battle.

"I don't think I'll be any different," I say and tighten my grip on Bridget's hand just in case she decides this is the moment to pull away and protect her heart.

She squeezes back.

The nurse steps into the room, and a crease appears between her eyes as her lips thin. "Visiting hours are not for another half an hour."

"Come on, Mary, you know Tom's my brother," he says, rolling his eyes at her. I didn't realize he knew the nurses by name, but I guess with Valerie's connections, he probably knew most of the hospital staff by first name.

"Do I have to call your wife?" Her arms cross.

CJ does that puppy-dog eyes thing. "Can't you just bend the rules for today? I'm already here, besides I brought him some clothes," he says, holding up my duffel bag, and gives her that signature smile I have seen on television more than a dozen times over the years. It always causes a collective sigh from the female audience and this situation is no different.

She makes that sigh and comes to my side, breaks the grip I have with Bridget, and checks my pulse. She glances at the coffee in my free hand and plucks it out of my hand.

"No caffeine until the doctor reviews your results."

I balk, but don't say a thing. We are already pushing our luck at this point, and I'd rather have Bridget and CJ here than a coffee, anyway. Instead, I ask, "Can I take a shower and put on some real clothes?"

"As soon as the doctor looks at you," she says. "He should be in here within the next half hour."

"Okay," I say, dropping my gaze. The need to feel clean is becoming as dominant as my need for food, and my stomach growls in response.

She pulls out a small vial syringe and attaches it to the open port in my IV, decompressing the handle until the vial is full. "Just checking your blood count," she says when she unclips it and then she disappears out of the room.

I glance back at CJ and Bridget.

"I really want to get the hell out of here."

CJ's expression sobers up, and he glances out the window. "Valerie explained the seriousness of your heart injury." He shifts and looks at the floor before meeting my gaze again. "You need to make sure your heart is as close to normal as possible before you check yourself out of here."

I bite my lip, trying to read into his mind, but he's blocking me.

Bridget turns and stares at CJ. "Why?"

"He could have a heart attack if he's not careful. That's why they are dancing around his aggravation and sedating him when he gets too... excited." CJ looks from Bridget to me. "You aren't out of danger yet." His hands slide into his pockets. "And Valerie's magic can't fix it."

The seriousness in both his features and his tone makes me nod slowly.

"So, if I push my luck, my ticker gives out?" My hand rises to cover my heart and I flinch at the pressure against the cuts underneath.

"Pretty much," he says.

"For how long?" I glance at Bridget for a moment before I meet CJ's gaze. He just shrugs.

"I'm not a doctor," he says.

"This isn't... permanent?" The monitor echoes the increase in my heart rate at the idea of being limited for the rest of my life, in ways I can only imagine.

Again, that fucking shrug. Before I can get any more uncomfortable with this conversation, the doctor waltzes in.

He is studying his tablet, swiping from screen to screen before he takes a seat on the rolling chair. He rolls to the ECG output as we all watch him. His mental narration is too clinical for me, so I glance at CJ. He gives me the *I have no fucking clue* shrug.

The doctor whistles, and my heart leaps into my throat. The auditory trigger catapults me back to the carving table in Georgia and terror grips every cell. My hands tighten on the rails of the bed as the pain spirals from my heart outward.

The whistling stops and he jerks his head towards me as the ECG goes haywire. He didn't quite understand why his whistling knocked me into cardiac arrest, but my frightened stare meets CJ's and the sound in the room fades to a high-pitched buzz.

I'm spinning, and my chest feels like someone just punched through it. I wonder if this is what Damian felt when I blew up his ribcage. My vision tunnels, darkening at the edges.

"You promised me!" Bridget's scream breaks through and my gaze snaps to hers.

"I'm not going anywhere." I try to speak, but I can't, so I send the thought to her as CJ grabs her and drags her from the room.

It takes me a minute to realize I am not observing the room from the bed, from my wide-open and unfocused eyes.

Shit.

I am not in my body and that high-pitched buzz is the heart monitor flat lining.

I promised Bridget I wouldn't die, and here I am, breaking her heart yet again.

"This is not happening," I say, willing my spirit to meld with my skin.

When nothing happens, aggravation flushes my vision. "Goddamnit! Do something!" I yell at the roomful of doctors.

"Clear!"

The electricity buzzes through my body and my viewpoint changes with the jolt. The doctor holding the paddles goes flying across the room, and I sit up, feeling every ounce of Raphael's angel grace melding inside me. It's just as painful as absorbing Lucifer's grace was, but this comes with an agonizing side benefit, the mending of my heart. I curl into a ball as light pours from me, blinding everyone in the room, and I don't realize I'm bellowing through the suffering until both the light, and my voice, fade.

I pant, scanning the shocked group of doctors and nurses, wondering why this didn't happen on the battlefield when CJ pushed the grace inside me. My gaze stops at the open doorway and both CJ and Bridget standing with open mouths. Everyone is staring at me with open mouths.

"You could catch flies with that," I say to my brother, resurrecting one of our mother's lines from when we were little. His mouth pops closed.

I glance at the doctor who was thrown across the room. "Are you okay?"

He utters a high-pitched laugh as he climbs to his feet. Everyone in the room takes a shaky step backward. All of them have eyes locked on my chest, and I glance down. A sigil is burned right through the bandage covering my heart. I recognize it immediately and glance at CJ as I claw at the dressing covering Lucifer's damage, ripping it from my skin.

I stare at the place previously marred by Lucifer's nails, and only Raphael's sigil remains, burned into my skin like a tribal tattoo. The heart monitor registers a strong and steady beat and I'm not sure what to say.

"I guess I should *not* stand outside in an electrical storm," I finally say, and eyes widen before CJ's chuckle rolls over the room and the tension splits into nervous laughter.

Angel Fury Chapter 16

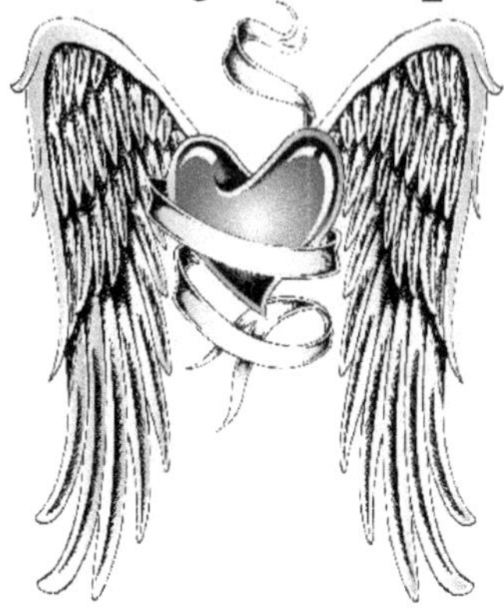

THEY HAVE NO IDEA what the fuck to do with me. I've succumbed to all of their tests after I took a shower and cleaned off any remnants of the horror I endured. Nothing remains of the damage that was there when I was brought in last night.

"We'd like to do more tests," Dr. Wallace says as he flips through my chart.

"No disrespect, but none of your tests is going to provide you with the logical explanation you're looking for." I lean back in the chair and cross my arms. "This one isn't explainable."

"I need to know what happened," he says, pulling his glasses off and pinching the bridge of his nose.

"Divine intervention," I say.

"Bullshit!" He glares at me from across the room.

I lean over and finish lacing my boots. I climb to my feet and grab the duffel bag CJ brought this morning.

"I'm leaving," I say and start out of the room.

"This hospital will not be responsible for any relapse if you leave right now," he snaps.

I glance over my shoulder at him. "I'm pretty sure that's something that will not happen for another forty years or so," I say, and I know it's flippant, but I am tired and hungry and want to eat a fricken moose, and then take a nap in a regular bed, not a hospital cot where they can observe the freak.

I walk outside, expecting CJ, but Bridget leans against her car instead.

"I don't smell like death and coffee anymore," I say and spread my arms out, giving her my signature grin.

Her lips spread into a tight smile and she nods, slipping into the driver's seat without a word. I toss my bag onto the back and then drop into the passenger seat with a huff.

"I need to eat," I say through a yawn.

"I'm sure your brother has something you can grab." The chill in her voice hits and I glance at her.

"You're pissed at me?"

She sends me a sideways glare. "Is this the way it's always going to be?" she snaps the question out.

"I didn't plan on dying, Bridget. It just fucking happened, okay?"

"What exactly happened in there?" Her hands grip the steering wheel so hard her knuckles are white.

I take a deep breath, calming myself. "You didn't get the tune he was whistling?"

She looks at me with a crease between her eyes. "Whistle while you Work from Snow White. Why?"

I just stare at her and cock my head.

She shrugs and looks back at the road. "Well?"

"Take a closer look at those memories of when I was nine." I glance out the side window.

We pass harbor beach and the church while she drifts through the memories. As we approach CJ's road, she gasps and nearly misses the turn. The car bounces off the curb before she gets control of it again and stops before we get to the curve in the road. Throwing the vehicle in park, she turns to me, her eyes wide enough for me to explain.

"It all came back like that." I snap my fingers. "So did the terror, and I guess CJ wasn't kidding about how fragile my heart was."

She quietly digests the new information, chewing on her bottom lip in a way that makes me want to kiss her, but I refrain. When her eyes drift back to mine, she says, "So, if we had taken you home and something triggered you, you would have died?"

I don't answer because she is probably right; instead, I look out the windshield. The electric shock did something, and if I hadn't been in the hospital... my mind doesn't even entertain the 'what if' involved, and I glance at Bridget.

"Technically, I did die." A chill skitters from my neck to my tailbone, and I grimace. "And you screaming at me was the only reason I didn't just fade to black."

She stares at me.

"So, thank you," I add.

She blinks and does a little shake of her head, as if something morbid crawled under her skin, before she focuses back on the road. With a deep breath, she puts the car in drive. "You're welcome," she says, without looking at me. "But it was the defibrillator, not me."

Her mind is swirling so fast that I'm only getting an image here and a thought there, and every memory is heart wrenching.

"It was you. Without your rant, I wouldn't have been trying to get back into my body at the precise moment they shocked me." I chew on the inside of my lip, debating on asking if I should really expect a future with her, especially after the pain I've caused.

She pulls through the broken gate and parks.

I grab her hand before she gets out, and she stops with one foot on the driveway and looks back at me. "What?"

The snap in her voice makes me let her go. "Nothing." I step out of the car and follow her to the door, where she waves for me to lead the way.

I open the door, and stare at the banner hung haphazardly across the living room. Noisemakers and streamers meet me, and if I *had* had a weak heart, the shock of the welcoming party would have put me into cardiac arrest. The words written on the banner pull a grin from me. Welcome back from the dead! I particularly liked the electrified skeleton they hung from one end, like a seriously twisted after-thought.

I meet my brother's gaze and he shrugs, looking over his shoulder at his handiwork, with the same stupid grin I'm sure I'm wearing. I turn on Bridget and point at her.

"You knew about this?"

Her light laugh caresses my soul and without her permission, I pull her against me and plant a serious kiss on her laughing lips.

I let more time pass than appropriate in a room full of onlookers before I break the kiss and step inside.

I stare at the sign and my smile fades. Everyone I truly care about stands in my brother's living room, and for a moment, I feel the loss of those who aren't here celebrating this moment with us. My gaze lands on Naomi and her family, and I give a nod.

Grace is the first person to approach, and she steps forward tentatively.

"Thank you," she says, and I just swallow the lump in my throat.

"I'm sorry your father wasn't here to see this day," I say, in a voice squeezed with emotion.

Her palm cups my cheek. "This was meant to pass," she says, and that age-old wisdom I remember clouds her eyes. "The righteous man has to fall in order to claim the light and banish the darkness." Her hand dropped from my cheek. "I never understood that until now."

"Where did you hear that?" I ask, and she gives me that soft smile that reminds me of both her mother and father at the same moment.

"The angels have been telling me that all my life," she answers, and I can't help but shiver and glance up at Naomi.

I utter a laugh. "So much for chance," I say, and Naomi actually allows a tight smile. She still does not like me, and being in the same room is painful for her.

"They also wanted me to let you know you've earned your salvation. Lucifer is no longer a threat to us, and for that, they are grateful."

I have to bite my lip against the sudden swell of emotion those words bring to the surface, and I give Grace a quick hug before crossing to Naomi.

"I know there isn't a thing I can do to fix what I've done to you and your family…"

She puts her fingers over my mouth. "It had to be you." She looks over my shoulder at Grace and then back at me. "And as much as I hate you for killing my husband, I know it had to be you, and it had to be him." Tears form in her eyes. "It was the only way for us to be free and that's all he ever wanted."

I drop my chin to my chest, fighting the burn in my eyes and at the back of my throat. "I miss him," I whisper, knowing my feelings on the matter are nothing compared to hers. He had been my best friend, my pillar when shit hit the fan, and he never once let me down. Killing him had nearly killed me. I meet her gaze and she rolls her lower lip between her teeth and nods before she pulls me into a hug.

When she releases me, I step back, scanning the room.

"Hey," I say to Paige and Austin. Outside of the small conversation at their house before hell broke loose, we hadn't really had a chance to talk. I was looking forward to getting reacquainted with them once things settled down.

"I guess this is all that is left of the angel bloodlines." Austin says, and I glance around the room.

"Twelve."

"The number of zodiac signs," Paige says with a smile.

I let out a laugh and turn back to Bridget, who stands right next to CJ. My gaze rises to the skeleton again just as another zap hits it. "Nice touch. Whose idea was that?"

The dimples carved in Bridget's cheeks give me the answer even before CJ points at her. I glance at our daughter.

"Your mother is seriously twisted," I say, and she just blushes and glances at Bridget with a nod.

"I have a bottle with your name on it in the other room," CJ says, and he shuffles his feet before he steps through the kitchen entry. The group flows through the door before I can, and I'm not sure if it's coordinated or just coincidence that I am left last with Bridget.

I grab her arm, stopping her from following the rest of the crew.

"So the car?" I hook my thumb over my shoulder. "You weren't really pissed?"

Her smile fades a notch. "CJ's been teaching me how to hide my thoughts, and it seems I'm most successful when I'm angry or hurt, so I just kept replaying those things in my head. And yeah, it still pisses me off that you left and made a conscious choice not to answer any of my calls, so I used it."

"Well, you did a great job. And that," I look up again at the extra special twist in the sign. "Is fucking fantastic," I add with a grin.

She takes my hand and leads me into the back room where everyone has gathered. I cross to the sliders and CJ hands me a glass of Dewars. I glance at the lawn and CJ wasn't kidding. It was a mess, with spots of black patches mixed with rust patches. "Did you try holy water?" I ask, nodding at the black mess.

CJ and Valerie exchange a glance and both of them shake their head.

"Neither of us even thought of that," Valerie laughs.

I offer my best 'maybe you should try' smile and focus back on the yard.

"We have hot dogs and hamburgers along with macaroni and cheese for everyone tonight," CJ says. "It's time to celebrate."

"Celebrating sounds great!" I say, and I'm not sure I mean it, but I sip my scotch and take a seat on the couch, observing the family dynamics I had missed for the last ten years. After a flurry of activity in the kitchen, the kids run downstairs with arms full of snacks and soda. CJ and Austin chat over by the refrigerator, while the women work as a team in the kitchen, putting together snacks for us.

Bridget catches me watching out of the corner of her eye and stops, turning towards me, and she just leans on the counter with a smile. I had her memories. I should know how close she has gotten to my family, but seeing it in action leaves an emptiness in my center, along with a sliver of envy. I raise my glass at her and down the scotch.

The warm flow spreads through me, and I close my eyes. The couch cushion shifts and I open my eyes, taking in Bridget's beautiful hazel eyes.

"Are you okay?" she asks softly, studying me, looking for any sign of weakness that might indicate a relapse of some sort.

"I'm fine." I look at the group continuing to talk and work together. "I just haven't been in a lot of social situations in quite a few years." When my gaze returned to hers, I press my lips together in a slight smile. "I'm not good at small talk."

"Since when?"

I laugh. "Since always."

"You used to be the center of attention," she says.

"That's only because people had to watch my hands to know what the hell I was saying." I chuckle, looking at her sideways.

"Yeah, well, your hands were magic," she mumbles and goes to stand up.

"What?"

She smiles. "All the girls watched your hands because we wanted them on us, and all the guys watched because your hands could catch a rocket at fifty yards."

"And here I thought it was because I had such interesting things to say."

"About what?" CJ says, and takes a seat on the other couch, looking between us.

"I was just teasing your brother," Bridget says, and wanders towards the kitchen and the cheese and cracker spread on the breakfast bar.

CJ watches her go and glances at me, tilting his head in her direction.

"I don't need dating advice from you," I say and lean forward, pouring another glass of scotch. "Besides, there's no rush. We'll eventually figure it out." I follow his gaze, and her light laugh drifts over the room.

The rest of the night passes in surreal slow motion. Laughter prevails, and it isn't the sarcastic or tension filled laughter of the last fifteen years. It's strange, and a part of me is uncomfortable with it, as if I am going to wake to find our peace is all an illusion.

Naomi has the same haunting in her eyes that I'm experiencing. She's been on the run a hell of a lot longer than any of us, so this has to be just as unnerving to her. She looks up from her conversation, meeting my gaze as if she can read my mind, and I send her a nod along with a closed-lip smile before I finish my drink.

"Did you ever think we'd see this day?" Valerie asks as she steps by my side, scanning the room with me.

"Honestly, no. I'm still waiting for the bomb to drop."

"I think we all are," she says and drapes her arm over my shoulder. "But for now, I say we seize the day!" Her grin is infections and I clink my empty glass against hers in a show of solidarity.

Angel Fury Chapter 17

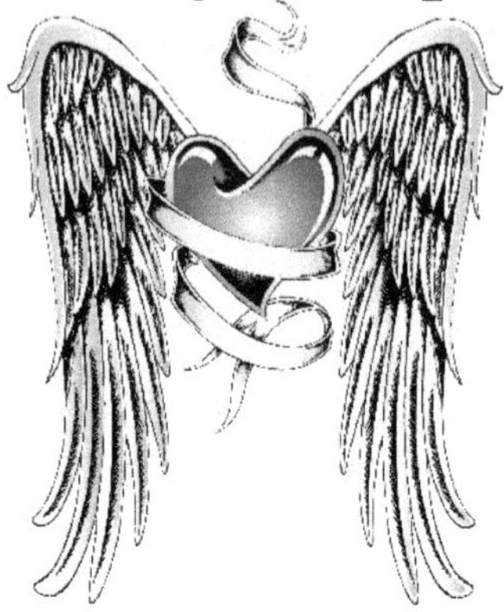

SUNSHINE WAKES ME AND I cover my eyes with my arm, but it's enough to get my mind moving, even though it's sluggish from alcohol consumption. I roll onto my side, even though I know it's useless. Once my brain shifts into gear, there is no more sleep coming until the most inopportune moment of the day.

After a shower and a change of clothes, I climb down the stairs and fix myself a cup of coffee, retreating outside in the cool morning sunshine. I find my perch on the rock wall and stare out at the water. Movement pulls my attention back towards the house and Naomi is a few feet away.

"Morning," I say and she takes a seat.

"Morning," she glances out over the water and turns towards me. "This is all too weird."

A low laugh comes from deep within my chest. "Very." My gaze drifts towards the damaged lawn. "I didn't expect to live," I say and meet her gaze.

"Neither did I," she says softly. "I guess now that this is all over, I should think about trying to move on."

I give her a slow nod. "Just don't let anyone take advantage of you."

Her curt laugh draws a smile and heat rises in my cheeks.

"You know what I mean," I say and roll my eyes. "Just out of curiosity, is there anyone in particular?"

Now it is her turn to blush, and she moves her hand back and forth.

I raise an eyebrow.

"One of the teachers at the high school has shown interest," she mumbles, and sips her coffee. "But he's a lot younger than I am."

"Look at you, going all cougar and shit," I say, grinning, and the look she sends me should have shut me up right there, but I've never been good with keeping my thoughts to myself since my wife's tongue replaced mine. "So, have you... um, sampled the goods?"

"Oh. My. God." She stands up and walks away.

"Naomi?" I ask, stopping her and she looks over her shoulder at me. "Damian wouldn't want you to be alone for the rest of your life."

She keeps her back to me. "I couldn't bring anyone into this nightmare."

I sigh, knowing exactly what she meant. "I ran from Bridget for the same reason."

She looks over her shoulder at me and her eyes sparkle as her lips twitch into a smile. "I think it's time we both sampled the goods."

I grin and sip my coffee as she wanders back to her house, laughing under her breath. The sea lulls me into thought, and they turn to Bridget, as they have since I drove away ten years ago. I glance at my watch. The bus has already come and gone, if my memory serves me and I head inside, retrieving the small box that I carried back from Greece.

"I'm borrowing the truck," I say aloud to the quiet house.

Okay, CJ's sleepy voice echoes in my head, and I grab the keys off the peg. The drive is short, and I sit in the cab, staring at the house, wondering exactly what I'm going to say. I can't exactly walk in the door and just blurt out the question on my mind.

I continue to stare at the house, inspecting my intentions a little closer, and then I slip out of the car and stroll to the door, looping the keys around my finger to settle the nerves biting at me.

I poise my hand to knock and then drop it, turning away. Staring at the river across the way, I can't help but wonder if Bridget is better off without me. I close my eyes and turn back to the door with my hands on my hips.

Now that the danger isn't lurking anymore, will she still see someone worthy of her love, or have I screwed this up so much that she'll finally see under the facade?

I grit my teeth and knock on the door.

The faint shuffle of feet on the wood floor drifts through the door, and when the wood door swings open, I offer an uncomfortable smile.

"Hi." I stare at her and lick my lips, unsure of what else to say. My eyes flow down the blue silk shirt to the cream skirt and the sexy open-toed heels. She makes me feel grossly underdressed in my jeans and flannel shirt.

"You don't need to knock. This is your business, too." She points up in the air and my gaze follows to the sign still carrying my name, while Bridget swings the door open for me.

"But you and April live here, and I don't want to impose." I know I'm reaching, but I can't figure out what her deal is today.

"Tom, you own the business and this house." She rolls her eyes at me when I step inside.

Technically, she's right. If I wanted to be a dick, I could insist on living here and she would have no choice, but I'm not. Nor do I want to be.

"Since you're back..." she hands me a stack of call transcripts and turns, heading into the only office left. I stare after her, and a low simmer burns at the sexy sway of her hips before she sashays out of sight. My gaze drops to the notes. I shuffle through them as I cross into Damian's old office.

I stop in the door and blink at the brightness before me. The only familiar item is the desk, and she slides into the comfortable looking ergonomic chair, turning towards the computer monitor. The rest of the decor has changed drastically from my old partner's dark tastes.

Now this space is light, almost too light, in my opinion. Even the furniture radiates a sunny disposition, which is in direct contrast to Bridget right now. She is all business, and I take one more scan, looking for an alternate workstation as if it would materialize out of nowhere.

"Where am I supposed to work?" I ask, and she looks up from the computer, nodding towards the couches.

"You can set up over there until we can get another desk." She turns her focus back to the computer.

Her lack of warmth has me a little confused, especially after the heat I felt from her yesterday when I kissed her at the house. I step closer to the desk. "Bri?"

Her hands pause over the keys, and she takes a deep breath before facing me and folding her arms on the desk. When she tilts her head and purses her lips, I'm not sure what to say.

It's been a long time since I felt like a scolded kid, but that's the vibe I am getting right now. I can't read a thing from her, which is more than frustrating.

I drop the pile of notes on the desk, meeting her hard and inquisitive gaze.

"I'm working, Tom," she says, and even her tone is terse.

That old familiar frustrated burn fills my stomach and I walk around the side of the desk. She swivels the chair, so she is facing me and crosses her arms. I lean forward, planting a hand on each chair arm, staring her down.

"You are right. This is my business, so stop treating me like I'm a junior intern on my first day."

The edges of her lips twitch.

"So, what exactly are you going to do to me, boss man?" Her voice fills with spitfire, but her cheeks flush in response to my close proximity.

My gaze drifts from her eyes to her now slightly parted lips, and then drops to the opening of her silk shirt, giving me a peek at her cleavage. I take a chance.

"What exactly would you have me do?" I ask in an equally terse tone.

A dimple appears before she locks it down, but the sparkle in her eyes tells me what I need to know. When she doesn't answer, I slowly drop to my knees.

"Would you have me beg for your forgiveness?" I ask, letting my hands drop to the side of the chair, my thumbs just barely grazing the outside of her silk-clad thighs.

"That's a start," she says.

"Perhaps instead of begging, I need to earn it." My hands move onto her thighs, drifting down to her knees before gradually moving upwards under the skirt. Her skin quivers under my touch.

"Perhaps." Her voice falls into that husky quality I remember from my dreams, and I stop.

The flare of wanting in her eyes resumes my momentum and I close in, meeting her parted lips with mine, just as my fingers graze her bare pussy. I chuckle against her lips.

"You are so very... naughty," I whisper and deepen the kiss, remembering the dream and the reality of her all at once. This time I do pause, and pull away from her mouth. Our eyes lock. My hand still plays with her and her thighs part, inviting me to do more than just caress her.

Heat fills my cheeks and I let out a laugh. "I don't have anything."

She smiles and opens the desk drawer, lifting out a strip of condoms.

"When did you pick those up?" I ask, hoping it wasn't some random time between when I left and today, but her answer just makes my heart pound faster in my chest.

"Last night on the way home," she says and tears one off; dropping it on the desk so I don't have to interrupt the slow stroke between her legs.

I stop long enough to push the silk up her thighs and then pull her to the edge of the seat. I'm in no hurry, and I do want to hear her beg for me until she's so wet she can't speak. I tease her, running my tongue slowly up the inside of her thigh before repeating on her other leg.

Her hand fists in my hair when my tongue rolls around her sensitive clit.

"Jesus, Tom," she whispers. "Just... just don't stop,"

I move away, sucking her thigh before returning to where she wants me. There is no level of control that can keep me from doing as she bids and I give in. She cries out under the manipulation of my tongue. Ten years of pent-up sexual frustration rushes out of her in waves and my build up is just as acute.

She whimpers in the chair. Her hands grasp my hair as if this is a dream she doesn't want to let go. The absolute rhapsody painted on her face makes me smile, and the salty-sweet taste of her drives me wild. My entire body pulses with the need building inside me and I pull away, climbing to my feet and fumbling with my belt. My breath matches hers, raspy and ragged, and she moves my hands away, unzipping my jeans and pulling my hard member out.

I squeeze my eyes closed, trying to hold on, but the moment her mouth wraps around the tip of my cock, I lose it.

"Oh, fuck." My whisper is enclosed in an exhale, and Bridget sucks with each spurt, stroking me with both her mouth and her hand. I finally pull away and lean against the desk, tucking my junk back into my underwear.

I open my eyes with a sigh, meeting Bridget's gaze. "Just give me a few minutes and then we can start over again."

She grins and stands up, placing her palm on the front of my pants, stroking.

I stare into her eyes and tuck a strand of hair behind her ears before I pull her into a gentle kiss. Just the friction of her hand against my underwear starts my revival and I pull away.

"I want more," I say and she smiles, misinterpreting my statement.

"In a few minutes, you'll get your wish," she purrs and leans in, kissing my neck.

"No, Bridget. I'm not talking about sex. I want more than just this."

She slowly pulls away and her eyes lock on mine as her hand slows.

"I want to wake with you by my side." I let out a laugh. "I want to continue sharing everything going on inside my head and my heart with you. I want to experience your joys and your fears firsthand, instead of through your memories, and I want to be a father to my daughter."

"How about we start out dating?" She interrupts me.

I raise my eyebrows. "You want me to wine and dine you?"

She blushes. "It would be kind of a nice change," she says.

"I guess I can do that," I say and bite my lip. Her hand is still pressed against me. "But I want to do it while under the same roof."

"Mmmm," she says and shakes her head. "That might send the wrong message."

"Really?" I lean away from her. "We can fuck until the cows come home, but the minute I hang my hat on the door, *THAT* sends the wrong message?"

Her eyes narrow and she pulls her hand away, crossing her arms. "You think you can just waltz back into my life and decide you want to shack up?"

"You're the one who wants to start with just dating," I say, using finger quotes around the words just dating, before I cross my arms. Whatever heat had been building between us was now as cool as the arctic.

I turn and pick up the unopened condom. "Am I just a good fuck to you?" I toss it at her and button my pants, escaping while I still have some dignity left.

"No. Tom, you know damned well you mean more to me," she snaps before I get to the door, and I stop.

"So, what is it you want? What does our future look like to you?"

Silence blankets us long enough for me to look over my shoulder.

"Everything we've done, we've done during a crisis. I don't know what we will be like without that," she says. "And if for some reason it doesn't work between us... I can't do that to April."

"Then what was all this about?" I turn and wave at the desk.

She raises her shoulders and they fall in defeat.

I'm not sure whether to stay or go.

"I stood outside for a good ten minutes before I knocked." I say, looking at the ceiling. "Because I wanted to make sure I was here for the right reasons." I drop my gaze to hers. "And not just because you are one of the sexiest women I know." I shift, uncomfortable with baring my soul with words. "I wanted to make sure that all that time away didn't make this more than it really was."

Her gaze bounces from my hands to my face and she sighs.

My hands are signing out of habit, even after this long, I fall into the same pattern when I'm out of my element. I let out a nervous chuckle. "I still sign when I'm nervous." I shove my hands into my pockets.

"Why are you nervous?" she asks.

"Because I feel like I've already lost you."

Bridget slowly lowers into the chair, studying me. "I'm scared," she admits, almost too softly for me to pick up, but the words echo in my head, melting my nerves.

"Why?"

"I can't handle another loss," she says, and the tears shining in her eyes squeeze my heart.

"Neither can I," I say. "But here's the thing. I can't walk away, either." I cross to the desk, and pull a small package out of my pocket and set it down on the wood between us. "You asked if there was anything I was hiding from you in my memories?" I point to the box. "I lied when I said no. I hid that."

Bridget's eyebrows rise, and she stares at the box before her gaze moves up to mine. "When did you get that?" she asks without reaching for the offering.

"I bought it in Greece before I came home, and I was hoping like hell I wasn't too late." I let out a nervous laugh. "That was before I found out Lucifer was still topside."

She leans back in the chair, staring at the tiny jewelry box, and my stomach flutters.

"Aren't you going to open it?"

She moves her gaze up to mine. "There's a part of me that is still pissed at you."

I reach for the box, intending to pocket it again, but she moves faster, covering it with her hand. The gesture is enough to inform me we are not done yet, but she doesn't pick it up. Instead, she moves it a little closer before taking a deep breath.

"How do you know you won't tire of me, or worse, get bored?"

"I highly doubt either of those things will ever happen."

"But how do you know?"

I lean my hip on the desk and study her chaotic aura. "Because you can still drive me bat shit crazy," I say, focusing on her in the center of the rainbow of contrasting colors. Her cheeks bloom red. "I'm not talking about our bedroom compatibility, Bri. Although, admittedly, if that had sucked, neither of us would be here right now."

"No pun intended?"

I grin and look down at my hands. "No, no pun intended." I close my eyes for a minute, calming the energy in my core. "If you want to date, that's what we'll do." I open my eyes, trying to squash the growing disappointment. "We have time."

"If I hadn't been such a bitch when you came in, what would have happened?"

I debate, and before I lose my nerve, I swipe the box from the desk and step around the corner in front of her. With my heart pounding in my throat, I drop to my knee and flip open the box.

"Marry me, Bridget."

She stares at me with her jaw hanging open. Her eyes never fall to the box or the engagement ring inside. There is a big nothingness in her mind, as if my actions short-circuited her.

I snap the box closed and stand up. "But you'd just like to date, so..." I turn around and she's on her feet, grabbing my arm and trying to turn me towards her.

"You really aren't kidding," she says with wide eyes.

"No, I'm serious. I'll date you if that's what you want," I say, trying not to let a smile surface.

"Was that a serious proposal?" Her voice rises to a near hysterical pitch, and panic of a lost chance flares in her eyes and her mind. She steps in front of me. "Tom?" she asks when I don't answer.

I open the box and hold it up within her line of vision. Finally, her gaze moves from me to the ring. Her hand flutters over her mouth as she stares at the white and black diamonds intertwined on the band and the sparkling one-carat rock in the center.

"Does that look like I'm kidding?" I say softly, especially since her eyes look as if they might pop out of her head at any second. "I want to make love to you every night, and then make you pancakes in the morning. I want to take you dancing, and to see a play on opening night in New York. I want to take you to Paris and Ireland, and anywhere else you want to go, just to see those places through your eyes. I want to be there with you through whatever kind of shit we get stuck in, and I'm sure we will see our fair share, but with you standing next to me, we can brave any storm they send at us. So, yes. I'm serious. I want to marry you. All you have to do is say yes."

She cocks her head. "Pancakes?"

"I make a mean stack of pancakes," I say with a smile. "So, can I take that as a yes?"

She looks at the ring and then back into my eyes and the slow smile spreading on her lips is my answer. If we needed some sign that this was right, it is delivered the moment I slide the ring on her finger. It fits perfectly.

Framing her face with my palms, I deliver a kiss that sears my soul to hers and she melts into me, lighting some of my more basic needs. We move this to the couch, and as she climbs onto my lap, I can't help but believe redemption exists and she's the catalyst.

"I love you, Thomas Patrick Ryan," she says, before she crushes my response with her lips.

The End

Continue with CJ and Tom's story in Hunting the Siren, the third book in The Paradox files.

About J.E. Taylor

J.E. Taylor is a USA Today bestselling author, a publisher, an editor, a manuscript formatter, a mother, a wife, a business analyst, and a Supernatural fangirl. Not necessarily in that order. She first sat down to seriously write in February of 2007 after her daughter asked:

"Mom, if you could do anything, what would you do?"

From that moment on, she hasn't looked back.

Besides being co-owner of Novel Concept Publishing, Ms. Taylor also moonlights as a Senior Editor of Allegory E-zine, an online venue for Science Fiction, Fantasy and Horror, and co-host of the popular YouTube talk show Spilling Ink.

She lives in New Hampshire with her husband and during the summer months enjoys her weekends on the shore in southern Maine.

Visit her at www.jetaylor75.com to check out her other titles.